ANN JEFFRIES

Southern Exposures

Family Reunion—In The Wisdom of the Ancestors Series

Copyright © 2013 by Ann Jeffries
annjeffries@newviewliterature.com
All rights reserved
Printed and Bound in the United States of America

Published and Distributed By
New View Literature
820 67th Avenue N, #7603
Myrtle Beach, South Carolina 29572
www.newviewliterature.com

Cover and Interior Design by:
TWA Solutions
www.twasolutions.com

ISBN: 978-0-9915003-0-7
Library of Congress Control Number: 2014907676

First printing June 2014

For inquires, contact the publisher.

ACKNOWLEDGEMENT

A Nigerian proverb says, "Hold a friend with both of your hands." To that, I would add, "Hold a friend with all of your heart." There have been true friends during each stage of my life that I hold in my heart with great and wondrous memories. One, in particular, was a working mother with a busy legal career and boundless energy to extend a helping hand to those in need. She made being a supportive wife, dedicated mother, caring daughter, faithful sister, great friend and hostess extraordinaire look like she was reading her many roles from newspaper headlines. She juggled all of those necessary roles, never dropping one of them. The mind boggled at all that she managed to accomplish with warmth and grace. Yet, this remarkable woman took time to read *Southern Exposures* while it was still in its infancy, and critiqued the manuscript in her (ha! ha!) spare time. That, in and of itself, was a daunting task. Still it only goes to prove further the point that she is the type of true friend that you hold with both of your hands and all of your heart through countless years.

Brenda Irons LeCesne, when I grow up, I want to be just like you, the epitome of the phenomenal woman.

"...I have this love-hate relationship with the South. Some of my best and worst experiences took place [there]. I believe that African Americans who have never had southern exposure have a limited prospective on racism. They think it's all about jobs, but it's not only about jobs. It's about land, ownership, and self-sufficiency. Our story might be different, if we had gotten our forty acres and a mule. People who can grow their own food and live independent of salaries are the ones who will survive. Everything else is fleeting...."

—Amanda Wheeler

Arms of the Magnolia
A Fawcett Gold Medal Book
Ballantine Books
Copyright 1994, p. 224

Prologue

August, five years earlier . . .

Summertime in the South. The heavy, salty, ocean air pressed the heat down to the fine, damp sand. Labor Day weekend couldn't have been better for the thirty-plus Cousins' Reunion. Five of the young men, surrounded by their history and their ancestry, lay on the sand at Atlantic Beach, South Carolina, whiling away the last vestiges of summer's magic. The big, four-level Victorian house owned by their Aunt Hanna Ivy was the perfect backdrop for the thirty-plus first cousins who flocked to the shore each year at the same time for a Cousins' Reunion. With only a few days left before they would go in different directions back to high school, college, graduate school or other institutions of learning, as the case may be, so many cousins had come from far and wide to spend the last five days of summer's splendor together.

Using his hand as a shield to block the approaching brilliant dawn, Kenneth James Alexander peered out over the Atlantic Ocean at the Air Force jets inbound on the horizon.

"What's that?" he asked his younger brother, Benjamin.

"Uh, sounds like the old F-14s, fighter jets. About six of them," he said without looking. Benjamin—Benny—occupied a blanket, his hands laced behind his head. His closed eyes hid behind sunshades that darkened the sun's brilliance, but not his daydream.

Seconds later, six F-14s streaked overhead, moving inland, the booming sound following in their wake.

"When you're good, you're good," his cousin, Donald Dixon, said dryly, watching the aircraft decorate the sky with their exhaust. "Sure are faster than that old crop duster you've been flying, Benny," he joked.

"Yeah, they'll be crossing over Goodwill in three minutes, on their way to Shaw Air Force Base," Benny said, smugly. "It would take me about half that time."

"He built that airplane all by himself, you know, Donald," said Gregory Alexander, Kenneth and Benjamin's youngest brother, in awe and pride for this older brother's accomplishment. "It's super-fast!"

"Kenneth designed *THE EXPLORER*, Gregory," Benny corrected. "She's fast because I followed his plan when I built her."

"You going to be an aerospace engineer, K.J.?" Gregory asked Kenneth, his oldest brother.

"No," Kenneth answered. "I'm getting my masters in electronics and telecommunications engineering, Gregory."

"How long will that take?" the bright youngster asked.

"I'll be finished this year," Kenneth said, yawning and propping his head on the palm of his hand.

"Man, that's pushing it, isn't it, K.J.?" Donald asked, sitting up on the blanket and hugging his bare knees to his equally bare, muscular chest.

"Look who's talking. You did MIT undergrad in three years. That's pushing it," Donald's twin brother, James Dixon, interjected as he rolled onto his stomach on the blanket and raised his upper torso, bracing himself on his forearms.

"Got things to do and people to see," Donald said, grinning. "I told you when I left home, MIT in three."

"What are you gonna do now, Donald?" Gregory asked.

"Just like K.J. I'm going to get my masters."

"And then what?" James asked his brother.

"Foreign service, FBI, CIA, NSA or maybe even the Secret Service. The possibilities are unlimited."

"Law enforcement?" James asked, surprised.

"Somebody's got to do it," Donald answered wryly.

"I thought you wanted to stay in Goodwill," Benny said to Donald.

"Nope, not yet. I want to see some of this world first. Explore like our grandparents told us to. Then someday, when the time is right, I'll come home for good. Until then, I'll leave my little brother in Summer County to take care of the farm," he said.

"Little brother?" James snorted. "Donald, you're five minutes older than I am, and I'm two inches taller than you. I don't know where you get that 'little brother' stuff from."

"Live with it, younger." Donald laughed.

"You're coming back home after graduation, James?" Benny asked.

"Hell, yeah. I'd rather be farming my own land, running my own business instead of working for someone else. When I finish my degree in animal husbandry and commercial farming, I'll work a few years to learn the business, and then I'll come home and help Dad and Uncle Bernard run the family hydroponics farm."

"Man, I love living in Goodwill, too, but we're related to everybody in town and half the people in Summer County. I want to meet some women that I'm not related to," Benny interjected. "If you don't get out there and explore your options, how are you going to find a wife, James?"

"First, I've got to get established. You know, build a home, continue to work the farm into a more productive business, have some roots. Something that I can be proud of. After that, I'll find her."

"Man, it's a wonder you two are twins because you sure aren't anything like Donald," Benny said.

"Good thing, too. I like the ladies now! Not later. I don't intend to wait to find Ms. Right. I'm going on my own reconnaissance mission, hunting for Ms. Right Now. Besides, I can't get anywhere with James around. He's wearing my face," Donald said.

"Maybe you've been hanging out with Benny too long, Donald," Kenneth said. "He seems to find more women than he can handle."

"Young blood," Donald deadpanned. "Last night, Benny must have thought there were two of him. He was at a club in Broadway at the beach and had a lady on both arms."

"Just copying what I've seen you do, cousin," Benny said, smugly, to Donald.

"If that was true, you should have had three ladies, not just two," Donald parried.

"I'm pacing myself," Benny said and grinned, his all too handsome face made more so by his youthful, rakish cockiness.

"Hey, you two, don't give Gregory any ideas," Kenneth warned. "Remember the reasons why all the first cousins come here every year for Labor Day weekend: to focus on our goals and directions for our family's future and to make sure that we're all on the right track. Not to get sidetracked on minor issues. We're supposed to be positive role models for our family members.

"I'm being a positive role model for G," Benny defended, mildly. "I'm teaching him restraint. I can't be held responsible when he's out of my sight. He's been on the road all summer playing basketball. Coach told me that he had to do bed check twice every night on G." Benny laughed. "Seems the ladies were crawling in through the window looking for him. After G and I had a little talk, Coach only had to do bed check once every night on him."

"That true?" Kenneth asked his youngest brother, his expression serious.

"K.J., it wasn't my fault," Gregory whined, with a sexy grin on his young, handsome face. "They be pressing me, man. Sweatin' me hard!"

"You're still young, Greg. If you don't control yourself better than that you might not fulfill your dream to make it into the NBA."

"I hear you, K.J.," Gregory said, sullenly. "I won't let it happen again, but it's not half as bad as Benny and Donald did when they were my age, I hear."

"Oh yeah," Benny said, demonstratively and laughed. "I remember that summer Donald and I went to New Orleans to play in this big basketball tournament."

"Uh, you would remember that one, wouldn't you?" Donald asked dryly, shaking his head.

"Hell yeah! I was what, fifteen or so? I was playing high school basketball and traveling with the team. Donald was captain of the team. Big time senior jock. That summer, I met this fine, fine, truly fine French mulatto girl...Cheri something, uh, Cheri DelaQuois, that was her name, Cheri DelaQuois."

"Ha! You mean woman, don't you, Benny?" Donald corrected. "She had to be at least twenty-five. She lived with her brother's family and he coached one of the other teams that we were playing against in the tournament."

"Yeah, now I remember. I met her the first day I hit town. The team had to go to this reception for all the basketball players in the tournament. Man, did I get a rush when I saw her! I hadn't had a lot of experience, but I couldn't get my hard off after I saw her. After the reception, Donald and I walked around the French Quarter and bumped into Cheri and an even more gorgeous friend of hers, Solonge. They asked us to join them. We did, but before long, Cheri and I were alone in a hotel room and I was learning a whole new language," Benny said and rakishly laughed. "Man, I just knew that this was it! This was the woman for me. It didn't matter that she was much older than I was or that I didn't know anything else about her. I just knew that I was in love. What Cheri taught me in those nine days could fill volumes of any *Encyclopedia*. My basketball game went downhill fast—it was lousy. I couldn't buy a basket with folding money, and I was averaging twenty points a game before that tournament. Don was getting more bedtime than court time with Solonge than I was with Cheri, but his game didn't suffer at all! He was still hitting twenty-five or thirty points a game! With no sweat!

"The night before the last game, I told Donald that I was in love with Cheri and that I wanted to marry her when I got out of high school. He told me to ask her to marry me *after* we beat her brother's team in the championship game. I didn't see then what that had to do with it, but I agreed to wait. We won the tournament. I had my best game ever. Man, you couldn't tell me anything! My head was in the clouds! As soon as the game was over, I found Cheri and asked her to marry me. She acted like I was first cousin to E.T., like I was some kind of alien. I was shocked, hurt, and very disappointed. My ego wasn't just bruised, it was crushed. I thought that she felt the same way that I did. Man, was I confused, but Donald knew what was happening all along. Cheri's brother had put her and Solonge up to distracting me, Donald, and a lot of other high scorers just so his team would win the tournament. Donald told me then never to think with the wrong head. He said that we were only having sex…not making love and that one day I'd know the difference between the two. I'll never forget that lesson."

"You are practicing safe sex, right, Greg?" James asked.

"I wouldn't call it practice, exactly," Gregory said and grinned smugly, "but, yeah, I remember what y'all taught me."

"Oh, so you think you've got pro status now, huh?" Benjamin asked.

"World class," Gregory said, all thirty-two showing on his handsome man/child face.

"That's your responsibility, Benny. You handle it," Kenneth directed.

Benjamin's long-suffering sigh was audible before he sat up, took off his sunglasses and looked his younger brother in the eyes. "Look, G, I think you missed the moral of my story."

"Oh, I got it all right," Gregory said, laughing. "I won't ask a hunnie dip to marry me until *after* I'm making big, stupid money. Then she'll think twice before she refuses. Everybody knows there ain't no romance without finance. And ain't no love without the glove," he said, as if it was one of the Ten Commandments.

"Greg," Benjamin said, shaking his head in frustration, "we're definitely going to have a little talk before I leave to go back to the Air Force Academy,"

"You still thinking about playing pro ball?" Donald asked Gregory.

"Only for a little while. After I get in and make some money, I want to go into business for myself just like James."

"Doing what?" James asked.

"Stocks and bonds. Investments, financial planning. Something like that," Gregory answered. "Uncle Calvin works on Wall Street and he said I could go into business with him."

"He's a good teacher, too," Kenneth added. "Three or four years down the road, I'm thinking about starting a computer software and hardware company.

Something I can make grow. Uncle Calvin is going to help me to do the finances."

"I thought that you were going to work for Sandoval Anniston Corporation in San Francisco after graduation?" Benny asked. "They've been after you for several years, since you were in undergrad."

"I am, but I'm not planning to make a career out of that."

"Whew! Glad to hear that!" Benny said demonstratively.

"Why?" Kenneth asked, confused.

"'Cause, there are some fine women in California! I was planning on visiting regularly."

"Maybe I better have a little talk with *you* before I leave to go back to Georgia Tech," Kenneth said, dryly. The young men all laughed. "Look, little brother, the same thing I told Greg goes for you, too, remember? You've got a few more years at the Air Force Academy, then flight training school and then I expect you to get a master's degree. Those are your only priorities for now, not the ladies."

"You include any time for me to breathe, K.J.?"

"I'm sure you'll find time to breathe in Colorado Springs. There's nothing but air up there. And, by the way, I expect your grades to stay above a 3.5 GPA this year unlike last year."

"Your grades dropped?" Gregory asked, surprised.

"Only in one subject, G," Benny said, reluctantly.

"What was it?"

"Physical Ed," he said, reluctantly.

"*What!*" the young men all said in unison.

"How'd that happen?" James asked.

"Claudette, Naomi, and Sarah, that's how," Kenneth added, dryly.

"Pay up, Benny," Donald said, holding out his hand, palm up. "You know the rule. Anybody gets lower than a 3.5 they pay."

"K.J., did you have to tell it?" Benny asked, reaching into his shorts and pulling out five dollars for each person.

"Those are the rules, remember?"

"I gotta cut back." Benny sighed. "This is costing me."

Everyone laughed.

"Hey, family!" Vivian Alexander, the third eldest of the Alexander's five children, and sister to Kenneth, Benny and Gregory approached the young men, carrying her sleepy baby sister, Aretha, propped on her hip. The six-year-old little girl reached out to Kenneth and he took his baby sister, readily kissing her chubby cheeks and hugging her close to his heart.

"Hey, Viv," they all said in unison.

"Is this a private conversation or can anybody join?" She flopped down on a space on the blanket.

"Hey, cousin, you're not just anybody, you be 'De Judge'," Donald joked and grinned.

"Uh-huh, I know what you're after, Donald Alexander Dixon. Her name is Dakota Sinclair."

"Who's that, Viv?" Benjamin asked his sister.

"Senior at Spelman. She's a runner. Could have made the U. S. Olympic team if she wanted to, but she decided against it. Donald has a thing for athletic women. He's been pressing me to get her contact information for him. He met her last year when he 'just happened to be in the neighborhood' with some of his frat brothers. Spelman wasn't ready for him and his friends, and it wasn't the same after they left," she said, followed by hearty laughter.

"Oh, so now you got my little sister finding ladies for you?" Benjamin asked Donald.

"Man, you ain't seen shit sharp sisters until you've been to Spelman," Donald said, dramatically. "In Vivian's dorm alone were the future Ms. Americas: JaiHonnah Hawkins, Savannah Logan, Kristen Bryant, Constantina Justice, Cheryl Lawrence. Man!" he said, shaking his head slowly. "Spelman women make you humble!"

"Oh yeah? How come whenever I'm there checking up on Vivian, these fine foxes aren't around?" Benny asked.

"Benny, you didn't have any trouble booking Spelman women. You've spent more time on Spelman's campus than I have, and I go there," Vivian teased.

"Oh, he does, does he?" Kenneth asked, with a raised eyebrow.

"Now you've done it, Viv," Gregory said, sighing. "You know what's coming next."

"Look, big brother," Benny began in his defense, "It's my responsibility to look after Vivian, right?" Benny reasoned. "That's what we were taught. We take care of each other. That's what I was doing. I had to go to Tuskegee for training, so I thought I'd check in at Atlanta and see how Vivian was doing."

"K.J., he was there for three days. Booked more women than Carter has little liver pills," Vivian said, laughing.

"Oh, like you've been so innocent. Listen up! I rolled up on Vivian in the gym playing basketball and beating the hell out of *three* brothers! One of them was this big time basketball jock, Carlton Andrews out of Clark Atlanta."

"I needed to make a point," Vivian defended. "The brothers were tryin' to play me, so I took them to the hoop."

"Yeah, you made your point alright and about thirty dollars, too," Benny said, snorted.

Vivian sheepishly looked toward her oldest brother. "K.J., you understand, don't you?" she pleaded. "Some people don't think bull horns will hook. The brothers needed to be taken to the clinic. You know, so I taxed them a little."

"Uh oh, here it comes," Gregory moaned.

Kenneth remorsefully shook his head. "What have I been trying to teach you?" Kenneth asked his family members. "Especially you, little sister. If you want to sit on the Supreme Court someday, basketball is only a means to an end, not a financial opportunity."

"You taught me that I don't have to prove who I am to anyone but myself, K.J., but—"

"No buts, Vivian Lynn. We all have to remember what our ancestors tried to teach us—all of us," Kenneth said, looking from face to face. He laid Aretha on the blanket and then stood with arms akimbo. "Donald. First principle."

Donald sighed and stood beside Kenneth. "We strive for and maintain unity in the family, in our communities, in our nation and in the human race."

"Benny. Second principle."

Benny stood next to Donald. "We define ourselves, create for ourselves and speak for ourselves."

"Gregory. Third principle."

Gregory stood next to Benny. "We build and maintain our communities together and make our sisters' and brothers' problems our problems and we solve those problems together."

"James. Fourth principle."

James stood up next to Gregory. "We build and maintain our careers, stores, and industries and profit from them together."

"Vivian. Fifth principle."

Vivian stood up next to James. "We use our collective vocations to build and develop our communities in order to continue our ancestors' traditions."

"James. Sixth principle."

"We leave our communities more beautiful and financially sound than when we inherited them."

"Donald. Seventh principle."

"We believe in our family, our parents, our teachers, our leaders and the necessity to improve ourselves to reach higher levels of understanding."

"The eighth principle is that we honor ourselves and treat everyone with love, kindness, and respect, learning always to appreciate another point of view." Kenneth thrust his fist into the circle. Everyone clasped hands on top of his. "That's why we all wear these gold chains around our necks as a symbol of what this family stands for and what we're all struggling and expected to achieve. What our ancestors struggled to make possible for all of us. We stand for something or we'll fall for anything. We are the links to an unbroken chain. We will not fail."

"We won't forget, K.J.," Donald said. "No matter what we do in life, we're a family."

"Let's wake up the rest of the cousins so that we can all renew our dedication to family unity and purpose."

The dawn's light rose on the gathering of family members united in their missions. Looking up at her family with big, smiling, bright eyes, little Aretha Alexander, the youngest of the cousins, stood at the center of the circle of thirty, first cousins. As bright as the dawn's early light and as knowing as the wisdom of their ancestors.

Chapter 1

A piercing scream followed by shrilled laughter tore Vivian Alexander's attention away from reading *Fahey: Treatise on Ethics*. She shifted *Black's Law Dictionary* to her side, and lifted her eyes to the little children playing raucous games with complete strangers, sending torrents of infectious giggles and laughter up to the high, cavernous ceiling. The vision brought a smile to her gamine face, bright brown eyes, and curved Cupie Doll mouth. She thought of her younger siblings—Gregory and Aretha—when they were at that age. She watched the children for a moment or two longer, hoping the little unguided missiles didn't fall flat on their faces or tumble over a piece of Samsonite luggage. The children were, however, under the watchful eyes of their parents who scolded them for making too much noise and, nodding toward her, smiled apologetically. Vivian acknowledged the parents with a smile and a shrug and turned her attention to the wintery scene unfolding outside the tall, wide window. Snow was still falling, blurring her panoramic view of the airport tarmac.

It was a very cold, grey, blustery day in Chicago. Muck-blotched snow was heaped high in places on the airport landscape at O'Hare International. Ground crews dodged arriving and departing international and domestic aircraft, as they scurried to load provisions, luggage, and/or fuel into waiting airplanes. In the background, deicing trucks spewed clear, slushy fluid on the aircraft fuselage and wings.

It was the Christmas holiday season, just before New Years' Eve. At any airport in the country, literally thousands of people were traveling. O'Hare Airport, still one of the largest and busiest in the world, was no exception despite the horrendous weather conditions. Controlled chaos would aptly describe the scene along the wide corridors of the airport's many concourses with passengers of many nationalities in a hurry to catch a flight to some distant destination. Little shops and food concession stands were bustling with activity. Airline flight crews briskly walked, pulling their rolling essentials behind them in black leather luggage not much larger than a breadbox. Passenger loading-bay areas were jammed with people sitting or standing guard over more carryon luggage than they probably needed. Ground-crew flight attendants scurried to their appointed posts, and were immediately mobbed by travelers looking for seat assignments, checking on connecting flight schedules, or asking questions about in-flight food service. Announcement after announcement chronicled the arrival and departure of many flights.

Some babies cried while others slept, nestled peacefully in their parents' arms. Little children continued their play, as if the melee were an extension of the just past Christmas morning enthusiasm. Occasionally, aircraft engines roared into action, as a ground crew released the front wheel of the aircraft and energetic hand signals sent it on its way.

Vivian quietly sat before one of the wide, ceiling-high windows in the airport on a padded bench with her long legs curled up under her. She was nearly oblivious to the chaos that surrounded her. She leaned back against a tall column, reading and occasionally observing ground flight crews, as they loaded baggage in steel cases into the belly of the airplane parked at the end of the long, slanted ramp. She, her parents, Bernard and Sylvia Alexander, her younger brother, Gregory Clayton, and her eleven-year-old sister, Aretha Grace, were waiting at Gate 6 for the United Airlines' attendant to announce that the flight was ready for boarding. They would continue their trip home to Goodwill, South Carolina, a small town located in Summer County, more than forty miles from South Carolina's state capitol of Columbia. Her return flight to Washington, DC, and Georgetown University Law Center, would not be leaving until 6:15 P.M. from Gate 23. The Alexander family was returning from San Francisco, California, where they spent the week of Christmas holidays visiting with Kenneth James, the eldest offspring of the Alexanders. Benjamin Staton Alexander, her twenty-eight-year-old brother, an Air Force jet pilot, managed to get some time off and fly himself to San Francisco from San Diego for a few days. It wasn't like being at home in Goodwill for the holidays, Vivian mused, but at least the family was able to spend another special time together.

They stayed at Kenneth's home in Marin County, outside of San Francisco. Vivian was enormously proud of her oldest brother, holding him and his accomplishments in awe. Before starting his own company, he worked as the lead electronics engineering specialist for Sandoval Anniston Corporation, a huge American aircraft and electronics manufacturing operation with corporate offices based in New York and other worldwide locations. Being the thorough researcher that she was, in undergrad she used Sandoval as an example in one of many business classes she took. The company had many military contracts for sophisticated and top secret surveillance and guidance systems, as well as doing some work for the FBI, CIA, Homeland Security, and the super-secret National Security Agency (NSA). She had done very well on that paper. Now Kenneth was the Executive Director of his own company, CompuCorrect, Incorporated (CCI).

For a few moments, Vivian allowed herself a respite from her intense focus on her reading of *Fehey's Treatise,* as she noticed her parents talking quietly together a short distance away from where she sat. She couldn't hear the conversation, but they always seemed to have so much to say to each other. She smiled, thinking that she couldn't have designed two more perfect parents. Her parents would have never permitted the raucous public display that she witnessed with the young parents seated nearby and their rambunctious offspring. Her parents could do more with one look than most parents did with a good scolding. She smiled again and turned her attention away from her parents and back to her reading.

"Bernard, did Kenneth James look too thin to you?" Sylvia asked her husband of thirty-plus years in a low, sotto voice laced with a syrupy southern drawl, as she sat next to him in the airport knitting a sweater.

"Ah, Silvy, honey, you always think that if our children aren't right up under you, they aren't eating right or taking care of themselves. Let the boy be. He's doing fine," Bernard answered with pride, flipping the page of a Chicago newspaper.

"I know that he's been very successful and all, and I'm as proud of him as you are, but that Tofu stuff and bean sprouts he had last night at that strange restaurant will not keep him from getting consumption," she declared. "It's cold in San Francisco this time of year and he never wears enough on his body. Did you know that he was not even wearing a T-shirt under that sweater he had on last night?" she rhetorically asked. "And, he had on those teeny-weeny underwear, and he wasn't even wearing warm sox? Just those thin-ribbed things that you could see through...and those loafers he was wearing won't keep his feet from getting frostbite and that—"

"Silvy, honey, please stop worrying about Kenneth James," Bernard interrupted, mildly. He knew his wife would not let up once she got started. "The boy's over thirty years old and he's survived living out from under our wings since the day he went away to college at Morehouse. He hasn't even had so much as a cold since he left home. He eats plenty and he works out all the time at his office and at that health and fitness club that he took me, Benjamin Staton, and Gregory Clayton to," Bernard said, shifting in his seat, still reading his newspaper and not looking toward his wife.

"I just don't think that he takes good care of himself," Sylvia continued, peevishly. "He ought to have a good woman looking after him. He could get sick and he probably wouldn't even tell me and—"

Bernard put down his newspaper and looked squarely at his wife. "Silvy, you've been a nurse for a very long time. Did Kenneth James have so much as a runny nose or a cough or even a sneeze while we were there?"

Sylvia smiled at her husband and pursed her lips. "No, but something is bothering him. I can feel it, Bernie."

Bernard briefly kissed his wife on her mouth, patted her hand. "No buts, honey," Bernard said gently, returning to reading the newspaper.

Sylvia was quiet for a few moments, knitting and purling the bulky sweater material, as she mulled over her husband's comments. "You know, Bernie, there's still a very high epidemic of HIV/AIDS in San Francisco. Do you think—"

"Sylvia, you know that you can't get AIDS from just living in San Francisco. We taught the boy a long time ago what to do to protect himself. We both talked with him and all the children about how to take precautions. He doesn't seem to have been seriously dating anyone for a while, and...and.... What time is it anyway? Shouldn't they be callin' that flight soon?" he asked, not wanting to lend any credence to his wife's concern that Kenneth might be ill. He, too, noticed that Kenneth seemed distracted, preoccupied, but had asked Kenneth about it, and was assured by his son that he was only concerned about his company. Something to do with military contracts, Kenneth said.

Bernard stood up, neatly folded his newspaper and placed it under his left arm. He stretched his lanky, six-foot three-inch frame, and walked around the energetic children toward the flight attendants' station.

"It's 1:30 P.M. California time," Sylvia called after him before talking aloud to herself. "So does that make it 2:30 P.M. Chicago time or 3:30 P.M.? And does that mean that our flight is supposed to leave at 2:30 P.M. Chicago time or...I get so confused with this time change business...Vivian Lynn, do you gain time going west or coming east?" Sylvia asked her daughter in a loud whisper. "Vivian Lynn...Vivian Lynn, do you hear me speaking to you?"

Vivian finally heard her mother and looked up. "Sorry, Mom, what did you say?" Vivian placed her finger on the spot on the book where she had stopped reading, trying to focus on what her mother was asking.

"Do you gain time going west or coming east?" Sylvia repeated in a slightly louder whisper.

"Going west, Mom. You gain time going west. Where did Dad go?" She looked around the crowded gate area.

"He's over there by the flight attendants' station. See? Right there talking on his cell phone." Sylvia nodded toward where Bernard stood, as she continued to knit.

Vivian spotted her father leaning against a telephone kiosk. He had one hand in his pocket, the other hand on the phone, head up, shoulders back and a wide stance; a familiar pose among the Alexander men. She put a bookmarker in the book, closed it, and walked toward her father.

He looked very distinguished, she thought, as she approached him, like professors on campus at Georgetown. He could have been a professor on any college or university campus with his doctorates in education and in business, but he chose to remain in South Carolina as the principal of Goodwill High School, one of two high schools in Summer County. His close-cut hair wasn't even graying at the temples, and his warm, nut-brown skin was still tight and wrinkle-free. His deep-set, dark brown eyes still had a sparkle in them, too. He could have easily passed for a man twenty years younger. Hugging his upper lip was a thin mustache awaiting the first opportunity to enhance a smile, which he did, as she approached. His broad nose held his glasses just above his full lips. He was wearing a grey pinstriped suit with a vest, watch pocket, a gleaming white shirt, solid grey tie and highly shined black wing-tipped shoes. He took off his stylish, black, square-rimmed glasses and pinched the bridge of his nose while he talked. From the watch pocket of his vest, he pulled a heavy, solid-gold watch by its long gold chain to check the time. A gold pendant, with the word **FAMILY** also hung from the chain.

"Okay, Carlton," Vivian heard her father say, as reached him. "It looks like we will be later than we thought getting into Columbia. I'll have Vivian Lynn call you when we take off and you can meet us at the baggage pickup area... Yes, that's right, Flight 7375... No, it's just the four of us.... No, Vivian Lynn is going straight to Washington from here.... Well, I don't know, why don't you ask her? She's standing right here."

Vivian tried to signal her father not to mention her, but it was too late.

Bernard handed his cell phone to his daughter. "Vivian Lynn, it's Carlton. He wants to know why you're not coming home with us for New Year's." He picked up his paper from the telephone shelf and playfully popped her on the head with it.

Vivian made a funny face at her father, as he smiled at her, tucked his paper under his arm, and leisurely strolled away. She took a deep breath, collecting her defenses in a neat, concise, and articulate fashion to counteract what she knew was coming. Now prepared, she said, with a cheerful voice, "Hi, Carlton, how ya doin'?"

"I was doin' just fine until your father said that you weren't coming home for New Year's. What's up with that?" Carlton Andrews was clearly very annoyed.

She squared her shoulders and began. "You know that I couldn't promise that I would be coming home. We talked about this before Thanksgiving. I've got so much to do before classes start and I've been off from work too long already. It costs money to go back to Washington from home and I don't have money to burn, you know. And besides, you know I'm volunteering some time at the homeless shelter. They really need the help during the holidays and I'm going to do some research for Professor Fehey in my free time. And I left the Snowman with some friends while I was away and he's probably getting on their nerves by now." She recognized that she was speaking in a rambling sort of way, not clearly and concisely as she intended.

"Snowman?" he shouted. "You're going back to Washington because of a dog? Ah, c'mon, Viv, you can do better than that! Tell me anything but that you're putting your dog before me!"

Vivian held the cell phone away from her ear and grimaced. She knew that he'd be angry when he found out that she wasn't coming home, but she wanted to avoid another argument. Things weren't going well between them and on the decline for nearly a year.

"No, Carlton, you've got it all wrong. Didn't you hear what I said?"

"Yeah, I heard you all right. So let's see how we can fix these little problems," he said, preparing to erase her cogent arguments. "I'll buy a ticket for you to fly back to D.C. I'll pay for your dog to stay in a kennel. I'll ask one of my frat brothers in DC to help out at the homeless shelter and I'll reimburse you for the time you lose at work. I know that Kenneth gave you a new laptop for Christmas and a membership to his on-line computer network. So that means that you can do your research in my bed while I make love to you. How's that? Now will you come home?"

Vivian rolled her expressive eyes up to the cavernous ceiling. He wasn't going to make this easy for her. Making love to Carlton was the last thing on her mind. She had to think faster.

"I've made commitments that I have to keep. Not someone else. I can't just pick up and go, and leave people hanging...And, besides, you can't afford all that on an assistant college coach's salary, and you know it."

His voice dropped an octave and became even more intimate. "I'll do whatever I have to do, if it means that we get to spend some quality time together. I'm willing to make the sacrifice."

"Carlton..." She sighed, searching her usually agile mind for other legitimate arguments that she could use.

"Come on, baby," he crooned. "I got lasagna cooking in the oven. Asti chillin' in the frig. Kenny G blowing on the CD. A Caesar tossing in the bowl, as we speak, with, I might add, those nasty anchovies that you like so much. And, I kicked Ray out of the apartment for three whole days. I've even got a couple of New Year's Eve parties lined up. I need to see you *bad*, baby!" He added great emphasis on the 'bad'.

Vivian could hear the music of Kenny G in the background when over the airport loudspeaker a female voice said:

"Ladies and gentlemen...Ladies and gentlemen, may I have your attention please? Due to the weather conditions, there will be another brief delay in boarding Flight 7375 to Columbia, South Carolina. We will be boarding through Gate 6 in approximately forty-five minutes. Please remain seated in the boarding area for further announcements. Your patience is appreciated."

"Carlton, listen," Vivian continued, "all that sounds great, but I couldn't get on this flight if my life depended on it. You should see this airport. It's packed, the weather conditions here are pretty bad, and I'm sure that the flight is full."

"Take a later flight. I'm picking up your family at the airport in your dad's van and then they are going to drop me off at home. I'll get my car and come back to the airport for you whenever you get in. Please baby, please baby, baby, baby, please," he pleaded mimicking Spike Lee. "I want to sport my super fine lady and have you in my arms on New Year's Eve kissing you into our future together."

Vivian exhaled deeply. Nope, this was not going to be easy. Why couldn't she just bring herself to tell him that maybe they didn't have a future? At least, not together. That would have been the truth, at least, but she didn't say it. She let the opportunity pass. As usual, she acquiesced under Carlton's relentless pressure just as she had always done. Maybe it would be better to talk with him face-to-face, she reasoned.

"Okay, Carlton," she relented with a long-suffering sigh. "I'll check the flight schedules and get back to you, but if I come, it can only be for a day or two. I really have to get back to D.C."

"I'll be waiting right by the telephone, so hurry up, baby. I've got a surprise waiting here for you, and, maybe once you get it, you won't want to go back to D.C.," he added cheerfully.

"What surprise?" she asked suspiciously.

"You'll see when you get here," he said in a silly singsong manner

"C'mon, Carlton, tell me now," she insisted. "You know I don't like it when you do that. You just gonna' leave a sistah hangin', my brother?"

"You gotta come here to get it and to get me, my Nubian Queen. Now go change your flight...hurry, hurry, chop, chop," he teased.

"I'll see what I can do," Vivian answered soberly, but hastened to add, "but I'm not promising anything."

"I love you, baby," Carlton said quietly.

"I hear you, Carlton," Vivian answered, closing the cell phone. She stopped a moment, leaned against the telephone stand and wished she could tell him she loved him, too, but things had changed for her. Carlton had changed...or had he?

An airline attendant confirmed that there were no available seats on Flight 7375 and, in fact, due to the inclement weather conditions, United Airlines cancelled all further flights to Columbia that day. Vivian walked away and sat next to her father, passing his cell phone to him.

"What's up, Vivian Lynn?" Her father put his arm around her shoulder and placed her head against his chest.

"Carlton wants me to come home with you today or catch a later flight. He's made all these plans for us over the next few days, but I need to go back to D.C." She leaned further into her father's embrace. "He even has some big surprise he wants to spring on me. I can't get a seat on this flight and after your flight takes off United doesn't have any more flights to Columbia today. Maybe I can get on another carrier, but that means that I have to pay for the ticket."

It all came tumbling out all at once without even a second wind.

"I know," her father said, gently stroking the wisps of hair sticking out from under the inverted baseball cap Vivian wore on her head. "He's going to ask you to marry him. He spoke with me when he took your mama and me to the airport before Christmas."

"I was afraid of that." Vivian inhaled and exhaled slowly, as she snuggled even closer to her father. "It's not that I don't care about him, because I do...but I'm not ready for marriage yet, Dad. I'm only twenty-three. I've got two and a half years of law school in front of me. When I got accepted into the Public Interest Scholars Program, I made certain commitments. Georgetown is already one of the toughest law schools in the country, but the expanded courses under the scholars' program are real brain busters. I'm competing against nearly three thousand other law school students just in Georgetown alone, not to mention a zillion other law schools in the USA. The competition at G'town is fierce and I want to make Law Review, if I ever master the Socratic Method, that is." Sighing heavily, she continued. "Course work in the next semester is going to be tougher than it was in the first semester. Former Senator Fehey is one of my professors and he's asked me to do some legal research on a book that he's writing about his life in the Senate. He could have picked a third-year student to do this for him, but he didn't. He picked me. That's quite an honor. I don't want to let him down. This could help me with my career. Someday I want to clerk for a federal or Supreme Court judge for three or four years or work on Capitol Hill for a Senate or House Subcommittee and then I want to go into private practice or become a state's attorney. I even want to be a judge one day, Dad, but I know that Carlton wants to get married right away, have beaucoup babies, and move back to his home in Dallas, Texas. He wants to coach basketball at the college level or even in the pros. That's why he's taken this assistant coach's job with the men's basketball team at the Grand Strand University. I can't see myself as a coach's wife, baking cookies for the men's basketball team, can you, Dad?"

Raising five children had schooled Bernard Alexander about giving unsolicited advice. Deftly, he avoided his daughter's question. He trusted her and knew that she would make the right decision regarding her relationship with Carlton. He was not going to try to influence her in any way. He also knew that if she wanted his advice, she would ask for it. He changed the subject.

"You can do anything that you set your mind to, Vivian Lynn. Of that I'm sure, but you can't cook worth two cents," he teased with a smirk. "By the way, what was that limp chicken dish you cooked and tried to get us to eat at Kenneth James' house?"

"Oh, Dad," she whined, sitting up and looking at her father, "that was coq au vin and you ate every bit of it and loved it."

"All I want to know is how you coaxed those half-dead chickens to get up and walk into the pot without their feathers on?" He continued to tease, trying not to laugh aloud at her mutinous expression. "Or were those feathers that I saw swimming around in the pot?"

"Stop, Dad," she playfully protested. "Those were bay leaves, not feathers. Tell him, Mom. You have to put bay leaves in coq au vin, don't you?"

"Yes, Vivian Lynn, but only one or two, not twenty or thirty," her mother answered, still knitting without even looking up.

"Oh, well," Vivian said demurely. "I thought it needed more flavor."

"Next time, baby, ask me before you add more of anything. Okay?" her mother asked, peeking over the rim of her stylish eyeglasses, which were perched ever so neatly at the end of her broad nose.

Bernard cupped his hand over his mouth to stifle his laughter. "Where are Gregory Clayton and Aretha Grace?" he asked, gaining his composure and looking around the gate area. "Where did they go? Vivian Lynn, go find your brother and sister, please."

"Dad, they're right over there by the pinball machines in the arcade," Vivian said, spying her younger brother's thin, six-foot frame and her sister's nearly five-foot-five frame on the other side of the wide concourse.

"Would you please go and get them and tell them that I said to come here and pick up this stuff?" He nodding toward Gregory's coat and book bag and Aretha's computer game that were laying in disarray across two seats in front of where he was sitting.

Dutifully, Vivian rose and crossed the wide walkway, dodging the travelers who were dashing in each direction toward their appointed destinations. She could see Aretha playing the electronic pinball machine and scoring big. Gregory was standing by, watching her score with his hands dug deep in the pockets of his over-sized, low-hung, faded jeans. He was wearing K.J.'s black crew-neck sweater that was so large that it hung down below his butt. The white X on his black baseball cap turned backwards on his head seemed to glisten as she approached. He was wearing thin, wire earphones and was swaying slightly, but rhythmically, to the music playing on the iPod attached to his belt. Vivian crept up behind him and pressed her knee into the back of his left leg, causing him to buckle slightly. He smiled broadly at her, as he put his long, lanky arms around her head, pulling her face into his armpit.

"Sup, V?" he cheerfully asked.

She playfully grabbed him around his waist and gave him a big squeeze.

"C'mon, little brother," she said, pulling her face away from his armpit and looking up into his light, cinnamon-brown face and dark, bedroom eyes.

"Little brother? Little brother?" he protested, releasing the bear hug he had around her head just slightly. "Who's looking up to who, you little shrimpette?" he joked, pulling the baseball cap off her head and holding it up in the air beyond her reach.

"All right, you! You're only a few inches taller than I am, but you're still my little brother," she said, tickling him in his ribs and forcing him to bring his arm down within reach. She was over five foot nine inches and grabbed for her cap. With his wide hand and superior height, he jostled her close-cut hair that was plastered to her head.

"All right, you long-legged, pigeon-toed, knock-kneed, gooseneck-looking refugee from the funny farm," she joked.

"Yeah? Well the hunnie dips like all that," he retorted, with a devilishly captivating smug smile, holding his long arms spread wide apart.

"Yeah and when Leslie finds out what you've been doing with Charlotte, Ellen, Ann, Regina, Jennifer, Geneva, and Lucille, you'll be looking for another beehive to be buzzing around, looking for some hunnies," Aretha sarcastically deadpanned without heat while still concentrating on her mounting pinball score.

"You've got my back though, don't you, Retha?" Gregory grinned at his younger sister.

"I'm not going to give them the 411 on you, if that's what you mean, but you better not slip up or somebody's going to be dialing 911 for you," she said, rolling her head on her neck.

"Give a brother a break, Retha!" Gregory joked, feigning innocence.

"Yeah, right," Aretha said flatly, rolling her impressive big brown eyes and pursing her lips.

Vivian laughed at her younger sibling's antics and noticed that it did not appear as if Gregory had shaved in weeks. She put her hand to his smiling, boyish, but handsome, face.

"What's this dirt on your face?"

"Dirt?" he exclaimed. "That's hair, baby! It's a man thang, ya know?" He broke out into his rendition of the latest dance.

"Come here, you nut. Let me talk with you." Vivian laughed, pulling him toward her by the front of his brother's pirated sweater. "Here…here's some money," she said, reaching for twenty dollars she had in her pocket.

He pulled the earphones off his head and draped them around his neck. "What's this for?" he asked, curiously eyeing the money in her hand.

"I want you to buy yourself some condoms and make sure you wear them any time you get busy with a girl."

"Dag, V! You and Mama must think I'm some kind of Olympic-class lover or some kind of cock hound like Benny. Mama's always buying condoms and sticking them in my drawer, in my wallet, in my book bag, in the glove compartment of my ride. She even put one in my lunch bag! Imagine how I felt when I dumped the bag on the table in the school cafeteria. That was embarrassing! I was hangin' with my boys and they all fell out laughing at me! K.J. even bought me this big box of those freaky, glow-in-the-dark condoms. Even Retha took her babysitting money and bought a box of those double-strength joints for me! I'm good, V. I mean, I gets my share of the hunnies, but I ain't crazy. I told Mama last month that she had better save some of those condoms for her and Dad. They're the ones knocking the boots all the time. They be goin' for it all night. They even started going to bed at seven-thirty and gettin' up hittin' it again early in the morning. Mom and Dad ain't that old, ya know. There could be six of us next year if they keep that stuff up. It's fierce around there sometimes! A brother can't even get any sleep no more." He eyed the twenty-dollar bill Vivian was holding and quickly plucked it from her hand. "But I'll keep the twenty anyway to take my hunnie dip out after the game next week."

"Young blood, G, but I'd rather have you safe than sorry. I don't want anything to happen to you, you know?"

"I love you, too, sis. I'm always careful. I don't want to bring home anything that I can't take care of with an aspirin, but I'm gonna save a whole lot of those ribbed condoms for when I come up to visit you this summer in D.C. I hear those Howard U hunnie dips are all that! I'm gonna get me some of that!" A devilish smile stroked his budding mustache.

"Yeah, you better be an Olympic-class lover to go up on Howard's campus 'cause they take no prisoners on Howard Hill. You had better just keep slow walking with some of those little high school girls and leave those college girls for when you fill out this sweater you *borrowed* from K.J."

"*Borrowed?* I was desperate. You need to check your little sister. She stays in my closet! She wears everything I own. She might even have on a pair of my jockeys!"

Aretha rolled her expressive eyes at her brother, but never stopped playing the pinball game.

"Do I look like I'm wearing *your* brother's clothes to you, V?" Aretha dramatically asked, rolling her impressive, brown eyes again.

Aretha was wearing a faded jean outfit from head to toe; one of many Christmas presents from Benny. Her faded denim apple cap was turned sideways on top of her long, black, thick hair. She wore a white *I Am Woman, Hear Me Roar* T-shirt that hugged her budding breasts and a faded jean jacket. Faded jeans hugged every curve of her young, nubile body. She may have only been eleven years old, but her body was beginning to look like that of a teen-aged model.

"Ah! When you're good, you're good!" Aretha exclaimed, as she scored a perfect game on the electronic pinball machine.

"Way to go, Retha!" Vivian exclaimed with a proud smile.

"Yeah, I taught her everything I know," Gregory added, sticking out his chest.

"Yeah, you taught me how to put the quarters in the machine," Aretha dryly said.

"You didn't have to go there, Retha," Gregory said, jokingly, as he pulled his younger sister's head into his armpit.

They all laughed and Gregory draped his long arms around his sisters' shoulders, as they walked back toward their parents who were sitting huddled together in conversation. Vivian smiled, as she thought of her parents "knocking boots." Well, they had knocked boots at least five times, accounting for the number of children they had. Of course, they must have practiced a few times to have five perfect children. Practice did make perfect after all. Their parents were a handsome pair, Vivian thought. Her mother's beautiful round face, doe-like dark brown eyes, and smooth supple skin. Her dark brown, full, long hair attractively framed her face. She didn't look a day over thirty-five, though they recently celebrated her fifty-fourth birthday.

None of them noticed the man who watched them intently.

"Look at those three," Sylvia Alexander whispered to her husband when she saw her youngest children approaching. "Just look at them! They look like ragamuffins! I don't understand why Vivian Lynn cut off all her hair. She's bald, I tell you, just plain bald about the head. The child doesn't even wear makeup. Not even any jewelry, except her gold family chain. And why can't she carry a purse like normal people? Even that man sitting over there is carrying a purse. Not a bad looking one either. He must be from San Francisco. And look at that boy of ours, with those clothes hanging off him. He doesn't even have those big old brogans he's wearing laced up. Didn't you tell him to shave that nest off his face? And Aretha. You need to speak with her, Bernie. She wears more of her brother's clothes than he does. At least she hasn't cut off all her hair yet. It's a shame! A crying shame how those three dress out in public!"

Bernard didn't answer his wife, but he did peek over the top of his glasses and observe his children, as they approached. He noticed that Vivian was smiling broadly about something. She and Aretha had beautiful smiles, he thought, just like Sylvia's.

"What are you smiling about, Vivian Lynn?" her father asked.

"Nothing, Dad, just something G said."

"What did he say that was so funny?"

"He said—."

Gregory suddenly clamped his hand over Vivian's mouth and said, while grinning, "Nothing, Dad. Just a joke between me and big mouth here."

"He said that you and Mama are always making love," Aretha supplied, with a big, bright smile.

Bernard looked at his children, smiled, shook his head, and continued reading the paper. He couldn't deny his daughter's statement. He made love with his wife at every opportunity and, God willing, he would continue to do so until he drew his final breath.

Sylvia blushed, and started knitting faster, as she squirmed in her chair. Quickly, she decided that it was time to change the subject. "Vivian Lynn, where is your purse?"

"I don't carry a purse, Mom."

"Where do you keep your money, your ID cards and makeup...you know, lipstick?"

"My money is in my pocket. My ID is in my book bag. My makeup, such as it is, my dear mother, is in my luggage. You know I don't wear a lot of makeup. I don't carry it around with me everywhere I go."

"See what I mean, Bernie? Ragamuffins!" Sylvia quietly mumbled, still knitting.

The Alexanders sat and talked about what everyone would be doing in the New Year. Sylvia continued to knit the sweater and mumble something under her breath about shoelaces.

Vivian sat, watching her mother's hands skillfully purling and looping with her glasses still perched at the end of her nose.

"Mom, who's this sweater for, King Kong?" Vivian asked, as she noticed how large the sweater would be, given the length it had already attained.

"It's for whoever wants it and whoever it fits. I don't force anybody to wear my sweaters. I just make them so anybody can wear them if they want to... You know Mabel Johnson's daughter? You remember her, Caroline Ann, I think her name is. She was in the same high school class with your brother, Benjamin Staton." Vivian didn't have a clue where her mother was going with the abrupt switch in topics, but she listened nonetheless. "Well, anyway, Caroline Ann went out to Minnesota to go to school. She met some young man out there, dropped out of college, got married, had two quick babies and Mabel told me last month that Caroline Ann has already filed divorce papers. Three years of college and she couldn't hold on just a little longer to get her degree. Now she's been married for only three years and already she's on her way back home, babies and all."

"All right, Mom, I know that there is something in this soap opera that you want me to understand, but, frankly, my dear mother, my brain went on download and stopped working about four hours ago."

Sylvia looked at her daughter, caressed her face, and said, with a knowing, warm smile, "Don't ever let someone force you to wear something that doesn't fit you, Vivian Lynn. Whether it's too small or too big. If it don't fit, don't force it. Keep trying on new and different things until you find something or someone that fits you."

She kissed Vivian gently on the forehead. Vivian put her arms around her mother's neck and laid her head on her mother's shoulder while her mother continued to knit.

"What Mama is trying to tell you, V, is—" Aretha said, as she played with her computer game seeming not to have been paying attention to her mother and sister's conversation.

"Aretha Grace, your sister knows what I'm talking about. She doesn't need it translated," Sylvia gently said, while still knitting.

Vivian did understand. She wondered whether her mother knew about how badly Carlton treated her and whether that was the reason for the parable. Although she could usually talk to her parents and the rest of her family about anything, the deteriorating relationship between her and Carlton was too painfully devastating and humiliating to share. Her mother had an uncanny insight and the wisdom of the ancestors. She smiled and hugged her mother tighter.

"I love you, Mama," she whispered.

Sylvia patted Vivian's cheek and kissed her forehead again. "I love you more, baby," she said, as she continued knitting. Well, maybe Vivian's new hairstyle wasn't *that* bad.

There were kisses and hugs all around when the flight attendant finally announced that the United Airlines' flight to Columbia, South Carolina, was ready for boarding. Vivian noticed how her father reached for her mother's hand, as they headed for the ramp. They always held hands, she recalled, and they always seemed to be so happy to be together. She wondered whether she and Carlton would ever share that level of intimacy if they were to marry. That seemed so improbable now. Carlton was her first real love, but she wondered if it was enough to overcome the pain that he caused her?

Vivian waved goodbye to her family, as they went down the ramp to the aircraft. Standing by the window, she watched as the ground crew backed the plane away from the gate and signaled the pilots to taxi to the runway for takeoff. She watched as the plane disappeared out of sight behind the large, plowed mountains of snow. The snow was still falling in Chicago, blanketing everything in its path.

Vivian remembered that her father called to her, as he was leaving and reminded her to call Carlton. She opened her cell phone, and speed-dialed his number. As Carlton's telephone began to ring, she remembered her mother's words: "If it don't fit, don't force it." To her surprise, her call went to voice mail, so she quickly said, "Sorry, Carlton. It's a 'no go' on the flight to Columbia, but my family just left. I'll call you when I get back to D.C."

She slung her leather book bag over her left shoulder, tucked her dark-blue hooded parka under her arm, dug her hands in her pockets, and headed for Gate 23. As she walked along, she checked the bulletin board for departing flights and noted that the message next to her flight still read DELAYED. When she reached the gate, she found a comfortable spot, opened her books, and started to study again. It wasn't until she began to get thirsty that she looked out the window and noticed how it had grown dark. The agent at the Airlines' desk told her that all flights to the Northeast were delayed because of the snowstorm that covered the airports. Everywhere from the Deep South to the far North was covered in some areas with at least ten to fifteen inches of snow.

While she was in San Francisco, Vivian vaguely remembered something about the storm on the news, but it did not phase her, as she swung bundled up in a hammock on the deck of her brother's home, watching clouds slowly, but steadily, moving across the azure blue sky and pondering what she wanted her life to be and whether she should permit Carlton to be in it.

The flight attendant could not tell her when her flight would be able to leave. Her flight was scheduled to leave at 6:15 P.M. She looked at her watch; it was already 8:30 P.M. She found a snack shop and bought bottled water and a salad bowl. When she returned to the gate area, there were no seats available. She perched on a wide, padded ledge by the window, stretched her legs out before her, and started to read.

"Georgetown! Hey, Georgetown!" a deep, melodic, baritone voice flew at her. "You mind if I share your bench?"

Vivian's eyes climbed up and up at the tall, thick mountain of a man standing before her. Finally, his question registered. She quickly scanned this vision standing over her, but didn't answer him. He looked like he had not shaved in weeks. Black, shiny hairs masked his face. He was wearing a dark brown Stetson pulled down low over the dark sunglasses that covered his eyes. Protruding from under the hat and tied into a ponytail at the nape of his neck was black curly hair. A brown and white plaid, wool shirt, unbuttoned at the neck, revealed a profusion of black hairs flooding over his even whiter chest. An oversized brown buckskin cowboy jacket, complete with rawhide tassels, hung over his thick body, draped nearly to the floor. Tight faded jeans hung low on his hips, held up with a cowboy belt and large silver buckle. The brown Timberland boots he wore were similar to the ones that she was wearing; a Christmas gift from Kenneth. She then glanced quickly around the passenger-loading bay and noted that there were no other seats available. With a long-suffering sigh, she swung her legs down off the window bench and pulled her possessions closer to her, making room for the mountain to sit down. He slung his nap sack off his shoulder and placed it near her feet. His canvas duffle bag made a loud thump, as he dropped it next to the window. He propped his skis against the wall and sat down with a thud. When he reached between his legs into his nap sack, he turned toward Vivian, and said, "Thanks, Georgetown. You want a brew?"

"No, thank you," she said, as she wondered how he knew she was at Georgetown. *Oh, yes,* she thought, *duh!* She was wearing a grey warm-up top with Georgetown Hoya written across the front. She reopened her book and continued reading, dismissing his presence from her mind. She sat there for what seemed like an eternity. She was getting weary sitting cramped in one position for so long, so she stood up to stretch.

"So, you're at Georgetown Law, huh?" the skiing cowboy asked. "This your first year?"

She wondered whether he was psychic or something. Then she remembered that the dark blue, baseball cap that she was wearing in reverse had the words, GEORGETOWN LAW, boldly printed across the brim.

"Yes," she answered.

"Yes, what?" he asked with a lopsided grin on his firm lips.

"Yes, I'm at Georgetown Law and, yes, this is my first year."

"Thought so. You look like a One L sitting there with your nose buried in that law book. I'm a second-year resident at Georgetown University Hospital."

"That's nice for you," she said, not wanting to make a conversation out of this. This is too far out, she mused to herself. A skiing-cowboy, second-year resident doctor. She absently shrugged mentally and returned to her reading. More time passed and Vivian checked her watch. It was 9:30 P.M., she noted. *Come on, people*, she thought, *when is this flight getting off the ground?*

As if by magic, the PA system kicked in. *"Ladies and Gentlemen.... Ladies and Gentlemen. May I have your attention please? United Airlines wants to thank you for your patience. We are ready to begin boarding Flight 627 to Washington Reagan National Airport. We will begin by boarding rows 35 to 50. Please have your...."*

When her row was called, Vivian picked up her belongings and headed to the gate. The skiing-cowboy, second-year, resident doctor was lying on his back, head propped up on his duffle bag, face covered with his Stetson, knees up in the air, and snoring loudly. She did not bother to wake him.

Vivian boarded the plane, found her seat, placed her parka in the overhead compartment, slid in next to the window, and placed her book bag under the seat in front of her. She pulled *Dante: Civil Procedure* from her book bag and placed it on her lap, as she buckled her seat belt. The plane was filling up quickly. She was losing hope that the seat next to her would remain empty. Then she briefly looked up and did a double take. The skiing-cowboy, second-year, resident doctor was the last one to enter the cabin. He ducked his head to avoid colliding with the low ceiling in the plane. He looked around for his assigned seat. *Oh, no*, she thought, *please don't let him be sitting in the seat next to me! Keep going! That's right, keep going!* She thought that she was safe and the seat next to her would be empty after all. Shifting her books to the seat next to her, she bent to retrieve a hi-lighter from her bag when she heard...

"Hey, Georgetown! Why didn't you wake me up? I almost missed this flight." He stored his duffle bag in the overhead compartment and dropped his nap sack on the seat.

Vivian dropped her head briefly and shook it in frustration. Then she looked up at the powerhouse and pursed her lips. "I go off duty at 9:50 P.M., doctor, and it's now 9:51 P.M.," she quipped. "You'll have to see Nurse Ratchet about your wake-up calls."

A slow, rakish grin hitched up one corner of his mouth. A knuckle kicked up his Stetson and then he drew his sunshades to the tip of his nose with one finger. Vivian almost gasped, looking into the most mesmerizing pair of ebony eyes she had ever seen. His face took on a new glow—devastatingly handsome. He could have passed for the movie-TV star Matthew Bomer who played Neal Caffrey on the television series White Collar. It finally registered with her where she had seen that fantastic physique before and who he was. He leaned in closer to her, peering at her over the top of his sunglasses.

"Cute, Georgetown—but no cigar," he retorted, standing now almost full height, stuffing his bag into the overhead compartment and closing it. He picked up his nap sack and plopped down on the seat, rocking it backward. His knees jammed into the back of the seat in front of him. The man sitting there turned slightly and looked back between the seats.

"Sorry, pardner," he said in a pseudo-cowboy drawl. "Bad knees."

Vivian observed the exchange, feigning total disinterest. Cute and a wry sense of humor too, she noted. She reached up and turned on the overhead reading light, opened her book again, and began to read. The engines started to hum, the plane backed away from the gate, and the cabin began to pressurize. She peered out the window and rubbed her eyes. She had read over three hundred pages of text and her eyes were getting tired.

The flight attendants finished their instructions on how to use the seat belt and floatation device. They pointed to the exit rows and demonstrated how to use the oxygen cups. Then they were off, scurrying to assure that everyone was buckled up for takeoff. Of course, the skiing-cowboy, second-year, resident doctor had to be awakened and asked to fasten his seat belt and return his seat to an upright position. Grumbling, he complied.

Vivian wasn't really a drinker, but when the flight attendant reached her row with the beverage cart, she quickly asked for a Bloody Mary—and no ice. The cowboy slept through the entire exchange. Reclined, with his Stetson covering his face again, he snored so loudly that Vivian couldn't concentrate on her reading. She turned out the overhead light, rested her head against the window, and peered out into the clear, moonlit sky. It looked so quiet and peaceful out there above the clouds. The moon brightly shone on the grey clouds below. Occasionally she could see tiny lights flickering far below. The steady hum of the engine and the Bloody Mary, with no ice, lulled her to sleep.

Vivian snuggled closer to the warmth, woke lazily, and yawned when the flight attendant reached for her empty cup and napkin. She found herself covered with a blanket and her head resting on the cowboy's chest. She moved away quickly, hoping that he hadn't noticed. He was turned toward her, but he didn't stir when she moved. The pilot was talking over the intercom system, saying something about being on the ground in five minutes and instructing the flight attendants to prepare for landing. Vivian peered at her watch through bleary eyes and noted that it was 11:55 P.M., but couldn't recall whether she had reset her watch. Nor could she recall who covered her or when she had laid herself against him. She returned her tray to its rightful position, placed her book in her bag—dismissing the unintentional show of intimacy—and looked out the window. Washington was lit up all around her like a bunch of diamonds glistening and flickering on a blanket of white. They were coming into the airport from the south, over the Potomac River, then the Anacostia River.

Suddenly, the plane began to shake violently and bank sharply to the right, tossing her back against the cowboy. The wind current and turbulence tossed the 727 from side to side, as the landing gear locked into place. The descent seemed too fast and too violent. Vivian tensed when the seatbelt sign came on, beeping incessantly, as they began to lose altitude. The dark waters came up fast beneath them. Vivian unconsciously tightened her hand on what she thought was the padded armrest. The tires hit the runway, then bounced up, finally touching down on the icy surface. When the wheels touched down the final time, the pilot put on the brakes so sharply that everyone lunged forward in their seats and she squeezed harder. It wasn't the armrest, she soon realized, when the plane began running smoothly down the runway and slowed. The skiing-cowboy, second-year, resident doctor covered her hand in his lap with his Stetson and quizzically looked at her. "Uh, was it something you wanted, Georgetown?"

Vivian flushed and quickly removed her errant hand. The embarrassment was complete when she heard the low rumble of laughter from the cowboy. She couldn't look him in the eyes.

As the plane taxied to the gate, the pilot said, "Welcome to the Nation's Capital. The ground temperature is fourteen degrees. Please remain seated until the plane comes to a complete stop and the seatbelt sign is turned off. Thank you for flying the friendly skies of United Airlines. Hope to see you all again soon on another United Airlines flight."

Before the plane came to a full stop, people began leaping to their feet and flooding the aisles. Overhead compartments flew open. The skiing-cowboy, second-year, resident doctor rose slowly, filling the isle with his bulk, stretched his huge muscular body, and began removing his bag from the overhead compartment. With his massive arms extended over his head, Vivian noticed the large bulge in his jeans that she had mistook for a padded armrest. Rolling her eyes, she silently berated herself.

"This your coat, Georgetown?" he asked, noticing Vivian's line of sight resting on his midsection. "What, no emblem—no insignia?" He hung his arms on the overhead and leaned in conspiratorially lowering his voice. "You know, Georgetown, you could get arrested for wearing a naked coat with no Georgetown insignia on it," he quipped.

Vivian rose slowly and defiantly met his gaze with her own studied stare. She leaned toward him. "Clean off your shades there, Doc," she intoned. "You see it says right there 'Polo.' P-O-L-O."

"Oh, now my life is complete. You used me as a pillow, tried to steal my family jewels, and now I know that you cannot only read, but spell too." He winked. "Real good, Georgetown. Real good. You'll go far," he replied with sarcastic humor. Vivian's eyes widened in embarrassment and her mouth gaped as he cleared a path for her to exit, blocking the other weary travelers' attempts at a hasty escape. "After you, ma'am," he said, taking off his Stetson, swinging it away, and bowing at the waist. A mass of curly hair flopped around his face.

Vivian slammed her mouth shut and breezed by him without so much as a backward glance. No man had the right to be that handsome.

Later, Vivian stood at the baggage carousel waiting for her luggage and looking at her watch. She would have to take a taxicab home. The subway system had shut down for the night. Buses were not running on schedule and it was well past midnight before the conveyor belt spit out her luggage most unceremoniously. She headed for the door, pulling her large bag behind her.

There was a long line at the cabstand—thirty or more people—and very few cabs were in sight. She heard a porter say to some of the people in the crowd that it was now twelve degrees outside with a wind chill factor of minus sixteen. The temperature was dropping. She put on her gloves and parka, turned her baseball cap around on her head, and pulled her hood of her parka tightly around her face. She pulled a long, gray, wool scarf from her pocket and wrapped it around her head, covering most of her face below her eyes. The wind whipped and the blowing, shiny snow stung, as it hit her cheeks. *Who left the back door to the North Pole open?* she wondered. People ahead of her in line danced back and forth from one foot to the other, trying to brace against the swirling snow and cutting wind. She turned her back to one swirl of wind while another bounced off the walls and stung her face from the other direction. Tears were freezing to her cheeks, her fingertips were numb, and her feet felt like ice. The line was moving slowly. A red pickup truck pulled up to the taxi stand and blew its horn. She ignored the noise of the truck, as she continued her wind dance, trying desperately to stay warm. A few more cabs pulled up. There were still more than twenty people ahead of her in line. This was going to take all night. Then she heard…

"Hey! Georgetown! Do ya need a lift?"

She noticed that the skiing-cowboy, second-year, resident doctor was honking the horn of the red, extended cab, pickup truck. His skis were mounted on the roof of the extended cab. A CB radio antenna, with a green tennis ball wrapped around it, was whipping in the wind. He got out of his truck and approached her.

"C'mon, Georgetown. Me an Ol' Reds here will get you to the big city," he said in a pseudo-cowboy drawl, easily lifting her heavy piece of luggage and placing it on to the back of his open-bed truck.

It was too cold to refuse the ride, she thought. She turned to a young, attractive blonde-haired woman standing behind her in line. "I want you to remember this cowboy's license plate tag, '**BFRINZ**', if you hear on the news that some poor, black, female, Georgetown law student was found murdered in the woods."

"Yeah, lady," the skiing-cowboy, second-year, resident doctor said to the lady, "and I want you to remember this woman if you hear that some poor, white, male, Georgetown doctor was found flailed, fricasseed, and hung by his gonads."

Vivian's eyes widened and her mouth, covered by her scarf, gaped. The cowboy grinned at her with a twinkle in his mesmerizing eyes.

The blond woman looked at both of them and said, through chattering teeth, "Georgetown, huh? Well, if you're going anywhere near Wisconsin Avenue and M Street, we will all be safe, if I can catch a ride with you?"

"Me too!" piped in a man standing in front of Vivian in line. He looked wildly from one face to the other. He appeared to be of East Indian descent, Vivian thought. Egyptian perhaps. "I go to Georgetown too, please, yes?" His voice shivered as much as his body.

"Well sure, ma'am and sir. Let's head 'em up and move 'em out," the cowboy said, picking up the woman's luggage and placing them onto the truck. "After you, ladies."

After the lady, Vivian climbed into the backseat of the extended cab. Her feet were frozen and her fingers were numb. The male rider got into the front seat with the skiing-cowboy, second-year, resident doctor. It was a bit cramped in the backseat of the extended cab for her long legs, but it was warm. Vivian had no fear of getting in the truck with the cowboy, particularly since she recognized him. He had an annoying, dry humor that had bested her more than a few times in their short acquaintance, but she didn't feel threatened by him. In fact, she enjoyed the repartee between them. The fact that she would not be alone on the ride to Georgetown and the fact that it was extremely cold outside also convinced her to accept his offer.

The snow was deeper in some places than others. The wind whipped and swirled around them, obscuring the view of the road. The truck's headlights did not improve the visibility, as it slowly crept along the ice-slick highway, as they departed the airport terminal and began to merge onto the George Washington Parkway North. The cowboy handled the truck masterfully, Vivian noticed, as if it was his love. She never would have thought that a man of his celebrity would be so comfortable in anything less than an expensive and flashy sports car. *Humph*, she thought, *interesting dichotomy*. She found herself wondering what other departures from the norm this enigma entailed.

"My name is Chuck. Chuck Montgomery," the cowboy said, as he shifted the truck into four-wheel drive. "You folks can call me Chucky."

Vivian's thoughts were verified. Chuck Montgomery was a former, all-pro basketball player who had a stellar career rivaling and bettering that of Aakeem, David Robinson, Patrick Ewing, and Shaquille O'Neal. He left the game on his way up the ladder to stardom.

As Chuck reached down to shift gears, the blonde-haired woman, who was squeezed into the corner, announced, "I'm Shelly Davis."

Vivian noticed the barely-veiled seductive way Shelly was eyeing Chuck. He did have that kind of effect on women—black, white, or other—and Shelly was clearly affected.

"Pleased to meet you, ma'am," Chuck said.

"I'm Ahkmed-Sudah Ryheme. Ahkmed is just fine with me," the East Indian man said, with a heavy Arab accent and a beautiful wide smile.

"Pleased to make your acquaintance, sir," Chuck said and then eyed Vivian in his rear-view mirror. "And you, Georgetown? What's your handle?"

"Just call me Annie. Annie Oakley, partner," Vivian said sarcastically in a western accent.

Chuck simply grinned, shook his head and said, "Okay, Shelly, where to?"

"I'm registered at the McCoy Hotel near Wisconsin and M Street," Shelly said, her breathless velvet voice waffling in the small enclosure, "all week," she breathed.

Vivian thought she might gag from the syrupy flood dripping from Shelly's lips. *He's not the man I've heard he is*, she thought, *if Chuck fell for that line.*

"And you, Ahkmed, where can I take you?" Chuck asked.

"I stay with friends on Wisconsin Avenue and 30th Street. You know this place, yes?" Ahkmed asked.

"Sure," Chuck said, "that's near the hospital where I work. It's right on my way home." Then he turned his attention to Vivian. "And you, Ms. Oakley? Where's your bunkhouse? Do you live in the dormitory across from the school on New Jersey Avenue or somewhere on Capitol Hill?" Chuck asked in his best western accent.

"Well, we can just mosey on up to R Street and Wisconsin near the main campus, a couple of blocks from the hospital, and I'll unsaddle my pony there."

"Sure thing, ma'am. Sure thing. We aim to please. We sure do." Chuck grinned at her in his rear view mirror. "By the way, it's going to take some time to get there in this weather so I hope that you don't mind if I listen to some good ol', down-home music on the way," Chuck said, as he lifted the top of the center armrest, pulled out a CD, and slid it into the CD player.

No one objected, of course. After all, it was his vehicle.

A rather up-tempo country and western tune began to play. Vivian thought that she recognized the voices of the vocalists. *Could that be the Pointer Sisters? No. No way. They don't sing country and western.* Later, on the same CD, she thought, *Gee, that sounds like The Staple Singers.* She knew that she must be really tired when she started hearing The Staple Singers or the Pointer Sisters singing with Travis Tritt, Garth Brooks or Tammy Wynette. Boy did she need some rest soon. Yet the music was interesting and she tapped her thawing toes a bit to the beat, especially when she heard Ray Charles crooning about Georgia.

Vivian sat quietly while Chuck, Shelly, and Ahkmed talked about the terrible weather conditions and themselves. It would take almost an hour and a half to reach the McCoy Hotel; a trip that would usually only take fifteen minutes. Shelly's barely-veiled interest in Chuck was now blatant. She made her interest in seeing him again crystal clear. When they reached the hotel, Chuck carried Shelly's luggage into the lobby. Vivian could see through the glass doors that Shelly was trying to offer Chuck something and she didn't think that it was money for being such a gentleman and giving her a ride. Chuck appeared to decline whatever the offer was, but what did she know, or even care, for that matter. Men, like Chuck Montgomery, usually had a harem standing around waiting for him to favor them with his presence. She was an expert on that topic. Carlton's basketball career wasn't nearly as illustrious as Chuck's was, but the groupies were always around Carlton—ready, willing, and able to service his every need. She noticed that Chuck shook Shelly's hand and, without a backward glance, walked back to his truck. Shelly stood at the glass doors, staring at his massive frame. His virile agility was not lost on Vivian either.

Chuck climbed back into the truck and began driving slowly up Wisconsin Avenue. He took off his Stetson, placed it on the seat beside her, and asked, looking at her through his rear-view mirror, "Is there something about me that riles you, Ms. Oakley?"

Vivian was caught off guard and in a surprising flash of heat from his gaze. She marshalled her thoughts. "Well, pardner," Vivian began in a Western drawl, "long time ago in the wild, wild west, I saw a poster hanging in the post office that sure did resemble you. It read: WANTED DEAD OR ALIVE.'"

Chuck gave out a full-throated laugh. "Well, Ms. Oakley, that there was my Pa. My ma put up a reward for his arrest for leaving her with me and the other young'uns back on the ranch. When my ma caught up with my pa, she whipped him to death with her razor sharp tongue and collected the reward herself, but if you want to take me in, I'll go willingly," he grinned, "but I'll be totally alive and willing for a tongue lashing."

Vivian's eyes widened. The double-entendres not lost on her. He was flirting with her! The surprise made her tingle uncharacteristically.

"Wanted poster?!" Ahkmed spoke and seemed suddenly alarmed. "Whipped to death?!" *Ahkmed obviously heard about American street violence*, she thought.

"Not to worry, Ahkmed, old pal. Just a little American humor. Bad humor, that is," Chuck sarcastically said, still grinning at Vivian in his rearview mirror. "Another triumph in poor taste there, Ms. Oakley,"

Vivian averted her eyes and had no reply. *PMS is a bitch on wheels*, she thought, but Chuck gave as good as he got and she knew, without question, that those sexy eyes of his had gotten him more than his share. Carlton and her brother, Benny, weren't the only men who could make a woman sweat in a blizzard with a look.

Chuck turned the truck right onto R Street, which had not been plowed. The truck swayed, jostling its passengers from side to side, as it lumbered up the street. The icy wind caused a hard crust to form on the top of the deep snow. The crust cracked and broke, as the big wheels of the truck forged a trail through the unblemished snow. Cars had not been moved. Walkways were not visible. Street lamp beams bounced off the white snow, illuminating the narrow street for blocks. Tree limbs hung low, weighted down by the heavy snow and ice.

"Turn left here at Madison. It's that house there on the corner," Vivian said, pointing to the large brick row house at 1825.

There it stood, 'Benny's Bordello,' Vivian dubbed it when her brother lived there. Their aunt, Hanna Ivy Benson, inherited the house from an elderly woman who she had worked for as a private duty nurse and companion. The woman died, leaving no relatives, but bequeathing this property, and one that she owned at Myrtle Beach, South Carolina, to Hanna. Aunt Hanna Ivy chose to stay in Myrtle Beach, preferring the warmth of the South to the cold and ice of the North. She sold the house in Georgetown to Benny for a ridiculously low price, far below the market value for a thirty-five-hundred-square-foot, four-level house on a corner lot in the heart of the fashionable Georgetown area not far from the famed Embassy Row. Benny had always been her favorite nephew, so when he graduated from flight training school and received his posting to Andrews Air Force Base in Maryland outside Washington, D.C., Aunt Hanna Ivy gladly sold the house to him. He lived there for nearly three years and remodeled most of the house to fit his robust lifestyle.

There were four floors in the house. The basement level had a separate entranceway, both in the front and back of the house, under the long concrete steps. It was perfect for an income unit, but Vivian had yet to finish some of the work on the space and rent it out. The main kitchen was her favorite room in the house, Vivian thought, with the huge, curved, window wall that Benny installed, overlooking the huge back yard, Rock Creek Park, and beyond. He put in a modern kitchen and bathrooms each with whirlpool tubs and large, frameless glass-enclosed showers. There was a kitchenette on the lower level and a full out-door kitchen on an expansive patio at the rear of the house. He removed the old cracked plaster from the interior walls down to the brick and threw out the old carpeting, revealing the beautiful Brazilian Cherry hardwood floors. This was 'Benny's Bordello' all right, but now Vivian and her four housemates called it home.

Chuck parked his truck in the middle of the street, left the motor running, and took Vivian's luggage up the two levels of long, wide, and snowy steps to the porch. Ahkmed got out of the truck and held out his hand to help Vivian climb out of the truck. She reached into the back of the truck and retrieved her book bag buried below Ahkmed's luggage and the snow. Vivian shook Ahkmed's hand, turned, and started toward the steps. She slowly pulled herself out of the deep snow that had accumulated between the parked cars on the street. She stepped into a deep snow bank that held her fast, but her long, strong legs finally plowed her way to the front of the house. She reached for the pole that held the **'Rooms for Rent'** sign in the front yard, which was barely visible above the crusty snow line. Vivian's journey to the porch took much longer than Chuck's, who's longer legs and thick muscular body aided him in maneuvering through the deep snow while carrying her luggage. Chuck stood nonchalantly, leaning on a porch column, Stetson pulled down over his eyes, with his arms folded and legs crossed at the ankles. He did not offer her a helping hand. When Vivian finally ascended the steps to the covered porch, she pulled a twenty-dollar bill from her pocket and offered it to Chuck.

He plucked the money from her fingers, moved within a whisper of her, and said, in a low, sexy growl, "Thanks, ma'am. I've earned this sawbuck for all the grief I've taken from you, Ms. Oakley. Happy trails." He tipped his hat, bounded down the steps through the snow before she could think of a pithy remark.

"All the grief he took from me?' What a crock!" she fussed, as she turned the key in the front door and pulled her luggage inside. She made the mistake of looking back and her eyes locked with Chuck's for what seemed like an eternity before he got back into his truck and drove away. She shook her head, as if to clear it then closed the door at her back, effectively dismissing the arrogance of Charles Montgomery and the entire episode.

Home at last! Vivian sensed that none of her four housemates were at home. The steps had not been cleared of the snow, none of their cars were parked on the street, and a pile of unopened mail claimed prominent position on the floor in the expansive entrance foyer. The house was dark and quiet, but warm. She could hear only the sound of the bitterly cold whirling wind outside. She headed up the wide, oak staircase to the third floor, leaving her luggage and books on the floor in the foyer. She flipped on the light in the bathroom and turned on the water faucet in the whirlpool tub for a bath. Next, she started pulling off her clothes, letting them drop anywhere they landed on the floor.

Sixteen messages on the answering machine, she noted, but did not attempt to retrieve them. She poured a glass of white wine for herself, sat bare-bodied on the table by her bedroom sofa, and started looking through her CD collection. She wondered absently whether she had any country and western music in her collected works, then dismissed the thought with a snort, continuing to look for her favorite musical artist.

"That's the one I want," she said aloud. *"Kemistry!"* She found the long, white, hooded terrycloth robe that she had 'borrowed' from Benny and wrapped it around herself, then set the timer on the scented body oil to warm. She slipped the CD into the player, picked up her glass of wine, and headed for the bathroom. The steam was filling the room, as she entered. Lighting candles that surrounded the tub, she turned out the lights. The room took on a surreal glow. She took another sip of wine, sprinkled bath salts into the hot, churning water, and slid in ever so slowly. "Ah," she moaned, pleasurably. The hot, scented water felt so good on her tired, aching body. Reclining in the tub, she looked up at the skylight above her head, listening to the wind rattle the windows, the melodious vocals of Kem, and feeling the water churn around her, releasing all tension that the long day's journey from San Francisco had caused. In the flickering candlelight, her thoughts went to the handsome, skiing-cowboy, second-year, resident doctor, former superstar ball player, as she let her head slip down below the water line. She was home and every fiber of her body began to relax.

When the timer on the whirlpool clicked off, Vivian released the water to the drain, stepped out of the tub, and wrapped herself in the terrycloth robe. She padded barefoot into her room and rubbed her body with warm, scented oils. She crawled between the silk sheets, found a comfortable position, and pulled the comforter up over her head. Her bed had never felt so good as it did at that moment, but why in the world was she thinking how much better it might feel with Chuck Montgomery in bed with her? "You're just a little horny." She laughed aloud at herself before sleep claimed her.

* * *

She had an interesting style about her Chuck Montgomery thought, as he drove to the hospital. An attractive, but unpretentious style. A little on the young side, but yet not immature. The Georgetown Law baseball cap turned backward on her head said that she had a quirky personality. Her loose-fitting

Georgetown Hoyer sweats. Her Timberland high-top boots. He had watched her standing at an electronic pinball machine hugging a young man with a long lanky build. Definitely ball players, both of them, he thought, by the way she moved effortlessly and easily, a woman comfortable in her own skin. A younger girl was playing the electronic pinball machine and racking up high scores. They were laughing and smiling at each other. His Georgetown girl had an infectious smile. Her face glowed when she talked to her young companions. They all did. That was what initially captured his attention. He guessed they were related. Though she looked like the actress Jada Pinkett-Smith in her young days, they had similar facial features and body builds. He had dubbed his Georgetown girl 'poetry in motion', as he watched them cross the airport's wide concourse walkway toward two other people—a very distinguished-looking older man and a mature, attractive, stately looking woman. They must be her parents, he thought at the time. He watched, as they huddled, talking together smiling and laughing. They seemed to be a very happy family, much like his own family, he thought before sleep overtook him.

When he woke up, they were gone. He stood up and looked around the airport gate area where they were sitting, but he didn't see them. He gathered up his things and headed for his departure gate. And, there she was again; his Georgetown girl. His heart skipped more than a few beats seeing her sitting on a wide, padded ledge by the window with one leg up, bent at the knee and the other leg stretched out before her. She was engrossed in her book. He scanned the area through his sunshades, but didn't see the rest of her family. He could have found somewhere else to sit, but he sensed something intriguing about her. Her big, bright eyes. Her sparkling smile. Her tall, slender, slightly muscular build. Her casual, unpretentious style. The way she moved. Something. Something that was so palpable that he could feel it in his gut and lower. He wanted to meet her so he approached her.

When the young woman looked up at him standing over her, his heart had stopped beating. She was even more beautiful up close. Not gorgeous like, Susan Churchill, a porcelain fashion model he dated off and on over the past several years, but this Georgetown Law student was earthy, appealing, like someone with inner strength, exuberance, vitality and beauty. He knew what he probably looked like to her, particularly since he was coming back from a skiing vacation and he had not had a shave in a week. She quickly glanced around the area, he noted, obviously evaluating whether it was possible for him to find a seat somewhere else or perhaps to take flight herself to some other remote area of the crowded airport. Finally, she swung her legs down off the window bench, pulled her possessions closer to her, and made room for him to sit down. He put his nap sack on the floor, his canvas duffle bag next to the window, stood his skis up next to the wall, and sat down. He was feeling like a real klutz and incredibly insecure about meeting this woman. He had just broken off his relationship with Susan and was feeling as if he should swear off all women for a while, but something about this beautiful young woman captured his interest for some reason. The fact that she was Black wasn't even a consideration. He tried to think of something to say to her, but she wasn't making it easy on him. When words failed to materialize in his head, he gave up, propped his head up against his duffle bag, and gone back to sleep, but not before her soft scent sent his senses into erotic orbit.

When he woke up, she was gone again and the ground flight attendant was giving a final boarding call. When he entered the aircraft cabin, he had done a double take when he glimpsed her sitting in coach class. This time he wouldn't leave their meeting to chance. His ticket was for the connoisseur class seating, but he spotted a vacant seat in coach next to the young woman, so he talked the flight attendant into letting him switch. He summoned the courage to try to talk to her again, but again he was rebuffed.

When they landed, he saw her standing at the baggage carousel waiting for her luggage and looking at her watch. He went to his pickup truck and drove around to the front of the airport, waiting to see whether someone was meeting her. Then he saw her come out of the airport alone and get in line at the taxicab stand. Okay, he thought, as he pulled his red extended cab pickup truck up to the taxi stand and blew his horn. He would give this one more try. She ignored his horn, as she continued her wind dance in the frigid night air. A few more cabs pulled up, but there were still more than twenty people ahead of her in line. *This was going to take all night,* he thought. So he finally got out of his truck and approached her. This time he was successful and she accepted his offer of a ride. He frequently looked at her in his rear view mirror, but she was still ignoring him. Well, he had thought to himself, maybe she just doesn't like white people. On the other hand, Shelly Davis had made her interest in him perfectly clear and explicit bordering on a proposition, but he wasn't in the market for that, especially since sitting in his truck was a rare diamond in the rough. She wasn't impressed or star struck even though she clearly recognized him. Rather, she was hell bent on squashing any attempt he made to get to know her better. He drove Ahkmed to his destination and then he drove directly to the hospital.

It was nearly three-thirty in the morning when Chuck pulled his truck into the nearly empty doctors' parking lot. He knew that there would be a shortage of doctors and nurses on duty on such a hazardous night and he was right. His life-long, best friend, Dr. Derrick Jackson, was the first person he saw when he checked in. He couldn't shake the thought of the woman whom he had given a ride home. He assumed that maybe she just didn't like him, yet someone whose family all looked like very pleasant and happy people couldn't be racist, he thought.

"Hey, buddy, what's the word?" Derrick Jackson asked when he saw Chuck entering Georgetown Medical Center.

They gave each other a power handclasp, bumping chest to chest.

"Snow," Chuck deadpanned, as he released Derrick's hand and signed in. "How is it going?"

"Not bad, but we're shorthanded. How were the ski trip and your lady....? Uh.... Susan, right?" Derrick asked, as he continued to check his patients' charts.

"Skiing was great, but Susan, well, that's history."

Derrick finally looked up into Chuck's eyes. "Sorry to hear it. You really liked her."

"Yeah, but it wasn't me that she liked. It was all that NBA glitz and glitter." Chuck took off his coat and gloves and blew into his hands.

"You're a doctor now. Doesn't she think that that's more important than being an NBA icon?" he mused.

"Hell no. She prefers me like I used to be—available. Not someone who spends twenty-five hours a day, eight days a week, and three hundred sixty-six days a year in a hospital. Man! How stupid could I be!"

Derrick laughed. "She's the one who's lost out on a good thing, buddy. Someone else will take up her slack."

"Naw, man, this is it for me for a while. I can't keep up. Although," he said, as the Georgetown Law school student's image flashed in his mind, "I don't know, I met someone at the airport in Chicago...naw. Don't let me even start thinking...."

"Who is she?"

"I don't know her name."

"I thought that you said that you met her?"

"I did, sort of; I mean, I sat next to her in the airport and on the flight back to D.C. I even gave her a ride home in this blizzard, but.... well, the lady wouldn't give me the time of day if her life depended on it," he said and laughed.

"So why are you even thinking about her?"

"Something about her…I don't know, she moves like a ball player; has these bright brown eyes, real good looking…nice body, too. A little bit country and a little rock and roll. She's in law, first year."

"She's a sistah?"

"Yeah, man. She took one look at me and acted like I was the man who killed Travon Martin."

Derrick laughed. "Told you about trying to hit on a sistah wearing that cowboy get up. You can't catch a cold looking like Willie Nelson on drugs." He laughed. "Sistahs don't usually go for the country-cowboy look. Maybe she's married or engaged or something."

"Naw, I checked. She wasn't wearing a ring or any other jewelry except a necklace that read **FAMILY** when she tried to relieve me of my family jewels."

Derrick quizzically looked up at Chuck. "Was this a mile-high quickie or what?"

"Naw, man." He laughed. "She fell asleep and I covered her up with a blanket. She ended up sleeping on my shoulder and…well, uh, never mind. I'll tell you later."

"Maybe the sistah knew that you were trying to hit on her."

"Wasn't like that. I mean she wasn't the kind of woman you'd want to hit on just because…I mean, she's something special; has this real quick wit about her. Made you think twice, told me her name was Annie Oakley with a straight face…. tough," Chuck said and laughed. "The woman's got it going on!"

"Sounds like she made an impression on you, all right."

"Yeah, she did, but she's not even going to…well, hell…let me get my mind off her. You say we've got a shortage of staff?"

"Yeah, looks like we're going to be on duty for the next thirty-six or forty-eight hours before we get any relief."

"Together again, huh, Derrick?"

"As usual, Chuck. As usual."

* * *

Vivian slept soundly until she heard someone frantically ringing the front door bell. Then pounding on the door. She squinted at her clock. It was 5:30 A.M.

"Who the hell?" she said aloud, as she crawled out of her warm, comfortable bed. She thought that perhaps it was one of her four housemates who had forgotten his or her key. She rose, put on her damp robe, grabbed her baseball bat, just in case, and crept slowly and quietly down the steps. The banging and ringing continued and grew louder and more frantic, as she reached the door. She flipped on the bright porch lights and could not believe her eyes. She must be dreaming! It couldn't be him! She opened the door. There stood Carlton Andrews holding a large yellow cooler.

"It's dinner time," he said, as he entered the house wearing a smile that lit up the room. He placed the cooler on the floor, shook off his coat, and engulfed Vivian in his powerful arms. "I'm hungry, let's eat," he said, devouring her mouth, her neck, and then her shoulders.

"Carlton, how in the world did you get here?" she asked, still amazed that he was there and somewhat dizzy from the force of his kisses.

"I was in the shower when you called and said that you weren't coming," he said, still holding her and kissing her wildly as he talked. "I sent Ray to the airport to pick up your family while I packed up the lasagna." He kissed her chin. "Asti." He kissed her ear. "Caesar." He kissed a bare spot on her chest. "Then I threw some clothes in a bag and jumped into my Pathfinder." He kissed her breast. "There weren't any flights, buses or trains moving so I simply headed North." He kissed her lips. His tongue circled the outline of her mouth, then slipping inside, probing even more deeply. She could not focus on what to ask next. She felt his breathing quicken, as he held her tightly against his chest, moaning his pleasure.

"Forget the lasagna. You taste better," he whispered against her mouth.

The muscles in his broad chest rippled, as he cocooned her, his engorged phallus protruding against her.

Vivian could feel herself being lifted from the floor. She let the baseball bat that she was still holding fall. She wrapped her arms around Carlton's neck and legs around his waist. She lost all sense of herself, melting into his blatant sexuality. It had been a long time since she let Carlton make love to her. She didn't know whether she wanted to try again, but, at the moment, the heat of his passion overwhelmed her. They reached the bedroom, still kissing passionately and locked in a strong embrace. Carlton's tongue skipped gently over Vivian's neck, as he lowered her against his body to the floor. Vivian watched, as Carlton very slowly and methodically unbuckled his belt and unzipped his jeans letting them fall. She spread her fingers and gently moved them up his back until his sweater cleared his head. They gazed into each other's eyes. She stroked his hair and bit softly on his earlobe and Carlton's body tensed, ushering forth a ragged shudder from his soul. He sat Vivian on the edge of the bed and knelt between her legs. Her robe fell from her shoulders. He kissed her left knee, then her right and moved on to her supple, slightly muscled inner thighs. Her body tensed, as his hands molded her thighs in his powerful grip. She ran her fingers through his jet-black, naturally curly hair. He kissed her navel, then her abdomen and buried his face between her thighs. The hair from his mustache excited her, as he lathered her pubis. Her toes involuntarily curled, as heat rushed up her outstretched legs. Moving up to her abdomen, lathering her with kisses, he stretched her arms apart above her head, interlacing their fingers, and they glided along the silk sheets toward the center of the bed. She kissed his eyes, the right and then the left. Carlton kissed one shoulder and then the other. He buried his open mouth under her chin. His body tensed, as he lowered himself into position. Now the heat she felt was rising to her hips. His body was moist, ready, and inviting. She kissed his chest, the nipple on the right and then the left, biting playfully. His butt muscles constricted under her grip and then something flashed in her head.

"No," she said.

"You don't mean that," he groaned lustfully, still trying to arouse her. "Let me love you. It's been so long, baby. I need to be inside you. I love you."

"No!" she said more forcefully, pushing away from him.

Carlton forcefully grabbed her arm, halting her retreat from him. Anger was apparent in his eyes. "I know you want me! I can feel it! I'll make you forget. Just let me...."

"No, I can't! I won't!" she hissed, pulling out of his grip and pushing beyond his reach.

Carlton balled his fist and gritted his teeth. "How long are you going to make me pay?!" he asked vehemently. "How long are you going to punish me?!"

Vivian looked away, rubbing the spot where he had gripped her arm. She said nothing more and covered herself in the bed linen. It was over. She believed, at that moment, that they were through.

Chapter 2

"Did you have a hard time getting home, Dad?" Benjamin "Benny" Alexander asked.

"We were delayed in Chicago for a while, but we finally arrived in Columbia late yesterday," Bernard Alexander answered. "Carlton's friend, Ray LaForge, picked us up at the airport, and then we dropped him off at his and Carlton's apartment, before we drove home."

"What happened to Carlton? I thought that he was meeting you at the airport."

"Ray said something about Carlton having to make an emergency run."

"Is it anything serious?" Benjamin asked.

"I don't know. Ray didn't say too much. Probably something to do with one of the boys on the basketball team or something. He's always having to yank someone's chain for one thing or another."

"Have you heard from Vivian, Dad?"

"Not yet. We called her last night and left a message on her cell phone and house phone. According to the news this morning, they're pretty well socked in up there in D.C. Twenty to twenty-four inches of snow in some areas. Looked like a lot of blowing and drifting snow was going on, too. A real blizzard."

"Yeah, Dad. I tried to call her last night, too, and so did K.J. Doesn't seem like the telephone lines are down, but, if she doesn't get back to one of us soon, I'll have one of my buddies at the Pentagon check on her."

"Benjamin Staton, you're just like your mother. Always worrying about somebody. Vivian Lynn will get back to us as soon as she can, I'm sure," Bernard said and laughed. "She's a grown woman capable of taking care of herself. You and Kenneth James hover over her like she's still a little girl."

"What are you saying about me, Bernard?" Sylvia asked from the kitchen.

"I'm telling Benjamin Staton that he's a worry wart just like you. Here, talk to your son," Bernard said, handing the cordless telephone to Sylvia, kissing her quickly on the lips, and sitting down at the large kitchen table to continue his backgammon game with Aretha.

"Benjamin Staton, did you get back to the Air Force base on time?" Sylvia asked.

"Yes, Mom, everything's cool. Did you have a good time in San Francisco?"

"It was great to have us all together. Looks like there won't be too many more of these holiday get-togethers when all of you children can come home."

"Don't worry, Mom. We have a lot of good times ahead of us."

"I hope so. I miss all of you so much. Seems like just yesterday that Kenneth James was around here working on some electronic gadget or other for a high school project. You and Vivian Lynn were running around here trying to throw pieces of peanut butter and jelly sandwiches into each other's mouths and messing up my kitchen."

"The things you remember, Mom." Benjamin laughed. "I hope that you remember that Viv always started it."

"If you didn't start that one, you probably started something else. You two were always getting into something and then you would try to cover up for each other. I sometimes think of you two as unguided missiles."

"You were time enough for us then, Mom, and you still are. Where's G? I've already talked with Retha."

"In his room on that new cell phone that you gave him for Christmas. That young man hasn't even been to the table for breakfast. He's been returning all these girls' telephone calls all morning," she fussed. "Hold on. I'll get him. Gregory Clayton! Gregory Clayton! Come to the telephone. It's your brother, Benjamin Staton."

While she waited for Gregory, she asked, "Benjamin, did you think that Kenneth James seemed disturbed or distracted while we were there?"

"No, no more than usual. He is building a very successful business. Why do you ask?"

"Well, maybe it's that, but...."

"Mom, dad is right. You are a worry wart," he said, laughing.

"We'll see," she said when she noticed her youngest son approaching.

Gregory lumbered down the hallway to the kitchen, rubbing his bare chest with one hand, the other hand dug deep in his low riding jeans. A gold chain that read **FAMILY** gleamed against his light, brown-sugar skin. He took the telephone from his mother, stealing a kiss from her cheek. Sylvia smiled at her handsome youngest son.

"Boy, put some clothes on your body before you catch your death," she gently scolded.

"Yes 'sum," Gregory said, winked at his mother and then turned his attention to the telephone in his hand. "Sup! Big Ben!"

"You got it, G! You the man!" Benjamin responded.

"I know I got it like that! All the hunnies were calling me, leaving messages while I was away. They had to cancel Christmas 'cause I wasn't here!" he boasted jokingly' as he strolled into the dining room and then the living room. He plopped down in an over-sized easy chair and hung his right leg over the armrest.

"Stop tripping, G," Benny said and smirked. "I want to hear that your head is going to be in some books and out of those clouds. You know that Dad's talking about sending you to prep school after graduation, if you don't get a 3.0 GPA this year. I hear you made honor roll last semester in Math, but the rest of your grades leave much to be desired. Two-point-five isn't acceptable in this family."

"You don't have to have a 3.0 to be a star in the NBA, Benny," Gregory answered smartly. "Dad said you had a 2.75 GPA and look at you…a big time fly boy!"

"That was in my freshman year in high school. Not my senior year. At the Air Force Academy, I busted a 3.5 every year. Vivian had a 3.4 at Spelman. K.J. had a 3.8 in undergrad at Morehouse and a 4.0 in grad school at Georgia Tech, and Retha's grades have been off the scale since she hit kindergarten. You gotta keep up the family tradition, even if you think you're going to play professional basketball. You've heard some of those guys who get interviewed after a game. They can't even carry on a decent conversation. But then you see and hear a brother like The Admiral, David Robinson. Now he's really had it going on! The man graduated from the Naval Academy in Annapolis, Maryland. You know it's not easy to get good grades and play basketball in college. That takes a real star. An educated star."

"Yeah, but, Benny, money talks and talks loud. You don't have to speak French to buy a Benz if you're LeBron James."

"Yeah, but you better be able to read the contract before you sign on the dotted line."

Gregory was quiet. "Okay, Benny, I hear you."

"By the way, G, how are you fixed for protection?"

"Dag! Why is everybody worried about me and my johnson? V was on this trip yesterday. She gave me twenty bucks to buy some condoms. K.J. got me some freaky neon-light looking condoms. Mama puts condoms everywhere, including my lunch bag. Retha bought the condoms-of-steel and now here you come! Can a brother catch a break?"

"So Mom's still pulling that old condom-in-the-lunch-bag trick, huh?" Benjamin mused. "Well, just having it is one thing; make sure you wear that protection."

A telephone rang in the background. "Gotta' go, Big Ben. My public is calling!"

"All right, G. I've already talked to Aretha so I'm out. Love you, bro," Benjamin said. "Back at you."

* * *

"So now is there any member of your family you still have to call, Benny, or can we pick up where we left off?" Stacy Greene asked seductively, as she stroked Benjamin's naked body.

"I still haven't talked with my sister, Vivian, and neither has anyone else," he said, placing his cell phone on the nightstand by his bed. "She's in D.C. and there was a big snow storm on the east coast yesterday. I need to call some people and make sure she's all right." He kissed Stacy sensuously on her lips. She tastes like more, but he had to make sure that Vivian was safe. He eased back from Stacy, intent on continuing his enjoyment of her as soon as humanly possible. He picked up the phone again and punched in some numbers. "K.J. called her several times and so have I and all I get is her voice mail." There was a pause and then, "Hello, this is Captain Benjamin Alexander. Is Colonel Baker available?" He paused. "Let me speak to him, please." He paused. "J.C., this is Benny…Yeah man, how ya doin'?" Pausing, he nodded his head. "Yeah, I'm livin' right. Look, J.C., I haven't been able to reach my sister, Vivian. She flew into D.C. yesterday and no one has been able to get in touch with her. What's the situation there? Really? Twenty to twenty-four inches, huh? That's more than what I heard on the news. You got anybody you can send over to her place and check on her? Great! You know the address…Yeah, call me at the crib or hit me on ComLink when you've got something. Thanks, my man."

Benny hung up the telephone, rolled over toward Stacy, and began kissing and stroking her body, enjoying the feel of her smooth, supple skin under his fingertips.

"Now what was that you were saying about 'Picking up where we left off'?" he growled lowly, kissing and sucking her taut nipples.

"That was then, Captain Alexander," she said and laughed. "You desert me for Christmas and fly off to San Francisco to be with your family. Okay, I say.

He didn't ask me to go with him. It's his family and we've only known each other for eleven months. I can cope with that. Then you blow into town, show up at my barracks unannounced, at who knows what time of the night, and ask me to come over, and I come. Then we get here and we spend half the night talking about your family and what a great time you had in San Francisco. It's now 0515, I haven't had any sleep, and I have formation at 0600. You've been on the telephone with one person or the other for over an hour," she playfully bristled.

"I love the way you get me up in the morning. How did you like the other half of the night?" he asked, still kissing and stroking her body.

"I would have liked it a lot better if, after all of this time that you've been away enjoying yourself in San Francisco, I could have gotten, at least, a whole night with you."

Benny looked up into Stacy's beautiful, light, crystal-brown eyes with a grin on his face.

"Why, Lieutenant Greene, are you trying to tell me, in your own sweet way, how much you missed me?" he asked, slowly pulling Stacy toward him.

"No, Captain Alexander," Stacy said, as she leaped out of bed, wrapping the sheet around herself. "I didn't miss you one little bit."

Benny smiled and rested his head on the palm of his hand, his eyes washing over her sexy body.

"I'll make it all up to you, baby, I promise. You can have me all night tonight. I'll even cook," he said, grinning. "And maybe we can plan something for New Year's Eve together. How does that sound?"

"Sorry, Captain Alexander, you're too late to ask me out for New Year's Eve. I'm going out with this Marine from Camp Pendleton, Ted Peterson. At least *he* wants to put me in first place on his agenda," Stacy said, as she turned on her bare feet, dropped the sheet, and sauntered into the bathroom. Benny watched the sway of her sexy butt, as she walked out of sight. Then he heard the sound of the shower start.

Huh, I wonder what brought that on? Benny wondered. *Put her 'in first place'.* He didn't like the sound of that. He and Stacy had a loose, intimate relationship, but he didn't like the idea that she was seeing someone else, especially not a Marine! *Sounds like we need to talk.* Benny made a few more quick calls and then crept into the shower behind Stacy.

"Stacy, baby, let's talk about this," he said, folding her warm, wet body into his arms.

"Talk about what?" she asked, tilting her head up to look into his eyes.

His breath caught every time he looked into her light brown eyes and fresh, clean smile.

"Let's talk about your wanting to be put 'in first place'. Isn't that what you said?"

"No. I said that I'm going out with someone who wants to put me in first place. I didn't say that it had to be you."

"Oh. Okay. Then, if I understand you correctly, you don't want me to put you in 'first place' in my life? Did I get it right that time?"

"Can't we simply drop this subject? I have to finish my shower. I've got to be out of here like yesterday." She eased out of his arms.

"Let me explain something to you," he said, reaching for her and holding her close. "I have a wonderful family and I love them very much, but I'm not putting them before my relationship with you. You didn't tell me that you wanted to meet my family. In fact, you've made it abundantly clear from the beginning that you did not want to get too entangled. 'Keeping it loose,' you said. Your words, not mine. When I take someone home to meet my family, it's because I've made a commitment. There's nothing 'loose' about it. Do you think that we're at that place in our relationship to be talking about commitment? Are you ready to put me in 'first place' in your life?"

"I don't know where we are in this relationship, but one of the things that I love about you, Benny, is the fact that you do care so deeply for your family. Like the good advice you gave Gregory about getting a good education regardless of what career he thinks he wants now. Like this gold chain that you wear around your neck all the time. It says who you are: FAMILY. I don't have much of a family to speak of, so I enjoy listening to you talk about your mother and father, and Aretha, Gregory, Vivian, Kenneth, your aunts and uncles and cousins, particularly the twins, Donald and James Dixon. You should see yourself. You actually light up when you talk about all of them. Maybe someday I'll want someone to light up like that when he talks about me, but for now, I like our relationship just like it is."

"You're giving me mixed signals. I'm not the one who wants to keep this relationship loose, you are."

"Is it all about the sex for you?"

His brows beetled. "No, it hasn't only been about the sex, Stacy. What's going on?"

"It's nothing, really. Probably just the holidays or being alone. Maybe it's PMS. Who knows? I do know that I don't want to feel like I'm only your lover and not your friend. That I'm only one of your bed partners whenever the mood hits you, which, by the way, has been often and continuously lately."

"That's not the point. Yes, I love making love with you, but—"

"We've both got our careers ahead of us. You're Air Force and I'm Navy. There are no strings attached to this relationship—whatever it is—but I resent not being considered your friend, Benny. That's why I wanted to meet your family, because we're friends, not because we're lovers looking to take this relationship to another level. Do you understand what I am trying to say to you?"

Benny put his hand to his chin quizzically, as the water beat down on his bare chest. "No, but go back to that first part again."

"What first part?"

"The part about 'one of the things you love about me.'"

"Sorry, Fly Boy. That just meant that you're special to me in that way," Stacy said dispassionately.

"What way, Lieutenant?" Benny asked, still smiling.

"You know what I mean. A special friend," she said, with a slight smile.

"So does that mean that you don't love me, Lieutenant? Or does that mean that you are ready to take this relationship to another level and meet my family? Are you ready for me to put a gold FAMILY chain around your pretty neck and a gold wedding band on the third finger of your left hand?"

"Captain," she said, with a crisp salute. "Permission to be dismissed, Sir."

"Permission denied, Lieutenant. At ease," Benny grinned. "I'll never dismiss you, and you know it."

Stacy placed her hands behind her back, as Benjamin thoroughly kissed her. She returned his kiss with equal measure until she felt his nature begin to rise.

"Lower your flaps, Fly Boy, and find another runway to land on. This one is going out of commission," she said, quickly stepping out of the shower.

"We'll pick this up again, you know, Lieutenant. Say about 1800 in my quarters? Full-dressed uniform will *not* be required, and, Lieutenant..." Stacy stopped. "I thought that we were friends—good friends—friends with benefits, not just lovers. Nevertheless, message received loud and clear."

Stacy smiled and disappeared through the bathroom door.

Benny heard Stacy say "good bye" and closed the door to his condo. He let the warm water rush over his body longer than usual, as he thought about Stacy's comments. What was she really getting at and what did he really want from her? No question that she was every man's fantasy. She's beautiful, bright, funny, intelligent, and filled out a uniform like...like...*Man!* Still, where were they taking their relationship? Stacy was calling the shots, as far as he was concerned. She didn't want to fall in love. She made it clear from the beginning that she had dreams of moving up through the military ranks. She wanted to have options in her life and especially in her career. One of only a few Black women who graduated from the Naval Academy in Annapolis, Maryland, with high honors. She is a Black, female senior communication's officer on a Navy aircraft carrier. She fought hard to keep from becoming some Admiral's over-qualified secretary at the Pentagon.

Benny let the water run down his face and remembered that the Pentagon is where they met for the first time. She was working late at the Pentagon on that night. She was taking special courses and working long into the night to prepare herself for active duty aboard a ship. He and his team had flown in some new F15 and F16 fighter jets to Andrews Air Force Base. He was running late for a scheduled meeting with his friend, Colonel John Calvin Baker, who was attached to the office of the Joint Chiefs of Staff. He and J.C. planned to do some serious partying at some clubs in D.C. While he was waiting for J.C. to come out of a meeting, he went to one of the cafeterias for coffee. There were a handful of people in one of the large, nearly empty Pentagon cafeterias and plenty of places to sit. However, he spied a woman wearing a naval officer's uniform in a deserted and dimly lit part of the cafeteria. She seemed to be fighting hard to stay awake. He watched her for a while, as she stood up and stretched. *Ah, nice body*, he thought, as she walked around trying to shake off the sleep that was overtaking her. When she sat down to read again, her eyes closed, and she fell asleep with her head face down in her books. He poured two cups of coffee and walked over to where Stacy was sleeping.

"Heads up, Lieutenant! Incoming!" Benjamin said loudly in his deep, military command voice.

Stacy woke with a start, leaping to her feet and knocking over her chair and her cold coffee. When she focused on the insignia on his uniform, she snapped to attention.

"Excuse me, Sir!" she had said. *"Would you repeat your orders, Sir?!"*

"At ease, Lieutenant. Take a load off," he said to her, amused by her very polished salute.

"Yes, Sir! Thank you, Sir!" Stacy relaxed her stance and found her seat.

They carried on a general conversation while sipping the coffee that he brought. He asked her why she was there so late and what she was working on. She explained the series of special advanced courses that she was taking, which she thought would improve her credentials and prepare her for positions with real challenge, responsibility, and authority. At least something more challenging than what she was doing as a US Navy Liaison Officer and Protocol Administrator to the Japanese Embassy. She talked about her experiences at the Naval Academy and how some of the people in her class received interesting commissions with high promotion potential while she received an assignment to the Pentagon as one of Admiral Gordon's six Liaison Officers. In her opinion, her assignment amounted to nothing more than a glorified office manager. Though she was not complaining, she felt that she needed to improve her standing so that when the opportunity presented itself, she would be qualified to move into a more challenging field position. In the meantime, she was meeting some very influential people who she thought might be willing to assist her with her career aspirations.

Benny listened and thought of how professionally she handled herself. Although she was very attractive and very young, she was beginning to impress him in other ways. Very articulate, aggressive, no nonsense, he thought. Different expectations for herself. Ready for challenges and new discoveries. An explorer, in a sense, like himself. He liked her and he wanted to get to know her better. She was easy to talk with and he wanted to talk more, but, as fate would have it, Colonel John Calvin Baker, III, showed up at the table. Stacy snapped to attention when she saw Colonel Baker approach. He also snapped to attention and smiled broadly at his friend J.C. They embraced and chatted, exchanging barbs, as Stacy stood at attention. Benjamin introduced Stacy to Colonel Baker who said, *"At ease, Lieutenant Greene."* He extended his hand and she shook it forcefully.

"It's a pleasure to meet you, Sir! I've read your articles in the Stars and Stripes. I especially like the one you wrote about the naval communications contribution during Desert Shield and Desert Storm," Stacy had said.

"I didn't know that you could write, J.C.," Benjamin interrupted. *"Back at the Air Force Academy you were always getting us underclassmen to do your dirty work for you. Well, I guess we did a good job, since Lieutenant Greene seems to think that you have something significant to say."*

"Is that any way to speak to a superior officer, Captain? What kind of example are you setting for this young officer," Baker said, with a straight face, nodding toward Lieutenant Greene.

"A good example, Sir!" Benjamin said, with a salute and a smile. *"Telling the truth is always a way of setting a good example, wouldn't you say so, Lieutenant?"*

"Yes, Sir!" she snapped.

Shortly thereafter, he left the cafeteria with J.C., but not before he got Stacy's contact information. He called her the next day after trying to get over a fierce hangover. He and J.C. partied until early in the morning with three gorgeous women who they met at the Hanger Club, but Stacy Greene made an indelible impression on him, not just his libido. By the time Benny woke up, kissed his female over-night companion goodbye, J.C. was gone. J.C. had to fly to San Francisco. Something about multi-billion dollar defense contracts and cutbacks at the Presidio. J.C. was then a light colonel assigned to the Joint Chiefs of Staff. General Colin Powell had long since stepped down as Chairman of the Joint Chiefs, leaving J.C. well positioned in his military career. J.C. left a note for Benny, telling him that the keys to his car and condo were on the kitchen table and for him to enjoy himself while he was there in Washington. Benjamin took that as an order and did just that. Stacy ended up being the first and last mission on his agenda during his brief stay in D.C., he recalled.

In the eleven months since he met Stacy, their friendship grew into a relationship and the relationship—to his way of thinking—was working just fine. He wasn't crazy about the fact that she still dated other men and wouldn't take their relationship seriously. In fact, at times, it wrenched his gut, but Stacy was not a woman who would let you tie her down. She was fiercely competitive and independent. She had that kind of city quickness about her and seemed to be in full possession of herself at all times.

Those were some of the traits that attached him to her. He saw Stacy at a naval base Halloween party with the Marine from Camp Pendleton who she mentioned and he and Stacy talked about her relationship with him. He also saw her on other occasions with other military officers. No strings. No pressure. Just great fun and a lot of laughs. He and Stacy saw each other when the opportunity presented itself. Now they were both stationed in San Diego. Stacy at the North Island Naval Air Station in Corona and he was at March Air Force Base in Moreno Valley. On occasions, he and his flight team were on exchange duty at the Naval Air Station in San Diego.

Although he and Stacy had been seeing each other more regularly, they had only been sleeping together for three months, and that was not frequent. At least, not frequently enough for him. His relationship with her, he thought, was uncomplicated. He had no clue that she was getting serious enough to want to meet his family.

As he got out of the shower, he decided that he wanted to delve into this situation a little more closely that night at dinner. If she was ready to make a commitment exclusively to him, it would be none too soon for him. He had long since been ready to make a commitment to her alone. The telephone rang taking his thoughts from Stacy.

"Captain Alexander," he answered, while he toweled himself dry.

"Benny, I've dispatched a couple of aides to check on Vivian," J.C. Baker said.

"Thanks, man. I owe you one."

"No big thing, Benny. You know how I feel about your family, especially that fine, foxy sister of yours. She seeing anyone these days?"

Something in J.C.'s tone bothered Benny. Maybe that's why Kenneth and J.C. seemed to be at odds. His brother was a good judge of character. Then he thought of his mother's question about his brother. She was usually right with her premonitions and, actually, when he thought about it, Kenneth did seem distracted. He wondered absently whether it had anything to do with the rift between Kenneth and J.C. He'd have to talk with Kenneth again about it. Besides the fact that they were brothers, they were also best friends. For the moment, however, he had to deal with J.C.'s interest in Vivian. He and J.C. partied together often and he knew how J.C. viewed women: Body by Fischer, brain by Mattel. J.C. Baker was a user. Vivian was not going to be one of the women Baker used.

"Yeah, she's got a man and don't forget that she's also got three over-protective brothers, J.C.," he said, laughing.

"Wouldn't touch a hair on her head, my man," he said unconvincingly.

"Yeah, right," Benny said, snorting.

"Speaking of your family, what's up with K.J. these days?"

"Why don't you call him and ask him?"

"Yeah, yeah. I might just do that," J.C. answered. "Well, I'll let you know when I hear something from your sister."

"Thanks, man," Benny said and then hung up.

Chapter 3

"Greetings. This is CompuCorrect. How may I direct your call please?" a pleasant female voice answered.

"This is Colonel J.C. Baker. Is Mr. Kenneth Alexander available?"

"No, I'm sorry, Colonel Baker, but Mr. Alexander is in conference. Could someone else help you? Mr. Jenkins perhaps?" There was a long pause. "Colonel Baker, are you still there?"

"Yes. Let me speak to Thomas," he answered annoyed.

The receptionist connected Baker to Kenneth's business partner, Thomas Jenkins.

"J.C., how are things at the Pentagon? Need my advice on military affairs yet?" Thomas jovially joked.

"I'll let you know when we need you, but I'm fine, Tom, and you?"

"I'm doing just great, partially because of you. I've been meaning to call you to say thanks."

"Thanks for what? I really didn't do anything."

"Sure you did. If you hadn't shown that Request for Proposals (RFPs) in the General Services Administration's news release to me, I might not have found out about the opportunity to bid on the Presidio's computer contract. I say you did a hell of a lot."

"I'm not going to take any credit for your success, Tom. I wasn't the Contracting Officer. You prepared the bid and, from what I hear, you did a great job. The brass at the Presidio is very impressed by your presentation and they're very impressed with the company. People at the Government Services Administration (GSA) said that it was one of the best bids that they received. I think that your company is going to be on their A List for a long time to come."

"Thanks, J.C., I appreciate your comments. It means a lot to a small company like CompuCorrect to get such high praise from people who have looked at a lot of companies and know which ones can deliver—and we can deliver. Kenneth is meeting with the Superintendent and the Budget Director from the San Francisco County school system now. They're going over the details for the computer network system we'll be installing throughout the county. Part of the government's initiative toward wiring all schools and libraries for access to the Internet. As you know, he's big on the Wired Nation stuff and letting everyone, particularly children, have access to the Information Super Highway. Kenneth really is the one who sold the deal on closing the digital divide. Our office party went over big with them too."

"Office party?"

"Yeah. Kenneth's family was in town for the holidays and he had the bright idea to invite not only our families, but also our clients and their families to the holiday office party. That gave our clients an opportunity to look at our operation on a personal level in a relaxed atmosphere. We've been getting nothing but rave reviews since then. The theme of the party was unity—family unity, company unity and customer unity. Kenneth was even forced to broker some new deals during the party," Tom chucked. "Everyone came away feeling that this company is united on a lot of different levels. Ergo, we would be united with our customers and assure them of our dedication to their success. It was a stroke of pure genius. Kenneth's got the Midas touch, all right," Tom said proudly.

"It sounds like Kenneth is really clicking on all cylinders."

"He sure is. The man is a workaholic. He eats, sleeps, and drinks CompuCorrect, Inc., but it's really paying off. Shirley Taylor, our comptroller, tells me that our revenue projections for this month alone are already up twenty-two percent over last year, without including the two, new, large contracts. Kenneth held a staff meeting this morning and he's already talking about contracting to refurbish the upper floors of this building. He was very excited about our corporate future. He wanted everyone's suggestions by January 1," Tom said and laughed, "but we had to remind him that January 1 is a holiday."

"What did he say then?"

"He said *okay, have them in by January 2*." Tom mimicked Kenneth and laughed again.

"Really doesn't sound like Kenneth has much of a social life going on outside of the office."

"If he does, I sure pity his partner. Kenneth is the first one in the office in the morning and the last one to leave at night. I was surprised that he took some time off to show his family around the area. After I met his parents, I understood."

"What do you mean?"

"His parents are 'the buck stops here', 'just do it' kind of people. His father had me to go over the whole operation with him and then, as we were talking, he was taking notes. When I finished he discussed, in detail, mind you, some things that could be done to minimize the burden on the staff. I was very impressed. There were some great suggestions in what he had to say. Then Kenneth's mother, even though she was a guest of honor at the party, made sure that the decorations were done well. She even sent Sara, our receptionist, to a shop for some more flowers. She and Shirley supervised the arrangement of the food on the table and even made us decorate the men's and ladies' rooms with fresh flowers, softer lighting, and little holiday hand towels. The woman is a dynamo."

"That's Sylvia Alexander all right," J.C. said, laughing. "I'm surprised that she didn't give knitting lessons during the party."

"Oh but she did!" Tom said, laughed. "In fact, she found the wife of the Superintendent of Schools, Tess Braxton, sitting in a corner alone. She's a somewhat shy woman. Mrs. Alexander sat beside her, talking for over an hour. They were acting like old friends before that hour was up and Tess Braxton was knitting like a champ before the evening was over. Mrs. Braxton was having so much fun that she didn't want to leave. She sent a huge bouquet of flowers to us and a note saying how much she enjoyed the party and the family atmosphere. Her daughter, Karen Braxton, tried to monopolize Gregory Alexander's time at the party and afterwards, but Juan Garcia's young twin sisters were dead on his case." Tom snorted. "Ah, youth."

"Sorry I missed it. Sounds like it was great fun."

"It was. I'm still jazzed, but I know that you didn't call to get a blow-by-blow on the CompuCorrect holiday festivities. Was there something specific that you wanted to talk with me or Kenneth about?"

"I just wanted to congratulate you on the contract and to wish you all a Happy New Year."

"That's good of you, J.C. If you'll hold on one minute, I think Kenneth's meeting is breaking up. I'll get him on the line. Can you hold?"

"I don't want to disturb him if he's busy."

"No. Please hold on. He's walking back toward my office now." Tom called to his partner. "Kenneth, pick up on line 4, would you? It's J.C. Baker." There was a pause. "He'll be right with you, J.C. He's heading back to his office. I'll talk with you soon and let us know when you're going to be in town. We at least owe you dinner and a few drinks. Okay?"

"Sure, Tom, you take it easy."

Tom hung up, as Kenneth picked up the telephone. Kenneth stood in his office looking out of the window.

"Alexander," he answered sternly, gripping the telephone.

"Hey, my man, how are you?"

"What do you want, J.C.?" Kenneth asked tersely.

"I wanted to congratulate you on your big successes. Tom tells me your company is really growing."

"I've warned you before. Stay away from my company. So, if that's all...."

"So tell me about it."

"You just said that Tom has filled you in on all the details and I'm sure that you didn't call just to hear about CompuCorrect's business ventures." There was tension in his voice. "So what's this about?"

"I've wanted to talk with you for some time. I wasn't sure whether you would be willing to talk with me. Is this any way to treat an old friend? It seems that things still aren't right between us. Even Vivian picked up on that. I want to get together and talk this whole thing over. I'm sure that we can work out something that will be mutually agreeable and profitable for all concerned. I can be in San Francisco next week. Maybe we can just kick back. You know, check out some happenings. Find a few women. How is your schedule?"

"Forget it. There is nothing to talk about."

"What do I say to your family about our friendship? I have to talk with Benny later today and he's asked me to check on Vivian. I thought that, if she had time, I'd take her out to lunch or dinner next week."

"You figure it out, but I don't want you anywhere near my sister or my company. Am I making myself clear?" he said tightly.

"Okay, Kenneth. We'll let it rest, for now, but you know that this isn't the last of it. The big boys have their eyes on you. You're playing a dangerous game and the odds aren't in your favor."

"I don't give a damn what the military or Sandoval Anniston Corporation want. You just remember what I said. Stay away from my family and my company."

"Fat chance," J.C. said, laughing derisively. "You're doing too well. People notice. See you soon, Kenneth."

Kenneth hung up the telephone and sat down in his glove-leather executive chair. He put his head back, swiveled around in his chair, and stared out of the large picture window behind his desk. His head was pounding. He unconsciously balled up his fists. *I've got to get a grip. I'm not going to let J.C. throw me off track. I've got too much to do.* His eyes dropped to the framed pictures of his family sitting on his credenza. He couldn't stop J.C. from contact with Benny, since he was in the line of Benny's commanding officers, but he sure as hell wouldn't permit him anywhere near the rest of his family.

There was a knock on his door and Kenneth swiveled back around to face his desk.

"Come in," Kenneth called out.

Tom stuck his head in the door. His round, cherubic porcelain cheeks held noticeable dimples. His eyes were an interesting shade of moss green and his hair was a curly, dark blonde. He resembled the actor Simon Baker. Not a very tall man, barely six feet tall, but a man with a sunny, cheerful personality. What he didn't have in the height department was more than compensated for by his personality and integrity.

"Hey, Kenneth, I see you're off the phone. It was great to hear from J.C., wasn't it? He had some good things to tell me about our proposal. You two sure had a quick conversation."

"Uh, are you ready for the meeting this afternoon?" Kenneth asked sidestepping any conversation about Colonel Baker. "I want to go over the details for our displays for the Small Business Expo."

"Sure. Who else do you want in on this meeting?"

"See whether Shirley and the other department heads are available. That should be enough for this meeting. We'll include the rest of the staff in on the planning after the holiday."

"Okay. You still want to meet at two o'clock?" Tom asked.

"Yes. Let's do it in Conference Room C. I've got too much confusion going on in my office."

Tom quickly glanced around Kenneth's rigidly neat office. Kenneth's desk was orderly. His round conference table only contained a few reports, all of them neatly stacked. The credenza behind his desk had pictures of his family nicely arranged. The coffee table in front of his sofa was orderly. If this was confusion, Tom thought, his office was a disaster area by comparison. Tom scratched his head and said, "Okay, two o'clock in Conference Room C. I'll tell everyone."

"Thanks, Tom. I'm going to lunch. See you later."

Kenneth got up from his desk and walked out of his office.

Shirley Taylor was standing in front of her office talking with Tom when she noticed Kenneth leaving. She called to him. "Kenneth, do you have a minute?"

"Yes, Shirley, what is it?"

"Tom says that you want to meet at two this afternoon about the Expo and that's fine. Do you want the cost projections ready for the meeting? I haven't quite finished them yet."

"Do the best you can, Shirley. I'm going to lunch."

Kenneth walked away. Shirley stood and looked after him, as he left the building. 'Do the best you can,' she thought. What did that mean? Either he did or he didn't want the cost projections. Wonder what's eating him? She flicked her wrist and noted that according to her watch it was eleven-thirty in the morning. She knew that Kenneth rarely ate lunch unless it was business. He usually worked out during the lunch period. He seemed to be in a foul mood, though, something else that was uncharacteristic of him, but then something seem to have been bothering him for months. Shirley shook off the unsettling feeling and returned to her office.

Kenneth got into his SUV and drove away from his office. It was a chilly day in San Francisco with grey, broken clouds moving swiftly across the sky. There was very little traffic, but when a car horn sounded, he realized that he must have been sitting at a stop sign too long. He drove down the street looking for some place to eat. McDonald's, Burger King, Dominos, Hunan House. Nothing seemed appetizing. He turned his SUV around and headed toward his home in Marin County. Perhaps he would make a light lunch and then go back to the office in time for the meeting. He had plenty of time to do that before two o'clock.

Fifteen minutes later, he pulled into his driveway and sat there with the motor still running. "I've got to snap out of this," he said aloud. He got out of the SUV and started up the walkway.

"Mr. Alexander?" A female voice called from behind him.

He turned quickly to see a young woman dressed in a Post Office uniform standing nearby holding mail in her hand. "Yes. I'm Kenneth Alexander."

"Your mail, Sir. I tried to get your attention before. You seemed to be— well—upset about something. Are you all right?" she asked.

"Sure, I'm fine." He said dryly taking the mail and walking to his front door.

The mail carrier watched him walk away. "You sure are one phine specimen of a man, but you sure don't look fine," he heard her grumble, as she jumped into her vehicle and drove to the next house.

Kenneth walked into his home and tossed the mail on his desk in his den. He loosened his tie, unbuttoned his shirt at the neck, and took off his suit jacket. The house was cold and still. He went into the expansive living room, started a fire in the fireplace, and turned on a few ceiling fans to help circulate in the air. The clouds passing swiftly before the sunlight caused the living room to appear to lighten then darken periodically. He walked into the ultra-modern kitchen and opened one door of the side-by-side, zero-temperature refrigerator. Plenty of leftovers, he noted. He thought about his family's visit. Of course, he would have to dump Vivian's Coq au Vin Nouveau concoction. *She's a great sister*, he thought, *but a lousy cook. Mom really can cook though,* he reminisced around a smile. He recalled how she spent the last day of her vacation cooking several different meals and packaging them individually in little covered Styrofoam trays. *"All you need to do, Kenneth James,"* she had instructed, *"is to take one of the trays out of the freezer and pop it in the microwave to heat."* She worried too much about him, he mused, and she had made a lot of meals. His freezer was full top to bottom with trays of food, but nothing appealed to him. He took a can of tomato soup out of the cupboard and poured it into a soup mug. Sprinkling it with fresh basil from his kitchen garden, he put the cup in the microwave oven. There was still fruit salad left in the refrigerator, so he scooped some onto the lettuce and fresh, raw spinach he placed on a plate. He got the sea toast from on top of the breadbox and headed for the living room. Putting more old shredded newspapers and logs into the fireplace, the flames catch quickly and blazed up around the logs. Kenneth gazed into the flames, as the edges of the logs began to pop and crackle. He returned to the kitchen and retrieved his hot soup.

Now back in the living room, he sat on the floor on a stack of cushions between one of the sofas and the highly polished coffee table that he built and placed directly across from the fireplace. The flames were spiking as he intently gazed at them. Warmth from the heat exchanger flooded the room while the ceiling fans evenly spread it. Kenneth sat in the silence, deep in his own thoughts.

Later, the phone on Kenneth's belt vibrated. He looked at the text message. It read 'call the office'. He got up from the floor, flipped open his cell phone, and speed-dialed his office.

"Greetings. This is CompuCorrect. How may I direct your call?" Sara's pleasant voice came through the telephone at him. "Oh, Mr. Alexander, I just noticed your phone number on the caller ID box."

"Sara, who's texting me?"

"Ms. Taylor and Mr. Jenkins asked me to get in touch with you. I tried to reach you on your cell phone, but I didn't get any answer. They're waiting for you to start the meeting."

"Meeting? The meeting isn't until two o'clock."

"It's two-forty now, Mr. Alexander. Do you want me to get Mr. Jenkins or Ms. Taylor on the phone for you? They're all in Conference Room C."

Kenneth looked at his watch. Sara was right about the time. Where had the day gone? This thing with Baker had to be settled, he thought, and soon.

"Mr. Alexander, are you still there?"

"Yes, Sara, I'm here. Put Shirley on the line please."

Sara connected Kenneth to Shirley in the conference room.

"Kenneth. This is Shirley. Are you all right?"

"Of course, I'm all right. Why does everyone keep asking me that?" he snapped, then sobered. "I'm fine." He caught himself. "Damn! I'm sorry. I didn't mean to snap at you."

"No apology needed. You've been working too hard the last few months." Shirley now whispered so that the other staff could not hear her conversation. "You seem a little distracted today after your meeting with Superintendent Braxton. Did everything go well in the meeting?"

"Yes, everything is fine. We start wiring all of the schools in the county, as soon as school lets out for the summer." Kenneth grabbed the back of his neck and stretched. "Look, Shirley, I have a headache." He stammered. "You, Tom, and the other managers go over the details for our Small Business Expo exhibit. Record the meeting and I'll listen to the tape later. I'm going to take the rest of the afternoon off and you all do the same after the meeting. Let the staff go home early too and enjoy what's left of the holiday season. They deserve it."

"Take the rest of the afternoon off? Are you sure you're all right? What's going on here? You haven't really taken time off in years."

"I told you, I have a headache."

"Okay, I'll tell everyone. I know that they'll appreciate it."

"Thanks, I'll see you tomorrow."

Kenneth closed his phone and collapsed onto the sofa. The soup was cold and the salad wilted. He hadn't eaten any of it. He placed more logs on the flame, as the old logs began to breakup into large pieces of glowing embers. He stood beside the fireplace. "Damn! Damn! Damn!" he muttered pounding his fist on the mantle so hard that it jarred the framed pictures of his family. He picked up the most recent family portrait made on their recent holiday visit. His family was precious to him and Baker was a threat to them and many more. Baker had to be stopped by any means necessary.

* * *

Someone rang the doorbell and Kenneth got up from the sofa where he was reclining to answer it. He looked at his watch. It was late. He wondered who would be stopping by at that hour.

"Shirley. Uh...how are you? Uh, is something wrong?" he asked with concern finding Shirley Taylor, a five-foot, five Halley Berry look alike with calm brown eyes and a slender build standing at his front door.

"No, Kenneth, nothing's wrong. Are you busy?" she asked.

"Oh, no," he said stepping aside. "Please come in. Have a seat in the front living room. May I get something for you to drink?"

"No, thank you. I was on my way home from work and I thought that I'd drop off the disks of the meeting so that you could listen to what we came up with for the Expo."

"You're just leaving the office? Shirley, it's nearly nine o'clock. Why were you there so late?"

"I wanted to finish the cost projections for the Expo exhibits. I also started work on the Annual Report. It's going to be quite impressive. I thought you might want to use it as a marketing tool during the Expo."

"I told you to let everyone go home early. That 'everyone' included you too."

"I'm on my way home now. Here are the disks. I've marked them in chronological order."

"Shirley, I'm the boss, remember? When the boss says take the afternoon off, I mean take the afternoon off," Kenneth said jokingly.

Hands to hips, Shirley huffed. "You can be the boss anytime you want to Kenneth James Alexander, but I know that you have worked all night sometimes. And if you can do it, *partner*, so can I," Shirley said firmly, but spoiled it with a smile.

Kenneth put up both hands in mock surrender. "Okay, I should have known better than to try to boss *you* around. Have you had dinner yet?"

"No and I missed lunch thinking that I needed to be ready for that two o'clock meeting that you called."

Properly chagrined, Kenneth said, "I'm sorry about that. Let me make it up to you. Have dinner with me. My treat. I haven't eaten today either."

"Do you want to go out somewhere?"

"Not necessarily. I have plenty of food in the freezer. It certainly wouldn't take long to prepare. My mother stocked it before she left and I couldn't possibly eat everything she cooked. Here, sit down. Relax," Kenneth said showing Shirley to one of the sofas in the living room. "What would you like to drink?"

"White wine, if you have it."

"Imported or domestic?"

"Domestic, of course. You can't live this close to Napa County and not drink its wine. You'd be kicked off the board of directors for the Chamber of Commerce for high treason," Shirley joked.

Kenneth filled two, fine-crystal glasses and handed one to Shirley.

Silently saluting each other, they sipped the wine.

Kenneth smiled. "You're right, this is good wine. Would you like chicken, beef, fish or pork for dinner?"

"Your mother really must have laid out a spread. That's a lot to choose from," she said laughing.

"She did, but her Chicken Florentine is world renowned and I have a taste for that. How about you?"

"Sounds great."

Kenneth went to the kitchen and pulled two trays of Chicken Florentine out of the freezer and put them on plates and then into the microwave oven to heat. Then he got the ingredients for a salad out of the refrigerator.

Shirley slipped out of her shoes and went to the fireplace. She looked at each of the pictures on the mantle. There was one picture with all of Kenneth's family posing together. Shirley kissed her finger and pressed it over Kenneth's face in the picture.

"You have a nice looking family," Shirley called out so that Kenneth could hear her. "Vivian had a lot of hair in this picture. It's very different from how she wears it now."

He returned to the living room whipping his hands on a dishtowel and noticed that she was holding the family portrait.

"That's a picture from several years ago. Vivian has always had a lot of long, thick hair. She played basketball in high school and college and wore her hair long, but she cut it off before she went to law school. She said that she didn't have time to fool with it anymore. Now according to her all that she has to do is wash it and wear it. I think that she looks good with a close-cut hairstyle, but my mother was very disappointed. She preferred her with two big plaits, like this picture." Kenneth was pointing to a picture of Vivian at age ten with two thick plaits and two big bow ribbons in her hair. He noticed that the flames had died down in the fireplace, so he stoked it and added more logs.

"Wow, who are all of these people?" Shirley asked, pointing to a three-foot-long, oblong picture.

Kenneth chucked. "First cousins. About a hundred of them at last count. We took that picture years ago at Myrtle Beach, South Carolina. One of my grand aunts has a home there right on the beach. It's that big Victorian in the background. Once a year all of the first cousins who are still in school get together for a last hurrah on the Labor Day weekend and literally camp out on the beach in tents. Since I'm not in school anymore, I haven't been in several years, but it's still a family tradition," he said, smiling at the picture.

"Sure are a lot of cousins. Looks like these two are twins," she noticed.

Kenneth smiled affectionately. "There are an inordinate number of twins and even triplets in my family, but that's Donald and James Dixon—my Aunt Olivia's and Uncle Romelo's sons." He went on to name the other cousins in the picture. "What about your family?" Kenneth asked. "I've only met your sister, Eileen, her husband, Forbes, and your nieces and nephews."

"She's about all that I have. My family is from a small town in Texas called Baytown. We still have some cousins there, but we don't keep in touch. Certainly not the way your family does. I see my sister and her family from time to time, but she has five children and a husband to keep her busy. I can't take all of that commotion for long periods of time, so I just go to Sacramento to visit her occasionally."

Kenneth laughed. "You sure wouldn't survive an Alexander family get-together, if you don't like commotion. It gets pretty wild around the farm at home when we all get together, especially during the annual Fourth of July family reunion. Hundreds show up for that event. My parents' farm is very large and family literally comes rolling in from around the country in campers, RVs, mobile homes, and set up a village on the farm. My father put in a swimming pool several years ago just for that occasion. Everyone in the family loves to swim and that keeps all the little people in one place. We also use the high school campus for activities."

"He did that just for one day?" Shirley asked, surprised.

"'One day'? Oh no, Shirley, our family reunions are four-or five-day events, every year," he laughed. "Vivian, Benny, and I aren't there during the summer much anymore. Only Aretha and Gregory. When we start getting ready for the family reunion, my father always has Gregory working from can't see in the morning to can't see at night." He laughed. "My mother has Aretha in one program or another."

They both laughed.

"During the Fourth of July reunion, Aretha and Gregory get to go swimming, huh?"

"They swim every day in the summer. So do my parents. On his birthday, August first, my father lets Gregory have a pool party. Dad's not a hard man, but firm in his convictions. Mom is the strict one and she wears it proudly," he chuckled. "She was time enough for all of us and she still is. When she gets an idea in her head, there's no moving her. The problem is that she's usually right. She can be a pistol sometimes. Vivian gets her steel constitution from our mother and Vivian can have a razor sharp tongue too. We all toe the line around Sylvia Benson Alexander. Even my father. Still, I've never seen two people more in love than my parents. They fiercely respect and protect each other. They still hold hands after all these years."

"Sounds like you had a happy childhood."

"We did. We weren't wealthy by any stretch of the imagination, but we were always surrounded by loving family members. My grandparents, their sisters and brothers, cousins. It was great growing up in Goodwill, Summer County, South Carolina." His eyes lit with private, warm memories, Shirley noted. "Sometimes, as children, we would sleep outside and just count the stars. It's a vast universe," he said smiling at the pictures on the mantle. "It helped us to put things in prospective. We lived a very uncomplicated existence. Nothing like what children have to suffer through now. Vivian and I have a theory about what it's like to grow up now in the city as compared to growing up then in the country."

"What is it?" Shirley asked, sincerely interested. She loved to watch him, hear his deep mellifluous tones, warm like a liqueur when it smoothed its way through a body.

"We believe that if people can live less complicated lives, move out of the cities, build a life where you can see the sky and see what's really important in life. Know how insignificant the need to amass fortunes is, in the scheme of things, we all could resolve so much of the world's problems. Some children don't see the sky anymore. You remember this old movie, *Grand Canyon?*" he asked, looking into her eyes.

Shirley's breath hitched. "No, I haven't seen many movies," Shirley said. His face and body were a study in male perfection and he was clueless to the effect that his mere presence had on women.

"There is a scene at the end of the film where the characters with far different backgrounds journey to the Grand Canyon together. As they look out over its vastness of that natural wonder, you see how their lives pale by comparison. How they look at themselves and each other from a different point of view, metaphorically speaking. That's what we've had all of our lives in the South…a different point of view. Vivian and I call it our southern exposures. For all of us, there's nothing more important than to live and work for family."

"You and Vivian seem very close," she said, just above a whispered awe.

"We are, but Benny's her partner in crime," he mused, smiling. "She and I share philosophically most of the same positions about life and living. She and Benny actually live life. It takes all of us though to keep Gregory and Aretha on short leashes." His smile brightened. "I failed to do that this holiday. Gregory and Aretha raided my closet like they were shopping at Nordstrom with someone else's gold card," he said and laughed.

"You miss being at home with your family, don't you?" Shirley asked, her head tilting to one side.

" I do, yes," he said, somewhat sobered. "I didn't realize how much until this past holiday."

"But your family came to visit you here in San Francisco. Wasn't that like being at home?"

Kenneth smiled, but shook his head. "It was great having my family here for the holiday, but it wasn't like being at home with Vivian, Aretha, Gregory, and Benny all making much mischief. The family compound at home in Goodwill is not to be believed during the holidays. To me, it's what family truly means. Benny and I both miss it a lot."

"Speaking of Benny, he called you at the office late today. When I told him that you went home early with a headache, he said that he'd call you tomorrow."

"Did he say what he wanted?"

"No. He was just very surprised that you weren't at work and said that he'd call tomorrow," she shrugged absently.

Kenneth looked at his watch. "I know my brother. He's out on the town somewhere by now, partying with a woman on each arm. I don't know how the kid keeps up. He keeps getting excellent commendations and promotions, so I know he's competent when he's flying his jet and leading his team, but how he does it with his social life is far beyond me. He loves women and they seem to love him." Kenneth shook his head and smiled.

"What about you, Kenneth? Do you have a social life?"

Kenneth shrugged absently. "Not much of one, I guess. According to Benny I don't. He says that I need 'balance' in my life," he said and laughed.

"Is he right?"

"When I'm working on all cylinders, I have balance. Doing what we're doing, creating jobs, breaking into new business areas, closing the digital divide is exciting to me. I love it. Right now, that's all the 'balance' I need or want. I still take time to look at the sky though."

They both laughed.

Kenneth returned to the kitchen and Shirley followed him. She sat at the center post, cooktop, breakfast bar in the homey, but large, modern kitchen while Kenneth tossed the salad. He talked while he worked, but Shirley was looking at his beautiful cinnamon brown skin, dark brown eyes, and full lips. A five-o'clock shadow had formed and accentuated his strong, square jaw and white teeth. His broad sculptured shoulders and arms were not hidden under his sleeveless Georgia Tech crew-neck warm-up that followed loosely the curvature of his broad chest and narrow waist. A gold chain that read "FAMILY" hung around his neck. Athletic-cut jeans that were cut off just above the knee, was fitting him loosely, but Shirley could see the outline of his long, sinewy, muscular thighs. She had seen him wearing only a jock strap and spandex with loose-fitting workout shorts on many occasions. The sight of him excited her. The confidence in his stride. His easy smile and hearty laughter. The sincerity in his voice and demeanor. The bravado in the entire package that was Kenneth James Alexander that people naturally gravitated toward and basked in his geniality. To her, he was Alexander the Great, the Phenomenal Man.

Kenneth took the hot plates of food out of the microwave oven and placed them on the round table in an alcove.

"Nothing fancy, Shirley," he said, seating her at the table.

"It smells great," she added, as she inhaled deeply.

They talked as they ate and drank wine. They laughed about the early days of CompuCorrect. How she found old, sturdy, wooden doors that she stained and converted to work stations, comfortable sofas from a hotel that was remodeling, and remnants of upholstery that she stretched over wooden frames and made large pictures for the otherwise large, bare warehouse walls. She hung vertical blinds at the oversized windows and placed big potted plants at strategic locations throughout the office. Those plants were now large, potted trees. She had personally supervised the reconstruction of the restroom facilities paying special attention to the women's room. She had scoured the junk yards and found old bar stools that she painted and reupholstered for work stools and some old wooden desks from a Stanford University dormitory that were badly discolored and scratched, but she thought, salvageable. Kenneth refinished each one beautifully. The office smelled of bees wax and lemon oil. No sterile office dividers, but real wood and pleasing fabrics. She had done a lot on the budget that had been allotted for the furnishings. Indeed, she even had enough left over to buy a brand new 20-cup coffee center for the office, complete with reusable coffee cups. No Styrofoam cups for this outfit. No, sir! She was not going to spend the better part of her day cleaning up the makeshift lounge area. *"If you drink the coffee,"* she had announced one day to the staff, *"you had better have your own cup."* She was the *"business manager, not the hostess,"* she announced, and she was not making the coffee or cleaning it up. And she never did.

Those were the early days of CompuCorrect. Now the company was very profitable thanks to Kenneth, but it still looked like someone's comfortable home heated and cooled with stained concrete floors and hanging studio lighting and ceiling fans. And, indeed, it was to the staff.

Then Shirley said, "This is the most I've heard you talk about non-business matters since I met you six years ago. I was a little concerned about you today. You really didn't seem like yourself. A little distracted, detached."

Shirley detected a change in Kenneth's mood, as he abruptly rose from the table and picked up their empty plates. He didn't comment until he returned to the table.

"You're a good listener, Shirley. I'm not sure why I chose tonight to talk so much."

"I've enjoyed it. You really light up when you talk about your family. Besides, I like to think of myself as your friend, not just your business partner."

"You are a friend and maybe we should do this more often, but now it's very late. I'm concerned about you driving around this time of the night. I have several guest rooms if you'd like to stay overnight."

The thought appealed to her. She wanted nothing more than to spend a cozy night wrapped in Kenneth's arms, but his mood and demeanor told her that this would not be the night to broach the subject with him.

"Nothing to worry about. I don't live that far from here, but I'd like to take you up on your offer of dinner sometime soon. Maybe at my place. What are you doing for New Year's Eve?" She smiled at Kenneth, but he seemed distracted, again as if he hadn't heard her. "You're right. I should be going."

Kenneth's thoughts were back to J.C. Baker. On his day off, he finally resolved in his mind what had to be done. It could be dangerous for so many people, but the thought of doing nothing at all would be worse. It could be catastrophic.

Shirley, moving toward the door, snapped his attention back to her.

"I'll walk you to your car," he said helping her with her coat.

Kenneth and Shirley walked out of the front door and down the driveway to her car. It was a clear, cool, comfortable night. Rare for San Francisco in late December. All of the clouds had passed away.

"Goodnight, Shirley," Kenneth said, as he opened her car door for her.

"Goodnight, Kenneth," she said, as she turned and hugged him, kissing him on the cheek. "I'll see you in the morning."

Kenneth was surprised at the show of intimacy from Shirley, as he watched her drive away. They had been friends when they and Tom worked for the Sandoval Anniston Corporation, but, although Shirley was a very bright and attractive woman, he never had amorous feelings toward her. Shaking his head, he grabbed the back of his neck and stretched, as he walked back into his home. "Women. Go figure," he said to the air. Unlike Benny, he had not made much time in his life for women having been considered pretty much of a nerdy type in his youth. It certainly wasn't that he didn't desire women because he did, but he hadn't made it a mission to seduce every woman who crossed his path the way Benny did. The few affairs that he had were physically satisfying, but not emotionally stimulating. Physical beauty and/or satisfying sexual needs alone simply weren't what he wanted in a woman. He wanted much more. Someone who stimulated his intellect, as well as his loins, but he hadn't found anyone like that, and at the moment, finding a woman to share his life was the last thing on his agenda. The first thing was dealing with Baker and the military industrial complex and corporate interests that he represented. Baker was right about one thing though. He was dealing in a dangerous area, but it was worth the risk. He could let nothing, absolutely nothing, stand in his way. The stakes were entirely too high.

Chapter 4

Vivian squinted through one bleary eye, as the sun reached an uncovered part of her bedroom window. Pulling herself from sleep's grasp, she tried to move, but Carlton's arm was draped across her waist, his chest to her back, and his leg across her thighs. Sometime in the night, he had come to her bed, but, thankfully, he had only held her.

"Don't go yet, baby," Carlton whispered groggily, as she shifted. Kissing her bare back, he crooned. "Let's just lay here like this a little longer? I want, no, I need to make—"

"I'm not up for that, Carlton," she said and sighed. "I had a long trip home and not much rest."

"Neither have I, Viv," he groaned, still feathering kisses across her back. "I drove all evening and all night in that blizzard to be with you." He held her tighter against his body. "I'm sorry about last night. I don't want to fight with you."

"That's all we seem to do, Carlton. It isn't getting us anywhere and it isn't getting any better."

His heated body, his phallus was, hard and strong, against her bare butt. "We'll make it better, baby," he groaned, kissing her shoulder and moving to her ear. "I promise. We'll make it better."

Vivian stiffened when his hand cupped her breast. She wanted to pull away, but couldn't, as he enveloped her with his powerful arms and legs. One arm held her in a loose choke hold while, with his free hand, he kneaded her abdomen to her pubis. She clamped his roaming hand and pulled away.

"I'm going to make breakfast," she said, planting her feet on the floor and looking over her shoulder at him.

The look of anger mixed with frustration was apparent in his eyes, as he leaned back against a pillow, a large hard hand coming down over his face.

"I'll do that," he said tightly. "I'll take a quick *cold* shower and I'll have breakfast…uh, lunch," he said, looking at his watch, "ready in thirty minutes." He pulled the covers off his nude body and stood to stretch.

"No one seems to want me to do any cooking. Why is that?" Vivian asked, as Carlton headed for the bathroom.

"Well, babe, suffice it to say, it wasn't your culinary technique that I fell in love with. You need a recipe to boil water," Carlton offered with a sly smile and a wink. He picked up the robe from the floor. "This looks like a man's robe. Whose is this?" Carlton asked with a raised eyebrow. "And by the way, I saw two sets of footprints in the snow last night. Who was the guy?"

"Oh, uh, Benny left the robe here the last time he was in town. He must have forgotten where he left it because he hasn't asked me to send it to him. Not that he'd need it," she muttered.

"Oh?"

"Can I be held to blame for my brother's absentmindedness? I'm sure that he never remembers where he's left articles of his clothing."

"I'll be sure to mention to him that I saw his robe in Washington. I'll let him figure out where," Carlton said, as he slipped into the robe. "And the man?"

Vivian's brows drew together, puzzled. "What man?"

"Big footsteps in the snow?"

"Oh, uh, a couple of people caught a ride home from the airport with this guy who had a four-wheel-drive truck. If he hadn't given us a ride, I might still be stranded at the airport."

"A brother? In a four-wheel-drive truck? Odd."

"No, he wasn't a brother," she said absently.

"I see…" He folded his arms across his chest. "So why did he come in? If he only gave you a lift?"

She rolled her eyes, silently praying for patience. "He carried my luggage through the snow up on to the porch and then he left."

"He didn't come into the house?"

Her prayers weren't answered and she snapped. "Look, Carlton, I don't know what you're trying to say in this situation, but let me clear something up real quick. Number one. I resent being questioned. Number two. You're the one hung up over skin pigment, not me. And number three. Don't you *ever* accuse me of being a liar."

"I never said—"

She held up one hand to forestall his retort.

Guaging her anger, he continued to the bathroom.

Vivian sank into the warm bed and stared blankly out of the window. The wind was still fiercely blowing, but the sun was brightly shining. The old fears about Carlton returning, his jealously wasn't endearing him to her. She had been completely faithful. Carlton was still trying to make her feel loved. There was no mistake about that. He still didn't understand. Neither did anyone else. Everyone tried to tell her what a lucky woman she was to have him care so deeply for her.

She grabbed the pillow where his head had rested, pulled it close to her body, and squeezed it tightly. Carlton is handsome, articulate, and bright, but they hadn't worked out their problems. She wasn't ready to make a commitment to him. She knew what he wanted. He wanted her to trust him again, to depend on him, and to give up her career goals for him. He promised that it would never happen again. That he would not hurt her again. That, when she married him, he would be a faithful husband and good father, too. There must be some flaw in her character, she surmised, that would not let her trust him fully. Not permit her to make a commitment, give up her career goals, and follow him around the country. She knew that she would have to be careful over the next few days while he was with her. If her father was right, and Carlton was going to propose marriage to her, she would have to be on her guard and choose her words carefully in telling him that she was not ready. In the meantime, she would swallow her fears and try to enjoy having him there. After all, he had driven so many hours through a blizzard to be with her. They had not been together in over six months.

"I'm through in the bathroom," Carlton said, returning freshly showered. "You got some lotion I can use? I left my bag in my car."

Vivian reached for the lotion on her nightstand and spurted some in Carlton's outstretched hand. He sat on the bed, as she pulled up behind him to massage the lotion over his smooth, thick, broad shoulders. His bunched muscles flexed, as he vigorously rubbed the lotion on his legs and feet. Kneeling forward, she massaged lotion on his broad chest and hard, concaved abdomen.

Carlton leaned back against her and closed his eyes. "Mmm, I love it when you touch me like that. It turns me on."

"You can do the rest," she said, covering herself with the silk sheet, stretching out across the bed, and resting her head on the palm of her hand.

Carlton glimpsed at her over his shoulder, but otherwise said nothing.

She watched him, as he continued to rub lotion on the rest of his body, and marveled at what a beautiful physique he had. Not an ounce of fat anywhere on his finely sculptured torso. Why couldn't that be enough for her? Many women loved their men for one-dimensional reasons—pretty eyes, tall frame, bowlegs, broad shoulder, or a handsome face—but that had not been enough for her and it never would be. In some important areas, they were as philosophically different as night and day. She didn't mind little differences, enjoying a healthy debate on issues was stimulating, but there were some very deep-seated differences that she had difficulty reconciling.

Carlton finished putting lotion on his face and noticed that she was staring at him. "What?" A questioning smile graced his lips.

"You're quite a sexy hunk, you know?" To admit the truth didn't cost her anything, she reasoned. Carlton's blush made her feel better and, apparently, him, too. That broad smile and sparkle in his eyes could even brighten a sunny summer day.

"Are you flirting with me, I hope?"

"Just an observation," she said absently.

"Vivian, I swear, I never know what you are going to say or do next." Carlton shook his head, amused at her directness. "Now what am I supposed to say to that comment, 'No I'm not a hunk' or 'I work out regularly' or 'I've seen better'? Sometimes you really catch me off guard. I always have to be on my toes around you." He crawled onto the bed and kissed her quickly. "Brunch in thirty minutes." He kissed her again more hungrily. "To be continued," Carlton said, as he gazed into her eyes. "And, Viv, please, don't give up on us. Give our love another chance. You won't be sorry this time. I promise." He kissed her again, slipped into the robe, and left the bedroom.

Vivian groaned her frustration into her bunched pillow.

After Vivian showered and dressed, she was feeling better about Carlton, but not comfortable. Why did breaking up have to be so painful? For months, he had been trying so hard to keep them together and she felt guilty not telling him how she really felt. He deserved to know the truth: That if they couldn't work out their problems in the relationship, how could they ever make a commitment as important as marriage? Yet, she felt something akin to pity that she hadn't tried hard enough to make the relationship work. Too many Black women gave up too soon and left their men. She wasn't that type of woman. Maybe she should try harder. At least while he was there. She owed him that much. After all, he had changed a lot over the years for her. She exhaled slowly, but resolutely. One more effort wouldn't hurt, would it?

Vivian whizzed through her housekeeping chores. Sitting on the sofa bed near a window in her bedroom and admiring her work, that pesky thought came to her again. Chuck Montgomery. She shook it off and pushed a button on her cell phone. Nine messages from her family. She'd have to call all of them back after brunch. Two messages from the Family Homeless Shelter confirming that she would put in a few hours on the twenty-ninth and thirtieth to screen new residents. One message from each of her four housemates—Gloria Towson, a Black female from Santa Barbara, California, called to wish her a happy holiday and to get Benny's phone number in San Diego. Melissa Charles, a white female from Providence, Rhode Island, called to say that she was back in town, but that she would be spending some time at her boyfriend's apartment. She left a number where she could be reached. William "Bill" Chandler, a bisexual, White man from Bronx, New York, said that because of the storm, he would stay in New York until after the holiday. Lastly, David Carter, a Black man from Minneapolis, Minnesota, called to say that he was going to stay a few extra days in Miami, Florida. Well, she thought, she and Carlton would be alone for a few days. Not a particularly happy prospect.

Something delicious filtered up from the kitchen. Vivian brushed her damp, short hair flat against her head and bounded down the steps. Carlton was tossing a salad, as she came into the large, airy, and sun-filled kitchen. She peeked into the microwave oven through the glass door and sniffed deeply.

"Ah, that smells good. Is that the lasagna that you made yesterday?"

"Yes it is. That cooler kept it cold and the Caesar salad was still crisp when I opened it. The ice packs hadn't even melted. Now, my dear, Ms. Alexander, you get to set the table. Brunch should be ready in a few minutes." Carlton finished pouring his homemade salad dressing over the Caesar salad.

Vivian pulled two, bright-red, lunch plates and matching salad bowls from the drying rack above the double sink, and walked to the twelve-seat, butcher-block, kitchen trestle table beside the curved wall-to-wall, ceiling to floor window. The snow-filled, expansive backyard and Rock Creek Park lay beyond. She flipped on the audio system to her favorite Howard University jazz station and found Paul Taylor's soulful sounds filling room. She pulled two water goblets and two wine glasses from an overhead swinging rack and placed them on the table. At the double-door refrigerator, she placed the water goblets under the ice shoot. Several cubes bounced into each goblet. She filled them both from the bottled water stand by the refrigerator.

"Okay, what else do I need?" She turned toward Carlton.

Carlton quickly scanned the table and mused sarcastically, "I think silverware and napkins might be useful."

"Carlton," she lamented, "you know that I don't do domestic stuff well."

"I know, baby, but you do try and I appreciate that." He smiled at her. "Would you get the wine out of the cooler and pop the cork?"

"You didn't bring some kind of wine that has to breathe or something, did you?" She lifted the lid on the cooler. Then audibly gasped. Her eyes widened and her mouth dropped open, as she lifted and opened a small, clear, square flower box. A beautiful white orchard, a baby-blue silk ribbon, and a diamond ring perched in the middle sparkled in the sunlight. Suddenly, she had no appetite. Her mouth went dry. She heard no music playing. She was numb.

"Soups on! Let's eat!" Carlton purposefully ignored Vivian's surprise and bewilderment. He lifted the lasagna from the counter and walked to the table. "Are you going to stand there with your mouth gaping or are you going to get that wine that I asked you for?"

"Wine? Wine? Oh, yeah," she muttered. She picked up the wine bottle and walked to where Carlton stood plating lasagna and putting the salad into the bowls. He took the wine from her and kissed her on the cheek.

Snapping his finger in front of her face, he asked, "Silverware, Vivian. You do remember silverware, don't you?"

"Oh, yeah, silverware," she muttered, laconically.

She turned robotically, gathered a handful of silverware and handed them to Carlton.

Shaking his head at the assortment she handed to him, a smile creased his face. "Here, baby, you sit right here." He placed her in a chair. "You seem to be a little out of it. I'll get the silverware, napkins, and...uh...do you have any butter?"

"Butter? Butter? I think so. Oh, I don't know," she said, flustered, raking one hand through her damp hair. "Uh, look in the cupboard. I mean, the stove. The refrigerator," Vivian stammered, still in a daze.

Carlton laughed. "Get it together, old girl." He returned to the oven, retrieved a long, silver wrapped package of steaming hot garlic bread, and placed it on the table. "Cork screw, cork screw." He looked around the kitchen. "Ah, yes, here it is." He grabbed the bottle of wine and began to screw the device into the top. He glimpsed Vivian's still stunned expression and grinned. "No, this doesn't have to breathe, baby," he sniffed the cork, "but you have to breathe sometime soon, don't you think?" He sat down across from her. "Come on and eat before your food gets cold." He grabbed Vivian's right hand and bowed his head. "Lord, bless this food and the wonderful woman who I am sharing this meal with today. She is my life's blood, Lord, and I love her more than my next breath. I know that I am not worthy of receiving her love in return, but please, Lord, help her to make the decision to be my wife and I will cherish her all the days of our lives. Amen."

When Carlton looked up from his prayer and looked directly into her eyes, she could feel the tears rolling down her cheeks. She heard his fervent prayer, but did not shared the sentiment. Instead, her prayer was for the strength of courage to weather what was to come.

Carlton poured the wine into their glasses, handed a glass to her, and then held his glass up to her, as if to make a toast. "If you didn't recognize it, Vivian Lynn Alexander, that was a proposal. I know that you've been having some doubts about us lately, but we can work through that as long as we're together. We've been together and in love for nearly three years. I've disappointed you before, but I'll never hurt you again. I'm committed to you and I want us to spend the rest of our lives together. I do love you. Just say, yes, baby."

Vivian didn't know what to think, what to feel or what to do. As she looked into Carlton's pleading eyes, she wished this moment never happened. Her heart was racing and her head was pounding. She had to focus on the good things about their relationship. It was hard to do now, but there were good things. Were they enough? They had to be. There would be time, she assured herself. Time to work things out.

"Please try, Vivian. I promise you won't be sorry. I need you. Only you," he said, gazing lovingly and longingly into her eyes.

"Yes," she heard herself whisper, regretting it the moment the single syllable slipped from her lips.

"Yes!" he said loudly, balling his fist and yanking the air. He untied the ring from the silk ribbon and placed it on the third finger of her left hand. It was a little too tight, but it finally slipped on.

Sitting back in her chair, Vivian looked at the ring on her finger and suddenly remembered what her mother had cautioned. *"If it don't fit, don't force it." What have I done? What in the world have I done?* Carlton had taken her completely by surprise. She lost her appetite, but not her mind. She forced herself to eat, but she couldn't taste anything. Her mind was blown. She could not speak. Across from her, Carlton was chatting away, talking about all the people they needed to call to announce their engagement. They would have a formal engagement party at her parents' home sometime in the spring, he was saying. Then something about a fall or winter wedding.

"Hold on here, Carlton. What did you say?" She finally snapped out of her near trance.

"I said we should have a formal engagement party at your parents' home in May and then have the wedding in the fall. Maybe September or October before the basketball season starts. That way we can take a two-week honeymoon so we can get pregnant and it won't interfere with the start of the season. We'll have plenty of time to get you moved on campus in the next few months after March Madness...."

"Move on campus? October wedding? Engagement party? I can't get married right away, Carlton! I'm in law school! Remember? I've got two and a half years to go before I can even think about wedding plans and engagement parties."

"Baby, in two and a half years I want us to be working on our second child. Why do you think I want a two-week honeymoon?" He grinned. "We'll start our family right away. You can handle a lot, V, but law school and babies? I don't think so. Besides, I don't want my wife to have to work. That's what a husband is for, to provide for his family. Your role is to raise the children, take care of the house and your husband. Once I make it to the NBA as a coach—."

Something inside Vivian snapped. *"Hello! My role?* Time out, Andrews. We've got a foul on this play. You've got me engaged, married, with one baby and another one on the way?" she bristled.

"Of course, Vivian, our time is now. We're young and healthy. What better time than the present to start our family? I want us to grow together. To grow old together and more in love, just like your parents are." He took her hands in his and kissed her ring. "My father died when I was very young. A little bit of my mother died with him. I don't want to waste one moment of the life we can have together. You have a big family with lots of people to share your happiness with. You wear that gold chain around your neck that says that you're a part of a family. I want us to begin the Andrews-Alexander branch of that family. Do you understand?"

Vivian's thoughts were racing and her heart was pounding. She tried to calm herself. "I think you've hit the nail on the head."

"What are you talking about, V?"

"Growing. Growing up. Growing older. I don't want to look back on my life and wonder what else I could have been or what else I could have accomplished. Being a wife and a mother are very important. Being your wife and the mother of your children someday, I think I can do, but our dreams aren't always in the place we expect them to be, Carlton. I've dreamed of practicing law since I was seven and Kenneth read the Thurgood Marshall story to me. Now, that dream may come true in just a few more years. You've dreamed of being a college coach or even coaching in the pros. You've told me that was your dream from the time you were ten years old. I couldn't and wouldn't ask you to give up your dreams for me. Are you going to ask me to give up my dreams now that I'm so close to making those dreams a reality? Besides that, Carlton, you and I both know that we have some very serious problems to resolve. That takes time; certainly more time than either one of us can give at the moment. If we wait to get married, we'll have time to pursue our dreams, then we can discuss when to marry and later, five or six years from that, we can talk about having a family, but marriage right now is not in the cards for us."

She was calmer now. Her words hung in the air. There! She had said it. She wasn't ready to become Ms. Vivian Lynn Alexander-Andrews just yet with all that title would entail. Her words were still hanging in the air when someone rang the front door bell. Vivian quickly rose from the table, avoiding Carlton's eyes, and went to answer the front door. When she opened it, a cold blast of arctic-like air rushed past her. Shivering, she wrapped her arms around her body. Two men stood in front of her wearing military fatigues and hooded parkas.

"Ms. Alexander?" one of them asked with a decidedly heavy Southern accent.

"Yes, I'm Ms. Alexander. Please, come in."

The two men stepped inside and Vivian closed the door behind them.

"I'm Corporal Yeager, ma'am. Colonel Baker sends his regards, ma'am. He has asked us to assure that you're safe," the young man said, looking around the area.

Confused, Vivian asked, "Safe? Well, of course I'm safe. What did J.C., I mean, Colonel Baker think? That I was being held hostage by terrorists or something?"

"I don't know, ma'am. He sent us over here to be sure that you were safe and to ask that you call him at this number as soon as possible." The Corporal held out a business card.

"Thank you, Corporal Yeager." Vivian took the card from his hand. "I'll call him right away."

"You're sure you're all right, ma'am?"

"Yes, Corporal, I'm fine, but, Corporal, where are you from? Do I detect a Southern accent?"

"Yes, ma'am," Corporal Yeager said, with a glowing smile. "I hale from Holly Hill, South Carolina."

"I thought so." She smiled.

Vivian offered the two soldiers coffee, which they declined. She talked with them for a while and they discovered that they knew some of the same people. The two soldiers left and Vivian closed the door behind them. She walked slowly and quietly back to the kitchen. Carlton was still sitting at the table looking out the window with his chin resting on this right hand. He had not finished his food. Vivian stood quietly at the door, looking at him. He seemed to be so deep in thought that he did not notice her standing there. He just stared motionless out the window.

"Carlton," she said, finally breaking the silence, "Thanks for brunch. It was delicious." Feeling a bit uncomfortable, she hastily added, "I need to make some phone calls. I'll clean the kitchen when I come down."

Carlton turned and looked toward her. "Don't worry about it. I'll clean up the kitchen. You make your phone calls."

He seemed so dejected that her stomach quivered. Quiet. He was too quiet. The only sounds were the wind whipping furiously outside and the music from the audio system playing softly in the background.

Vivian stood in the doorway and watched Carlton for a few seconds longer not knowing quite what to do, as he continued to stare out the window into the cold, blustery day. She began to feel the full effects of the words that she left hanging in the air. How could she hurt this man so deeply? A man who she loved and who obviously loved her so much. How many people find what she and Carlton had, even if they searched for a lifetime? A strong relationship built on mutual trust, respect, and admiration. She wondered how many women find someone like Carlton, with his character that was totally unselfish and romantic during intimate moments. She felt the urge to run to him, hold him, and tell him that it was all a mistake. That she would marry him any time and any place that he wanted. Yet, something prevented her from returning to the kitchen, prevented the words from coming out of her mouth. That same something kept her anchored to the space where she stood. Finally, she turned, walked down the wide hallway, and scaled the steps to use the telephone in her bedroom. When she reached her room, she sat on the sofa bed and took a deep breath.

"God, I don't want to hurt him. What am I doing?" She looked at the ring on her finger. She shook off her self-recriminations and picked up the bedside phone. "Colonel J. C. Baker, please. This is Vivian Alexander. He's expecting my call. Thank you, I'll hold."

"Hi, Viv. Where have you been?" Colonel Baker asked. "Your family is looking for you."

"Is anything wrong, J.C.?" she asked, concerned.

"No. You've apparently been incognito."

Her concern eased. "How could I be incognito with you around?" she teased. "When the military police showed up at my door—two of them—I thought that I was really in some trouble. I thought maybe you and Benny stored some top-secret weapon system information in the walls when you two lived here. I'll bet Benny put you up to calling out the National Guard to look for me. Does the government know how you're spending its money, sending two soldiers out on a day like this to look for a civilian?"

"Sure," J.C. said, chuckling. "We do it all the time. It's our military duty to make sure our country's citizens are safe from aggression."

"That's foreign aggression, J.C.," Vivian retorted.

"Same difference these days."

They both laughed.

"Are you okay, Viv? You don't sound like your usual snappy, erudite self."

"I'm fine," she said and sighed. "Just a long delay in Chicago yesterday and I didn't get home until early this morning. I'll get back to my family shortly. How are you? I haven't seen you for a couple of years now."

"Great! Doing just fine. How is the rest of the family? Kenneth, your parents, Aretha and Gregory. Aretha must be ten or eleven now and Gregory must be what, sixteen or seventeen?"

"K.J. is busy with the new company. My parents are fine. We all had a nice time in San Francisco. Aretha is doing everything better and faster than any of us did at her age. And Gregory, well he's in his teens, but he thinks that he's going on thirty-five. He thinks that he's God's gift to women. He's trying desperately to develop a reputation with the ladies that surpasses yours and Benny's."

"Speaking of Benny, he and I didn't get much of a chance to talk this morning. Is he still seeing that cute, little Lieutenant?"

"Beats the heck out of me. He didn't mention anyone special, but you know Benny as well as I do. The original rolling stone that gathers no moss."

"And K.J., is he involved with anyone?"

"He didn't introduce us to anyone. Why don't you call him and say hello? Do you have his phone number?"

"Yes. I think I have it. Let's get together for a meal sometime soon. How's your schedule?" J.C. asked.

"I'm pretty flexible this coming week. Classes don't resume until the following week. Give me a call when you know your schedule and we'll work something out. Okay?"

"Sounds great. I'll call you next week. Uh, Vivian, let's not mention our rendezvous to Kenneth. You know how overprotective he is. Take care of yourself, Viv, and let me know if there is anything that I can do for you."

"Okay, J.C., I'll see you sometime soon."

That's odd, Vivian thought when she hung up. *Wonder why J.C. hasn't talked with Kenneth? And why did J.C. want to keep our meeting a secret?* Kenneth and J.C. seemed to have been very good friends at one time. Well, she would just have to figure that one out later. First, call the parents.

She spoke to her parents, Aretha, and Gregory and recounted her journey from the time they left her in Chicago. She apologized to them for not getting back to them sooner and letting them know that she was fine. She mentioned, Chucky, the skiing-cowboy, second-year, resident doctor, and the other strangers who shared the perilous journey from the airport. Gregory was awed that his sister met one of his basketball idols, Chuck Montgomery. She mentioned her conversation with J.C. and questioned whether something happened between Kenneth and J.C. that she didn't know about. Her parents knew of no reason why Kenneth and J.C. weren't in contact. She mentioned that Carlton surprised her by driving for hours from Columbia, South Carolina, through the hazardous conditions to Washington. She even mentioned how good the lasagna was, but she never mentioned the ring on the third finger of her left hand.

Next, she called Kenneth, who was happy to hear from her, but scolded her for not calling sooner until she explained about the delayed flight. She told him about Chucky, the skiing-cowboy, second-year, resident doctor, her conversation with J.C., and Carlton's drive from South Carolina to Washington. He questioned her more closely about her conversation with J.C., but he never said that there was any problem between them. He dismissed his failure to keep in touch with J.C. as simply a problem of scheduling. Still, she never mentioned the ring on the third finger of her left hand.

Next she called Benjamin.

"Benny!" she said, as soon as he answered the phone.

"Hey, V! It's about time someone heard from you."

"Benny, I've got a big problem. I need your help."

"Hey, kid, what's the matter? Are you all right?" he asked, concerned.

"Yes, physically I'm fine. I'm just not ready for marriage and I've hurt Carlton, and I just don't know what to do. He's talking engagement parties, a fall wedding, two babies in two years—."

"Whoa, Counselor! Could we start with the subject of this conversation and then the predicate? You lost me somewhere around you're 'physically fine'."

Vivian took a deep, calming breath. "Carlton has asked me to marry him."

"That's great, isn't it? I knew that he bought an engagement ring and was planning to ask you when you got home from San Francisco. So what's wrong?"

"He wants to get married this coming year! I'm not ready for marriage, yet. When I was at Spelman, all I could think about was marrying Carlton, having babies with him, and hanging curtains. I thought that was what I wanted. That's all we talked about. Now he's making all these plans for engagement parties, fall wedding, and even babies over the next two years and I'm not ready. I have a lot of living to do before I get married. Now he's ready to settle down and he wants me to move on campus with him before May. I feel like I must have been giving out mixed signals."

"It must be something in the air," Benjamin mumbled in frustration.

"What does that mean?"

"I'll explain later. I see the problem. Does he understand that you want to finish law school and get your career going first?"

"Apparently not. He doesn't want me to work. He probably thinks that I would be willing to give up my career goals to be his wife. He wants me to be barefoot, pregnant, and living on the outskirts of town!"

"That's not you, V. You two have been together for what three or four years now...since your sophomore or junior year at Spelman. Doesn't sound like he knows how you have grown since those early days of your relationship. Has he given you the ring yet?"

"He sprang it on me today."

"And? What did you tell him?"

"I told him I would marry him, but before I could say anything about *when* I would marry him, he was off and running to the wedding chapel. I tried to explain to him that I needed to fulfill some of my own personal goals before I become a wife and mother. That seemed to hurt him even more. Then too, we've got issues."

"Are you asking for my advice?"

"Yes, I don't know what to do and I don't want to hurt him."

"V, in my opinion, you already know what you want to do with your life, at least, in the immediate future. So you have to lay it on the line and let the chips fall where they may. If he's the man for you, he'll understand your needs and want to help you reach your goals, even if that means putting some of his plans on hold for a while. If he's not, then you have to be prepared to let him go. You know what Mom says about relationships, 'If it don't fit, don't force it.'"

"I know you're right. I've come to the same conclusion. I just needed to talk to you about it. You know, say it out loud so that I could listen to myself think."

"Have you told anyone else about this?"

"No. I had to work it out in my own mind first. You know, get my head on straight."

"I never worry about your head being on straight, V. You're one of the most level-headed people I know, even though you are my little sister." He chuckled. "You'll simply have to find a way to help Carlton to understand your position."

"I'm going to try. He'll be here through New Year's Day. Maybe we can get this all sorted out by then. Now, back to the comment about 'something being in the air.'"

"You know, you're going to be a great attorney one day. You never forget anything."

"Don't try to change the subject, Benny. What did you mean?"

"I've been seeing someone for a while. Nothing structured. Just good fun and a lot of laughs here and there. It was her idea, from the very beginning, to keep the relationship loose. She didn't want any entanglements—just sex. She's very career oriented just like you are, but this morning, she told me that she was disappointed because I didn't ask her to come to San Francisco to meet all of you. Frankly, I was surprised. When I tried to explain to her what 'taking a women to meet the family' meant to me, that it was about having a committed relationship that was expected to lead to marriage, she clammed up. Talk about getting mixed signals! It's not that she isn't special. She just caught me off guard and didn't or wouldn't explain what she expected or where she wanted this relationship to go."

"Sounds like I'm not the only one who needs to have a little heart-to-heart talk. At least I know that Carlton loves me. What are your feelings for this woman?"

"I really hadn't given it a lot of thought," he hedged. "I want to take our relationship to another level. The sex is great! It's the best! As I said, she's special, but I'm not in love, or, at least, I don't think that I am. She and I are supposed to have dinner together tonight. I hope that I'll find out more then."

"If you are in love, my housemate will be crushed."

"Which housemate?"

"Gloria Towson. She left a message on my voice mail. She's in Santa Barbara with her family for the holidays and she asked me for your telephone number."

"Gloria? Gloria?" he said, trying to remember her. "Oh, *G l o r i a.* Tall, long legs up to her ears and lashes. Stacked. The one who won some contest—Ms. UCLA or something two or three years ago. That Gloria?"

"Yes, Benny, *that* Gloria. She was a runner up in the Miss California contest two years ago. She graduated from UCLA."

"And she wants my number?"

"Yes, Benny, that's what she said."

"She's a little young, but, sure! Give her my cell phone number and my ComSat number, too, if she wants it!" Benny said, eagerly.

"Gee, Benny, I don't even have your ComSat number," Vivian said, laughing. "Are you sure you're ready for Gloria now, given this current situation?"

"By the time I hear from Gloria, maybe I will have figured this all out. By the way, I forgot to ask you about the house. How are things going?"

"I haven't rented the four bedrooms downstairs. That's hard to do at mid-year, but we finished the tile work in the bathrooms and it looks great. K.J.'s idea to put in heated floors was great, too. It's nice and warm down there. The kitchen appliances and cabinets are installed and look great. We still have to paint all the rooms down there, clean the floors, and maybe put in some area rugs. We already have the paint for the walls and ceiling. The only thing that I'm concerned about is the door on the front. It doesn't seem to close tightly. I feel a draft when I'm working down there and I think that's where it's coming from."

"Sounds like you have accomplished a lot. Put some weather stripping around the door. I'll look at it the next time I'm in town. Have you sent the January mortgage payment in yet?" Benjamin asked.

"No, not yet. Don't you want me to send the payment to you? It's your house, you know. Maybe you should send the payment to the mortgage company?"

"It's my tax deduction, but you're my landlady. That's what I pay you those big bucks to do." He laughed.

"Big bucks! Big bucks! Surely you jest!" Vivian scoffed. "I haven't seen 'big bucks' since Hector was a pup and he died of old age fifty years ago!"

"There you go using Grand Aunt Hanna Ivy's old saying."

"Still rings true though."

"If you need anything else for the house, just let me know. I've got to get up out of here. I'm supposed to be on the flight simulator over at the naval base in thirty minutes. You okay?" Benny asked.

"Yes. I think I know what I have to do. Wish me luck."

"You'll handle it just fine."

"Thanks, Benny. I love you."

"Hang in there, kid. I love you more."

"Oh, Benny."

"Yes?"

"Do you know whether something went down between Kenneth and J.C.?" Vivian asked.

"No. Why?"

"I talked with J.C. and Kenneth both today and it seems that they have not been in touch for some time, years in fact. Baker seemed a little evasive when I suggested he call Kenneth."

"And Mom says I'm a worry wart! Huh!"

"Well, I was just curious."

"I don't know of anything, but I haven't been focusing on it. I'll bet J.C. steered Kenneth toward that big military contract he got though. J.C. and Kenneth probably haven't had much time to hang out. They're both dedicated to their jobs and careers, but you be careful around Baker. He goes through women like Jackson through Vicksburg."

"Look who's talking," she said and laughed, "but I'll be careful. If there's one thing I don't need in my life, it's another man with a hidden agenda. I'll see J.C. for a meal soon, but that's all. Any messages for him?"

"No. I'll talk with him later today I'm sure. We have to go over some details about field maneuvers next month."

"Okay, go fly your simulator."

"Take care, little sis."

They hung up.

Talking with Benny always helped Vivian work out her problems. He knew how to listen and he only gave his advice when or if she specifically asked for it. He was always there for her no matter what. Even when they were little kids they were close, but now she couldn't even tell him the truth about her relationship with Carlton or the real reason that she was reluctant to marry him. She never lied to Benny before, but she felt that she was being disingenuous now.

Chapter 5

The sun beamed so brightly against the unsullied snow that Vivian had to shade her eyes from the glare, as she stood at her front door watching the street scene. The snow removal along R Street was beginning to take place. The District of Columbia was alive and beginning to dig itself out. Noisy trucks scrapped the street, while little children screamed and frolicked in the deep, white snow. Some children built snowmen. Others built snowballs and tossed them at each other. Adults shoveled steps, walkways and sidewalks, as the wind blew half the snow back toward the places they had just cleared.

The city was a wonderful place to be sometimes, Vivian thought. Neighbors helped each other dig cars out of the snow that was banked up against them. Mrs. Milton, an elderly neighbor, who lived alone except for her cat, made hot cocoa for the three men who cleared her walkway. Her eyes sparkled when Mrs. Kurts, another neighbor, brought a quart of milk and a loaf of bread to her, and asked whether she needed anything else. Mrs. Kurts would not accept any money for her trouble from Mrs. Milton.

Mr. Jones, a middle-aged music teacher and concert violinist, who lived next door to Vivian, cautioned his piano student to be careful, as she and her mother climbed the steps to his home for her piano lesson. Two young boys, who both looked to be about thirteen years old, were clearing his steps and walkway—for a price, Vivian was sure. She'd better get going, she thought, before they came pounding on her door looking for work.

Vivian could hear the dishwasher working, as she approached the kitchen. The kitchen was clean, the terracotta tile floor had been scrubbed, and the food had been put away, but Carlton was not in the kitchen.

"Carlton," she called out.

"Yes," he answered.

"Where are you?"

"I'm in the front living room."

Vivian opened the large, sliding oak pocket doors that led to the front parlor and saw Carlton sitting in a corner of the deep burgundy, leather sofa, holding a glass of wine. A fire blazed in the fireplace.

"I didn't know that you were in here. What are you doing?" She approached him.

"Just regrouping. I started a fire; I hope that you don't mind."

She sat down beside him and put her head in his lap.

"No, of course, I don't mind. It feels good in here. Thanks for cleaning the kitchen. You did a great job."

Carlton stroked what was left of her hair, but said nothing. He didn't like her new haircut. He preferred it long and thick, hanging down her back near her waist. He just sipped his wine and watched the flames. The silence was deafening.

"What are you thinking about?" Vivian asked, even though she knew the likely answer.

"You," Carlton said barely above a whisper, still stroking her hair.

"And what are you thinking about me?"

"How much I love you."

His words grabbed her in the heart. Vivian sat up and looked at Carlton. "Please don't...." she started to say.

He pulled her toward him and placed her head on his chest. His arms felt comforting. "I can't stop loving you," he said. "And I'm not going to try. No matter what it takes, we're going to be together."

Vivian lifted her head to look into his eyes. "I'm sorry if I seem less than enthusiastic about—."

"Shhh," he whispered, putting a finger to her lips. "Let's not spoil this time together with another argument. I just want to hold you." He brushed his lips against hers.

"Still, we have so much to clear up—."

"Not at this moment, we don't. We're alone together for the first time in over six months. Let's make the most of it before your housemates get back. I drove here because we needed to be together. I love you, Vivian." He pulled her into his lap, kissing her hungrily. "I love you."

Vivian's head was beginning to throb, but she didn't pull away. Carlton held her, crushing her body to his. For a moment, she let herself melt into his embrace, his urgent need. A moan grew from deep in his chest, as his hand kneaded her breast through the fabric of her sweater. Then he deepened the kiss, slipping his hands under the sweater and releasing her breasts from her bra. Her arms hooked around his neck, as he took the hardened nipple of one breast between his fingers, squeezing then rubbing the pain away with the palm of his hand.

She couldn't even psych herself up to be aroused by his passion anymore. There had been a time when his touch thrilled her, but that too had been cooled by their inability to work out their problems. Sex had never before been an issue between them, but now it seemed that it was all that was left. Sex and her feelings of guilt for wanting a career more than wanting to be with him.

"I love you, baby," he crooned in her ear. "Work with me. You seem to be a million miles away."

Vivian brought her thoughts back to the moment, as Carlton laid her on the sofa and covered her body with his. He removed her sweater and bra, trailing hot kisses along her neck, down her chest, feasting on her breasts. "Work with me, baby," he said again against her abdomen, pulling her loose-fitting warm-ups down to her knees.

Vivian closed her eyes and stroked his think, curly hair, as he tried to arouse her. Tears of regret fought to spill, but she held back.

Carlton stripped the robe from his body and then removed her pants. She lay bare before him, but she felt naked and almost ashamed, as his eyes and hands washed over her. Her head was pounding, as he nibbled at her pubis. She wanted to scream at the intimacy, but not in ecstasy. She exhaled a ragged breath of discontent, but Carlton mistook it for an indication that his foreplay was having the desired effect. It wasn't. Instead of her body heating from desire, it heated from the temperature in the room. She turned her head and looked at the blazing fire in the hearth while Carlton continued his attempts to arouse her. The flames danced and her mind cooled. Cold, she thought, as cold as the biting wind outside. The wind that danced around her at the airport before Chuck Montgomery took her into his warm truck. The warmth enveloped her there. His friendliness touched her, and she wondered absently what he was doing at that moment.

Someone knocked loudly on the front door. Carlton spit out a curse, got up, and tightly wrapped the robe around him.

"I'll get it. You hold the thought," he said, as he went to the front door.

Vivian took that opportunity to gather herself, dressing quickly.

"Okay guys, thirty it is, but do a good job."

"Thanks, Mister," the boys said in unison, as they began shoveling the snow.

Carlton closed the door and went back to the front living room where Vivian was sitting with her clothes back in place.

"Viv . . ." his voice trailed off in disappointment.

"It's not the time.... I mean, things were getting out of hand and we weren't being responsible—."

"I'm going to get dressed. Do you want this suitcase here in the hallway taken upstairs to your room?" he asked, his anger barely veiled.

"Yes, I forgot all about it. Leave the book bag. I'm going to do some reading."

"Fine," Carlton said through gritted teeth, handing the book bag to her and closing the pocket doors to the front room behind him.

Vivian heard Carlton climb the steps, as she emptied her book bag on the coffee table. Her lipstick slipped out through a slit in the bag. She shook the bag vigorously and searched among the books and papers for her wallet. Unzipping her laptop bag, she searched inside. She looked under the coffee table and the sofa. Then she retraced Carlton's steps to where the bag laid all night. No luck. Maybe she put it in her luggage, she thought, as she climbed the stairs to her bedroom.

Carlton was looking around the room, as she entered.

"Did you see my wallet anywhere? I can't find it and it has my identification cards in it."

She went to her luggage and opened it.

"No, but I have a question for you," he said.

"What is it?" she asked, as she pulled clothes out of her luggage and dumped them on the floor.

"Where are my clothes?" he asked, puzzled.

"Oh, I cleaned up the room and put the clothes in the laundry basket in the bathroom closet."

Carlton went to the basket and there, beneath the damp towels were his clothes.

"Vivian, I don't mean to discourage your attempts at domesticity, but maybe I had better do the laundry after we're married. You shouldn't put wet towels in the hamper on top of my jeans and my wool sweater," he said, lifting the crumpled up clothes from the hamper.

Vivian had to stifle her amusement at seeing Carlton standing there holding up his soggy, crumpled clothing. The expression on his face was priceless, she thought, but when he retrieved his shoes out of the hamper, she could not hold it back. She fell on the bed in uproarious laughter. Carlton held his clothes and shook his head. She calmed herself enough to say, "Well, you said that you loved me for trying to be more domesticated."

Carlton had to smile and let the clothes fall to the floor. Vivian rolled off the bed and walked over to him, stepping over the piles of clothes on the floor. She hugged him and planted a kiss on his cheek.

"I have some of Benny's things in the closet. You should be able to wear something of his."

Vivian felt the heat of Carlton's gaze washing over her. Swiftly, he pulled her into a hard embrace, his powerful phallus thrust forward. She knew that she could no longer delay or deny him. Roughly, he took her in his arms, placing a bruising kiss on her mouth. His hands worked deftly to shed her clothes until she stood bare before him again. He carried her to the bed and deposited her there, his eyes ablaze.

"Carlton . . ." she started in a vain effort to stall, her words lost in the fire in his eyes.

"No, Vivian, no more delays. No more excuses. I've been patient long enough," he growled, snatching a foil pack from her bedside stand. "I'm your man, damn it! And you and I aren't leaving this room until you show me that you're my woman!"

Condom in place, Carlton kneed her thighs apart, feasting his eyes on her bare body like a hungry animal. In one swift move, he lowered himself into position, raised her thighs to his waist, and entered her roughly without preamble. His blazing eyes bore into hers, as he thrust himself into her.

"You're my woman," he bit out, each thrust becoming harder and more intense. "Stay with me, baby. I need you."

His plea was so urgent that it reached out and wrenched her heart.

"Please, baby!" he pleaded. "Help me!"

Vivian closed her eyes against the anguish that she saw in his face. Slowly she began to ungulate her body beneath him. His muscular arms rippled in her hands, as she tried unsuccessfully to capture his mood. Her sex drive was as normal as any woman's, but try, as she may, she could only move her body to meet his urgent heat, not her heart to meet his need.

"That's it, baby!" he bit out, as a mantra in labored breaths. He swallowed her mouth, stabbing his tongue against her lips until she opened to him. He lay heaving on her chest, his virile body pumping harder and harder against her.

"Touch me, baby," he hissed through gritted teeth against her throat, his unshaven face scratching her chest.

She wanted to cry out to stop the hopelessness of his endeavor, but she bit back her desire and clasped his butt in her hands, helping him reach for his elusive ecstasy. It seemed like an eternity was passing, as he pounded against her. Her mind began to wander to things at the top of her thoughts. The research she had to begin for Professor Fehey, the hours she would volunteer at the family homeless shelter, picking up her dog from her friends' house, meeting with J.C. Baker....

"Oh, baby!" Carlton moaned, as his body stiffened in reflexive jerks, spasms that seemed to go on forever.

He collapsed onto her, breathing heavily and squeezing her tightly, as the last violent shudders gripped and released his damp, hot body.

Vivian breathed a heavy sigh of relief when she heard his breathing quiet to a snore.

Later, Vivian and Carlton were greeted at the front door by a blast of arctic air.

"Let's go and get 'em," Carlton said, as he stepped out onto the porch.

Vivian looked at Carlton, turned back toward the house, and said, "Maybe not."

Carlton grabbed her by her shoulders and redirected her down the steps.

"You can handle it, Viv. I've got faith in you."

When Vivian and Carlton descended the steps, the two boys had cleared the first set of steps and were well on their way to clearing the walkway to the second set of steps and the public sidewalk beyond. Vivian pulled two snow shovels out from under the front porch and tossed one to Carlton.

"Okay. Your car or mine?" she asked.

"Let's dig yours out first. I'll start at the other end of the driveway," Carlton said, as he wrapped a scarf around his face and moved toward the driveway.

Vivian started closer to her car and began shoveling snow away from the tires. She was clearing the snow from the last tire and bent over just before a snowball whizzed past her. She looked up at Carlton, but he was still shoveling at the other end of the driveway with his back turned toward her. She noticed no one else around. She continued to work when another snowball splattered against the car.

"Okay, Carlton," she yelled, "you asked for this!"

Vivian balled up some snow and threw it at Carlton. It hit him squarely in the back of his head.

"Vivian! What the hell did you do that for?" he asked, confusion bunching his face.

"What's wrong? Just 'cause you missed and I—."

SMACK!

A snowball smashed Vivian squarely in the face.

Carlton stood laughing and holding up both hands. "Wasn't me," he said, nodding toward the front of the house.

Vivian moved forward and ducked, as another snowball whizzed by.

"Melissa!" Vivian yelled, as she balled up more snow and tossed it at her housemate. She missed Melissa, but hit Stan Cavanaugh, Melissa's boyfriend, in the chest. Poor Stan stood holding three large bags of groceries.

"That's not the right flavor, Vivian," he said sarcastically, licking the snow from around his mouth. "Try a little raspberry on the next one. I'm partial to raspberry."

"Sorry, Stan. I was aiming at your crazy lady friend," Vivian said. "And I do use that term 'lady' loosely."

Just then, Melissa peeked out from behind Stan; devilish, deep blue eyes brighten her translucent, porcelain face scanning the snow to find more mischief. Her rich, silky black hair was fanned by the icy wind.

Vivian deftly calculated the imp's next move. "Don't even think it, Melissa! You'll never make it into the house!" she warned.

Melissa giggled, balled the snow, threw it at Vivian, and made a mad dash for the steps. A grave miscalculation on her part. She wasn't fast enough. Vivian fired a snowball catching Melissa, as she reached the top step of the porch. The snow smacked Melissa right in the ear.

Leaning on their shovels observing the exchange, the two boys yelled, "Way to go, lady!" They gave each other high fives, laughing robustly. "You sure got some arm!"

Melissa stopped dead in her tracks, turned toward Vivian, and narrowed her pretty, blue eyes menacingly. "I owed you that one, but I want a rematch!"

Vivian laughed and gestured with her arms held wide apart. "Anytime, Melissa. Anytime."

Carlton helped Stan with the grocery bags and they all went inside, laughing. They shook off the snow and unwrapped. Vivian pulled off her gloves and hat and threw them on the closet shelf.

Melissa suddenly gasped. "Vivian, what is that rock on your finger?" The words were slow, but expressive. Melissa grabbed Vivian's hand, yanked her toward the light, and slipped into her best Valley Girl impression. "Oh, my God. Oh, my God, it's like an engagement ring or something!" Her head snapped back and forth between Vivian and Carlton. "Okay. Okay. Is someone going to explain what's going on around here?" Hands on hips, she was patting her foot on the floor.

"No." Vivian nonchalantly shrugged, tossing her head in the air, turning on her heels and heading for the kitchen.

Melissa was in hot pursuit. "No? What do you mean, 'no'?"

Vivian laughed at the incredulous disbelief on Melissa's face. Carlton smiled, as Melissa approached him in the kitchen.

"Okay, Carlton, confession time!" Melissa demanded.

Carlton was putting the canned goods from the grocery bags into the pantry. "Melissa, do you want this creamed corn on the second or third shelf?" he asked, ignoring her obvious question.

"Isn't anybody going to tell me anything around here?" Melissa huffed, arms akimbo, stamped her feet, and pouted.

Carlton and Vivian glimpsed each other and snorted, "No," with a shrug of their shoulders.

Even Stan had to laugh at the scene. He decided to give Carlton an escape route. "Come on, Carlton. I'll help you finish shoveling the snow."

No sooner had the door closed behind Carlton and Stan, Melissa darted to Vivian.

"Please, please, please, Vivian. You've got to tell me what's going on!" she begged.

Vivian exhaled deeply. "Carlton asked me to marry him."

"And? And? What did you say?" Melissa asked excitedly.

"I said yes."

"You said *what?*" Melissa yelled in disbelief.

"I said yes."

"You didn't?"

"Okay. I didn't."

"Vivian!"

"Okay, I did say yes. Are you happy now?"

"Vivian, the question is not whether I'm happy. The question is, are you happy? I know you care about Carlton—he really looks rad in a pair of tight jeans and all—but I didn't know that you were ready to marry him. How did this all happen? Are you having some type of out-of-body experience?"

"Inquiring minds want to know," she exhaled, putting water into a kettle to boil.

Melissa pulled four mugs from the drying rack, placed them on the table, and sat down hanging on every word Vivian uttered.

"Do you want herbal tea, cocoa, or coffee?" Vivian asked.

"An explanation will do for now," Melissa said. "Tell me all!"

Vivian sat down at the table and described the events of the morning. Melissa's deep blue eyes grew wider, as Vivian talked. Her jaw dropped open when Vivian described Carlton's plans for a May engagement party, fall wedding, and babies. Melissa sat back in her chair with her eyes wide and mouth gaped.

"Geez-o-flip, Vivian! What are you going to do?" Melissa exclaimed.

"Pray," she said and snorted cynically.

The kettle whistled and Vivian rose to remove it from the flame just as Stan and Carlton re-entered the kitchen.

"Do you guys want something hot to drink?" Vivian asked.

"Yeah, is there anything to eat?" Stan asked, rubbing his stomach. "Melissa is trying to starve me to death."

"There's a tray of lasagna on the second shelf in the refrigerator," Carlton said.

"Great, I'll have some of that myself," Melissa chimed in.

They sat in the kitchen eating lasagna, Caesar Salad, drinking wine, and talking about their vacations for several hours. Melissa kept eyeing the ring, then eyeing Vivian. Finally, Carlton rose to clear the dishes from the table.

"I'll do that, Carlton," Vivian said, as she also rose from the table.

Carlton sat down and handed the dishes to Vivian. Melissa was sipping her glass of wine, but nearly choked. Even Stan looked surprised. Vivian's lack of domestic skill was legend.

"I need a stronger drink," Melissa said blithely.

Vivian gave her a dirty look and Carlton, Stan, and Melissa broke out into uncontrollable laughter. They all knew that domesticity and Vivian Alexander didn't mix.

Chapter 6

Benny dropped the convertible top on his sleek, jet-black Mercedes 500 SL, with a license plate that read: EXPLORE. He loved the southern California weather in the winter—seventy degrees, bright sunshine, and no humidity. A far cry from the sub-freezing temperature on the East coast. He put on his sunshades, flipped through several CDs selecting Four Play, and drove to the security exit gate at March Air Force Base. An attractive female military police officer snapped a salute, as he came to a stop, waiting for sliding gate to open.

Returning the salute, Benny grinned. "You're looking pretty snappy there, Soldier."

A sexy grin split her face. "Not bad yourself, Captain," the woman said, and winked. "Not bad at all."

Benny flashed a smile. "Carry on, Soldier."

"I'll be carrying on at 2300 hours at the Bay House in San Diego, Sir," she said still saluting expressionless, "If you're free tonight, that is?"

"We'll see, Soldier," he said and drove away from the base toward San Diego.

Life was great. On the way home, he stopped at Michelangelo's, a trendy restaurant, bar and carry out in the Gaslight District of San Diego. He had called ahead and placed a triple order of **gazpacho**, duck à l'orange, braised asparagus spears, parsley potatoes, and strawberries with Grand Marnier sauce for dessert. He had a healthy appetite and an abhorrence for cooking. He always ordered more than he needed for one meal. He stopped at Michelangelo's often to pick up dinner. The Italian manager always beamed when Benny came in and usually added something extra to the order. Tonight it was fresh cut flowers and a bottle of Cabernet Blanc.

"Captain Benny! Captain Benny!" Milo San Angeloe, a short, robust, Italian man greeted him gaily in a thick accent. "Good to see you, Captain Benny. You been aways?"

"Yes, Milo, I was in San Francisco with my family for a few days," he said, smiling. "Is my order ready?"

"Sure, sure, Captain Benny. You gonna have some hot date tonight!" he said, with a wink of his dark eyes and a sly smile on his large, round face with thick mustache.

"I'm working on it, Milo." He returned the winked with a cocky grin and a pat on the older man's back.

Benny drove to his high-rise condo building and slid his key card into the slot that opened the underground garage's gate. Two women in a late model, forest-green Jaguar, with the convertible top down, pulled up behind him. He drove to his parking spot and put the top up on his car. As he grabbed his flight bags, briefcase, and groceries, the two women approached him.

"Hi, Benny," they said in unison, not hiding their flirtatious smiles and glances.

"Cecil, Janice," Benny said, admiring their attire and statuesque bodies, "you ladies sure look lovely, as usual."

Cecil Jordan and Janice Atterly were both dressed in attractive business suits with short skirts showing long, shapely legs. They walked with Benny to the elevator where other residents were standing. Cecil, Janice, and Benny were good friends who often partied together and the two women loved to play practical jokes on him. Cecil was the taller of the two women, with an athletic, shapely physique, and short, silky hair the color of cinnamon that matched her skin tone. Light-brown eyes, narrow nose and a wide, sexy mouth, her beauty was staggering.

Janice, shorter by three inches, was no slouch either. She wore her curly hair longer, but clamped in a barrette. Bright, brown eyes, a wide nose, and small mouth, her skin was like the color of teakwood with red undertones.

"We missed you at the mixer, Benny," Cecil said, while still standing waiting for the elevator.

"I was out of town for a few days. How was the mixer?"

"The building management went all out. There was a great band and the food was delicious. It wasn't as much fun without you there, Benny," Janice said.

"Sorry I missed it."

"You'll probably have to pay for it in increased condo fees," Cecil said dryly.

The elevator finally arrived, the doors opened, and the crowd parted to allow the two women to enter. Benny followed, juggling groceries in his arms and holding his flight bags and briefcase. The doors closed and they were jammed into the elevator like sardines in a can. As the elevator began to rise, Benny felt a hand cupping his butt between his legs. Then, another hand squeezing his crotch. He couldn't move. Cecil and Janice were standing on either side of him, both smiling and staring straight ahead. They fondled him shamelessly, as the elevator stopped on nearly every floor to let passengers off or on for twenty-two floors. Fortunately, no one else on the elevator seemed to notice what the two women were doing to him because he was beginning to get an erection. Finally, on the twenty-third floor, the two women released their captive and walked out of the elevator without a backward glance. Benny leaned back against the elevator wall and breathed an audible sigh of relief. The other passengers turned and looked at him.

"Long ride," he said, smiling sheepishly.

When Benny reached his condo, it was 6:30 P.M. He was late, but a quick call to Fred, the desk clerk, confirmed that Stacy Greene had not yet arrived. Quickly he transferred the dinner to his black onyx dishes and set the table. He put the wine on ice to chill and put five CDs in the changer—all of Stacy's favorites. He looked around. Carmella, his favorite housekeeper, had done a good job cleaning his place, he thought. He put the flowers that Milo had given him in a vase and placed them on the table. The mood was set. The sun was beginning its descent into the deep, blue ocean outside his wraparound windows. One last glance around assured him that everything was ready, as he awaited Stacy's arrival.

Grabbing a Corona from the wet bar refrigerator in the media room, he walked out onto the terrace overlooking the City of San Diego, San Diego Bay, and the Pacific Ocean beyond. Sitting at the glass-topped, wrought-iron table, Benny flipped through his mail and opened a few belated Christmas cards. One was from Deborah in Boston. Cross-country skiing in Maine has been...interesting, he recalled. Another card was from Melanie in Jacksonville, Florida. Ah, Melanie, he thought. Some woman she was on their long, lost weekend in Jamaica. Teresa's name was on the last of many cards. She lives in Portland, Oregon, and loves to water ski, he remembered. Fond memories there, too, he mused, but none could hold a candle to Stacy Greene.

Of all the women he had known, and there had been many, Stacy had his number. She alone lit a fire within him that could not be doused, but she would not commit to him or anyone else. With all that he had learned from many liaisons with women, nothing that he did brought her closer to him. Her desire was for a successful military career. He knew that it had fueled her passion. He also knew and understood that need. He had it, too. That was one of the things that attracted him to her. While it was less than a year since they met, they spent much of their limited time together putting into focus a master plan to prepare themselves for more professional challenges. Stacy wouldn't spend time working toward solidifying their relationship though he was beginning to want that from her. They had a good and solid friendship though and they were lovers. For now, he would accept her position, but one day—very soon—they were going to have to talk about a future—a future together. Since they opened the topic for discussion that morning, tonight would be a good time to broach the subject, once again.

He downed the last of the Corona and headed for the shower while checking his watch. It was well after seven o'clock. As he passed the telephone, he noticed that he had messages. He pushed the button and Stacy's voice was the first one he heard. *"Sorry I can't see you tonight, Benny, but I got this chance to ship out on maneuvers for three days. See you when I get back. Have a Happy New Year."*

"Ah, damn!" he groused, frustrated by all the preparation, his desire to be with her, and now no Stacy. He headed for the shower anyway. Maybe he'd go to the Bay House after all or maybe to Jason's Nightclub. While he was shaving, he heard the telephone ringing. He dashed for it just as the answering machine picked up.

"Hello, Benny, this is Gloria Towson, Vivian's housemate. Sorry I missed you, but if you get—."

Benny picked up the telephone. "Gloria, how are you? This is Benny."

"Hi, Benny," she said, giggling. "What are you doing, monitoring your calls?"

"No, no. Not at all. I was shaving when the phone rang. Vivian told me that you might call," he said, walking back to the bathroom. "What's up with you?"

"My sister and I drove down to San Diego this morning for a little rest and relaxation from our parents, so I thought that I'd give you a call. If you're shaving this late in the evening, you must have plans for tonight, so maybe we'll catch up with you another time."

"Plans? Me? No, I was just going to have a little dinner and spend a quiet evening at home. Where are you?"

"We're in my sister's car driving south on Park Boulevard near Broadway. We were looking for somewhere to have dinner. Do you have any suggestions on where we should eat?"

Benny smiled to himself. "Sure, *Chez Ben-nay*, at your service."

"Your place? Are you sure that this wouldn't be an intrusion on your quiet evening?"

"No problem. I have no plans and I have plenty for dinner."

"Okay, Benny, if you say so. How do we get to your place?"

"Stay on Park and make a right on Market Street to Harbor Drive and turn right. The Harbor Towers. The address is 45323. Pull up to the door and the valet will park your car. I'm in the North Tower on the 28th floor in 2814. The desk clerk will ring me when you arrive. You're only about ten minutes away."

"Okay, Benny. See you in ten minutes."

Benny hung up the telephone, dashed down the steps to the kitchen to load the food into the warmer, lit a host of aromatic candles, and added another place setting on the dining room table.

"There is a God!" he shouted, as he dashed up the steps taking them two at a time. He dressed in a pair of grey, silk-blend, Jordache slacks and a white, Polo, short-sleeve, knit shirt, with gunmetal grey, thin-ribbed sox and maroon, Italian loafers. He was splashing on Cool Water cologne, as the telephone rang.

"Captain Alexander, you have two guests in the lobby. A Ms. Gloria and a Ms. JeNelle Towson."

"Thank you, Fred. Please have the ladies come right up."

Benny dashed down the steps again, grabbed the remote control and slightly dimmed the lights. With the same device, he started the CD player and opened the draperies to display the panoramic view of the now brightly lit City of San Diego. The aroma from the kitchen was filtering out into the living room, as the doorbell rang. He dashed to the door, calmed himself, taking a deep breath, and casually slipped one hand in his pants pocket.

"Good evening, ladies," Benny said in a very relaxed tone, as he opened the door. His eyes widened, as the two women came in. *Whoa*, he thought, Gloria was gorgeous, but her sister was a knock out! She looked a little like Beyoncé, but much more beautiful. She took his breath away.

"Hi, Benny," Gloria cooed, as she hugged him and gave him a kiss on the cheek. "I don't think you've met my sister, JeNelle. JeNelle, this is Vivian's brother, Captain Benjamin Staton Alexander, US Air Force."

JeNelle extended her hand and Benny took it. When they touched, he got a rush that sent his senses racing. Her fingers were slender, her hands soft as butter. He brought her hand to his lips and kissed her knuckles.

"It's a pleasure to meet you, Captain Alexander. I've heard a lot about you from Gloria." Her voice was melodic and soft, like warm honey.

"I'm pleased to meet you, too, JeNelle, but, please, call me Benny, and I'm innocent of all charges. It wasn't me that committed those crimes that you may have heard about. I wasn't even there," he joked, regaining his composure.

"That's unfortunate. I've only heard good thing about you," she said and smiled.

"Oh, you mean *those* things. Sure. I confess. It was me after all," he said leading JeNelle into the living room. "Please come in and have a seat. What can I offer you two ladies to drink?"

Benny's eyes followed JeNelle, observing every sweet curve of her voluptuous, hourglass shape, as she moved across the spacious room. And he thought that Gloria was stacked! *Wow!* JeNelle was clearly older than he was, perhaps in her early thirties, but that didn't matter. She had real curb appeal. He liked that in a woman.

"I'll have a Stoli straight, if you have it," Gloria said, seating herself at one end of the grey, soft-leather sofa. She crossed her shapely legs and her short skirt rode up her firm thighs.

"I'll have an Amaretto on the rocks," JeNelle added, as she strolled over to the terrace door, not looking in Benny's direction.

He was looking at her though. He could barely say, "One Amaretto and one Stoli, coming up."

He stepped behind the wet bar in the far corner of his living room and could see JeNelle's reflection in the mirrors behind the bar. Her long, dark-bronze, curly locks fell softly on her smooth bare back and shoulders. Her backless jumpsuit made his heart pound in his groin, as he drew his eyes along her shapely form until his eyes again settled on her stylish hair. No weave there, he thought, as he poured the drinks. He was observing JeNelle so intently that he over poured her Amaretto. He picked up the glasses and walked over to Gloria first and then to JeNelle. He handed the glass to JeNelle, as she continued to look out of the sliding glass doors. He caught a whiff of her Boucheron perfume. Stacy sometimes wore that scent, he thought absently and smiled. The scent was intoxicating.

"That's a beautiful view," JeNelle said, as she accepted the Amaretto. She looked up at him briefly and then smiled when she noticed how full the glass was that he had given to her.

"Thanks, I wish that I could take credit for it, but the city painted this landscape. It makes it worth the property tax though," he said sharing her view of the city and the naval base. His mind skidded to thoughts of Stacy, the disappointment fresh. Stacy opted again for a chance at career enhancement over spending time with him.

Gloria, flipping through the large, hardcover book, *I Dream A World* brought his thoughts back.

"Benny, I love your place," Gloria said. "Would you take us on a tour?"

"Sure, Gloria," Benny said, still agog at JeNelle.

"You two go ahead. I would like to go out on the terrace, if that's all right with you, Benny?" JeNelle asked.

"Sure you don't want to come along?"

JeNelle shook her head. "No, you two go," she said and smiled, but he noticed that her smile didn't quite reach her eyes.

"Gloria and I won't be long," he said quietly.

"Let's start upstairs with the bedrooms," Gloria suggested with a devilish gleam in her eyes.

Benny led Gloria to the second level and into his bedroom. She marveled when he opened the double doors that led to his huge bedroom suite with its thick plush carpeting. She was even more impressed when he opened the double doors that revealed a deep, wide Jacuzzi whirlpool tub surrounded by mirror and marble walls. In another room was a large, frameless glass, rectangular shower and the double sink and mirrors all around the room. He had walk-in closets, one side filled with his uniforms hung in precision military fashion, the other side filled with very stylish, custom-made, clearly not off the rack clothes, highly polished shoes, and an array of designer ties. The bedroom with the leather-textured wallpaper matched perfectly with the love seats and small coffee table in the sitting area off the master bedroom. The sleigh bed with large posts and a large wooden canopy with other matching furniture ensemble was a particular hit with Gloria. She sat on the high bed and looked up to see the mirrors overhead in the canopy. She gave Benny a coy smile and he covered his face briefly with one hand and looked away. "I love these satin sheets, comforter and pillows, Benny, and that audio/video cabinet are fabulous, but I'm surprised that you don't have a bar in here."

Benny walked to the cabinet, pushed a button, and the bar doors opened up and a soft light popped on. "My brother, Kenneth, built this and the rest of the furniture for me several years ago. I added the mirror."

Gloria blushed, went to the terrace doors and opened them. There was another panoramic view of the city from a different angle. "If I were you, Benny, I'd spend all of my time in here. This is a great grownup's play room," she said and smiled when he joined her on the terrace.

"It has its moments," Benny said, taking Gloria's hand and leading her to the spare bedroom with its private bathroom, and then back to the staircase. Gloria stood at the top of the staircase overlooking the huge living room area toward his media room. Benny could see JeNelle standing on the lower terrace looking out over the city. He was anxious to get back to her.

Back on the first level, he took Gloria into the media room, the den, two smaller bedrooms—one with double beds, with full Jack-and-Jill bath—the dining room and the kitchen in record time.

"Something smells great, Benny. What did you cook?" Gloria asked.

"Oh, yes, uh dinner. Well how does...." he went through the list.

"I'm impressed. You cooked all of that for a quiet dinner alone at home, Benny?" Gloria skeptically asked. "Why didn't you teach your sister to cook? She tells me that you taught her everything else. She's lousy in a kitchen."

"Well, I have to confess that Vivian is great at a lot of things, but she was absent the day my mother passed out cooking talent. I'll put the food on the table, if you're ready to eat?"

Whew! He successfully navigated through that, he thought. He never said that he actually *cooked* the meal. He wanted to impress JeNelle, but lying never came easy to him.

"I'm ready. What about you, JeNelle?" Gloria asked, as JeNelle joined them in the living room.

"Yes, thank you, Benny. This is very nice of you. May I give you a hand?"

"No, uh, you ladies just relax. I've got this all under control." Benny headed for the kitchen.

Moments later, the round, smoked-glass dining table was ready. Benny lit the candles and dimmed the dining room lights.

"Dinner is served, Mademoiselles." He seated Gloria and then JeNelle at the table.

"Benny, this is beautiful," Gloria said, with her eyes shining in the candlelight.

"Thank you." He uncorked the wine and poured a small amount into JeNelle's glass. She tasted it and nodded her approval. Then he filled everyone's glass and placed the bottle in the ice bucket.

"To good friends," he said, holding up his glass.

"And new memories," Gloria added, looking at Benny.

Benny smiled briefly at Gloria, but his attention was drawn again to JeNelle.

Her light brown eyes were magical in the candlelight, he thought. Not as exotic as Stacy's though. It was difficult for him to take his eyes off her. Her smile grabbed him in the pit of his stomach, which felt like taking a header off a high diving board. There seemed to be so much beauty, but he sensed something very reserved or aloof perhaps, in her demeanor. Older women sometimes struck him that way. As if they knew something about life that they were unwilling to share.

"What do you do for a living, JeNelle?" Benny asked conversationally, so that he would have a legitimate reason for gazing at her.

"I own a small shop in Santa Barbara."

"Small?" Gloria balked. "JeNelle owns INSIGHTS, the third largest bookstore, art gallery, and gift shop in Santa Barbara. It's very chic and exclusive. She or her shop have been featured in the city newspaper three times this year alone. She's also the President of the Santa Barbara chapter of the Business and Professional Women's League and she's on the Board of Directors of the Santa Barbara Chamber of Commerce. She does a lot of other stuff that I can't remember. My sister is a true example of today's successful businesswoman and a master of understatement."

"And my little sister is given to overstatement," JeNelle flushed slightly and then added, "This is very good food, Benny. How did you learn to cook so well?"

"I learned at my mother's knee," he said, "She's a great cook."

Well he didn't say that he actually 'cooked' the meal. He just didn't correct the impression that they obviously formed. Lying certainly didn't get any easier, he thought.

"I've heard a lot about your family from Gloria. I understand that you were all in San Francisco for Christmas. How was it?"

Benny began to talk about his brief, but enjoyable, trip to San Francisco for Christmas. He watched every expression on JeNelle's face, as he talked. Her creamy, light-bronze complexion was blemish free. Very little make up; just accents all in the right places. Her full lips, her perfectly shaped nose, and those beautiful eyes with long, thick lashes, just like Gloria's. JeNelle was twice as beautiful as Beyoncé all rolled up into one, he thought in awe.

As they ate, they had a lively and interesting conversation. Benny brewed coffee and served the strawberries with Grand Marnier Sauce. JeNelle had a little sauce on her chin, and before Benny realized what he was doing, he took his napkin and dabbed her chin. JeNelle blushed and when the full radiance of her beautiful smile burst through, his breath anchored in his throat.

Benny knew that Gloria had noticed his reaction to JeNelle, but there was a real chemistry there for him. He thought that she seemed a bit perturbed, but when she didn't say anything, he let the thought pass. Gloria still seemed to be having a wonderful time even though he was paying more attention to JeNelle than to her.

"Let's have more coffee and some brandy in the living room," Benny suggested.

The women agreed and rose from the table.

"Let me help you clear the table, Benny," Gloria said. "It's the least that I can do for this wonderful meal."

"Okay, Gloria, if you insist," he said, watching JeNelle float out of the dining room.

In the kitchen, Gloria and Benny chatted, as they loaded the dishwasher.

"I didn't realize that military people were paid well enough to afford a place like this, Benny. Vivian mentioned that you recently bought a new Mercedes, two-seater," Gloria said, with a curious expression.

"Ah, the military can be a great life, but you won't live on easy street in public service. Fortunately, my brother, Kenneth, made very wise investments for me that have had very good returns. I bought this condo from someone who was desperate to sell before he was transferred overseas. That fact coupled with the downturn in the real estate market—," he said and shrugged. "It's been a good investment."

Then Gloria asked, rather abruptly, "What do you think of JeNelle, Benny?"

Benny felt suddenly trapped. What did he think? He wanted to shout her name aloud from the rooftops! Write her name across the sky in fireworks! The vision of her was etched on his mind's eye.

"Why did you ask me that, Gloria?" he very calmly asked.

"Well, you seemed...I don't know...attracted to her."

"Did I? I hope that I didn't offend you or your sister," he said, as he stacked another dish in the dishwasher.

"No, I'm not offended and I don't believe JeNelle is either. She seems to be enjoying herself considering the fact that I had to literally drag her down here."

"Drag her?"

"If it were up to my sister, she'd still be at her shop working. I made her promise to spend the day with me doing something that I wanted to do," she said, as she handed another scraped plate to Benny.

"And you wanted to visit me?" he asked, his grin curious.

"Well, yes," Gloria said slowly, as she eased closer to him. She ran a leisurely finger across his chest and seductively smiled up at him. "I like you, Benny. I wanted to get to know you better."

She had a familiar gleam in her eyes that Benny recognized in the eyes of some women he dated. Now he really felt trapped and somewhat guilty. Gloria certainly would have made any man's temperature rise, but JeNelle would break the thermometer.

"Let's see how we can get to know each other better. Do you like to dance?" he asked.

"Sure," she said and smiled, easing back.

"How about going to Jason's with me tonight? It's a club in the Harbor District. Usually have a good crowd, band, and a nice dance floor."

"Sounds great. Can we take JeNelle with us?"

"Of course we can. Do you think that she would be willing to go?"

"I'll ask her. No, I'll make her go," Gloria said, as she left the kitchen.

Benny put more coffee in a small pot and loaded a tray with cream, sugar, cups and spoons. His mother's home training certainly was paying dividends. He carried the tray into the living room and sat it on the large, glass, coffee table. Gloria and JeNelle were standing on the terrace. Gloria came inside and closed the door behind her.

"She's being stubborn, Benny. Can you try to convince her to go with us?" Gloria asked, stroking his chest.

"I'll try, Gloria," he said, as he poured a cup of coffee for her. "How does JeNelle like her coffee?"

"Black, no sugar, no cream."

He poured another Amaretto into a snifter and went onto the terrace, closing the door behind him. He approached JeNelle.

"Ms. Towson, you have three options to choose from," he said, standing next to her.

JeNelle looked toward Benny, a puzzled expression on her gamine face. She was even more beautiful in the moonlight, he thought.

"Options?" she quizzically asked.

"Yes. If you pick the right option you get the other two free of charge," he said and grinned.

"And if I pick the wrong option?"

"Then you have to suffer the consequences."

"What are my options?" she asked with a curious smile.

"You can have coffee, brandy or whatever is behind curtain number three. You're a risk taker, aren't you? How lucky do you feel?"

"What's behind curtain number three?"

"Oh, no, you must choose first," he insisted smugly.

She looked at Benny with a questioning smile, pondering the options and said, "I'll take the coffee."

"*Bong!* Wrong answer. You lose. You have to pay the consequences."

"I'm afraid to ask. What are the consequences?" she asked, laughing while taking the cup of coffee he offered.

"You must go out with me and Gloria tonight to do a little partying."

"I'm getting the distinct impression that this game of yours is rigged. I want to see the gaming official," she joked.

"Sorry. Once you choose, you can't renege."

"You always get your way, don't you?"

"I hope so. This time, I really hope so," he said and grinned.

Benny, Gloria, and JeNelle were on the elevator when it stopped on the twenty-third floor. The doors opened and in walked Cecil Jordon and Janice Atterly decked out and looking totally correct. You could have sold Benny for two cents and gotten change. He wanted to melt into oblivion.

"Hi, Benny," they both said, as they entered, smiling at him and his two companions. "Hi, I'm Cecil Jordon," she said, holding out her hand to JeNelle.

"Pleased to meet you, Cecil. I'm JeNelle Towson and this is my sister, Gloria."

"Hi, Gloria. I'm Cecil and this is my condomate, Janice Atterly."

"Nice to meet you both," Gloria said, as she shook their hands. "You two look like you're headed out for a good time."

"Yes, we're going to Jason's, a club in the Harbor District."

"That's where we're going," Gloria added. "Do you want to go together?"

Cecil and Janice looked at each other and then at Benny who was silently praying that they would decline Gloria's spontaneous offer, but he knew that they wouldn't. They were enjoying watching him sweat.

"Sure, why not," Janice said, shrugged.

Benny's heart sank.

"We can take JeNelle's car. She has room for all of us," Gloria piped up.

Benny was really feeling trapped now. Four women! He wondered what he had done to deserve this punishment. Two is company, three is a crowd, but four is a harem! On any other night, he would have enjoyed the company of four beautiful women, but tonight his mission was JeNelle Towson.

The group got off the elevator in the lobby and went to the front desk to order JeNelle's car. Fred, the desk clerk, said, "Oh, Captain Alexander. I was just about to call you. These flowers arrived for you." He lifted a vase filed with two dozen, long-stemmed, red roses onto the desktop. "Here's the card that came with them."

How could it get any worse? Benny wondered. All four women were standing around him and watching, as he opened the card.

Benny—
Sorry about today. Of course, the sex was great! It always
is. These flowers are a small indication of how much I
enjoyed you. Looking forward to more. We'll finish that
conversation when I get back. Keep it warm for me, baby.
Stacy

All eyes were on him, including Fred's. Benny felt a twist in his gut. He wished that Stacy were there with him, but he was looking forward to her return. Trying to appear innocent, he looked around at everyone. "They're from my mother." Although no one said a word, he had the distinct impression that no one believed him.

Cecil and Janice snickered.

JeNelle's brand new Champaign-colored Mercedes Benz 520 SEL with all the bells and whistles rolled up outside the lobby under the portico. JeNelle and Gloria got into the front seats while Cecil, Benny, and Janice got in the backseat. Cecil and Janice put Benny in the middle between them. He had to straddle the drive shaft with his long legs and place his arms on the seat behind Cecil and Janice. There he was spread eagle between two gorgeous women with two more in the front seat. No sooner than he got comfortable, Janice and Cecil started plucking his feathers. Each one placed a hand on one of Benny's knees and started massaging them. As they rode along, their hands massaged further up his thighs. He could not move. They had him trapped again. He had to remain unaffected by the motion, but it was getting tougher. Chills were climbing up his back when JeNelle looked at him in her rearview mirror to ask for directions. He tried to comply, but was beginning not to know his right from his left. Cecil and Janice looked out of their respective side windows, but continued to arouse him unmercifully. When they arrived at Jason's, he nearly leaped out of the car. He turned his back to the women, pretending to have to brush lint off his slacks, but, in fact, he was desperately trying to reposition his full erection, which was clearly bulging from his slacks. He closed his sport jacket and ushered the women ahead of him, as he tried to refocus his thoughts. That didn't help much, as he saw the four shapely bodies moving rhythmically ahead of him. It was not a warm night, cool in fact, with a chilly breeze off the ocean, but perspiration was forming on his brow. This was going to be a very long, tough night. Perhaps the toughest in his twenty-eight years.

Jason's—a multi-level club, well decorated and a great view of the dance floor from every angle—had a very congenial atmosphere. As they entered the club, the place was packed and the music was bumping. Several people spoke to Benny, as he entered with his companions.

"Good evening, Captain Alexander. Are there *five* in your party tonight?" the maître'd asked with an amused look on his smug face.

"Good evening, Ray," Benny said. "Yes, a large table, please."

A waiter led the way. Benny stopped to acknowledge several people, as he walked. A large group of players from the San Diego Chargers' football team was clustered around the bar. When they saw Benny enter, escorting four beautiful women, they all let out yelps, whistles, and calls.

Tony Jamerson, one of the Chargers who Benny sometimes partied with, jumped down from his barstool, gave an exaggerated stiff salute, and yelled, "Attention! There's an officer on deck!"

Another large group of military men and women also joined in the friendly, but exaggerated chastisement and snapped to attention, as Benny walked by escorting the women.

"At ease, brat pack!" Benny yelled good-naturedly toward both groups and threw his hand up at them, as if to dismiss them, but the whoops and hollers continued.

"*Four* women, Benny?! Can't you give the rest of us poor slobs a break?!" someone yelled.

"Now that's what I call an Officer and a Gentleman!" someone else shouted.

"I'm in the wrong line of work, Benny," one of the Chargers yelled out. "Where can I go to sign up for the Air Force?! I like the way you guys get to serve our country!"

"Do I have to take a number and get in line again, Benny?!" one of the Navy women yelled.

"Naw, it's going to take an Act of Congress to get into his lineup," another female officer yelled, "and I'm writing to my congressman tonight!"

Benny tried to ignore his friends, but they weren't about to let up on him. They teased and taunted him most of the evening. His companions loved every minute of it. Men kept falling all over themselves and each other asking his companions to dance or to buy them a drink. The females, sometimes two at a time, kept him on the dance floor doing some very seductive dance moves. Benny kept his eyes on JeNelle, as she danced with other men.

Later in the evening, Tony Jamerson walked up to Gloria and said, "I'll have your baby, if you will just dance with me one time."

Gloria rose and sauntered to the dance floor, giving JeNelle a sly wink over her shoulder. Now it was just Benny and JeNelle sitting alone at the table. Another Air Force pilot approached to ask JeNelle to dance. Benny quickly pulled rank on him and ushered him away.

"It's my turn now," Benny said, looking at JeNelle. "I've been waiting for this all night. May I have this dance, Ms. Towson?"

JeNelle rose from the table, as the band began to play "You Give Good Love." The vocalist led into the song with a rhythmic monologue. Her voice was melodic and sensual. Her words seemed to express every emotion that

Benny was feeling, as he held JeNelle in his arms. Her body matched every movement of his. He could feel the tingling beginning in his spine that always gave rise to his nature. He was powerless to stop it. He thought, perhaps if he opened his eyes and tried to focus his attention on something else he could control himself. Do calculus in his head. Fun flight maneuvers. Nothing. It didn't work. JeNelle's soft, fragrant hair against his cheek smelled fresh and invigorating and felt soft on his neck and chest. Her perfume took him outside of himself, but for some reason reminded him of Stacy. The vocalist wasn't helping matters either. Her soulful rendition went on and on, each chord and each phrase more soulful than the one before it. He was fully erect now. JeNelle had to have noticed the change, he thought, but she did not backed away from him. She continued to move with him, her full breasts pressing against him and her taught nipples teasing his chest. Her bare back felt as smooth and soft as velvet under his hands. When the music ended, Benny suddenly feared what the erection in his slacks would reveal.

JeNelle looked up at him. Her face was even lovelier and her eyes more radiant.

"You do that very well," she said. "Was it hard?"

"Hard?" he asked, suddenly feeling embarrassed, as they left the dance floor. *'Hard'* was the operative word to be using at that moment. He was hard as an oak.

"Was what hard?" he asked, feeling some concern about her answer.

"Was it hard for you to learn to dance so well? What did you think that I meant?"

"Dance, uh, I knew that you meant dance. Uh, no, you're a good teacher."

"I'm sure you've had plenty of experience before. It surely felt like it to me."

"No, uh, I was merely following your lead all the way. I was inspired."

JeNelle smiled and looked squarely at Benny. "You were the pilot, I was merely the crew."

He wanted to tell her that she could throttle up his engine anytime she was ready! But he held back. Instead, he signaled the waiter to bring another round of drinks.

"How is it that a fascinating woman like you isn't married with a house full of children?" Benny asked.

"I've been married. I'm divorced," JeNelle said, without expression.

"The man was a fool to let you get away. Was he crazy or just plain stupid?" he joked.

"I was lucky."

Benny was puzzled. "Lucky?"

"Yes, lucky that we made a clean break of it and that there were no children involved," she said, looking away from him.

"How old were you when you got married?"

"Seventeen, but it's not a topic that bears discussion."

He sensed a shift in her demeanor and felt as if an invisible curtain had just been dropped.

The waiter brought two new rounds of drinks and announced, "Last call." Gloria, Cecil and Janice were all still on the dance floor. JeNelle looked at her watch. It was 1:45 A.M. and many of the patrons were beginning to leave. JeNelle noticed that Benny had been drinking Saratoga Mineral Water all evening.

"You're not drinking?" JeNelle asked, curious.

"I can't drink and fly within twelve hours. I have to be on the flight line by 0930 tomorrow." He checked his watch. "Uh, I mean today."

"Then we should go so that you can get some rest. You shouldn't have let us keep you out so late."

"I'll be fine," he chuckled. "I only need a few hours of sleep." He took her hand in his. "I've enjoyed being with you tonight. I hope that we can do this again very soon," he said an octave lower, mesmerized by her beautiful eyes.

Before JeNelle could answer, Gloria returned to the table with Tony Jamerson close behind. They were obviously exchanging contact information, as they stood whispering beside the table. Then Tony gave Gloria a little kiss on the cheek and was having a hard time releasing her hand.

"See you at the game," Tony said, as he finally began to depart.

Benny raised an eyebrow, as he looked up at Gloria who smiled and shrugged. "A woman's got to do what a woman's got to do," she said.

Benny just shook his head and smirked. He called for the check, but their waiter told him that the Chargers had covered their tab.

Cecil and Janice were still being courted by several admirers. They weren't going straight back to the condo. Benny sighed in relief. Benny, Gloria, and JeNelle drove back alone with Benny behind the wheel and JeNelle beside him. Gloria sat in the back seat smiling as if she had some guilty secret, he noticed.

"You're not going to try to drive back to Santa Barbara tonight, are you?" Benny asked.

"Sure. It's only a few hours up the coast from here."

"Oh no, I've got a couple of spare rooms and one with twin beds. You can have your pick. You two are staying over."

"I have to open the shop in the morning."

"Sorry, JeNelle. I'm a country boy. You'll have to accept my Southern Hospitality and call one of your managers or employees and get one of them to open up for you. I wouldn't be able to sleep thinking of you and Gloria on the highway at this time of the morning. How could I explain this to Vivian if anything happened to you and Gloria? She'd kill me."

"But—."

"No 'buts'."

"Come on, JeNelle. You can go in late just one day, can't you?" Gloria whined. "Plus we've both had a lot to drink and I'm too tired to drive home tonight."

"Speak for yourself. I only had a few drinks." JeNelle knew that it was not wise to drive even after one drink, particularly when she was unaccustomed to drinking at all. She sighed in resignation. "Okay, Benny, I can't argue with both of you. We'll accept your 'Southern Hospitality' and stay over. Gloria and I will leave in the morning."

They drove to Benny's and the valet opened the car door for them to get out. As they walked toward the elevator, the ever efficient and helpful Fred said, "Captain Alexander, your flowers, remember?"

Benny turned around, accepted his flowers from Fred, and put his electronic key card in the elevator slot, punching his access code into the security pad. The doors opened and they went in. Benny stood between JeNelle and Gloria, holding the flowers and feeling very foolish.

"Your mother really must think a lot of you to send you two dozen, long-stemmed, red roses, Benny," JeNelle said, smiling knowingly.

Gloria covered her mouth to hide her amusement. Benny didn't say a word.

Once in his condo, he gave the women fresh towels and silk nightgowns that he claimed Vivian brought and forgot to take with her on her last visit. The women weren't convinced, he noticed, particularly since Gloria knew that Vivian rarely wore anything to sleep in. Benny strongly suggested that JeNelle might be more comfortable in the spare bedroom that adjoined his because it had a queen-sized bed in it. JeNelle and Gloria opted to stay in the spare room on the main level that had two full-sized beds. Benny said goodnight, went up to his room and closed his door. He speed dialed Vivian's number. It was 6:15 A.M. in Washington, D.C.

"Hello?" Vivian answered very groggy and not really conscious of what she was doing.

"Vivian, wake up!" Benny insisted.

"Benny, is that you? Why are you calling me so early? Is something wrong?"

"I think I'm in love," he enthusiastically said.

"That's nice, Benny," she mumbled. "I'm glad you two worked it out. Have a nice life."

"No, Viv. I'm not in love with Stacy. I'm in love with your housemate's sister."

Vivian didn't hear the 'sister' part. She was still sleeping.

"You're in love with my housemate? Who Gloria?" she asked with some surprise.

"No, with JeNelle."

"Benny, I don't have a housemate named JeNelle."

"No, you don't understand. I went out with Gloria, Cecil, Janice and JeNelle—."

"Wait a minute, Benny. It's a little early in the morning for me. Just give me the facts. Who's on first, where is second, and what the heck happened to third? And, oh, who's at bat?" Vivian was struggling with the lineup.

"While I was dancing with her I realized that she had to be the one."

"Which one? Who are Cecil and Janice?"

"They live in the building on the twenty-third floor. You remember. You've met them before."

"So who's the one?"

"JeNelle! Aren't you listening? See, Stacy sent these flowers to me, and JeNelle . . ."

"Stacy? Who's Stacy?"

"Stacy's the one I told you about."

"I thought that we were talking about JeNelle or Cecil or was it Janice?"

"No, no, you've got it backwards!"

"Benny! Brother, I do love you! I swear I do! But I can't keep up! Can you call me back during the daylight hours? And in the meantime, brother, get a grip!"

Benny laughed. "Okay Viv, I'll call you later today."

"Thanks, my brother. I'm out."

Chapter 7

Vivian hung up the cell phone.

"Who was that, Viv?" Carlton asked.

"I think it was my brother," she moaned trying to recapture the sleep that she lost.

"Which one?"

"Benny, I think. He says that he's in love," she groaned.

"With who?"

"I'm not sure. There seemed to be a long list to choose from."

"Well, you know Benny. You can't tell who the players are without a score card," Carlton said, folding Vivian into his arms. "I'm glad that you're a one-man woman."

Vivian snuggled close to her pillow, trying to sink back into a strange dream about a cowboy, skis and a Stetson. Carlton found her buried beneath the covers and kissed her passionately. She was still groggy and could have used four or five more hours of sleep, but Carlton was wide-awake and feeling amorous. As he reached for the nightstand drawer and pulled it open, Vivian thought, *I'm going to kill Benny. Just wait until I get my hands on his scrawny neck.* Carlton and Vivian had sex for hours the night before, not falling asleep until well after 2:00 A.M. She was not feeling particularly amorous at that time of the morning, but she submitted and responded to Carlton as best she could. It wasn't the same for her anymore. She felt like she was only going through the motions, because her mind and heart weren't in it. For some reason that she couldn't understand, the skiing-cowboy-doctor crossed her mind just as Carton was about to reach his climax. She tried to refocus her thoughts away from Chuck Montgomery, but somehow he was in her head.

Vivian's alarm sounded at 9:00 A.M. Carlton reached across her and hit the snooze button. Vivian didn't even move. She was buried somewhere under the thick comforter. Carlton shook her.

"Vivian, wake up. It's nine o'clock."

"In a minute, Carlton. Give me just a minute." The muffled sound came from beneath the covers.

"Vivian, you're going to be late if you don't get up now. You agreed to go to the shelter today, remember?"

"I'm going, I'm going," the sound said. "Just give me a few more minutes."

Carlton got up and walked to the foot of the bed. He reached down, grabbed the comforter and yanked it off the bed. Empty condom wrappers flew everywhere. Vivian still didn't move. She stayed curled up in a fetal position hugging her pillow. Carlton opened the door between the bedroom and bathroom, picked up Vivian, and carried her into the shower. The water charged out of the shower nozzle. That got her attention.

"*Carlton!*" she screamed, as the water hit her body, "I could learn to hate you real easy for this!"

"You'll thank me later," he said, pouring shampoo on her hair and vigorously rubbing it in. He soaped her body and then his, rinsed himself off, and stepped out of the shower, leaving Vivian to finish the rest.

"Breakfast in five minutes," he said, as he closed the bathroom door.

"Yep, I'm going to kill Benny and it will be ruled justifiable homicide. No jury in the country would convict me!" she said aloud with much emphasis then turned her face up to the full-force shower spray.

Carlton was dressed, putting cream cheese on two hot onion bagels when Vivian dragged herself into the kitchen. Grapefruit was already sitting on the table, perfectly sectioned, and the table was set for two. The aroma from the fresh-brewed coffee was permeating the air. Vivian sat down at the table and buried her face in her hands. She was wearing a dark blue Georgetown hoodie. The bottom of her pants were stuffed down into her new Timberland high-top boots, a Christmas gift, which showed no sign of water spots from her previous experiences in the snow.

Carlton placed the hot bagels on a plate in front of her and poured the coffee into the waiting mugs.

"Don't you two ever sleep?" a voice grumbled from the kitchen door.

Vivian and Carlton looked up to see Melissa come in wearing a one-piece plaid pajama with feet in them and pompoms on the toes. They looked at each other and burst out laughing at Melissa, as she shuffled across the kitchen and picked up a coffee mug from the rack. She sat down at the table with a thud.

"Don't you two dare laugh at me!" she scornfully mumbled. "You kept me up half the night! Telephones ringing at ungodly hours of the morning. Sounded like Carlton was auditioning for a hallelujah choir. Then you two hitting it again and again and again this morning. Then there's water running, people yelling in the shower. If this is what engaged people act like, I want no parts of it! Pour some coffee for me, you sex fiend!" Melissa ordered, shoving her cup at Carlton.

"Who's a sex fiend?" Another voice entered the conversation from the kitchen doorway.

In walked William "Bill" Chandler dressed in his traditional *GQ* attire. The man was built like a Greek God and had a face like a Botticelli painting. A young Tom Selleck look-alike, but better. He had been a professional male model since he was sixteen, and a male prostitute before that. His picture was always adorned by some haute couture's wardrobe in *Esquire, GQ,* or *Playgirl*. In addition to being a high-priced model, he was an actor, but he made more money posing nearly nude or nude in the gay trades. He was certainly a favorite. The camera, and most of the cameramen, loved to photograph him. He was hung like a stallion. He reeked of an edgy sophistication and charm with matinee-idol good looks. Unless he told you, no one would have suspected that Bill was gay or "bisexual," as he preferred to call it. He looked equally as comfortable with a woman as he did when he was with a man. His dark eyebrows against his fresh, white skin and deep blue eyes stopped both men and women in their tracks. He also possessed one of the best legal minds of their group of scholars.

Bill came into the kitchen and unwrapped his six-foot, four-inch frame from under a black cashmere Adolfo coat, cream-colored Polo scarf, and black fedora with a small feather in the band to reveal a beautiful grey Armani silk-blended suit, and cranberry turtleneck that hugged his pecks, as if he had been poured into it. He hung up his coat, suit jacket, hat and scarf, tucking his black calf's skin gloves into his coat pocket.

"Who's a sex fiend?" he repeated.

"Carlton," Melissa chirped.

"What are you doing here, Bill?" Vivian asked. "I thought that you were going to stay in New York through New Year's?"

Bill picked up a cup and poured coffee for himself. Then he walked to the table and kissed Melissa and Vivian on their foreheads, before sitting down.

"I got bored. I sat around for two days waiting for my agent to ink the deal on Sergio's fall collection and the bastards couldn't agree on who would do the make up!"

"Didn't you enjoy spending time with your family?" Melissa innocently asked.

"Oh sure!" he facetiously intoned. "My father sat around the house all day wearing the gold Rolex that I gave him for Christmas and telling me how I ought to buy a house for him in the Catskills. My sister was bitching about why I gave her a diamond tennis bracelet for Christmas instead of a BMW. She's only fifteen. My dear, absentee mother, wherever the hell she is, didn't even bother to call to say Merry Christmas or kiss my ass. Some Norman Rockwell portrait that was. I had had it. I just got out of there on the first available flight I could get and came home."

"Sounds like you had as much fun as I did," Melissa sighed. "My parents must have paraded every eligible bachelor in the State of Rhode Island through the house, extolling each one's virtues. I never did get to see any of my friends. I couldn't wait to get back to Stan."

"Stan? Where is he anyway, Melissa?" Carlton asked.

"He left last night after you two went to bed. He had to take his kids to the dentist at eight o'clock this morning."

"*Kids?* Stan is married?" Vivian asked, shocked.

"Well, technically, yes."

"I'd say kids and a wife are a bit more than a technicality, Melissa," Vivian drolly said.

"Well, they've been separated for three months. They just need to work out the details for their divorce."

"*Divorce?*" Vivian asked. "How long have they been married?"

"Seven years," Melissa said matter-of-factly.

"Speaking of marriage, Vivian. I love a great segue. Is there something that you want to tell me?" Bill asked, lifting her left hand to inspect the ring on her finger from several angles. "I'd say about two carats, blue-white stone, with what, fourteen carat gold setting? Yes, I think that there is definitely something that you want to tell me."

"It's an engagement ring, Bill," Melissa cheerfully chirped.

Carlton beamed, but Vivian blankly stared at Bill.

"Oh really, Melissa, and what was your first clue?" Bill asked with acerbic wit without heat. "Now, Vivian, I thought that you were going to tell Carlton about our affair. I remember specifically that, after we made love last weekend, you swore your undying love for me. Now I see you sitting here wearing another man's engagement ring. Yes, I think that you have some 'splaining to do, Lucy."

"*Affair?*" Carlton exploded.

"*Love making?*" Melissa questioned. "Where was I during all this?"

"He's joking! You know…pulling your leg?" Vivian leered at Bill with her infamous *'you're dead meat'* expression and said, "In your dreams, Chandler! In your dreams!"

"That's what it was, Carlton, I'm sorry to say, my man. A dream come true."

"I'm out of here!" Vivian said still leering at Bill while pointing two fingers at her eyes and then at his. "I'll deal with you later, Chandler!"

"I'll be waiting, my pet. I love it when you're forceful. No chains this time. Just bring your whip," he responded smugly.

Vivian rolled her eyes, popped Bill on the head with one of his magazines, and left the kitchen. Carlton followed her and heard Melissa and Bill talking.

"I didn't know that Vivian had a whip!" Melissa incredulously said.

"It's a long story, Melissa. I've been Vivian's love slave all along. Pour another cup of coffee for me and I'll tell you the whole, sad story."

Carlton was silent, as he drove Vivian to the shelter. She curled up in the passenger seat and dozed off. He finally had to ask.

"Vivian, Bill was just joking, wasn't he?"

Vivian didn't even open her eyes, but said sarcastically, "No, baby, he and I have been kicking the covers for months now. You know gay guys make great lovers. And he's mesmerized by this chocolate body of mine. He calls me his 'Chocolate Syrup' because I just ooze all over him when we make love. Got the picture?"

"He's not gay, he's bisexual!" Carlton insisted, desperately trying to search Vivian's face to discern the truth while he drove.

"Get over it, Andrews! You've been beaten out by a white, bisexual, movie idol, male model in drag!"

Carlton was now quiet. Vivian opened one eye and peeked at him. She could almost see the wheels turning in his head. He suddenly swung the car over to the curb and put it in park. Vivian sat straight up.

"What are you doing, Carlton?"

Carlton forcefully grabbed her by the shoulders. "Vivian, tell me the truth! Is there something going on between you and Bill?! I mean, he's with you all the time! He's got money and—."

"Carlton Andrews, you're acting like a fool!" she said, breaking his grip on her. "I told you that Bill was yanking your chain! I was in San Francisco last weekend, remember? Get a grip! Bill and me? It ain't happening!"

Carlton faced her squarely. "There is a lot of race mixing going on at SCU. White guys coming on to black women all the time. Some of them even date openly. It's not as rare as you think!"

Calmly, Vivian said, "I'm not the one whose fidelity is in question, remember? I do care about you, though. I—."

"You're going to bring that up again?" he exploded.

"Enough said! Now start this car and take me to work," she ordered.

Carlton complied, but Vivian felt that he still wasn't convinced. *Another case of justifiable homicide*, she thought. *Benjamin Staton Alexander and William Anthony Chandler.*

Moments later, Carlton pulled up in front of the Family Homeless Shelter.

"I'm going back to the house and do the laundry," Carlton said, somewhat dejectedly. "Call me when you're ready to be picked up."

Vivian frowned and rubbed her arms where he had held her roughly.

"I've got some errands to run after I finish here. I've got to go to DMV and get a new driver's license and over to Administration and get another ID card or I won't be able to use the library. Then I have to pick up the Snowman. I'll get home on my own. I do it all the time."

"No," he said forcefully, "you call me and I'll take you on your errands."

There was that 'don't mess with me look' in Carlton's eyes, so Vivian agreed to call him when she finished work. She didn't kiss him goodbye when he leaned toward her. She got out of the car and headed into the shelter.

Betty Foster, one of the shelter agents, was obviously glad to see her come through the doors that led to the Clearing Center. She grinned broadly and nodded toward a long line of people who were waiting to be interviewed by the law school students whose primary function was to help applicants fill out forms for jobs, public assistance, Medicare, housing, food stamps, green cards... whatever the need. The law school students were there to help. Vivian could see it was going to be a long day.

Vivian had been there for over six hours and was beginning to feel weary. Fortunately, she and Alan Lightfoot, another law school student, were working together with their last client of the day, a Peruvian woman, Signora Anna Menendez-Gaza. She had two young children, Angelique and Miguel, and spoke very little English. Alan Lightfoot, a Native American, who was older than most One L's at Georgetown, helped translate for Signora Menendez-Gaza. Alan grew up on the Navajo reservation in New Mexico, but he only knew a little Spanish. They could barely make out that Anna had come to Washington looking for her husband who had been sending money home every week until about four months ago. The last address that she had for her husband was for a place in the Adams-Morgan area of Washington, but when she finally arrived, the building was a burned-out heap. There was no sign of her husband, she had no relatives or friends in Washington, and she had no money.

Vivian and Alan were working with Anna so intently that they didn't notice the figure of a man standing just outside of the cubical where they were sitting with Anna and her two children. Anna's son, Miguel, was playing quietly on the floor with a small plastic truck, but her daughter, Angelique, who appeared to be about twelve years old, was leaning against her mother, nodding off to sleep. Alan finally noticed the man standing there and said, "Can I help you, sir?"

"I'm waiting to see Ms. Alexander," said a voice that Vivian thought she recognized. She turned around and there stood Chucky, the skiing cowboy, second-year, resident doctor wearing that same cowboy getup complete with sunglasses.

Something welled up in Vivian at the sight of the handsome, somehow sexy vision standing before her. Her breathing quickened and her pulse raced for some inexplicable reason. Vivian excused herself and walked toward Chuck.

"What are you doing here?" she asked.

"You left this wallet in the truck. I found it under Ahkmed's luggage. I thought that you might need it," he said, handing the wallet to Vivian.

It was hers all right. "Thank you," she mumbled, still amazed at how he had found her and how he made her feel. "How did you know that I was here?"

"Your housemate, I think her name is Melissa, told me that your fiancée took you to work here at the shelter. Your other housemate called the shelter, I think his name is Bill, and verified that you were still here."

"I left the wallet in your truck two days ago. Why are you just now getting in touch with me?"

"Look, Ms. Oakley. Holster those six shooters. I've been on duty for forty-eight hours straight. I just got some relief. There was no telephone number in your wallet and you're not listed in directory assistance. I tracked you down as soon as it was humanly possible. Now is there anything else that you need to know?" Chuck Montgomery was clearly annoyed.

Vivian was beginning to feel ashamed of her incessant questions and the tingle of excitement creeping up her spine. She realized that she was cranky because of a lack of rest or sleep and her annoyance with Carlton. PMS was a bitch on wheels, too.

"I'm sorry. I do appreciate your taking the time to bring this to me, especially since you've obviously been working since we flew in from Chicago." Stuffing her hands in her pants pockets, she relaxed a bit. "I never really said how much I appreciated your kindness for taking me home from the airport."

"That's better," Chuck said, now visibly calmer. "All that you had to do was say 'thank you'." Chuck looked past Vivian at the little girl sitting with her mother. "By the way, I think that little girl is sick. She needs to see a pediatrician. If I'm right, she's running a high fever."

Vivian looked over her shoulder at the little girl. Although Vivian had not noticed it before, the little girl did look ill. Vivian tried to ask Anna whether her daughter had been ill, but was getting nowhere. Even Alan didn't know the right words. Chuck stooped down before Angelique, felt her head, and took her pulse. He talked with Anna in fluent Spanish and, apparently, asked questions and got answers that he didn't like.

"She needs to see a doctor immediately," Chuck said, standing.

"They don't have medical insurance or any money," Vivian answered, frustrated.

Chuck reached into his pocket and pulled out a pad. On it, he scribbled the name and address of a doctor in the Georgetown area.

"Here, take her over to this address. I'll call ahead and tell them that you're coming," he said, handing the note to Vivian.

"I don't have my car here," Vivian said, with growing concern, "and even if I could get a cab it would cost a small fortune for all of us."

Without a moment's hesitation, Chuck took off his long buckskin coat, wrapped it around Angelique, and said something to Anna in Spanish. He picked up Angelique in his arms and headed to the door. Anna grabbed her son and followed. Vivian and Alan grabbed their coats and headed after them. Chuck put Anna in the back seat of his truck and Miguel on her lap. He handed Angelique to Alan. Vivian got into the front seat. As they drove away, Chuck pulled a cell phone from his pocket and speed dialed a number.

"D.J., I've got a twelve-year-old female, her pulse is...."

Vivian couldn't understand the medical discussion Chuck was having, but Chuck's haste, as he drove through the streets of Washington, D.C., on a workday during rush hour, clearly evidenced that there was some urgency in the situation.

"...ETA five minutes," Chuck said before he closed the cell phone.

"Where are you taking her?" Vivian asked.

"I have a buddy who's a pediatrician. His office is around the corner from the hospital. He's waiting for us."

Shortly thereafter, they pulled up to a very posh-looking building and Chuck got out of the truck. He took Angelique from Alan's arms. They all scrambled into the building, following Chuck whose long, ground-eating strides made them have to trot to keep up with him. He entered two, big, carved-oak doors on the first floor that had a gold plate affixed to the wall. The plate read: *"Doctors' Offices. Goldmahn, Fitch, Bellingham, and Jackson."* The office was a sumptuously furnished enclave, but comfortable. The nurse at the desk ushered Anna and Chuck carrying Angelique directly into an examination room while another nurse asked Vivian, Alan, and Miguel to have a seat in the waiting area. They all took seats and while Alan tried to comfort Miguel, Vivian glanced around the room. There were six or seven young patients seated with their parents who looked like they were all born with silver spoons in their mouths. Gold draped from the women's necks and wrists. They wore very chic, expensive clothing with bright, white diamonds on their fingers. Clearly, they must have looked like escapees from a refugee camp in Nicaragua as compared to these well-clad patrons. They sat in the waiting area while doctors went in and out of the room where Angelique was being examined.

Later, one doctor came out of the room, as ambulance drivers hustled through the oak doors. In a flurry of activity, they went into the room where Angelique was being examined and returned with her moments later accompanied by a Black man who could have been Denzel Washington's double, Vivian thought. He talked with Chuck, as they walked to the waiting ambulance. The sight of her daughter being wheeled out on a stretcher with a gas mask over her nose and an intravenous bag dripping fluid into Angelique's small arm frightened Anna. She began to weep. Alan was still trying to comfort her, as Chuck motioned for everyone to get into his truck.

The ambulance driver did not turn on the siren, but in moments Angelique was being wheeled into Georgetown University Hospital's Emergency Room entrance. Angelique seemed barely conscious. Chuck spoke to the six-foot, eight-inch Denzel Washington look-alike and then brought him to speak to Anna. Chuck translated what the Doctor Denzel look-alike was saying. Anna looked no less afraid, but seemed to understand what the doctors were telling her. The initial diagnosis was that at a minimum, Angelique was suffering from starvation and dehydration. She also had a high fever, 106 degrees, which the doctor felt had to be reduced or Angelique could be in serious danger. Vivian watched Chuck, as he took care in how he spoke to Anna. Although she did not seem to understand the medical terms, Chuck seemed to be giving Anna support and reassurances that all would be well. His attention was totally focused on Anna, Vivian noticed, and she responded to him even though tears were streaming down her face. She looked directly into Chuck's eyes with hope evident on her face. Dr. Denzel was finishing his discussion with Anna when Chuck brought him over and introduced him.

"D.J., this is Annie Oakley, Alan Lightfoot, and Angelique's little brother, Miguel. Everyone this is my best friend and mentor, Dr. Derrick Jackson."

"It's a pleasure to meet you, Denzel, I mean, Dr. Jackson," Vivian said, feeling quite embarrassed for her faux pas, "but my name is not Annie Oakley, it's Vivian Alexander." *His smile is radiant*, she thought.

"Somehow the name Annie Oakley didn't seem to fit you, Ms. Alexander, but I've known Chuck a long time. I know what to expect from him. I do want to thank you for getting Angelique to us so quickly. You probably saved her life."

"I had nothing to do with it, Dr. Jackson. Chuck was the one who spotted the problem. The credit belongs to him."

Alan agreed.

"Good look, Chuck," Derrick said, patting him on the back. "We may make a doctor out of you yet."

"Or kill me trying," Chuck added.

Then Derrick turned that radiant smile back on Vivian and an unexpected thrill ran up her spine. *What the hell is the matter with me? Just because two, handsome, physically appealing men smiled at me, I am feeling like some silly adolescent with raging hormones.*

"I've got to get back to my patient. It was a pleasure meeting all of you and especially you, Ms. Alexander," Derrick said, as he flashed that true Denzel Washington smile. "I hope to see you again under more favorable circumstances very soon." Then turning to Chuck, he said, "Chuck, may I speak with you for a moment?"

Derrick didn't know what hit him, but something about Vivian Alexander had paralyzed him. She was a dream come true. He had noticed her in his office, but now she captivated him. When she extended her hand and released an award-winning smile, he knew that he was sunk.

Walking away, Chuck and Derrick quietly spoke together. Occasionally Derrick would glance at Vivian while he and Chuck talked. Vivian became a bit selfconscious and wondered what they were discussing. Dr. Jackson took Anna with him to be with her daughter. Chuck started back to where Vivian, Alan, and Miguel were sitting, but before he reached them, an elderly nurse intercepted him.

"Dr. Montgomery, I can't read your instructions on this chart. I've been trying to page you for over an hour."

"I turned off my pager, Lucy. Officially I'm off duty for the next forty-eight hours," Chuck said, as he rewrote his instructions more legibly.

"I know that you've been on duty for the last two days, Doctor, but this is a good example of why we need to be able to reach you. You should never turn off your pager or your sell phone. Your handwriting gets worse every day," the nurse scolded.

Chuck leaned in close to the nurse with a salaciously naughty grin on his face. "Why don't you give me private handwriting lessons at your place, Lucy? Say about eleven o'clock tonight? I'll bring my pen."

The elderly nurse blushed. "Doctor, if you don't stop flirting with me, I'm going to have to bring you up on charges of sexual harassment."

"Meet me at your place, Lucy, and I'll really give you something to charge me with," Chuck said, with a sly smile and a wink.

The elderly nurse cupped her hand over her mouth, hiding her smile and scooted away. Chuck returned to the waiting area.

"Now, posse, all we can do is wait. Angelique will be taken upstairs, as soon as she's stable. In the meantime, I'm going to catch some shut eye," Chuck said, as he stretched out on one of the long, wide, waiting room benches next to Vivian and put his Stetson over his face.

She immediately lifted the hat. Although his eyes were closed, she spoke in a rush. "Chuck, you know that Anna doesn't have any insurance. How is she going to pay for this?"

"I've worked it out. It's handled. The next step is yours," he said cryptically.

"What are you talking about, 'the next step is mine'?"

"Give it a rest, Annie. I'll explain later," Chuck muttered groggily

Vivian was tempted to insist on an explanation at that moment, but Alan put his hand on her arm and shook his head. Just then, Vivian heard Chuck snoring. She dropped Chuck's Stetson back over his face. His snoring could still be heard. The man could fall asleep anywhere—in a busy airport or an emergency room.

"He's dead on his feet, Vivian. He's done a lot. Let him rest now," Alan cautioned.

Vivian took another long look at Chuck's prone body. He certainly was a big man and nearly seven feet tall. She relented and talked with Alan whom she did not know very well. Of course, she had seen him at the shelter whenever she was there and they did take honors classes together. She learned that Alan had gone into the Marines when he was seventeen years old. He served four years and fought in both Iraq and Afghanistan. Later, he left the Marines and attended the University of Texas at El Paso. He was new to Washington, D.C., and had no friends or family in the area, but whenever Vivian encountered him at the shelter, all the residences seemed to know him and trust his guidance. They talked about their feelings about the wars. Vivian told Alan that her brother, Benny, was with the 1st Tactical Fighter Wing. They talked until they saw Dr. Jackson and Anna approaching.

"Chuck," Dr. Jackson said, as he shook him, "you can go now. Angelique is resting comfortably. Her temperature is down to 104°. Take these people home. They all look beat. And you go get some rest. It's already after ten o'clock."

Chuck lifted his long legs off the bench and pulled his massive, but agile frame to a standing position. He stretched his arms out, twisted his neck from side to side and cupped his hands over his face, rubbing his eyes.

"All right, DJ, I'll call you later around 2:00 A.M."

"Oh no. You heard me. You've been at it for several days. Get some rest. Doctor's orders."

Chuck and Derrick exchanged a manly embrace.

The tired, and now hungry, posse piled into Chuck's truck again. Vivian suggested that they all go to her place for lasagna and everyone agreed. As they approached her door, she heard a dog barking and scratching.

"The Snowman's home!" she yelled.

Alan carried a sleeping Miguel on his shoulder, as he and Chuck looked at each other. "Snowman?" they mouthed at each other and shrugged their shoulders. Before Vivian could unlock the door, it flew open and there stood Carlton with his hands on his hips, eyes flashing, and obviously upset.

"Where the hell have you been?!" he stormed. "Do you know what time it is?! I have been all over this damn town looking for you! I want an explanation, and I want it now!"

Vivian was too tired to cope. "I'll explain later," she said, as the Snowman, a pure white, Alaskan Husky, jumped and pranced around her. She hugged her dog and then got to her feet.

"Carlton Andrews, this is *Señora* Anna Menendez-Gaza and her son, Miguel, Alan Lightfoot and Chuck Montgomery. We're starving. Is there any lasagna left?"

"Sure, there's plenty of food, but you and I need to have a talk about...." Carlton said, stumbling to a halt and then suddenly his demeanor changed. *"Montgomery? Did you say Chuck Montgomery?"*

"Yes, Chuck Montgomery," Vivian repeated.

"Are you the same Charles Montgomery who played power forward and center for Boston College?"

"The same," Chuck said, extending his hand.

"Of course, you are," he enthused. "You play in the pros out west somewhere... Denver or Utah, then the Celtics, right. I remember when you got drafted! You are awesome on the court! Where are you playing now? You here to consider playing for the Washington Wizards? They certainly could use a strong center like you," Carlton asked, excitedly pumping Chuck's hands.

Carlton was over the moon, Vivian noticed. She gaped at his changed comportment. She barely recognized this instantaneously changed personae.

"No. Bad knees. I'm trying to learn to practice medicine," Chuck said.

When Vivian finally closed her mouth, she took their coats and showed them into the back family room where Melissa and Bill were watching the video, *Tombstone*, Bill's favorite movie. They introduced themselves while Vivian excused herself and dragged Carlton away from Chuck and to the kitchen.

"What do we have in the house to eat?" Vivian asked, as they reached the kitchen.

"Well, there's baked chicken, mashed potatoes, green beans, salad and rolls left over. And, of course, lasagna and...."

"Would you help me set it all up?" Vivian asked.

"Vivian, do you know who that is in there?" Carlton asked emphatically. "That's Charles Montgomery! He's a multimillionaire! The man plays some ball! The leftovers are fine for those other people, but you can't feed him just anything. Don't you have any steaks? Or maybe lobster? He's used to the best!"

"I don't care how rich he is and maybe that's what he did before to make that kind of money, but tonight he saved a little girl's life. I think that's more important than his wealth or bouncing a basketball. Besides, he's tired and hungry. We all are. I don't think that it would matter much to him what he ate at this point. A Happy Meal would taste like pheasant under glass right about now."

"Uh, Vivian," Carlton looked at her and frowned, "You don't get it, do you? He's got connections. He's got big bank! He's got juice! He *knows* people. *Influential people.* He could introduce me to all the *right* people. That could get me into coaching in the pros. I've got to make a good impression on him." He put his hands on her shoulders. "You're going to be my wife, Vivian. You've got to learn to...uh...support me when it comes to making the right impression. Tonight could lead to something big for me...I mean, us." He looked at

Vivian's clothes. "Why don't you go change your clothes and put on something, you know…uh…pretty, sexy. Maybe fix up your hair and…uh…put on a little makeup or something."

Reigning in a rude remark, she tried patience. "Carlton, it's late. I've been on my feet all day. I'm tired, cranky, and hungry. We've all had a drain on the body systems today. All anyone wants at this point is some food and some rest. No one is here for a social affair or a career opportunity."

"I have to take whatever opportunity I can get! When opportunity knocks, *open the damn door!*" he said demonstratively and frowned at her.

Vivian could see that she wasn't going to get her point across and she was too weary to keep trying. She thought if Carlton only knew what kind of impression she had already made on Chuck Montgomery a few days earlier, he'd probably have a coronary. She decided that telling him that she had also just met *the* basketball icon Derrick "Dunk and Jam" Jackson it would truly push Carlton over the edge. Derrick Jackson, or DJ, as he was affectionately known in the basketball world, was even more famous than Chuck Montgomery. Nope, this was not the time to mention DJ Jackson though her thoughts were on him and on Chuck Montgomery a little too much for her own comfort.

"Let's just see how fast we can get some food on the table, Carlton. We'll worry about 'impressions' later," she said, frustrated.

Vivian started placing the plates and glasses on the table. Carlton busied himself pulling food from the refrigerator and desperately searching in the freezer for some steaks. When she finished setting the table, she decided to go into the back family room and see what everyone wanted to drink. She approached the room expecting to hear people talking, but there was dead silence except for the cracking sound coming from the burning logs in the fireplace. The television was still on and Val Kilmer (playing Doc Holiday) was sitting at a piano, noodling some tune. As Vivian's eyes rounded the room, she saw Alan asleep on one of the recliners with his feet up. Chuck was in the other recliner snoring. Anna was sitting on the sofa clutching a pillow and nodding off. Bill was lying in the middle of the floor with a sleeping Miguel nestled in his arm. Bill was stroking Miguel's curly brown locks and said, "I'm your huckleberry." Miguel had his tiny arm draped across the Snowman. Her dog uncharacteristically did not move when she entered the room. Melissa was snapping pictures of Bill, Miguel, and the Snowman with the fireplace in the background. She quietly tiptoed toward Vivian and whispered, "Now that's a Norman Rockwell portrait." The fireplace logs continued to pop and crackle. Vivian and Melissa covered their guests with blankets, but they did not bother to awaken anyone for dinner.

Chapter 8

Benny woke early, showered, dressed in his flight uniform, and was downstairs microwaving bacon when JeNelle entered the kitchen.

"Good morning," he said, with a bright, cheery smile and tone in his voice. "Did you sleep well?"

"Yes, very well, thank you. What are you doing?" she quizzically asked.

"I thought that I'd make breakfast for you and Gloria before I left. How do you like your eggs?"

"Benny, I usually don't eat breakfast and, uh, I don't like eggs. I'm sorry that you've gone to all of this trouble," she said, smiling.

A knot tightened in Benny's chest. Her smile was so beautiful. "You have to have something. How about juice, coffee, and toast?"

"All right, Benny, since you've gone to all this trouble. Is there something that I can do to help?"

"Oh no, I have everything under control. You just sit at the table by the window and look beautiful...I mean, relax. The morning newspaper is on the chair and your juice is on the table."

Benny watched JeNelle, as she moved across his expansive eat-in kitchen and went toward the table to sit down. The sun began to rise and shine through the east windows. The hues of early morning light made a perfect backdrop, but could not compete with JeNelle's beauty, Benny thought. He kept glancing at her out of the corner of his eye, as she sat reading the Business Section of the newspaper. He didn't notice that the toast was starting to burn in the toaster until JeNelle looked up over the newspaper at him and caught him staring at her.

"Benny, I think you have a problem," JeNelle said, with a slight smile.

"Me? No. I'm an uncomplicated person. No problems to speak of," he said, jovially.

"No, Benny, that's not what I mean."

Suddenly the smoke alarm went off. Benny dropped the bowl of eggs, splattering its contents over the counter top. The toaster finally released its grip and the toast popped up and out of the toaster, but not before it filled the kitchen with smoke. Benny began fanning the smoke away from the ceiling alarm. He flipped on the exhaust fan over the stove and then dashed to the sliding glass door in the kitchen. He fumbled around trying to open it.

"I'll do that, Benny," JeNelle said calmly. "You need to catch the eggs."

Benny dashed back to the counter where the eggs were dripping down the face of the cabinet onto the floor. He grabbed the paper towel so forcefully that it broke away from the holder and rolled across the room right up to JeNelle's feet. The microwave bell sounded and Benny opened the door to find overcooked bacon. He closed the door without removing the food. It was a colossal fiasco. Benny was trying to make a good impression on JeNelle and he was beginning to feel like a total klutz.

JeNelle noticed his embarrassment. She opened the full-view glass door and picked up the paper towel, which had rolled out to at least ten feet.

"What's going on in here?" Gloria asked, as she came through the kitchen door frowning and fanning the smoke away from her face. "What's burning?"

"Benny was making breakfast for us and overdid it a bit," JeNelle said, with a wry smile on her face.

"Breakfast? I don't eat breakfast, Benny," Gloria said, still fanning the smoke. "You shouldn't have gone to the trouble."

"Now you tell me," Benny muttered, dejectedly.

"I'm going to take a shower. Just juice for me, Benny," Gloria said, leaving the kitchen, still fanning the smoke.

JeNelle replaced the paper towel in its holder, smiled at Benny, shook her head, and returned to the table to read the newspaper.

Benny cleaned up the eggs, trashed the bacon, poured two cups of coffee, and sat down at the table across from JeNelle.

"You like it black, no sugar, and no cream, right?"

"Yes, you remembered. Thank you," she said, taking the coffee, but her attention seemed to be on an announcement that she was reading in the newspaper.

"What are you reading?" Benny asked.

"This article about a Small Business Expo in San Francisco next week. Looks like it's going to be a big one."

"Are you exhibiting?" he asked. "I know that my brother is."

"Your brother? What's his line?" she asked.

"He and two partners own a company called CompuCorrect, Inc. They design computer networks, service, repair and recondition computer systems, and other electronic equipment. They also design computer software systems for small businesses. It's a full-range information technology company—computer-telephony integration systems, interactive voice response and other artificial intelligence systems. He's been doing quite well."

"CompuCorrect. I read about that company last week. They won a very lucrative contract with the military and another one with a county school system. I hear that they do very good work. They have a good reputation, according to the article that I read."

"That's my big brother, Kenneth. He earned that reputation honestly. He's a workaholic and his partners and staff are just as fanatical as he is. I mean, the man has no life outside of his business. I took him to some clubs while I was in San Francisco for Christmas. I think that he danced once and that's only because I forced him into it. It was party time…you know, Miller time, and all that he did was talk about the business. Don't get me wrong though, I do love my brother, and I respect and admire what he's accomplished, but what do you do with the rest of your life? You have to have some balance. Life means living it. Go for the gusto. Enjoy your accomplishments, don't just work for them."

"Your brother doesn't enjoy his accomplishments?"

"I've seen no evidence of it."

"Sounds perfectly normal to me. He's set some goals and he's dedicated to achieving them."

"No question! But I don't want to sit here and squander what little time I have with you talking about my brother. What's more important to me is: when can I see you again?" He smiled at her.

"Benny, let me be frank. I think you know that my sister has a crush on you. I'm not going to interfere with that."

"Gloria? A crush on me?" he said in all innocence. "I don't think so! If last night was any indication, I'm the last person on her mind. I'll bet that on New Year's Day she'll be in San Diego Stadium sitting in the VIP section reserved for guests of the San Diego Chargers watching the game and one special person on the team."

"I'm not going to run the risk of doing something that might hurt her."

"Okay, you ask her what her feelings are about me. Then you have three options."

"Options again. I lost at this game last night, remember?" She chuckled.

"I won," Benny said softly, reaching for JeNelle's hand. "Now, your options are these: You can have a friend, a romance or whatever is behind curtain number three. It's your call, but remember, if you pick the wrong option, you'll have to suffer the consequences."

"And what are the consequences?"

"That's not how we play the game. Remember, you have to take risks."

JeNelle looked at Benny for a moment and said, "Let's try friendship."

"Bong! Wrong answer. You have to suffer the consequences."

JeNelle smiled. "And what are the consequences?"

"You have to have dinner with me on New Year's Day while Gloria is at the game."

"You certainly are sure of yourself about Gloria. And what if you're wrong and she's interested in you?"

"Trust me. I know what I'm talking about," Benny said, with a knowing smile.

Right on cue, Gloria entered the kitchen brushing her long, black, thick hair. "What are you two talking about?"

"Options, Gloria. Options." Benny grinned, looking at JeNelle and sipping his coffee.

JeNelle removed her hand from Benny's and picked up the newspaper. Gloria looked at them both, shrugged her shoulders, and said, "Is there any juice left?"

"Sure," Benny said. "Here, you sit down and I'll get it for you."

"Thanks, Benny. You've been such a great host. You're really set up for overnight guests, too. Hair dryers, flat irons, nightgowns, robes, slippers, toothbrushes, shampoo and conditioners. Even women's underwear with the tags still on them."

Benny cleared his throat uncomfortably and flushed. "Uh, Vivian left a lot of that stuff here. I just left it for when she, my sister, Aretha, or my mother visit. You know, just in case they forget something they won't be inconvenienced. Of course, I do have a lot of male buddies who stay over sometimes. Mostly military."

"I'm sure that your male buddies appreciate the silk bras and panties," JeNelle quipped, looking away from Benny, as she sipped her coffee.

Benny took a quick look at JeNelle, as he poured the orange juice into a glass and handed it to Gloria. He knew how to handle this situation. He had a lot of practice.

"Uh, Gloria, I had a great time last night. I have some mandatory downtime coming up and I wondered what you're doing on New Year's Day? I thought that we might all get together and have dinner. You pick the place and time."

"Oh, I'm sorry, Benny. I have plans for New Year's Day, but why don't you and JeNelle have dinner together."

"Are you sure? We could eat late if you want. It's your call," Benny said, confident of what Gloria would say.

"Oh no. You and JeNelle go ahead. I'm going to the Chargers' game and I don't know what time I'll be free. In fact, JeNelle, would you drive me down here to the game? I can get home on my own. You and Benny can spend the time together."

"That's a great idea," Benny said, grinning at JeNelle.

JeNelle pursed her lips. "I'll see what I can do," JeNelle said, avoiding Benny's smug stare. "But I'm thinking about exhibiting in this Small Business Expo next week, if it's not too late. I may have to work New Year's Day. If so, I'll let you use my car to go to the game. That way I'm sure you'll be able to get home."

"What about dinner with Benny?" Gloria asked. "You're not going to leave him all alone on New Year's Day, are you? How am I going to explain this to Vivian? I'm living in Benny's house in D.C., dirt cheap, I might add, with his sister. Benny goes out of his way to make dinner for us, take us out to a great club, put us up overnight, and then serve us breakfast, and we're going to leave him, a military man, stranded on New Year's Day? The least you can do, JeNelle, is buy dinner and a few drinks for him to say thank you. Besides, JeNelle, nobody works on New Year's Day. It's downright unAmerican!" Gloria joked.

"I'm sure that Benny would have no trouble filling his time on New Year's Day. Any one of the women at Jason's stated that they would pay for his company," she mused.

"JeNelle—," Gloria huffed, frustrated.

"All right, all right, Gloria, you're going to be some attorney. You've even got me convinced that it's my patriotic duty to take Benny out to dinner. I get the impression that I'll be drummed out of the family and shot at sunrise, if I don't," JeNelle said, as she looked across the table at Benny who looked very smug.

"I'm glad that you see the wisdom of your sister's argument," Benny said, with a wry smile, as he sipped his coffee. "I'll call my brother later today and see what he knows about the Expo and whether you can still get into the exhibit?"

"That's not necessary, Benny. I'll call the Expo officials when I get back to work today. They'll know whether it's too late or not. Please don't go to any more trouble on my account. I might not be able to pay the tab," JeNelle said, nonchalantly.

"It's no trouble at all," Benny said, as he rose from the table. "I have to get going or I'm going to be late. You two take your time. *Mi casa es su casa.*"

"Thanks again, Benny," Gloria said, giving him a big, but friendly, hug. "Now I know why Vivian thinks that you're so special."

"Does Vivian know that you're psychic, too, Benny?" JeNelle added. "I'll call you about dinner when I know more about my plans."

"It's a date," Benny said, with a wink at JeNelle, as he headed through the kitchen door.

Gloria and JeNelle cleaned up the kitchen and started the dishwasher. As they were about to leave, the telephone rang. The answering machine picked up and JeNelle heard a woman's voice say.

"Sorry, I missed you, Benny. I'm also sorry that I couldn't make
it for dinner last night. I hope that you weren't too disappointed.
I know that the roses that I sent to you won't make up for everything,
But I'll be back soon and we can pick up where we left off.
Ciao, Baby."

The person hung up.

JeNelle shook her head and smiled. "So he had no plans, huh? Just made a small dinner for himself, huh? Quiet evening at home. Benjamin Staton Alexander, you may be more than a notion and some piece of work," she said aloud and chuckled.

Chapter 9

"Hey, Man! Benny! Wake up!" Kenneth said when Benny picked up the telephone.

"K.J.?" Benny grumbled. "Only you would call someone at five-thirty in the morning. On New Year's Eve at that! This had better be important."

"Are you alone or should I call back?" Kenneth asked, laughing.

"Wait a minute, let me check," Benny said, as he put the telephone down and walked around his condo. Shortly, he crawled back into the bed between the billion-count sheets and noticed a note pinned to one of his pillows. His evening's companion had left her kiss on a note:

Benny—
Had to run. Thanks for a really good time. Here's
another kiss for you until the next time.
Beth

Benny smiled and picked up the telephone.

"Yeah, I'm alone, unfortunately," he said, remembering fondly what an exciting lover Beth had been. "What's up?"

"You tell me. I'm returning your telephone call. Didn't you call me at the office the other day?"

"Oh yeah, but Shirley said that you went home with a headache. I hope that she was gorgeous and built," Benny said, yawning and trying to wake up.

"Benny, your mind goes in only one direction most of the time."

"If you want, big brother, I can give you lessons on how to—"

"Never mind, little brother." He chuckled. "I've seen you operate. Most women don't stand a chance when you're around."

A beat later, Benny said, "I hope that's true because I think I've met the right woman for me."

"Is that who you were looking around your condo for?" Kenneth wanted to laugh it off, but he heard something disquieting in his brother's voice.

"No, that was someone else," Benny said, somewhat chagrin.

Kenneth laughed loudly. "Does Ms. Right know that you're spending your nights with Ms. Right Now?"

"I'll explain all that later. First let's talk about G."

Benny explained what he had in mind for Gregory and asked for Kenneth's thoughts on the matter. Kenneth agreed that it would be a good idea, but wondered whether Vivian, with her hectic schedule, really had the time to devote to Gregory all summer. He offered to let their younger brother come to San Francisco and work at CompuCorrect, if Vivian needed a break. Benny told him that Vivian was in agreement with the plan and might even go home with him to talk to Gregory about it. Kenneth said that if he needed him, he too would fly home for Easter. Benny agreed to let him know.

Benny then began to relate the story about his trip in the elevator, being stood up, the evening with four women, the roses from Stacy, and the morning with Gloria and JeNelle. The comical way in which Benny told the story had Kenneth rolling in laughter. Every time Kenneth thought that he had himself under control, Benny would tell him more and he would lose it all over again.

"I can just see *you* in the kitchen trying to make breakfast," Kenneth said, laughing. "You know that you can't cook. You're as bad as Vivian. And you really thought that you were going to impress this JeNelle Towson? I guess that kitchen drama left some impression on her all right. Smoke everywhere, huh?"

"It was a disaster area!" Benny exasperated at the memory. "Then, when I got home, I found a message from Stacy that must have come in before JeNelle left my condo. I don't know whether JeNelle heard the message or not, but I got a single red rose from JeNelle yesterday and a note that said: *I'm not going to try to compete with your mother's roses. See you for dinner at 5:00 P.M. at Michelangelo's.* My cover is blown! Michelangelo's is where I picked up my carry out the day that JeNelle and Gloria dropped by!"

Kenneth couldn't hold it in. He laughed uncontrollably. "She's got your number, little brother. Sounds like some lady. If you think that she's Ms. Right, you'd better play it straight with her from now on or you'll be picking up Ms. Wrongs for a long time to come."

"That's where you come in, K.J."

"*Me?* What do you want me to do?"

"She's interested in exhibiting at the Expo that you were telling me about when I was there for Christmas. Maybe you can help her register for the Expo and while she's there, take her out to dinner or for drinks to give her a better impression of me. You know…tell her that I'm not such a bad guy."

Kenneth noticed the seriousness of his brother's tone. "This is very important to you, isn't it?"

"It is, yes."

"Okay, Benny, I want to help, since it's so important to you, but I'm not going to tell any lies just to get you in tight with her. I don't like the idea of manipulating anyone under any circumstance and certainly not just to get you into her bed."

"I know, K.J., but I may have made such a fool of myself trying to impress her that she won't take me seriously."

"I'm no miracle worker, Benny, but if she decides to come, I will try to point out your good qualities."

"K.J., you're my man, my ace! I knew that I could count on you, big brother!"

"Don't thank me yet. Just don't screw up at dinner tomorrow or I won't be able to do any damage control for you."

"I'm going to take this one real slow and easy. No more posturing for effect. I promise. By the way, have you talked with J.C. Baker lately?"

Kenneth's mood changed. "Why do you ask?"

"Viv was wondering why you two hadn't been in touch. I told her that I thought that maybe J.C. got you that contract and that you two just haven't had time in your schedules to get together."

"He didn't get us that contract! He gave a news release from GSA to Tom and Tom took it from there. I didn't know where Tom's lead came from until after we won the contract, but you're right, our schedules don't coincide. Nothing to worry about."

Benny noticed something in Kenneth's tone, but decided not to press it. He changed the topic.

"Look, what's up for tonight, K.J.?"

"What do you mean?"

"It's New Year's Eve, remember?"

"Oh, I hadn't given it much thought."

"K.J., one of these days you're going to wake up and find out that your entire life has passed you by and you'll probably say *'oh, I hadn't given it much thought.'*"

"You're probably right," Kenneth said and snorted.

"I know I'm right. Why don't you give that private life of yours a little attention? Go out and have some fun! Snuggle up to something other than your computer keyboards!"

Kenneth laughed. "Okay, little brother, I'll think about it. How are you going to spend New Year's Eve?"

"I haven't made any plans."

"What? That doesn't sound like you. I would have expected you to have women lined up to take out."

"There is someone who I wanted to spend New Year's Eve with, but she's out of town on a mission."

"Benny, I can't keep up. Now which one is this?"

"Stacy. Stacy Greene. She's the one who sent the roses to me."

"Is this Stacy Greene someone special, too?"

"Yes, but—."

"But what?"

"Stacy's not making any commitments. She's still seeing other men and insists that I still date other women. In fact, until this mission came up, she already had a date for New Year's Eve with a Marine from Camp Pendleton. Someone she said wanted to put her in first place in his life."

"I don't understand. If she's special, why are you so hot for this JeNelle Towson? And don't tell me that you're going to let a Marine beat you out for Stacy's attention! Aren't you willing to put Stacy Greene in first place in your life?"

"JeNelle is different. Wait until you see her. Man! She's gorgeous! Body by Fischer!"

"Oh, so Stacy isn't gorgeous and she doesn't have a great body?"

"No, Stacy's got it all and more, but like I said, she won't make a commitment."

"Have you talked with her about it?"

"We started to have a conversation the day after I got back from San Francisco. That was the first time that Stacy mentioned the word 'love'."

"She told you that she loves you?"

"No, not exactly. What she actually said was that one of the things that she loved *about* me is the fact that I care deeply about my family. Then she started talking about our friendship and she said that I was special to her. When I asked her whether she loved me, she clammed up and left. I was ready to talk to her about taking our friendship to another level that night at dinner, but she shipped out and Gloria and JeNelle showed up."

"Sounds like you and Stacy have some unfinished business. Are you experiencing one of your infamous unguarded moments with JeNelle because you can't be with Stacy?"

"I don't know…I don't think so, but JeNelle did hit me like I was pulling 100 G's in an inverted position on a high dive! Man, did I get a rush!"

Kenneth laughed. "She must be some woman if she knocked you for a loop."

"Yeah, that's why it's so important that I make a better impression on her than I did before."

"And what if Stacy finds out about JeNelle?"

"I wouldn't hide anything from Stacy. I never have and neither has she. We're friends with benefits and I respect her. We talk to each other about everything, including the other people that we see… that is, when I can get her alone. Besides, if I didn't tell her about JeNelle, the Sin Sisters would."

Kenneth laughed aloud. "The Sin Sisters?"

"Yeah, Cecil Jordan and Janice Atterly. Stacy and I call them the Sin Sisters. They live in this building on the twenty-third floor," Benny said, frustrated.

"Okay, I may regret this, but I have to ask. Why do you call them the Sin Sisters? This has got to be good."

Benny laughed. "Next to Stacy, Cecil and Janice are two of the most brilliant women that I know outside of our family. They're also two of the most uninhibited women I know. They aren't related, but they were at UC-San Diego together and they're good friends. Both are doctoral candidates now. Cecil is an oceanographer at Scripps Institute of Oceanography and Janice is a biochemist at the Salk Institute. They get some perverse pleasure out of tripping my trigger, if you know what I mean. They're always playing practical jokes on me, like what they did to me in the elevator and in the back seat of JeNelle's car, but that's light stuff compared to some of the other things they've done to me.

"When Stacy came to San Diego, she asked me to go sailing and told me to bring a date. I took Cecil and Janice with me. There were about twelve of us. Stacy was with this Lieutenant Commander who was teaching her how to sail. We sailed up to Mission Bay and had a party on the beach. We did some swimming, skin diving, and some scuba diving. While we were swimming, Cecil and Janice relieved me of my swimming trunks. I couldn't come out of the water! The fish were beginning to mistake my johnson for a worm. Well, you get the picture."

Kenneth howled.

"Another time, I took this young lady out to dinner. I didn't know her very well. I brought her back to my place later, you know, to get better acquainted. When I opened my glove compartment to get the garage key, a zillion condoms fell out all over the young lady's lap. Man! Was that embarrassing or what?! I knew immediately who had done it.

"Another time, Cecil and Janice threw this big surprise birthday party for me down at the pool, and they had almost every woman I've dated in the last three years, about eighty of them at the party, and as if that wasn't enough, they hired these professional belly dancers to...well, you get the picture. Stacy was even in on the planning. That's why we call them the Sin Sisters."

Kenneth was rolling in laughter, as Benny told the stories of other tricks that Cecil and Janice had pulled on him. Benny laughed, too.

"They are totally uninhibited for two young women with such impressive credentials, but I wouldn't trade either of them for anything and neither would Stacy. We've had some good times together. I'd like for you to meet them the next time you're in town."

"Uh, I don't think so, Benny. I can't think that fast. I'm still a country boy, remember?"

"You'd like them, K.J. Both would be considered nerds just like you were. They're very attractive and good people too. You know, like family."

"I'll take your word for it."

Kenneth and Benny talked for a while longer and then they hung up. Benny went back to sleep.

Later that morning, the doorbell rang. Benny looked at the clock. It was nine o'clock in the morning. He dragged himself out of bed, put on his short robe and tied it loosely around his waist.

"*Whoa!*" he said, as he opened the door.

"Hi, Benny," Cecil and Janice said in unison in very seductive voices.

"Oh no you don't! Not again! I already gave at the office," he said, as the two women sauntered into the vestibule. They were wearing string bikinis with see-thru jackets that looked like they had left most of the material in the store. He backed up, tied the belt on his short robe into a knot, and put up both of his hands in mock defense.

Cecil and Janice laughed at his antics.

"We're going to the pool to swim, Benny," Cecil said. "Why don't you and Stacy come with us?"

Benny let out a sigh of relief. "Stacy's not back yet. She's still out on a mission."

"Then what did you mean by that remark that 'you gave at the office?' Don't tell me that JeNelle Towson is here?" Janice asked.

"No, I was with someone else last night. She must have left sometime early this morning. I'm seeing JeNelle tomorrow."

"I've never met a man who is always in the load-and-lock position the way you are," Cecil said.

"Yeah, me and Mike Tyson. What do you expect when women, as beautiful as you two, show up at my door wearing dental floss and a smile at 1:00 A.M.? She wasn't selling Girl Scout Cookies and I checked; her name wasn't Desserie."

They laughed.

"You and Stacy have a very open relationship," Cecil said.

"I'd call it totally unique," Janice said.

"Yeah, Stacy's great," Benny answered, with a broad smile.

"The sister's got a lot going for herself. She knows her stuff, too. We had lunch last week at the Naval Officer's Club with Stacy and some of her shipmates. She's into that telecommunications stuff deep. She's been working on some of that super-secret sonar equipment that we keep hearing rumors about over at Scripps. I think it was designed by Sandoval Anniston, that big conglomerate outside San Francisco. She couldn't talk about it, but she sure loves her career in the Navy," Cecil said.

"Sandoval Anniston, huh? My brother used to work for that company before he started CompuCorrect. Stacy didn't mention anything to me about new systems, but that's one of the things that's so unique about her. She's extremely competent. She loves what she does and she does it very well. Stacy's going to make everyone proud of her. I'm proud to call her my friend," Benny said.

"You two act more like pals or buddies then two people in love," Cecil said.

"That's the way Stacy wants it. We haven't moved to the love and commitment stage…I don't think. Plus, Stacy's still seeing other people, too."

"Yeah, Cecil, like that fine specimen of a Marine from Camp Pendleton, Ted Peterson! He's really got the hots for her," Janice said.

"Or that Black Adonis she was with when we all went sailing. The one who said that he would give up a year's pay if Stacy would date him exclusively. What was his name again? Lieutenant Commander something?" Cecil asked, trying to remember.

"Bruce Payton," Benny supplied dryly.

Both women looked at him.

"You two do have a unique relationship," Cecil said, with some surprise in her voice.

"So I guess you know that Stacy hasn't been seeing anyone since your birthday party," Janice said.

"She hasn't had time. I barely get to see her," Benny said. "Just like now. She's off on another mission. One that she probably asked for. She's been taking on the toughest assignments that she can get."

"Yeah, you two and your rushes! You get it when you fly and she gets it when she sails," Cecil said.

"That's not the only time we get a rush," Benny said quietly to himself with a knowing smile.

"So why are you still seeing other people, like JeNelle Towson?" Janice asked.

"Stacy says that Benny is the dangerous type...the type of man that women fall head over heels in love with and goes crazy over. She says that insanity doesn't run in her family," Cecil said, laughing.

"Like I said, that's the way Stacy wants it. She wants to keep it loose. No strings. No bonds. Just good friends with benefits. Now, JeNelle!" he said, with a big smile and a gleam in his eye, "I could get real serious about her!"

"Yeah, we noticed at Jason's. You were really on a mission that night," Janice said.

"Yeah, now JeNelle's the dangerous type," Benny said. "I get a rush whenever I see her!"

"JeNelle's got it going on all right, but I don't see you two together," Cecil said, with a shrug, "but a man's got to do what a man's got to do."

"Benny, my friend," Janice said, "You know a lot of women, but you don't *know* women. What you and Stacy have going on is rare, believe me. I'm a woman. I know these things. It's going to take you eons to get to that same place with someone like JeNelle Towson. You two don't speak the same language."

"We'll see about that. It all starts with dinner tomorrow at five o'clock," Benny said, with a smug grin. "And I'm not telling either one of you where we're going. Who knows what you two might decide to do."

Both women laughed and just shook their heads.

"So are you going to swim with us or what, Benny?" Cecil asked.

He looked at them both. "Only if you two promise to be on your best behavior."

Cecil and Janice looked at each other. *"Not!"* they said in unison.

"That would take all of the fun out of it," Cecil said, with a coy smile.

They all laughed and Benny went swimming with them anyway.

Chapter 10

Vivian opened one eye and saw the Snowman patiently sitting by her bedside with his leash in his mouth. His little companion, Miguel Menendez-Gaza, was gently stroking the dog. Vivian reached for her robe, but it was nowhere to be found.

"I'm coming, Snowman. You go wait downstairs by the door," she said and yawned.

The dog left the room with his companion. She found her robe and slippers and washed up. Carlton was still soundly sleeping. As she went down the steps, she heard people talking in the kitchen and smelled wonderful aromas filling the air.

"*Hola,*" Anna happily said, as she stirred the eggs and checked the flame under the other pots on the stove.

Melissa, Bill, Alan and Chuck were all sitting at the long, trestle table drinking coffee and laughing. Her favorite radio station was playing some great jazz music, as usual.

"*Hola,* Anna," Vivian replied, "and a good morning to all of you," she said and smiled. Her eyes went to Chuck and locked. He was more handsome than she had realized before. Something grabbed at her heart and squeezed, as he gazed at her.

"It's about time, Vivian," Melissa said. "I thought that you and your sex-fiend fiancée weren't ever going to get out of the bed."

Vivian momentarily flushed. Melissa had a heart of gold and innocent sweetness, but wasn't the most discreet person. She was glad that she had something to do. Looking at Chuck was making her nervous.

"Who can sleep with Snowman around," Vivian said, as she opened the back door and attached the dog's leash to a tether in the back yard. Snowman went romping around in the snowy yard like a crazed animal. Miguel stood at the window, giggling, as he watched the dog play.

"Any coffee left?" Vivian asked, averting her eyes from Chuck's heated gaze. "And what is that wonderful smell?"

"Anna has been driving us crazy for the last hour with those wonderful aromas. She wouldn't let anyone near the stove," Bill said.

Vivian sat down at the table and noticed that Chuck was clean-shaven and he had changed his clothes from the night before. So had Alan. In fact, Anna was wearing some clothes that resembled some that Melissa owned.

"You all look like happy campers this morning. Have we heard from the hospital yet?"

"I called the charge nurse at seven-thirty this morning and Angelique was doing better. Her temperature was still high, but that's to be expected with Scarlet Fever," Chuck said, noticing how beautiful Vivian looked in the morning light. Yet, she always looked beautiful to him. "She's going to need a long period of convalescence and that's where you come in, Annie."

"Annie? Who's Annie?" Melissa chirped.

"Your housemate," Chuck responded, a grin crossing his lips and thinking, yep, she's one fine looking lady.

"Vivian, I didn't know that your name was Annie. I thought that it was Lynn, Vivian Lynn."

"I'll explain it to you later, Melissa," Vivian deadpanned while still looking at Chuck. "So what is it that I can do to help?"

"You've got a great four-bedroom, two bath apartment downstairs. Bill and Melissa took me and Alan down there and showed us around. It's warm, dry, comfortable, and clean with plenty of space for the kitchen, dining and living room with ample storage. There's a draft coming in through the front door down there, but I can fix that. The back door and windows are secure with no leaks. A little more work and some furniture and it would be quite comfortable. Bill, Alan, Melissa and I have talked it over. We'll finish up the work that needs to be done. Bill has offered to furnish it, at his own expense. Alan will rent one of the rooms, so he can move out of the shelter—"

"*Move out of the shelter?*" Vivian questioned, momentarily stunned. "Alan, I didn't know you were living there. I thought that you just volunteered time there just like the rest of us in the law school program."

"Stay with me here, Annie," Chuck interjected, bringing her attention back to him. "Here comes the kicker. You let Anna, Angelique, and Miguel stay here, rent free, in exchange for working around the house. You know cooking and cleaning."

"I can't ask her to do that, Chuck. I would have to pay her something; at least minimum wage, her social security taxes, and Medicare benefits. You remember what happened to Zoe Baird? I may be up for appointment to the Supreme Court someday and it would be just my luck to have something like this pop up."

"We can all help, Vivian," Bill added. "We're living here very cheaply, so we've decided to up the rent to everyone, including Alan, and that should be enough to pay Anna a salary and pay the taxes. Just don't charge her rent for the three rooms," Bill added. "Her room and board can be a part of her compensation package."

"That's a new twist, the tenants upping the rent on the landlady. What about Gloria and David? They live here, too, you know. What if they don't want me changing their lease agreements in midstream like that?" Vivian asked, with some concern.

"If they don't want to go along with it, then I'll put up the extra money, myself," Bill said, without hesitation. "I've checked the grocery and utility budgets and we have more than enough to feed and house four more people. Hell, we end up throwing out more than we eat or eating out because none of us can cook!"

"What about medical care? How do we handle that?" Vivian asked.

"That's my department," Chuck said. "I'll take care of it. Derrick's not billing for his services or Angelique's care and I've already talked to the hospital administrator about her bill."

"Well, they need clothes and shoes. They only have what's on their backs. How do we handle that?"

"That's my department," Melissa happily chirped. "You know that I love to shop," she beamed. "So I'm taking them shopping later for some essentials. Anna is a bit smaller than me, but I have a whole trunk full of brand new clothes that my parents sent to me and I haven't worn any of it. Anna is handy with a needle and thread so she can make any alterations she needs. The children should be real easy to clothe. We can hit Target or Walmart."

"Sounds like you've worked out all the details," Vivian said, her brows furrowed in concentration.

"Still, it's up to you, Vivian," Alan said, without expression. "None of this works unless you agree. You're the landlady. You probably could make more money renting the whole apartment to three more paying students. This house is in a prime location of the city right around the corner from Embassy Row and within easy walking distance of campus."

Vivian sensed that Alan's caution was related to his heritage. She wanted to assure him that his heritage was not an issue in the household. That he was welcomed to live there.

"Alan, this is all so overwhelming, but it's not about the money. I'm from a big family. I love to have friends around. Especially people who are in the

Scholars Program like you, so I'll give it a try," Vivian said. "I do want to help Anna find her husband. She's going to need a sponsor so that Immigration doesn't try to deport her. I'll talk to my father—"

"Way to go, Ms. Oakley!" Chuck said, excited. "I knew you had grit!" And he felt something more, listening to her and watching her get caught up in the plan.

"Who's this Ms. Oakley person, Chuck?" Melissa asked, with an innocent curiosity typical of her.

"I'll explain that later, Melissa," Chuck said, with a broad smile, patting her hand.

Everyone laughed except Melissa. She looked at the smiling faces, but still didn't get it.

"What's everyone laughing about?" Carlton asked, as he entered the kitchen. "And what's that I smell?"

Everyone looked at each other. Vivian said, "I'll tell you later."

Everyone laughed. Carlton looked confused, but Chuck and Vivian looked at each other.

Anna served breakfast and everyone agreed that it was well worth the wait. They complimented her profusely and Chuck translated what they were saying. Tears formed in Anna's eyes and she rushed over to Chuck and hugged him tightly. He returned her hug. She turned to the group and said, in English, "Thank you."

With tears rolling down her cheeks, Melissa managed to say quietly. "There's another Norman Rockwell moment for you."

Miguel had climbed into Bill's lap and he was feeding himself and Bill from Bill's plate of food. Bill stroked Miguel's hair and said quietly, "I'll be your huckleberry."

Vivian left the crew hard at work, painting walls and scrubbing floors. Even Carlton was too busy talking to Chuck to drive her to the shelter. She was happy for the time alone without Carlton. Alan said that he would meet her at the shelter later to pick up his things. As Vivian drove along the streets of Washington, she felt good about what this small group of people from very diverse backgrounds accomplished in twenty-four hours for three people who were complete strangers the day before. When she stopped at a red light, she looked up at the sky and smiled.

"It all depends on your point of view," she said aloud to herself.

Later that night, other law school students in their study group and some doctors and nurses from Georgetown Medical Center joined the housemates. About thirty people stood holding each other about the waist or shoulders huddled before the large flat-screen. They started counting down, as the ball atop Times Square began its annual descent.

"Five, four, three, two, one. Happy New Year!!" they all yelled in unison.

Kisses and hugs abound. Chuck and Vivian found themselves face to face. Their eyes met and held. Vivian had felt Chuck's eyes on her all evening, as the house filled with party revelers. Anna had made a feast and while Carlton partied, Vivian and Chuck filled the dinner table with food, picked up empty beer bottles, emptied the trash, and performed other chores, as if they were the host and hostess of the party.

"Happy New Year, Annie Oakley," Chuck said, his eyes captivating hers.

"Happy New Year, City Cowboy," she intoned quietly in a western accent, her eyes locked with his. "I hope that this New Year brings you everything that you want."

"It already has," he said, smiling at her, and then quickly corrected, "I mean, I have new friends to start the year with. That's important to me. Very important."

"To me, too," she said, transfixed by his overwhelming impact on her from the very moment that they had met four days earlier.

They moved toward each other and hugged, brushing lips against each other's cheeks, but the moment was pregnant with what was not said between them.

Chapter 11

Benny arrived at Michelangelo's early on New Year's Day. He wanted to make sure that everything would be perfect for his date with JeNelle. When she arrived, Benny left the bar where he was sitting, talking with some friends of his, and walked toward her to greet her. Milo San Angelo reached her first and greeted JeNelle warmly, speaking to her in Italian.

"Ms. JeNelle, Ms. JeNelle. Long time no see you. You still beautiful lady. *La Bella, La Bella. Muie Bella.* And your friend, Ms. Carson, she too is well?"

Benny was surprised at how Milo greeted JeNelle and even more surprised when JeNelle spoke to Milo in fluent Italian. He did not understand what they were discussing, but that didn't matter. He stood by observing how spectacular JeNelle looked in her ivory-colored silk suit. Her hair was swept up in the back and an ivory comb could be seen beneath her bronze locks. Her makeup was in rich earth tones, just perfect, and accented her full lips. Her legs were long and shapely. Clearly, she worked out regularly, he thought. Though she looked beautiful, she was dressed for business, he noticed, not casually for an evening of seduction. He knew that he had his work cut out for him, but she was worth it, he thought. He was ready to make a commitment to someone and at the moment that someone was shaping up to be JeNelle Towson. Although the thought pained him, if Stacy was unwilling or unable to move to another level in their relationship, maybe he should be the one to move on....without her, he thought.

Milo noticed Benny standing beside them. "Captain Benny," he said, "I not know you wait for Ms. JeNelle. Ms. JeNelle a longtime friend and customer. I not see her and her friend Ms. Carson many years now. *Labella, Labella.* I give you best seat in house. Make extra special for you and *Labella* JeNelle," Milo effused.

Milo led them to a table overlooking the waterfront. He lit the candle on the table and whispered something to a waiter who scurried off toward the bar.

"*La Bella* JeNelle, Captain Benny, I plan whole meal! You see! Only the best!" He kissed his fingertips, tossed the kiss in the air, and scurried away.

Benny turned his full attention toward JeNelle when Milo left the table. "I was beginning to believe that Milo was going to keep you captive all evening. I can understand why. You look stunning, JeNelle."

"Milo and I are old friends. I used to come here often when I lived in San Diego."

"He mentioned something about a Ms. Carson."

"Yes, Beverly Carson. We were at San Diego State together. This is a great restaurant. I would recognize Milo's cooking anywhere," she said, smiled knowingly.

Benny noticed how JeNelle deflected questions about herself and her past. He wanted to press her to get to know her better, but at the moment he had more pressing matters to discuss. He took a deep breath. "Uh, about that, let me clear up some things right away. I was trying to impress you the other night, so I let you and Gloria believe that I had cooked the dinner that we ate. Actually, I got it from here on my way home. Someone who I was supposed to have dinner with when Gloria called stood me up. That same person actually sent the roses to me to apologize for breaking our date. Not my mother. My mother loves me, but she wouldn't send two-dozen, long-stemmed, red roses to me." Benny was watching JeNelle's expression very closely, but she gave no sign as to how she was receiving his confession. "And, no, my sister didn't leave her clothes at my place. I bought those things for overnight guests—female guests, not males—and, yes, I have dated a number of women. I have a very good friend who is very special to me, but our relationship hasn't moved to the love and commitment stage. So, if you're not thoroughly appalled at my confession, can we just start over today, New Year's Day, and wipe the slate clean?"

The waiter brought a bottle of champagne—not the one that Benny had ordered—but better. He poured the wine into JeNelle's glass after Benny approved of the vintage.

"Hello, Captain Benjamin Staton Alexander, my name is JeNelle Elise Towson. My sister, Gloria, is your sister's, Vivian, housemate."

"I'm pleased to meet you, Ms. Towson. May I offer you a drink to celebrate the New Year?"

"Thank you, Captain Alexander. I would like that and may I make the first toast of this New Year?"

"Certainly, Ms. Towson, you have my full attention."

"To clean slates," JeNelle said, as she touched her glass to his, "and new beginnings. Happy New Year."

Dinner was as delicious as they had expected it would be since Milo supervised each dish as it was delivered. Time seemed to speed by. When they finished eating, they sat talking over snifters of Amaretto.

"I talked with my brother, Kenneth, about what a jerk I had been with you and he warned me that I should be straight with you or I would regret it. I've even enlisted his help to convince you that I'm not a complete jerk all of the time, even though when I'm around you, I do tend to have my moments."

JeNelle's brows bunched. "What have you asked your brother to do?"

"To take you out to dinner while you're in San Francisco and to tell you about some of my more positive, socially-redeeming qualities, as you're already far too familiar with my shortcoming."

"And he's agreed to this?" JeNelle asked, with more surprise and trepidation.

"He made it clear that he would do it only on the condition that he would not lie to you for me under any circumstance."

"Why did you feel that you needed to call in reinforcements? We're just learning how to be friends. I'm not intimidating by any stretch of the imagination. At least not in my opinion."

"No, I haven't observed that in you, but you certainly are formidable. I know that I can't put anything over on you and expect you to tolerate it. I want to be completely candid from this new beginning."

"You're right, Benny, I had formed certain opinions about you, but not to the extent that you seem to think."

"You mean that I've gone through this confession of all of my sins and you didn't think that I was a complete jerk-off anyway?" he asked, feigning shock.

JeNelle grinned. "I doubt seriously that you have 'confessed all of your sins' to me, Benny, but I am impressed. Not many men run the risk of being completely honest with a woman they've just met and that's much to your credit. It does take character to say what you have said to me tonight. So no, I don't think that you are without some 'socially redeeming qualities,'" she said, smiling.

"Only 'some' socially redeeming qualities?" Benny asked, with a wry smile, as he placed his hand on hers across the table.

She patted his hand in a motherly fashion and smiled. "Don't push it, Captain, you're already flying on one wing," JeNelle joked.

They both laughed and talked about what JeNelle planned to exhibit at the Small Business Expo. She said that she would have to work fast to get geared up. She had faxed her registration and it had been accepted, but she was too late to get a prime spot on the Expo floor. She was on the waiting list for rooms at several hotels near where the Expo would be held and she could only take two staff people to help her with the booth. That meant that she would be on her feet from 7:00 A.M. until 9:00 P.M. for five days straight. It would be a grueling schedule and she wasn't sure that she'd have time to have dinner with Kenneth since she needed to keep tabs on what was going on at the store in Santa Barbara. She did agree to try to make time.

"Benny, you've made it clear to me that you're interested in getting to know me better, and I don't reject that idea, but I feel that I have to be candid with you."

"This sounds ominous. I don't know whether I'm ready for all this honesty."

"You're a very attractive man, charming and attentive."

"Do I hear a *'but'* coming?"

"Yes, *but* for some time now I've not made room in my life for close friendships or intimate relationships. I'm not looking to jump into anything. I don't make promises that I don't plan to keep. And I can't promise you that this new friendship we're starting to work on today will ever develop beyond this point."

"Is it the difference in our ages that makes you have these reservations?"

"That's a consideration, because I'm not a cougar-in-training," she chuckled, "but certainly not the main one."

Leaning forward with his forearms folded on the table, he intently gazed into her eyes. "Then what is it that would keep us from just letting go and letting our relationship...excuse me, friendship develop?"

"I'm not sure, at this point, but I think that it's a difference in philosophy." She took a cleansing breath and returned his direct gaze. "We have different points of view about some very basic issues. For example, you sacrificed yourself to party half the night with Gloria and me, showing us a great time when you knew that you had to fly seven hours later. I never would have done that. I rarely go to parties or even to clubs. I enjoy spending time alone, regrouping. You never seem to have down time. You're obviously very popular in this town. You're on all the time. When do you shut off? Power down?"

"I 'power down,' as you put it, when I fly. That's when I regroup."

"That's scary," she said, incredulously.

"I don't even think about the fact that I'm moving at six hundred or nine hundred knots at sixty thousand feet. It's where I love to be. Nothing compares to it. It's a rush that I don't know is there until I'm on the ground, and then I want to feel that rush again. Still, I can't log more than twelve to fourteen hours of flight time per week before I have to go to a mandatory crew-rest period, so I look for substitutes. I got that same rush when I met you," he said seriously, looking into her eyes.

"I don't want you to depend on me to be your 'rush', Benny," JeNelle said, with an equally serious tone.

"I get that rush whenever I see you," he said honestly. "It's not something that I can control. You have that kind of effect on me."

"That's just it. I'm not looking for a lover, but I would be willing to see you as a friend. A purely platonic friend," she emphasized. "I can't even see you often. Even if I didn't live in Santa Barbara and you're here in San Diego, I have a business to run and other business and organizational commitments to keep. Like your brother and other small business people, ninety-nine percent of my time is spent doing what I have to do to be successful."

"Then let me share that one percent of the time that you do have left and maybe—just maybe—the chances of improving on that small statistic might change," he said, smiling warmly.

"You are persistent," JeNelle said, flattered, but not sold.

The moment was pregnant with unspoken truths between them, as they gazed into each other's eyes. Fortunately, the music began to play in the background and several people got up to dance. The restaurant was very crowded now and people lined up at the door waiting to get in and be seated.

"Obviously, the football game is over," Benny was saying, as a photographer came to the table and asked whether he could take their picture. He said that there would be no charge because Milo wanted a picture of them for the collection of pictures of regular customers that were prominently displayed at the entrance to the restaurant. JeNelle and Benny agreed to have their picture taken together and Benny asked the photographer to make additional copies of the picture. He generously tipped him for the favor. The photographer scurried away, vowing to return soon with Benny's copies. When the man left, Benny heard the beginning of the song, *Evergreen*.

Benny stood and extended his hand to JeNelle. "Ms. Towson, may I have this first dance of the New Year with you?"

"Are you sure that you want to dance to a slow song, Benny? You seemed uncomfortable when we danced at Jason's the other night," she said, grinning.

"Uncomfortable? Me? Uh, how could you tell?"

They both smiled and went to the dance floor. As Benny took JeNelle in his arms, he felt calm and totally relaxed. As they danced, they talked like two old friends. He was responding to her and her to him, but he could not focus on the conversation. She looked up at him and, her eyes twinkling in the dimmed light of the restaurant, made his imagination soar. *I could look at her forever*, he thought. The highlights of her flowing hair, the natural arch of her eyebrows, the softness of her cheeks, the shape of her nose, the fullness of her mouth and those eyes. Not just the shape or the length of her eyelashes, but the depth that he found in her eyes. There was beauty in those eyes, but there was something there that he could not read—could not touch or feel—aloof, distant, detached—a sweet sadness. It made him want to protect her from whatever caused her melancholy. He pulled her closer.

Too soon to Benny's way of thinking, it was time to go, as the photographer brought the pictures framed in cardboard to the table. Benny signaled the waiter for the check and reached for his wallet, as the waiter approached.

"No, Benny. Remember this is on me," JeNelle said, as she pulled out her Gold Card. Benny threw up his hands. "Whatever you say, Ms. Towson, but don't think that I'm an easy score just because you bought my dinner and a few drinks. It's going to take a lot more than one wonderful meal and a quick trip around the dance floor for you to get me into your bed."

"But I'll still respect you in the morning, Captain Alexander," JeNelle said, jokingly with a wink and a sassy smile.

Benny's heart warmed. He wanted her respect, but, at the moment, he just wanted her— badly.

The waiter overheard the conversation and looked curiously at them. They both noticed the waiter's bewilderment and laughed. When JeNelle tried to hand her credit card to the waiter, he said, "No, no, Ms. JeNelle. No bill. Mr. Milo say, 'It on the house'!"

Benny palmed money and shook the waiter's hand. The waiter peeked at the gratuity, smiled broadly, and left the table.

JeNelle and Benny made their way through the crowded room. As they passed, men openly looked or stared appreciatively at JeNelle. She seemed oblivious to their glances and looked straight ahead, but Benny noticed their furtive looks and felt a strange sense of resentment. He had been out with other beautiful women who turned men's heads—that was nothing new, but these men, Latino, Black, white, oriental, and others were ogling JeNelle and he didn't like it. JeNelle reached the stand where Milo was placing the photoshopped picture of her and Benny in the center spot on a board among many pictures of other patrons. He positioned it just right. JeNelle gave her business card to Milo and thanked him in Italian for his kindness. She kissed him on both cheeks and he beamed with tears forming in his eyes. He hugged JeNelle and whispered something in her ear. JeNelle whispered something back to him.

He was still beaming at JeNelle when Benny shook his hand. Benny sensed there was more to Milo's relationship with JeNelle, but couldn't figure out what it was.

In the parking lot, Benny was talking with JeNelle, as she unlocked her car. She was headed to pick up Gloria and then go home. She told Benny that she would have to get an early start on the day since she wanted to leave on an early afternoon flight to San Francisco.

"So when do I get to see you again, JeNelle?"

"I don't know, Benny. I do have to go to a social event in six or seven weeks, Valentine's Day weekend. It's a black tie gala that the Santa Barbara Chamber of Commerce is putting on to raise seed money for new businesses. Would you like to be my escort?"

"Six or seven weeks? I can't see you again for another six or seven whole weeks?"

"Remember, Benny, one percent shared," JeNelle said firmly, with a smile.

"Okay. Never mind. I'll think of something, but, yes, I do want to be your escort. Just let me know when and where. I'll be there with bells on."

"It's black tie, Benny," JeNelle said sarcastically without heat.

"Okay, with bells and a black tie. See how easily I conform to your wishes?"

JeNelle hugged Benny and her lips grazed his cheek. "Happy New Year," she whispered.

He wanted to possess her mouth and taste her tongue, but he sensed that she wouldn't be receptive to that...yet. She looked toward a spot in the parking lot and something painful crossed her face, Benny noticed.

"What is it, JeNelle?" he asked with concern.

"Nothing," she said abruptly and climbed into her car.

She put the window down and he leaned in.

"Are you sure you're all right?"

"Yes. Goodnight, Benny. I had a nice time."

She started the engine.

"Happy New Year, JeNelle."

Then she was gone. Benny watched her car speed out of sight and said to himself aloud, "Six or seven weeks? Not a chance, Ms. JeNelle Elise Towson, not a chance."

Even though it was late on New Year's Day, Benny drove to his condo. At a florist shop on the ground floor of his building he ordered that a single white rose be delivered to JeNelle's store no later than two o'clock the next day. He scribbled out a card to be included with the flowers. He also bought a gold Florentine picture frame and immediately put his copy of the picture of them together at the restaurant in it. Once he arrived home, he stared at the picture and placed it on the nightstand beside his bed. He picked up the telephone, made several calls, and then turned out his bedroom light.

He lay naked in the near darkness, looking at JeNelle's picture, listening to music, and replaying the evening in his head. A few women called to entice him to come out with them, but he turned them down. The glow from his clock illuminated JeNelle's face. He could still feel her in his arms, as they danced. His naked body against his silk sheets recalled the feel of her silk suit to his mind. The scent of her hair was vivid in his memory. His thoughts began to surge ahead. He could see himself making love to her for the first time. How that would feel. How she would taste. And the ecstasy and orgasms that they would share. He could feel her beneath him. On top of him. Caressing her breasts, her thighs, her hips. He closed his eyes and pictured every feature of her face. He stroked his body. He was fully erect. He whispered, "JeNelle, JeNelle, JeNelle," over and over until his body relaxed and he fell asleep.

Chapter 12

JeNelle's van left Santa Barbara for San Francisco at 6:00 A.M. driven by the Marketing Manager, Barry Kennedy, and the Arts Manager, Felix Olson. Luke Malone, the Sales Manager, would stay in Santa Barbara and run the operation. JeNelle personally supervised the packing of the truck. Later in the morning as she sat in her office, she received a call from one of her store floor clerks, Wanda Willis.

"Ms. Towson, there's a delivery for you at the front of the store," Wanda said over the telephone.

"Sign for it please, Wanda. I'm trying to inventory the books and pictures that need to be reordered."

"I can't, Ms. Towson. The delivery man said that only you can sign for it."

JeNelle looked out the glass wall in her office on the second floor that overlooked the entire store. The store was bustling with customers buying up merchandise from her New Years' sale. A deliveryman and Wanda were standing at the front desk. Several lines of customers were at various checkout stands.

"Okay, Wanda, I'll be right there," JeNelle said, as she rose from her desk, walked out of her office, down the steps, and toward the front of the store weaving around customers.

"What is it, Wanda? Where is the delivery?"

"Are you Ms. JeNelle Elise Towson?" the deliveryman asked.

"Yes, I am."

"Sign here, please, ma'am," he said, handing a clipboard and a pen to her.

JeNelle signed the receipt and the deliveryman handed a flower box to her.

"Have a good day, ma'am," the man said, as he left the store.

JeNelle opened the box to find one single white rosebud surrounded by greenery and baby's breath. Wanda peeked over JeNelle's shoulder, as JeNelle opened the small card.

"You don't have to compete with anyone. Ever.
Very truly yours, Benny."

"Mmmm, that's *some* card, Ms. Towson," Wanda commented with a gleam in her eye and a sly smile on her round, brown face. The jewelry in her million micro-braided hair and extensions musically tinkled.

JeNelle pursed her lips. "Uh, Wanda, don't you have some customers to help or something?" JeNelle chided, half-jokingly nodding toward the long lines.

"Yes, Ms. Towson, that's *some* card," she said, with a wink, as she sauntered off to open another register for checkout.

JeNelle went back to her office, placed the flower in a small vase, and placed it on her desk. She opened her desk drawer and pulled out the picture of herself and Benny. She looked at it, smiled, shook her head, placed his card inside, and put it back into her desk.

It was after noon when Gloria knocked on JeNelle's office door.

"You're taking me to lunch, aren't you, JeNelle?" Gloria asked, as she stuck her head inside. "I've brought your car back, full of gas, I might add."

"What time is it?" JeNelle asked.

"It's almost one o'clock and I'm starving."

"Frankly, I was going to try and catch an early flight to San Francisco. I don't have hotel reservations there yet, so I have to scout the area before Barry and Felix get there with the van. I don't think that I have time for lunch. What time is your flight to DC? Perhaps we can catch a cab to the airport together and have something there."

"Oh, no. The food at the airport is terrible. My flight leaves at three-thirty this afternoon. You can take a later flight. Let's go somewhere nice, like Maison's."

"The Country Club? Ah, so you only want the best, I see?" she chuckled.

"Yes, and I'm worth it." She spotted the rose on JeNelle's desk. "Where did you get that?"

"Someone sent it to me."

"Oh, it's pretty," she said. "Can we eat now?" Gloria pressed.

Gloria insisted on driving them to the restaurant. "After all," she told JeNelle "I won't be able to drive this fabulous car again for a long time."

They arrived at the Country Club's five-star restaurant and went inside. There was a short line ahead of them when JeNelle walked up to the maître'd.

"Ah, Ms. Towson. How are we today?" the maître'd greeted her warmly.

"We are fine, Jerrod. I didn't make a reservation for lunch. Is it possible to be seated?"

"Of course, Ms. Towson. We always have room for you. Are we a party of two?"

"Yes, Jerrod, just two," she said and smiled.

"Then we can seat you immediately," the maître'd said.

Jerrod led them through the opulent restaurant with Greek frescos painted on the walls and ceiling to a table near a tall silk draped window. The other patrons—mostly males and some females—glanced at them and nodded as they passed by. Two men, who were also on the Chamber Board with her, stopped her briefly to say hello. She saw other people who she knew or with whom she had worked on various occasions or committees. The Mayor and two City Council members briefly cornered her. After she and Gloria were seated and started looking at the menu, a very stylishly dressed, middle-aged woman approached the table.

"Ms. Towson? You are Ms. JeNelle Towson, aren't you?" the woman asked.

"I am, yes," JeNelle said, and smiled curiously.

"Well, I'm Mrs. Johnston White Worthington, IV. I'm Judge Worthington's wife."

"It's a pleasure to meet you, Mrs. Worthington. This is my sister, Gloria. Would you like to sit down?"

Mrs. Worthington nodded at Gloria with a quick smile.

"No, no. I just wanted to say hello to you. The Judge talks about you all the time. My friends over there pointed you out to me as you came in. That's a stunning winter-pink, French-silk suit that you're wearing. Is it an original?"

"Yes, in a manner of speaking," JeNelle answered.

"Well you must give me the name of your couturier, but, as I started to say, we want to make sure that you will be attending the Chamber of Commerce Gala. I'm on the planning committee and we haven't received your acceptance. Are those cultured pearls that you're wearing? Who's your jeweler?"

"I'm not sure about the pearls, but I put my acceptance in the mail this morning. You should receive it in a few days."

"That's wonderful. And, of course, you will sit at our table at the Gala, won't you?"

"Thank you. I'd be delighted."

"Wonderful, the Judge will be very pleased. Is that a Hermes purse you're carrying?"

"I'm not sure."

"Well, I must run now, but don't forget to give me the name of your couturier. It was nice meeting you, too, Gloria."

"Certainly, Mrs. Worthington. Goodbye."

After Mrs. Worthington left the table, Gloria leaned over toward JeNelle and whispered, "Wouldn't Mama be surprised if Mrs. High Society Johnston White Worthington, the fourth, called her to see her spring collection?" She stifled her amusement.

"Mama could be a very successful designer. She makes beautiful clothes and she still makes most of my clothes. She's fantastic."

"Yes, but who has time to wait to have something made. When you need something to wear, you need it right away, not a week from now," Gloria said.

"Mom puts her love into everything that she makes. You can't buy love off the rack. She's designing my dress for the Gala, as we speak. That's worth waiting for and besides, I think she'll do a wonderful job on it, even better than any famous couturier."

Gloria huffed and rolled her eyes. "JeNelle, wasn't it you who came up with the idea to have this Gala in the first place?" Gloria asked, with her nose positioned up in the air.

JeNelle marveled at the way her younger sister could change direction in midstream when the conversation wasn't going her way. It was a familiar ploy and JeNelle generally tolerated it and so did their parents. These days, however, her patience with her sister was wearing a bit thin. Gloria's behavior over the holidays swung, at times, from arrogant to asinine. "It doesn't matter who gets credit for the idea. I just want it to be a big success so that the Chamber can provide seed money for new businesses," JeNelle answered, her tone telling her annoyance with her sister. While it was true that she spawned the idea, many people came together to make it happen.

"You mean *Black* businesses, don't you?" Gloria retorted.

"No, any small business man or woman, Black or white or anything in between."

"You were the one who got all those Black women's organizations to join the Chamber and support this fundraiser. I thought that you were working your butt off for 'our' people," Gloria huffed.

"You and I don't agree on who 'our' people are. I don't always look at things in black or white. If we can put more people into businesses, then we can put more people to work, and then you'll have more people to represent when you start practicing law." Gloria was plucking the proverbial last nerve. Her sister, in her view, was an immature, spoiled brat, but she had helped to make her that way, which was what tempered her ire.

"I could care less about passing the bar. I don't have any real aspirations to practice law and I'm not real interested in having a career."

JeNelle almost lost it. "Then why the hell are we spending all this money on you for law school?"

"*Duh!* To find a man, what else?!" she asked flippantly. "Wake up, JeNelle. I don't want to be working at a 9 to 5 from 7 A.M. to 11 P.M. like you do! I want someone else worrying about paying the bills for a Mercedes Benz and my trips to the islands and shopping on the European Continent! All I want to have to do is look pretty driving the car, wearing fabulous clothes and sitting on the beach!"

Of all the foolish, immature, childish…JeNelle bit back the expletive and fought to cool her temper. Her sister needed guidance, not scorn. She tried to take a positive approach.

"You have to learn to depend on yourself to achieve your goals—not on a man. What happens when the man is gone? What do you do then?"

"Get another one!"

"And what do you do when you run through a whole legion of men and you're older and not as attractive and firm as you are now?"

"If I work it right, this body will last me a long time. Don't get me wrong, JeNelle, I'm very proud of what you've accomplished. I'll write 'MY SISTER IS JENELLE TOWSON' across the sky for everyone to see, but I would never do what you're doing. I don't ever want to have to do what you're doing. You threw the good life away when you divorced Michel. You had it all—beautiful cars, diamonds, furs, houses all over the world, trips to fabulous places—everything! That man laid the universe at your feet and you walked away. Now you have no joy in your life. You've dated maybe three people since you came back to Santa Barbara and none of them were important to you. What kind of life is that? When was the last time you had some fun, took a real vacation or, for that matter, took a weekend getaway with some hunk with ways and means? You get up in the morning, go to the gym, go to work, go home, and go to bed—alone. You're still an attractive woman, JeNelle, even though your birthday is just around the corner. You wouldn't have to work that hard to find yourself someone to take care of you again."

That cut it.

"I take care of me, Gloria! I don't have to have a man in my life to know who I am! For your information, I have joy in my life! Far more joy than I had when I was married to Michel! You and I simply don't define that word 'joy' in the same way! I have down time, time when I can enjoy myself. I go out with my friends. I even went skiing last year…."

"That was business, JeNelle, and you know it! The ski trip was a business trip! When you get together with your friends, it's to talk about some deal you are planning to make or some program you want to initiate! You can't snuggle up to a business deal in the middle of the night and I doubt that you're into electronic love toys! I know that you don't think much of the way that I live my life, but at least I have one! I've got talent with men that you wouldn't even dream of! I can make a man beg or cry and make him feel like he's King Kong if I want to. You sit in your ivory tower and dare any man to climb your damn wall!"

"May I take your order now please, Ms. Towson?"

Gloria and JeNelle were startled by the waiter's question. They didn't realize that he was standing there or even knew how much of their conversation he may have overheard. They were at each other again, JeNelle thought. They could rarely spend time together without an argument, although she had tried to keep the peace between them. JeNelle now knew that giving Gloria whatever she wanted and acquiescing to her every whim had been a grave mistake. She regained her composure and quickly scanned the menu.

"I'll have the chicken salad and a glass of white house wine, please," JeNelle said.

"I'll have the filet mignon, rare, with two shots of scotch—Pinch—straight," Gloria added, as she noticed JeNelle's expression. "Don't look at me like that, JeNelle. You know that airline food is terrible and I hate to fly, so I'm going to be ripe by the time the plane lifts off."

JeNelle looked at her sister and thought that perhaps she was really seeing her clearly for the first time. There were only seven years difference in their ages and they were raised by the same two loving parents, but they were worlds apart in their points of view, she thought, as she continued to talk with her sister. Perhaps Gloria was right about one thing. She had not taken a hiatus since Michel...but she didn't want to think about that. That was many painful years ago and it had no relevance to her life now. Gloria was wrong, that's all. She did have 'joy' in her life. She was doing all the things she wanted to do. She had no regrets, except maybe one.

Gloria was chatting away while she devoured her steak. She was excited about Tony Jamerson, the star wide receiver. She reminded her sister of which one he was.

"You remember, JeNelle. He came up to me at the club and said, 'If you'll dance with me just once, I'll have your babies'. Real corny line, but boy is that country boy built! Baby's got back, too! And a whole lot more! He's making stupid money, JeNelle; eight figures, and I'm just the woman he should be spending it on, too. He's already asked me to come to his games—and he's paying for the airline tickets and the hotel rooms. After the season is over, he wants us to go to Cozumel for a month of R&R."

"What about Benny Alexander? He seems like a nice enough guy. I thought that you had the hots for him?"

"Benny's a great looking guy, real sexy, got body, and rumor has it, he's hung like a horse and that he's a great lay, but he's not making multiple eight figures on an annual basis like Tony. Benny can't keep me in the style to which I want to become accustomed. Why don't you use him as one of your boy toys? Might at least take the edge off or melt that frost that surrounds you these days," Gloria said sarcastically.

"He's a person, Gloria! Not a toy to be played with! I don't use men for what I can get out of them or just for sexual gratification. When the time is right, there has to be some type of commitment, love, respect, trust, and understanding. Men are people, too, you know! They don't deserve to be used just for what they have swinging between their legs!"

"Is there anything else I can get for you, Ms. Towson?" the waiter asked.

Gloria and JeNelle had not noticed him standing there—again.

"Do we have time for another drink, JeNelle?"

JeNelle looked at her watch. "No. You've already had two double scotches and I just have enough time to get you to the airport."

JeNelle signed for their lunches and included a handsome tip for the waiter. Gloria had a little trouble steadying herself, as she stood up.

"Whoa, who's moving this room around?" she asked, as they headed for the door. The valet brought JeNelle's car and they sped off toward the airport. JeNelle checked Gloria's luggage at the ticket counter and warned the ground flight crew that perhaps her sister would need some assistance boarding the plane because she was "overmedicated." Aided by an attendant, Gloria staggered through security. She blew kisses at JeNelle and was giggling, as she turned the corner, disappearing out of sight.

JeNelle thought about her sister's comments. *I'm not going to let Gloria fall into that same trap that I did! She's not going to let anyone use her and nearly kill her!* JeNelle hurried back to the store to finish some last minute details. Her staff kept her busier than usual that day. She was just finishing and about to call for a cab to take her to the airport when her telephone rang.

"Yes, Wanda, what is it?" JeNelle asked.

"Your cab is here, Ms. Towson."

"My cab?" she said, but then shrugged and shook her head. "Thank you, Wanda. I'll be right out."

JeNelle was confused and thought that maybe she already asked someone to call a cab for her. "JeNelle, old girl, you're truly losing it," she said aloud. She picked up her luggage, her briefcase, and headed down the steps toward the front of the store. A number of her female clerks were giggling and smirking, as she walked by, but she disregarded their behavior. When she did not see a cab driver, as she reached the front desk, she went to Wanda.

"Where is my cab, Wanda? I thought that you said that the cab was here?"

Wanda giggled and nodded toward one of the aisles of books. JeNelle turned in the direction of Wanda's was nod.

"Your chariot to the airport awaits you, Ms. Towson. May I take your luggage for you?"

It was Benny Alexander wearing his full-dressed uniform complete with an extraordinary and impressive array of ribbons and insignia, his cap, and flashing a million-dollar smile. He had been leaning against a high bookcase out of sight. There he stood with his arms folded across his impressive chest and one leg crossed over the other. Gloria was right about another thing, JeNelle thought. Benny did have real sex appeal. The female clerks and some of the female customers couldn't take their eyes off him. There was something about a handsome man in uniform that just caught the eye. The women were even swooning openly. Even one of her male clerks, who was openly gay, twirled around and swooned.

"There is one thing that I can say about you, Captain Alexander," JeNelle said, grinning.

"And what is that, Ms. Towson?" Benny asked, as he moved so close to her that she could feel the heat from his body.

"You certainly are persistent."

"You ain't seen nothing yet, Ms. Towson. I can be downright tenacious when I want something and I'm not even trying hard yet. I intend to have my one percent of your time whenever and wherever I can get it." He picked up JeNelle's luggage, briefcase, and opened the door for her. He turned to the clerks huddled nearby and winked at them. "Thanks for all your help. I'll take care of Ms. Towson's travel arrangements from here."

The women squealed with laughter and stamped their feet. Wanda said very demonstratively, "God! He so *phine!*"

The gay clerk snapped his fingers in the air and said, "I'll press that uniform with him in it any time he wants," and twirled again.

Benny opened the car door for JeNelle and put her luggage in the trunk of a rented convertible. The top was down, the late afternoon air was balmy, and the sun was still shining brightly.

"Would you like to get something to eat before you leave, JeNelle?" Benny asked.

"No, I had a late lunch with Gloria before she left for Washington. I'll get something on the plane or when I find a hotel in San Francisco."

JeNelle put on her sunshades, as Benny started the car.

"You aren't going to deprive me of looking at your beautiful eyes during my one-percent period of your time, are you, Ms. Towson?"

"That's *shared* one percent, Captain," she corrected him with a teasing smile. "I'll take them off when we get to the airport. Then you may have your share of that one percent. In the meantime, you keep your eyes on the road."

"You sure know how to hurt a guy, Ms. Towson, but, at least, you're willing to share your time with me." He winked at her and grinned. "That's a start," he said, as he put on his sunshades and drove away.

He frequently looked at JeNelle, as they drove and talked. Her hair blew freely in the breeze and her skin shone so clearly healthy, he noticed.

She slipped out of her shoes and stretched out her toes along the plush carpeting. She leaned back against the headrest and closed her eyes. The balmy breeze rushed over her body. She didn't notice immediately that Benny had driven into a restricted area of the airport until Benny came to a stop and a man dressed in a security guard's uniform approached the car. Benny pulled out an identification card and the guard signaled to open the gate. Benny drove through and parked inside a large hanger next to a twin-engine Cessna. JeNelle watched Benny, as he walked to an office and signed some papers. He then came back to the car.

"Are you ready to go, Ms. Towson?"

"Yes, Benny, get in. I need to check my luggage at the PSA terminal."

"No you don't. We're here," Benny said smoothly.

"We're where?" JeNelle looked around the hanger.

"This is your flight and it's ready for boarding." He opened her car door and extended his hand. "Please step out of the car and be careful as you enter the cabin. You may stow your luggage in the under seat compartment. Buckle up and no smoking please," he said, mimicking a flight attendant.

JeNelle was overwhelmed. "Benny, what are you going to do?"

"I've told you before. I'm going to get my share of that one percent of your time any way that I can."

He smiled and led her to the aircraft. She followed his instructions and found herself sitting in the cockpit. Benny put his hat behind the seat, his sunglasses on, and a headset on his head. The ground crew pulled the plane out of the hanger and onto the tarmac. Benny started the engines and took over lining up behind a group of planes that were waiting for departure.

"Santa Barbara Tower. This is Cessna November 1120 Romeo. How do you read? Over"

"Cessna November 1120 Romeo. This is Santa Barbara Tower. We read you five-by-five, Captain Alexander. Did you get your lovely lady? Over."

"Roger that, Santa Barbara Tower. Cessna November 1120 Romeo, ready for takeoff. Over."

"Roger that, Cessna November 1120 Romeo. You are cleared for departure. Over."

Benny revved up the engines and the plane sped down the runway. The ground fell away below it. The plane roared, as it ascended through some wispy clouds, climbing higher and higher into the sky.

"Santa Barbara Tower, this is Cessna November 1120 Romeo. I have cleared the runway on heading 124 mark 1. Over."

"Roger that, Cessna November 1120 Romeo. Climb to 30,000 feet. You are cleared to San Francisco International. Hope the lady likes the ride. Over and out."

Benny took the headset off his head and draped them around his neck.

"Now, Ms. Towson, what was that you were saying about eating on the plane?"

JeNelle was still a little dazed. "Benny, at this point, I would believe that some cute, little, female, airline attendant is going to roll a cart up between these seats and offer me a cocktail!"

"Not quite, but if you'll reach behind my seat, you'll find a picnic hamper. Sorry I didn't have time to get swizzle sticks, but you can have that small bottle of champagne in the cooler. Unfortunately, I'm the designated driver. I can't join you for the champagne toast."

JeNelle opened the hamper and there was that familiar aroma of food from Michelangelo's restaurant. The hamper was neatly packed and came compete with napkins, plates and eating utensils. JeNelle looked around in the hamper and then glared at Benny.

"What, no Italian olives?" she chided good-naturedly.

"Sorry, baby. I was a little pressed for time this trip, but I'll have them on the return flight."

'Baby!' The word jabbed into her chest. No one had called her 'baby' since she was at Julliard. She was unaccustomed to hearing the word used to refer to her.

Even the few men who she dated never called her 'baby'. It didn't feel right. It didn't fit her. She was not someone's 'baby'.

"What are you thinking about, JeNelle? You've been quiet for nearly twenty minutes."

"I'm taking this all in. It's a little overwhelming, to say the least, Benny, don't you think?"

"Nope. This is how I've chosen to get my one-percent share of your time."

"Is there more to this than I'm already aware of?"

"Well, yes and no."

"Give me the 'yes' part first. I'm bracing myself for the impact."

"Yes there's more. K.J., I mean, Kenneth James, my brother, is meeting us at the airport, but no, don't worry, I'm not staying with you this trip. I could only swing enough time to fly you to San Francisco. I have to be back tonight and scramble by 0500 hours; that's five in the morning in civilian time. Oh, and K.J. is going to put you up at his place since you couldn't get the reservations you wanted. Your staff already knows about it. They're staying there, too. You won't even have to rent a car to get to the Civic Center since you'll have your van at your disposal and K.J. has to go to the same place every day anyway."

"That's a hell of an impact. I'm beginning to feel like I'm ground zero and the missiles are inbound. Is there any other parts of my life that you've already arranged and that you care to share with me now?"

"No. Not now, baby. I'm still working on it," he said, grinning.

There was that word again. It didn't feel any better the second time he said it. It still didn't fit, she thought. "Are you sure that this is not going to inconvenience your brother? Did he agree willingly to all of this?"

"My brother is a bachelor. Looks like for life. He has no cats, no dogs, and no other pets, if you know what I mean. And yes, I cleared all of this with him. He may have a surprise for you, however."

"You and your brother give new meaning to the phrase, 'double impact'. You're more than a notion, Benjamin Alexander. I know that I'm ill equipped to handle two of you. What has he got planned? Move the Expo to Santa Barbara or some other Herculean feat?"

"No, but 'move' is the operative word. I'll let him tell you the rest. Now, how about some food? I'm hungry, but you're going to have to feed me. I have my hands full at the moment."

"Isn't there an auto pilot button somewhere in this cockpit?" she asked, looking at all the buttons, switches, dials and gauges on the dashboard and overhead.

"I thought that you didn't know anything about flying?"

"I know you can feed yourself and fly, too."

"Rats! Foiled again!" he joked.

The bright lights of San Francisco at dusk with a light fog rolling in over the Bay were mesmerizing, JeNelle thought. Benny landed the plane at San Francisco International Airport and taxied to a General Aviation hanger. JeNelle could see the figure of a man leaning against a SUV in the same way that Benny had a tendency to stand. The man approached the plane, as Benny cut the engines and got out. When Benny was on the tarmac, he embraced the man and then helped JeNelle out of the cockpit. When they moved into the light, she was reminded of a scene in an old movie, *Lady Sings the Blues,* when Billy Dee Williams first meets Diana Ross playing the role of Lady Day. There was that same million-dollar smile that Benny usually wore, but this man was even more handsome than Benny. She took in a quick breath, as if something had struck her. She felt her heart rampaging in her chest and felt the blood draining from her head. His smile could melt the polar ice caps, she thought. He had a different style about him than Benny—less flash and boyish charm, but much more depth and sophistication. She had to force herself to breathe.

"JeNelle Towson, this is my big brother, Kenneth James Alexander, the world's brightest up and coming entrepreneur. Better known as K.J. to those of us who love him. K.J., this is JeNelle, the brightest star in my universe."

"Enough already, Benny," Kenneth said, as he extended his hand to JeNelle. "It's a pleasure to meet you at last, JeNelle. Needless to say, Benny has done nothing but burn up my phone line talking about you. I'm glad to finally meet you in person."

His voice was deeper than Benny's with more resonance and confidence, she thought. His presence struck something inside her that she thought was long dead and buried. She was awed by his geniality, his caressing, deep melodic voice, and his soft touch. Realizing she was staring at him, she snapped back to attention. No man had ever had that effect on her before.

"Kenneth, I've gotten the same treatment you have. Benny has talked quite a bit about you and the rest of your family. Now I understand that he has commandeered your home. I'm sorry that he's put you to so much trouble. Really, I could find a hotel or motel for the time that I and my staff will be here."

She realized that she was still holding Kenneth's hand. Strangely, she was reluctant to let go. It felt warm, strong, and comforting. His touch was sending shots of electricity through her body.

"Please, don't think that Benny had to twist my arm to do this. He'd do the same thing for a friend of mine if I asked him. I'm glad that I could help. Are you comfortable with the arrangements?"

She wasn't comfortable at all when Benny told her what he had arranged. She had decided to politely refuse Kenneth's offer, but now..."I am, yes," she said, as she took in his entire presence. It wasn't just his physical attributes, of which there were plenty to behold, it was more. Much, much more. Kenneth was tall, with broad, straight shoulders covered by a brown, leather, bomber jacket. He wore comfortable looking jeans and boots.

"Good. Barry and Felix arrived and were sitting down to eat when I left my house. They'll probably be waiting for you to arrive. I hope that you don't object, but I've taken the liberty of working out a new location for your exhibit booth. I know that you registered for space late, but, in my view, the location you were assigned was unacceptable. There was no electrical or telephone access and it was in an isolated area on the Civic Center floor. The space for your booth is going to be larger, at no extra cost, and it's on the aisle directly behind where we're setting up our booth. I rented that space already for storage purposes, but I've made other arrangements to store my products.

"Barry told me that you didn't have time to arrange for your computer and network hookups, so I've arranged to have our engineers set up three computers for you. You should be on-line and networked with your store by eight o'clock in the morning. Also, since you were unable to arrange to bring additional staff, some of my staff have volunteered as relief workers for you. You and your managers will meet with them tomorrow morning at seven to go over your inventory and to prep them so that they can be useful to you. Do these arrangements meet with your approval?"

JeNelle was overwhelmed. She was having some disquieting thoughts, as he spoke, but he spoke with such confidence and well-reasoned deliberation. There was a meticulous attention to details, but without being overbearing. He had a gleam in his eyes—more of a twinkle she noted. No one had controlled her life so completely since... She had to gather herself to speak.

"You've been busy and indeed, very thorough. I don't believe you've overlooked anything. Of course, it certainly does meet with my approval."

Benny noticed that JeNelle seemed a little off center, but he could not glean the cause. He anchored his arm around her waist.

"It looks like I'm leaving you in good hands, baby. Now you play nice with the others and try not to hurt anybody with that devastating smile of yours,"

Benny said, as he embraced JeNelle and kissed her softly on the cheek. "I'll see you in five days."

There was that word again, she thought. She wanted to stop him in his tracks and tell him not to call her "baby," but this was not the time. All that she could manage to do was to say "thank you" and return his kiss on the cheek.

Benny noticed rigidity in JeNelle's body language. He released her and turned to Kenneth. "Okay, K.J., I'm out. You take good care of my lady or there will be hell to pay," he joked.

Benny and Kenneth hugged and Benny winked at JeNelle. He climbed back into the Cessna, waved to them and taxied to the runway. Kenneth and JeNelle watched until the plane climbed through the clouds and out of sight.

"Well, JeNelle, let's get you home, so that you can relax and get ready for tomorrow," Kenneth said, as he opened the door to his vehicle for her and put her luggage and briefcase into the back. He got in and started the engine.

JeNelle was surprised somewhat that he drove an extended cab truck, given what she knew about Benny's fairly lavish lifestyle, but it seemed to fit Kenneth. He had his own style. Very unpretentious. She hoped that he wouldn't be offended by what she was about to say, but it had to be said, the air had to be cleared. "Kenneth, I don't know how to say this—."

"You feel that Benny has taken too many liberties," he interrupted and smiled indulgently.

JeNelle was amazed at his insight. It seemed that he was reading her thoughts. "Yes," she stuttered. "I mean, I'm not accustomed to anyone taking charge like this. I hope that you're not offended."

"Of course, not. If you feel the slightest bit uncomfortable, just let me know. Benny and I sincerely want you to enjoy your time here. Have you been to San Francisco before?"

"Only a few times, but I've never really seen the city. Usually all I get to see is the airport and the hotel."

"Would you be willing to make time to see some of it before Benny picks you up? It's an interesting city."

"Yes, I would," she said, amazed at her answer. "The way you've worked things out, it looks like this will not be a draining experience after all."

"Good. We'll see how the timing works out."

They drove along the streets and talked. JeNelle noticed a sign that read: Marin County Limits. Eventually, they pulled onto a tree-lined street with well-manicured lawns and tasteful, but large, uniquely designed homes. As

Kenneth pulled into the driveway, she spotted her van parked in front of a triple-door, side-load garage. Lights popped on outside, as they approached the huge, California ranch-style house and went inside.

"I'll take your things into your bedroom. Make yourself comfortable," Kenneth said.

JeNelle went into the front living room and was immediately warmed by its comfort. Beautiful wood furniture set off the otherwise masculine room. It was very pleasantly decorated, she thought. Very different from the way Benny's condo was done. Kenneth's home was designed for comfort, not seduction—warm, vibrant colors, a fireplace that actually had been used, pictures on the mantle. She could see a den and maybe what might be an office. Also very tastefully done and neatly arranged. The artwork on the walls was not overstated. It fit perfectly with the decor.

"Would you like something to drink or eat, JeNelle?" Kenneth asked, entering the living room.

"No, nothing to eat, thank you. Benny had a picnic hamper of food on the plane, but I'd like a glass of wine, preferably white."

"I have some very good wine from Napa County."

"That sounds fine."

"I'm afraid that Barry and Felix are asleep already," Kenneth said, pouring two glasses of wine. "If you're tired, I'll show you to your room?"

"No," JeNelle said, walking to where Kenneth was standing before a beautiful wooden étagère with a small bar area tucked behind glass doors. "I'm not tired."

"Good. I'll light the fireplace to knock the chill off this room."

JeNelle ran her fingers over the fine grain of the beautiful piece of furniture.

"Kenneth, this is a very unusual and beautiful piece of furniture. Where did you find it?"

"Uh, well, actually I built it myself. Something I like to do in my spare time."

JeNelle was impressed. The piece showed the love and care that he had worked into the design. She gazed around the room at matching pieces. "Did you make all of this?"

He nodded and shrugged. "Uh, yes, as a matter of fact, I did."

"Did someone teach you the art of woodworking?"

"Yes," he shrugged absently again. "My paternal grandfather. He was a master craftsman when he wasn't working on the railroad. He came from a long line of ship builders. Once he retired from the railroad, he made furniture full time. He taught all the kids in the area the art."

"Benny, too?"

"Well," Kenneth hesitated, "Benny's patience goes to mechanical things. He built an airplane, instead. Said he'd get where he was going faster that way." Kenneth laughed.

"But where do you make all of this beautiful furniture?'

"I converted my garage—."

"May I see?"

Kenneth smiled skeptically. "Are you sure you want to do this? It's not much—."

"I'd love to see it."

"Okay," Kenneth said reluctantly.

He led her through the expansive kitchen and family room though a mud room that contained a full bath to the garage. When Kenneth flipped on the light, JeNelle gasped audibly. The triple garage was lined with beautiful old pieces of sturdy furniture in various stages of restoration or construction. A large frame and headboard sat in the middle of the garage. JeNelle approached the beautiful piece, running her fingers its surface.

"Kenneth, this is the most beautiful sleigh bed I've ever seen." She was overwhelmed by its beauty.

"Thank you. It's a replica of my maternal grandparents' bed."

"So that's why you drive a—."

"A truck? Oh," he smiled, "I do have a car and a SUV though. I just rarely drive them. The truck is much more comfortable and practical. When I have time, I drive upstate looking for trees that I can buy and have milled. That's where I was earlier today before I met you and Benny at the airport. An old post-and-beam tobacco barn was going to be demolished, so I bought it and I'm having it deconstructed and shipped. It has some beautiful old growth redwood that I'd like to preserve and use to build a home someday on land I own in Goodwill, Summer County, South Carolina. My family has tree farms all over the county and a sawmill, but we don't have redwoods. My cousin, James Dixon, and his father, my Uncle Romelo, run our family's businesses, including a Hydroponics farm, fishery and livestock. We do a fairly brisk business at home. I guess I'm still a country boy at heart." He smiled. "I enjoy working with my hands."

"I must say, I'm very impressed. You're quite a craftsman."

"Thank you. It's just a hobby that I enjoy. But enough about me and the Alexander clan. Tell me about you, JeNelle," he said, guiding her back to the living room.

Kenneth started the fire and then sat on one of the sofas across from her. She talked about things that had not come to mind in years. She wasn't just talking about her business experiences either, but about her personal life, too. Something that she rarely did. She talked about her family and thought how easy it was to talk with Kenneth. She watched the expressions on his handsome face. He was a good, active listener and an interesting conversationalist. She was never this animated even with people who she had known for a long time, but here she was talking, as if they were old friends.

Kenneth had that same glow about him that she saw in Benny when he talked about his family. Kenneth focused heavily on Benny's character. He shared some of their childhood antics and how well Benny had done at the Academy, finishing in the upper five percent of his class and how proud he and his entire family were when Benny made captain and got his own jet fighter team. He talked about how much he had learned from Benny considering that their mother was always promising that Benny would not see his next birthday if he didn't work harder and longer.

"Yet Aretha and Gregory have us all beat, hands down. They've got more talent in their little fingers than all of us put together. Vivian, Benny, and I had to work long and very diligently to succeed in school, but not Aretha or Gregory. Gregory puts in as little time as possible and still manages to do well when he wants to, especially in Math and Economics. We all played basketball, even Vivian, but Gregory has got all the moves, except Vivian's three-point shot," he said, snorting. "She still hits ninety-nine percent of her shots from three-point range. She murders all of us. She's probably financed her college career from money we've lost to her betting her that she couldn't hit a tough shot.

"Aretha is amazing. She's been a straight-A student all of her life. She doesn't understand why everyone didn't get grades like hers. She plays the piano and has a voice like an angel, but she'll whip you without a blink at chess, checkers or backgammon. She can entertain herself for hours just reading anything and everything that she gets her hands on. She's already read all of the great American and European classics, even Shakespeare and Tolstoy. When we ask her what career she's thinking about, she simple says, 'I'll tell you later.' Until then, she says that she has to keep Gregory in check."

Kenneth found himself gazing at JeNelle while they talked easily and comfortably. Something he had never felt before began to overtake him. She was a masterpiece, he thought to himself. She was bright, interesting and devastatingly beautiful. His thoughts were moving in dangerous directions and his efforts to hold himself in check were disintegrating the more they talked. He wanted to know everything about her, and it wasn't because of Benny, it was for himself.

The telephone rang and Kenneth got up to answer it. He moved so smoothly with such ease of motion for a man with his stature. JeNelle began to force herself not to look at him so frequently, opting instead to gaze into the fire or the incredible furniture that he designed and built. His talent was enormous.

"….no, Benny, she's not asleep yet. I've been boring her with family fables. JeNelle's right here," Kenneth said, as he handed the cordless telephone to her.

"Benny, where are you?"

"I'm at home, but I wanted you to know that I miss you already."

"At the condo? What time is it?" JeNelle asked with great surprise.

"Same time as it is there, JeNelle, twelve-thirty in the morning."

JeNelle looked at her watch. It was, indeed, half past midnight. She was surprised at how fast the time had flown by. Talking with Kenneth was effortless and easy. They had been at it for hours. They finished two bottles of wine and a large pizza that Kenneth had built himself and baked in a pizza oven in his spacious backyard. She had been awake since 4:00 A.M., but because of Kenneth's easy manner, she didn't even feel fatigued.

"Is everything all right, JeNelle?" Benny asked with concern.

"Yes, Benny, everything is fine. You get some rest. You've had a very long day and so have I. I'll see you in five days."

"Goodnight, baby. I'll see—."

Four strikes and you're out. JeNelle got up from the sofa and walked out of Kenneth's earshot. She lowered her voice. "Benny, we're going to have to talk about this 'baby' business. Friends, remember?"

"JeNelle, it feels good to me to call you my baby. Can't you let go just a little?"

"You're flying on one wing again, Captain," she admonished lightly. "I'm not at that point in our friendship, yet. Don't push it."

"'Yet?' That sounds promising. Okay, I won't say it, but you sure can't stop me from thinking it. Goodnight, JeNelle."

"Goodnight, Benny. Thank you again for everything you've done."

Chapter 13

It was nearly nine o'clock in the evening when Gloria Towson dragged herself into the house in the fashionable Georgetown area of Washington, D.C. Her housemates, except David Carter, were assembled in the front living room watching the video, *A Few Good Men*, and filling up on applesauce cake.

"God, I hate flying!" she said, dropping her belongings on the floor in the foyer.

"Hi, Gloria," Vivian said, without rising from her comfortable position on the sofa.

"Hi, Gloria," Bill and Melissa chimed in unison, equally unfazed by her return.

Gloria leaned against the living room door, feeling the wrath of the two double scotches that she consumed at lunch and more on the flight. "Don't bother to get up, anybody," she cracked sarcastically.

"Okay, we won't," Bill shot back, still not looking in her direction.

When no one moved she said, "Well, isn't anyone going to help me with my bags?"

"I'll help you later, Gloria, but it's getting to the good part," Vivian said. "Wait a minute…here it comes,
*'If you handle this case with the same kind of
fast food, slick ass, Persian bazaar….'*
"You tell him, Demi!" Bill shouted.

"No, wait a minute," Melissa said, "listen to this, when Tom Cruise says,
'Why Lieutenant, I think I'm starting to get aroused….'
"Oooh, he's soooo kool!"

"No the best part is when Tom Cruise says,
'I want the truth!' and then Jack Nicholson says, *'You can't
handle the truth!'*

Alan chimed in. "You're all wrong. The best part is when Tom Cruise says,
'Did you order the code red!' and Nicholson says
'You're damn right I did!'

Tom Cruise is blown away. He got Nicholson to crack on the stand. Man, that's controlling a witness! He suckered Nicholson right in!"

"You people watch too much TV," Gloria said sarcastically, starting up the steps.

"Oh, Gloria," Vivian yelled, "Don't go yet. We have something to talk with you about."

"In the morning, Vivian. I'm too tired to talk tonight. All I want to do is sleep."

Gloria proceeded slowly up the long staircase to her room. Moments later, she made a hasty return and flew into the living room. She was alert now and whispered rather frantically, flapping her hands to get her housemates' attention, as she looked from face to face.

"There's someone sleeping in my bed!"

"Said the Mama Bear to the Papa Bear," Bill added glibly.

"That's what we wanted to talk with you about," Vivian said, scooping another piece of applesauce cake into her mouth and still watching the movie.

"Well talk!" Gloria demanded.

Moments ticked by. Everyone was still engrossed in the movie and motioned for Gloria to be quiet. Gloria wasn't having it. She marched over to the ultra large, flat-screen and turned it off. Her hands gripped her impressive hips while everyone railed and moaned.

"We're missing the good part, Gloria," Melissa whined.

"It's a DVD, Melissa!" Gloria shot back.

"Okay, Gloria, sit down. This is the deal," Vivian began.

Vivian explained the events that transpired in Gloria's absence. As Vivian talked, Gloria looked from one person to the next, as they added their piece of the puzzle. They introduced Alan who Gloria had already seen in classes. As they finished the saga, Gloria looked at all of them.

"Is that all that we have to pay? And this Anna person can cook, clean and run the house, too? Are you kidding? That's a bargain! That's okay with me. All I want to know is: where am I sleeping tonight and when do I get my bed back?"

"With me, as usual, Gloria," Bill said, stroking her arm.

"Bite me, Chandler!" Gloria shot a menacing look at Bill and rolled her eyes.

"Again?" Bill grinned. "God, you're insatiable, Gloria."

Melissa's eyes popped. "Have you been sleeping with Gloria, too, Bill?"

"Sure I have, Melissa. Didn't you know that?" His grin became more mischievous.

"No, but...but if you can sleep with Vivian and Gloria, what's wrong with me? Am I chopped liver or something?"

"I have to build up to you, Melissa." Bill winked. "They're just getting me ready for my big score with you." Bill leaned over toward Melissa in a mock whisper and said, "By the way, have you played with those electronic sex toys that I gave you for Christmas yet?"

"Bill!" Melissa flushed. "You weren't supposed to tell anybody about that!"

Vivian sat straight up in her chair, eyes narrowed. "You gave electronic sex toys to Melissa for Christmas?" Vivian asked incredulously.

"I'll explain later," Bill said glibly.

A beat later, everyone fell out laughing, except Melissa, of course.

When Vivian composed herself she said, "Gloria, I'd suggest that you sleep in David's room, but that's where Alan is sleeping. You can sleep in my bed. I'll sleep on my sofa bed. The furniture is coming tomorrow at nine o'clock in the morning, right Bill?" Bill nodded in agreement. "Then you can have your bed back."

Gloria was satisfied and went back upstairs to Vivian's room. Bill flipped on the television and they all began to watch the movie again. Then out of the blue, Vivian suddenly sat up in her seat again.

"Melissa Bernice Charles and electronic sex toys. Now that's a scary thought!"

Everyone fell out laughing again. Even Melissa laughed, as she threw a pillow at Vivian.

After the movie ended, Vivian went up to her bedroom where she found Gloria wide-awake, sitting in the middle of the bed talking on her cell phone. As Vivian came into the room, she overheard Gloria saying, "And just how much do you miss me?.... You want to do what to me?.... Ooh, baby, that sounds so good.... I can't wait!.... I'm wearing a blue see-thru nightgown.... I can't do that right now...." She giggled. "Vivian just came in.... I'm going to rock your world, baby.... Yeah, that too, baby.... Tell me that one more time.... And then what are you going to do?.... Ooh, baby, that's real freaky...."

Vivian was pulling her sweater over her head, as Gloria talked. She stopped, looked at Gloria, and shook her head. Then Gloria said, "Okay, baby. See you in two weeks. Stroke it one more time for me, baby. Goodnight, lover."

Gloria purposefully shuddered and squeezed herself. "Oooo, he's sooo bad," she cooed.

"Gloria, you give new meaning to the phrase 'oral sex'. Are you going into a new line of work...telephone porn?"

Gloria grinned devilishly. "No, that's my baby, Tony Jamerson."

"The guy who plays wide receiver for the San Diego Chargers?"

"Yes! He's so fine! And body! The man's built like a Sherman Tank and he's got a big gun, too, if you know what I mean!" Gloria used her hands to demonstrate the approximate length of Tony's 'big gun'.

"I get the picture, Gloria. I've met him. He and Benny party together sometimes."

"I know. That's how I met him. I was out with Benny, JeNelle, and some other people at Jason's Night Club and Tony came up to me and said *'I'll have your babies, if you'll dance with me just once.'*"

Vivian shook her head. "And you fell for that weak line? I thought that you were interested in Benny? You were pressing me hard for his contact information."

"Frankly, Vivian, I was, but I think that your brother is more interested in my sister, JeNelle, than he is in me. He's flying her to San Francisco today and she's staying with your other brother, Kenneth, at his house."

Vivian thought a moment. "Benny did call me one morning talking about someone, but I thought that it was you he was talking about. It was all so confusing, but how do you know that Benny is flying JeNelle to San Francisco and that she's staying with K.J.?"

"Benny called me after his date with JeNelle and told me what he was going to do. He had it all planned. All I had to do was to make sure that JeNelle didn't take an early flight to San Francisco, so that Benny would have time to get to Santa Barbara and surprise her. I kept her car all day and then I got her to take me to a late lunch. Everybody in JeNelle's store, INSIGHTS, was in on it. They kept her so busy that she couldn't leave until late. Benny called before JeNelle and I left for lunch and asked Wanda to make sure that JeNelle didn't take a cab to the airport. I don't know all of the details after that. JeNelle took me to the airport and then she went back to work."

"And you were in on this scheme?"

"Sure. I think that Benny and JeNelle make a hot couple. She's just a few years older than Benny, but that didn't seem to matter to him. But let me tell you what else happened."

Gloria began to relay the story about Benny and the roses, Cecil and Janice, breakfast the next morning, and getting JeNelle to have dinner with Benny on New Year's Day.

"Sounds like Melrose Place West to me," Vivian said. "I hope that JeNelle is up for the hunt. If Benny is in hot pursuit, the fox hasn't got a chance. And if he's got K.J. involved, there's no contest!"

"Benny's smooth, all right, but he's up against my sister, JeNelle, the iceberg and you know what happened to the Titanic when it hit an iceberg." They both laughed. Then Gloria said, "I see that Carlton was here."

Vivian shot a quizzical look at Gloria. "What business are you going into now, Gloria, a revival of Psychic Friends with Dionne Warwick?" Vivian climbed onto the sofa bed and turned out her light.

"No. I have the evidence right here in my hand." Gloria produced an empty condom wrapper. "It was stuck in your pillowcase. What are all these little holes in here for?"

"Gloria, just toss the damn wrapper in the trash, turn out the light, and let's get some sleep. Goodnight!"

Chapter 14

JeNelle woke early the next morning and headed to the bathroom to shower. As she passed Kenneth's bedroom, she noticed his door was slightly ajar. She saw his reflection in a mirror, as he stood drying himself and talking on a cell phone. She caught her breath and shuttered involuntarily. His body was more magnificent nude than any sculpture she had ever seen. She knew that she should simply pass by and take her shower, but the sight of his tall, lean, muscular, body caused something else to stir in her. She felt something when she met him for the first time, something disquieting, but then, as they sat on the sofa and talked, and now—it was all too perplexing, she thought.

"Shake it off, JeNelle," she whispered to herself, as she continued toward the guest bathroom.

Kenneth introduced JeNelle and her staff to everyone at CompuCorrect, Incorporated. Assembled by 6:45 A.M., they were having a light buffet breakfast and making plans for the day. Kenneth led the discussion. JeNelle watched how he talked with his employees and how they responded to him. It was clear they had more than just a work-place relationship with each other; obviously, they were friends as well. Everyone seemed eager to help. Even the receptionist, Sara McDougal, was anxious to contribute, she thought.

JeNelle was very impressed with Kenneth's business operation housed on the ground floor of a twelve-thousand-square-foot warehouse as well. Although he constantly gave the credit to his business partners, Shirley Taylor and Thomas Jenkins, she could see who provided the moving force, Kenneth James Alexander, Executive Director of CompuCorrect, Incorporated.

When they arrived at the San Francisco Civic Center, there was already a bustle of activity. Although the press and news media would not be permitted into the Expo until after 3:00 P.M., exhibitors were hard at work setting up their booths. The public would be permitted in the following day after a breakfast ceremony for the exhibitors to be hosted by the Mayor and the Governor.

Electrical wiring was being taped to the floor; banners were being hoisted in the air into position, trucks with products of every type and description wheeled in and out of the Civic Center. There were more than fifteen hundred exhibitors. Kenneth and his crew had their exhibit constructed by eleven o'clock. CompuCorrect's exhibit booth was a dazzling array of thirty, large, flat screen, video monitors stacked six across and five high forming a collage of panels and connecting the user to information services worldwide. All the video, voice and telephony data at your fingertips. The archway that stood in front of the booth read: CompuCorrect—The On Ramp for the Worldwide Information Super Highway in dazzling, eye-catching colors and lights. There was also a miniaturized model displaying how the multidirectional computer, security and video systems worked to form a Smart-House and to connect the users to homes, schools, hospitals, libraries, corporations, utility companies, and a myriad of other businesses and even to the White House and other world capitals. There was something for everyone from the homeowner to the largest corporations.

Underneath three, round, glass tables that sat four people comfortably in ergonomic chairs that beckoned the customer's to relax, was thick, deep maroon carpeting.

Once Kenneth's exhibit was completed, he and his staff moved on to help JeNelle, Barry, Felix, and some of Kenneth's other staff people to stack books, art, videos, and other products on displays in what appeared to be a cozy room complete with tables, sofas, chairs, bookcases, and lamps in someone's home. JeNelle thought that he must have visited her website to have crafted the tableau to replicate her shop's décor so closely. Kenneth was right about the location, JeNelle agreed. It was on a primary walkway and her products did not have to compete with the plumbing supply company on her right or the natural fruit juices company on her left. He also had her exhibit networked to her store so that she would be in a position to check her inventory and supplies as she talked with potential buyers and distributors. She was totally impressed by the efficiency with which Kenneth's technicians, computer specialists, and engineers handled their tasks. By lunchtime, everything was completed and they had three hours to kill before the Expo planners did a walkthrough with the press and other news media.

Local television stations' trucks and other national and international news gathering organizations were setting up in the parking lot, as JeNelle and Kenneth left the Civic Center with their staff members. A female reporter, followed by a camera crew, rushed up to JeNelle and Kenneth just as they were about to get into Kenneth's truck and asked whether she could briefly interview them. They agreed and answered questions on camera for fifteen minutes.

When JeNelle and Kenneth arrived at CompuCorrect, a buffet lunch was underway. A feast, JeNelle thought, that did not seem like an unusual event for the company—very relaxed atmosphere in a very well decorated, comfortable, employee lounge area of the warehouse. JeNelle commented to Kenneth that the exercise equipment and the basketball hoop in a time-out room of the office were very pleasant additions. She had noticed his staff members, like Sara, a stout, young woman with naturally bright red hair and pretty blue eyes, working out on the equipment earlier that morning. Now others were working out during lunch and Kenneth was one of them. He had changed out of his tailored Italian business suit and was wearing loose workout shorts and a cut-off muscle shirt. She watched him do one hundred sit-ups. Then he lifted weights. While she was watching him on the rowing machine, she caught a glimpse of Shirley Taylor out of the corner of her eye. Shirley was watching her. JeNelle felt a little embarrassed so she turned her attention away from Kenneth.

"Shirley, do all of the employees use this equipment?" JeNelle asked, covering her embarrassment.

"Yes, everyone comes in here at some time of the day. It helps to work off the tension and stress of the long hours we all sometimes put in and the tedious work. Sara says that she started working out when she saw how much better people seemed to feel and how much energy they had after a good workout. Since then, she tells me that she's lost fourteen pounds and trimmed three inches off her waistline. Now she doesn't miss a day working out." Shirley sized up JeNelle with a critical eye. "You look like you work out, JeNelle."

"I do, yes. If I had known that this equipment was here, I would have brought my gear with me."

"If you'd like to work out, I have some extra clothes and a pair of shoes that I think would fit you. We have a dressing room, lockers, and showers in the Ladies Room. Come with me and I'll get them for you."

JeNelle undressed quickly, plated her hair, twisted it into a ball and pinned it up. First, she headed for the free weights. She worked out with Tom on the bench press and then on the mechanical bike. Finally, she got on the rowing machine for ten minutes. Kenneth was playing one-on-one basketball with Juan Cuero, one of his top engineers and losing badly.

Kenneth was shooting baskets with Juan when JeNelle and Shirley left the dressing room. Suddenly, he missed a shot—one that he rarely missed—but the sight of JeNelle in scant workout clothes caused him to inhale sharply and lose his focus on the game. She was magnificently built. She took his breath away. His attention to his game continued to falter and he lost the game to Juan, something else that he had not done in four years.

Being around JeNelle was rocking him to the core. His attempts to stifle his attraction to her mentally, emotionally and physically were working havoc on his integrity. She was his brother's lady, he kept telling himself. Just watching her, gazing at her, was a betrayal of his brother's love and trust, he thought, but his engorged phallus was speaking to his heart, and not his head. Workout longer and harder, he told himself, but it was painfully obvious to him that even a thorough workout wouldn't quell his growing desire for JeNelle. He had to try though. Benny asked him to look after her, and he made it clear that JeNelle was very important to him. Kenneth vowed that he would do nothing to betray his brother's trust, but he knew that his years of sexual hiatus had ended with the sight of JeNelle Towson. His private life needed attention. Perhaps he'd be fortunate, like Benny, to find a JeNelle sometime in his future, though he doubted whether any woman would ever be as appealing to him as JeNelle was proving to be. As he took his gaze from JeNelle, he noticed that Shirley was watching him. He averted his scrutiny from JeNelle and went to work out on the Stairmaster.

When JeNelle finished her shower and was dressed, she felt revived. She tingled all over. Shirley sat on a bench in the dressing room. JeNelle was applying makeup and checking her appearance in the mirror.

"I understand that Benny Alexander flew you to San Francisco last night in a private plane," Shirley said.

The mention of Benny's name while her thoughts were on Kenneth caught JeNelle off guard. "There really are no secrets around CompuCorrect. You all seem to share everything." JeNelle laughed.

"Not everything," Shirley said, with a curiously tight tone in her voice, "but we try to make it a pleasant place to work."

"You've succeeded and done a wonderful job. Kenneth says that you and Tom deserve all the credit. The art on the walls is very impressive. I understand that was your handiwork."

"Some of it was, but everyone chipped in something."

"If you ever feel the desire to do some moonlighting as an art dealer, please call me first. I'd hire you in a heartbeat."

"I'm very happy right where I am. By the way, will Benny be joining you here during this week?"

JeNelle thought Shirley's question was a bit curious. Especially for someone she hardly knew.

"Joining me here? Why would you think that Benny would be joining me here?"

"I understand that you're staying at Kenneth's place."

"And?" JeNelle asked, with one raised brow.

Shirley shrugged. "And Kenneth is Benny's brother. They're very close."

"Okay, I'm staying at Kenneth's, Kenneth and Benny are brothers, and Benny flew me up here. I still don't understand why you think that Benny would be 'joining me' here."

"You two are seeing each other, aren't you?"

JeNelle turned around, looked squarely at Shirley, and asked, "What on earth gave you that idea?"

"It seems that both Benny and Kenneth have gone out of their way for you. Kenneth's on the Chamber of Commerce's Board of Directors and he moved heaven and earth to make the officials change your exhibit location and to give you his prime spot on the exhibit floor. It's a space we were going to use for storage equipment. He was here at the office late with Juan several nights before you arrived to work out the computer connections, software programs, and a few hundred other details so that your booth would be ready on time. He even called in a favor of an interior decorator he knows to design your booth and furnish it. It just seemed to add up that you must be very important to Benny."

"Look, Shirley, if you're trying to discover whether I'm your competition for Benny's time and attention, I promise you that I am not. I met Benny just before New Year's. My sister, Gloria, introduced us. She's a student at Georgetown Law and she lives in Benny's house in Washington with Kenneth's and Benny's sister, Vivian. Benny and I are just friends. He saw a way to do a favor for me and he did it—all without my prior knowledge or consent. It seems to be a family trait. I did not ask Kenneth to do anything. I didn't even know what was going on until I was at the airport in Santa Barbara and I didn't know Kenneth or what Kenneth had done until I landed in San Francisco last night. That's when I met Kenneth for the first time at the airport. So please, stop worrying, Shirley, and redo the math here. In this case, one and one don't equal two."

This revelation did not seem to lighten Shirley's mood at all. In fact, she seemed more disturbed. JeNelle couldn't understand it. She sat next to Shirley on the bench. "Shirley, I'm not your competition for Benny."

"Thank you, JeNelle, I do believe you. I hope that you don't think me rude for questioning you that way?"

"No, in fact, I want us to be friends. This is one way friends get to know each other better. They ask questions, so ask anything that you like."

While JeNelle finished putting on her makeup and Shirley finished dressing, they chatted companionably, but JeNelle fervently hoped that Shirley didn't ask what she thought of Kenneth. JeNelle didn't think that she could be as detached talking about her feelings about Kenneth as she could about Benny. She was amazed at all the trouble that Kenneth went to in order to help set up the booth for her and allowing her and her managers to stay at his home for the week. Something about Kenneth mesmerized her—hell, *everything* about Kenneth mesmerized her, but she had to stifle that growing desire within her. Her life would never again include a man, not after what Michel had done to her. She could no longer trust any man and she no longer trusted her own judgment. She learned the hard way and it was a painfully devastating lesson. No man had touched her since then and she privately vowed that no man ever would again, but Kenneth had awakened something in her that she thought she could never feel again.

JeNelle studied Shirley in the mirror. Shirley was very attractive. Fair, fresh skin, almond shaped eyes, oval face, with a cute haircut that really complimented her appearance. She dressed stylishly, which enhanced her thin build and legs. Her nails were nicely manicured and her makeup applied not to excess. She was tall and model statuesque. *Yes*, she thought, *just the type of woman who would be interested in Benny.* Maybe she could do something to put them together when Benny returned. As a rule, she never meddled in anyone else's life, but she'd have to think about that carefully.

Everyone left CompuCorrect after lunch and returned to the Civic Center. The press corps was in full attendance and photographed everything and everyone. JeNelle watched from the sidelines, as the press interviewed Kenneth with Shirley and Tom by his side. Cameras were rolling, lights were flashing, and questions were coming at him fast and furiously from every direction. Kenneth was handling it all as if he were reading it all off a cue card. He even managed to make the press corps laugh heartily several times. He was relaxed, confident, and firm. He made very clear, concise, and direct statements, and there was that ever-present, million-dollar, polar-ice-cap-melting smile. Even when some reporters asked the dumbest questions, he handled it all with ease and aplomb. He was enormously articulate with a slight hint of a Southern Gentleman's demeanor behind the cultivated charm of an urbane man. Feet apart, head up, shoulders back, and hands in his pockets, he was magnificent. She was totally impressed and more than a little smitten.

That evening, at Kenneth's house, JeNelle was lying across the queen-sized bed jotting down some notes when Kenneth knocked at the open door and peeked in. He stood with his hands in the pockets of his gray Calvin Klein casual slacks. JeNelle looked up and saw his million-dollar smile, complimented by his navy blue cashmere V-neck Adolpho sweater, and dark grey POLO leather jacket. He was leaning against the doorjamb when her eyes washed over his fine physique. She could see a gold chain around his neck that read FAMILY tangled in the hair on his chest. *Benny isn't the only one in that family who has real sex appeal*, she thought, as she looked at Kenneth in the doorway. Kenneth had it in spades.

"Shirley and Tom are here and we're all going out to the Empress of China restaurant in Chinatown to have dinner. Felix and Barry are going, too. Would you like to join us?"

"Yes," she managed to say, as she snapped her focus back to what Kenneth was saying. "Give me five minutes to slip into something more comfortable and I'll be right there."

"Great," Kenneth said, as he started to leave the doorway. Then he stuck his head back into the room. "Uh, you may want to put on some comfortable walking shoes and bring a jacket, too. It can get chilly in San Francisco in the evenings this time of the year."

When they reached Chinatown, they parked and walked around the area for a while, sightseeing. The restaurant was very nice and the group was joined by many of the other employees from Kenneth's company and their families in a private dining area. That made for many funny stories around the dinner tables, as the group shared different dishes—some that JeNelle had not tried. They didn't talk about business or the Expo. Felix and Barry told some funny stories about JeNelle and she retaliated by telling some even funnier stories about them. Kenneth's staff and partners roasted him, too, and he blushed at what some were saying about him. Tom could mimic Kenneth perfectly and the tables roared in laughter all evening. Kenneth and JeNelle caught each other often gazing at the other one. Those in the party seemed to sense something, too. JeNelle insisted on picking up the tab for everyone. It was a fun evening that broke up at about nine o'clock.

After dinner, Kenneth decided to take JeNelle on a night tour of the city and offered to take Barry and Felix along, but they declined saying that they were going with Tom to watch a basketball game on television at a local sports bar. Shirley decided to go home. After bidding everyone goodnight, JeNelle and Kenneth drove alone through the city and Kenneth pointed out some of the famous landmarks. They ended up walking along the Embarcadero with Alcatraz Island barely visible in the dark distance across the water. As they walked, Kenneth talked about all the shops and restaurants along the way, how his mother visited each one at least twice and, of course, about Benny. Then they drove to a spot in Golden Gate Park overlooking the Golden Gate Bridge. JeNelle thought the bridge and the view were breathtaking, but Kenneth was even more so. Kenneth told her that next to his home in Goodwill, South Carolina, this was his favorite spot to look at the universe, but he didn't add that viewing it with her made everything else pale by comparison. He pointed out constellations until the fog rolled in and obscured their view.

JeNelle found herself standing shoulder to shoulder with Kenneth, as they leaned against the car absorbing the night. Kenneth's manly, understated fragrance sent waves of pleasant chills surging through her body. JeNelle shuddered visibly and Kenneth noticed.

"Are you cold, JeNelle? We could go—."

"Just a little chill, but I'd like to stay a while longer, if you don't mind." She smiled up at him. "You warned me that the nights here could get cold."

Kenneth's heart was pounding like a slow motion jackhammer. JeNelle's soft natural scent was wreaking havoc on his senses. He started to take off his jacket to put around her shoulders, but when he opened his arms, JeNelle moved inside and, after a moment's hesitation, he closed his arms and jacket around her. Standing with her back to his chest, he had to modulate his breathing, as she laid her head back against his chest. Her body pressed against his sent heated shockwaves careening through him, his blood warming. Every inch of him came alive. He turned his head up to the sky and squeezed his eyes shut against his rising desire.

JeNelle didn't know or understand what came over her, but moving into Kenneth's embrace to share his heat seemed such a natural act. She had never been held with such gentleness or warmth, but she had very little experience with a man. Michel was the only man to touch her and that was more than ten years ago. What was happening to her now did not resemble anything that happened between her and Michel. Kenneth was warm and protective. She felt safe from harm in his arms and though she thought her action inappropriate, she didn't want the sweet ecstasy to end. Feeling his masculine body wrapped around hers caused her core to ache with a desire that she had never known. She squeezed her eyes shut, bracing against her mounting desire for a man who she had just met.

When JeNelle looked up over her shoulder at Kenneth, the overwhelming desire to capture her sweet mouth was nearly his undoing. Her mouth was a breath away from his and the sparkle in her eyes sent him soaring. He had to look away abruptly before he did something that he might regret.

"It's getting late. We'd better go," Kenneth said, finally finding his control.

They drove into Kenneth's driveway at about 12:15 A.M. and went inside. Barry and Felix had returned and they were already asleep. Kenneth and JeNelle said goodnight and went their separate ways.

Chapter 15

It had been four days since Benny had seen JeNelle. He was looking forward to tomorrow. When he reached his condo it was nearly 7:00 P.M.. He was busy all day in strategy sessions for an upcoming, all-out military drill and massive maneuvers involving all uniformed branches of the service. Since September 11, 2001, these sessions had taken on a sense of urgency. The date for the maneuvers had not been announced so all pilots had to be ready to move at a moment's notice. Military personnel were restricted to their various bases and most long-term, none medical leave was being cancelled. Benny had gotten J.C. Baker to amend his orders so that he could fly to San Francisco to pick up JeNelle. J.C. was going to be in San Francisco, too, but not when Benny was scheduled to arrive.

This was going to be Benny's last night in his condo for a while and he was looking forward to a long, hot bath in his Jacuzzi (cold showers were not helping his disposition) and he wanted some real food from Michelangelo's. After he relaxed in the Jacuzzi, he wrapped himself in a robe and stretched out in the media room to watch a basketball game on the giant, flat-screen television. Stacy Greene crossed his mind. He didn't notice that he was stroking himself until a commercial came on. "Damn!" he said aloud. Just the thought of her had him hot. He placed the still chilled empty bottle between his thighs against his nuts. He had to stop thinking about Stacy now that he met JeNelle.

Benny was working on his second Corona when the doorbell rang. He assumed that it was a neighbor, since he was not expecting anyone, and Fred had not announced the arrival of any guests in the lobby. He tied the sash around his waist and opened the door.

"Hi, handsome," Stacy Greene said, seductively and lowly, as she opened her overcoat. She was completely nude.

His reaction was immediate and his body betrayed him, as his phallus stood at attention and saluted her through the fold in his robe.

"Stacy, what are you doing here?" he asked, as he attempted unsuccessfully to avoid looking at her nude body.

"I've been calling you for days. The question is where have you been?" She stood on her tiptoes, brushing against him and licking her tongue against his lips.

"Restricted to base, but how did you get in without Fred announcing you?" he asked with great difficulty, as her tongue flickered down his neck.

"The Sin Sisters, Janice and Cecil. I had dinner with them today. They checked with Fred to make sure that you weren't entertaining any guests. Fred told them that as far as he knew, you were alone and that you told him that you weren't expecting anyone tonight." She looked up at him and grinned devilishly. "The Sin Sisters told me what they did to you in the elevator and in the back seat of a car." She chuckled. "That was terrible of them. They also told me that you claimed that your mother sent you my roses. Are you angry with me for standing you up? You know that I had no control over that." She moved to lick his now hardened nipple.

He closed his eyes, desperately trying to maintain his composure, but her hand had answered his salute and she untied the belt on his robe.

"Mmmm," she moaned, as she stroked him.

"I wasn't jumping with joy when I got your message. We had some unfinished business, remember, but I did understand," he said, as he tried again desperately to avoid looking at Stacy's nude body, but she took off her overcoat, dropped it on the floor, and wrapped herself around him inside his robe.

The long bath was now a thing of the past, as the beads of sweat rolled off his heaving chest. Stacy was driving him crazy, but she always did.

"Janice and Cecil told me that you had two women with you when you left the club. Really, Benny, you do have a hell of an appetite! Two women in one night!"

Stacy was kissing his chest and stroking him unmercifully, as she had often done before. He managed to say with great difficulty, "Stacy, that was not what it seemed." She was guiding him backward up the staircase toward his bedroom. She was arousing him more and more each step of the way.

"Do I look intimidated to you?" she asked, pushing him backward on to a step.

"I told you to keep it warm for me and it feels like you followed my orders, Captain."

Her tongue teased his navel, as she spread his thighs apart. He gripped the wrought iron rails of the staircase and his head fell back on the carpeted step. A moan escaped from deep in his throat. He lost his breath, as she licked his inner thighs.

"Aren't we…uh…going to…uh…finish our…uh…conversation? I think… that we…were about…to…discuss something…important," Benny groaned deep in his throat, as he tried to maintain some semblance of his composure.

"Yes, I think that we should," she cupped him, "but talking is the last thing on my mind right now, Captain, and it feels like it's the last thing on your mind, too. So let's talk in the morning, unless you have other plans that I don't know about tonight."

"Plans? Plans? Whatever they may have been, Stacy...I've already... forgotten...about...them."

Sheathing him, Stacy's mouth replaced her hand and he lost his resolve, spread eagle on the staircase with Stacy aggressively working his muscle in a slow steady cadence. He had not had sex for four days, cold showers were failing him, and Stacy showed no mercy. She never did. He loved to have sex with her. She excited him beyond any experience that he had ever had before. She was an assertive lover who played his body like an old, sweet, love song, and she didn't miss a beat. Every touch a familiar refrain. His muscle was her microphone, as she blew the chorus that tugged at his heartstrings. He had real passion for her and he never failed to let her know it. He craved her and her touch.

"Oh my, God!" he yelled, as she mounted him, "please, give me strength!"

"Baby," she urged him, riding him slowly, but forcefully against the steps. "I need you."

That did it! He couldn't hold off any longer. He released his grip on the rungs of the staircase and cupped her butt, moving her rhythmically against his body to an initially slow cadence, but then quickening the pace to the drum of his heart as penetrating as Tyco drums. She swept the moisture from his brow, while she whispered wants in his ear, sending messages of throbbing ecstasy to his loins. His breath baited, as he mouthed her left nipple and suctioned it, her coaxing causing his head to spin. Her moans of pleasure thrilled him. His hand found her inverted Y-axis, as he massaged between the moist folds worrying her sweat spot. He had to have more of her. To taste her. He hoisted her up the stairs and rested her thighs on his shoulders until he felt her heave against his cheeks. He still could not let her go. He had more to give and she took it speaking her ecstasy. After her second climax, he slid from beneath her trembling body. She laid her head against a step, as he smoothed the muscles of her back with his tongue and kneaded her breasts. Her outstretched arms gripped the railings, as he positioned himself behind her and began the cadence anew. New moans began to build in them.

"Show me, Stacy. Show me you need me," he moaned against the back of her neck with each stroke.

"I know, baby," she panted. "Not yet."

His body strained to its limits, but finally she eased from the third to the fourth climax. Then she broke their union and mounted him driving her tongue deep into his mouth.

"God, woman, you're killing me!" he groaned against her. "I can't hold on much longer! What are you doing to me?!"

"Give it to me, Benny!" she implored. "Benny!"

"Stacy!"

They yelled in unison; their wet bodies slamming against each other, as Benny lay back on the steps holding her against his heaving chest. Their unions were always cataclysmic and beautiful. They were totally attuned to each other.

"So much for small talk," she panted.

They both began to laugh uncontrollably in their euphoria savoring the afterglow with tongues dancing together in sweet celebration and in anticipation of more to come. Benny lifted Stacy in his arms, as she wrapped her thighs around his waist and he carried her to his bed.

Sex with Stacy was always an all-night, erotic adventure and this was even more passionate. JeNelle's face was etched in his mine, as he performed. Thoughts of her every movement flooded over him. Dancing with her at the club, sitting with her at the breakfast table the next morning, dinner at Michelangelo's, her hair blowing in the wind on the way to the airport, and sitting close and talking with her in the cockpit on the plane. Each vision brought forth torrents of his nature.

The sound of the early morning news program on the television set that he had left on in the media room woke Benny from a dead sleep. He was spent. Every muscle in his body ached. Even some that he didn't know that he had. Stacy shifted her body beside him. He put his arms around her, pulled her close to him, spooning her, as he began to stoke her. She felt warm and right beside him. He kissed her back between her shoulder blades and then moved to reposition his legs. He hit a wet spot on the sheets and then another, and another. There didn't seem to be any dry spots left. Suddenly he began to focus on the previous night and realized that he had not been wearing a condom. He had not had unprotected sex since his parents discussed HIV-AIDS with him and his siblings. He regularly had himself tested and he knew that Stacy did as well.

Stacy rolled over, raised her head, and looked at the clock. She noticed the picture in the beautiful gold Florentine frame on the nightstand by the bed and she picked it up. She turned to Benny and said rather matter-of-factly, "This must be JeNelle."

Benny shot a look at Stacy holding the picture. "Why did you say that?"

"Well, Fly Boy, you called her name a few times last night. You've never done that before and you've never had a picture of anyone, except your family, displayed in frames. You do the math."

"I'm sorry. I didn't mean to call...I mean, I didn't realize that I was saying—."

"Stop stuttering, Benny." Stacy smiled, caressing his face. "Last night and this morning you took me—or JeNelle—to someplace I've never been before. It was a hell of a rush!"

"You're not offended by what I've done?" he asked in disbelief.

"I'm not thrilled that you were fantasizing about another woman while you were having sex with me, but I have to admit, I've done the same thing from time to time myself. It happens. Sometimes a woman's got to do what a woman's got to do to get a rush."

Benny's heart sunk. He kissed her on her neck. "Even with me you've fantasized about another man?"

Stacy sensed his disappointment. "Now who's getting offended? I've never lied to you, Benny. I'm not going to start now. Yes, even when I've been with you, but you're the best and my best friend."

He collapsed on to Stacy's breast and buried his head.

Stacy laughed and stroked him playfully.

"Just pour a little more salt into that open wound or twist the knife a little deeper, why don't you?" Benny asked jokingly.

"We've had a totally open and honest relationship, haven't we? The most open relationship that I've ever had with anyone. Neither one of us has any illusions about the other nor have we hidden the fact that we see other people. That's what I was trying to explain to you before I left. We've been having sex a lot lately, and I do enjoy it and you, but I don't want the sex to get in the way of our friendship. From my perspective, we're friends first and lovers second. I can't even begin to see beyond that point and I don't necessarily want to."

"Why is it that all of a sudden women just want to be my friend?" he lamented.

"Sounds like you haven't made it with JeNelle yet. Stop feeling so insecure. It's not your style. Half the women on military bases in the area are trying to get into your bed, including the married ones. Your reputation is legendary and your technique is lethal."

"Only 'half' the women on base?" he asked, his brows beetled.

"See, that's better," she said, smiling brightly. "Now that's the Benny that we all know and love, but if you're really serious about this JeNelle person, maybe we should go back to being platonic friends again. Some women prefer to have an exclusive relationship. She may not be into sharing you with other women and you may not want to complicate your relationship with her. Continuing to sleep with me or other women won't help you focus on her. If she's been able to withstand your many charms, Fly Boy, you may really have your work cut out for you."

"I'm flying to San Francisco to pick her up later today and take her back to Santa Barbara where she lives. I hope that K.J. has been able to convince her that I have some socially redeeming qualities."

"Why did you think that you needed your brother to do that for you, Benny? You're a warm, giving, charming and wonderful man."

"JeNelle doesn't seem to want to take me seriously. I was a real jerk when we met a couple of weeks ago. I was sure that I had blown it with her."

"You're the closest that I've ever come to calling someone my best friend, so let me let you in on a little secret about women."

"What's that?" he asked caressing her face.

Stacy kissed the palm of his hand and cupped his face in her hands.

"Be yourself," she said, searching his eyes. "Every woman that I know would kill to find an honest man like you. Someone who's not trying to run games on them all the time. Professing undying love one minute and then sneaking around knocking boots with someone else the next minute behind her back. You're always up front with women. You're not a user. You don't tell a woman that you love her. You tell no lies. I can depend on you to tell the truth and that's very important to me, and most other women, but if you can't do the time, baby, don't do the crime. If you can't give a commitment, Benny, don't ask for one."

Benny lay back lacing his fingers behind his head. "Commitment? I can't get JeNelle past the acquaintance stage. I called her 'baby' and she shot me down cold."

Stacy laid her head against Benny's bare chest smoothing the thick soft hairs gently.

"Hang in there, Benny. Remember, I told you that you're the dangerous type. Don't rush her. You said that it's only been a couple of weeks."

"Well what do you suggest I do in the meantime?" he said, lazily stroking her back with one hand.

"With your unquenchable nature even cold showers aren't going to work for long. I think that you're going to have to evaluate what it is that you want from JeNelle. Is it live or is it Memorex. Is what you're feeling love or is it lust. Is it just sex, sex and commitment, marriage, what? Then you'll have to find out what she wants from you. If you both want the same thing, then work from there. The rough part is finding out what you both want or don't want. Getting there is the easy part if you both want the same things."

"That may be difficult with JeNelle. She doesn't give me much to go on. She doesn't talk about herself. She'll talk about her business or her family, but she holds back about her personal life. There seems to be so much there that she's not willing to reveal."

"My dear friend, you may have lucked up on a nut that you can't crack, metaphorically speaking, that is. Pun intended. There are places in a woman's sole that not just any man can reach; no matter how much love and attention he's willing and able to give. Men are no different. Reaching below the surface into the very soul is a scary proposition. It's not for the faint-hearted. You have to be ready and able to deal well with what you find there."

"What about us, Stacy?" he asked raising her face to see her eyes.

"We are as we have been, Benny. Very good friends. Your traffic pattern is full."

"I don't want to lose what we have and I'm not talking about what we do in bed."

"I know what you mean. You're my best friend. We won't lose that."

"Is that as far as we can go, Stacy, best friends?"

"Fly Boy, you're pushing the envelope already."

Stacy's calm with Benny was a learned response. She had been secretly trained for the dangerous encounters. Her missions were in preparation for the possibility of top-secret excursions into war-torn places. Her training was serving her well now in Benny's arms. She had fallen in love with him and she could no longer deny it to herself. Every man that she had ever known paled by comparison to him. She had to let him go though. She couldn't make Benny a part of her life. A choice had to be made. Her love for Benny or a career—there were no other options for her. She had chosen her career, but her need for and intimacy with Benny was great and all encompassing. The dull ache that she felt now that she had made the decision to give him up tore at her. She would never love again, but in her sorrow, she was glad that he had found someone to make the center of his existence.

Benny was a lovable man who women had used for their intimate pleasure. He gave without looking into his heart and soul. She had looked into his heart and she had captured him in hers. That would have to be enough for the rest of her life, but for the moment, she wanted to love him and let him love her in the final moments of their last time together. After the upcoming military drill, she knew that she would never see him again. Her secret orders had already been cut.

Stacy would never know how her rejection had staggered him, Benny thought. The one woman he wanted above all others would not be his, by choice, her choice. She didn't, wouldn't or couldn't love him and that realization choked him and caused a dull ache in his heart. They had their long awaited conversation and he sensed that he had lost her. He closed his eyes tightly and pulled her to his body. He needed to hold on to her before she slipped away again into her dreams for her future. A future that didn't include him. What he had not told her was that he needed her in his life. He sensed that she was still not ready for that next step in their relationship and probably would never be. It was his pain that he felt churning inside him and mixing with his craving for her. No matter what she meant to him beyond their deep and abiding friendship, he had to support her goals and desires. What was important to her was important to him. She was his center.

Benny laced his fingers through Stacy's silky hair and hugged her close to his body. His heart was breaking, as he kissed the top of her head, lifting her chin to meet his kiss. A needful groan grew around the lump in his throat, as he captured her mouth. So sweet, so lush, so warm and giving. He rolled on top of her, moving her thighs apart. Her soft whispers against his ear sent chills up his spine.

"Benny, maybe we shouldn't—"

He closed off her words with his kiss. He couldn't take another rejection of his affection for her.

"You needed me last night. Now I need you, Stacy," he whispered against her mouth. "You know what I need."

"Benny," she whispered softly.

"Until you have to leave…" he whispered, as he captured her mouth again.

Stacy put her arms around Benny's muscular frame, kneading his back. He knew what set her ablaze and how to ignite her core. She was eager to please him and to be pleased by him. She raised her knees and widened his area to advance. She could not say no to him even if she wanted to—and she didn't want to. Leaving him would be the hardest thing that she ever had to do, but at the moment he was rocking her core. She shuttered, as he entered her for the last time.

Chapter 16

The Expo was a great success. JeNelle made a lot of new contacts and her merchandise and products were nearly depleted. She had done a handsome business and was very pleased by what she had learned from other entrepreneurs. There were also so many new books on the market written by talented authors. She also purchased a new line of greeting cards and picked up a new art collection.

Kenneth and CompuCorrect also did well. Entrepreneurs from the Expo were lined up each day in three rows patiently waiting to make appointments for one of CompuCorrect's sales staff to visit them and evaluate their businesses for computer network systems and software applications. On the very first day, Kenneth called more staff in to handle the flood of requests. Six more employees arrived carrying laptop computers, hooked into CompuCorrect's internal network and were ready to schedule appointments in record time. Kenneth observed his staff at work that first day and answered a myriad of questions for the potential clients. Whenever Shirley and Tom came to relieve him, he sought out JeNelle.

During the week, Kenneth managed to show JeNelle around the city quite a bit. They had lunch or dinner together, sometimes alone and sometimes with others at some great restaurants. The Equinox, which revolves above the Hyatt Regency, The Donatello, and the Top of the Mark. They even left the Expo early to go shopping together, something that JeNelle admitted that she hated to do, but she enjoyed going with Kenneth.

At Tiffany & Company, they both saw a beautiful covered crystal jewelry box, but JeNelle said that, although it was breathtakingly beautiful, it was too expensive. At the chic clothing shops, she even found a few new outfits that she liked and a pair of shoes at some chic boutiques. Kenneth tried on a few new suits at a famous haberdasher. JeNelle liked two of them. He bought them both. She helped him pick out three new ties and five new shirts. He agreed with her selection of scarves, but Kenneth didn't like the monstrous floppy hat that she tried on, but she knew that he wouldn't. She just tried it on to get a rise out of him. He was usually so diplomatic, but he roared with laughter when she tried on that floppy hat. She loved to see him smile. It elicited such shattering emotions from deep within her core.

The computer network setup and software package that Kenneth quickly designed for her was far superior to the one that she was using. Kenneth agreed that he or one of his sales staff would come to Santa Barbara to look at her operation and make some proposals about upgrading or redesigning her computer programs, security system, and equipment. Juan was sure that they could improve upon her inventory tracking system, the speed of the access to data, and perhaps save her as much as thirty percent on the cost of a new state-of-the-art system. JeNelle thought the new system would be crucial to the mail-order business that she was thinking of instituting over the Internet. She needed a new web page to make it happen. Juan had some good suggestions about a new web page to include her new business. Both CompuCorrect and INSIGHTS had accomplished a lot by the fourth day.

Before the Expo closed for the day, Kenneth and JeNelle left their employees working and took a ferryboat ride to Sausalito. As Kenneth and JeNelle rode atop the ferryboat main deck, sea gulls soared just slightly above. One or two even plucked popcorn out of JeNelle's hand, as it hovered above her. Kenneth held her steady, as the wind whipped and swirled around them. JeNelle's soft hair blew freely in the cold breeze, as Kenneth held her close to him.

It was a beautiful, bright, windy late afternoon and they both commented how the San Francisco skyline was breathtaking. When the ferryboat docked, they walked through the Sausalito Village Fair and looked at the many handicrafts on display. JeNelle found a vendor with handcrafted baskets. In a short time, she negotiated a deal to sell the baskets in her gallery as art.

Kenneth and JeNelle had dinner at Scoma's, an enchanting Sausalito restaurant that sat right on a peninsula in San Francisco Bay. JeNelle thought Sausalito was a very scenic area. She could see homes that were tucked between the trees up steep inclines and along hilly terrain. For a long time she just sat in the restaurant, sipping an Amaretto before the large picture windows looking at San Francisco's skyline across the Bay and the Golden Gate Bridge, as it began to dawn its evening glow. She watched the waves break against the sea wall below. Seagulls perched on the dock or floated on the water.

"A fortune for your thoughts, JeNelle," Kenneth finally said.

"I wish that this was not so relaxing. I wish that this was not so peaceful," she said, wistfully. "I wish that I didn't feel like I've been on a vacation. I wish that I didn't want to bottle this all up and take it with me. I wish that the Expo wasn't going to end tomorrow." She turned and gazed into his eyes. "I wish that I wasn't going home tomorrow."

"That's a lot of wishes. Which one is most important to you?"

JeNelle smiled at Kenneth and took a deep breath. "I'm just feeling very happy." She avoided his question because if she had answered him truthfully, she would have said that staying in the protective cocoon that he spun since they met would have been where she longed to be. Safe in his embrace and in his heart.

Kenneth sensed that his question made her uncomfortable. He changed the subject. "You've been doing deals for four straight days like there's no tomorrow. You completed another just a few moments ago. And people call me a workaholic. I can't hold a candle to you. You had buyers eating out of your hands and begging for more. You really know how to work a crowd. Yours was the busiest exhibit on your aisle."

"I feel wonderful though. I don't remember the last time that I felt this relaxed or had this much fun on a business trip. I don't know how I'm going to repay you and your entire staff for what you've done. I want to do something special for each of you. Everyone's been so kind and helpful, especially Shirley."

"You make it easy to do nice things for you, JeNelle. You've got the entire office wishing that you weren't leaving tomorrow. I've enjoyed having you here. Benny is a very lucky man."

That comment got JeNelle's attention and snapped her back to reality. "Kenneth, your brother and I are just friends. Nothing more. I think that Shirley might be interested in him though."

"Shirley? Not likely," Kenneth said and snorted. "Benny made a play for Shirley two years ago and again at the last Christmas party. Benny told me that she turned him away flat both times. Shirley's not your competition for Benny. Of that I'm sure."

Now JeNelle was really confused, but she felt it necessary to deal with another issue that was more important to her.

"I don't think that you understand my friendship with your brother. We're not involved and, frankly, are not likely to be. Benny is aware of that."

"I'm sure that Benny's point of view is quite different. I've never known him to be this excited about someone. Try not to judge him on the basis of what your first impression of him must have been. He told me about what he did. Not being honest about his culinary skills of which he has none," he said and laughed. "Lying about the flowers that he received. There's more to Benny than he has shown you so far."

JeNelle laughed. "You're a good brother to Benny, you know, Kenneth. He told me that he enlisted your help in his campaign to change my first impression of him. He also told me that your agreement to support him was conditional."

"I love my brother, not just because we are related, but because we're also best friends. I would want to be his friend even if we weren't related. I like the person that he is. He has a good, but tender heart. Still, he's right, I told him that I would not lie to you just to further his 'campaign'. That wasn't hard for me to do. Benny wouldn't ask me to lie for him. He's a very honest man."

"You've done your duty, both as his brother and as his friend. I do want to get to know him, but I don't want to mislead him. I'm really concerned that he will misconstrue anything that I do or say."

"That's certainly a risk that you'll have to consider. As you probably already know, Benny lives life to the fullest. He always has. That's why he chose 'EXPLORER' as his Air Force Code Name."

"I didn't know that. Explorer, what does it mean?"

"He's an explorer in the sense that he's fascinated by new challenges, professionally and privately. He has that kind of unlimited energy and passion that leads men to make great discoveries. If he were a scientist, I'm confident that he would have discovered a cure for HIV/AIDs, cancer, or even the common cold. Or if he were a statesman, he would have found a solution to the Middle East crisis before he was forced to participate in an Iraq or Afghanistan operation. Or if he were a business person, like you or me, he would have found a way to end the economic crisis that this world is in. Benny throws his entire essence into everything that he chooses to do and when he does that, he is relentless and unstoppable until he reaches his goal. The word failure isn't in his vocabulary. He will never live a mundane existence. It's all out, full throttle, power up in every facet of his life all of the time. I admire those qualities in him."

"I know. I've witnessed that about him. He seems to be exhilarated by every challenge, triumph or discovery."

"That's Benny," he said and smiled, but he wished down deep in his soul that his brother wanted someone other than JeNelle. Some inexplicable need made dropping his almost uncontrollable interest in her totally impossible.

JeNelle listened to Kenneth talk about Benny and pondered everything he said, but it was not Benny who she found so intriguing, it was Kenneth. She listened to the words that he spoke, but she found herself being fascinated by him. She had the distinct impression that he was consciously blocking her questions about him at every turn. He could be cleverly ambiguous and affable simultaneously. It was as if there existed an invisible wall between them. She could not see through it, climb over it or go around it. And she was beginning to want to try.

It was late in the evening, nearly midnight, as JeNelle and Kenneth pulled into his driveway. A man wearing an Air Force uniform emerged from the back seat of a car parked in front of Kenneth's house. Initially, JeNelle and Kenneth didn't notice the man. They were laughing about a humorous incident at the Expo until they heard the man call out.

"Kenneth, I've been waiting to see you," J.C. Baker said, walking up the driveway.

JeNelle opened her car door and got out.

"Oh, I didn't know you had company," J.C. said, seemingly somewhat startled by JeNelle's appearance at Kenneth's side.

JeNelle sensed Kenneth's mood drastically changed when the military man spoke to him. She could feel the barely-veiled tension in Kenneth. She suspected that Kenneth was very angry and not at all pleased to see this man.

"Baker, what are you doing here? I told you that I didn't want to see—" Kenneth broke off his conversation because JeNelle was within earshot. The moment was awkward, but Kenneth reined in his anger. "Uh, JeNelle Towson, this is Colonel John Calvin Baker, one of Benny's commanding officers. Colonel Baker this is JeNelle Towson," Kenneth said, with no smile and that barely veiled anger growing in his demeanor.

"I'm pleased to meet you, Ms. Towson," Colonel Baker said, as he extended his hand to JeNelle.

"Thank you, Colonel Baker, but has something happened to Benny?" she asked, concerned, as she shook his hand.

"No, oh no. Benny is fine. I spoke with him yesterday, in fact. He needed permission to fly up here tomorrow. He didn't say why he needed the leave, but knowing Benny, there's always a woman involved," Baker said and grinned unctuously with a sly wink.

Neither JeNelle nor Kenneth smiled or volunteered any information. JeNelle didn't say anything because she didn't feel comfortable with this Colonel J.C. Baker. Kenneth's reaction gave her more reason for concern.

Kenneth turned to JeNelle. "JeNelle, it's late. The house isn't locked. You don't have to wait for me. Why don't you go in? I'm going to speak with Colonel Baker for a few minutes and then I'll be in," Kenneth said dryly.

JeNelle clearly felt that she was being dismissed. She also knew that this was unlike the Kenneth Alexander who she had spent nearly every waking minute with from the moment that she arrived in San Francisco. The Kenneth that she was growing to respect and admire would have extended himself even to total strangers, but this Kenneth had not even extended himself for a handshake or offered the hospitality of his home to Colonel Baker. She was startled by Kenneth's abruptness, so she merely said goodnight and went into the house. It was a very perplexing situation, but she did not feel that she had the right to pry.

JeNelle put some logs into the fireplace, lit a match to the kindling, and watched as the flames began to blaze up. She could faintly hear the voices outside being raised, perhaps in anger. Kenneth, she observed, had a hardy laugh; he enjoyed laughing and joking with people, even strangers, but the sounds that she heard coming from the driveway were clearly no laughing matter.

As she sat on the floor before the fireplace, she hugged her legs close to her chest and rested her head on her knees. Sitting before the now blazing hearth, she felt a chill in this room that was not present before in the late evenings when she and Kenneth would spend time sitting there and talking or when he entertained her and her managers in the family room or game room. It was a stark contrast to what she had experienced when she and Kenneth were together. Kenneth, she realized, communicated very little personal information about himself although he spoke volumes about his family and friends. There were some basic things about him that she did not know. For example, whether he was currently involved with a woman. It was obvious that women found him extremely attractive. Enough of them had flirted with him during the week, but he was ever the gentleman easing himself out of sticky situations without being blunt about his disinterest. Nevertheless, no one seemed to have penetrated that ever-present wall that he seemed to have around him. She now knew that she was experiencing, perhaps, some indication of what lay behind the wall. J.C. Baker clearly aroused in Kenneth something that few people had probably ever seen in him—rage. Kenneth was in total control of himself every minute that they were together even when he was in the midst of the dense and hectic pace that seemed to orbit around him. He exhibited a quiet-spoken unassuming control; nonabrasive, nonthreatening, and non-manipulative. It was a positive, reinforcing influence that seemed innate, not developed artificially. A comforting presents often surrounded by chaos—a port in a storm or at least that's what she had observed.

When Kenneth entered the house, he slammed the door so forcefully that the windows rattled. JeNelle jumped, but did not otherwise move from her reflective position or even acknowledge his presence. Kenneth started down the wide hallway toward his bedroom when he noticed a figure sitting before the lit fireplace in the darkened room.

"JeNelle? Are you still up? I thought that you would have gone to bed by now. Why are you sitting here in the dark? Are you all right?" Kenneth asked with great concern, as he came into the front living room."

"I'm fine, Kenneth. No need to be concerned," she said quietly and unemotionally, "but don't let me keep you up."

"No, I'm not quite ready to sleep yet. I think I'll have a brandy. May I get anything for you? "

"A brandy would be nice. Thank you."

Kenneth poured two drinks and handed one to JeNelle.

"Do you want to be alone, JeNelle? I'll go—"

"No, Kenneth, please stay and keep me company, if you'd like."

"You seem to be deep in thought, sitting here in the dark like this. I don't want to intrude."

"You're not intruding," she said, looking up into the warmth in his eyes.

Kenneth sat down beside her on the floor. "I'm sorry about the scene outside. I hope that you weren't offended by my abruptness or J.C.'s comment about Benny and other women. J.C. and Benny have been friends for some time. They were at the Academy together. He was one of Benny's instructors when they were both posted in Washington, DC. They even lived together in Benny's house in the Georgetown for a while when they were both stationed there. I don't believe J.C. would have been so callous if he knew what you mean to Benny."

"You and Colonel Baker aren't friends?"

The question startled Kenneth. "Friendship is a fragile commodity, JeNelle. You have to spend it sparingly. You can't squander it."

JeNelle felt that invisible wall grow higher, wider and thicker. She knew that was not the time to probe deeper. They sat together companionably in the stillness of the night, watching the fire devour the logs.

* * *

The last day of the Expo was as chaotic as the first. After the doors closed to the public, the legions of exhibitors and crews began dismantling and demolishing the exhibits and packing up what was left of their brochures, fliers, visitors' business cards, samples, merchandise and products. Banners came down, electrical wires were ripped up, and wall dividers disappeared. Barry and Felix packed up the remaining merchandise and stored it in their van for the trip back to Santa Barbara, while JeNelle talked with some of the other exhibitors. She had a briefcase full of business cards, which she had been given by people interested in keeping in touch with her or wanting to do business deals. She even met people from Santa Barbara who she did not know previously. Paul Garrett, a man who owned a printing and engraving business in Santa Barbara, and Cheryl Blackstone, a woman of Native American ancestry who owned her own jewelry store, designed and manufactured her own jewelry and was a licensed goldsmith. Some other exhibitors were discussing the possibility of doing a smaller version of the Expo in Santa Barbara. JeNelle was busily jotting notes and didn't notice Benny standing nearby. It wasn't until Kenneth walked by her, smiling broadly that she turned to see who had put that smile on his face. Benny leaned against her van in that same familiar sexy stance that the Alexander men—at least Benny and Kenneth—had risen to an art form. She was still engrossed in her conversation, but she flashed a quick smile and a wink at Benny, as he and Kenneth talked.

Benny never took his eyes off JeNelle, as he and Kenneth talked.

"She is some kind of perfection, isn't she, K.J.?"

"She's a great lady, too, Benny. It's not just the wrapping on the package. There's great value inside the package," Kenneth said, standing beside Benny and gazing at JeNelle.

"Then you like her?"

"What's not to like?"

"Did you talk with her about me?"

"Yes, I did my best and I never lied."

"Your best has always been good enough for me. Maybe now I can get to first base with her."

"She doesn't play games, Benny. She's honest and forthright very much like you are. So if you're thinking of running any games on her, I'd change my game plan, if I were you. She's got depth. Something drives her to achieve as much as she has. I couldn't discern what fuels that fire, but there's a quiet storm raging beneath that polished, articulate exterior."

"You sensed that about her, too? I was beginning to believe that I was imagining things that weren't really there. Sometimes I see something in her eyes or her demeanor one minute and then it disappears the next."

"You've got a lot to learn about her, and may I give you some advice?"

"Yes, sure, what is it?"

"Take it easy. Know what you want from her before you jump into this and take off on your usual all-out campaign to seduce her. You might win a few battles, if JeNelle is not focusing on what you're up to, but you sure as hell will lose the war if you're not careful."

"A friend of mine—you know, Stacy, the lieutenant I told you about who sent the flowers—said something similar to that last night or rather this morning."

"Last night or this morning?" Kenneth asked, annoyed. "What happened last night or this morning?"

"Stacy surprised me last night, my defenses were down, I had JeNelle on my mind and..." He shrugged laconically.

"And you had Stacy in your bed. So while I'm here telling JeNelle what a great guy you are and asking her not to judge you prematurely, you're at your place sleeping with Stacy."

"Believe me, K.J., when Stacy's around, sleeping is the last thing on my mind. I told you, she caught me at an 'unguarded moment'."

"Benny, you are one walking, talking unguarded moment. I've never known you to be able to last for more than twenty-four hours without surrendering to an 'unguarded moment'."

"I tried cold showers all week and it was killing me until Stacy showed up. She gets my afterburners fired up! She gets my adrenalin going and takes me into orbit. Sometimes I can't get enough of her. She's a phenomenal woman. She knows about JeNelle. She gave me the same advice that you did."

"Was that before or after you slept with her?"

"Both."

"*Both?*" Now Kenneth was really annoyed. "What do you mean '*both*'?"

"We had sex most of last night and again this morning. Stacy told me this morning that I kept calling JeNelle's name in my sleep last night. Then we talked about what was going on or rather *not* going on between me and JeNelle, and we had sex again," Benny said rather matter-of-factly. "Stacy's cool. She's the type of woman that I would like to take home to meet the folks if she would permit it. We need the same kind of stimulus. She's uncomplicated and she's not possessive. Sometimes I wish that she wasn't so independent. Unfortunately, she's not carrying around a torch for me or any other heavy emotional baggage. She insists that we're just good friends first and lovers second. I can only take so much rejection before I get the picture."

"Benny, I'm sorry. I didn't know that you were..." Kenneth groped for the right words.

"Hurting?" Benny supplied.

"Well, yes, I suppose, but I'm sure that you'll bounce back. You never cease to amaze me. Are you going to tell JeNelle about Stacy?"

"I mentioned my relationship with Stacy to JeNelle the night that I met JeNelle for dinner. If she asks me about Stacy or any other relationship, I'll tell her. I'm not going to lie to JeNelle. That's what Stacy says is the worst thing that I could do to her—gain her respect, her trust, and then let her find out I've been less than honest with her. Stacy's right, it would destroy any chance that I've got, and right now my chances with JeNelle fall somewhere between slim and none."

"So what are you going to do with that overactive libido of yours while you're trying to earn JeNelle's trust and respect?"

"I'm going to obey my thirst!" Benny joked. "I'm not capable of doing anything else the way you are. Your water bill must reach astronomical proportions for all the cold showers that you must have been taking."

Benny and Kenneth were both laughing when JeNelle approached them. Both men were drop-dead gorgeous, JeNelle thought, but Kenneth's presence did something to her that her body couldn't deny. Her brain fought a valiant effort, but she was losing her grip when she was around him. She had to steel her emotions though. Kenneth had given her no reason to think that he wanted anything more than to help his brother do a favor for a friend. That's as it should be, she thought, but she wondered consciously what it would feel like to be in his arms, to kiss his mouth and to stroke his body next to her... *Get a grip!* she chastised herself, as she walked toward the two handsome brothers who were still laughing together.

"What's so funny, you two?"

"My brother, JeNelle. I've been discussing his water bill problem," Benny said, with a smirk.

"Water bill problem?" JeNelle asked quizzically. "How is that funny?"

"It's a brother thing, JeNelle. Don't *even* try to understand it." Kenneth blushed.

Barry and Felix said their goodbyes to Kenneth and his staff and drove away in the van, heading for Santa Barbara.

"JeNelle, it's been a pleasure meeting you and having you here. I'll have Juan get in touch with you next week and set up a time when it's convenient for him to come to Santa Barbara and look at your operation," Kenneth said.

"Why don't you come down, Kenneth?" Benny asked. "Maybe we can spend some time talking about how to cure your water bill problem."

"Yes, Kenneth, if you can spare the time, I'd like to repay your hospitality. In fact, there's going to be a Chamber of Commerce Gala in Santa Barbara that you might find interesting. Benny's going to be there as my escort and I can get a couple of tickets for you, too," JeNelle added.

"I can't promise anything at this point, but—."

"But nothing. You're coming because I'm asking you to," Benny insisted, "and don't plan on just a one-day visit either. Captain's orders!" Benny chuckled.

"Looks like I'll be there, JeNelle." Kenneth relented.

"Great, we'll see you then," JeNelle said.

Benny and Kenneth embraced. Kenneth embraced JeNelle and as they brushed each other's cheeks with their lips, Kenneth whispered, "Thanks for not asking."

JeNelle knew immediately that Kenneth was referring to the argument with J.C. Baker. She did not respond and she sensed that she should not mention the incident to Benny.

As Benny drove away, JeNelle watched Kenneth in the side view mirror. She was looking forward to seeing him again.

"So, are you hungry? We could stop for dinner before we leave," Benny said, driving through the streets of San Francisco toward the airport.

"You mean Milo didn't pack a picnic hamper for you this time?"

"Of course he did. Including the Italian olives that you like, but, if you prefer, we have time to eat here."

"No. I'm anxious to get back to Santa Barbara."

"Then Santa Barbara, it is."

When the plane lifted off, JeNelle looked down at the City of San Francisco below her and recalled the now precious moments that she spent with Kenneth roaming the streets of that city. The Golden Gate Bridge faded from view, but not the memories of Kenneth James Alexander.

Chapter 17

"Hi, Honey, I'm home," David Berham Carter, III, called out, as he entered the Georgetown house, but no one answered him except a woman who was speaking Spanish and wearing an apron. He did not recognize her.

"Who are you?" he asked, perplexed, staring owlishly through his large, horn-rimmed glasses.

The woman said, "No speak Americano," and then something in Spanish.

Snowman came galloping down the steps followed by a little boy. Vivian peeked over the railing above. "Is that you, David?"

"Yes, but who are all these people?" he asked incredulously blocking his face from the white wolf whose tongue licked out. Vivian's dog frankly scared him, but he'd never admit it.

Vivian loped down the steps in navy blue warm-ups and bare feet to introduce David to Anna and Miguel. Then she took him into the front living room to explain the circumstances.

Chuck appeared at the living room door covered in paint. "The painting is finished, Annie. It's your turn to clean up."

"Annie, who's Annie and who's the cowboy?" David asked rather confused.

"I'll explain later, David." She brushed him off. "David Carter, this is Chuck Montgomery. He's the doctor who saved Angelique's life."

"Angelique? Who's Angelique?" David asked, becoming even more confused.

"I'll explain later," Vivian said, again.

David shook hands with Chuck and got paint on his hands. David was totally unaccustomed to manual labor. Though of African-American descent, he had grown up in a predominately white, upper-class environment where he began wearing three-piece suits, even in grade school. His parents were both prominent professors currently in residence at the University of Minnesota. His mother taught classical music and was one of the first female conductors of famous orchestras worldwide and his father taught English literature, but had directed classical plays in both London and New York. David did not grow up around many other Black children and, though he was Black, had assimilated much of the culture that surrounded him. He was an only child, but, unlike Melissa, he never regretted it. He was aristocratic in his appearance and carriage and would often speak in Old English. He could be found playing Chopin on his violin in his bedroom, while Gloria, who occupied the bedroom next door to his, was singing *"She's a Brick House"* or some other raunchy Rick James tune at the top of her lungs. David was the most rhythmless Black person Vivian and Gloria had ever met. They tried to teach him popular dances, but he always looked like someone having an epileptic seizure when he tried to mimic what they were doing.

David would be considered 'odd' by most people; a Black Republican, but his housemates did not view him as a curiosity. Rather, he was their leader when it came to reading the law. He was simply brilliant with an extremely high IQ, but low people skills. Though he rarely digressed from agreeing with a conservative position decided by the courts, he could argue with equal conviction and rather forcefully, the other issues of any case. A card-carrying member of the ACLU, he possessed a vast knowledge of vocabulary and would not hesitate to correct his housemates on their elocution or diction or pronunciation. He had, in his view, a lot of molding to do to correct Melissa's Rhode Island 'twang', Bill's New York 'nasal' tones, Vivian's southern drawl, and Gloria's Valley Girl influences. He often sighed, "there's no rest for the weary" after a study session with his housemates, but he would begin again with new vigor at the next session.

* * *

"Okay, Vivian, you had United States v. Contento-Panchon, 723 F. 2d 693 (9th Cir. 1964)," David said, as the housemates and some other first year law students sat or reclined in the Georgetown house library going over their assignments in the study group. Anna served warm applesauce cake and coffee to the students. "Has everyone read the case?" The twelve study group members all nodded or mumbled in the affirmative. "All right, then we need not describe the circumstances. Vivian, state the case."

Vivian began to brief the case.

"BACKGROUND: The United States accused Juan Manuel Contento-Panchon of unlawful possession of a controlled narcotic substance with the intent to distribute in violation of 21 USC Section 841(a)(1). Contento-Panchon argued and attempted to offer evidence to prove in his defense against the charges that he was operating under duress, which necessitated his behavior. The United States countered and convinced the court that the duress and necessity defense should be disallowed because Contento-Panchon had not submitted substantial evidence to support his allegation for that defense. Contento-Panchon was convicted.

"RULE OF LAW AT ISSUE: Whether evidence of duress and necessity are admissible as triable issues of fact? If so, whether the lower court's ruling, as inadmissible as a matter of law, was appropriate.

"CONCLUSION: Yes. Evidence of duress and necessity are admissible as triable issues of fact to be judged by the jury. The elements of the duress defense and the necessity defense criteria were present and should have been admitted into consideration as factual evidence. Fact-finding is within the province of the jury. These defenses should not have been excluded as a matter of law.

"Therefore, the lower court erred in its decision not only to rule these defenses inadmissible, but also by its failure to recognize that the elements of the defenses were clearly present.

"KEY FACTS: The trial court found Contento-Panchon proof insufficient in two areas: (1) immediacy and (2) inescapability. Contento-Panchon had, in fact, met both criteria. He knew that Jorge, an unsavory character who had lured him into becoming a carrier for a known drug dealer, had the means and ability to harm him and his family and had made specific threats. Jorge also had the opportunity to do so at any point in the trip that Contento-Panchon made to the USA until he (Contento-Panchon) arrived at a place of relative safety. Moreover, Contento-Panchon voluntarily agreed to be x-rayed by the US Custom's officials with the certain knowledge that the cocaine that he had in his stomach would be found which gives further support to his defense.

"HOLDING: The trial court, in this instance, should not have ruled on the admissibility of the evidence as a matter of law since elements of the defense arguments were clearly present. When the elements of duress are present: (a) an immediate threat of death or serious bodily injury, (b) a well-grounded fear that the threat would be carried out, and (c) no reasonable opportunity to escape the threatened harm, these defenses must be considered viable.

"The lower court excluded the evidence of duress and necessity because the court believed that Contento-Panchon failed to offer support for the immediacy and inexcapability issues of the duress and necessity defenses. The lower court failed to recognize the clear presents of the supporting evidence.

"REASONING: There is no clear basis here to rule on a question of fact as if it were a question of law. Were it not for the lower court's inappropriate ruling, the jury would not have been denied its fact-finding obligations, including its opportunity to review all facts involving whether the proof of immediacy and inescapability were sufficient to support the proffered defense. Had the jury heard the defenses it may have reached a different verdict.

"The defenses were appropriate and supportable based upon the facts. Contento-Panchon and his family were in immediate danger of death or bodily harm from Jorge if Contento-Panchon did not go through with the plan to smuggle the drugs into the USA. Contento-Panchon and his family had no reasonable opportunity to escape the reach of Jorge leaving his home and job. Finally, Contento-Panchon, although not required to do so under this defense, took the first real opportunity to cooperate with authorities with whom he felt safe without alerting any observer."

"You were doing great, Vivian, up until the point at which you reached the court's holding," David said. "Remember that your holding must include all of the key facts of the case, but in your reasoning, you have to leave out the facts and only focus on the legal reasons why…you know, what legal standards did the court apply?"

"But I reached the same conclusion," Bill interjected. "The lower court erred in its decision."

"You're right, Bill," Alan added. "I read it the same way you did and I reached the same conclusion, but, David is right, too. It's not that we reached different conclusions; it's in the construction of Vivian's brief. All of the elements are there."

"Well, looks like it's back to the laptop for old Contento-Panchon and me." Vivian sighed. "I'll redraft the brief and have it ready in the morning. I'll e-mail it to everyone."

"Are you feeling all right, Vivian?" Melissa asked. "It's not like you to have a problem briefing cases for us, but you haven't been looking at all well the past couple of weeks."

"How can you tell? Vivian never looks 'good'," Gloria added sarcastically, "but she hasn't had much of an appetite. The way Anna has been feeding us around here, it's hard to stay out of her kitchen. I've even gained an ounce or two of unwanted fat."

Anna beamed at the compliment.

"I want it! I want it!" David said eagerly, nearly salivating over Gloria's voluptuous body.

"Down, David," Alan said, "if you get started craving Gloria's body again we'll never get through the next case."

David calmed himself with difficulty. "All right, let's move on to Contracts, then Property Law. I want to save Civil Procedure for last because Professor Fahey is exhilarated by the systematic contemplation of our demise," David said.

Everyone looked at him except Melissa.

"In English, the translated version of what David said is that Professor Fahey is going to eat us alive tomorrow if we don't know Civil Procedure backwards and forwards," Melissa said.

"Oh," everyone responded blankly.

"That's what I said. Wasn't anyone listening?" David retorted defensively. "All right, Bill, you have the floor. Enlighten us with your exorbitance of manner and magnificently electrifying insight into contracts."

Bill stared blankly at David.

"State the case, Bill," Vivian said informatively, "and electrify us."

"Oh, is that what David meant?" Bill devilishly grinned. "I thought that he wanted me to do this new dance that they're doing in the gay bars that I've been taking him to. They do this thing with lights around your—."

"Never mind, Chandler. I think that we all get the picture. I love a double entendre, pun intended," Vivian quipped.

Everyone laughed and then Anna spoke. "This man, this Cabrera, he innocent. He only try to save his family. These men come and make honest men in our village carry drugs like, uh, *el burro?*"

"You mean, like mules?"

"*Si*, yes, like mules. If they do not go, they would be killed and their families left to die. My Miguel, we tell him to go and find work away so he would not have to be a mule like Cabrera." She continued giving life to a textbook study. Her words had a sobering effect on the law students, yet causing them to appreciate more fully the intricacies of the law.

This was the typical scene around the Georgetown house. The twelve-member scholars study group met twice a day, four out of seven days a week. Usually the sessions could be characterized as intellectual melees. The housemates and other study group members worked themselves into near states of total exhaustion. The second session of law school was turning out to be even more demanding than the first session. Free time was nearly nonexistent. They all still volunteered at the Family Homeless Shelter though and worked part time at other jobs to have a little extra spending money. Of course, all that Bill had to do was one photo spread a month, and make ten times more than they all did combined. He still devoted some of his spare time to an HIV/AIDS program for young children. He always pretended to have such a hard shell, but they all knew how warm, loving, and giving he was under that hard exterior. Miguel could pull him out of that hard persona with a smile and Bill would melt right before their eyes. He tried to cover it, but it never worked. Miguel had Bill and the rest of the housemates twisted around his six-year-old little finger.

As the weeks passed, it was clear that David had a mammoth crush on Gloria. However, Gloria was far from interested in him. She was usually on a jet somewhere to watch one of Tony's football games leading up to the Super Bowl. Melissa was still seeing Stan Cavanaugh now and then, but was not interested in anything long-term. Alan didn't date much. Rather, he stuck close to the house studying and doing odd jobs for Anna as necessary.

Anna kept them all fed, washed clothes for them when she knew that they were stressed, and cleaned their rooms. She was usually the first one up in the morning with a good, hot nourishing meal on the table when they came down to leave for class. No one, no matter how rushed they were, passed up on Anna's meals. She was often up until the wee hours with the study group making coffee, or tea, cocoa or bringing water, sodas, or beers. She even made them take regular breaks from studying and always tempted them with some new delicious dessert. She mothered them as if they were her own children and they all appreciated everything that she did for them. Each of them would occasionally show her their appreciation by bringing a small gift or a token to her from time to time. She beamed no matter what it was. Flowers, a small box of chocolates, a Spanish comb for her hair, a pretty tube of lipstick, some nail polish or a book of Spanish poems.

Chuck Montgomery became a regular part of the household, too. He sat and talked with Anna and, of course, ate many meals at the Georgetown house, regardless of whether any of the housemates were around. He kept close tabs on Angelique and took her and Miguel to their regularly-scheduled appointments with Derrick Jackson. He got the kids enrolled in a Catholic school a few blocks away from the house and paid for their tuition, uniforms, and books. In his free time, Chuck taught Anna how to get around the city and where to shop for groceries. When Anna knew that Chuck had pulled long hours at the hospital, she would force him to take a nap in Miguel's room, and Chuck knew not to disobey Anna. She'd threaten him with a rolling pin in one hand and a big slice of homemade apple pie or some other delectable treat in the other hand. He always complied with her wishes.

Chuck bounded up the steps of the Georgetown house and entered without knocking. After working a double shift, he was in need of some of Anna's good cooking. He was late, but he knew that Anna would have left a plate of food for him and he knew that her cooking wasn't the only reason for his visit. Vivian would be there studying with the group. He missed seeing her over the past couple of weeks. Between his long hours at the hospital and her hectic schedule, he felt lucky to catch a glimpse of her in passing. He made every opportunity to see her and spend time in her presence.

Approaching the library door where Vivian and the other members of the study group were sitting, Chuck stopped. It was obvious to him that Vivian's feelings for Carlton were not as strong as Carlton's were for her—and after all, why should they be?" In his view, Carlton was a jerk, undeserving of a woman like Vivian. Still, he recognized that his feelings toward Vivian were not altogether innocent or altruistic. The feelings that encased him when he was near Vivian fired his imagination. Never before had he encountered a woman of any heritage or age, which, through no effort on her part, sent adrenalin coursing through his veins or stimulated his desire. Though she was much younger than he was, she need only look at him to turn his senses loose—just as she did when she spotted him at the door watching her.

Vivian looked up at Chuck's smiling face and her lips parted in an uncontrollable broad smile. She smiled a lot when Chuck was around. He plucked up his Stetson and winked at her. Why did he have such a wonderful smile? Why did he have to be the perfect gentleman? So warm and giving? Why couldn't she find anything about Chuck that didn't send her heart soaring whenever she saw him? Not even his cowboy getup or green hospital scrubs turned her off. He was a total man no matter what he wore, and she imagined all too vividly and far too often what he would look like wearing nothing at all. She glanced away from Chuck's handsome face and redirected her attention to her readings and the study group. The engagement ring on her finger still did not feel as if it belonged there. She turned it around on her finger and continued to study.

* * *

Easter was still some weeks away, but the cold February winds gave no indication that spring would ever arrive. Angelique was released from medical care, and Gloria and Alan took it upon themselves to tutor her, Anna and

Miguel in English. Of course, David was supervising the whole program. Chuck was making regular visits to the house whenever his schedule permitted and the housemates often noted that he was making time to see Melissa now that Stan Cavanaugh had moved back in with his wife and children. Melissa was not upset about the turn of events. She knew that if things had gotten serious between her and Stan that she would have to deal with his two children. Melissa acknowledged that she wasn't ready for that.

On one of Chuck's visits to the house to see Angelique, shortly before Valentine's Day, Anna mentioned to him that Vivian was ill and that she was making some hot, homemade, chicken noodle soup for her. Chuck volunteered to take the soup and a large bottle of ice water up to Vivian's room. When Vivian told him to come in, he opened the door.

"Wow! Annie you're really sick!"

Vivian could barely lift her head from the pillow. She rolled her eyes at him, blew her runny nose, and, with a hoarse voice, sarcastically said, "And what was your first clue, Montgomery?"

"I see you haven't lost your grit. How long have you been sick?"

"I've been feeling ill for some time. I must have the flu. I've been coughing, sneezing, and throwing up all over the place and I need some rest," she whined. "I can't sleep at night, I'm bloated, and my head feels like it's going to explode. I can't keep anything on my stomach, I'm urinating all the time, and the slightest smells, like those roses that Carlton sent to me for Valentine's Day, make me sick to my stomach. One minute I want one thing to eat, the next moment I don't want anything. Somebody ought to just shoot me and put me out of my misery," she lamented.

"Come on, Annie, you're a fighter. You can beat this thing. You look like hell now, but you'll be fine in a couple of days."

"Thanks, Chuck, I know that I can always depend on you for a kind word," she hissed sarcastically. "I know I look like hell. I feel like hell. You didn't have to confirm it. Why don't you just go torture one of your patients or something and let me die in peace?"

"Whoa, Annie, you must have a little PMS thrown in there with all your other symptoms. You came out shooting, both barrels blazing, the minute I walked in the door. Here, I brought you some of Anna's homemade chicken soup. Doesn't this smell good?"

Vivian took one whiff of the soup and, before she could control herself, she vomited all over Chuck's pant legs.

"Way to go, Annie! Just 'cause I said you had PMS, you go and ruin my best slacks."

Vivian composed herself. "Take that soup away. It's making me nauseous!" she demanded.

All of Chuck's years of medical training and instincts crystallized and his fears along with it. His muscles clenched. "Well, partner, I think you've got more than the flu going on. Have you had a period lately?"

"That's a hell of a question to ask a dying woman," she moaned.

"Check your dates, Annie. I think you're pregnant."

"Go to hell, Charles Montgomery! You go straight to hell! Don't even joke like that! It ain't funny!"

"I'm not joking with you, Vivian. Some of your symptoms don't sound like you just have the flu."

Vivian looked at Chuck and saw that he was serious. "I can't be pregnant, Chuck. That's impossible. I don't believe in the Immaculate Conception, I haven't been with anyone except Carlton, and that was six or seven weeks ago... before New Year's, in fact. We always use condoms. What are they teaching you at that hospital—witch doctoring?"

"Vivian, you need to get a home pregnancy test and check it out."

Later that day, Vivian asked Anna to go to the drug store for the home pregnancy kit. When the test showed positive, Vivian sat in the bathroom in a daze and said over and over again, "I'm dead. The rabbit's dead and I'm dead."

Later, Chuck sat in his apartment, as memories of seeing Vivian for the first time flashed in his head. He swallowed his can of beer and remembered. The pain gripped his heart, as he crushed the empty beer can in one hand.

Chapter 18

It was the all-out drill for which everyone at March Air Force Base, North Island Naval Air Station, Camp Pendleton, and Fort Rosecrans Military Reservation had been waiting and planning. Benny learned that he would probably be away for four to six weeks on the day that Kenneth arrived in San Diego. He only had time to meet Kenneth at the airport and have Kenneth drive him back to the Air Force base. Benny called Fred, the desk clerk, from his car and told him that his brother would be staying at his condo for a few days. He then called a jeweler and a florist to order two dozen, long-stemmed, white roses to be delivered to JeNelle for Valentine's Day. The florist was already familiar with her address. Benny sent bouquets to JeNelle over the past six weeks. He also sent flowers to Stacy. Although Benny was able to see JeNelle only a few times since she returned from her trip to San Francisco, they talked on the telephone rather frequently and he felt that he was making progress with her. Stacy, on the other hand, was making herself uncharacteristically scarce, and that bothered Benny a great deal, but Stacy was not a woman who would permit him to pin her down.

Benny then tried to reach JeNelle to tell her that he would be away, but was unsuccessful. Benny told Kenneth that the woman he arranged for Kenneth to escort to the Gala, as a blind date, was also involved in the drill. He asked Kenneth to call JeNelle and let her know what was going on and to escort JeNelle to the Gala in his place. Kenneth agreed, reluctantly, to take Benny's place as JeNelle's escort since he would be in Santa Barbara primarily to see JeNelle's computer setup. Kenneth drove away from March Air Force base as sirens blared, alerting the air base that the drill was commencing.

* * *

"Stand still, JeNelle or I won't be able to get this dress to lay right by tomorrow night," Canty Towson fussed, as she fitted the evening gown on her daughter. "You've been acting very strange lately. What's going on with you?" she asked not looking up.

"Nothing special, Mama. I'm just very excited about the Gala."

"Is it the Gala or that nice young military man, Benny Alexander, that you've been seeing lately?"

"Not exactly."

"Not exactly what, JeNelle?"

"Not exactly the Gala or Benny Alexander."

"Then exactly what is it?"

"Well...I met someone."

"JeNelle, stop making me dig for this information. Just tell me what it is. If it's not Benny Alexander, then who is it?"

"It's Benny's brother, Kenneth Alexander."

Canty Towson rose from where she was kneeling, pinning the hem of her daughter's evening gown and looked at her, cocking her head to the side, grinning.

"He must be a very special man to have you this hot and bothered. I have not seen you this excited about a man in a very long time. Too long, in fact."

JeNelle pursued her lips. "I'm not 'hot and bothered', as you put it."

"You haven't dated anyone seriously since you divorced that deranged animal, Michel, and that was nearly eleven years ago. You started INSIGHTS and you've had your head buried in purchase orders, stock supplies, payroll taxes, employee insurance, and hospital plans, or some community service project or the other. You haven't even taken a day off, not to mention a vacation, so don't tell me you're not hot and bothered. You're as nervous as a priest in a whore house."

JeNelle looked at her mother head on. "You know why I've worked so hard."

Soberly, she shook her head. "Yes I do, JeNelle. You've been trying to show your sister that you're super woman."

"No, Mama, that's not it. I just want to be a good role model for Gloria so that she'll see that a woman can make it on her own. That she can be self-sufficient, independent. That she doesn't always need a man around. I don't want what happened to me to happen to Gloria."

The older woman folded her arms over her full breasts; her carriage erect. "Gloria is a full-grown woman, JeNelle. She's my daughter and I love her, but she's been hardheaded all of her life. She got worse after she was a runner up in that Ms. California contest. Running around with all those men with their fancy cars and big money. She don't believe that bull horns will hook! She ought to be grateful that you're even speaking to her after how she behaves toward you sometimes."

"She just doesn't understand why I left Michel. She was so young and impressionable back then. I didn't want to disillusion her. She misses all of the things that I was in a position to do for her when I was married to him. Someday I may explain it to her; tell her what truly happened that made me leave him."

"Humph! You're still doing for her and she doesn't appreciate that either. You paid her tuition at that fancy, private, prep school, you paid for her to go to one of the most exclusive colleges in the country, and now you're paying for her to go to Georgetown Law School. And don't think that your daddy and I don't know that you put money in her bank account, too. That girl hasn't ever hit a lick at a snake and she's walking around wearing designer this and couture that. You do too much for her, JeNelle. You ought to let her fall on her face a few times and then maybe she'll learn the value of what you've done for her. And maybe she'll learn to stand on her own two feet!"

"Gloria is a good person. I can't let her suffer just to prove a point."

"You're the one suffering, JeNelle. You have no life, child, outside of your company and your community projects. You need to find yourself a good man and give me and your daddy some grand babies. Maybe this Kevin Alexander is the one you ought to be concentrating your energy on...not your sister. What does this man do for a living?"

"His name is Kenneth, Mama, not Kevin. He owns a very successful computer software, hardware, and networking company in San Francisco with two partners."

"He's not married is he?" She raised a brow.

"No, Mama, he's single and he's never been married."

"How old is he?"

"I'm not sure. I'd say early thirties."

"What does he look like?"

"He's very handsome, very well built, a real heart stopper."

"Is he gay or bisexual?"

"No, Mama."

"Does he do drugs?"

"No, Mama. He doesn't even smoke, and before you ask, he doesn't chase women, have any illegitimate babies, and he's never even had a parking ticket."

"Wait a minute! You're telling me that, in this day and time, you've met a man who's successful, not gay, not married, in his thirties, and he's handsome, too? Well what's wrong with the boy?"

"He's no boy. There's nothing wrong with him. He's a wonderful man."

"Then what's wrong with you, girl? You still having problems getting over what Michel did to you?"

"I've put all of that behind me."

"No you haven't, JeNelle. Gloria told me that you're still having nightmares. I think that you need to go back to seeing that shrink, the one you were in college with...what's her name?"

"Dr. Beverly Carson."

"Yes, her. You've been too long without a man and love in your life. It ain't normal. You're a young, beautiful, and vital woman, JeNelle, even if I do say so myself. You ought to have someone other than me and your daddy telling you that. Someone who can make you feel like a woman again."

"Are you nearly finished with this dress? I've got to get back to the store."

"I'm finished with the dress, JeNelle Elise Towson. It will be ready for the Gala tomorrow night, but don't you think that I'm nearly finished with you, young lady!"

JeNelle kissed her mother and hugged her. "I love you, Mama."

"I love you, too, baby. But you heed what I'm telling you!"

Meeting Kenneth was like someone turning on a bright light in the darkest night. With so much darkness in her life, JeNelle spent years trying to avoid her former husband, Michel San Angeloe, and his threats and harassment, not knowing when or where he would attack next. He neither accepted nor honored the terms of their divorce. He still considered her his wife, his possession, like chattel, and she had to admit, at least to herself, that she was afraid of him. He told her that it would never be over between them; that, one day, she would be with him again. He reminded her that no wife of an Italian man was ever divorced. His threats frightened her more than she had ever told her family or friends. Thankfully, she had the support of his family to shield her from him and her growing business to occupy her time, so she didn't think about him much. He was busy, too, building his many businesses and investments into an empire.

Michel taught her a valuable lesson though. She could not trust her judgment when it came to men. She surrendered herself to that prophecy and vowed never to put her judgment to the test or herself in jeopardy again.

Her family and friends tried to convince her that one bad experience with a relationship should not make her adamant against having others, but she was not able to do it. Having no relationship was safe for her and any man that she might become involved with; safe from Michel San Angelo and his violent threats. She found comfort in her career, satisfaction in the struggle to build her business, and love from her family. That was all working well for eleven years.

Benny Alexander was in hot pursuit though. He would not let her reticence dissuade him. He found any excuse to spend time with her and he had been a seemingly incurable romantic, often sending flowers, cards and notes. Visiting with her and planning interesting and romantic outings. Introducing her to his friends and intimating that she was something more to him than just a friend. Of course, on each opportunity, she set the record straight both privately and publicly—they were friends—platonic friends.

Kenneth. Well, that was a completely different story.

* * *

"JeNelle Towson, please. This is Kenneth Alexander," he said over the cell phone, bracing himself for the jolt he knew would come from hearing her voice again. Since she left San Francisco, he thought of little else except her.

"Kenneth, how are you?" she said very happily.

"I'm fine, JeNelle. And you?"

"Just great, but I've been so busy since I got back to Santa Barbara. I'm looking forward to seeing the designs for this new computer system and software package. I've been periodically talking with Juan to keep him up-to-date with my expansion project. He's really very competent. He even gave me some ideas that I hadn't considered." She knew that she was babbling, but couldn't get herself under control. What she wanted to say was that she was looking forward to seeing Kenneth, but she didn't.

"I know. He's been keeping me apprised on your discussions. I have the three proposals that he believes will be best for your operation now and in the foreseeable future. What time tomorrow do you want to get together?"

"Is lunchtime all right with you? I can pick you up at the airport and we can go over the proposals over lunch."

"I'm in San Diego, JeNelle. I flew in a day early to spend some time with Benny. I'm at his condo now, but I have some disappointing news for you."

"What is it, Kenneth?"

"Benny's been called away for a massive military drill and he'll be gone for four to six weeks. He's asked me to be his standin and escort you to the

Chamber of Commerce Gala. I hope that you're not too disappointed. There was nothing that Benny could do. He tried several times to reach you before he left, but you were out of the shop."

"I was probably at my parents' home being fitted for my gown for the Gala. I'm sorry to hear that Benny's been called away, but I'm glad I won't have to go to the Gala alone."

"We're all set then. I'll drive up to Santa Barbara tomorrow morning and meet you at the store. Then we can talk about the proposals over lunch."

"Thanks, Kenneth. I'm grateful to you for making this effort. If my committee meeting were going to end early tonight, I'd ask you to drive up and have dinner with me at my place. That way we could get a fresh start in the morning."

"I know how committee meetings can go."

"Thanks for calling, Kenneth. I'll see you tomorrow."

Kenneth closed his cell phone and loosened his tie. He looked around Benny's condo and mused, *This is a den of iniquity, if I've ever seen one. It's clear, from looking at this place, what my brother's master plan is.* Kenneth walked up the stairs and into Benny's bedroom, and sat down on the bed. Immediately, he saw the framed picture of JeNelle and Benny at a restaurant. It was hard to miss it, as it was promanately displayed on the nightstand. Picking it up, he lay back across the bed. He looked up, saw himself in the mirror over the bed, and shook his head. Thoughts began to flood his mind, as he gazed at JeNelle's picture. Perhaps Benny had slept with JeNelle in this bed. Held her tight and made love with her. Kenneth closed his eyes against the suddenly painful thought. Cursing himself for wanting JeNelle, he looked at the picture again.

JeNelle looked radiant. Just as she had the very first time that he saw her when she emerged from the airplane with Benny. It was like the opening of a rose to full bloom. She was breathtaking, soft and delicate. He recalled how he had to force himself not to reveal how instantly attracted to her he was right from the moment he first saw her. She stirred something within him, something unexplainable and deep. Still, as the week they spent together in San Francisco progressed, he knew that it was not only her physical beauty that attracted him to her. It was her spirit, her energy, her enthusiasm, and her intellect. She had such a keen sense of who she was. A polish that could not be learned that he found so intriguing. He recalled how affected by her he was when she walked out of the dressing room at CompuCorrect to work out on the exercise equipment that first day of the Expo. The moment she walked by and mounted the stationary bike, he could barely contain himself. He recalled playing basketball with Juan and missing nearly every shot, and he had never lost a game to Juan before. He forced himself to work out even longer and harder so that he would not overtly watch her. He wasn't sure, but he thought that Shirley might have caught him watching JeNelle when she was on the rowing machine. JeNelle was pure poetry in motion. Who could blame him? Half the men in his office were thunderstruck by her beauty.

All that week, he caught glimpses of her, as JeNelle worked with potential buyers and distributors and other customers. She had them mesmerized with her crisp, clean smile, and that ever-present twinkle in her eyes. Later, as she toured the city with him, he had to restrain himself, on more than a few occasions, from reaching for her hand, as they walked or caressing her face as they talked. It was uncanny how their tastes ran in the same direction. Particularly when they both spotted that beautiful piece of covered Waterford crystal jewelry box with many facets of light that shone brilliantly, but when the salesperson told them the price, JeNelle put the covered crystal down and directed him to another piece. He noticed how JeNelle kept looking back at that same piece of crystal. She was hilariously comical in that floppy hat, but she even gave that hideous hat a touch of class.

Dining with her alone was the hardest thing that he recalled having to do, but he would not have traded a moment of the time they spent together for anything in the world. He made a point of engaging her in conversation about business when they were alone, but she even made that subject sound poetic. She had a way of moving her head and sticking her fingers in her hair and raking them through when she talked. She was so clear in her understanding about economic concepts that affect small business; what needed to be done to help them succeed. Then, on other occasions, specifically at the Chinese restaurant, she kept the group in uproarious laughter over what were seemingly ordinary events in her store. She could be unbelievably funny and everyone in his office loved her. He thought he would not be able to bear it when they rode to Sausalito on the ferry. He held her in his arms while she fed popcorn to the sea gulls. Her soft hair blew against his face and her delicate perfume excited him. As she sat across from him at Scoma's Restaurant in Sausalito and said she didn't want the week to end, her vulnerability overwhelmed him. He recalled her serenity when they sat before the fireplace on her last night in his home. His naked want for her coursing through his body. He also recalled how stark reality gripped him, as he watched her walk away with Benny.

CompuCorrect's staff was ecstatic when they received a case of Chardonnay, Pinot Noirs, and Sauvignon Blanc wines from Santa Barbara County's Santa Ynez Valley Vintages as a gift from JeNelle, Barry and Felix. In addition, JeNelle sent a gift from her store to each person at CompuCorrect and a personal note, thanking each one for being so supportive during the Expo. No two people received the same gift and note, but everyone proudly displayed his or her gift. She sent the coffee table book, *Feeling the Spirit*, to him. It contained beautifully photographed pictures of the South. Places that resembled Goodwill, Summer County, South Carolina. He recalled sitting in his office on the day the gifts arrived, sipping a glass of Au Bon Climate Chardonnay and being lost in each page of the book. He didn't even want to work anymore that day. His only thoughts were of her, of JeNelle.

Kenneth sat up on the bed and placed the picture of Benny and JeNelle back on the nightstand. It was a good thing he wasn't going to see JeNelle tonight. His defenses were low and she inspired him to want something more from her than just her friendship. He had to stop thinking about her that way. He had to stop thinking about her. Period. She was Benny's lady and nothing was going to change that.

He changed his clothes and headed for the swimming pool in the exercise area of the condo complex. Perhaps some laps in the Olympic-sized swimming pool would serve to clear his mind of JeNelle. He had such mixed emotions about seeing her again. He tried to avoid coming to San Diego for that very reason. He wanted to refuse his brother's request, but Benny was adamant, and he never denied Benny anything so simple to give. Kenneth feared that Benny might sense something if he protested too much. They were very close and could easily read each other's feelings. He had to avoid that at all costs. He forced himself to put his relationship with JeNelle Towson into perspective. She was strictly a client, like many others that CompuCorrect served. More importantly, Benny was crazy about her. Kenneth thought that if he could manage to get through these next couple of days with JeNelle, he could begin the process of distancing himself from her. He could not and would not fail. Benny's happiness was at stake.

"You must be related to Benny Alexander," a sultry woman's voice said, as he finished forty laps and emerged from the pool. The water was dripping into his eyes and down his muscular body, as he sat on the side of the pool and reached for his towel.

"Yes, I am. I'm his brother, Kenneth," he said, standing up and extended his hand. *Whoa!* he thought. *She is gorgeous!* "And you are?"

"Cecil Jordon. I live in the building on the twenty-third floor. I've known Benny since he moved here."

"Oh, yes, Dr. Jordon, Benny mentioned you and, I think it's your condo mate, Dr. Janice Atterly, to me some time ago." He also remembered the tricks that Benny told him that Cecil and Janice were famous or infamous for pulling on him.

"Please, just call me Cecil. Are you visiting Benny for the Valentine's Day weekend?"

"I was, but he's been called away unexpectedly. I have some business to take care of in the area and then I'll be going back to San Francisco. But tell me, how did you know that I was related to Benny? Am I wearing a tag that says Benny's brother or are you psychic?" he joked.

"Psychic, no, but a tag? You could say that. I'd know that finely sculptured Alexander body anywhere. I spotted you when you got off the elevator and I've been watching you swim. Benny swims in this pool all the time. I'd call the shape in those swimming trunks that you're wearing a tag. You two look alike, but you're even more handsome than Benny is, if that's possible. Tell me, are there any more like you at home?" she asked, grinning.

Kenneth chuckled and nearly blushed. "Benny said that you were...uh... uninhibited. I'm not sure how I should respond, but we have a younger brother, Gregory...he's only sixteen," Kenneth hastened to add. He wasn't sure what to expect next from Cecil Jordon, but Benny was right, she was a stunningly beautiful woman.

"I'll bet that he's a heart stopper, too. Are you sure that you can't spend more time in San Diego? Janice and I would love to show you around. It's the least that we can do for Benny."

"Uh, no. I have a business meeting in Santa Barbara tomorrow, so I'll be leaving here in the morning and staying there overnight. I'll only be back in San Diego briefly to bring Benny's car back."

"Santa Barbara? That can mean only one thing: JeNelle Towson."

Kenneth's heart nearly stopped at the mention of her name. "You know JeNelle?"

"Sure, I met her, quite by accident, with her sister, Gloria, and Benny before New Year's. We ended up going out together that night. Last Friday was JeNelle's birthday and Benny arranged a surprise party for her at Michelangelo's. Some of the people from a club called Jason's, where we partied the night I met JeNelle, were there, and people from her store and some of her friends and business acquaintances. A bunch of Benny's friends from March Air Force Base and a lot of the San Diego Chargers were there, too. She didn't have a clue what he was up to. We had a great time."

"That sounds like something that Benny might do."

"Yeah, it was a great night for everyone. JeNelle ended up getting a lot of us to purchase tickets to attend the Santa Barbara Chamber of Commerce Gala. Then Benny gave JeNelle a pair of spectacular diamond earrings for her birthday and JeNelle was speechless the rest of the evening." Cecil laughed.

Kenneth thought about JeNelle, as Cecil talked. It made him even more determined to distance himself from JeNelle. He ended up having dinner with Cecil and Janice. They proved to be very interesting dinner companions and he actually enjoyed their company. He understood why Benny liked them so much and why he tolerated their antics.

Early the next morning, Kenneth drove the to Santa Barbara, checked into a hotel, and then went to JeNelle's store just after it opened for the day. One whiff of the intoxicating scent permeating the air and his senses went into overdrive. The store was beautifully decorated much like walking into someone's private sanctuary. The glass shelves gleamed with pretty pots and bottles of exotic fragrances. People sat on comfortable sofas that looked like a library surrounded by books. Others strolled aisles of tastefully displayed collectables, furniture and art. Fine China and flatware was in another alcove where bridal couples met with consultants. The store was chic with strong Old World influences. Garden frescos were hand-painted on the charmingly cracked plaster walls and ceiling. Kenneth felt as if he were coming home. Pleasant music, something with mandolins and harps lulled the senses and made you want to take off your shoes and get comfortable among the many treasures that he could see.

An obviously gay man approached him, as he stood in reverent awe. "May I help you, sir, I hope?" The man eyed Kenneth suggestively.

"I have an appointment with Ms. Towson. My name is—"

"Don't tell me," the man interrupted. "You're related to Captain Alexander."

"Yes," Kenneth said surprised at the man's statement. "I'm his brother, Kenneth Alexander. Is Ms. Towson available?"

"Not according to Captain Alexander, she's not." The man giggled.

"My question referred to whether Ms. Towson is physically present in the store. I have an appointment with her," Kenneth said, clearly annoyed.

"Yes, she's here," the man said, noting Kenneth's change in demeanor. "I'll announce you."

The man switched away and telephoned JeNelle. Shortly, she emerged wearing a big, bright smile and that ever-present sparkle in her beautiful eyes.

He masked his emotions at seeing her again. This was going to be harder than he realized. He wanted to take her in his arms and kiss away the cinnamon-colored lipstick on her mouth, run his fingers though her flowing, bronze locks that bounced on her shoulders, caress the mounds of her... Kenneth braced against the jolt of lightening that struck him, as JeNelle approached. He was trying to cope with the feelings that engulfed him. Feelings of disappointment that he had not met her first and joy for his brother because she was clearly an important part of Benny's life. Her picture at Benny's bedside, the surprise party Benny arranged, and the diamond earrings. Kenneth knew and understood his brother's needs and desires for JeNelle. He was fighting his own needs and desires for her, too.

Approaching Kenneth, JeNelle swallowed hard and felt her body temperature rising. She couldn't help gazing on his handsome face. Memories of her week with him in San Francisco invaded her. She knew that lifting her eyes to meet his spelled trouble for her and she was right. Painfully so. His maleness enticed her to thoughts that she had never had before. Her eyes briefly rested on his mouth, but even his full lips enticed her when they curved into that polar-ice-cap-melting smile of his. She found herself wondering what it would feel like to kiss him. To have his arms wrapped around her. Emotional turmoil churned through every fiber and sinew of her body. This couldn't be happening! Not to her! She guarded against wanting a man in her life or a relationship for many years, but since the day she met Kenneth James Alexander her life turned on its ear. She wanted Kenneth, but the thoughts of Michel San Angelo reaching his ugliness and cruelty into her life again squashed her dreams. Yet, how, after two years of pain, suffering disillusionment and degradation of marriage with Michel, had Kenneth made her feel warmth and other emotions that were all too foreign to her? The emotions simultaneously frightened her and elated her. Watching Kenneth move toward her, she was lost in a quandary.

She guarded against involvement for so long that she didn't know how else to react in the presence of a man like Kenneth. She had no frame of reference. She had never met a man like him before.

"Kenneth, it's good to see you." She smiled, extending her hand. "Please, come up to my office."

They started toward her office and she led the way. As they walked up the steps, JeNelle's voluptuous body swayed naturally ahead of him. He could feel his nature rising and pulsating against his tailored suit. He placed his briefcase in front of his growing erection. Once inside JeNelle's office, sparsely furnished, but tastefully decorated, they exchanged pleasantries and talked about her business operation and her plans for expansion.

Kenneth was unyielding in his business-like approach. After one cup of coffee, he opted to wander around her store alone, without her assistance, hoping that to be out of her presence would help him gain some control over his emotions. However, that effort was for naught. Everywhere he looked in the chic store was JeNelle.

JeNelle watched Kenneth from her windowed office. His rejection of her assistance, as he toured the store and talked with her employees and managers startled her. She couldn't get a take on him or his reaction to her. It was cordial and business like, of course, but somehow distant, dispassionate and aloof. She knew those emotions well. She practiced them most of her life since Michel. Even so, Kenneth's tall, sculptured physique excited her beyond belief. She exhaled slowly, trying to deny the electricity that streaked through her body whenever she was in his presence. This wasn't normal for her. No man had ever caused this type of reaction in her, not even Michel. She didn't understand what was happening to her; it even frightened her. Not like Michel had inspired fear in her. No, what she felt for Kenneth was something strange, but exciting.

When Kenneth returned to her office, he suggested that she review the proposals and let Juan know which one she preferred. That's when JeNelle noticed something in Kenneth's demeanor that worried her.

"Kenneth, have I done something to offend you?" With concern, JeNelle looked directly into his eyes.

The question startled Kenneth. He was afraid that he had unintentionally let his emotions show. He quickly dismissed that thought. If anything, his thoughts of loving her endlessly would have offended her considering her relationship with Benny. "*Something to offend me?*' No, JeNelle, of course not."

"You seem so distant. Not like yourself."

"I apologize. Perhaps I'm overtired. I spent last evening with Cecil Jordon and Janice Atterly. I believe that you know them. They're Benny's friends. We were up pretty late talking and I got a very early start this morning."

"Yes, I know them. Cecil and Janice are two very interesting women," she said and chuckled. "They had us all in stitches talking about Benny last Friday. They even made him blush. They're very good friends of his and I like them both very much. They treat him like a kid brother."

"Interesting,' that's an understatement," Kenneth said and snorted.

JeNelle laughed. "Well, if you spent the evening with them, no wonder you're over tired. Why don't we just get out of here and have a relaxing lunch?"

Kenneth wanted desperately to refuse, but JeNelle seemed so concerned about him that he agreed to go along. He was going to have to control himself better if he was going to get through these next few days with JeNelle. Her very presence electrified him. The sensuousness of her tightly formed body, the curl in her flowing hair, the shade of her eyes, the tilt of her head, the fullness of her mouth, the roundness of her breasts, the sway of her hips, the touch of her hand, the curve of her bottom, the strength of her legs, the arch of her feet—everything about her spelled trouble—with a capital T for Towson. He had to look away from her to maintain his composure, but he was falling hard for her and he knew it. Taking the drive with her didn't help. Her skirt moved up her firm, well-shaped thighs when she sat behind the wheel of her car and inched up more as she shifted her foot from the gas pedal to the break. Her soft scent danced in his brain, firing his emotions and causing his core to ache. This had never happened to him before. Unlike Benny, he did not take advantage of every sexual opportunity that came his way, but over the years, he had known the tenderness that a woman would offer. None of his affairs, brief though they were, had ever inspired him in the way that JeNelle managed to do. He was glad that there was only a brief ride to the restaurant. Trying to keep his nature under control was hard to hide. He wished they had gone in separate cars.

When they arrived at Maison's, some of the patrons greeted JeNelle. As she and Kenneth passed through the opulent dining room, she introduced him to everyone who stopped her.

During lunch, Kenneth tried to keep the conversation light. He purposefully stuck to the script that he had rehearsed in his mind so carefully on his drive from San Diego to Santa Barbara. He did not look into her eyes. Instead he looked at the proposals, pointing out the advantages and disadvantages in each one based on what he saw on his tour of her business. When their meals arrived, he kept his mind on his food. That was very tough to do, since he did not regularly eat lunch, opting to exercise instead, but on this day, he forced himself to eat.

"JeNelle, how are you?" An attractive woman approached the table where Kenneth and JeNelle were sitting.

"Lisa, I'm fine. Lisa, may I introduce you to—?"

"This man needs no introduction," Lisa Lambert said, extending her hand. "You're Kenneth Alexander, aren't you?"

"You must know my brother, too?" Kenneth rose from his seat and shook Lisa's outstretched hand.

"Your brother?" Lisa asked, puzzled. "No I don't think we've met. I'm Lisa Lambert."

"Have a seat, Lisa," JeNelle said, indicating a chair between her and Kenneth.

"Thank you. I can only join you for a few minutes. I have to get on the phone with the Governor in about fifteen minutes. He'll be pleased that I've run into you, Mr. Alexander."

"I'm at a loss, Ms. Lambert. How did you know who I am?"

Lisa was immediately all business. "I read about you several times in the Business Section of the San Francisco newspapers and then I saw you being interviewed at the Small Business Expo. You were with JeNelle. Later I read some other reports from the Expo that indicated that your company, CompuCorrect, made one of the best showings at the Expo and that you were a man on the rise and one to be watched."

"Oh, I see," Kenneth said.

"Lisa is Special Assistant to the Governor for Economic Affairs. She and I have been talking about some exciting plans for instituting more business courses and opportunities into the junior and senior high schools in the state," JeNelle explained.

"Yes, and I've had you on my list of people to call, Mr. Alexander. The Governor liked what he saw in the interviews you've had with the press and news media. We're looking for bright, young, role models to work on our projects to interest young teenagers to consider business and economics as career options. We're convening a special Blue Ribbon Panel in Sacramento beginning in the spring to work on how to institute the program. Then, the Panel Members will give speeches, hold workshops, and do other public appearances around the state to encourage school systems to participate and to encourage students to enroll in a special business and economics partnership program with small business entrepreneurs in their communities. It will be a work/study program where the students will actually work for certain small businesses to learn business management first hand in exchange for course credit.

"JeNelle has been very instrumental in getting this project off the ground and she's agreed to be on the Blue Ribbon Panel. The Governor would like you to join the Panel as well, Mr. Alexander. You have a natural tie-in with the work that you're doing for the San Francisco County schools and library systems. Superintendent Braxton and his wife, Tess, speak very highly of you and your family."

"Thank you, Ms. Lambert. I'm very flattered by the Governor's offer. This sounds like a very worthwhile program, but I'm not in a position to give you an answer today."

"That's fine. Take all the time that you need, but the Governor is not going to take no for an answer from you, of that I'm sure," she said and smiled. "I'm often in San Francisco. I'll call you for an appointment and we can discuss this further at that time." Then turning to JeNelle, Lisa said, "I'll see you at the Gala, JeNelle. It's been a pleasure meeting you, Mr. Alexander. I look forward to seeing you again soon."

"Kenneth will be at the Gala, Lisa. We'll be at Judge Worthington's table."

"Great! So will I. Then I will see you both at the Gala."

Lisa rose, shook Kenneth's hand again, and left the table. Kenneth remarked to JeNelle that Lisa was certainly a formidable person and JeNelle agreed. They finished their lunches and JeNelle took Kenneth back to his car parked at her store.

Kenneth arrived at JeNelle's home at 6:45 P.M. Cocktails were being served at 7:00 P.M. at the Gala and dinner would begin at 8:00 P.M. A ceremony was to be held after dinner and the dancing would follow thereafter. Kenneth was wearing a black Perry Ellis tuxedo with shawl lapels and white cotton pleat shirt, black onyx studs, and black tie. He also wore a double-breasted tuxedo coat, a Gucci watch, DNA fragrance and Lorenzo Banfi shoes.

When JeNelle opened the door and smiled brightly, as she invited him in, she gave him a quick hug and kiss on the cheek. He prayed that she would not look more beautiful and stunning than usual. His prayers were not answered. Her long, black, sequenced gown lay softly on every perfect curve of her hourglass body. A long slit on the left front side of the gown revealed her long, firm, shapely legs up to the thigh. Her shimmering, black-tinted stockings had an embroidered rose at the ankle and her shoes had a single, diamond-studded strap at the ankle and one across her perfectly pedicured toes. The bodice of the dress was strapless and its ability to remain in place, cupping her full breasts, defied the laws of gravity; especially, considering the fact that the dress was backless to the waist except for a tiny string that held it all together. Her hair was mounted gracefully atop her head in a Georgian style with wisps of tendrils dangling around her lovely oval face and onto her neck and bare shoulders. A diamond choker graced her neck and a single diamond hung down her bare back. She was breathtaking, incomparable.

"Kenneth, I'm usually not this disorganized," JeNelle stood before a full-length wall mirror in her living room trying on different earrings. She could see Kenneth's full body reflection behind her. "Which pair of earrings do you think are more appropriate?"

Kenneth was so overwhelmed with her and her beauty that he gazed at her unknowingly. He covered her body with his eyes and felt the emergence of his rising nature.

"Kenneth? Which pair?"

He had to force himself to breathe. He cleared the large lump in his throat. "Diamonds," he managed to say, not sure of where the thought had originated.

JeNelle looked very surprised, even though she tried to hide it.

"I see that you've heard about Benny's birthday gift," she said and sighed. "I was furious with him for giving me such an expensive present. I didn't want to make a scene at my birthday party, considering all the trouble that he went to in order to surprise me. I could barely contain myself the rest of the evening. Later, when we had a moment alone, I refused to accept the diamond earrings and I gave them back to him. Tonight, just before you arrived, I received those roses from Benny," she said, pointing to a box of roses on top of her grand piano, "and the same diamond earrings were in the roses. If he were here tonight, I'd return them to him, again. He doesn't seem to understand that I only want to be friends."

"May I see the gift?"

JeNelle looked at Kenneth's reflection in the mirror for a moment. She seemed tense and uncomfortable with his request. Then turning away, she went to the boxed flowers, retrieved the earrings, and handed them to Kenneth.

He took them out of the black velvet box and held them up to her ears, as she looked at them and him in the mirror.

"They look a little better than that big, floppy hat that you tried on, wouldn't you agree?" He smiled, as he stood so close to her that he could inhale the essence of her delicate perfume. They gazed at each other in the mirror for a pregnant moment and then they both laughed.

"That was an awful hat, Kenneth." JeNelle laughed and was more relaxed.

"These earrings suit you much better. I think that you should wear them. Benny gave them to you in friendship. I know my brother, JeNelle. It's not the value of the gift that's important to him, it's the value of the person to whom he has given this small token of his friendship."

JeNelle continued to gaze at Kenneth in the mirror, as she put on the earrings. Although they were gleaming brilliantly, Kenneth thought that they paled by comparison to her beauty. She pinned a single white rosebud to his lapel and kissed him on the cheek. She thought his smile could melt both polar ice caps.

* * *

The Chamber of Commerce Gala was not a small town affair. After all, it was Santa Barbara, one of the wealthiest sites in the state. There were top executives from some of the most prestigious and influential companies in the state in attendance. Foreign dignitaries were also there looking to find business opportunities. The Hollywood and political elite also flocked to the Gala. After all, Douglas Fairbanks, Sr., and Zelda and Scott Fitzgerald led many Hollywood notables to Santa Barbara County with its opulent mansions, zillionaire Republicans and movie stars. Ronald Reagan's ranch in the Santa Ynez Mountains and Michael Jackson's Neverland Estate also drew quite a bit of attention to the area. John Fitzgerald and Jackie Kennedy spent their honeymoon there and Jimmy Cagney owned Sterns Wharf. Posh residential enclaves housed Charlie Chaplin, Michael Douglas, Jeff Bridges, Geena Davis and John Cleese, among other notables. The searchlights gave the Gala a feel of an Academy Awards night with all of its glitz, glitter and glamour.

The indomitable press corps buzzed around each arriving vehicle. A valet opened the car door for JeNelle and helped her to her feet while a second valet whisked the car away. Kenneth put her matching, floor-length wrap around her shoulders and offered JeNelle his arm, as they climbed the wide, white marble steps amid flashing bulbs that led to the Atrium Manor, a huge structure for a city of only eighty-six thousand residents. The whitewashed building had a decidedly Spanish flare with its red tiled roof, an intertwining of New England, and adobe architecture. Cascading gardens in front and down the gradually rising stairway, perched in the hills overlooking the City of Santa Barbara and the Pacific Ocean beyond.

The Mayor of Santa Barbara, his wife and their entourage greeted each person as they arrived. Inside the glass-enclosed Atrium Anteroom, people milled around greeting each other and talking about the topics of the day. Huge ice sculptures placed strategically around the room between lush foliage adorned in red roses and greenery silently glistened and melted in the ambient light from the massive overhead crystal chandeliers. An army of young wait staff skillfully moved among the throngs of people offering trays of hot and cold hors d'oeuvres. Other waiters carried, on one hand, champagne glasses perched precariously on trays.

Women clad in beautiful and expensive evening regalia glided around the room accompanied by male companions who looked quite dashing in their couture tuxedos and black or white ties. None looked more elegant than Kenneth and JeNelle, as they entered the room. Heads turned, both men and women, as they advanced through the crowd. They were met every step of the way by people who approached and warmly greeted them. Photographers seemed to dog their every footstep and flash pictures with each word that they uttered and with each greeting. Kenneth and JeNelle were impervious to the cameras that constantly surrounded them, as they sipped a very fine champagne and chatted with other guests.

Judge and Mrs. Johnston White Worthington, III, followed by their entourage, approached JeNelle and Kenneth.

"JeNelle, how absolutely lovely you look," Mrs. Worthington enthusiastically emoted, looking JeNelle from head to toe.

"Thank you, Mrs. Worthington. You are always so very complimentary and gracious," JeNelle demurred honestly.

"Are those one or two carat diamond earrings you're wearing, my dear?" she asked, moving closer and squinting at each earring.

"I'm not sure, Mrs. Worthington," JeNelle chuckled, "but may I present my escort, Mr. Kenneth J. Alexander of San Francisco? Kenneth, this is Judge Johnston White Worthington and his wife, Constance."

"A pleasure to meet you, Mr. Alexander." Judge Worthington grinned, extending his hand, forcefully pumping Kenneth's. "Alexander? Alexander? Didn't I read something about a Kenneth J. Alexander in the newspaper recently? Something to do with a big military contract?"

"Yes, sir. My partners and I have recently been granted a contract for certain computer services at the Presidio."

"Ah, yes." He smiled. "Fine bit of work I hear your company is providing in the San Francisco Bay area. We, in the judiciary, need to look at upgrading our intrastate computer network." He cupped Kenneth's elbow, moving a few steps away from the group. "Let me tell you some of what we have in mind and perhaps you can give us some pointers…"

The Judge and Kenneth were involved in conversation while Mrs. Constance White Worthington introduced JeNelle to her entourage, the Santa Barbara elite, and continued to grill her about her jewelry, her dress designer, and her hair stylist.

Kenneth was never far from JeNelle, however. No matter how interesting his conversation with others, for him, she was the only other person in the room.

Big doors opened and the throngs of people swarmed into the ballroom, which had been set up as the dining room for the evening. There was a large stage and orchestra playing beautifully as people dined on a seven-course meal amid lavish decorations. Throughout the fabulous dinner, people at the round table of twelve kept Kenneth and JeNelle engaged in lively conversations.

A press table was positioned nearby and reporters took notes, as Kenneth or JeNelle spoke. One reporter overheard Kenneth mention something about a proposal to JeNelle and the fact that they had recently been together in San Francisco for a week. The reporter could not hear all the details clearly, but she could see the excitement in Kenneth and JeNelle's eyes.

Kenneth and JeNelle were relieved when the Mayor of Santa Barbara took to the podium to announce awards for community service. The room darkened and a single, bright spotlight grew, as the mayor said, "And now we come to the part of the evening that you've all been waiting for. We will announce the recipient of the Santa Barbara Chamber of Commerce's highest and most prestigious 'Man of the Year' award. Here to tell us about this year's recipient is an esteemed member of the California State Supreme Court, Judge Johnston White Worthington, III."

While the Judge read an enviable list of accomplishments of the person selected for the high honor, JeNelle took the opportunity for a mental escape and focused her attention on Kenneth in the darkened room. He looked so very handsome that she couldn't blame the other women for swooning every time he smiled. He was warm and affable. His conversation kept everyone enthralled. He was the epitome of graciousness and panache. Her heart was pounding against her chest just sitting next to him and then she heard the Judge say, "Ladies and Gentlemen, I give you the *Woman* of the Year, my close and personal friend, Ms. JeNelle Elise Towson, owner of INSIGHTS, Inc."

Thunderous applause rose, as people leaped to their feet. A spotlight in the darkened room shifted to JeNelle, who was sitting in absolute shock and awe. She was stunned. She had no idea she was even under consideration. Kenneth stood, applauding her, and helped her from her seat. He escorted her to Judge Worthington at the podium and she held his arm tightly. He felt her trembling. Clamorous roars went up, as she took the stage and continued long after the Judge handed the crystal and gold figurine to her and she embraced him. None of the applause was more enthusiastic than Kenneth's. Each time the clamor started to wane so that she could speak, it would start up again more enthusiastically than before. Finally, JeNelle put up her hands to quiet the crowd and they took their seats. She began,

"In the now famous words of my idol, former Congresswoman, Barbara Jordan, in her Keynote Address before the National Democratic Convention of 1976, I say to you, *'that there is something different about tonight. There is something special about tonight. What is different? What is special?'* I, the daughter of a seamstress and a city bus driver, am standing here to receive the 'Woman of the Year' Award. A lot of years have passed since the first award was given and during that time it would have been most unusual for any major organization to select me, JeNelle Elise Towson, to receive this prestigious award, but tonight here I am. *'And I feel that notwithstanding the past that my presence here is one additional bit of evidence that the American Dream need not forever be deferred.'*

The audience was silent. A pin drop from any area of the room would sound loudly. Waiters and waitresses stopped in their tracks. Kitchen workers stopped their tasks and lined the walls, listening to every word JeNelle spoke.

Her performance was seamless, standing before more than two thousand people assembled, delivering a moving, extemporaneous, acceptance speech in strong and confident voice with tears rolling down her flawless face. The audience was spellbound by her words and no doubt by her beauty and her demeanor. Kenneth's eyes never left her, as he stood with Judge Worthington slightly behind her and to the side, while she spoke. During her oration, she challenged the crowd to support the Governor's plan for Youth in Business and Industry, by all means necessary.

The throngs of people leaped to their feet again with even more fervor than before. The clamor continued long after she reached her seat. The Judge finally quieted the crowd and when he had their full attention he said, "And now you know why no words I speak could ever aptly describe this Woman of the Year. JeNelle, would you take the floor with your escort, Mr. Kenneth J. Alexander of San Francisco, and lead with the first dance of the evening?"

Kenneth led JeNelle to the center of the dance floor while the orchestra began to play, "You Are So Beautiful to Me." The audience was silent, as Kenneth took JeNelle in his arms and danced in the glow of the single, white spotlight. The moment was pure magic. As other people began to take the floor, they whispered their congratulations to her, but Kenneth never took his eyes off JeNelle. She looked up at him, as they danced. His adoration for her grew by leaps and bounds, as they glided around the floor and gazed into each other's eyes. Kenneth took a deep breath.

"Benny would be very proud of you tonight, JeNelle. I'm sorry that he's not here to share this moment with you."

"Benny? Oh, uh, yes," she said deflated. "Thank you, Kenneth, but I didn't know anything about this. I thought that I would faint when I heard my name announced. I'm so happy that you were here with me to give me moral support. I don't think that I could have gotten through this if it weren't for you. You keep coming to my aid at such critical times."

"You deserve all of the accolades that have been bestowed upon you tonight. You were brilliant. Congresswoman Jordon was one of my idols, too. Although I wasn't born when she gave that speech in 1976, my parents often talked about her and read her speeches to us. So I remember it and her vividly. She did so much in her lifetime to shape the national agenda. She is sorely missed."

JeNelle laid her head against Kenneth's chest. She could feel his heart beating rapidly, but outwardly, he was cool as a cucumber. She looked up at him again with dewy soft eyes. Accolades were sincerely appreciated, but what she wanted most was to feel Kenneth's mouth on hers.

Kenneth fought the desire to envelop her mouth in his. Her flawless face grabbing at his heart, his mind and his soul. The way she tilted her head. The sparkle in her eyes. The feel of her body against his. The velvet smoothness of her skin. The fullness of her breasts riding high on her rib cage nearly brought an audible moan from his core. It was becoming too much to bear. He had to look away from her before his body betrayed him.

Throughout the rest of the evening, people came to the table where they sat to ask her to dance or to congratulate JeNelle. She put her hand on his, as they talked and he had not the strength to withdraw. Her fresh, clean smile was alluring and her conversation enchanting. Cecil and Janice, with their escorts in tow, screamed wildly, all decorum abandoned, as they hugged JeNelle like old sorority sisters who were seeing each other after a long separation. Their intervention gave Kenneth the reprieve he so desperately needed to refocus his thoughts. He could not succeed if JeNelle kept looking at him.

Lisa Lambert, who had been periodically observing JeNelle and Kenneth throughout the evening, took Kenneth aside to dance.

"Now I think you see why the Governor and I believe that JeNelle should be a member of the Blue Ribbon Panel. She has real star quality and people respond positively to her. We see the same characteristics in you, Kenneth. I hope you won't let us down."

"I will certainly consider the offer very carefully, Lisa. You'll have my decision when we have a chance to meet in San Francisco."

Kenneth's gaze repeatedly, but unintentionally strayed toward JeNelle, as he danced and talked with Lisa and others. Often he noticed that JeNelle was also glancing at him. When the music ended, Kenneth and Lisa talked privately for a while. When they rejoined JeNelle, Cecil, Janice and company, Kenneth heard Cecil saying, "I can't wait to tell Benny all about this, as soon as he gets back." She was very animated. "And when you said, *I challenge business owners to put your shoulders to the wheel along with the youth of our state and bring us out of this dark recession that affects every living being in this state*', girlfriend, I had tears in my eyes and I was ready to shout hallelujah and I'm not a religious person."

People laughed.

"No, no," Janice interrupted, "when JeNelle said, *'Some of us have come from a low dark place in this society and we were not there alone. We cannot, indeed, we must not, leave anyone else in that place. This society, we men and women, us, you and me, are the ones who know where that low place is in each of our lives. We must go back there and form a link, a sturdy chain, that leads ahead out of that low dark place into a new and brighter future,'* I was ready to get on the telephone and start looking for those people I know who are still in that *'low dark place in society.'* Girl, you've got it going on! Benny's truly got his hands full! I'm buying the video from the videographer and playing it every time I feel like I can't take another step!"

Others picked out their favorite parts of JeNelle's unrehearsed and totally extemporaneous oration, each reciting it verbatim.

Fully flushed with embarrassment, JeNelle said, "It was all an act."

Everyone laughed, except Kenneth who said adoringly, "It was an Academy Award performance." He noticed something about her speech that captured him. A deep sadness that rose to the top, but she suppressed it as if, had she let it go, it would have overwhelmed her. It seemed almost out of place in her presentation. He met her parents at the Gala, and heard stories of her youth from them. Happy stories about their daughter, a very talented and accomplished piano virtuoso who studied at Julliard in New York City, but that was where the happy stories ended, almost as if a dark cloak covered her life beyond that point. Her sadness was almost palpable and he wanted to hold her and convince her that her life ever after would be full and joyous, but Benny's affection for her kept him grounded, rooted in his determination to steel his feelings and bury them deep inside himself.

As the evening was ending, Kenneth picked up JeNelle's award and they began to head for the door. The Judge and Constance followed. Kenneth went to retrieve JeNelle's wrap and to order the car. While he was waiting for the hatcheck person to return and talking business with other guests, he observed two men who appeared to be of Italian or Spanish descent, approach JeNelle and lead her away from the group. A third man approached from a different direction. The third man was older, polished, but in some ways seemed almost sinister. He whispered something to JeNelle, but Kenneth could sense that something was wrong—terribly wrong. His jaw clinched and his fist balled. He was about to excuse himself from the crowd that surrounded him and go to her until he noticed that Judge Worthington went to JeNelle's side. The Judge's face was soon beet red and he was clearly quite angry with the men who exchanged heated words with the Judge and then left. Kenneth could not hear the conversation, but when the men left, JeNelle seemed to stagger into the Judge's arms. He led her to a bench at a remote area of the Atrium Room. The Judge pulled his handkerchief from his pocket and handed it to JeNelle.

JeNelle noticed Kenneth watching, as she talked with the Judge. She gathered herself and kissed the Judge on the cheek. He escorted her back to the small crowd of people, none of whom seemed to have noticed the commotion. JeNelle summoned a smile, bidding them all goodnight as Kenneth led her from the building and helped her into the car.

Mrs. Worthington rushed to the car and knocked on the glass. "JeNelle, are those shoes Italian or Parisian?"

"I'm not sure, Mrs. Worthington, I'll have to get back to you on that."

Constance Worthington was indomitable, nonetheless giving a cheery wave, as Kenneth drove away. How Judge Worthington managed to survive thirty-plus years of his wife's effervescence was no less a miracle to Kenneth.

Kenneth and JeNelle drove to her home in near silence. It was clear to Kenneth that JeNelle was shaken by the experience with the three men. She was not herself. The sparkle that was ever present all evening seemed to have dulled. Kenneth parked the car in front of JeNelle's home.

"Would you come in for a night cap, Kenneth?"

"I'll stay for a few minutes, but you must be exhausted after a full day at work and then this evening. It's already little after two-thirty in the morning."

"Really, I'm not tired. I'd like the company."

Once inside, JeNelle poured two glasses of brandy and sat at one end of her sofa pit. She took off her shoes, loosened her hair, and let it fall to her shoulders.

"As usual, Kenneth, you managed to charm everyone in the room." She smiled warmly. "You had a lot of people trying to close deals with you tonight, I noticed."

"I apologize for that. It wasn't my intention to use this evening as a networking opportunity. I was enjoying the event with the most celebrated entrepreneur in San Barbara." He raised his snifter in toast and returned her smile.

"Nevertheless, you do have an effect on people. A very positive effect. Johnston Worthington was very impressed and it's not an easy task to impress him."

"I enjoyed talking with him and all of your friends and admirers. Your parents are wonderful people. They remind me so much of my own parents."

She leaned her head back against the sofa cushion and stretched her neck from side to side.

"Admirers," she said lowly, with some disdain.

Kenneth noted her tone and placed his brandy on a nearby table. He rose from his seat, positioned himself behind her, and began massaging her neck and shoulders. She closed her eyes and moaned lowly. Kenneth began to feel her tension dissipating. The soft light in the room caught the glint of her diamond earrings and Kenneth stopped the massage.

"Okay, lady," he joked. "That will be fifteen cents for fifteen minutes."

"You really drive a hard bargain, sir. Put it on my tab," she retorted with a smile. They laughed and talked for a while longer. Kenneth downed the last of his brandy and rose to leave.

"Do you really have to go so soon?" she asked her concern showing.

"Yes, it's very late. I don't want to wear out my welcome."

"You're perfectly welcome to stay here tonight. I have three spare bedrooms."

"Uh, thank you, but I'm already booked at the hotel and I want to work a little before I sleep."

"I can't thank you enough for being there tonight for me."

"It was my pleasure. I enjoyed myself. I'll see you at your office tomorrow morning before I leave and we'll finalize the deal."

Kenneth started to leave, but JeNelle caught his arm and hugged him tight. He cradled her in his arms and closed his eyes. He did not want to let her go now or ever. It felt so natural to be holding her in his arms. She kissed him on the cheek so close to his lips that he felt himself giving way to his emotions. He fought even harder and returned the kiss on her forehead.

"Get some rest, JeNelle. I'll see you later today."

As Kenneth drove back to the hotel, he replayed the evening in his mind. The vision of them dancing in the single beam of light took his attention away from the road. A car horn sounded and startled Kenneth back to reality. He swerved the car just in time to avoid a head-on collision and pulled to the side of the road. He put the car in park and leaned his head against the headrest. The scent of JeNelle's delicate perfume was still present in Benny's car. He looked at the rosebud in his lapel and shook the steering wheel violently.

"Get a grip, Alexander!" he shouted at himself. "Just one more day! You can do this! It's for Benny, remember!"

He started the car and drove to the hotel, determined to put everything, including JeNelle Towson, behind him.

The next day, Kenneth and JeNelle were leaving her office and Kenneth was putting the signed proposal in his briefcase when a woman he had not seen before called to JeNelle.

"Ms. Towson, there's a reporter on line three who wants some background information for an article she's doing on the Gala and your award."

"You handle it, Wanda. I'm going to walk this gentleman to his car."

Wanda picked up the telephone and said, "Ms. Towson asked me to give you any information that you need.... Yes, her escort was Mr. Alexander.... Yes, they've been seeing each other for some time now and he gave her diamonds for her birthday...You can describe it as spectacular.... He's always sending her flowers or cards and calling.... They get together as often as they can, I guess, but they live in different cities. He flew her up to San Francisco for five days last month. She stayed at his house in San Francisco, I think....How do I know? Well, because Mr. Alexander left that number with us, but once we tried to reach her and the answering machine said, 'This is the Alexander residence'. Her sister, Gloria, lives in his house in Washington, D.C., with his sister, Vivian, I think her name is. I think he has a condo in San Diego, too. I know because Gloria told me they stayed there.... Sure we all love him. He's so phine and sexy....Yes, they do make a great couple.... Yes, my name is Wanda Willis with two l's.... You're welcome and thank you for calling INSIGHTS."

Kenneth put his briefcase in the car and stood on the curb, talking with JeNelle.

"Kenneth, I really wish that you didn't have to go back to San Francisco so soon. I wanted an opportunity to take you on a tour of Santa Barbara. It doesn't compare with San Francisco, but it has its moments," JeNelle joked.

"Maybe another time, when Benny gets back, we can sit on your deck overlooking the ocean and you can serenade us on your piano."

"It's a deal then. Give my regards to Cecil and Janice when you see them later and to your staff, too. I got that gigantic thank you card they sent to me and please tell them that I miss them, too."

"I'll tell them, JeNelle. Juan will call you tomorrow about the installation of your new computer system and software programs. The Purchase Order should be completed within the next three to five days."

"Take care of yourself, Kenneth, and drive carefully."

She hugged him tightly and whispered, "And thank you for not asking."

Kenneth drove out of the city limits of Santa Barbara and onto the Pacific Coast Highway that would lead him back to San Diego. With the top down on Benny's convertible Benz, Kenneth prayed that the beauty of the landscape would erase JeNelle from his mind. Again, his prayers went unanswered.

He reached Benny's condo and parked the car in Benny's assigned spot. He noticed that Cecil's parking spot was empty. Cecil and Janice insisted on taking him to dinner at Michelangelo's and then to the airport. He went up to Benny's condo to await their call. He was standing on the terrace when the telephone rang.

"Hello, Benny? I'm glad I caught you! I've got to talk with you! It's very important!"

"Whoa, this isn't Benny. This is his brother, Kenneth. Benny's out of town."

"Oh, Kenneth, uh, hello, uh, this is Lieutenant Stacy Greene. I'm a friend of Benny's. It's imperative that I speak with him. Do you know where he is or when he'll be back?"

"No, Lieutenant, I don't know where he is. He left unexpectedly several days ago on some massive military maneuvers. He said that it will be four to six weeks before he gets back."

"Damn!" she muttered and then caught herself. "I'm sorry, Kenneth. I'm out at sea on those same maneuvers. I'll try to find him some other way. I'm sorry if I disturbed you."

"Not at all, Lieutenant. Sorry I couldn't be of more help."

They hung up and Kenneth returned to the terrace. Before he could sit down, the telephone rang again.

"Benny! I'm in deep trouble and I don't know what I'm going to do!"

"Vivian? Is that you? What's wrong? You sound terrible."

"Kenneth?" she squeaked. "Did I dial your number by mistake?"

"No, honey, I'm in San Diego at Benny's condo. He's not here. What's wrong?"

"Oh, uh, nothing much. Uh, I forgot to send the mortgage payment to the bank and, uh, I got an overdue notice. Uh, I have to pay late charges and uh, I'm a little short of cash." She lied to Kenneth, something that she had never done before.

"That doesn't sound like you, Vivian. You never forget details. How much do you need? I'll send it to you."

"Uh, I've been in with the flu and I just let things slip. No need for you to send money. When will Benny get back?"

"He said that it would be about four to six weeks."

"Four to six weeks?" she hoarsely screamed. "I'm dead!"

"Vivian, tell me how much you need. I'll put the money in your account today, immediately. You don't have to wait for Benny to take care of this problem."

"That's not necessary, Kenneth," she said, calmer. "Uh, I'll call you if I need the money immediately."

"Okay, Viv. Just let me know what you need and take care of that flu. You really sound terrible."

"Thanks, K.J. I love you."

"I love you, too, kid. Goodbye."

As soon as Kenneth sat down, the telephone rang a third time and Kenneth picked it up.

"This is Kenneth Alexander, not Benny Alexander. Benny is not here, so if you have any minor or major crises going on at the moment, you'll have to wait four to six weeks for him to return."

"Kenneth? This is Cecil," she said, laughing. "I already know all that. Benny's women must be giving you a fit. It sounds like we'd better get you to a bar real soon before you become unglued on us."

Kenneth laughed. "Sorry, Cecil, I've had two very strange telephone calls in the last few minutes. I'm ready to go. I'll meet you in the lobby in five minutes."

On the way to the airport after dinner, Kenneth stopped at an overnight mail service, wrote a check and sent it to Vivian with a note that read: *Love from one of your other brothers.*

*   *   *

Kenneth awoke late and looked at his clock. It was nearly nine-thirty in the morning. He bolted out of bed and rushed into the shower. He had no time for a cup of coffee or even time to read the paper. He dressed casually in just a sweater, jeans and some running shoes and sox. He grabbed the newspaper from the bushes alongside his driveway. He'd have to speak to the paperboy about his aim, he thought, and jumped into his SUV. He pushed a button on the radio and it automatically began to search the stations. He was looking for business news reports, but when the radio momentarily stopped on a jazz station, he heard the song, "You Are So Beautiful to Me." He stopped the search and listed, as he drove through the streets where he had wandered aimlessly for hours with JeNelle by his side.

There it was again; the vision of them dancing in the beam of light. He couldn't take it any longer. He continued the search for the news station before the music ended.

When he arrived at his office, the staff members were huddled together in small clusters. Sara noticed Kenneth come in the door and cleared her throat rather loudly, alerting the others of his arrival.

"Uh, good morning, Mr. Alexander. Welcome back. Did you have a good trip?" Sara asked more demonstratively than usual.

"Good morning, Sara," he answered, eyeing her curiously. "Yes, I did. Have there been any calls for me?"

The clusters broke and greeted him. Most of them were grinning at him strangely and scurried back to their appointed posts. Copies of newspapers were everywhere. He noticed that something was amiss, but didn't have time to talk to his staff members about it.

"Yes, sir," Sara said, turning on her computer, before going over the list of telephone calls and handing a stack of mail him to him. She had that same strange grin on her face that he witnessed on the faces of his other employees. Kind of moony-eyed with a soft sigh.

"What's going on, Sara? Is it the way that I'm dressed? Do I have shaving cream on my face? What?"

"Oh, no, Mr. Alexander." She perked up, straightening things on her already neat and tidy desk. "You look just fine as usual." Then she giggled and returned to her computer.

Kenneth shrugged, shook his head in confusion, and went to the lounge to get a cup of coffee. Other employees in the lounge snickered and grinned, as Kenneth passed by. He shook his head again. It wasn't as if he had never dressed casually for work before, he thought. He then went into his office and closed the door. He placed the stack of mail on his desk and opened his briefcase. Just as he was about to sit down, the door flew open and in walked Shirley and Tom.

"Way to go, old man!" Tom exuberantly shouted, extending his hand and with a broad smile on his face and a twinkle in his green eyes. "You sure do work fast!"

Shirley didn't look very happy, but Kenneth didn't bother to ask why. Kenneth assumed that Tom was referring to the signed proposal and Purchase

Order to install new computer equipment at JeNelle's store or the other deals he had closed in San Diego.

"Thanks, Tom. JeNelle was very pleased with the proposal. I've assured her that everything will be in place in three to five days. I was about to give the agreement to Juan when you two came in."

"The question is, Kenneth, old friend, old buddy, old pal, did she accept your proposal?" Tom asked with a twinkle in his eyes and a sly grin on his face.

Kenneth looked at him quizzically. "Of course she did, Tom. I just told you that. Weren't you listening?"

"So when's the wedding?" he asked jovially.

"That's a strange way to refer to a contractual agreement to install new computer equipment and software packages. What kind of joy juice have you been drinking?"

"Me?" Tom shouted. "What kind of joy juice did you give JeNelle to get her to agree to marry you?"

"*Marry me?*" Kenneth shouted. "What the hell are you talking about?"

"It's in all the newspapers, Kenneth!" Shirley said, slapping a copy of the *San Francisco Chronicle* newspaper down on Kenneth's desk. She seemed truly upset.

"What's in all the papers?" Kenneth picked up the newspaper. There it was again. A large picture of him and JeNelle dancing together in a beam of light gazing into each other's eyes. There were other snapshots of them together, talking and laughing with other guests at the Gala and one of him looking at her adoringly, as she gave her acceptance speech. Kenneth read the caption aloud:

THE WOMAN OF THE YEAR AND HER MAN FOR ALL SEASONS

Ms. JeNelle Towson, respected entrepreneur of INSIGHTS, President of the Santa Barbara Business and Professional Women's League, and a Member of the Santa Barbara Board of Directors for the Board of Trade, received the Woman of the Year Award from the Santa Barbara Chamber of Commerce at a Gala held in that city on Valentine's Day. She is pictured here with her adoring fiancée, Mr. Kenneth J. Alexander of San Francisco.

Mr. Alexander is the owner and Executive Director of CompuCorrect, Inc., a computer and information technology company, which recently received a very lucrative military contract and a contract to design, install, and service a new computer network for the San Francisco County's public schools and libraries.

Considering their very busy schedules, a reliable source confirmed that Ms. Towson and Mr. Alexander have been spending what precious little time they have together at Mr. Alexander's condo in San Diego and that he recently flew his bride-to-be to San Francisco for a five-day rendezvous—perhaps to purchase the engagement and wedding rings for Ms. Towson, and to purchase her trousseau.

Our sources also confirmed that Mr. Alexander frequently showers his future bride-to-be with flowers and cards. The same sources also confirmed that Mr. Alexander made a proposal to Ms. Towson, which she accepted. A source close to Ms. Towson described the diamond engagement and wedding rings as 'spectacular'.

Obviously, Ms. Towson and Mr. Alexander will become weary of the frequent flier miles that separate them. The question on everyone's mind is, 'who will move for love?' Will Mr. Alexander give up his very prosperous company and move to be with his true love or will she give up her very lucrative business to move to San Francisco to be with her Man for All Seasons? Or perhaps they both move to Washington, D.C., to his home in the fashionable Georgetown area. Their sisters, Vivian Alexander and Gloria Towson, are currently law school students and housemates at the Georgetown location—family ties are always so very important in these affairs of the heart.

The beautiful and charming Ms. Towson gave a powerful acceptance speech at the Gala with her fiancée at her side. The Honorable Judge Johnston White Worthington, Ms. Towson's close friend and mentor, seemed to bless the upcoming nuptials when he asked the handsome couple to take the floor and begin the dancing. Ms. Towson was a vision in her black lame sequenced gown and Mr. Alexander made a very handsome escort in his couture tuxedo with a single white rose in his lapel and his true love in his arms.

This reporter has it on good authority that the Governor has asked both Ms. Towson and Mr. Alexander to become members of his recently announced Blue Ribbon Panel on Youth in Business and Industry. From the looks of things, it doesn't appear that their rendezvous could come any too soon for this happy couple. Stay tuned for the continuing saga of JeNelle E. Towson and Kenneth J. Alexander."

Kenneth sat down with a thud, as if his legs had been cut off from under him. He could not believe what he had just read. He was dumbfounded.

* * *

Meanwhile, back in Santa Barbara, JeNelle was working in her office when Wanda rang her on the telephone.

"Yes, Wanda."

"Mrs. Johnston White Worthington, III, is on line one for you, Ms. Towson."

JeNelle braced herself. She knew that Constance Worthington was probably calling to find out who did her makeup or what brand of toothpaste she used.

"Good morning, Mrs. Worthington. How are you today?" she asked brightly.

"I'm fine, JeNelle, but please, do call me Constance."

"Certainly, Constance. What can I do for you today?"

"I just want to know who's going to do your gown? Johnston and I want to give you a formal engagement party as soon as we can arrange it. You sure can keep a secret, JeNelle. Oh, hold on, Johnston wants to talk with you."

"JeNelle, congratulations!" his voice boomed through the telephone. "I'm so very happy for you and Kenneth. He's a fine man. I was extremely impressed with him and he's a perfect choice for you. In fact, I'm going to meet with him and see if he won't consider redesigning the judicial intrastate computer network. Install that Internet stuff, you know? He had some excellent ideas for improvements. Still, I'm disappointed that you didn't let me in on your secret. You haven't even mentioned that you were dating again. That's all right, though. I'll forgive you this time, but Constance and I insist on giving you and Kenneth an engagement party. When can we arrange it?"

"Johnston, what the hell are you talking about? Engagement party—for what? I'm not engaged."

"Oh, you can tell me now, JeNelle. It's all over today's newspaper. Haven't you seen it?"

"Today's paper?' she asked just above a whisper. "What's in today's newspaper?"

"Look at the front page of the Style Section, JeNelle. It's all there in black and white." Then he whispered lowly, "Have you told Kenneth what happened to you when you were younger? I truly believe that you should tell him before you're married. As I said, he's a fine man and I know that he'll understand." Now raising his voice to a normal tone. "I've got to run now, but I'll give you a call later and we'll arrange to have lunch. I want to talk with you about what happened at the Gala. Goodbye, for now."

Judge Worthington hung up and JeNelle sat for a minute in complete and utter confusion looking at the telephone in her hand. Then suddenly she leaped from her desk and started tearing up her office looking for the newspaper. She rarely read the Style Section unless she had placed a store ad in the paper. She found it in her trash can below a half consumed cup of cold coffee, the torn stockings that she had to replace, and a mountain of shredded paper that she had discarded that day. Finally, she found it and began reading the cover story. She batted her eyes to make sure that she was reading what was actually printed. Her mouth dropped open.

"Where the hell did this come from?" she asked aloud in absolute amazement and sheer terror. She thought about the details reported in the newspaper. Then she recalled Wanda telling her that a reporter was on the telephone and telling Wanda to handle the call.

"Wanda!" she screamed at the top of her lungs, as she opened her office window. People in the store were startled and Wanda cringed. "Wanda Willis, you get into my office, now!" she bellowed.

Wanda was frightened out of her wits. She had never seen JeNelle angry ever. She couldn't imagine what she had done. Except, perhaps, that she had taken a long lunch hour or she was late getting to work one day last week. Her mind raced, as she very timidly approached JeNelle.

"Yes, Ms. Towson?" she asked in a barely audible whisper, as JeNelle slammed the door behind her. "Ms. Towson, I'm sorry I was late coming back from lunch the other day and I'll make up the time because I was late coming to work and—"

"Wanda, be quiet and read this!" JeNelle said sternly, as she handed the newspaper to her.

Wanda read the article and her mouth flew open and her eyes widened. "Ms. Towson, I didn't know that you were getting married and who's this Kenneth Alexander? I thought you were dating Benny, I mean Captain Benjamin Alexander."

"I'm not getting married, Wanda!" she said still very angry.

"But it says so right here in the newspaper, Ms. Towson," Wanda said, pointing to the article.

"Never mind what it says in the paper, Wanda! What I want to know is: did you give this story to that reporter who called?"

"No, Ms. Towson, I mean, uh, yes, I did say that Mr. Alexander was your escort, but I thought the reporter was talking about Captain Alexander. Who is Kenneth?"

"Kenneth is Captain Alexander's brother and he escorted me to the Gala, not Benjamin!"

"I didn't know that. I thought Benny was taking you. You're going to marry this Kenneth instead of Benjamin—he is good looking and he's built real well—"

"Wanda, stop tripping! I'm not getting married to Benjamin or Kenneth! You got that?!"

"But the article says, Ms. Towson—"

"You saw Mr. Alexander the day of the gala, didn't you? He walked the showroom floor and talked with the employees."

"No, see, it was like this, that day, I had my dentist appointment? Are you sure that you're not going to marry him?"

"Wanda, go back to work…*n o w!*" JeNelle railed, pointing an arrow-straight finger toward the door.

Wanda left the office and, as she closed the door and went down the steps, the other employees rushed to hear what was going on. She told them to read the Style Section and then said soberly, "I don't know what's going on. All I can say is believe half of what you see and none of what you read. It's all so confusing."

So many people were calling JeNelle to congratulate her and she had to repeat her denial so many times that she finally gave up and refused to accept any more calls. The same thing was going on at CompuCorrect. Finally, Kenneth told Sara to hold all of his calls. When Sara rang him again, Kenneth was not pleased.

"Sara, I told you to hold all calls!"

"It's your fiancée, Mr. Alexander, on line 2."

"*My what?* Oh, all right, Sara, but Ms. Towson is not my fiancée!"

"Whatever you say, Mr. Alexander, but she's still on line 2."

"JeNelle, this is Kenneth. Have you seen today's newspaper?"

"It's not JeNelle, Kenneth. It's Lisa. Lisa Lambert in the Governor's office. I had to use a little subterfuge to get past your receptionist. Sorry about that."

Kenneth expelled a weary breath. "Lisa, I haven't had time to consider the Governor's offer yet. It's been a little crazy around here today."

"I can imagine," she said and laughed. "The Governor and I have been talking about your impending marriage to JeNelle Towson and we think that a husband and wife team would be a real asset on the Blue Ribbon Panel. Could we release an item to the press stating that you'll be expecting your first born by Christmas or is that a little premature?" She teased and laughed again.

"Lisa, the article is a complete fabrication. JeNelle and I aren't engaged. Actually, she's seeing my brother and when he sees this, he's going to go ballistic!"

"Can't he take a joke?" She laughed again.

"A joke? Lisa, this is really no laughing matter!" Kenneth said annoyed.

"Calm down, Kenneth. I've already talked with JeNelle and she's hopping mad, too. She's not concerned with how your brother is going to take this news. She's concerned about what impact this is going to have on you and your business. The article implies that you might be willing to leave your company and move to Santa Barbara to be with her. She's worried that your clients might see that as a betrayal or that your company is unstable."

"I'm not worried about that. CompuCorrect will survive this, but Benny and JeNelle are just starting their relationship."

"JeNelle said that she and your brother are merely friends, but she doesn't want to be the cause of any dissension between you two over the article. The Governor and I both had a good laugh about the whole thing. We knew that the report was false, but it sure got a lot of good press for the program."

"I'm glad that you and the Governor were amused," Kenneth said sarcastically, "but if JeNelle and I don't take some kind of action, this whole thing could get blown out of proportion."

"Let me give you some unsolicited advice, Kenneth, from someone who has to deal with the press and news media on a daily basis. Don't do anything. This will all blow over in a few days. I told JeNelle the same thing. She was ready to file suit against the newspaper and the reporter. That only adds fuel to the fire. If the press sees a spark, they'll fan it into a raging inferno. Just let your family and friends know the truth. Everyone else will forget in time."

"I'll have to talk with JeNelle about this before I do anything, but I do appreciate the advice."

"Good. Then are we still on for our meeting this week?"

"Sure, but I can't promise you that I'm going to agree to anything."

"I'll see you on Wednesday, 1:00 P.M. at Lion d'Or, Private Dining Room A."

Kenneth checked his calendar on his computer.

"All right, Lisa. See you Wednesday."

Kenneth called JeNelle, but she wasn't taking any calls.

"Tell Ms. Towson that it's her fiancé, Kenneth Alexander."

The person answering the telephone gasped and then a pause before she made the connection.

"Kenneth, have you lost your mind? I've been trying to convince my staff and everyone else all day that you're not...I mean, that we're not.... oh, you know what I mean . . ." she said, flustered. "And then you call and say you're my...Oh, Kenneth, what a mess! I'm so sorry. I was too embarrassed to call you. I just didn't know what to say."

Kenneth laughed. "I've never heard you at a loss for words, JeNelle."

"But, Kenneth, what is this going to do to your business?" she asked with great concern.

"Don't worry about that, but how are we going to explain all of this to Benny?"

"*Benny?*" she shouted. "What's Benny got to lose? You could lose clients and business opportunities over this!" JeNelle said, obviously annoyed.

"He may think that he could lose you, JeNelle. I don't think he's going to be very understanding."

"Lose me? Benny doesn't have me to lose, Kenneth! We're just friends and if he blames you in any way for this fiasco, he and I won't even be friends! I will not be the cause of any problems between you and Benny."

"Let's hope that by the time Benny gets back, this whole thing will have blown over and we won't have to mention it to him."

"I've already received a call from Cecil and Janice who thought that this whole thing was hilarious. I'm sure that he'll hear about it from them and others, as soon as he returns."

"Then we will have to face him together and explain what really happened."

"No, Kenneth, this is my problem. I'll deal with it myself. I don't want to drag you into this any deeper. Benny will have to understand that you were doing a favor for me and that neither one of us had any control over what happened.... I mean, any control over how that reporter completely misread the situation."

"I'll follow your lead, JeNelle, but I know my brother. I may have to talk with him in any event, but I'll see how that goes."

"You're really wonderful not to be upset with me about the mess I've caused."

"You didn't cause it, JeNelle, the reporter did. I spoke with Lisa Lambert earlier. She put it in perspective and gave me what I think is some good advice. She told me that she had already spoken with you."

"Yes, she did call and I was calmer after we spoke."

"I'm meeting with her Wednesday. What can you tell me about her?"

"Lisa? Well, I haven't known her that long. She and I are members of the same Business and Professional Women's organization. I can tell you that she is very bright and competent. She has her undergraduate degree in Economics from the Wharton School of Business at Penn State, her MBA from Michigan and her PhD in Economics from Harvard. She's single, maybe thirty or thirty-one, and a real political animal. She's a mover and shaker. She had a stellar career at the Brookings Institute and then the ultra-conservative Heritage Foundation in Washington, D.C., until the Governor asked her to handle his economic agenda. If anyone should be guiding our economic policy, she should. She's dynamic, direct and astute. Real political savvy. Everyone I know has nothing but good things to say about her economic vision. She has some of the best contacts in the country and she knows everything there is to know about everyone. She doesn't take no for an answer and she gets what she goes after."

"I was correct, she is formidable."

"What have you decided to do about the Blue Ribbon Panel?"

"I'm not convinced that I can afford that kind of investment of my time at this point. We're getting a lot of new business and we're bringing in new staff people this week. I haven't rejected the idea. I thought that perhaps Tom or Shirley would be available and like the opportunity to sit on such a prestigious Panel. I'll have to discuss this with them before I make a decision. The program that Lisa briefly outlined for me is definitely worthwhile and I know that I can give the Panel my whole-hearted support, if not my time. I'll decide before I meet with Lisa."

"I'm glad that you're keeping an open mind about this, Kenneth."

"I'll see how things are after I talk with my partners."

When Kenneth and JeNelle hung up, Shirley knocked on Kenneth's door.

"Kenneth, I see you're off the telephone. May I see you for a minute?"

"Sure, Shirley. Please come in."

"I'd like to talk with you about the article in the newspaper."

"It's not true, Shirley. I thought I'd made that clear with you, Tom, and the rest of the staff earlier today. I even framed the article, hung it in the reception area with a sign across it that says, '*It's Not True*'."

"I know that, Kenneth, but how do you think Benny is going to take this report?"

"Not well, I'm sure, but JeNelle is going to handle it with Benny and she's threatening to dissolve their relationship if she believes that it will cause dissension between me and him."

"Then that would leave them both available to see other people?"

"I suppose it would, Shirley, but I thought that you weren't interested in my brother. He's tried to date you several times, I understand, and he's under the impression that you're not interested in him."

"He's right, I mean, Benny is a great guy, but he's not my type."

"Then I'm not sure I understand why you would be concerned about whether he's free to date other women. Do you know of someone else who is interested in him?"

"That's it. Someone I know is interested in dating Benny," she lied.

"Well, Benny is very interested in JeNelle Towson. I'm not sure where their relationship stands at this point, but tell your friend not to be too optimistic. JeNelle Towson is, as you've witnessed, a wonderful woman. Benny would be a fool not to care very deeply about her, and my brother is no fool."

"What about JeNelle? How does she feel about him?"

"I can't speak for JeNelle. Given time, Benny will either succeed or fail on his own merits, but I think that JeNelle will see what a fine man he is and perhaps give him an opportunity to show her that he does have 'socially redeeming qualities', as he puts it."

Kenneth laughed.

"What's so funny, Kenneth?"

"Something my brother said about my water bill."

"I don't understand."

"Don't try to understand, Shirley. It's a brother thing."

"Kenneth, are you working late tonight? I thought we might have dinner and see a movie or something."

"I'm afraid I can't tonight, Shirley. I have a lot to catch up on. I also need to speak with you and Tom later about a plan the Governor has for getting young people involved in business and industry. He's asking me to participate on a Blue Ribbon Panel."

"Then there was truth in the article. You and JeNelle will both be on the Panel."

"The program was JeNelle's idea so, of course, she's planning to do it. I haven't decided yet. I'm scheduled to meet with Dr. Lisa Lambert, the Governor's economic advisor on Wednesday. I want to discuss it with you and Tom before that. I have to consider a number of factors before I decide. We'll talk later, if that's all right with you, but right now, I need to get back to work. Is there anything else that we need to discuss immediately?"

"No, anything else can wait. We'll talk later."

Chapter 19

"You have a bogey at one o'clock, Explorer!" Benny remembered his Captain saying years earlier, as he flew his F-15C Eagle fighter at thirty thousand feet over Iraq. Then Benny was a lieutenant, fresh out of flight school. He was honored to have been chosen as one of the pilots for the 1st Tactical Wing of the 71st Tactical Fighter Squadron.

He had just flown over the Euphrates and Tigris Rivers when he saw cities all lit up before him. The Captain was leading them on a hunt for Iraqi aircraft and they found their prey. Captain took out the first aerial kill and now it was Benny's turn to score at airspeeds approaching six hundred knots. AWACS confirmed the bogey and Benny armed his weapons. He was carrying four Sidewinder infrared, heat seeking missiles, four Sparrow radar-guided missiles, and nine hundred forty rounds of twenty-millimeter ammunition. Benny jettisoned his external fuel tanks and prepared to fight. He pulled into a two-hundred-seventy-degree right turn to maneuver into position in front of the target. Benny called out to the leader, "I've got signal lock on the bandit at twenty-six Km." The Iraqi Mirage F1 showed up inside the target box of Benny's Heads-up Display projected on the windshield. "This is the Explorer firing the Sparrow." The rocket hit its target and within moments a huge engulfing fire billowed up.

Since that time years earlier, Benny had flow F-4 Phantom fighters, EF-111 Ravens and the Navy and Marine #A-6B Prowler. Now he was leading his own team in realistic combat training. Benny had flown hundreds of sorties in Iraq and Afghanistan. Now it was up to him to teach his team what he learned. In a six-week period, Benny had flown thirty-five missions logging over two hundred combat hours. His was a crack team. It gave new meaning to the phrase, "Benny and the Jets." The team, lead by The Explorer, performed extremely well during combat of this all-out, all services, military surge on the Pacific Rim. Now he was leading his team home.

As they flew over cruisers, destroyers, and frigates on the vast ocean below them, Benny noticed the battleships USS Idaho and the USS Arkansas, and he knew that Stacy Greene was aboard one of the ships below him. The Navy had conducted amphibious landings and assaults. Benny knew Stacy would be heading up any anti-submarine radar surveillance and electronic jamming. Also targeting information to feed into the guidance system of Tomahawk missiles and drones. That's what she had trained so diligently for when he met her that late night in the Pentagon cafeteria. And she was one of the best at what she did. She was well respected by her peers who learned to trust her judgment without question. To them, she was a top-notch Navy officer who happened to be a woman, but to him she was much, much more.

He looked at boundless blue sky ahead of his aircraft and visualized Stacy. Suddenly, he wanted her more than anything, but he reminded himself that she wouldn't consent to be his and his alone. He broached the subject with her often enough, but each time she turned him down and then proceeded to sap every ounce of energy from him when she made love to him. He didn't want to press his luck and say something stupid like I love you. He knew that would send her running for cover. She was a woman who could not be boxed or handled. She was independent and confident; very direct and often uncompromising. She had a career that she loved, and, as she often told him, that's all she needed or wanted. He gritted his teeth, as he flew, recalling that she had rejected him yet again. The time away from her was painful, but now he had a new perspective. Stacy had pulled away from him. He would focus on building a new relationship with JeNelle. Perhaps JeNelle's defense mechanisms wouldn't be as strong as Stacy's. Maybe he could find the love that he wanted from Stacy in a relationship with JeNelle. For sure, the torture that he felt had to end. Mentally and emotionally, he had to move on.

"Heads up, this is The Explorer! Mission accomplished, we're heading home! Let's push this envelope one more time!"

"Roger that, Captain. San Diego here we come!" One of Benny's pilots said.

"Yeah, I got a blond bombshell waiting for me at the Hootenanny on Elvira, table 6," another pilot said joyously with fervor.

"Bet you got that pretty Navy lieutenant waiting for you too, Captain! Man! Some people have all the luck! Sure wish she was waiting for me! I'd get out and push this baby all the way home!" another pilot said, laughing.

"This is The Explorer, cut the chatter! We've still got work to do! Let's get it done. Roll the ball and let her rip!"

Benny's team fell into position behind him at nine hundred knots and flew their usual triumphant pattern with wing tips inches apart approaching the landing strip.

"Explorer, this is ComSAC Base. Good Show! You've got the ball. Bring them in, Explorer."

"Roger that, ComSAC Base. I'm reading you five-by-five. Benny and the Jets are coming home."

The team set down in perfect, textbook style and rolled to their respective ground crews who were all standing and ready to receive the F-15C Eagle fighters. Cheers went up from the ground crews, as Benny and his pilots emerged from their aircrafts. Benny was proud of his team. They won the highest commendations of the simulated combat military training series against twenty-six other teams involved in the drill. There were handshakes, pats on the back, and well-wishers, as he led his team to the debriefing session.

This had been a long drill. In a few days, he would be back at his condo and back with JeNelle. He had not permitted himself to focus on her during the time that he was away. He worked himself and his team into a near state of exhaustion to avoid the dreams of her that would seep into his sleep, as he lay alone on a bunk in the officers' quarters at Hickam AFB in Hawaii. But now the excitement began to grow. He was feeling the rush. Not just from flying, but from visualizing JeNelle in his mind, in his arms and in his bed.

He and his team had a ten-day liberty pass coming, as soon as they hit March Air Force Base. Benny began to plan how he would spend that time with JeNelle. He called a ski resort in Vail, Colorado, to check on the availability of a suite or a chalet. He was taking no chances. The suite he ordered had two bedrooms, a living room with a fireplace and a kitchenette, wet bar and liquor cabinet. It overlooked the North Slope where he visualized himself with JeNelle on the night run down the slopes. He ordered flowers to be sent to her at the store and more to be placed in the room, with a light dinner and a magnum of Champaign. He called the airport and reserved a plane. He would fly to Santa Barbara, pick up JeNelle, and fly to Vail; all in the space of a few hours. He wanted his reunion with JeNelle to ignite into a relationship like what he had with Stacy, an intimate relationship, and he was setting the stage for that to happen.

Benny contacted his allies on JeNelle's staff to work out the details of freeing her from the store. Barry was willing to help by covering the store and Wanda knew how to work JeNelle's schedule. He would be home soon to put his plan into action. He would check his mail, call his family, shower and change, pack his clothes, grab his skis and gear, and be on his way. He only had one mission in mind and that mission was JeNelle Eliese Towson.

The cab let Benny out in front of his condo. Fred greeted him and handed him stacks of mail.

"You've been away a long time, Captain Alexander. You have a huge stack of Valentine's Day cards. The postman said he couldn't get it all in your mailbox. You also received these boxes of candy and a lot of flowers and balloons. I had to throw the flowers and balloons away, but I saved all the cards that came with them and I wrote down exactly what each woman sent to you—either the balloons or flowers. Oh, and your brother, Kenneth, told me to tell you that he left your car keys on the bar in your media room. Real nice man, your brother. Dr. Jordon and Dr. Atterly kinda took him under their wings while he was here. They said they want to see you soon as you get back."

"Thanks, Fred. I would appreciate it if you wouldn't mention to anyone that I'm back in town. I'm just going to be here for a few hours and then I'll be gone for the rest of the week."

"Sure thing, Captain, but what should I tell Dr. Jordon and Dr. Atterly?"

Benny took some money out of his pocket, palmed it, and shook Fred's hand.

"I'm sure you'll think of something, Fred."

Fred peeked at the gratuity and smiled broadly. "You got it, Captain!"

As soon as he entered his condo, Benny dropped his flight gear on the floor. He glanced at the envelopes of the Valentine's Day cards he received. Nothing from Stacy. *That's odd*, he thought. Then he finally found something else that he was looking for; a card from JeNelle. He dropped all of the other mail and the boxes of candy on his desk and tore open the card. The front of the card was very elegant, Benny thought, but he was disappointed at the inscription inside, which read:

Dear Benny,
Thank you for all that you did for me to make
my exhibit at the Expo a huge success and arranging for your brother to be my escort. You
are a true friend and I owe you one. Have a
Happy Valentine's Day.
Your friend,
JeNelle

It wasn't gratitude that he wanted from JeNelle. But he would change all of that with this surprise trip to Vail. He checked his answering machine. There were forty-two messages. He was exhausted though and did not bother to read any of the other mail or listen to the messages. Instead, he decided to take a short nap before he left to be with JeNelle. He flipped through his CD collection and found one of Stacy's favorites, Al Jarreau. He slid it into the CD player and crawled into bed.

Benny had only been asleep for an hour when the telephone rang. He was tempted not to answer it. No one knew that he was there except Fred. He waited for the answering machine to pick up the call.

"Benny, if you're there, please pick up the telephone. It's Stacy and it's urgent that I talk with you right away."

She sounded upset so Benny picked up the telephone.

"I'm here, Stacy. What's so urgent?" he asked groggily.

"This is not something we should discuss over the telephone. May I come over now?"

See her? He couldn't see her and not want to touch her. Not want to make love to her. He was trying to respect her decision to back away from a sexual relationship with her. He couldn't very well do that if he was with her. No matter how hard he had tried, not loving Stacy was impossible to fathom. Never the less, he had to try. "I'm going away for a few days. Can this wait until I get back?"

"No, I need to talk with you now. Immediately."

"You're not going to tell me that you're a deserter or something, are you?"

"No, but this is just as important."

When he heard the hitch in her voice, alarms went off in his head. Stacy never asked him for anything before. It wasn't in her nature to do so. If she actually needed him for anything, he would always be there for her. "All right, come on over. I'm going to take a shower. I'll tell Fred to send you straight up and I'll leave the door unlocked. How long before you get here?"

"I'll be there in fifteen minutes."

"See you then, Stacy."

Benny got out of bed and put on some more CD's to play while he showered. He was singing "Just the Two of Us" at the top of his lungs when he heard the telephone ring. It was Fred announcing that he was sending Stacy up to his condo. Benny put the shaving cream on his face and he was almost finished when the doorbell sounded. He pushed the intercom button.

"Come on in, Stacy," he said still humming and shaving. "I'm upstairs."

Stacy came up the steps and into his bedroom. She stood by the bathroom door, as Benny continued to shave. He quickly looked at her. She really looked upset to him, but he was trying hard not to think about her. Rather, he steeled himself to focus on JeNelle.

"Now what's so urgent, Stacy? You sounded very upset on the telephone."

"I'm pregnant."

Benny never noticed the pain when he cut himself on the chin. Red blood mixed with the white saving cream and dripped onto his bare chest. He looked at Stacy, excitement building in his body. A baby! Something shifted in his world. Suddenly he felt happier than he had ever felt before in his life. He was going to be a father. Stacy Greene was going to be his and they were going to have a family!

"Are you sure?" he asked, his voice just above a whisper. When she nodded, a smile began to bloom on his face.

"I'm sure, yes. The damn rabbit died twice," she groaned.

Benny wiped the remaining shaving cream and blood off his face and chest, went to Stacy, and held her at arm's length and searched her face. He could barely contain his enthusiasm. Unbelievable joy nearly took his breath away. Lifting her in his arms, he found her sweet mouth. All was suddenly right in his universe. "How did this happen? We always use condoms and you're on the pill."

Stacy wiggled out of his arms and began to pace. "When I shipped out in a hurry for that three-day tour of duty, I forgot my pills. I was so engrossed in the mission that I really didn't think about it. We didn't use condoms the last time we were together; remember when we were on the stairs? We went bareback. That's the only time that it could have happened. I haven't slept with anyone else."

"When did you find out?" he asked, beaming; loving more and more the thought that his baby was growing inside the woman he loved. He reached for her, but she stepped away from him.

"Shortly after you left for The Surge. I had to ship out the next day," she said, sulking, her hands dug deep into the pockets of her uniform. She began to pace again.

"That was four or five weeks ago. Why didn't you get in touch with me?" It was beginning to annoy him that each time he tried to touch her she would move out of his reach.

"I tried, Benny!" she snapped, spraying her hands. "I called you here. Your brother answered and said that you were already gone. Then I tried to reach you on CommNet, but they would only permit emergency calls to go through. I got in touch with J.C. Baker, but even he wouldn't get a message to you. He told me that your team was in the number one position and that you were in line for highest honors. He said that unless it was a matter of life or death he didn't want you distracted. I wouldn't tell him why I needed to talk with you so I just gave up trying. I know what your career and your team mean to you. Colonel Baker was right. You didn't need to be distracted. And this is a hell of a distraction."

Finally, Stacy stopped moving long enough for him to pull her into his embrace, rocking her gently. He could not have been happier.

"The fact that we're going to have a baby is a new and very exciting feeling for me to digest, but I certainly would have wanted to know about it as soon as possible. I'm sorry that you had such a hard time getting in touch with me."

Stacy backed away from Benny and looked him straight in the eyes. "I said, I'm pregnant, Benny. I didn't say anything about having a baby," she said, frowning.

Benny stepped back. What was she talking about? "You just told me that you're carrying our baby inside you. Of course we're going to have it."

"Are you crazy? No, Benny, I want to have an abortion," Stacy said emphatically.

It took a moment for her statement to register. The smile slipped from his face. "*What?* You can't be serious about this!" Benny's ire was building. The veins in his neck stood out in stark relief and pulsated.

"Oh hell yes I am! You can take that to the bank!" she shouted and began to pace again.

"Forget it, Stacy!" he hissed. Turning on his heels, he marched to his audio system and switched off the music. "It ain't happening! No abortion! No way! No how!"

"I'm not ready to have a baby and neither are you!" she implored.

"I'll be ready by the time our baby is born!" he snapped.

"I won't be!" she snapped back.

Stacy was clearly upset, Benny noted. This highly emotional argument couldn't be good for their baby.

"An abortion is the only option," she continued. "I need your moral support, not your permission to do this. The longer I wait, the more dangerous it becomes to go through the procedure. I've found a reputable doctor to do it and I've already paid for it. I've got a ten-day leave. According to the clinic that should be more than enough time to recuperate after the procedure. No one else knows about this except you and I want to keep it that way. No one, not even your family. I'm asking you to give me the moral support that I need to get through this."

His look was incredulous. Could she really believe that he would go along with this craziness? "Believe me when I tell you that there is nothing that you could ask of me that I wouldn't do for you in an instant, but not this. An abortion is *not* the only option and, from my perspective, it's not even a consideration at all!" He had to calm himself and her, too. Taking a cleansing breath, he decided to try to reason with her. "You're not looking at this thing clearly and I don't think that you're considering my feelings in this at all. Stacy, I want our baby. I don't want you to have an abortion. Trust me, please. We will work this out together."

Stacy threw up her hands in frustration. "You are the one who can't be thinking about this clearly!" Ticking off reasons on her fingers, she continued. "First, we're not in love with each other. Second, this baby was conceived in lust. Third, I damn near raped you! And finally, do I have to remind you that it was JeNelle you were thinking about while we were having sex? I can guarantee that having a baby with another woman is *not* the way to endear yourself to JeNelle."

That last comment hurt because it was partially true. He was thinking about JeNelle. She was wrong, though, about whether he was in love or in lust. She never would have been able to seduce him if he wasn't in love with her. This was not the time to tell Stacy how much he was in love with her. She would never believe him now. The issue was their baby. He may never win Stacy's love, but he'd be damned if he'd give up their child. "Our baby won't know or care whether she or he was conceived in love or lust! All that our baby will need is two parents to love and take good care of him or her. And, Stacy, that's us. You and me!"

"We can't have a baby together! What would we do with a baby?!"

"Raise it, Stacy! You and me together! We did this together. You weren't the only one there, you know. I was there, too, and I'm very happy about this."

"*What?* Think about what you're saying! We're in the military at the beginning of what may end up as two very successful careers! We can't just throw all of that away now!"

"We aren't throwing anything away. We can both still have interesting careers. There are thousands of people in the military, including the Air Force and the Navy, raising their children and having successful careers. Why should we be any different? Sure, we'll have to make some adjustments. I understand what you're feeling. I love what I do, too. I enjoy my life and my career, but I'd sacrifice all of that in a heartbeat for our baby."

"I care about you and what you think and feel, but the sacrifice is too great for me to even consider. I don't want my life to change now. Especially not now. I've got to think about my future. I can't do this to a child. I'm not mother material. God! I don't even have a frame of reference because my mother left us when I was very young!"

"You are important to me, too. I know about babies. I helped raise my sisters and brother. It's not that hard. You just have to give them a lot of love and everything will work out," he pleaded.

"No! I'm not even going to consider this! I don't even want to talk about it anymore!"

"Tough! We are going to discuss this until you understand how important having our baby is to me!"

"I believe you. I know what family means to you. I thought of not telling you and simply going through with the abortion alone. I couldn't do that to you, especially after I made such a big deal about friendship. You had a right to know about this, but I expected you to support my decision to have an abortion and not try to change my mind."

"How could you even consider not telling me and why in the world do you think that I'd support you in having an abortion? If you had the abortion and didn't tell me, in my view, you would have been lying to me! Hiding the truth! And we don't lie to each other, Stacy! We never have and we never will!" He took a more conciliatory tone. "Look, we are on opposite ends of the spectrum on this, but we only have to figure out *how* to work this out."

"To you, 'work it out' means to have this baby, Benny, but it means not having this baby to me! There is no way to reconcile that!"

Before Benny could answer, the telephone rang. Benny and Stacy had been shouting at each other and they were both feeling frustrated. Benny ignored it until he heard Barry Kennedy say, in a whisper, "Benny, JeNelle is back in the store. She'll be here until closing at 9:00 P.M. If you're going to put your plan into action, meet me at the store before closing and—"

Benny picked up the telephone. "Barry, this is Benny. I've had to change my plans. I'm not coming up to Santa Barbara tonight. I'll get in touch with you later."

"Is something wrong, Benny? You sound upset."

"I'm all right, Barry, or at least I will be very soon."

"Okay, Benny, let me know what I can do to help."

"Thanks, Barry."

Benny hung up and looked at Stacy. There were both drained. They never raised their voices at each other or had an argument before. Moreover, he was worried about what the stress of their argument might do to their child. Benny was agitated and he paced the room contemplating the situation. They were both calmer, but the frustration was still present. Stacy stood up and started to leave.

"Where do you think you're going?" Benny asked when Stacy moved toward the bedroom door.

She didn't turn to look at him. "I'm sorry, Benny," she said more calmly. "You did tell me that you were going away. I didn't mean to keep you this long. I'll take care of this alone."

"I'm not going anywhere, Stacy, and neither are you! Take off your coat and hat, get comfortable! What do you want to eat for dinner? I'll order whatever you want. Sorry no alcohol for you, but I'm having a beer!"

Benny dressed in a pair of sweat pants and a t-shirt. He walked down the steps to his living room and over to the wet bar. Stacy slowly followed him.

"Who can eat at a time like this? We're both upset. I should go. Think about what I said. I'll call you—"

"You got a problem with short-term memory or something? I said you're not going anywhere until you agree to have our baby. Now I'm hungry," he said after he swallowed half of his Corona. "All of a sudden I'm starving and you will be, too! I'm on leave and so are you! If we have to stay in this condo throughout the entire time to work this out, that's what we are going to do!"

"You have not been listening to me! I'm not going to have this baby!"

"You haven't been listening to *me!* You're going to have *our* baby! Not 'this' baby! Not just your baby, but *our* baby!"

He calmed himself, approached her, and guided her toward a chair in the living room. "If you're not hungry, then you can sit here and watch me eat. If you're tired, take a nap. You know where the bed is. Until we agree on this, you're stuck with me!"

The telephone rang again and again Benny ignored it until he heard his sister's voice.

"Benny? Are you there? Pick up the telephone if you are, it's important."

Benny picked up the telephone. "Hi, Viv. What's wrong? You sound strange."

"I'm in trouble."

"What kind of trouble?"

"I'm pregnant." There was a long pause. "Benny, are you still there?"

"There is definitely something in the air!" he said under his breath. "Vivian, how did this happen?"

"Of all people, Benny, I shouldn't have to draw a picture for you. Suffice it to say, it was not the Immaculate Conception! And what's with this 'in the air' business?"

"You certainly don't have to explain how it happened. I am completely familiar with the process...especially tonight. The question that I'm trying to ask is: why did it happen? Weren't you and Carlton using protection?"

"Every time! We never made love without it! I don't know why it happened!"

"How is Carlton taking the news?"

"I haven't told him. Only you and Chuck know about this."

"Why haven't you told Carlton and who is Chuck?"

"I'll explain about Chuck later, but I'm afraid to tell Carlton. This is just what he would want to happen. He's been pressing me about setting a wedding date."

"You love him and trust him, don't you?"

"Of course...well, maybe I do."

"You don't sound very convincing, but, nevertheless, you have to tell him about this. You can't keep something like this from him. He has a right to know."

"And then what?"

"And then you'll work it out."

"Work it out?" she shouted. "I'm in my first year of law school. Work it out means I have to have an abortion. It's killing me to even think of doing that."

Where have I heard this before? Benny wondered rhetorically.

"You can't think only of yourself, Vivian. You have to include Carlton in on this decision. Look at it this way. You love him and trust him and he feels the same way about you. Could you face him if you had an abortion and didn't tell him?"

"No," she said somberly.

"Then I think that you know what you have to do."

"Benny, I can't do this by myself. I know that it's asking a lot, but would you meet me at home? If I've got to do this, I need your moral support."

"Yes, I can do that. In fact, that will work out fine, Viv. I've just decided tonight to go home anyway. When can you be there?"

"Whenever you can be there."

"I'm on a ten-day pass, but I have some things to work out myself. I'll meet you there on Friday. How is that for you?"

"That's fine. I'll drive down on Friday morning. I'll see Carlton before I come home to talk to Dad and Mom. I can't tell Kenneth about this yet. I lied to him and he's not going to be happy with me at all, especially since he sent money to me when I really didn't need it."

"Do you want me to talk with him for you?"

"No. It's my responsibility. I have to do that myself. I'd rather face Mom and Dad first and build up to K.J. He's going to crucify me."

"He loves you, honey, but I've got your back if he comes down on you."

"You always do and I love you for it. I needed to know that you're in my corner."

"I'll always be in your corner, Vivian, no matter what. Now who is this Chuck?"

"Charles Montgomery. He's the skiing-cowboy, second-year resident doctor who I told you about. Remember, the one who brought me home from the airport in the blizzard?"

"You don't mean Chucky Montgomery, the guy who played at Boston College and then played pro ball, do you?"

"Yeah, that's the one. Why? Do you know him?"

"Sure I do. I played against him in the Boston Shootout back in the day, my last year of high school. Nice guy, too. We hung out together. He had all the ladies after him. Wore a cowboy get-up; drove the women wild. I lost track of him after college. He played in the NBA for a while; made a boatload of cash. I heard he left the game—bad knees, I think. I'm glad that he landed on his feet. He was awesome back in the day. He used to tag after this kid from Philly— big time ball player, DJ—"

"You don't mean Derrick "Dunk and Jam" Jackson, God's Gift to Womankind, do you?"

"Yeah, that's the guy. He's about K.J.'s age or a little older, maybe Donald's and James' age. He played in the pros for four or five years. Made a lot of money and got out. Do you know him, too?"

"He's a very successful pediatrician here in DC. He's the one who took care of Angelique. He and Chuck saved her life."

"Who is Angelique?"

"I'll explain when I see you at home, but what is this 'in the air' business about? You sounded upset when you answered the telephone"

"That's going to take a little explaining, too. I'm bringing someone home with me and we'll talk about it all then."

"Ah, so now we get to meet the fabulous JeNelle."

"No, not JeNelle. Someone else."

"Someone else?" she yelled. "Benny, I can't keep up anymore. I'll wait for Friday night. If you're bringing someone home to meet the family, this promises to be interesting."

"Little sister, you won't believe how interesting this is going to be."

"I'll take your word for it. See you Friday night."

"I love you, Viv."

"I love you more, Benny, and thanks, big brother. Goodbye."

Benny and Vivian hung up. Stacy was not paying attention to Benny's conversation until he mentioned something about taking someone home with him…someone other than JeNelle. She didn't have to wait long for Benny to confirm her worst fears.

"All right, Stacy, you'll have to be packed by Friday. We're going to take a little trip to Goodwill, Summer County, South Carolina. So now, getting back to where we left off, what do you want to have for dinner? Our baby's got to eat, you know. Let's name her Whitney or Janet or Alisha or Mariah. With a mother like you, she's sure to be a real knockout."

"I can't do this! You're talking crazy! You're talking about names for this…I mean, *our* baby and I'm trying to get it through your head that there's not going to be any baby! What do I have to say to convince you of that?"

"You really do have a short-term memory-loss problem, huh? Okay, so listen carefully. You're not going to convince me that an abortion is the right thing for either of us. What you need is a little southern exposure. Perhaps that will help you understand what family means to me and how important the principles that my family holds sacred are in our lives. You're coming home with me to meet our baby's grandparents, aunts, and one of her uncles. You can try to convince all of us at the same time."

"Come home with you? You've been sniffing too much pure oxygen up there in that rarified air for too long! Come home with you? As what, your friend, your lover? I can just see the scene now. Hi Mom, Dad, I'm home and here's my walking, talking, baby factory, Stacy. She happened to be in my bed when I was dreaming about another woman and she got the long end of the stick, so to speak, pun intended. Stacy, take a bow. Welcome to the rest of your life milking cows and slopping pigs deep in the heart of Dixie. Sing hallelujah, chillins. Let the peoples say Amen! Alls God's chillins got shoes."

Benny laughed at Stacy's animation and then took her in his arms. He tilted her head up and kissed her gently on the lips.

"You've been watching too much TV," he said and grinned. "It's not like Mayberry, RFD, at all. We actually have indoor plumbing in the kitchen now. You don't even have to go to the outhouse anymore. So you're not going to get out of this by portraying it as the backward South. Come home with me as my best friend and the mother of our child and I promise I won't ask you to milk one cow or slop one pig, but there are a few rows of cotton I want to introduce you to," he teased.

"Now you've got jokes? I can't go to your parents' home. Not like this. What would I say if they asked me how this happened?"

Benny laughed. "Tell them that you seduced me or better still, tell them the truth. You were having your usual way with me, forcing me to have unbelievably great sex with you against my will, and that it was a stellar event. Much better than we realized at the time. According to Gregory and Aretha, my father and mother still know what great sex is and they practice making it better all the time the same way we do."

"There's a difference, as you've told me many times, your parents are very much in love. We aren't. We're just good friends, nothing more."

"Best friends with benefits," he corrected, "but that's your decision, not mine and I've respected your position. You didn't want to fall in love. You've made that painfully clear since we met. You've insisted that I see other women when you know that's not what I want. I'll live with that, but I won't live without our child, no matter how you feel about our relationship. It's not about us anymore. It's about our baby. You don't want me to be in love with you so I won't press the issue.... for now. I'm doing as you requested and seeing other women, JeNelle Towson, in particular."

"That's good, Benny. I understand from Cecil and Janice that she's a very fine woman and you deserve the very best."

What could he say to that? JeNelle was, indeed, a very fine woman on so many levels, but he wasn't in love with her. He was in love with the finest woman he had ever met, Naval Lieutenant Stacy Greene. The woman who was now carrying his child. The woman he wanted as his wife. The woman who didn't love him in return. He had charmed so many women in his life, but not the one he truly wanted. What irony?

The telephone rang again, and again Benny ignored it until he heard JeNelle's voice. He picked up the telephone.

"JeNelle, I was just sitting here talking about you to my friend, Stacy, and you called me. This is a first! You're not calling to tell me that you're expecting our first child, are you?" he joked.

JeNelle laughed. "We haven't been intimate, remember? It's me, JeNelle Towson. Remember me? I'm one of the few women left in this hemisphere who hasn't succumbed to your charms."

"You forgot to add the word 'yet'."

"I'm not even going to go there with you. You're too swift for me. I can't keep up, but I do want to see you as soon as possible. When can we get together?"

"You want to see me?" he asked skeptically. "Are you sure that you know who you're talking to? Did you dial the right number?"

"All right, Benny, stop joking. Yes, I want to see you and don't push it. Remember, you're still flying on one wing, Captain Alexander."

"Well, should I play hard to get?"

"No, but may I suggest that you meet me at my house tomorrow. I'll take the day off so that we'll have plenty of time to talk."

"JeNelle...are you sure that this is the real JeNelle Towson, woman of my dreams, the apple of my eye? You're going to take tomorrow off to spend it with me—at your place? There is a God!"

"Well, I didn't want any distractions."

"This is sounding better and better. Your place is fine. I'll fly up in the morning. I'll see you at your place at ten o'clock."

"Great, I'll make lunch."

"You mean you even know how to cook, too? Using real pots and pans and everything?"

"Yes, Benny, what would you like for lunch?"

"JeNelle, at the risk of having my other wing cut off—or some other precious parts of my anatomy—I'll just say that what I want for lunch, you can't cook on the stove, and leave it at that."

JeNelle laughed. "One wing, Captain. I'll look forward to seeing you tomorrow at 10:00 A.M."

Benny hung up the telephone.

"Yes!" he yelled, yanking the air with his fist.

"Please don't tell JeNelle about this. I don't want anyone else to know."

"You were the one who told me to be honest with her, remember? Your exact words were 'Be yourself, Benny.'"

"I know what I said," she groused. "You don't have to repeat it, but just don't mention my pregnancy to her tomorrow. Please, Benny."

"All right, but JeNelle is going to have to know about this eventually. A baby does tend to grow up, you know. JeNelle's swift. I think that she might notice something like that."

"There you go with that baby stuff again!"

"Yes, and again, and again and again!"

"You're really not going to give up on this no matter what I say, are you?"

"What? Did you hear me stutter? No, I'm not giving up. Get over it. We are going to have a baby, Stacy, whether you like it or not."

"I've got to think about this, but I'm too exhausted to do it now."

"Then there's the bedroom. Get some rest. I'm going to order Chinese. I'll be up later."

"I don't exactly feel very amorous tonight. That's what got me into this jam in the first place."

Benny took Stacy in his arms. "I haven't touched you or anyone else in over five weeks and right now I'm so happy that I want to share that with you. I want to make love with you like never before. I'm only a mere mortal, but I won't touch you if you don't want me to. I just want to listen to our baby grow. But, Stacy, the dye has already been cast, so to speak. What could it hurt?"

"*Benny!*"

Stacy wrapped her well-toned thighs around Benny's waist and locked her legs at her ankles. Lifting her bottom, she met his downward thrust, stroke for earth-shattering stroke.

This was pure, unadulterated madness on her part. How could she distance herself from this wonderful man if she could not stay away from him? God knew that she had tried, but as her hands scrambled to keep a firm grip on his muscular, sweat-slicked body, she had to admit at least to herself that she had once again failed.

Weary from their argument, when Benny settled in to order dinner from a nearby restaurant, she had gone to one of his guest rooms to rest. In no time, she had fallen off to sleep. Who could blame her? She had been on an emotional rollercoaster ride from the moment that the home-pregnancy strip turned from clear to blue. Not believing the first results to be accurate, she had taken the test again with a different product. Same results. Morning sickness was bad enough. Then came four weeks of agony on a rolling and pitching Pacific Ocean off the coast of some disserted island during a few days of a violent storm. Afraid that someone would notice her frequent trips to the head, she had played it off as seasickness.

As the war games were winding down, she called in every favor she could to be relieved of her post early, to get a hop in a helicopter supply ship so that she could get to Hawaii in time to catch a Navy transport to San Diego. When she landed, the tower acknowledged that the Explorer Squadron had set down a few hours before her own arrival.

Stacy was afraid that Benny wouldn't listen to her many messages on his voice mail. He usually wanted to decompress after a long mission with a brew and a long nap. Afterwards, he'd been out and gone on leave.

Fortunately for her, she caught him before he left. She did not expected him to argue so vehemently against her decision to have an abortion. Truth told, for a fleeting few moments after realization struck, she contemplated the thought of having a baby. The hurt and disappointment that she saw in his eyes stunned her. Why would a warm, fun-loving and fatally attractive man like Benny want her to have his child?

Stacy's thoughts scattered when Benny kissed her long and deeply. It was hard to think at all when Benny was hot and sweating, wrapped around her, and buried deep in her core. All she wanted at those times was more. Then, her vision began to dim, and her body alerted her that she was again headed down that slippery slope to ecstasy. She tried to scramble back up, to savor more of this last time that they would ever be together, but Benny could not be resisted or denied. He dragged her into that same euphoric orbit with him. Involuntarily, her inner muscles clamped around him tight as a fist. For what seemed like a lifetime, their bodies experienced uncontrollable spasms. His mouth swallowed both of their shouts of blissful release.

Slowly, by degrees, her body muscles began to relax. When Benny gathered her in his arms, she knew why she had to leave him. She was hopelessly in love with him. Then she drifted into sleep.

Chapter 20

It had been more than six weeks since Kenneth met Lisa Lambert. Leaning back in his office chair, while she worked on her laptop on his sofa, he reflected on their first of many business meetings. Who is Lisa Lambert? He still questioned after all of this time. Standing, he paced and stood at his window, hands dug deep into his pockets. From the moment that he entered the private dining room at Lion d'Or he struggled to answer that question.

"Good afternoon, Kenneth. I'll be with you in a moment," Lisa had said, as she continued a conversation on her cell phone.

Lisa Lambert, he had observed, was an attractive woman—not a beautiful woman like JeNelle. No, where JeNelle seemed soft and feminine, Lisa had an edge about her. Where JeNelle had welcoming, smiling eyes, Lisa had piercing eyes like someone who could look right through him, and did not suffer fools readily. Lisa could easily be mistaken for the Chairman of the Board of any corporation—Bendix, IBM, even General Motors. He sensed that she possessed that kind of aggressive and dynamic personality. When he spoke with her, he had the sensation that she was not only dissecting each word that he uttered, but also reading his mind before he even formed the thought. She would definitely be ten steps ahead of him before he even realized that he was ready to take a step. To describe her as "assertive" or "aggressive" would have been gross understatements; carnivorous came to his mind.

As she talked on the telephone, she took copious notes and entered data on her iPad. He could see through her stylish eyeglasses that those piercing eyes were searching and digesting information thoughtfully, as each word was being uttered. She was definitely a woman who knew no bounds or impediments to her professional skills and abilities.

Her business attire was very stylish, even a bit sensuous. Her navy-blue, skirt-length jacket, with one gold button at the hip line, was open and revealed a short, above-the-knee straight skirt that rose to the thigh line, as she crossed her leg at the knee. The soft, white blouse that she wore had no collar, but drew the eye downward toward her small, but shapely breasts. A small-link, gold chain hung from her neck and her gold earrings matched the stunning, gold, abstract pin on her jacket. Her hands were graceful with clear polish on her manicured nails. Her complexion was honey-toned and fresh; very little makeup and lipstick that was barely there. Her short, crinkle-cut hairstyle was parted on the left and swept to the other side of her head, covering the earpiece, as she talked. Clearly, he thought, she did not make her attire an issue to be reckoned with—you had to deal with her unencumbered by unimportant distractions.

"I apologize for that, Kenneth," Lisa had said, as she tapped and removed the earpiece, closed her iPad, and placed her earring on her earlobe. *"Modern technology isn't always a benefit, but now I have turned off all of my communications equipment. I have instructed the waiter not to disturb us until I call for him. I've also taken the liberty of ordering this white wine before you arrived. We've had to delay this meeting several times over the last couple of weeks. I want no distractions during this luncheon now that we've managed to synchronize our schedules."*

Lisa poured two glasses of wine and handed one to Kenneth.

"I understand how necessary it is to be able to reach out and touch someone at a critical moment. It's not necessary to apologize for having important work to do, Lisa."

Kenneth took a sip of the wine.

"The only person I want to reach out and touch at this moment, Kenneth, is you."

Kenneth nearly choked on the wine. He realized that she was being purposefully provocative and wondered what she had in mind.

"I've told you of the Governor's desire to have you on this Blue Ribbon Panel. He's authorized me to make the offer to you and he and I both expect an answer in the affirmative."

Kenneth breathed a sigh of relief. *"As I mentioned before, Lisa, I am very interested in the program and I am willing to support it fully. I suggest, however, that you and the Governor consider using one of my partners to actually sit on the Panel. I've met with them and discussed the plan; both of them have indicated a willingness to serve in my place."*

He took another sip of wine.

"If JeNelle Towson were not a Panel Member, would you be offering up your partners for the task or would you then be willing to serve?"

The question startled Kenneth. He nearly choked again. *"JeNelle? What does her participation have to do with this?"*

"It's obvious to me, Kenneth, that you are very attracted to her, but you're looking for ways to distance yourself from her because of her relationship with your brother, Benjamin. Your family is very close and you would do anything in your power to avoid hurting Benjamin in any way."

"The newspaper article was false! Moreover, that incident occurred over a month ago. As you predicted, it all blew over. I thought that you believed me about that?"

"The man doth protest too much. I was at Maison's and at the Gala. I observed you and JeNelle on both occasions. The article about your involvement may have been a fabrication, but your feeling for JeNelle spoke volumes of truth. I'm not going to put you on the spot and try to force you into a confession. My question is unchanged, however. Would you join the Panel if JeNelle were not a member?"

Kenneth put down the wine glass. He was rarely at a loss for words, but Lisa had thrown him off balance.

"JeNelle's participation or nonparticipation makes no difference."

"Then what can be done to get you to agree to participate?"

"Nothing at the moment. I have an incredible workload at this time and I have to share the load with my other partners. You've seen an example of that since it's taken so long to work out our schedules. It would be unfair of me to saddle them with more work, especially now. I also have a private life that needs some attention."

"Let's stop dancing around this issue. Your partners gave you the green light on your participation on the Panel and fully support it. Tom sees it as a golden opportunity for CompuCorrect, Inc. to further establish the company's reputation and credibility. That's only to be expected because he's a public relations, sales and marketing expert. Although Shirley agreed, but was less supportive of the idea, I suspect that her hidden agenda is not to share you with JeNelle or any other woman, if she can help it.

"As for your private life, well, I think the word 'nonexistent' is apropos. You've dated only four women in the nearly seven years that you've been in the area and none of them seriously. You don't even own a CD player and your audio collection is woefully out of date. You're very much a family man and very supportive and protective of your siblings. You're one of the most sought after bachelors in the area, but you've chosen to live a life that could only be described as 'monastic' in stark contrast to your brothers, Benjamin and even Gregory. Your sister, Vivian, has been involved with only one man for the last three years, Carlton Andrews, who recently, I might add, proposed marriage to her. You sister, Aretha, well, let's just say that I would not want to compete with her when she's older. She's a young genius. Your parents, Dr. Bernard and Sylvia Benson Alexander, have had a very fulfilling life together for thirty-five years. Your father is overqualified for the position that he has held for many years. God only knows why he chose to stay in a small town like Goodwill, South Carolina. He could have gone anywhere in the country with his credentials. That's been your life...family life.

"Your financial life does not need attention. You don't spend money frivolously. You have a comfortable home in one of the premier counties in this state that you

got for a bargain because of the downturn in the market. You have remodeled it and raised its value to substantially more than your original purchase price. You're well invested in state municipal bonds, a nice stock portfolio, mutual funds, and a 401K plan. You have ample money market accounts, both savings and checking, and you don't live above your means. You've made some very wise and lucrative investments for yourself and you've parlayed Benjamin's income from five to six digits in less than three years. You've established hefty stock and bond trust accounts for Benjamin, Vivian, Gregory, and Aretha, which you have not told them about. The sizeable gift that your parents gave to you to help you start CompuCorrect has been repaid with interest and you've established accounts for your parents in which a part of your profit goes into a separate account for them.

"You occasionally drink wine or brandy and have never had so much as a parking ticket. You have a light breakfast, usually just coffee and toast—no butter—sometimes country jam or jelly, and juice. You rarely eat lunch, unless it's a business-related event, because you usually exercise during the lunchtime period. You're partial to salads, which you often eat alone at home while watching the National Business Channel until approximately 11:00 P.M. when you generally work on your woodworking projects or go to bed. You are almost always the first one in your office in the morning and usually the last to leave at night.

"Professionally, you graduated from Morehouse, in the upper one percent of your class, and received your double masters from Georgia Tech. You're essentially a science and technology prodigy who often wrote a column for Science Today while you were in high school through college and grad school. You were immediately snapped up by the Sandoval Anniston Corporation, primarily because you're Black, a damn good industrial engineer, and you had designed and patented some nasty little spy gadgets that they were very interested in. You quickly won the respect of your colleagues and your superiors and were a rising star moving swiftly into more challenging work and a higher income bracket then your white counterparts. You were the lead engineering specialist on several sensitive and top-secret NSA and CIA projects during the last administration although you are not a political animal. You are, however, politically astute. You chose to leave Sandoval, and your six-figure salary, to start your own business when you began to get pressure from your superiors and certain military officials to inflate the costs of the government projects that you were responsible for. You consistently refused to do that. The straw that broke the camel's back, so to speak, was the pressure that you got from, your then close friend, Colonel John Calvin Baker, who has, I might add, tried to influence you to take more military contracts as his way of bringing you back into the fold. You've steadfastly resisted and refused him

vehemently and consistently, but you have not told your family, including Benjamin, about Baker pressuring you, primarily because he is your brother's friend and one of his commanding officers.

"You haven't taken a real vacation in years although you enjoy skiing, swimming, and playing basketball. You've donated many pieces of furniture that you designed and made to charitable organizations to help them raise funds. You're on the board of directors of six corporations and charitable groups. You hold a pilot's license and an Amateur Radio Station license, Advanced Class. You're not gay or bisexual and you've never been caught with a dead girl or a live boy. Now does that about sum it up or did I miss something?"

Kenneth was dumbfounded, but he managed to say, *"You missed the color of my toothbrush."*

"Red, compact head and hard bristles," Lisa responded without a thought and with an unfazed look on her face.

They both laughed. She was right, he thought, about the toothbrush, but he'd have to check when he got home.

"You have certainly done your homework. I'm not sure how accurate this all is, particularly your mention of Shirley not wanting to 'share me'. She and I have a purely platonic, professional, business relationship."

"You're right, but did you really think that your background and current activities wouldn't be completely and thoroughly vetted for a panel appointment as important as this one? And as for my comment about your partner, from your perspective that's all it is, but trust me. I'm a woman. I know these things. My question is still on the table. What is it going to take to get you on this Panel?"

"If I said that it's going to take an 'Act of God,' I believe that you'd arrange it."

"You're right! 'One Act of God' coming up!"

Kenneth shook his head, thought for a moment, and then looked thoughtfully at Lisa. *"All right, Lisa, I'll do it, but you and the Governor must agree that, should my participation on the Panel cause any problems either professionally or personally, I'll be permitted to withdraw with no questions asked."*

"Done!" Lisa said emphatically. *"Now what would you like for lunch?"*

"You tell me. You obviously know me better than I know myself."

"All right. We'll have the tomato bisque and Caesar salad with broiled chicken, no anchovies. House wine and French bread. How's that?"

"Fine with me," Kenneth said, still somewhat dazed and unnerved by Lisa's accurate summary of his life. Knowledge of his finances was difficult to come by. She could gain access to records filed each year, both corporate and personal,

with the state and IRS. Moreover, any company that dealt with government contracts would have to have an FBI clearance. She could also gain access as a state government official. What did concern him was how she knew about J.C. Baker. No one knew about that except for himself and Baker. At least that's what he believed. Something was not right. He didn't know at that moment what it was, but he would continue to play along until the picture became clearer.

Two waiters served lunch as skillfully as brain surgeons ply their trade. As they finished their meals, Lisa looked at Kenneth intently. He noticed her watching him, but he could not read her expression. He sipped his wine.

"*Now,*" she said, "*let's get to the most important topic of conversation.*"

"*I thought that we had? What's left to discuss? My views on the NBA season?*" he asked somewhat sarcastically.

He sipped his wine.

"*How I can get to know you better?*"

He almost choked. He put the wine glass down. "*You recited my life story in painful detail. If there's something left that you aren't already aware of, I certainly don't know what it is.*"

Lisa sat back in her seat, laced her fingers and stared directly into Kenneth's eyes. "*Kenneth, that was the easy stuff. Your life is so open and squeaky clean it whistles. What I want to know is why haven't you dated more? You're a very attractive man. Successful, intelligent, energetic, dynamic....*"

"*Keep going, I'm beginning to enjoy this,*" he said, chuckling.

"*You haven't answered my question,*" she said and grinned.

"*I don't know what I can tell you other than I, frankly, have been engrossed in getting CompuCorrect off the ground. I can't afford the distraction. My parents made a substantial investment, not only in the company, but more importantly, in me. I don't want to disappoint them. I'm not suggesting that they are interested in the monetary rewards, because they're not, but they have instilled in all of us a strong work ethic and a sense of responsibility and commitment. They expect to see a return on that investment. I feel that spending my time chasing women or taking expensive vacations or spending money foolishly is a betrayal of their investment and confidence in me. Therefore, I simply have not focused on that aspect of my life.*"

He decided to try another sip of the wine. After all, it was very good.

"*And perhaps you had not met the right woman—until JeNelle Towson.*"

He choked. "*Lisa, I haven't admitted to anything concerning my feelings about JeNelle.*"

"And you haven't denied it either."

"I thought that you weren't going to try to force me into a confession?"

"I'm putting all the cards on the table, Kenneth, so that there are no hidden issues. I like what I see in you and I know what I'm up against. JeNelle Towson is a formidable competitor, but she has one major impediment that works to my advantage and her disadvantage."

"I'm not admitting to anything, but what major impediment are you referring to?"

"You, Mr. Kenneth James Alexander. No matter how attracted to her you are, you'll never do anything about it because of your relationship with your brother and the rest of your family. The irony of the situation is that, although your brother met her first, I believe that you're better suited to her needs than he is. But you'll never know that because you will not let yourself become intimately involved with her, although it is clear to me, and to any other close observer of your behavior when you are near her, that you want to be with her desperately."

"Ergo?"

"Ergo, I may benefit from JeNelle's impediment. It's a win/win situation for me. That is, if you are serious about wanting to give your private life a little attention. I'm not going to press the issue. You're not a man who can be manipulated. You've proven that with your fierce defense against your former friend, J.C. Baker. I would not be interested in you if you didn't have strength of character and a strong sense of loyalty. I'll simply leave you with this thought: What better way is there to shield yourself from any innuendo concerning JeNelle than to become involved with another woman? I'm qualified for the position, as the woman in your life. Here is my card with my cell number and my private numbers both at the office and at my residence. I frequently come to San Francisco on business and I'll be in town for a few more days. I'm at the Fairmont Hotel and Tower on Nob Hill at California Street, Bentley Suite 1140. I'm single, unattached emotionally to anyone, I play a mean game of racquetball, and the ball is in your court."

He stared at Lisa's business card and studied it for a while, considering the possibilities and pitfalls. What could it hurt to get to know her? At least he would find out how she obtained so much intimate and private information about him and his family. Ultimately, he had made the only decision that had seemed viable at the time.

"Lisa, this is Kenneth Alexander. I'll see you on the racquetball court at the Health and Fitness Center on Edison at 1:00 P.M. sharp tomorrow."

He stood at this same window while replaying his conversation with her in his head. He marveled at the way she dissected him and thought how he never felt the blade of the knife, as it cut through his flesh. He since learned that she did, indeed, play a mean game of racquetball and she played hardball with the greatest of ease and with the best of them. He also wondered how he could have failed so miserably at covering up what had become an unmanageable desire to be with JeNelle. He thought he had done everything in his power to mask it. Still, each day, without warning, she would creep into his conscious thoughts. He'd see the book that she sent to him that sat on his coffee table at home, and think of her. Or he'd see the gift that she sent to someone else in his office and she would spring to his mind. Business associates would ask him about her, or the staff would repeat something humorous that she said. Or he would sit at home before a roaring fire tasting one of the Santa Barbara wines that she had sent to him, and visualize her sitting in the dark, as she had done that night with only the flames from the fireplace to illuminate her face.

No matter how much time passed, JeNelle was still on his mind where she didn't belong. Lisa was in town again today. She called him earlier to schedule another racquetball game. They had been seeing each other frequently over the last six weeks. Though they had not slept together, it was getting more difficult to deny his needs and her open invitations. Something was holding him back. Something in addition to his desire to be with JeNelle. That's what he had been pondering for the past few hours. He knew that he had to figure out what it was about Dr. Lisa Lambert that bothered him.

Chapter 21

Stacy was still sleeping when Benny returned from the grocery store with breakfast foods and plenty of milk. He boiled an egg, made toast, poured a glass of orange juice and an even bigger glass of milk. He cut the fresh strawberries in halves and scooped yogurt over top. He placed fresh flowers on the tray, along with a copy of *The Baby Book* magazine that he found at the grocery store, and the breakfast that he had prepared. He wrote out a greeting card, placed it strategically on the tray, and went up to his bedroom.

Benny kissed Stacy gently on her cheek, her neck and then her lips and sat on the edge of the bed, watching her, as she began to awaken.

As she awoke and yawned lazily, she found him sitting next to her. "Benny, what time is it?"

"It's 0730 and its time for you and our daughter to have some breakfast," he said, reaching for some pillows to put behind her back. "You didn't eat anything last night."

Stacy sat up in bed, cupped her hands over her face and rubbed her eyes.

"I wasn't hungry. I hoped that this was all a bad dream, but here you are, bright and early—after keeping me awake half the night having sex—talking about 'our' daughter before I can even have my first cup of coffee. I never noticed it before, Benjamin Staton Alexander, but you have a mean streak in you," she joked and yawned again, stretching lazily.

"You were as spectacular as ever as far as I was concerned, but sorry, no coffee for you for the next seven months. It's not good for our daughter."

"No *coffee?*" she scoffed. "That's the life giving fluid that runs through my veins! I'll cease to exist without at least four cups of coffee per hour!"

"I'm not impressed, but I'll see whether you can have decaffeinated or herbal tea."

"*Tea?*" she squeaked, bewildered. "Benny, nobody drinks tea!"

"It will be an acquired taste and you'll survive it," he said dryly.

"The question is, Benjamin Staton Alexander, will I survive *you?*"

"We'll talk about that when I get home tonight. I'm on my way to see JeNelle. Now, here is your breakfast. Our daughter is hungry so you must eat it all."

Stacy noticed the card with her name on it propped up against the flowers. She opened it and read:

To the Mother of Our Child.

Only you, Stacy, can carry our child in your body, but I'll be there to carry you in my arms. I'll rub your back when it's sore and your feet when they ache. I'll make midnight runs for pickles or ice cream or even chocolate soda if you like. I'll hold you when you need comforting and support you when you want to share a special moment. I'll be there to share each movement of our tiny gift, as we prepare for her arrival. You will grow lovelier in my eyes than ever before, and I'll be there to help you with each and every chore. Your waistline may blossom along with your breast, but you'll never look more beautiful to me.

You make things make sense, Stacy. I respect and appreciate your opinion because I trust you without question or forethought. You make me come alive because you understand me and care about me no matter my faults or shortcomings. Thank you for being my best friend.

From the Father of Our Child,
Benny

Stacy closed the card and tears formed in her eyes. She reached for him and he hugged her and kissed her on her neck. She put her arms around him and wept.

* * *

As Benny landed the Cessna at the Santa Barbara Airport, he wondered how he would be able to avoid telling JeNelle about Stacy and his baby. He wanted to skywrite it across the heavens the length of the California coastline. He felt that it would be a betrayal of his friendship with JeNelle to withhold the truth from her, but he had promised Stacy that he would remain silent and he felt a deeper commitment to her. He would do nothing until she agreed.

In the short time since he gave her a surprise birthday party, Benny had talked with JeNelle rather frequently by telephone, sharing with her everything about himself, holding back nothing and answering any question that she might ask. They shared the trials and tribulations of her busy schedule. Listening to the excitement in her voice, as she talked about the success of a plan or a program that she was a part of and asking his views or advice on matters gave him better insight into who she is. They were closer. He could feel it. She was not as guarded with him as before. She relaxed more and more, as they talked and got to know each other. She loved to hear the stories of his life in Goodwill, South Carolina, and about Vivian and Kenneth and Gregory and Aretha. They would laugh for hours over the Alexander children's youthful antics and she listened closely, as he talked about the close relationship that they had with their paternal and maternal grandparents.

His excitement grew, as he bounded up the steps to JeNelle's home. He was early, but he couldn't wait to see her.

Opening the door and wiping perspiration from her face and neck with a towel that was draped over her shoulder, JeNelle cheerfully quipped, "Benny, you're early."

He rushed to her and lifted her in his arms, turning her around and around. Finally, he let her slide down his firm, muscular body until her feet touched the floor. He kissed her with passion, but he didn't feel it the way it felt with Stacy.

"*Whoa*, Captain Alexander. You certainly are flying high today." JeNelle laughed, as she backed away from him. "Are you feeling that infamous 'rush' that you're always talking about?"

"I told you. I feel a rush every time I see you," he said still loosely holding her in his arms. "It's been exactly seven weeks, three days and seven hours since I last saw you and you still have the same effect on me. I couldn't wait to see you."

He was flashing that million-dollar smile she noted, but it only served to remind her of his brother's, Kenneth's, all-engrossing smile. His body felt warm against hers just as Kenneth's body had felt and the powerful muscles in his arms flexed, as he held her fast just as Kenneth's muscles had felt, but she realized that she did not feel the same way she had felt when Kenneth held her in his arms. It wasn't even close to the sensations that caused her to tingle from head to toe when she was near Kenneth or heard his name or thought of him.

Benny was dressed casually in a light blue pullover Calvin Klein sweater pushed up at the sleeve, and an open collar that revealed the same gold chain that Kenneth wore tangled in the soft hairs that lay against his muscular chest. His slacks were Calvin Klein casuals with an athlete's cut that still revealed the shape of his thick, heavy and long muscles, firm butt and thick thighs just like Kenneth's frame. She never fantasized about Benny, but Kenneth had a starring role in her dreams both day and many sleepless nights.

JeNelle was dressed in her exercise gear—a cut off T-shirt that barely covered her full breasts. A pair of runner's shorts clipped high on her upper thighs. A pair of aerobic shoes with white socks rolled down to her ankles. A sweatband around her head and her hair plaited and twisted into a ball on top of her head. Her body was moist and her clothing was damp. Her face glistened and her eyes were wide and shinning.

"I'm sweaty, Benny. I was working out when you arrived. I didn't expect to see you until ten o'clock," she said, backing further away. "Let me take a quick shower, wash my hair, and then we can catch up on all the news since we last talked."

"I can be pretty handy in a shower. I could scrub your back for you or wash your hair. I could make a career out of just holding your soap," he said, still holding her hands in his.

"I'm beginning to see cracks forming in the fuselage, Captain. That one wing might just break off, if you're not careful," she said jokingly with a broad, menacing smile.

"I'm landing, I'm landing, Ms. Towson," Benny said, releasing JeNelle, raising his hands in a playful motion of mock surrender, and backing away from her.

"That's better, Captain. Now you can repair those cracks in your fuselage," she said, with a smile and a twinkle in her eye. "I thought that we'd have lunch on the deck. It's a beautiful day and the ocean is calm. Just a gentle breeze blowing," she said, scurrying into her bedroom. "Make yourself comfortable. I won't be very long."

Benny went out on the deck that overlooked the vast Pacific Ocean with the Channel Islands clearly visible in the far distance. Sea gulls glided overhead, or walked along the beach picking at the sand. Joggers jogged in the distance far up the beach. A man walked his dog, as it ran to the edge of the surf and hopped playfully out of the way, as the tide rolled into the shore. Sailboats gracefully moved on the glistening water far out in the ocean; their sails billowing in the breeze. It was a beautiful morning. One that he should have been spending with Stacy, but he didn't want to crowd her. He was grateful that she had agreed to spend the weekend with him at his home in Goodwill, South Carolina.

Benny was still standing on the deck when he heard JeNelle turn off the shower. He could see her faintly through the sheers on the French doors of her bedroom. Her hair was wrapped in a towel and another towel was wrapped around her body. She sat in a chair near the doors rubbing lotion on her body, but she did not notice that he was watching her. When she stood up and pulled the towel off her head, her wet hair fell around her shoulders and down her back. In another motion, she removed the towel from her body, but she was quickly out of his view. A short time later, he heard music playing inside the house and through the speakers mounted under the eaves on the deck. JeNelle emerged from the house holding two mimosas. She was dressed in a pair of peach-colored harem pants pulled tight at the ankle, matching halter top and flat black sandals with a thong between her pedicured toes. She was not wearing makeup. Her hair was still damp and brushed away from her face. The wet curls hung down her back.

"That was quick," Benny said the mimosa and taking a sip. He was pleased that the drink contained Sparkling Cider and not Champaign.

"I've had plenty of practice recently of getting dressed in record time. I've raised it to an art form. I thought that you might like something to drink. It's not made with alcohol; its sparkling cider and orange juice. I know that you can't drink and fly. I remembered what you said."

"You certainly have and may I make the first toast of the day, Ms. Towson?"

"You certainly may, Captain Alexander," she said, smiling at him.

"Here's to art. I love the form it takes." He eyed her shapely body.

"I see I'm going to have to be on my toes with you today, Captain. You are really in rare form. What's got you so excited, and don't tell me it's me. I've heard that line from you before. And how did you cut yourself? Were you trying to shave and fly your jet at the same time or something?"

At that moment, he was tempted to tell her about Stacy and their baby. He ached to share the news with her, with everyone, but he thought of his promise to Stacy and held back.

"I'll tell you later," he said.

They stood on the deck talking about his recent missions during the all-out military drill or her expansion projects for her business, and watching the beach scenes as the sun rose higher in the sky. Leaning against the railing, the gentle breeze blew through JeNelle's hair, as it air-dried. A few strands of her hair blew across her face. Benny captured them and moved the soft tendrils gently away, tucking them behind her ear. Her profile was as alluring as her full face, he thought. He watched how she tilted her head as they talked and her body language as she pointed to distant boats or ships at sea. He heard her words, but he was looking at her. He missed being with her more than he would permit himself to realize.

"JeNelle," he said spontaneously, as he rested his arm on the deck railing, turning his head, and looking directly at her. "I've made no secret about my feelings for you and I know that you have told me that all that you're willing or able to give, at this time, is friendship. I've tried to hold back. Not to let myself rush too far ahead of where you want this friendship to be, but I have to be as honest with you as I know you have been with me.

"I've reserved a chalet in Vail for next week. No pressure to make love with me. The chalet has two bedrooms, but I want this friendship to move forward to a relationship and maybe, someday, even to a commitment. I believe that I'm ready for that. I want someone in my life that I can love and who can love me in return. I believe that I want that person to be you, but I have to be honest with you. I believe that I've fallen—"

JeNelle put her soft fingers to his lips and moved into his arms. She laid her head against his chest. She said nothing. He held her in his arms. She would not hear the words that he wanted to speak. He was going to tell her about Stacy. How he felt about her, but not about their baby. He kissed the top of her head. He recalled how Stacy had wept in his arms just hours earlier because she felt that she could not give him what he wanted—their child. He knew now that JeNelle could not give him what he wanted from her now—her trust. Yet he would wait until she could. Just as he would wait for Stacy's decision. JeNelle's trust and his child with Stacy were both equally as important to him.

Later, JeNelle set the table on the deck for two and they talked, as she stirred the homemade clam chowder, and scooped the shrimp and lobster seafood salad onto beds of romaine lettuce and leafy spinach. She cut up the fresh cantaloupe and honeydew melon, scooped it into serving bowls, sprinkled fresh raspberries and blueberries, and ground nuts over top. Nothing more had been said about Vail and the week that he had planned.

"I know it was over five weeks ago, but you haven't mentioned how the Chamber Gala went," Benny said, cutting a piece of sour dough bread from the loaf and buttering it. "I'm very sorry I missed it."

"It was a very successful event. We raised nearly three million dollars in seed money."

"Did K.J. enjoy himself at the Gala?"

"Yes and no. I believe that he enjoyed the Gala. Everyone who met him was impressed and certainly enjoyed his company, but the aftermath didn't turn out to be any fun for him. An unfortunate and embarrassing situation developed that put him in an untenable position," she said, with great concern.

"What happened, did the waiter spill that one-thousand-dollar-a-plate meal all over his tuxedo or something?" Benny asked jokingly.

"No, that would have been a blessing."

"This is beginning to peak my interest. What happened?"

"Wait here, I'll show you."

JeNelle went into her study and returned holding a newspaper in her hand. She handed it to Benny and he began to read the cover story. He saw the picture of JeNelle and Kenneth dancing in a beam of light and slumped back in his chair. His million-dollar smile disappeared and his eyebrows narrowed as he read in silence. He looked at the other snapshots of Kenneth and JeNelle together and read the other articles. All of them were filled with innuendo, gossip and supposition about Kenneth and JeNelle. From reading the newspaper account, one would think that they had lit the sky that night. Every article seemed to be about them.

"Congratulations on your award, JeNelle," he said dryly. "You're obviously held in high esteem by your colleagues and rightfully so."

"Is that all you're going to say, Benny?" She was tense and uncomfortable. "I've embarrassed your brother and you terribly. This was such a fiasco that I can't even think about it without getting angry all over again. After all that you and Kenneth have done for me, look at how I repay your kindness. I'm still sick about the whole thing."

She looked at him with such anguish in her eyes, he thought.

"What did Kenneth have to say about this?" Benny asked his voice uncharacteristically monotone.

"He said not to do anything and that it would all blow over in time. I'm surprised that he still spoke to me after this hit the newspaper. He's a highly respected and admired businessman. His company could have suffered financial losses because of this fiasco. His clients probably were ready to take their business elsewhere and it all would have been my fault."

Benny saw how upsetting this article was to JeNelle. He put his arm around her and placed her head on his shoulder.

"Don't worry about Kenneth. He didn't get to where he is today without knowing how to avoid a few pitfalls. I know my brother very well. If he said not to worry, believe him. He'd handle it. I'm glad that he got you to wear my birthday gift though. When I tried to return the earrings, the jeweler thought that I was losing my touch with women and that if that happened, he'd have to close up shop and go out of business," Benny said jokingly, blowing on his fingernails and brushing them mockingly against his chest.

JeNelle sat up and looked at Benny's smug smile. She punched him in his rock hard stomach. He jokingly doubled over, holding his stomach.

"Whoa, JeNelle, if you wanted your undigested lunch back, I could find a less painful way to return it to you—*hara-kiri* would have been easier. That's a mean right hook that you've got there, baby...I mean, Ms. Towson. Ever consider Golden Gloves as a career? I'm sure that we could make a mint off of you, champ!"

She punched him again and he cradled her in his arms. This time she hugged him and he felt her body relax.

Benny cleared the runway and turned the plane southward toward San Diego. Then, putting his headphone in place, he signaled the tower. "Santa Barbara Tower, this is Cessna, November 2020 Bravo. How do you read me? Over."

"Acknowledged, Cessna November 2020 Bravo. We read you five-by-five. Are you reporting a problem? Over."

"That's a negative, Santa Barbara Tower. Request a change in my flight plan. Get me a clearance to San Francisco. Over."

"That's an affirmative Cessna November 2020 Bravo. Permission granted. Climb to 30,000 feet. The pattern is clear. Turn left on heading Mark 240 to San Francisco International. Over."

"Acknowledged, Santa Barbara Tower. Cessna November 2020 Bravo executing a one-hundred-eighty-degree left turn and climbing to 30,000 feet. Altitude and course achieved. Over and out."

As Benny flew into the airport in San Francisco and taxied the airplane to the General Aviation hanger, he remembered landing there with JeNelle by his side only a few months earlier. Now another vision flooded his mind. The telling newspaper image of JeNelle and Kenneth gazing into each other's eyes, embracing in a beam of light.

Benny barely spoke to people, as he entered CompuCorrect and headed straight for Kenneth's office. He didn't bother to knock, but barged straight through the door. Kenneth looked up from the contracts he was signing, as he stood behind his desk. His eyes narrowed.

"What are you doing here? I didn't know that you were in town," Kenneth said shocked to see Benny barging through the door. Kenneth's sense of Benny's anger, mixed with pain and indignation, were immediate.

"Are you making a play for JeNelle?" Benny demanded. "Are you in love with her, Kenneth?"

Kenneth rounded his desk. "Wait a minute. You're wrong."

"I should say that he has it all wrong," a female voice purred from one side of the office.

Benny had not noticed the attractive woman sitting on the leather sofa working on an iPad and wearing damp workout clothes and a towel around her neck. She rose from the sofa, walked over to Kenneth, and passionately kissed him.

"This sounds like a personal matter. I'm going to take a shower, Kenneth," she cooed, rubbing his chest. "I'll be ready to leave for dinner any time that you are. Just pucker up and whistle for me whenever you want me."

She seductively glanced at Benny, picked up her clothing bag, and left the office.

Benny's eyes followed her across the room. *Damn, she's sexy*, he thought, his ire dwindling. He turned to face Kenneth.

"Damn, K.J., who was *that?* You really know how to solve a water bill problem!"

"Her name is Lisa Lambert."

"Lisa? Have you been holding out on me, K.J.?"

"Lisa and I are just business acquaintances, Benny. She's the Governor's Advisor on Economic Affairs. We just got back from playing racquetball."

"K.J., that didn't look like a little kiss between acquaintances. I know a friendly kiss when I see one, and that one was off the Richter Scale!" Benny was totally relaxed now. He noticed that Kenneth was also wearing his exercise clothes. "And racquetball, at this time of the afternoon, on a business day? That must have been some game or did some of that sweat you're wearing come from a little afternoon office romance?"

"No, Benny, I told you. Lisa works for the Governor. She's only here for a few days. She has a very busy schedule. Whenever she's in town and has the time, we have a friendly game of racquetball. We started playing at 1:00 P.M. and we've been at it all afternoon."

"Who won?"

"We tied, as usual. She's a hell of a racquetball player," Kenneth said dryly.

"And a hell of a woman, I might add. I hope that you were wearing a new jockstrap. She looks like she could really bust some balls. Figuratively speaking, that is, K.J."

Benny was smiling now. Kenneth gave Benny a quick look and just shook his head.

"Benny, when you came in, you seemed upset," Kenneth said, looking down at some papers on his desk and avoiding Benny's eyes. "You must have seen that ridiculous article in the newspaper. I hope that you didn't draw the wrong conclusion. It was all a big mistake."

"I admit that at first I did believe that something was going on between you and JeNelle—that is until I saw Lisa. But I know you, K.J. I don't know how I even thought that you would do something like that to me. I'm sorry that I doubted you and especially for embarrassing you in front of Lisa."

Kenneth looked at Benny. "You're my brother and my best friend. I promise you that I will never do anything that I think will hurt you. I want you to known that and believe it."

"I do know that, K.J. I just left JeNelle's. I spent part of the day with her. She still wants to keep our friendship where it is—purely platonic—but I'm working on that," he said, grinning and winking. "When I saw the pictures of you two together, and read all of those articles, I thought that was the reason she would not let me fall in love with her. I thought that maybe she might be falling in love with you."

Kenneth could not look into Benny's eyes. His head was pounding and he felt terrible for being disingenuous with his brother; something that he had never done before. Still, his heart swelled with the knowledge that JeNelle still wanted a platonic relationship with his brother. He looked down at the papers on his desk again, as if what he was saying was of minimal importance.

"Give her time. JeNelle's not going to move at 900 knots the way you do. She's a very special lady. If you're falling in love with her, don't fall too fast. Wait for her to catch up. It's only been a few months."

"I want…rather, I *need* someone in my life; someone who cares about me, not just someone who wants a boy toy. I've been with more women than I can remember and I've respected all of them, but today's women don't seem to have dreams of love and romance anymore. They seem to give it all at the office and don't save enough of themselves for men in their lives. I haven't met or been with anyone who wants what I want: the simple pleasures like a happy home and a family. A life that doesn't involve closing a big deal, or becoming famous, or making piles of money, or making all the right career choices like my friend Stacy. I keep looking for the new woman with old fashion dreams and values and I keep coming up empty. JeNelle is a few years older than I am, about your age, but she's as close to the kind of perfect relationship that I'm looking for. That's not to say that she's not ambitious, but she's made it. She's already who she wants to be and she's comfortable with that. I want her to be comfortable with me. To trust me."

"You're an explorer; a risk taker. I know you want someone who is just as daring as you are and maybe that's JeNelle, but she's a tough read. A relationship isn't only about one person's agenda. Make sure you're what she's looking for. I like her and respect her and she would make any man she chose to be with very proud to be with her. I love you and I want it to work out between you and JeNelle, if that's what you both want. Still, before you try to move to the next level, make sure of what JeNelle wants; not just your needs. When you do that I'll give you all my support toward that end."

Benny embraced Kenneth and they talked about other things. Kenneth told Benny how much he enjoyed meeting Cecil and Janice. He described his meetings with them and Benny roared with laughter. Benny wanted to tell Kenneth about Stacy and his baby, but he held back. He wanted to tell Kenneth about Vivian, but he held that back, too. They were laughing loudly when Lisa knocked on the door and peeked in.

"I'm sorry to break up what appears to be a happy reunion, but, Kenneth, the limo will be here shortly. We have dinner reservations at 6:00 P.M. and the theater doors open at eight o'clock. I'll keep your friend company while you shower and change."

"Oh, I'm sorry, Lisa. Please come in. You two haven't been formally introduced. This isn't just my friend; this good-looking kid is one of my brothers, Captain Benjamin Staton Alexander, US Air Force. Benjamin, this is Dr. Lisa Lambert, Special Assistant to the Governor for Economic Affairs."

When Lisa stepped inside the door, both men's eyes bugged and their mouths flew open. Kenneth dropped the pen he was holding and it rolled off his desk and onto the floor. He did not attempt to retrieve it. Lisa was decked out and looking totally correct in a very chic, sheer black body dress draped over one shoulder and held up only by one silver button. She had a diamond-studded comb in her hair that was pulled back in a French roll. Her long shapely legs were covered in black nylons and her black suede pumps had cascading diamond tips on the toes. She had a silver fox fur over her arm and she was unwrapping a shoulder-to-hip length sequenced evening bag, as she approached Benny.

"It's a pleasure to finally meet you, Captain Alexander," she said extending her hand. "Kenneth has often talked about you." Then turning to Kenneth, Lisa said, "Darling, limo? Dinner? Theater? Remember, Kenneth? I'll keep Captain Alexander company while you shower and change."

"Limo? Oh, yes, sure, uh, sure," he faltered, confused. "Let me get showered. I'll be ready shortly," Kenneth stammered, as he tried to tear himself away from the view of Lisa. She looked fabulous; simply attired, but very chic. He was seeing her from a different perspective. Not the calculating business persona he witnessed often on previous occasions. Not the relentless competitor he faced many times on the racquetball court. Now he saw a woman. A very sensuous woman.

"Please call me Lisa, Benny…I mean, call me Benny, Lisa," Benny stumbled, kissing her hand, very much affected by her appearance. "And may I say that you look stunning this evening."

"Thank you, Benny. Before I left to get dressed, I heard you mention JeNelle Towson. I understand from Kenneth that you're seeing her. She's a close friend of mine. She has been for some time."

"Yes, we are friends. I was with her earlier today in Santa Barbara."

"I haven't seen her since the Gala over a month or maybe it was as much as six or seven weeks ago now. How is she doing?"

"She's beautiful, as usual, but I didn't know that you were at the Gala too from the pictures that I saw in the newspaper."

"I hope that you're not referring to that dreadful article about JeNelle and Kenneth," she said and laughed.

"That's the one."

"Well, the photographers were supposed to shoot pictures of JeNelle because she received a very prestigious and well-deserved award. Kenneth was being a real gentleman since JeNelle didn't have an escort. It's a shame that her shining moment was marred by those stupid press articles. I was there all evening with Kenneth and JeNelle and they were both livid when the articles appeared in the newspaper. JeNelle was ready to file suit, but Kenneth's been rock solid through it all. He's quite a man."

"Kenneth didn't tell me that he had a date for the Gala. In fact, I had arranged a blind date for him. How long have you known my brother? He hasn't mentioned you to me before."

"Not nearly long enough to start bringing me home to meet your family," she teased.

"Oh, I see that you've heard about our family tradition."

"You'd be surprised at what I know about your family. Kenneth talks about little else. We don't get to see each other nearly often enough since I'm usually in Sacramento and his business keeps him on the go so much, but we're working on it."

Kenneth returned to his office dressed in a very handsome Italian suit and joined Benny and Lisa, as they talked on the sofa. Shirley knocked on the office door and came in.

"Oh, you're not working tonight, Kenneth?" Shirley asked. "Hello, Benny." Benny nodded his acknowledgement.

"No, he's not, Shirley," Lisa interjected smugly. "Not while I'm in town and he'll be late coming into the office in the mornings as well. I'm sure you'll agree, Shirley, that Kenneth works entirely too hard. You and I are going to have to work harder to free up his schedule more from now on."

Benny felt comforted by Lisa's obvious overtures of deep feelings about his brother and, since Kenneth didn't protest her behavior, he felt that his accusations about him and JeNelle were totally unfounded and without merit. He did wonder how Shirley was handling the relationship between Kenneth and Lisa. Shirley, to his way of thinking, was obviously infatuated with Kenneth and wondered whether his brother had a clue.

The limo arrived and Kenneth helped Lisa into the car. He turned to Benny and said, "See you next time, little brother, but call before you come."

They embraced and Benny watched, as the limousine drove out of sight. He said to himself, "Yep, Big Brother, no more surprise visits. You've got your hands full and so do I."

"You know you're really quick on your feet, Lisa. I appreciate what you did for me back there. I wasn't sure that Benny was going to believe me. You can have the limo driver drop me off anywhere. I'll take a cab home so that you won't be late for your appointment tonight."

"That was no act just for Benny's sake. You're coming with me tonight. The Governor is in town for a dinner with the California State Manufacturer's Association. That's the reason that I've been in town this week working with the Association's Board of Directors. The Governor is giving the keynote address and he wants to meet you in person. I was going to tell you about it just as your brother burst through the door."

"It's a good thing that I keep a change of clothes at the office. I usually need more notice than that, Lisa, so that I can be prepared in advance."

"The only thing that you need to be prepared for tonight, Kenneth, is to work on that kiss. Now let's try that again. This time with a lot more energy."

Kenneth complied and kissed Lisa long and sensuously until he began to feel something that he had only felt for JeNelle—his nature beginning to rise for someone other than JeNelle.

"That's more like it," Lisa whispered, as he released her. "I've wanted to do that for a very long time. We'll just have to keep practicing this move all night so that it will be perfect by the morning."

Kenneth kissed her again. It had been too long since he had held a woman in his arms like this, and Lisa was no ordinary woman. She handled him as skillfully as she handled her iPad. It was as if she knew all the right buttons to push. There was no hunt and peck. All ten fingers were manipulating him. Throughout the formal dinner, Lisa would whisper something to him that would get a rise out of him. She rested her hand on his inner thigh and massaged it under the table, as they both carried on conversations with other people, including the Governor. He had great difficulty concentrating on his conversation. At one point, as her hands reached his crotch, he placed his hand on top of hers to stop her. In the darkened theater, she moved close to him, and her lips would graze his ear or his cheek.

Later that night when the limo driver let them out at the Fairmont Hotel on Nob Hill, Kenneth was reluctant to go in. Lisa pushed another button. She wasn't taking no for an answer. She took his hands and held them behind her back inside her silver fox fur. She shifted her body against his, and licked and kissed his neck, his chin and his lips. As they went through the lobby, she told the desk clerk to place no calls to her suite. In the vacant elevator, she cupped his face in her soft hands, licked his lips and his tongue, and pressed him against the elevator wall feeling his chest and abdomen. She didn't release him even as he opened the door to her suite and she flipped on the 'Do Not Disturb' light. She began to undress him sensually and skillfully. He loosened the one button on her dress and it slid down her body to the floor. She was not wearing a bra and the tips of her breasts stood at attention. He embraced her and kissed her repeatedly, feeling the smoothness of her back and spine. Cupping her butt in his hands, he brought her up flush to his raised, hardened ridge. His reluctance dwindled in equal proportion to the rise in his nature. She skillfully set about her task of seduction. Tying his hands above his head to the bed, Lisa covered each inch of his body with her tongue, teeth and mouth. He called for divine intervention, but there was no reprieve. He was powerless to resist her. Their sexual prowess was as intense and all-consuming as their racquetball games were. Every nerve ending of Kenneth's body was exposed. There was no place on his body that Lisa did not turn into an erogenous zone.

In the morning, Kenneth awoke and could not remember feeling so relaxed or so spent, but unfulfilled emotionally. The sheets were still damp from their heated night of passion. Lisa sat writing near a window at a small, round table. She was wearing only a short, satin robe tied loosely at the waist. Long, silky and muscled, her legs were crossed above the knee and revealed her firm thighs and bare feet. Kenneth sat up in the bed and stretched. He could feel every muscle in his body, but none responded. He was totally spent. Lisa glanced in his direction.

"Good morning. How do you feel?" she asked with a sly, somewhat triumphant, smile on her firm lips.

"Like Samson after Delilah," he said dryly, trying to summon the energy to move.

"Well, Samson, I have just what you need to get your strength back," she said, as she brought a breakfast tray to the bed. She straddled him on her knees, as she placed several pillows behind his back. Her breast brushed against his cheek. She positioned herself until they were navel to navel. Her body felt warm and inviting.

The breakfast tray held an assortment of fresh fruits, blocks of hard cheeses, fresh bagels and cream cheese, and a mountain of fresh whipped cream. She began to feed him from the tray of fruits and lick any juice that dripped from his lips. She placed his hands on her hips and she began to move, as if she were on a rocking horse. She rocked slowly, methodically, but forcefully against him. He was lost in her motion against his rising nature, the fruits, her touch and her mouth all over him. He could not remember the exact moment that his nature reached critical mass. He closed his eyes and submitted to the sensations she caused in him. He didn't know how he was going to summon the energy to return the passion.

Lisa smeared a line of whipped cream on him and held down his hands, as she licked it all off his neck and chest. Then she licked and kissed his eyelids, his ears, his neck, his chin, his chest, his stomach, his abdomen and then attacked the hubs of his swollen muscle. She had a seemingly insatiable desire to extract every drop of life-giving fluid from his body. He tilted his head back against the headboard when he felt her roll the condom into place and mount him. Again, he silently called for divine intervention and again his cries went unanswered. For nearly an hour, Lisa kept up her manipulation of him and each time that he thought that he might recover, she would begin to excite him again with some new technique of which she seemed to have an endless supply. Finally, he could no longer hold back. Waves of emotion flooded over him. His muscles constricted and he exploded deep inside her. He thought that the spasms would never stop, but finally, his body began to relax. He felt about as strong as Jell-O when Lisa finally released her hold on him.

"Now, don't you feel better?" Lisa asked softly, her tongue still working his.

"Better than what, Lisa?" he asked breathlessly. "Better than a wet dishrag? A wet mop? What?"

"Ah, come on, Kenneth. You work out. You're a young, strong, virile man," she teased, kissing his chest, gnawing his nipples.

"That was then, but I've aged considerably since we've been playing racquetball and even more so in the last twenty-four hours," he said dryly.

"You matched me point for point. It was a hell of a match."

"Yeah, Delilah scores, Samson zip."

Lisa laughed. "Come on, Samson, let's get you into a nice, hot shower and see if we can't revive you."

"You mean I have to get up and walk?" he asked incredulously.

"Sure you do. You can handle it, Samson. I've got faith in you," she teased.

Lisa rolled out of bed and pulled Kenneth up by his hands. She led him to the bathroom to shower. Lisa sensuously soaped his back and his chest with each stroke, but when she reached for the area between his thighs the telephone rang.

Lisa left the shower and Kenneth slumped against the marble wall. *Saved by the proverbial bell*, he thought. Every muscle in his body ached. He could barely move. *Yes*, he thought, *this woman knows no bounds or impediments to her sexual skills and abilities either.* He let the water beat his body until it began to tingle. Then there it was again, the vision of JeNelle with him in the beam of light. He let the water beat him in his face, as if the force of the shower would wash her vision from his mind. It didn't. If anything, he wanted JeNelle more, but he realized that she could never be his. He promised his brother that he would support him with JeNelle. That was a promise that he would keep no matter what. JeNelle was outside of his reach, where she belonged.

"That was my secretary, Jonathan. Apparently your office is trying to reach you," Lisa said, re-entering the shower.

"Did he say what it was about?"

"No, he didn't know what it was about, but your office has called twice."

Kenneth got out of the shower and wrapped a towel around his waist. He placed another one around his neck to dry his face and hair, then went to find his pager. Lisa followed him. The pager was turned off. He looked at Lisa quizzically.

"Yes, I turned it off," she admitted. "I told you that I've been waiting for you to make the first move for over a month, but since you didn't, I had to. I didn't want us to be disturbed."

Kenneth said nothing although Lisa's behavior annoyed him. He resented being manipulated in his business or his personal life. He would have to discuss this with her. If they were going to continue to have an intimate relationship, she would have to refrain from taking liberties with his life. He went to his cell phone, which was also turned off and dialed his office. When Sara answered, Kenneth asked whether he had received any urgent calls.

"No, Mr. Alexander. Your brother, Benjamin, called twice, but he didn't say it was urgent. In fact, he was laughing and saying something about racquetball and a water bill, but he didn't explain to me what he meant by that," Sara said. "He just left messages on your voicemail.

"Then who called Dr. Lambert's office looking for me?"

"Oh, that was Ms. Taylor. She had me call twice."

"Is Shirley there now?"

"Yes, Sir. She seems to be in quite a state."

"Connect me with her, please."

A pause and then.

"Kenneth?"

"Yes, Shirley, I understand that you have been trying to reach me. What's so urgent?"

"You didn't show up at work this morning and you didn't answer your telephone at home or your pager or your cell phone. Your van is still parked in the parking lot. I thought that something might have happened to you."

"Is that the only reason that you've been trying to reach me?"

"Well, our new employees reported for work today and I wanted to know whether you were coming in. It's already eleven o'clock," she said peevishly.

"I was not scheduled to meet with them today. Tom is handling the orientation. I thought that there was some emergency. I'm not at home, but I'll be in the office in shortly. I'll see you then."

Annoyed, Kenneth hung up the phone and looked quizzically at Lisa. Obviously, she had overheard his side of his conversation with Shirley.

"Don't say I didn't warn you," she said, as if reading his mind. "I just spent a spectacular night and morning with you. Something that Shirley wants desperately to do. Remember, I'm a woman. I know these things."

Kenneth shook his head. Lisa approached him and released the towel from around his waist.

Kenneth backed away. "Oh no you don't, Delilah. You're not sapping any more of my strength today. I'm getting dressed and going to the office."

Lisa kissed him and he returned her passion.

"Until the next time," Lisa whispered, reigniting his passion. He still had to talk with her, but he didn't have the time or inclination to do it at that moment. He needed to get back to work.

When Kenneth reached his office, the staff was a buzz. The new employees had reported for work and were being shown around by Tom.

"And here's our illustrious leader, Kenneth Alexander, now," Tom said, as Kenneth came through the door.

"Hello, everyone," Kenneth said. "Welcome aboard. I regret that I was unavailable to greet you this morning, but I will meet with you all jointly, as previously scheduled, tomorrow morning at eight o'clock and then individually throughout the day. In the meantime, I leave you in Tom's capable hands to continue with your orientation."

Tom said to the new employees, "I'll be with you all in a minute. I need to speak with Mr. Alexander. Juan will show you to the Break Room." Tom took Kenneth's arm and led him to a secluded spot while Juan took over. "Man! What happened to you?" Tom asked emphatically. "You look worn out."

"You wouldn't believe me if I told you, Tom," Kenneth said dryly.

"Well, my friend, you've done it again."

"What now?"

Tom opened the newspaper and there was a picture of him and Lisa at the Manufacturers' Dinner.

"Damn, it must have been a slow news day! Can't these society column reporters find anyone else to focus on except me?"

"Most men would kill to be in your shoes, Kenneth."

"And be killed in my shoes," he quipped, as he headed for his office.

Tom laughed and winked at Kenneth. "Go get them, Champ!"

Shirley stopped Kenneth in the hallway. "Are you going to work out now, Kenneth?"

"I already have, Shirley," he said cryptically, as he opened the door to his office, "but I think that we need to talk later."

He closed the door behind him. He immediately dialed Benny's number.

"Hello."

"Benny, what's up? I understand that you've tried to reach me."

"K.J., what's wrong with you? You sound tired. Have you been playing racquetball all night and again so early this morning with the lovely Lisa Lambert?"

"Not exactly, Benny."

"I tried to reach you at home last night at about two o'clock in the morning and again this morning at 6:30 A.M. Then I called the office twice and no one knew where you were. Then I saw the morning newspaper. What's happening, my brother?"

Kenneth groaned. "I'll tell you later. What was so important?"

"I wanted to apologize again for acting like a jerk. I spoke with JeNelle last night after I got home and I told her what I had done. To say that she isn't happy with me is putting it diplomatically. I also told her about you and the lovely Lisa. She seemed surprised about you two."

Kenneth felt a knot tighten in the pit of his stomach and suddenly his head began to pound. He sat down in his chair, closed his eyes, and leaned his head back against the leather.

"No need to apologize," he said, squeezing his eyes tightly closed. "If I were in your shoes and didn't understand the facts, perhaps I would have felt uneasy, too."

"Based on the pictures in today's paper and the sound of your voice, Lisa must have crossed the business acquaintance line at 900 knots. How many 'G's' were you pulling until eleven-thirty today?"

"No comment," Kenneth said dryly. "I'm not giving any exclusive interviews on that topic."

Benny laughed. "It's about time you got that monkey off your back! My money's on Lisa. She's a sure winner. Looks like I won't have to give you any lessons after all. She must have whipped you to a frazzle—on the racquetball court, that is." Benny laughed loudly again.

What Benny didn't know was that he was dying inside while his brother enjoyed teasing him.

"I told you, little brother. It was a tie."

"Sure you're right! Hang in there, brother. From the looks of the lovely Lisa, it's going to be a helluva match!"

"Now that you've amused yourself at my expense, may I get some work done?"

Benny laughed louder. "Sure, but before I let you go, I just wanted to tell you that I'm going home Friday for the weekend and I'm taking someone home with me to meet the folks."

The knot in Kenneth's stomach grew tighter and his head ached harder, as if someone was going mad in his head playing Tycoon drums.

"I thought you said that JeNelle wasn't ready for a commitment?"

"I'll explain more when I get back from Goodwill. I can't talk about this yet. I'll call you or come to San Francisco as soon as I can. My best to the lovely Lisa."

"Okay, Benny, I'll look to hear from you next week."

Kenneth hung up. He thought that the blood would rush out of his brain. Benny is taking JeNelle home to meet the family and he knew what that meant. No one took a significant other home unless he or she was very serious about the relationship. Benny said that he wanted a full-time relationship with a woman like JeNelle. She must have agreed. Something in his heart wrenched.

Chapter 22

Vivian was packing when Chuck Montgomery knocked on her open bedroom door.

"Hi, Chuck, how are things with Angelique?"

"She's coming along just fine, but how are things with you?"

"As well as can be expected under the circumstances," Vivian said sadly.

"Then the test was positive?"

"Yes, unfortunately, it was. You were right. I'm sorry for the way that I treated you. You didn't deserve that. I know that you were only trying to help me just like you always do."

She hugged him and laid her head on his broad, firm chest. He tightly embraced her and soothingly rubbed her back.

"You don't sound happy about this turn of events, Annie. I thought that you and Carlton were ready to take the big leap. You're wearing his engagement ring."

She released Chuck and returned to her packing.

"Carlton is ready, but I had different dreams for what I wanted my life to be before I marry Carlton. Children were definitely included in the picture after we were married, but not now."

"What are you and Carlton going to do?"

"I haven't told Carlton or anyone else except you and my brother, Benny, about my pregnancy. His team has a tough game today against an ACC top team. I didn't want to distract him with this news."

"You are going to tell Carlton about this, aren't you? He has a right to know what's going on. I don't have to tell you that this is something that two people in love should share."

"That's what my brother said. He agreed to meet me at home to give me his moral support. That's why I'm packing. I'm leaving today for the weekend. I'll see Carlton before I go to talk with my parents. He will want to go with me, I'm sure."

"Your brother is right. No matter what, Carlton deserves the chance to share this with you and your family. Your brother sounds like he's got his head on straight. I'd like to meet him someday."

"Apparently, you already have."

Chuck's brows bunched. "I don't understand."

"Benny told me that he played against you at the Boston Shootout years ago."

"Wait a minute. You don't mean 'Benny the Bruiser,' do you? Big, good looking kid. Had all the ladies after him."

"I've never heard anyone call him, 'The Bruiser', but that's his picture on my dresser. As for the women—no question. He hasn't lost his touch. That's why I call this house 'Benny's Bordello'. The house came by that name honestly. Benny owns it."

Chuck picked up the framed picture. "That's the same guy all right. This kid was a natural. I had my hands full with him, but I liked him even though he bowed me in the face and dunked on me twice. This kid was a real competitive, country kid. He was younger than me, but he had a big body. Strong as an ox. Couldn't move him off the blocks. I sure was glad that I didn't have to see him in the pros. Competition was tough enough. I lost track of him. What's he doing now?"

"He's a Captain in the Air Force stationed at March outside of San Diego. He flies jets and he loves it. He had opportunities to play basketball in the ACC or the Big East, but Benny's always been an explorer. He's wanted to fly jets all of his life. You know, walk the path less traveled. I think he's planning to move into space flight.

"When we were little, we'd swing in a hammock that my brother, Kenneth, made and just look up at the stars for hours. He's a Star Wars fanatic He said then that he wanted to be up there racing across the sky, traveling from planet to planet. That was his dream and now he's doing it. Not the interplanetary travel, of course, but he is living his dream. Life was so much simpler then, than it is now."

Vivian was suddenly sad. Chuck noticed, embraced her again, and turned her face up to his. He could see the distress in her eyes and he wanted to kiss away her pain. Even through her despair, she was so beautiful. Holding her in his arms was sending him into the danger zone, but he wanted and needed to be there for her now and in the future. Although they had only known each other for a short time, she was constantly in his dreams both day and night, but he had not told her how he felt about her. He respected the sanctity of her engagement to Carlton, but looking into her eyes now made him want to forget that. Her lips were but a breath away. He choked off his impulse.

"Come on, Annie. You'll live your dreams someday, too. You've got grit! I knew it the minute I laid eyes on you at O'Hare Airport. No one's going to stop you. I'm sure of that."

After a last squeeze, Vivian moved out of Chuck's embrace and returned to her packing. "Thanks, Chuck. I wish that it was that simple, but I know that once Carlton knows I'm pregnant, he'll try to stop me. *I'm* sure of that."

"He'll stand by you, Annie. If he's the man you think he is, he'll help you live your dreams. Don't worry about it."

He wanted to say that if Carlton didn't, that he would.

Vivian looked up into Chuck's warm, brown eyes.

"I don't think that you understand. I've thought about this situation for a long time. That's why I haven't done anything about it. Plus, we're in the beginning of March Madness. For Carlton that's the hunt for the Holy Grail. If they win today, they have a good chance of making it into the NCAA tournament. Carlton has already made it perfectly clear he doesn't want me to have a career other than being his wife, the mother of his children, and his biggest cheerleader."

"Then you'll have to convince him otherwise. If anybody can do it, Annie, you can. My money is on you, kid. You're not some trophy that any man could put on a shelf and take it down when he wants to shine."

Vivian finished packing and Chuck carried her bag to her car.

"Look after everyone for me, Chuck, and please don't mention the pregnancy to anyone. I don't want the housemates to feel like they have to start looking for somewhere else to live. This semester has been tough enough on all of us, except David, of course. They don't need any distractions now."

"Keep your powder dry, Annie. You'll be fine. Don't worry about anything. This is a sturdy house and so are the people who are in it. That includes you, too," he said, kissing her on the cheek.

Vivian drove away and headed for Interstate-95 South. She had a long drive ahead of her, nearly seven hours, but she needed the time to think about how to break the news to Carlton. How she was going to convince him that marriage and a baby were not what she wanted or what they needed now. Carlton should know that she was not rejecting him. He knew that she loved him.

As she drove the ribbon-straight highway with light traffic, she turned on her XM-radio to listen to the game, but the memories of how she and Carlton met at a frat party during Greek Week on Clark-Atlanta's campus came rushing back to her. Carlton was then a fifth-year basketball athlete at Clark-Atlanta because of an injury, which forced him to sit out of basketball for a year. It was her second year at Spelman. It was early in the semester. Her friends literally had to drag her with them to a party. Frat parties back then were notorious for being wild and raucous on Clark-Atlanta's campus. The party had been just as Vivian expected—a lot of noise, loud music, barks, and stepping. The smoke from marijuana and cigarettes was thick and pungent inside the frat house. At her friends' insistence, she had danced a few times, but the sweaty bodies, stifling heat, and smoke-filled room made her lightheaded and queasy, so she had gone outside to breathe and get some fresh air. She had only been out there for a few minutes when her friend, June Austen, had come down the steps looking for her.

"*Viv, this real cute, phine, super phine, built like a big dog, well-hung frat brother wants to step to you,*" she bubbled. "*He's been asking everybody who you are and all about you. He said that he saw you before playing basketball in the gym. C'mon back into the party. He's looking for a hook up with you.*"

"*June, you know that I don't do drugs and I can't stand the smell of pot. It's gotten in my clothes and my hair. All I want to do is go take a shower and wash my clothes.*"

"*C'mon, Viv. You've gotta do this if you want to pledge DST this year. You've got to be seen in the right places and with the right people. This guy plays basketball for Clark. All the ladies have been trying to tap this hunk. You don't want some AKA to get him, do you? It would be bad for your image.*"

"*No disrespect to the good sistahs in the Soros. They do good work, but I don't give a flying fig about pledging or my image on campus if I lose my self-respect. I'm not being someone's chameleon just so I can pledge. So you can tell this pretend cute, jive-talking basketball-playing, pot-smoking, frat-dog with the big balls to just go bark up some other tree.*"

"*You're such a naïve country girl that it's a shame. This is the big city, girl. Not some hick town in South Carolina. Competition for men around here is fierce. You'd better forget those antisocial ways of yours and step to the music. Otherwise you'll find yourself on the outside looking in on the good times.*"

"Good times?" she said. "*You call this the* 'good times'? *People spilling beer all over you. Trying to slobber you down. Sweatin' you. Talking about 'hey, baby, can I get with you tonight?' I may be a country girl, but I ain't giving it up out of both panty legs just so that I can be on the inside with the 'good times'. You stay here, if you want to. I'm going back to the dorm.*"

"May I escort you to the dorm?" a deep, melodic voice came at them from the steps above where June and Vivian were standing. "*A good-looking, stacked with tits and ass, fresh leggy hunnie dip like you needs protection. Nobody messes with Carlton Andrews' women."*

"*Oooh,*" June swooned, as she hunched Vivian, leaned toward her, and whispered, "*that's the guy that I've been telling you about. Ain't he phine?*"

Vivian rolled her eyes at June. "*You handle it, June. Take care of my light work. I'm looking for a challenge and he ain't it.*"

She turned on her heels and walked away toward Spelman's dormitories. It was one of those hot, sweltering September nights in HotLanta. Everybody was outside trying to keep cool. Vivian moved along briskly in her walking shorts and halter-top. Her Keds, with rolled down sox, made it easy to move swiftly along the paths that led to Spelman.

"*Hey, baby, what's your hurry, you phine mamma jamma?!*" Carlton asked, as he came up behind her. "*You're putting a hurtin' on those shorts. Do fries come with that shake! A sweet tasty hunnie dip like you shouldn't be out here alone.*"

Vivian didn't turn around. She just kept on walking.

"*Hey, baby, you phine thang. Didn't you hear me? I'm Carlton Andrews! I'm the man and I want to get witchu! Can't a brother get some digits?!*"

Vivian stopped walking, turned around, and put her hands on her hips. "*Look, I don't care who you are! Step off!*"

"*Whoa, baby, you didn't have to crack on a brother like dat. Chill a minute, baby,*" he said, bobbing and weaving around her, scoping her from every angle.

"*I'm not your baby! Don't step to me with that jive-ass, weak rap! I ain't about hearing it!*"

"*You gonna kick a brother to the curb like that, my sistah? All I want to do is get a straw and sip you up slowly. You know how it be, sistah. I been scopin' you out. You make me so hard I could break a brick! I wanna get witchu tonight. Show you how a pillow can talk. Make you wanna holla my name 'cause you love my game. I got your rock and I'm ready to roll.*"

"*I ain't your sister and hell will freeze over before you get next to me.*"

She started walking again.

"*Oh, so you one of those uppity Black bitches, huh?*"

That cut it. She stopped, turned around, and hit him dead in his jaw.

"*Who you calling a bitch?*"

The blow took Carlton by surprise. It was so forceful that it rocked him backward flat on his butt. Vivian stood over him, fuming, with her fists balled up at her sides ready for him to make a move. She was seething with anger and Carlton could see that in her flashing brown eyes. He got to his feet and backed away without another word. Vivian turned and stormed away, continuing her now angry pace toward the dormitory. She didn't realize how badly her wrist hurt until she slammed her door behind her in her dormitory room. She was still angry. She made an ice pack, tied it to her wrist to stop the swelling, and picked up the telephone.

"Benny!"

"Hey, Viv. What's wrong with you? You sound angry."

"I am! This brother called me an 'uppity Black bitch'."

"What? Why did he do that?"

"I wasn't trying to hear his lame chat. So he called me a 'bitch'."

"What did you say?"

"I didn't say anything until after I coldcocked him. Stole him dead in his jaw!"

"He didn't come back at you, did he?"

"No, he stepped off."

"Way to go, Viv! You handled him. I'll bet that he won't come at you like that again."

"He'd better not! I was ready to hurt the brother. Who does he think that he is, calling somebody a 'bitch'? Nobody's ever going to call me out my name like that and get away with it!"

"You tell 'em, slugger! You want me to come? Are you all right otherwise?"

"No, you don't need to fly here just for this. I'm all right. I might have broken my wrist though. It hurts like hell!"

"Put some ice on it, then heat if it starts to swell, and go get it X-rayed."

"I put ice on it already. I remembered what you taught me. If it's still hurting in the morning, I'll go to the infirmary before I go to class. Basketball practice starts next month so this has got to be okay."

"You get some rest, but if you need me, you call me. I can be there in a few hours. I'll call you tomorrow and see how you're doing. I love you, Viv."

"I love you more, Benny. Oh, by the way, were you with someone?"

"Uh, sis, there are some things that you don't need to know about," he said, laughing.

"What's her name?" Vivian laughed.

"Crystal, now go get some rest."

"Benny's Bordello," she said and laughed. "Last night it was Teresa. Night before that it was Alicia, and before that it was...."

"None of your business. Good night, Viv."

"Kiss, kiss," she joked.

The next day it was all over every campus that some woman had broken Carlton Andrews' jaw. June Austin had come running into Vivian's room, as she was preparing to go to the infirmary.

"Vivian, did you hear about Carlton Andrews?" she was so excited that she was nearly spastic. *"Some bitch broke his jaw!"*

"Who are you callin' a 'bitch'?" Vivian turned around, fuming.

June saw the ice pack on her wrist and jumped back. *"You did that?"* she asked with her eyes and mouth wide open. *"Are you crazy? That's Carlton Andrews! He's the man! He's a star on Clark's basketball team. You can't just go around slugging him in the jaw!"*

"I don't give a flying fig who he is! He called me a 'bitch'!"

"So? And your point is?"

"So? What do you mean 'so'? June, if you don't understand that is an insult to a woman, then I sure as hell can't explain it to you!"

"He could have you arrested, you know. They could charge you with an unprovoked assault or something like that. You could go to jail and then what would happen to your grandiose ideas about being a lawyer and a judge?"

"Unprovoked?" Vivian yelled. *"You'd let somebody call you a 'bitch' and do nothing about it?"*

"Niggas be doin' it all the time, Vivian. They don't mean nothing by it. I keep trying to tell you, Kunta Kinte Alexander, you'se in America now. You ain't back in them woods swinging from those trees."

"June Austen, let me tell you something quick, fast, and in a hurry. So listen up, sistah! I'm no 'nigga' and I resent your using that term about or around me! You're my friend, but if you think being called a 'bitch' or a 'nigger' is phat, then you're one more ignorant fool! I'm out of here!"

Vivian went to the infirmary. She only had a bad sprain. The doctor wrapped it and asked how it happened. She explained what she had done to Carlton Andrews.

"Good for you!" the young, male doctor said. *"It's about time that my brothers started treating their Black sisters with some respect. Women have it hard enough without having men put them down. Andrews was in here last night swearing that he had walked into a door. He's not badly injured, but he'll be feeling the pain for a few weeks. I didn't think that his injury came from a swinging door. I'm proud of you, sister! You did the right thing! Don't you ever let anyone put you down like that!"*

Vivian thanked the doctor. His comments just reinforced her belief that Carlton's behavior was totally out of place, unacceptable, and inexcusable. She hated resorting to violence. Under ordinary circumstances, she was a non-violent person. She vowed never to let anyone force her into violent behavior again. There were other ways to handle stupidity and ignorance and she was going to find a way to do just that.

Two weeks later, June came to Vivian's room and asked her to go to The Rathskeller, a club just off campus. At first, Vivian was reluctant, but June said that she just didn't want to go there by herself. Vivian agreed, since she and June had not been speaking since their argument. Vivian wanted a chance to patch things up with June, but she didn't really want to go to a club.

"Aw, c'mon, Vivian," June whined. "You haven't been out in weeks. All you do is study, play ball, and work on those committees for this cause or that cause. We never have any fun together anymore."

"All right, June, but I'm not going to be out with you all night."

They arrived at the club and Vivian was glad that the place was nearly deserted. Vivian started toward a booth in the front by a window, but June dragged her to a booth in a dark, secluded area in the back of the club. Vivian couldn't see anyone sitting in the booth over the high-back seats until she started to sit down and slide in toward the wall. There, sitting in the darkened area, was Carlton Andrews. She started to get up, but June blocked her in.

"What's going on here?" Vivian demanded, looking at June.

"Carlton has something that he wants to say to you, Vivian, so you just sit there and listen to the man," June insisted, as she slid out of the booth

"Thanks, June," Carlton said. "I owe you one."

"Anytime, Carlton, you know that." She grinned, preened, and then headed toward the front of the club where some other people they knew were sitting.

Carlton was a handsome man. Smooth, dark-chocolate complexion with black eyes and naturally curly, thick black hair. He had a strong face, square jaw, with white teeth and ebony black eyebrows and mustache. He took a cigarette lighter out of his pocket and lit the candle on the table. He had big hands with long fingers. The thick gold chain around his wrist and his neck, and the small gold hoop earring in his left earlobe, flashed against his black skin when he lit the candle on the table. He was wearing a gold watch that had brilliant stones where the hours were on the watch face. His Clark-Atlanta short sleeve white T-shirt clung to his muscular body like someone had painted it on. Yes, she could see why girls were ready to lay down for his favor, but she wasn't going to be one of them.

"All right, Mr. Andrews. You've gone to a considerable amount of trouble to get me here, so say whatever it is that you want to say so that I can leave."

He raised his eyes to hers. *"Coach says that I have to apologize to you for calling you a bitch or I'll sit the bench the whole season."*

"You mean that this was not your idea? Your coach is forcing you into doing this?"

"Well, yes and no," he said slowly, hunching his massive shoulders.

"Well, which one is it, yes or no? Either he forced you into this apology or he didn't. It can't be both ways!" Vivian snapped.

"Coach talked to me; said that I wasn't shit. Told me that you should have kicked my ass all over campus and charged me with sexual harassment and a few other things that I don't want to think about. He asked me whether my mama was a bitch, too. That made me angry. He wanted me to get angry and jump in his face so that he could have an excuse to whip my ass and kick me off campus. And he could do it, too. The man bench presses three hundred fifty pounds."

Carlton shifted, seemingly uncomfortably in his seat.

"I never thought about it when I called someone a bitch before. Everybody does it. It's like saying hello. It didn't mean anything. I was just pissed off because a fine hunnie dip...I mean, an attractive, young lady like yourself was kicking me to the curb. Hell, nobody ever did that to me before! Hunnies are always giving up the pussy...I mean, having sex with me and coming back for more. I could get any hunnie on this campus if I wanted to. They're always hanging around the team. This is my fifth year here, no hunnie ever turned me down...and nobody, especially no hunnie, ever broke my jaw 'cause I called her a bitch."

He shifted in his seat again.

"Now, some people are grittin' on me and booing me when I'm in basketball practice. Some people aren't even speaking to me anymore and Coach acts like I don't even exist. So yes, Coach told me that, if I was a man, I knew what I had to do, but he said he wasn't going to make that decision for me. I know that I'd be riding the pine until I made the right decision. I need Coach to help me play in the pros when I get out of here. If he's pissed off at me, then he's not going to do jack shit for me. So I talked to June about you and she said that you even called her 'ignorant' for letting a brother or anybody call her a bitch."

Vivian listened to Carlton Andrews, but she wasn't impressed.

"Look, Andrews, I could care less whether you get splinters in your butt from riding the pine or get into the pros. When you're ready to apologize to me for calling me a bitch because you know that you were wrong, then let me know. Until then, your Coach was right, you ain't shit!"

Vivian got up from the table and walked to the front of the club toward June who was standing at the bar. She pulled June aside.

"June Austen, your parents are spending a lot of money for your education and you haven't learned a thing. Don't you ever try to manipulate me into anything again! If you want to remain my friend, then you better start acting like it!"

Vivian left the bar and walked back to campus. She didn't hear from Carlton again, but she and June began to talk more about interpersonal relationships. They became better friends than ever before. June didn't press Vivian about going to any more fraternity parties or about joining a sorority, even though a number of sororities had invited Vivian to join.

It was Clark-Atlanta's opening basketball game of the season. The stands were packed and the band and the cheerleaders were revving up the crowd to a fever pitch. The visiting team had just been introduced and the Clark-Atlanta team was standing and clapping wildly. Each time a home-team member's name and number was announced, the crowd went wild. Carlton was the last of the starting team lineup to be introduced. He jumped up from the bench and jogged through the line, giving high-fives, as he passed. Then he suddenly went to the announcer's table and took the microphone. He quieted the crowd. His booming voice came over the loud speakers.

"As many of you already know, I made the mistake of calling one of my beautiful sisters a bitch a couple of months ago and she made me pay for it by breaking my jaw. Vivian Lynn Alexander, if you are in the house tonight, I want to apologize to you. I was wrong. I can't speak for my Black brothers, but in my view, no Black man who calls a Black woman a bitch deserves to be called a man. I'll never disrespect my Black sisters again, as long as there's breath in my body."

The crowd was stunned. Carlton returned the microphone and a thunderous standing ovation went up. Even the opposing team stood and cheered Carlton's remarks. People sitting near Vivian cheered her, too. June grabbed her and hugged her with tears in her eyes. Vivian was speechless all through the game. She watched Carlton intensely, as he played. He was a good basketball player, she thought, but not great. After all, she had seen better, literally, in her own back yard when she played with her brothers and cousins. Nevertheless, with very good teamwork, Clark-Atlanta won the game and Carlton was a hero. If not for his gamesmanship, certainly for his statement. After the game, people milled around outside the locker room door waiting for the Clark-Atlanta players to come out. When Carlton came through the doors, he was immediately mobbed by people wanting his autograph or to shake his hand, or to take a picture with him or to give him a telephone number and key to a dormitory room.

Carlton's eyes were scanning the arena while he obliged everyone's request, rejecting key offers. Then he spotted Vivian and June sitting high up on the bleachers. Their eyes locked. He kept his eyes on Vivian until he finished appeasing his fans, then he crossed the deserted gymnasium floor, and galloped up the bleachers to Vivian and June.

"*Hello, Ms. Alexander. My name is Carlton Andrews. I've wanted to meet you for some time,*" he said, extending his hand, "*so I asked June if she would make sure that you attended today's game.*"

"*Thank you, Mr. Andrews. It's a pleasure to meet you. I waited for you because I wanted to compliment you on your game and your courtside manner. Not bad for a start, Mr. Andrews, but we still have some work to do on you yet.*"

"*Why? What did I say this time?*" Carlton asked quizzically.

"*It isn't what you said, Mr. Andrews. It's what you didn't say.*"

"*All right, Ms. Alexander, you've got my undivided attention. What didn't I say?*"

"*What you didn't say was that no man who calls* a woman *a bitch deserves to be called a man.*"

"*I don't see the distinction.*"

"*You will, Mr. Andrews,*" Vivian said, with a wry smile. "I promise you that you will,"

After that day, Vivian and Carlton became good friends and then, a year later, lovers. Carlton graduated from Clark-Atlanta and was playing in the Continental Basketball League. He and Vivian didn't see much of each other during the basketball season, but after it was over, and Vivian was out of school on summer break, they would spend as much time together as possible. A year later, when Carlton re-injured his ankle, and it appeared that his basketball-playing career was at an end, he took an assistant coaching job at Grand Strand University, in part, because it was only a few hours away from Spelman and, in part, because it appeared to be a good career move.

Now three years had passed since they first met and Vivian was on her way to Carlton to tell him that she was pregnant with his child. Because of his upcoming important league game, she had not called Carlton in advance to tell him that she was coming. She also didn't want to answer any questions on the phone. This was something that they needed to discuss in person.

She pulled into the parking lot of the apartment complex where Carlton and Raymond LaForge shared an apartment. She saw Carlton's roommate driving away in a hurry. She blew her horn, but he was playing the car radio so loudly that he apparently didn't hear her. She spotted Carlton's vehicle in the parking lot and saw the lights on in his apartment. After parking, she got out of the car, and slowly walked up the steps, preparing herself for what she knew she had to do. Loud music seemed to be coming from Carlton's apartment and the closer she got to Carlton's door she could smell the faint, acrid odor of pot on the cool late afternoon air. She heard the frat brother's bark and assumed that Carlton and Raymond had company. She started to leave, but then decided that it had to be now no matter who he was entertaining. When she knocked on the door, a man, whom she did not recognize, opened it. He was only wearing a pair of Jockey briefs and pulling on a blunt. He inhaled the smoke deeply and held his breath.

"Well, hello, my lovely," the man said tightly. "Come on in and join the party. It's about time we got some color up in this mofo joint."

Vivian glared at the man, as she entered the apartment. She walked down the dimly lit hallway into a darkened living room area. The stench of pot, beer and other unpleasant odors filled her nostrils. The room was hot and muggy. She could smell the sweat. As her eyes adjusted to the dimness, she looked around the room and noticed ten or more people all nude or partially clad. The women appeared to be young coeds. They were laughing and giggling, as they pawed the nude bodies of the men who were reclining in different areas of the room. Most were involved in different sex acts. That's when Vivian realized that she had walked in on an orgy. Men and teenage girls treating sex as if it were a game where scoring had a different connotation. She did not immediately see Carlton in the dimly lit room, but she heard his moans and groans of ecstasy. She moved closer and looked down in the middle of the floor. She recognized Carlton's nude body humping away, as his bottle-blonde partner cheered him on. She was watching, but not really believing what was going on. The loud music seemed to be pressing her in her chest. The heat was stifling. The sight of Carlton, butt naked on the floor pillows having sex with a teenage girl, and the stench in the room, caused Vivian to want to vomit. Her head was pounding, as she heard Carlton repeating in a chant, as he began to reach climax, "Damn this is some good pussy, baby! Better than the last time! We gonna keep practicing this 'til you get it right! I want some head, too, baby! Damn, this is good! Whose pussy is this, baby?! Whose damn pussy is this?!"

Another woman said, "You promised to do me next, Carlton. I gave you good head all last week and all you been doing is fucking her all this week and all night. When do I get my turn, baby? You promised me!"

"I fucked you for a solid month, so shut up! There's enough of this dick to go around! I'll get to you next, baby. I need a little breather, but you can give me some more head while I take a break. I like the way you lick my balls and the crack in my ass for me, baby, doggie style."

Just as Carlton got to his knees, he looked up over his shoulder and saw her standing there watching him.

"Oh, shit! Uh, baby. Uh, what are you doing here?! Uh, I didn't know that you were coming! Uh, this is not what it looks like. Uh, we won the game today and, uh, we were just letting off a little steam."

He stood up and reached for Vivian. She stepped back out of his reach.

"I wouldn't do that if I were you, Carlton," Vivian said, her voice low and menacing. She looked down at his shriveled penis with the full condom still hanging off it. She glared up at him.

"Awh, c'mon, Vivian. I can explain. Don't jump to any conclusions about anything. This don't have nothing to do with me and you," Carlton pleaded. "I mean, I love you, Vivian! This is just something to do!"

Vivian's head was spinning, her heart was pounding rapidly, and she was trembling with anger. She turned on her heels and headed for the door. Carlton came after her and grabbed her arm. Vivian didn't turn around.

"Take your hands off of me *now*, Carlton!" she bit out through clinched teeth.

"Vivian, we have to talk! C'mon, baby. Let's go back to my bedroom. Just give me a minute to explain. Please don't leave like this."

"C'mon, Carlton," the young blue-eyed, blond-haired coed whined, as she pulled on Carlton's arm. "You promised to do me next. Who's this Black bitch, anyway?!"

"Who are you calling a bitch?!" Vivian asked in a low, menacing tone, as she turned to face the blonde girl.

"*Oh, shit!*" Carlton yelled, but it was already too late.

Chapter 23

Benny arrived at his parents' home in Goodwill, Summer County, South Carolina, with Stacy in the early evening just as the sun was beginning to desert the sky. It was a crystal-clear day and an easy flight from San Diego in a comfortable Cessna that Benny leased. Few clouds and a favorable jet stream put them there in record time. He stopped the rented SUV at the lane that led to the circular driveway of the Alexanders' home.

"Here it is, Stacy. This is where I grew up," Benny said, more in appreciation than as a boast.

There was pride and reverence in Benny's face, Stacy noticed. She took in the panoramic view that the car windows afforded. There was much to behold. The big front yard filled with Live Oak, Weeping Willow trees and shrubbery, a few brown leaves were scattered around the nicely manicured yard, and clung to the areas where she could see flowers would grow in the spring. Pine needles and pinecones lay in neat heaps gathered around the yard. The single-level, sand-colored, brick ranch-style farmhouse looked surreal in the setting sunlight with its earth-toned shutters and window boxes. The earth seemed to be poised waiting for the start of another spring to burst forth with all of its finery and surrounding the house and yard in its embrace. It was Norman Rockwell picture perfect even in late winter.

Benny pointed in the different directions to where his aunts, uncles, and cousins lived on the family compound. Their homes and farms were not in the line of sight, but seemed to surround them. Benny explained that his paternal great, great grandfather built the house many years ago and that, as the family grew down through the generations, additional rooms were built on to the original house. When the house became too small for everyone, his aunts and uncles moved out as they started their own families and built homes elsewhere on their farm. All of the children were raised together in their Eden-like compound much like a Hyannis Port of the South. One of his uncles and cousins ran the hydroponics farms as a collective and hired laborers to work the fishery, cattle and other livestock.

"Thank God it never changes," Benny said, with deep reverence.

"I don't know how or why I let you talk me into coming here. What am I going to say to your family?"

"Try, hello. They'll take it from there," he said and grinned confidently.

Benny started the car and drove into the driveway.

"Vivian must not be here yet," he said, as he spotted his parents' and Gregory's cars in the parking area. "Well, she'll be here soon though, I'm sure."

Benny got out of the car, grabbed their luggage and guided Stacy to the front door. He knew that the front door was not locked. It never was.

"Mom, Dad, I'm home!" he yelled enthusiastically, as he entered the house.

"Well, for lands sake, Benjamin Staton, is that you?!" Sylvia Alexander joyously shrieked from the kitchen, as she wiped her hands on a kitchen towel and hurried toward the front door. "What are you doing at home? You didn't even tell us that you were coming."

She beamed as she approached her son and his companion.

"Hi, there, you light-of-my-life," Benny said, scooping up his mother in his arms, swung her around, and gave her a big, sloppy kiss on her cheek.

"You stop that, Benjamin Staton Alexander!" she said, giggling. "You're too fresh for bread and you're not too big for me to spank you, you know." She gave him a big hug, cupped his face in her hands and kissed him on the forehead. "Gee, it's good to see you and who is this lovely young lady?" she asked, eyes sparkling.

"This is my friend, Lieutenant Stacy Greene, US Navy. Stacy, this is my mother, Sylvia Benson Alexander." He smiled, putting his arms around her waist.

"It's a pleasure to meet you, Stacy. Welcome to our home," Sylvia said, grinning brightly from ear to ear.

"Thank you, Mrs. Alexander. It's a pleasure to be here. I've wanted to meet you for a very long time. Benny talks about his family all of the time."

Stacy didn't know what she had expected, but the woman standing in front of her didn't resemble the stereotypes of the haggard Southern woman who had toiled in the fields. In fact, Sylvia Alexander didn't even look like she had been on earth that long. She didn't look tired like some woman Stacy knew who had raised five children. Her face was wrinkle free with big, bright, shining eyes and a welcoming smile. Stacy was amazed at her full, but shapely physique. No rolls of fat or unsightly grey hair. Not even a varicose vein or age spot on her butter-pecan complexion.

Just then, Bernard Alexander, Benny's father, emerged from his study and broke into a big, brilliant smile—Benny's smile, broad with perfectly shaped ivory white teeth. The bloodline was unmistakable, Stacy thought. Bernard could easily have passed for Benny's older brother. His shoulders were broad and straight and his build slim, but sturdy. Thinner than Benny's muscular frame, but just as pleasing to the eye.

"Hey there, son. This is a nice surprise. It's good to see you." Bernard beamed, as he hugged his son tightly and they kissed each other's cheek. "And you've brought a lovely friend with you, too, I see."

Benny introduced Stacy to his father, who immediately cocooned her in his arms, as he led her back to the kitchen.

"Come with me, Stacy. We have so much to talk about," Bernard said, with a broad smile.

Benny smiled, as his father whisked Stacy away. He gathered his mother into his arms for another hug, which she returned warmly.

"Where are Aretha and G, Mom?"

"Aretha Grace is still at her piano lesson, but she'll be home at any minute. Gregory Clayton is in his room. He's supposed to be studying, but I'll bet that he's on the cell phone, as usual. Go and get him, Benjamin Staton, and bring him into the kitchen to meet Stacy. She must be someone very special if you've brought her home to meet us," she said, hopefully, grinning with a gleam in her eyes.

"I'll explain later, Mom. I'll get G."

Benny went to Gregory's door and heard him on the phone.

"... Now you know that Charlotte doesn't mean what you think she means to me, Leslie. I was just giving a sistah a hand by giving her a ride home after the game. She's your best friend. She wouldn't hit on me if she's your ace, now would she? Besides, she knows that you're my main squeeze."

Benny leaned against the open door with his arms folded across his chest and shook his head with a big knowing grin.

When Gregory spotted his brother, his smile lit the room. "Big Ben, what up, my brother!" Gregory got up from his sofa. "Charlotte, I mean Leslie...let me hit you back later. My big brother's here!"

He hung up before he even heard the girl's reply and leaped across his bedroom.

"Hey, G," Benny said, embracing his younger brother. They kissed each other on the cheek. "You still trying to run that same, lame game on the ladies?"

"I gets my share, Big Ben," he said, with a devilish smile on his handsome face.

"I'm sure you do. We're going to have to talk about that while I'm home, but right now I have someone who I want you to meet."

Benny cradled Gregory's head under one armpit and led him to the kitchen. It was getting harder to do that. Gregory seemed to have shot up a couple more inches since he last saw him at Christmas. They were almost the same height.

"Stacy, this is my little brother, Gregory Clayton. Gregory this is a friend of mine, Lieutenant Stacy Greene, US Navy."

"Whoa! H e l l o, Stacy!" he said enthusiastically and seductively, as he grabbed her hand and kissed it. "Don't let my brother mislead you with that 'little brother' stuff. Looking at you, I'm ready to sign up for the Navy today!"

Stacy laughed at his antics. "It's nice to meet you, Gregory. Your brother talks about you all the time. He failed to mention how handsome you are."

"He can't stand the competition, Stacy. He's over twenty-five. That's elderly in today's market. He knows that I've got it like that, but I'd give it all up for you," Gregory said, kissing Stacy's hand again.

"You stop being so fresh, Gregory Clayton," Sylvia scolded jokingly.

"No, Mom, let him talk," Benny said confidently. "He'll soon find out how fast he can get kicked to the curb."

Stacy looked up at Benny with a sly smile and kissed Gregory on the cheek. Gregory beamed.

"Now who's going to get kicked to the curb, Big Ben?" Gregory asked with a sexy grin.

"See me in about ten more years, Gregory, and we'll talk about it then," Stacy said coyly.

"I'll wait.... uh, unless you've got a younger sister," he said, grinning.

Everyone laughed.

The front door opened and closed and Aretha walked into the kitchen.

"Benny!" she screamed, as she ran to him and jumped into his arms. He caught her on the fly and swung her around. She wrapped her legs around his waist and enthusiastically kissed him all over his face, as he squeezed her tight. "When did you get here? How long can you stay? Why didn't you call? You're not sick or anything like that are you? You didn't crash a jet, did you? Did you get fired or something? They don't fire you in the Air Force, do they? Well, anyway, Gregory has a game tomorrow at two o'clock. Will you come? Oh, and I have a piano recital on Sunday. Would you please come to that too?" Aretha's questions were coming fast and furiously.

"Whoa, Retha," Benny said, laughing. "And we thought that Vivian asked a lot of questions! *Wow,* kid, maybe you ought to be the lawyer in this family."

She didn't ponder that for long. "No, this week I'm considering becoming an investigative reporter. Being a lawyer is too boring to me, but next week who knows? Maybe I'll want to be a concert pianist or a stock broker or an astronaut—the options are unlimited for someone at my stage of life," Aretha said confidently, as her brother held her in his arms.

"Before you blast off, little astronaut, I'd like for you to meet a friend of mine," Benny said, lowering Aretha to the floor. He stood behind her with his hand on her shoulders. Wow, she was getting taller too. "Stacy, this little comet is Aretha Grace Alexander. Aretha, this is Lieutenant Stacy Green, US—"

"And I know, you're in love. I can tell," Aretha said, with all the wisdom of the ages. Then she stepped forward and extended her hand to Stacy. "Hi, Stacy, I'm pleased to meet you, but you look like a responsible, sensible, and intelligent woman, and you're really quite beautiful, too. You're really going to have to be very patient with Benjamin Staton after you're married. He doesn't know how to cook or clean a house. We've tried to teach him, Stacy, but he's still a work-in-progress—"

Benny clamped his hand over his little sister's mouth. "Hold on, you little comet. I said that Stacy and I are friends." He turned to his father. "Dad, where did you and Mom find this precocious, little comet, anyway?"

"She's got your Grandma Emma in her, Benjamin Staton. She's wise beyond her years."

Aretha leaned her head back against her brother's chest and looked up at him with her big, pretty, brown eyes. *Their grandmother's eyes,* he thought. Benny removed his hand from over her mouth and released her.

"As I was saying, Stacy, before I was so rudely interrupted," Aretha continued, locking her arm in Stacy's and walking toward the kitchen table, "Benjamin Staton may not be the domestic type right away, but he's trainable. You just have to lead him into things slowly at first, then, after you've been married for a while—"

Stacy looked back at Benny and smiled.

Benny threw up his hands, looked up at the ceiling, and put his hands on his hips. He shook his head. "Are we sure that she's an Alexander or did we have a visit from an alien from somewhere else in the universe?" Benny asked, exasperated.

"You think this is bad? Huh! You ain't seen bad, Ben," Gregory said. "I live with the little comet every day. You never know what to expect from her. It gets real scary around here sometimes."

Bernard kissed Aretha on the forehead and hugged her.

"She's just like her Grandma Emma. Out of the mouths of babes," he said, stroking her long, thick hair.

The family sat at the kitchen table and talked. Aretha made Benny and Stacy agree to come to Gregory's basketball game on Saturday and to her piano recital on Sunday. These were not optional plans that Aretha was making. Benny and Stacy knew that these were command performances. Aretha Grace Alexander was in control.

Stacy was the center of attention and she beamed with delight at the way that she was welcomed into the Alexander family home. It was a warm feeling sitting around the table in this big country kitchen, as mouth-watering aromas from the stove filled the air.

Benny gazed at Stacy and felt something strange come over him, as she interacted so effortlessly with his family. She had all of the requisite qualities that he admired in the many different women that he had known and many more qualities than he had expected. Not just surface qualities, she was indeed a beautiful and sensuous woman in his view, but there was much more. An openness that led her to be frank and honest. A vulnerability, but yet confident and self-assured. She, indeed, was a total woman, he thought, as he watched and listened to her.

Sylvia got up to check her dinner as it cooked. Benny got up from the table, grabbed her from behind, and enveloped her in his arms, she stirred the vegetables.

"Mmm, that smells good, Mom. What's for dinner?" he asked, rocking her in his arms.

"A little of this and that. I made baked chickens, rice and gravy, string beans, collard greens, a bit of left over macaroni and cheese. I'm making hot rolls, a carrot and raison salad and apple pie and ice cream for dessert. If you had told me that you were coming and bringing Stacy, I would have fixed something special for you."

"Everything you cook is special, Mom, even the left overs and so are you," he said, kissing her on the cheek and rocking her in his arms.

Sylvia leaned back against her son's chest and patted him on the arm, as he held her. Her children were very precious to her and she enjoyed the affection that they showered on her.

"Dinner will be ready shortly. Why don't you show Stacy where she can wash up and Aretha and I will get the dinner on the table."

Benny released his mother and asked, "When did you hear from Vivian last, Mom?"

"Sometime last week, why?"

"Oh, no reason. I was just curious."

Sylvia narrowed her eyes, her mother radar engaged. "Benjamin Staton, I know you. What are you and Vivian Lynn up to?"

Benny avoided his mother's question with a wink.

"Come on, Stacy, let's go wash up while Gregory sets the table," Benny said slyly.

"*Me?* Why do I have to set the table? Your hands aren't put on backwards. I'll show Stacy where she can wash up," Gregory countered.

Just then, they heard the front door open and close. Vivian appeared in the kitchen doorway and forced a smile.

"Hello, everybody. Surprise, I'm home," she said rather somberly.

As her family rushed to her, Benny, Gregory, and Aretha sensed that something was wrong. Then they noticed that Vivian was holding her wrist. Benny could see that she was in pain and that she had been crying. She looked drained and drawn.

"What happened to your hand, Vivian Lynn?" Sylvia asked, her mother radar registering trouble. "It looks swollen."

"I jammed it," she said trying to avoid Benny and Gregory's stares.

"Well, come on with me," Sylvia said, leading her daughter to the bathroom. "Bernard, please get an ice pack out of the freezer for me."

Stacy and Aretha followed to see if they could help. Bernard took an ice pack out and followed. Benny and Gregory remained in the kitchen alone.

"I'll bet that frat-dog, Carlton, had something to do with this," Gregory said through clinched teeth.

Benny felt Gregory's anger. It was very familiar to him. They were both angry. Spontaneously, without another word, they headed out of the front door together.

"I'll drive, Benny," Gregory said, jumping into his four-wheel drive Jeep. "I know exactly where Carlton lives and hangs out."

As they drove, Gregory told Benny about the rumors that he heard about Carlton and Raymond's wild, sex parties with women from GSU's campus. He also said that he had seen Carlton at GSU games and afterwards with other women, but didn't want to tell Vivian about it. He didn't have any real evidence that anything was going on. Benny told him that he should have called him about the rumors and that he could have checked it out. Gregory said that he did call twice, but Benny was not there. Then he called K.J. and found out that Benny was out of town. He didn't want to get K.J. involved. He knew that CompuCorrect was just getting rolling and Kenneth was so busy.

They pulled into the parking lot of Carlton's apartment complex and before Benny could get out of his seat belt, Gregory tore up the steps and banged on Carlton's door. Benny reached Gregory just as Carlton opened the door, but before Benny could get a hand on Gregory, he had socked Carlton in the jaw.

"What the fuck did you do to my sister?" Gregory yelled, as Carlton fell back into the apartment.

"Nothing, man! I didn't do nothing to Vivian! It was all a big misunderstanding! She caught me by surprise! Off guard, you know? I wasn't expecting it!" Carlton said, trying to defend against the potential for another fist in his face and recovering from Gregory's blow.

"My sister tells you that she's pregnant with your baby and all that you can say is that it's a *big misunderstanding*?" Benny yelled.

Dead silence reigned. Gregory and Carlton both stared at Benny with wide eyes and open mouths.

"Pregnant?" Carlton asked in disbelief. "Vivian didn't say anything about being pregnant. She caught...I mean, she found some lady friends over here with some of my frat brothers and she drew the wrong conclusion," he lied.

"Then how did she hurt her wrist?" Gregory snapped.

"Stupid woman made the mistake of calling Vivian a bitch and Vivian punched her in her mouth. I think Vivian broke her jaw. I know how that feels," Carton said, flexing his own jaw. "Her friends took her to the clinic. I never touched Vivian, but she was so angry that she wasn't hearing anything that I had to say. I swear, man, she never told me that she is pregnant!" Carlton said, getting to his feet and still rubbing his jaw. "It's about time though. My little maneuver must have worked after all."

"Maneuver? What maneuver? What are you talking about, Carlton?" Benny asked.

"You know how women are, Ben. You've been around the block a few times yourself. Your sister was giving me so much grief about not getting married right away, that I had to figure out a way to convince her to marry me now at the end of the basketball season and not wait. So, I stuck pin holes in all the condoms so that, if she got pregnant, I could convince her that we needed to get married right away. Vivian could stop all this bullshit about being a lawyer and a judge—"

POW!!

Before he knew what he was doing, Benny punched Carlton in the eye. Carlton went flying back across the coffee table, smashing it.

"You mean you planned this whole thing? That it wasn't an accident?" Benny yelled, as he started after Carlton again.

Gregory grabbed Benny and barely held him back.

"C'mon, Benny. He ain't shit and he ain't worth going to jail for. Vivian needs us now," Gregory said, with real disdain for Carlton in his voice.

"Mom, where are Benny and Gregory?" Vivian asked.

"I don't know. Your father said that they went flying out of here over an hour ago. They haven't come back yet."

"Oh, shit!" Vivian yelled, as she leaped from the bed where she had been napping. She ran to the telephone in the study and dialed Carlton's telephone number.

"Carlton, this is Vivian. If my brothers show up there, don't let them in."

"You're too late, Vivian. They've already been here and they're gone. Benny told me that you're pregnant. We've got to—"

Click! Dial tone.

Vivian hung up the telephone and slumped against the wall.

"What is it, Vivian? What's got you so upset?" Sylvia asked. "It's not like you to use profanity."

"I'm sorry, Mom. I'll tell you later. I just want to wait for Gregory and Benny to get home."

Sylvia saw that Aretha, Stacy, and Bernard were in the kitchen setting the table and engrossed in a heavy conversation about the family history. She took Vivian by the hand and led her into her bedroom. She closed the door and sat Vivian down on the bed. Then she took Vivian's face in her hands and said, "If it don't fit, baby, than fix it." She laid a hand on Vivian's abdomen.

Vivian looked into her mother's warm eyes and solemn face and tears began to roll down her cheeks. She hugged her mother and wept tears that she had refused to let flow uncontrollably before.

"I love you, Mom," she whispered.

"I love you more, baby."

Benny and Gregory drove back to Goodwill in near silence.

"That's a frat-dog for you," Gregory said sternly. "You don't do that to any woman just to get your way. No woman deserves that!"

"And I thought that I was going to have to talk with you about your attitude about women. Sounds like that would have been a wasted conversation."

"Dad and I talk about it all the time, Ben. He said to treat my girlfriends with as much respect as I treat Mama. That put a whole different light on the situation. Ain't nobody going to treat my Mama with disrespect, so I treat my female friends with respect. The only thing is, Ben, when I started treating them with all this respect, all of a sudden everybody wants to dig on me. Hunnies be coming after me and sweatin' me *harder* than ever, givin' me the full-court press, ya know? And I ain't even trying to get serious about nobody. But they be calling me up all the time wanting me to go out. And Dad and Mom ain't hearing that *'go-out-on-a-school-night'* stuff. After school, if I don't have basketball practice, Dad has me working in the Administration Office until he leaves and then Mom has me doing housework when I get home. Then I got to do my homework because Mom goes over my homework and Aretha's before she leaves for work in the morning. They got me off the telephone and asleep by eleven o'clock and I'm almost seventeen years old! And Aretha! She's on me like a hawk. She stands over me and makes me work out on the exercise equipment. She's worse than my coach! The only night that I get to hang out is Friday, but not if I've got a game on Saturday. I can hang out after the game, but Dad and Mom always seem to know when I get in. They must have parent radar or something," he grumbled.

"No, they had three children before you came along. You're getting the same treatment that the rest of us got."

"It sure cuts down on my social life. I don't have time to see a lot of hunnies and Dad and Mom know everybody's family history back to when they came through The Middle Passage. And what Dad and Mom don't know, Aretha tells them. They know everybody I talk to personally."

"You're not complaining are you?"

"Nah," he shrugged. "The folks and Aretha are cool. I know that they are doing it because they love me. I know that. K.J. said that I might not appreciate it now, but I will later. But if I ever did something like what Carlton did to Vivian, I'd be dead meat in this family and Aretha would personally slice me up. I'd never do something like that on purpose to a woman. He wasn't showin' Viv no respect. She's grown. She can make up her own mind, whether she wanna be with him or not."

"You're going to hear this when we get home, but Stacy and I are going to have a baby. That's why I brought her home to meet all of you."

Gregory sharply pulled the car to the side of the road and looked at Benny with a serious expression on his face. "Ben, I know you. This was an accident, right? You might be some super, Olympic-class lover, but you're not going to convince me that you did this on purpose. You're not like that frat-dog Carlton."

"God, am I glad I've got you for a brother!" Benny said, grabbing Gregory around the neck and kissing his forehead.

"Hold up, big brother! Don't be going all mushy and soft on me. You better save it for my niece or nephew," Gregory joked. "You're really in for it when 'Aretha the Hun' gets a hold of you though!"

Gregory and Benny pulled into the driveway and Vivian flew out of the house and grabbed them both. She kissed them all over their faces and they lifted her between them and swung her as if she were sitting in a swing. They all went inside and sat down to dinner. It was a relatively common occurrence and a funny sight to see three of Bernard and Sylvia's five children sitting at the table wearing ice packs on their right wrists, trying to eat dinner with their left hands. Sylvia remarked to Stacy that it was just like old times. That's why she always had several ice packs in the freezer. She never knew who was going to do what next, so she had to stay ready for any eventuality.

After dinner, they all sat in the living room talking and having coffee. Everyone except Stacy, Gregory, and Aretha, that is. Benny made tea for Stacy and Sylvia made cocoa for Gregory and Aretha.

"Dad, Mom, and the rest of you crumb snatchers, I have an announcement to make," Benny smiled, grabbing Stacy's hand.

"I know. You and Stacy are expecting our first grandchild," Bernard said rather matter-of-factly. Everyone, except Aretha, looked at him in amazement. "I knew it the first time that I laid eyes on you, Stacy. You have that same beautiful glow about you that my wife had when she was pregnant with each one of our children." He put his arm around his wife, kissed her gently on the lips, and said, "Well, Sylvia, here we go again."

Vivian leaped to her feet and ran to Stacy. She hugged her tightly and kissed her on the cheek. Then she went to Benny and jumped into his arms.

"You're going to be the second best father ever," she said. "I know what I'm talking about." Tears formed in Vivian's eyes and Benny held her close.

Stacy was overwhelmed by their excitement. She looked at everyone's smiling face and knew what she had to do.

Aretha walked to Stacy and hugged her. "I told you that Benny loves you and I was right. Now I'm sure that you love him, too. I can't wait! Now I won't be the youngest Alexander in this house anymore! Well, I guess I have to study up on the responsibilities of being an aunt."

Everyone laughed.

Later, as Sylvia brought fresh towels into Benny's bedroom for Stacy, she hugged her again and sat with her on the bed.

"Mrs. Alexander, I have to admit that I was very uncomfortable about coming here, but your son is very persuasive. You've all welcomed me so openly that I feel like I have to tell you the truth. I really don't want to have a baby. I wanted to have an abortion, but Benny wouldn't hear of it."

"Aretha was right, but, unfortunately, you two don't know you're in love yet. I hope that someday you will both realize it so that you and Benjamin Staton can give this baby inside of you a loving home."

Stacy was surprised at Sylvia's remark, but she looked into Sylvia's warm and loving face and felt relaxed and comforted.

"No, Mrs. Alexander, you don't understand what I'm saying. Aretha is wrong. Benny and I aren't in love. We are really just good friends who had an unguarded moment, but neither one of us is in love with the other one, and we're not likely to be. I'm not ready to be a wife or a mother the way that you are. You make it look so easy, but Benny and I are not going to marry. Benny really wants this baby and I believe that he's ready to be a father. That's the reason why I'm going to have his child. It's for him because he's my best friend. I can't raise this baby, but I'm not going to deny Benny the right to raise it."

Sylvia hugged Stacy again. "Mark my words, Stacy. Aretha is just like her grandmother. She has wisdom and insight far beyond her years. You two are in love, as sure as the sun rises in the East, and until you two figure that out, this baby will get all the love and support that we can all give it."

Stacy averted her eyes. "You know, I was ashamed of what has happened. Coming here like this. I don't want to embarrass you and your wonderful family. I mean, you can be completely candid with me, Mrs. Alexander. If you would prefer, I could go to a hotel...."

"Absolutely not, Stacy. My son is a grown man. Bernie and I have taught our children that they must learn to be responsible and never do anything out in the world that they couldn't or wouldn't do in this home. We're a family, Stacy. That means that we not only love each other, but we respect each other, too. We trust Benjamin Staton and we're very proud of him. Yes, we know that he's dated a lot of women because he's told us about all of them. It's his way of searching for the right one. We don't judge him or his behavior because we understand that he has a deep sense of affection, respect, and responsibility. We know that he would not have brought you here to meet us unless he's committed to you and your relationship. Bernard and I believe that he's made the right decision and no matter why this baby was conceived, it will be loved and cherished by him and all of us."

Stacy smiled shyly. "You didn't mention it, but he's cute, too."

Sylvia laughed heartily. "Yes, that's his father's fault. It's the curse of the Alexander men. Bernie is still a hunk, if you ask me," she said, giggling. "You should see how silly the women act around him. Humph! When all of the Alexander men get together, women drop at their feet." She laughed. "But they're all a loyal bunch. Once they make up their minds who they want to love, there's no shaking them. Benjamin Staton is no different. I'm his mother and I see it in his eyes, Stacy. He's in love…with you."

Benny walked into the bedroom and saw his mother and Stacy talking quietly.

"What's going on in here?" Benny smiled. "Are you two talking about my daughter?"

Sylvia looked up at her son quizzically. "And what makes you think that you're going to have a daughter, Benjamin Staton?"

"Aretha told me. And besides, the men in this family outnumber the women. It's about time to even the odds. I think that Whitney will do that just fine."

"Whitney? Who's Whitney?" both Stacy and Sylvia asked.

"My daughter, Whitney Alexander. Aretha and I will have to think of a middle name, but we'll deal with that later."

The two women looked at each other and shook their heads.

"Well, if Aretha Grace told you that, then a girl named Whitney it is!" Sylvia confirmed with a big smile. "Now you two get some rest. It's been a long day and we've got Gregory's game to go to tomorrow."

Sylvia kissed both Stacy and Benny, closed the bedroom door behind her, and went down the hall to her bedroom.

"You have an incredible family, Benny. I've never met anyone like them. And Aretha…she's too much."

"Yeah, family is something you don't get to choose in this life. I lucked up and got a great one. My grandparents used to say that the real source of inner strength comes from the sense of the family and that what you need to have in your life to succeed depends on the ability of the family to survive as a close-knit unit. It's the family that gives us all strength and commitment to struggle to succeed. There's no substitute for it. When you have the moral and emotional support of your family, there's no goal too lofty to achieve. I never take them for granted."

"Now I see why you're so determined to have this baby and I've decided to do it, but—"

"But what, Stacy?"

"I can't be a mother to it, Benny. I didn't come from where you did. I had to raise myself and I still do. So you're going to have to raise this baby alone... without me. I don't feel connected and intertwined the way that you do, but I believe we've reached a common ground. This is the only way that I can agree to go through with this pregnancy and that's final."

"All right, I'll agree to that, if you'll agree to see our baby often."

"I can't promise you that, Benny."

"Then until you're ready, I'll be there for our child. Maybe you'll change your mind later."

"No, Benny, don't count on it. Once *your* child is born, I want to put all of this behind me and get on with the rest of my life. If we're friends, you won't ask me for any more of a sacrifice."

Benny knew that Stacy meant what she said. He could have discussed it with her more and tried to win her over to his way of thinking, but then he thought of how Carlton had manipulated Vivian to get what he wanted. He wasn't going to ask Stacy to do more than she had already agreed to do. At least not at this point. He would have time with her later to show her how important and necessary family is. This weekend would be a good start. He also knew what else was coming. It always did when his family had something to celebrate and this weekend would be chocked full of good tidings. He kissed her and she returned his kiss.

Benny and Stacy lay in bed in his old bedroom looking up at the constellations that he had painted on the ceiling as a child. Stacy was laying in his arms, as he pointed to each one. Jet airplane and spaceship models hung from mobiles and turned slowly and silently in the air moved by the rotating ceiling fan. Different pictures of the solar system were pinned to the walls. In the distance, Benny began to hear the faint, but familiar sound of lovemaking. Stacy began to hear it, too. They heard Bernard Alexander calling for divine intervention and then silence.

"I don't think that they were praying, do you, Stacy?"

"They're *your* parents, Benny."

"Let's show them how you can make me plead for mercy."

"*Benny!*"

Early the next morning, Stacy smelled the aroma of fresh brewed coffee. Benny was still asleep when she pulled herself away from the warmth of his body, crept out of bed, put on her robe and slippers, and headed to the kitchen.

"Is that freshly brewed coffee that I smell?" Stacy asked, inhaling deeply.

"Yes, ma'am, it is," Sylvia said and smiled, as she hugged Stacy, "but I have strict orders from the Captain not to give you any. So I've made a small pot of freshly brewed decaf tea for you."

"I don't know whether I'm going to survive this pregnancy with your son around. He's bought every book that he could find on pregnancy and child rearing. He even scheduled us for Lamaze classes and doctor's appointments. He insisted that we see the obstetrician before we left San Diego and he asked her questions for over an hour. I've really got my hands full with him."

"Sure sounded like he had his hands full with *you* last night. We thought that the boy had suddenly gotten real religious and was starting to speak in tongues." Sylvia laughed. "He kept yelling 'Oh my God! Oh my God!' half the night. Such moaning and groaning, it's a wonder that you two have any voice left," she teased.

Stacy and Sylvia glimpsed each other and broke out in laughter. Vivian walked into the kitchen, yawning and rubbing her eyes.

"Don't you people ever get any sleep in this house? I heard you and Dad on one side of me and Stacy and Benny on the other side. Gregory couldn't sleep either. We both got up and went into the living room to get some rest. He's still sleeping on the sofa. Aretha slept through the whole thing. I've got to find out what her secret is."

Stacy and Sylvia glimpsed each other again and laughed.

Stacy poured a cup of decaf tea for herself and sat at the kitchen table before the big picture windows that overlooked the back yard, the farm, and the forest beyond. Grey ringlet moss hung like lacy shawls from the trees. A soft, white fog intertwined with the bushes and shrubbery, as the sun began to rise. Roosters crowed in the distance. She could see little furry creatures begin their daily chores. Squirrels hopped from one tree to the next. She spotted deer grazing in the low grass at the edge of the forest. Birds raised a cacophony of sounds, welcoming the morning. Cows mooed, sheep bleated, horses whinnied, and pigs oinked. The farm and the woods were alive, welcoming Mother Nature's gift of a new day.

"I don't think that I've ever seen a more beautiful and peaceful spot on land before," Stacy wistfully said, gazing out the window.

"It is special," Vivian said, sitting beside Stacy at the table. She pointed to two big Live Oak trees. "There's the hammock that K.J. made out there between the big oak trees. Mom and Dad used to let us sleep out there in the hammock on hot nights sometimes. We'd sing, count the stars, and listen to the crickets all night. Benny knew the names and places of every constellation. K.J. and I would say that the best thing in the world is looking at the sky at night."

"Now Gregory and Aretha hang out together in that same hammock," Sylvia added, looking through the window over the sink where she stood. "It's a special place, all right."

"This must have been a wonderful place to grow up. It looks so pure and clean and untouched. Very different from where I grew up in the old section of Cabrini Green in Chicago. I never knew anything but ugly, high-rise, tenement buildings. We didn't even have trees where squirrels or birds could nest. Just concrete and asphalt. I promised myself that if I ever got out of there, I was never going back. But *this!* I never even dreamed of a place like this. I didn't know that this type of life existed."

"I carry the images of this place in my mind wherever I go. Someday, I'd love to live on a farm and raise a family there just like the rest of my family," Vivian said wishfully.

Stacy turned, looked at Vivian's face, and said, "And you will, Vivian. I believe that you have the ability, strength and courage to do whatever you decide you want."

Vivian hugged Stacy, as if they were old friends. Though they had come from vastly different backgrounds, they were near the same age, Stacy a little older. Both sensed that they shared the tenacity to overcome any obstacle.

Sylvia was watching and listening to them talk, as she stirred the big pot of hominy grits on the stove. "And she thinks that she and Benjamin Staton aren't in love. Ha!" Sylvia mumbled to herself.

"What did you say, Mama?" Vivian asked.

"Uh, you two girls go get washed up and get those men and Aretha out of their beds. Breakfast is almost ready."

Stacy entered the bedroom where Benny lay sleeping on his back. His head was turned to one side with one hand above his head and the other cupping his penis, which appeared to be fully erect. She stood for a moment smiling and feasting her eyes on his entire, finely sculptured body. She had often watched him sleeping and felt the need to bury herself in his warm, sensuous embrace. He looked so peaceful, yet powerful. His massive arms and shoulders relaxed. The gold chain around his neck that said 'FAMILY'. The soft hair on his massive, muscular chest curled down to his lower abdomen and between his thick muscular thighs. He was a sexy and sensuous man, even when he was sleeping. He was the realization of every woman's fantasy of the perfect man, she thought, as she looked at him. She wondered why she couldn't make a commitment to him instead of pushing him away. What more lovingly, supportive being existed in the world than Benjamin Staton Alexander? She shook off her troublesome thoughts. She was in love with him. She would have no choice but to leave him. He stretched and started to awaken. Stacy took that opportunity to lie on top of him placing her chin on her stacked hands, and smiled broadly, as he opened his eyes. She felt his thick penis hardening against her.

"Well, good morning, Sunshine. What's got you looking so radiant this early in the morning?" Benny smiled, as he suggestively rubbed her back and butt.

Stacy kissed him, searching his mouth with her tongue. He responded to her heat, groaning his pleasure.

"Thank you for forcing me to come here, Benny," she said softly, tracing the outline of his mouth with her fingertips. "It's a wonderful place. I see why you love it and your family so much and why you always wear this gold chain around your neck." She kissed the chain with an open mouth against his chest.

"Yes, it is, but is that why you look so radiant this morning? Didn't last night add a little gleam to all this glitter?"

"Of course, it did," she said, snuggling against him. "It must be this good, clean, fresh country air. You were even more spectacular than usual." She stroked his chest lovingly playing with his flat, raisin-like left nipple. "Even your mother and Vivian thought that you were in good voice," Stacy said, still smiling.

"Oh, they did, did they?" He grinned, stretched his body fully, tightening his muscles and yawned again.

"Yes and your mother sent me in here to get you to rise and shine for breakfast," she said, switching to play with his right, flat, hard nipple while tonguing the left one.

Benny opened his thighs and raised his knees. Stacy fell between them, as he began rubbing her body more sensuously. He felt violently aroused at her ministration. He untied the sash on the robe that separated Stacy's soft skin from his. Just the heady scent of her heated his blood.

"Stacy, if you keep lying on top of me like this, something's going to rise all right. I love my mother's cooking, but breakfast may have to wait a while."

"Oh no you don't, Fly Boy. You brought me here and I'm not going to spend all of my time in the bed having sex with you, no matter how good it is. So fall in, Captain," Stacy said, rolling off Benny.

He caught her hand, put it on his now erect penis and brought her back to him, finding that place under her neck where he knew her sensitivity was the greatest. "I'll let you go for now," he moaned in a low voice against the hollow of her throat while she kneaded him, "but we country boys go to bed early and go to sleep late. So, I'm giving you fair warning, Stacy Greene, we're going to bed early tonight."

They were all at the table having a real Southern breakfast and there wasn't a bagel or cream cheese anywhere in sight. Stacy dug into the grits, thick link sausages, scrambled eggs with cheese, hot stewed sliced apples with cinnamon, grapefruit, applesauce, home-fried potatoes, and country bacon. Gregory took the piping-hot, baking-powder biscuits from the oven and yelled, "In coming!" as he tossed them one at a time through the air to Aretha, Benny, and Vivian. They caught them, as usual, and spread them with real fresh-churned butter and homemade apple butter that Vivian and Benny fought over constantly. Finally, Bernard picked up the jar of apple butter and put it in front of his plate. Vivian and Benny looked sheepishly at each other, pouted, and contented themselves with the assortment of other jams and jellies on the table. Gregory, Sylvia, Aretha, and Stacy roared with laughter at the sight. Bernard shoveled mounds of the chunky apple butter on to his third hot biscuit.

After breakfast, Bernard, Aretha, Vivian, and Gregory took Stacy on a walking tour of the farms, and to meet some of the aunts, uncles and cousins. Benny stayed behind, cleared the breakfast table, and loaded the dishwasher, as his mother supervised from her comfortable position at the breakfast table drinking her second cup of coffee. Eyeing her son, she knew that this sudden desire for domestic work was a ruse to have a private talk. Benny, more than any of her other children, had a harder exterior, but more tender core. Military life, having to take a leadership role, and make command decisions brought out a skill set that was learned through experience.

"Stacy's a very special young woman, Benjamin Staton, and she's going to be a wonderful mother. I like her very much and I think that you're very much in love."

"Yes, Mom, Stacy is very special, but she's not in love with me." He took a cleansing breath. It was hard to admit even to himself that he wouldn't have a life with Stacy, but she'd made it perfectly clear that she wanted a career more than anything that he could offer her, including himself. So he'd have to shoulder his hurt and disappointment and move on to someone who was perhaps more ready to settle down and have a normal family life. After all, JeNelle had already achieved her career dreams. She had only to accept him as a vital part of her life. Time would give them something to work toward. "I believe that I'm developing a closer relationship with someone else. Her name is JeNelle Towson. Her sister, Gloria, and Vivian are in law school together and housemates. When JeNelle's ready, I want to bring her home to meet everyone. She's already met K.J."

"What do you mean 'when she's ready'? You're in love with Stacy now, Benjamin Staton, and she's in love with you. The problem is that neither of you know it yet."

"You haven't met JeNelle yet, Mom. When she's ready I think that I want to ask her to marry me."

"What's holding up this romance with JeNelle?"

"She just wants to be friends for now. She's not ready for a real commitment yet."

"Does she know about Stacy and your baby?"

"I've told her about Stacy, that we're good friends, but Stacy doesn't want anyone outside of the family to know about her pregnancy. I want to tell JeNelle, but Stacy won't permit it. I have to respect Stacy's wishes even though I was recently on the brink of telling JeNelle everything. JeNelle is a wonderful woman. K.J. can tell you how special she is."

"I've heard all about JeNelle Towson from Kenneth. He sent a copy of that newspaper article to us, just in case someone asked us about him marrying JeNelle. You remember Tess Braxton, don't you? She's the wife of the Superintendent of Schools in San Francisco. You met her and her family at Kenneth's holiday office party. She called us to congratulate us on Kenneth's up-coming marriage."

"That was all a big mistake, Mom," he chuckled. "K.J.'s not in love with JeNelle, nor is she in love with him. In fact, K.J. is seeing a woman who works for the California Governor, Lisa Lambert."

"Uh huh," Sylvia said under her breath. Lisa Lambert? Not likely. Mother radar engaged.

"Stacy and I are just good friends and we enjoy each other's' company, but we're not in love, Mom."

"Uh huh," Sylvia said again. "Didn't sound like you two are 'just good friends' to me and your Dad last night."

Benny ran his tongue around his teeth. "You and Dad have got to do something about the echoes in the halls in this house. You know sound travels in both directions, remember?"

"You watch yourself, Benjamin Staton Alexander," she said, and laughed. "You're not too big for me to get a switch after you."

Benny went to the table and kissed his mother. She cupped his face in her hands and kissed him.

"Stacy fits you, Benjamin Staton. Don't lose her."

When the family members returned, Benny took Vivian on a long walk through the woods. As they walked, they held on to each other as they did when they were children. Dried leaves and twigs crunched under their booted feet.

"I really like Stacy, Benny. She's going to make a nice addition to this family." She squeezed Benny around his waist and grinned up at him.

"Not you, too, Vivian? I just finished explaining my relationship with Stacy to Mom. She has this crazy idea that Stacy and I are in love, but we don't know it yet. I told Mom that Stacy's not in love with me. She cares about me and I feel the same way about her. There's nothing that I wouldn't do for her. I'll admit that if Stacy had given me any indication that she wanted anything more than an intimate friendship, I would have been amenable, but she hasn't. I have strong feelings for Gloria's sister, JeNelle. But you know Mom. Once she gets something in her head, there's no moving her. She'll see, over time, how much JeNelle means to me," Benny said confidently. "That reminds me, Vivian, you can't mention Stacy and our baby to Gloria or anyone else. That's not the way that I want it, but Stacy's adamant about that."

"I know, Stacy told me. I won't say anything to Gloria, but Benny, from what Gloria tells me, JeNelle's not returning your feelings for her. Are you sure that you're getting romantically involved with the right woman?"

"Yes, Vivian, I am. But I didn't bring you out here to talk about me. I have something to talk with you about that I believe is going to hurt you."

"What is it?" Vivian asked with some concern.

"It's no accident that you're pregnant, honey. Carlton planned it that way. He put pinholes in your supply of condoms so that he could get you pregnant. That's how desperate he is to marry you this year."

Vivian couldn't believe what she was hearing. "How could he do that to me, Benny? People shouldn't just go around screwing up someone's life just to fit a timetable in their heads. I thought that he loved me and respected me as a woman. I should have known better. I've tried to love and trust him. I thought that in time he'd change and that we wanted the same things out of life: To support each other with the goals that we each had and to someday marry and have a family. How could I have been so stupid! So naïve! Such a fool!"

A flood of emotions overtook her. Benny felt her pain and her anguish, as he held her. She was crushed, demoralized, and angry. No man should ever do to a woman what Carlton had done to Vivian.

When she composed herself, Vivian told Benny about finding Carlton in the midst of an orgy and what she had done to the coed who called her a bitch.

"Carlton can't do this to me and disguise it as love. He's not capable of loving me the way that I need to be loved. He's proven that too many times before. This thing with the coeds wasn't the first time he's been dishonest with me, but I keep trying to be there for him. I can't put my trust in someone who professes love one minute and is out screwing someone else the next minute. It's not even about the sex. It's about respect and trust. Carlton wants me to fit some image in his head of the dutiful wife and mother of his children. I'm not that person."

Vivian's words struck hard inside Benny. It was as if she were describing his relationship with JeNelle and Stacy. How could he be falling in love with JeNelle and still desire Stacy so deeply? Had he created an image of JeNelle as the dutiful wife and mother of his children and the mother of his child with Stacy? During long conversations that he had with JeNelle, she never asked him whether he was sleeping with other women and he never brought it up. What impact would the knowledge that he slept with Stacy and was having a baby with her have on the relationship that he wanted to have with JeNelle? She knew that there were other women in his life. He told her about them, and he told her specifically about Stacy. Stacy was different—she was very special to him. Not like the myriad of other women he had known. Is that why JeNelle was unwilling to love him? Why hadn't JeNelle asked any questions? Why hadn't he told her?

"Benny, you have a strange look on your face. What are you thinking about?"

"Stacy and JeNelle."

"What about them?"

"I haven't worked some things out in my head yet. I'll explain later," he said thoughtfully, then turning his undivided attention back to his sister. "What are you going to do about the baby, Vivian?"

"I can't keep it. Not just because of Carlton and the kind of person he is, but because of me. I am not ready to be a mother. Mom and Dad understand. They've given me their permission to end the pregnancy if I want to. Even Gregory and Aretha agreed. Tell me that you won't hate me for doing this, Benny? Stacy told me how hard you've fought to keep her from having an abortion."

Benny hugged his sister close to him and kissed her on the top of her head. "I love you, Viv. I could never hate you no matter what the circumstance. The situation between you and Carlton is for you to decide. You do what you have to. I told you, I'm always in your corner…no matter what."

Gregory left early for his big high school basketball game and took Aretha with him. Aretha was his good luck charm. He knew that all the college basketball scouts from the Atlantic Coast Conference, the Big East Conference, and other athletic conferences would be at the game. Although he had another year of high school to go before he graduated, he wanted to make a good impression so that he would be offered a scholarship by one of the big universities. He knew that his parents planned for his college years, but he didn't want them to foot the bill for four years, especially since Aretha would also be going to college. He was determined to land an athletic scholarship.

The rest of the Alexander family, including Stacy, piled into Dr. Alexander's late model SUV to drive to the big game. Along the way, they stopped periodically to speak to a neighbor or to show Stacy some points of interest.

"That's the old loading dock where my grandfather would jump off the Old Silver Meteor train for his three days off during a fourteen-day period. They used to call it 'The Chicken Bone Express'."

"'The Chicken bone Express?'" Stacy said, laughing. "I've read a lot of history about the South, Dr. Alexander, but I've never heard of that."

"Now, Stacy, you're going to have to learn to call me Dad since you're going to be one of the family."

"Yes, sir."

"That's better. Well, everything didn't get into the history books yet, but I'm working on that. But I'll explain. You see, Black folks could ride on the train during my grandfather's time, but they had to ride in certain cars and weren't allowed to buy food on the train. So any Black person had to pack a lunch or dinner if he or she wanted to ride the Old Silver Meteor and most of the time it was a homemade, boxed meal that always included fried chicken," Bernard stated. "That's how it got its name, The Chicken Bone Express. My grandmother used to make the best boxed meals and sell them to people riding the trains.

That's how she helped make a living for her family. One of my sisters, Olivia, she's a Dixon now, and an older brother, Malcolm, and I would stand there, as the train went through town and wave at our grandfather on the caboose and help sell those boxed meals.

"That's the church over there where my great grand parents, grandparents and great parents were married and where my whole family was baptized. My parents had fourteen children and all of us are healthy and happy except for my sister Beatrice. She and her husband, Rick Johnson, died in a car accident out in California. They had nine children who now live here except for my niece Terri. She married her college sweetheart. They live in Los Angeles and have three children.

"And over here in the little house in the cornfield is where I was born. It used to be the home of a midwife.

"That's the Town Hall over there. One of my younger sisters, Olivia, is the Mayor of Goodwill. She has been for a long time. She does such a good job that no one ever runs against her. She and her husband, Romelo, we call him Romeo, have twin boys, James Edward and Donald Alexander Dixon. James used to be a big time lobbyist up in Chicago for the farm industry and Donald, well he works for the government. James heard the call of the South, came home, started our family hydroponics farm and other businesses while Donald heard the call of the wild. That boy rarely gets home.

"A cousin owns that little grocery store and we provide a lot of the produce and another cousin runs the laundry over there. Down this lane is Goodwill Institute, the elementary school where I and all our children attended grade school. Aretha goes to school there now. The Wilson brothers own that pulp and paper mill over there and Mr. Ezra Douglas owns the hardware store. The Newley family run the fish market and Ms. Bonnie Talbert runs the meat market. The corner drug store over there is where Benny took his first girlfriend, Caroline Ann, out for an ice cream soda. She's married now with two children. Mr. Joe Sephus owns the gas station and garage. His kids moved away.

"My brother, Malcolm, and one of his sons, Malcolm Junior, own the drug store now. Malcolm Junior is a pharmacist and married a wonderful girl from Tampa, Florida. They have two children and they're pregnant again.

"Mary McLeod Bethune was born just down that road. Bethune-Cookman University in Daytona Beach, Florida is named after her.

"And that's where our son, Kenneth James, built a gazebo in the town square as his senior project in high school. Still looks good, doesn't it?" Bernard asked with pride.

"There certainly is a lot of history in this little community. I didn't even know the names of any of the shopkeepers in the Cabrini Green area. It was just another big grocery chain or clothing store with graffiti on the walls and bars on the windows," Stacy said. "There was never any personal relationship with the store clerks. Most of them acted as if you should be honored to be served by them."

"Here in Goodwill, and even in Summer County, we get to know everyone pretty well. There aren't a lot of people, but they're all good, hardworking folks. We're related to so many of the people in the county that we told the children that they couldn't marry anyone from Goodwill because they were probably cousins twice removed," Sylvia laughed. "So the children have to go elsewhere to find their mates."

"But I don't see a jail or a police car," Stacy said.

Bernard laughed. "We don't have a jail or a policeman. There's a county sheriff and a deputy, but when someone has a problem, they just go talk to my sister, Olivia. She can usually take care of whatever it is. We haven't ever had anyone get into serious trouble around here. Once old man Taggard's brahma bull got loose and he ran through the gasoline station, but that's about as serious as it gets."

"You mean that no one's been shot in Goodwill?"

"Well, once Mrs. Ada Goings thought that her husband was fooling around with Mrs. Selah Jones, and Mrs. Goings got her rifle out, but she didn't shoot anyone. The rifle wasn't even loaded, but Mr. Goings got the message and he and Mrs. Jones have made a wide berth around each other ever since that day."

"Aren't there any liquor stores or shopping malls around here?" Stacy asked.

"Well, we suspect that Old Man Petrie has a still down in The Bottom; that's what we call the wetlands or the swamp, but no one has been able to find it. He keeps the locals supplied with white lightening though. He also makes a variety of wines that he sells legally at the grocery. We can usually get anything we need right here in Goodwill or in Summer County. Everyone in town has something they can do. We don't lack for talent." He smiled. "Yep, we've got everything we need right here: food, shelter, clothing and entertainment. If we want to do any other shopping, we go to somewhere else in Summer County or to Columbia or on the Internet."

Stacy was amazed. This was a whole new way of living in a stress-free environment.

Bernard pulled into the parking lot at Goodwill High School and right into a parking space with **Dr. Bernard Alexander, Principal**, clearly marked on a sign post. As they got out of the car, people warmly greeted them. Benny and Vivian introduced Stacy to classmates of theirs and there was Mabel Johnson and her daughter, Caroline Ann, who was carrying one baby and pulling another one behind her.

"Benjamin Staton Alexander, as I live and breathe! How are you, honey child?" Caroline Ann asked, with a broad smile.

"I'm fine, Caroline Ann. And you?"

"Fair to middlin', I think. And look at your lovely wife. My name is Caroline Ann Johnson-Plimpton," she said, releasing the hand of the toddler and extending her hand to Stacy. The little boy in Caroline Ann's arms reached for Benny who took him from his mother while she talked. "My daddy was third cousin to Fessor Alexander's brother-in-law, Rick Johnson, but I used to date this here buck. I want to tell you that you're a lucky lady to have landed this man. Just look at those broad shoulders and that big chest of his and that narrow waist. Baby's got back, too," she said, peeking behind him. "Let me look at your hands, boy. Mmmm, I never got that far with him, but I'll bet that he's a good husband. Those big hands really tell the story about the rest of the package…you must be carrying some heavy luggage, Benjamin Staton." She beamed at him, and then conspiratorially leaning forward, she said to Stacy, "You see, I was his first girlfriend, but we were only ten years old at the time." She giggled and nodded. "I lost track of you after high school and the Air Force Academy, Benjamin Staton. Where are you and your wife living these days? I know that Vivian Lynn is somewhere up in DC and I hear that Kenneth James is in California, but I'm not sure that I know where.

"Hear tell that we're gonna have a lot of those college scouts out here today after Gregory Clayton just like they did when you were playing basketball your junior and senior year. You were a great basketball player, Benjamin Staton, but I think Gregory Clayton has a few new moves on you. That Aretha Grace has been working on him something fierce, but that's what you have to expect from her. She's just like your grandmother used to be when she was living over on your farm.

"Well, it was nice meeting you, Mrs. Alexander, and it sure was good seeing you again, Benjamin Staton. I'm sure that your wife will pardon me for saying it, but I never should have let a good-looking man like you get away." She laughed. "Yep, you sure landed a good one, Mrs. Alexander. Looks like he's going to be a great father, too. My boy won't go to just anybody, but he sure likes you, Benjamin Staton, you can…"

Benny tried to interrupt Caroline Ann to explain that he and Stacy weren't married; that they were only friends, but that was an exercise in futility when Caroline Ann got going.

"...what did you say your wife's name was, Benjamin Staton?"

"This is Stacy—"

"Stacy, what a pretty name. Stacy Alexander. We'll have to put the announcement in the church bulletin tomorrow that Stacy and Benjamin Staton Alexander are here visiting their folks, Mama. Well, let's go see Goodwill High School beat the pants off whomever they're playing. Those boys are really...." Caroline Ann took her son from Benny and went away, still talking.

Both Benny and Stacy covered their mouths to hide their amusement.

Sylvia observed the exchange and mumbled under her breath, "And they think they're not in love. It's written all over their faces...everybody can see that."

"What are you saying, Mom?" Vivian asked.

"I'll explain it to you later," Sylvia said, cryptically.

The Goodwill High School gymnasium was filled to capacity. The band was playing loudly and the cheerleaders were revving up the crowd. Bernard Alexander led his family to their special seats just behind the home team bench. When they arrived, the teams were warming up. They spotted Aretha busily at work helping the other team managers set up the water, arrange the chairs, put out the towels, and separate the warm-up attire for the team members. She had one eye on Gregory, as he starting shooting around at the basket. Stacy was busily scanning the opposing team and comparing the players to their stats listed in the game program. She was sitting between Benny and Vivian, but she wasn't listening to a word that they were saying. As the game began and the teams were announced, Stacy was on the edge of her seat. When Gregory's name and number were called and he ran out on to the floor, Stacy was the first one on her feet, yelling and clapping. Vivian and Benny were astonished at her enthusiasm. They leaned back and looked at each other quizzically, as Stacy stuck her fingers between her teeth and loudly whistled.

The game continued and Stacy was calling the plays better than any color-commentary announcer.

"That's a foul on #22, Ref. Where did you get your patch, Sears and Roebuck?

"Aww, c'mon #30 get down low!

"That's right!

"Now work it inside so G can fire that rock!

"Way to go, G! Take him to the hoop! Give #30 some dap!

"Now steal the ball!

"Yes!

"Keep that man of the blocks, Gregory!

"Watch your back #7. He's going to try an alleyoop on you!

"Get back there and cover your man #12!

"Three seconds in the lane, Ref!

"#41 is holding! You got to call them both ways, Ref! Are you blind?

 "Come on Ref, can't you even count to a three-second violation either!

"He walked!

"Give up the ball!

"Ten seconds on the clock!

"Get across the line!

"That's right #7!

"Now pass it inside down low!

"That man can't handle you, Gregory! You handle him!

"Two points and a foul!

"Awe, come on ref! He ran out of real estate! No body touched him!"

Vivian and Benny just looked at Stacy. There was no reason to watch the game because she was calling it play by play. When the whistle blew for a time out, Stacy sat down in her seat. Benny and Vivian just stared at her. She noticed and looked from side to side at them.

"What?" she asked.

"Stacy, I didn't know that you knew anything about basketball," Benny said.

"There wasn't much else to do in my old Cabrini Green neighborhood. I grew up on the game and played it in high school. I was all-city champ at my position four-years straight and took the state championship my senior year. How do you think that I got into the Naval Academy? You can't grow up in Chicago nearly next door to the Bulls and not know the game."

She acted as if they should have known all of that. When the game resumed, so did Stacy. She was back on her feet again, calling the game and coaching from the sidelines. People sitting nearby were nodding and agreeing with her. Giving her high-fives and *"you tell em, sister!"*

Throughout the game, Vivian felt uneasy, as if someone was watching her, but she shook off the feeling and enjoyed the game with Stacy. They started comparing notes on the skills and abilities of the players, while they continually brought into serious question the heritage of the referees. Even Benny had to blush at their language. Stacy made a particularly colorful remark and Benny shot a look at her. She noticed and grinned.

"What do you expect, Fly Boy, I am a sailor!" Stacy said, with a shrug.

Aretha sat on the home team bench next to the coaches. All throughout the game the Alexanders could see her talking to the coaches and using her hands to demonstrate what appeared to be different strategies or plays. She never took her eyes off her brother and the other team members, as she talked to the coaches. Occasionally she would leap to her feet, cup her hands around her mouth, and yell something to Gregory. He seemed to acknowledge her and correct or change whatever he was doing. Whenever she sat down after coaching her brother, the official coaches would nod their heads in agreement.

During time outs, the coaches would huddle with the team members and Aretha was right in the thick of it. She didn't interfere with the coaches instructions to the team, but before Gregory returned to the game, Aretha would occasionally whisper something to her brother and he would nod in agreement. She popped him on the butt and he would take to the floor. Whenever Gregory sat down to take a breather, Aretha sat next to him, clearly strategizing what he should be doing or complimenting him on his performance thus far. Whenever he stood up to go back into the game, he put his hand on the top of Aretha's head and jostled her hair.

Gregory scored twenty-seven points, had fourteen rebounds and twelve assists; a triple double. Of course, Goodwill High won and Gregory got the most-valuable-player award. He beamed, as he held it up in one hand and hugged Aretha with his other arm in the middle of the gymnasium floor. He handed the trophy to Aretha, trotted to his mother and kissed her. He shook his father's hand and hugged him tight. There were tears of joy in Sylvia, Vivian, and Stacy's eyes, as they cheered Gregory.

As Benny and his father stood cheering Gregory, Benny recalled how he had felt playing basketball in this very same gym and what an incredible feeling it was to have his family there to support him. He understood just what Gregory was feeling. His eyes met Gregory's and gave him a thumbs-up. Leaping from their seats, they joined the crowd that surrounded the winning team. They would advance to the state championship games. March Madness was in full swing.

Benny and Vivian hugged their brother and congratulated him and the other team members and Aretha who they knew obviously played an important role in Gregory's performance and the team's victory. Stacy was Gregory's biggest cheerleader. As the team went into the locker room, the throngs of college scouts followed them. Some people began to leave the gym while others stood around in groups talking about the game. Vivian had reminisced with some of her former female high school team mates about their glory days playing on that same hardwood. She was a deadly three-point shooter in high school and in college and she still played as often as she could now that she was in law school. She loved the game and the exercise it provided. Then she sat on the bleachers alone while Benny introduced Stacy to some of his other high school friends. Bernard and Sylvia sat in another area of the gymnasium talking with other parents about the upcoming state high school championship games that would be held in Columbia, South Carolina.

"Vivian, we have to talk about this pregnancy," Carlton Andrews said. "I've been watching you from across the gym. Brings back old memories about how you used to cheer for me when I played ball at Clark-Atlanta. Those were some good times we had...."

She did not turn around to look at him.

"I love you, Vivian. You haven't given me a fair chance to explain. I know what it must have looked like to you and I know that you're feeling jealous and hurt. You're probably still pretty angry with me right now, but in time, I know that you'll see that no relationship should rise or fall based on who you screw or the foolish mistakes someone makes. It isn't as if those women meant anything to me. You and I have been together a long time. I know how much you love me and now that we're going to have a baby, we should try to work this out so that we can get married real soon. I know that you didn't want to get married this year, but now we have to, baby," he pleaded and rushed on. "You just set the date and we can start getting on with the rest of our lives together. We can put all this foolishness behind us. I've made some plans for us. You're home now. We don't have to wait and have a big wedding. Reverend Thomas said that he would perform the ceremony today. I already arranged to pick up the marriage license. Didn't want your family to go get a shotgun next," he said and laughed nervously. "So what do you say, baby?"

Benny noticed Carlton sitting behind Vivian pleading with her. He started to approach them, but Vivian looked at him and shook her head. He stayed where he was, but he positioned himself so that he could keep an eye on his sister and Carlton.

"Are you finished, Carlton?" Vivian asked in a low, calm voice.

He indicated that he was ready to listen to her.

With no detectable emotion in her voice or change in her demeanor, Vivian said, "I've been remembering how we met on campus, too, Carlton. I remembered how long it took us to develop what I thought was a relationship, a commitment to love, trust and respect each other. It's ironic that what we had between us started in a gymnasium and will now end in one. Still, you're right about one thing. I do love you, Carlton, in my own way. But I love you less now than I did an hour ago and I'll love you less tomorrow than I do today and I'll love you far less next week and next month than I do today, and one day soon, I won't love you at all." She removed the engagement ring from her finger with ease. She stood up, turned around, handed the ring to him, and looked him in his eyes. She saw his blackened eye and bruised jaw, but even seeing the man she once thought she'd live her life with battered and bruised stirred nothing; not even pity in her. "That day can't come too soon for me. I wish that I had stuck to it years ago when I told you to step off. I'm a little older and a lot wiser now. This time there is no coming back, so step off. I never want to see you or hear from you again. *Ever.*"

Vivian turned and walked down the bleachers and away from Carlton. She was calm and collected throughout the entire exchange. Surprisingly, she felt as if a weight had been lifted from her shoulders. She felt no regret and no remorse for leaving the man who she had loved unconditionally for nearly three years. When she approached Benny, she was able to smile at him without a hint of sadness. She felt free.

After the game, the Alexander family headed home for a victory dinner with the whole family, including the cousins, aunts, and uncles. As the Alexanders approached their home, Stacy saw that the once peaceful surrounding now resembled a parking lot. There were cars and people everywhere. People were carrying fat pots and pans full of food into the house. Children were playing catch in the backyard or jumping rope, or tossing horseshoes or playing hide-and-go-seek among the big Live Oak trees. It was pure pandemonium.

"Benny, what's going on here? Who are all these people?" Stacy asked, as Benny helped her out of the backseat of the car.

"Oh, just some of my family," he answered, as if there were only a few people.

"'Some of your family'? Benny, there's got to be over a hundred people here!" Stacy said awed.

"That's what I said, Stacy. Just some of my family. Everybody doesn't come to these little get-togethers."

"'Little get-together'! You call this a 'little' get-together?"

"Sure, some of my family live too far away to come every time that we get together. You'll see many more at the July fourth family reunion though. More than a thousand usually show up for that. This is small as compared to that. Come on; let me introduce you to them."

Benny took Stacy's hand and led her to each relative. There was uncle this, and aunt that, and cousin so and so. There were people everywhere. The kitchen and dining room were overflowing with food. Some people were setting up tables on the screened-in back porch. Others were spreading tablecloths on the lawn tables in the back yard. There were trashcans filled to capacity with ice and cold sodas and others filled with beer. Paper plates, napkins, and forks were piled high on one table and desserts of every type and description were on another. Children were taking turns making ice cream in an old-fashioned churn. A huge round metal drum was hoisted onto a metal stand and turned into a grill. Several men stood over the grill, sopping sauce on an assortment of meats. Fresh corn still in husk was being placed on another grill. White and sweet potatoes were being placed between the ears of corn. Large, whole fish were being stuffed with crabmeat, lobster, and other seafood delicacies freshly plucked from the family fishery, wrapped carefully in aluminum foil and placed on another grill.

Soul, rap, reggae and pop music could be heard in different rooms of the house or different areas of the yard. Other young people were huddled together harmonizing. Someone pulled out a guitar. Another one arranged pots and pans into a drum set. Yet, someone else was tuning up a clarinet and someone else a saxophone. Aretha set up her electric piano on some crates. Another crew placed folding chairs around the makeshift bandstand.

Basketball teams were being chosen for a game that included many age groups and both men and women. Vivian, Aretha, and Gregory were right in the thick of it with cousins who could have doubled as their sisters or brothers.

Older women were shepherding toddlers, as they tried to navigate on their tiny feet. Other women were cuddling babies on their laps and feeding them from bottles as the babies' eyes darted from one face to another. Older men sat huddled around card tables, slamming cards down and scooping up their winnings. Brown paper bags with unmarked bottles or jars sat at their feet and were occasionally lifted and poured into cans of soft drinks that the men had conspicuously set on the table while they played cards. Games of checkers, or darts, or chess or monopoly were being played in other areas.

Stacy was being introduced at such a dizzying pace that she could not remember whom she had or hadn't met. They all resembled each other and all the men were drop-dead gorgeous. They were hugging each other, especially Benny and Vivian, giving each other high-fives, and grinning from ear to ear. Joking with one another and laughing with full, hardy voices and sparkling eyes seemed to be a family trait.

"Benny! Slow down! I've never seen so many people who all resemble each other." Stacy pulled on his arm. "I can't remember all these names." She looked at Benny's face. She had never seen him so happy. He was beaming.

Benny pulled Stacy into his arms and kissed her, playing havoc with her senses.

"I'm sorry, Stacy. I haven't been home for a while and it's good to see my family again," Benny's excitement was unstoppable.

Stacy noticed a tall, very handsome man laughing and turning the meat on a grill. Her mouth gaped at his phine physique. She put her hand on Benny's arm to get his attention. "Benny, is that your brother?" she asked nodding toward the men at the grill.

Benny craned his neck, looking across the lawn. When he spotted the man Stacy was referring to, he laughed. "That's my cousin, James Edward Dixon. He and his twin brother are Uncle Romeo's and Aunt Olivia's sons. Come on, I'll introduce you to him." He took her hand and weaved through the crowd.

James noticed them approaching and a huge smile split his handsome face.

"Hey, cousin," Benny hailed, as the two tall men hugged each other.

He was so handsome that, just for a moment, Stacy just stared, with opened mouth, looking back and forth between Benny and James. They looked almost identical.

When Benny turned to her, she was still staring. He laughed and slipped his arm around her shoulders.

"Stacy Greene, this is my cousin, James Edward Dixon."

Stacy extended her hand her mouth still agape.

James ignored her hand and pulled her into a bear hug.

"Welcome home, Stacy," James beamed, and then he kissed her.

She blushed her thanks, but Benny pulled her out of his cousin's arms.

"Mine." He grinned at James.

James laughed. "Would I do something like that to you?"

"Uh huh." Benny grinned. "You're a Dixon. It's in the genes. Stacy thought that you were Kenneth."

Both men laughed.

"You look like twins," Stacy said, still awed.

"I am a twin. My brother, Donald, isn't here, thank goodness. He'd be trying to get you away from Benny. He's the one Benny has to keep you away from. Me? I'm harmless." He winked again, slipping his arm around Stacy. "I'm just a country boy."

"A country boy who has a double doctorate, lectures at South Carolina University, and runs one of the most successful hydroponics farms in the state for our family," Benny said, laughing. "He's been known to invite unsuspecting women to tour his sweet potatoes and sweet peas and talk them out of their sweetness."

James laughed. "Don't believe a word of that, Stacy. It was my brother, Donald, not me. I get a bad rep because we're identical twins and people can't tell us apart."

Stacy shook her head in awe.

"Benny! Stacy! James! Come on! The game's about to begin!" Vivian yelled, dragging them to the backyard basketball court. "Let's go, Stacy! It's you, me, Benny, Gregory and cousin James is going to take K.J.'s spot!"

"Wait a minute, Viv. Stacy can't play and neither can you. You're both pregnant, remember?"

"Oh yeah?" Stacy said, narrowing her eyes. "And who's going to stop us?"

"I am. I'm not taking any chances that you two could get hurt," he said, narrowing his gaze.

"Look, Fly Boy, just because I'm carrying this baby for you, don't you think that somehow I've lost my ability to think for myself," she quipped.

Benny relented. Stacy was getting into the flow of his family's tempo and that made him happy, but he was more concerned about her welfare.

"We're first up against the Lawson cousins again! But the bad news is that Aretha's one of the referees," Vivian interjected.

Benny and Gregory groaned. They knew how tough Aretha could be when she had that whistle in her mouth, refereeing a game.

They huddled and mapped out their strategy.

"Stacy, you've got point. I'll be two man. G, you take swing man. James you take power forward and, Benny, you've got center," Vivian said in their huddled. They put their hands in the circle, yelled "Go team!" and the game was underway.

Stacy brought the ball up court and passed it to Gregory who swung it to Vivian who shot it on the fly…three points! The game went to twenty-one. Team Alexander lost to Team Lawson, again. But, as expected, Aretha had called a tough game. She called infractions on both ends of the court. Stacy had five points. Vivian had nine—all on three point shots—Benny had four—both dunks—and their cousin, James Dixon, had two. Gregory bragged that he gave twenty-seven points at the office that day, so he only let them try to catch up with him.

Team Alexander retired and the next teams took the court. Team Alexander grabbed seats, cold drinks, and sat around watching the next game and grumbling about how the referee stole the victory from them.

Later, Sylvia Alexander rang a big, cowbell signaling that everything was ready for dinner. Everyone huddled and held hands while the eldest member of the family gave thanks for the good food and the privilege of sharing it with good family. As soon as the prayer ended, the elders of the family were ushered to the table first or were served by Aretha and other young people where they sat. Then the tables of food became mob scenes.

Benny sat quietly watching his family. Childhood memories of so many other family get-togethers filled his thoughts. The smell of hot apple cider and turkeys with all the trimmings. In his mind, he saw Grandmother Emma's black, pot-bellied pot still sitting in the yard where he had helped her make soap when he was a small boy. He glanced at the screened-in back porch and remembered the old washing machine and his grandmother, as she pushed heavy, wet clothes through a ringer that she insisted using rather than the band new one in the house. She was an independent woman just like Stacy. Perhaps that's why he admired Stacy so much, because she possessed the same qualities as his grandmother.

He looked at the sturdy old barn just a short distance outside of the perimeter of the yard where a new generation of children now played. He remembered holding his grandfather's hand outside of that barn and tossing feed to the chickens, as they cackled and scampered around when he was only about five or six years old. With a new coat of red paint that barn looked enormous when he was small. Now it had taken on a new, much smaller dimension. He sat and thought that he would one day walk with his soon-to-be-daughter and point out the old, black, pot-bellied lye pot and tell his daughter the stories of their ancestors in this place.

"They're still here, Benny, aren't they?" Vivian asked, sitting quietly beside him. She laid her head on his shoulder and his arm automatically came around her, holding her against him.

"You feel them too, don't you?"

"I remember them clearly. I'll never forget them or the stories that they told us about our heritage. About our ancestors from Egypt and Barbados. The images of Grandma Emma and Grandpa Bernard sitting on the back porch holding us and telling us the stories of their youth stay with me. Grandma Emma had the sweetest voice when she would sing to us and rock us in her arms and Grandpa Bernard would harmonize with her. It's so good to remember them. Aretha reminds me of them most of all. She's more like them than any of us. She has the wisdom of the elders. The ancestors have smiled on her."

Not much was left after the feast, but whatever leftovers there were, were carefully packaged in covered Styrofoam plates that relatives took home to enjoy another day. Nothing was thrown away. A brigade of family members washed dishes, cleaned the tables, and bagged the trash.

The bright, warm, sunny March day was beginning to give way to the cool of the evening, as metal barrels were loaded with trash and firewood and ignited. Lights were turned on around the back yard. The family sat together before the makeshift bandstand and listened to the music. Bernard, Gregory, Benny, Malcolm Senior and Junior, and Romelo and James Dixon did their rendition of "In the Still of the Night" a cappella. There were impromptu skits, dance routines and jokes, and comedy routines by still other family members.

Aretha beautifully and effortlessly played jazz, pop, rock and anything else that the crowd asked for on her electric piano. Young and old alike were on their feet when the band struck up "Rockin' Pneumonia and the Boogie Woggie Flu."

Benny was dancing with Vivian, but watching Stacy's sultry moves, as she danced with Gregory. A sensation came over him, as he looked into Stacy's clear, clean, fresh face. She was indeed a phenomenal woman—his woman. He danced Vivian to Gregory and took Stacy into his arms.

Stacy was surprised by the gesture, he noticed, and even more surprised when he gazed into her eyes, stopped dancing and lowered his head by degrees until he captured her mouth. The music swirled around them, but they were lost in the sweet ecstasy of their union.

The final event was the birthday cake decorated with the names of the seven family members who had birthdays. The band struck up a very up-tempo version of "Happy Birthday" and everybody sang to the seven family members.

Later, Stacy sat next to Vivian and looked at all the happiness and joy that this family shared. They had made her feel a part of it all. Sylvia Alexander stood behind Stacy with her hands on Stacy's shoulders.

Bernard stood before the group and quieted them for announcements. He started with news that the Farmer twins were accepted to Howard University in the fall; that Cousin Jasper Cooper was moving to Toronto, Canada, for his new job at a book publishing company; and that Cousin Edna Smith-Wilson was going to retire from her job at Pennzoil in Dallas and would be returning to Goodwill with her husband of forty years, John Wilson, by Christmas.

"Family is perpetual," Bernard continued. "Each generation of the family from the time of The Middle Passage has brought forth small gifts, which keep us strong and vital and vibrant. We watch these small gifts grow and develop and bathe them in the love of family. Being a parent is an honor, which celebrates the cycle of one's life. It makes all the rough times smooth again when we can rejoice in the joy and happiness of our offspring and continues the family tradition. We are fortunate, Sylvia and I, to announce that, our son, Benjamin Staton, and Stacy Greene, will bring forth another small gift and another generation in September. According to my son it will be a little girl who Benjamin and Stacy will name Whitney Ivy Alexander."

Everyone clapped and cheered Benny and Stacy. Sylvia was surprised that they were naming their daughter for her Aunt Hanna Ivy Benson, the woman who had raised Sylvia after her parents went on a European tour with the megastar, Josephine Baker. Sylvia's sister, Mariah, was still living in Paris after leaving her husband. She bent and kissed Stacy on the cheek. Vivian hugged Stacy. Gregory rushed to Stacy and led her to the place where his father stood. Benny followed and, as he hugged Stacy in front of his cheering family and kissed her, he whispered "Thank you" in Stacy's ear. Tears were streaming down Stacy's face, as she gazed into Benny's eyes. Bernard hugged her and then allowed the rest of the family members to welcome her. Everyone congratulated Benny and Stacy.

Night had overtaken daylight. As the Alexanders waved goodbye and the last car pulled down the lane out of sight, Benny enveloped Stacy in his arms and kissed her gently on the lips.

"You know, Navy, our daughter, Whitney Ivy, is going to share in all of this. Twenty years from now she'll be out there just like her mother playing ball, dancing or singing like her Aunt Aretha, or joking or blowing her own horn."

"My God, Benny. I just hope that she'll be able to remember the names of all of her relatives!"

They both laughed and went inside with the rest of the Alexander family.

As Benny had asserted, he and Stacy went to bed early. They lay together in the afterglow of another euphoric encounter that had lasted for hours. Benny lay with his head on Stacy's left breast, his left hand over his daughter in Stacy's womb, and his left leg across Stacy's thighs. He was drifting into sleep, as Stacy lazily stroked his arm and shoulder with her left hand, laid her head against the top of his head, and caressed his face with her right hand.

"Benny?" she said softly, as she held and caressed him.

"Yes, Stacy," he answered half asleep, "just give me a few more minutes to catch a nap. You're wearing me out."

"No, Benny, I want—"

"Baby, I know what you want, but I just need a little shuteye and then I'm all yours for as long as you want," he said, still drifting into sleep.

"That's not what I'm asking you about, Benny," Stacy said, correcting his obvious misconception.

"That's a relief," he sighed. "I didn't know that pregnant women had so much energy. It sure wasn't in any book that I've read about pregnancy."

"Benny, why do your parents use both your first and middle names?"

He spoke around a yawn. "Everyone does that, not just my parents." He shifted his body more securely against hers. "It's a Southern thing."

"But why, Benny?"

"Baby, do we have to talk about it right now?" he mumbled against her breast.

"Just tell me about this and I'll let you catch a nap."

"All right," he said, fighting to stay awake. "In the South, your first name is for the new person that you are and your middle name is for the person who passed before you came. Southern people want you to remember who you came from, remind you and themselves of who has passed on by giving their children the names of someone who was loved and who has now passed on. The spirit of the person who has passed on is always remembered from generation to generation."

"So who was Staton?"

"Kenneth James and I are named for our maternal great grandfather, James Staton Benson."

"Then who is Gregory named for?"

"Our maternal grandfather, Clayton Charles Benson."

"What about Vivian and Aretha?"

"Vivian is named for our maternal grandmother Anne Lynn Burley-Benson. Aretha is named for our paternal grandmother Emma Grace Smithy Alexander. Now can I take a nap?" He yawned.

"Who did you name Whitney for?"

"Whoever you want. Whitney Houston is one of my favorite vocalists, so I chose Whitney as our daughter's first name. Her middle name doesn't have to be Ivy. Pick someone who was important in your life and has now passed on. I suggest that you choose a woman since we're going to have a daughter."

"What name would you like?"

"I don't know. Aretha suggested Ivy for our maternal grand aunt, Hanna Ivy Benson. I thought that that would make Mom happy. Aunt Ivy raised Mom and her sisters and brothers after their parents and grandparents continued to tour the European continent with Josephine Baker. They were actors, singers, dancers, entertainers like Whitney Houston was. Aunt Hanna Ivy sold the house she owned in Georgetown to me when I was stationed there. She lives in Myrtle Beach in another house she owns. At the end of the summer, the young cousins to go there and camp on the beach for Labor Day weekend and do whatever maintenance needs to be done to the house. Aunt Hanna has arranged for the house to continue to be passed down through the generations so that the tradition will continue."

Benny knew his families' history well, but sleep overtook him. As he lay peacefully and comfortably in Stacy's warm embrace, she gently stroked his body.

Stacy was wide-awake, thinking of all of the generations of the Alexander and Benson families who contributed to the new person who she now carried in her womb. She knew very little about her own heritage. She had no middle name to lay claim on a connection to her past. It never seemed important before. She thought about it now, as Benny lay in her arms. *It must be a wonderful feeling to know whom you came from,* she thought. After the events of the day beginning with the walking and then riding tour, she felt a warmth and a connection to Benny's past and present. She caressed Benny's face and gently kissed his lips. He responded to her in his sleep. She shifted her body against his, feeling the need for him growing in her core. She kissed his right ear with an open mouth, sliding her tongue slowly down to his neck and under his chin onto his chest and lingered at the nipple on the left, as she gently rolled him onto his back. The feel of his warm, strong body excited her, as she shifted her body partly onto his. She massaged the growing fullness of his...

Benny's eyes popped open. "Uh, Stacy... Baby.... Uh.... Where are you getting.... all of this..... energy? You're insatiable! I can't keep up.... this.... pace."

"You must have overlooked that chapter in the pregnancy book," she said, as she continued to unmercifully arouse him.

"Stacy, uh.... I thought that.... you.... were going.... to let me catch.... a nap," he managed, as the sensations began to be more than he could bear.

"I lied."

On Sunday morning, Benny awoke as the roosters began to crow in the distance, one after the other, announcing the beginning of a new day. The sunlight began to flood into the bedroom where he lay next to Stacy. He turned toward her and propped his head up on one hand and gazed at her while she slept. He looked at every peaceful contour of her face. Her eyes, her eyelashes, her nose, her mouth, her chin, her cheeks, her eyebrows, her chin. Her curly, light, auburn hair was cut short into a bob and lay on the pillow framing her face. Again, the fact that Stacy looked almost exactly like Alisha Keys came to mind. She lay on her back with one hand behind her head. He looked at the slender column of her neck and her nicely muscled arms. Gently he pulled the sheet down until it cleared her firm, ample breasts. She shifted her body slightly, but did not waken. Her perfectly shaped breasts rode above her chest, as she breathed in and out. Her pecan-colored nipples were round and firm and blended with her smooth café-au-lait colored skin. He slid the cover down further to reveal her stomach, small navel, narrow waistline, and firm abdomen. Her body was smooth and supple, as his hand glided over the place where his daughter-to-be lay growing in Stacy's womb.

"Uh, Benny, what are you doing?" Stacy asked, as she awoke and found Benny kissing her abdomen.

"I'm saying good morning to our daughter."

"She's not old enough for you to talk to her yet," Stacy said, as she stroked the nape of his neck, her emotions tangled at his reverence.

"We're still communicating," he said, gently burying kiss after kiss in her abdomen in several spots moving downward.

Stacy gasped, as Benny's mouth moved around her inner thighs, his hand cupping her butt and positioning her to create an erotic arousal of her senses.

"I'm.... not.... sure.... whether.... she's getting.... the messages.... that.... you're.... sending.... but.... I.... sure...am...." Stacy panted, as Benny slipped his head between her thighs and lingered there. Stacy's breathing began to quicken in tandem with her racing heartbeat.

Benny slipped both hands under her butt, holding her quivering body steady and firmly. She closed her eyes and submitted to the sensations that were overtaking her. She moaned in ecstasy, as she reached climax. Benny rolled onto his back and brought Stacy on top of him. He sat up and began to swallow her breasts, allowing equal attention to both. Lowering her into position over his hardened erection, he slowly entered her. Her back arched, as he fit comfortably between her open thighs and began to move in rhythm with her. His kiss was wet, warm and sensuous. Opening her mouth, she received his tongue and gripped his back, as his muscles flexed beneath her hands and between her thighs. They groaned their ecstasy with each slow, methodical thrust, savoring the excitement within them. Soon their perspiration began to mingle, as Stacy reached another climax. Then they were again lost in the ecstasy of their union. Benny lowered her onto her back and mounted her. He slowly, but steadily, began to bring Stacy back to another heightened state. He knew her body well and read her body language as easily and as confidently as he could read the constellations in the sky. He moaned with the pleasure of their union. Stacy's whispers in his ear caused his body muscles to bunch. Benny tried to prolong the ecstasy of loving Stacy, but as sure as day follows night, they reached the dawning of their new day together with all the brilliance of the formation of a new sun. They were breathless, as their sensations continued to flood over them and began to subside.

"Where were we, Benny?" Stacy panted, as she struggled to catch her breath. Her body was trembling and tingling from head to toe.

"Somewhere I've never been before," Benny said, still having difficulty controlling his breathing. His heart was thundering in his chest.

They both went limp.

When they glimpsed at each other, they began to laugh. Benny swallowed her in his arms. She stroked his hair. They were both still breathless when they heard Sylvia knock lightly on the door to tell them that breakfast was almost ready.

A half hour later, Sylvia was pouring coffee, as Benny and Stacy entered the kitchen. She looked at them curiously and smiled. She tapped Bernard on the shoulder and nodded toward Stacy and Benny. He looked up at them and then back at Sylvia. A broad smile covered his face, as he sipped his piping hot coffee. Bernard's eyes met Vivian's over his coffee cup. He cut his eyes toward Benny and Stacy. She studied them momentarily then winked at her father, as she poured the orange juice. She caught Gregory's eye and nodded toward Stacy and Benny. Gregory looked at them and broke out into a broad grin, as he put the hot biscuits into the basket on the table.

Benny and Stacy noticed the glances and the silence in the room, as they sat down at the table. They looked at each other and shrugged.

Aretha entered the kitchen wearing a beautiful floor length, forest green, taffeta dress with long sleeves and an empire waistline. She twirled around so that everyone could see. They all applauded her and her appearance. Her hair was up in a ball on top of her head with a net of small, pale-pink, seed pearls woven through it. She was wearing a little blush, some lip gloss, and a radiant smile. Her eyes were shinning, as Gregory very gentlemanly seated her at the table. Aretha looked quizzically at Stacy and then at Benny and started to ask them something until she caught a glimpse of her mother who put one finger to her lips and shook her head. Aretha didn't ask the question that she had on her mind.

All through breakfast, the Alexanders would glimpse at Stacy and Benny, and giggle or grin. Gregory left the house early to take Aretha to Sunday school and then to her piano recital. Vivian, Benny, and Stacy packed their clothes and loaded them into their cars before they left for church.

As the Alexanders climbed the steps to the small Presbyterian Church, they noticed Benny reach for Stacy's hand. They held hands all through the church service. The sermon that day was on "The Unlimited Power of Love." After church, Reverend Johns greeted the parishioners and guests, as they left the church.

"Well, Benjamin Staton, it's good to see you sitting in the pew again and this time with your lovely wife. Caroline Ann Johnson-Plimpton told me that you two were visiting your parents. You two are simply glowing in the love that I spoke about today. I hear that you two are expecting your first child. I hope that you'll bring your baby home to Goodwill to be christened here in our little church. Well, I'll see you both at the recital. I hear that your sister is performing. Was nice meeting you, Mrs. Alexander. Stacy's your first name, isn't it? That's what we put in the Church Bulletin anyway. You and Benjamin Staton make a handsome couple. Please come back and see us soon."

Without taking a breath, Reverend Johns turned to the next parishioner. "Well, Mrs. Briggs, it's good to see you looking so well today. How is that knee?"

"Benny, doesn't anyone ever let you get an opportunity to get a word in edgewise around Goodwill?" Stacy was flustered, as they walked to the car.

Before he could answer her, other parishioners were surrounding and greeting them in the church yard under the big Live Oak trees. Although Stacy consistently introduced herself as Stacy Greene, the parishioners disregarded it and called her Stacy Greene-Alexander. Benny and Stacy gave up trying to correct the misconception, as they finally extricated themselves and walked hand-in-hand to the car.

The Goodwill High School Auditorium was packed. All of the churches in Summer County held early services so that the parishioners could attend the music recital at noon at the high school and the Sunday Social that would follow. For weeks, The Good Sisters of the Churches collected donations for the food that would be served at the Social that would follow the recital. The program listed twelve children of all ages who would be performing that day. The crowds quietly and attentively sat through each performance. They applauded loudly for each performer regardless of the quality of the performance.

Gregory was backstage helping to move equipment around, and opening and closing the stage curtains on cue, until he stopped everything and grabbed his video camcorder when he heard the Master of Ceremonies announce the last performer.

"And now, Ladies and Gentlemen, for our final selection of the day, Miss Aretha Grace Alexander will perform a medley of tunes from the opera, *Porgy and Bess*."

Gregory opened the curtain and, carrying a rose, Aretha entered from the opposite end of the stage. She winked at Gregory who returned the gesture, adding a thumbs-up before he began recording her performance. She walked to the piano, laid the rose on the empty, sheet-music stand, bowed to the audience, and took her seat. Her selections included, "Summertime," "Bess, You Is My Woman Now," "I Loves You Porgy," "There's A Boat That's Leaving," and other pieces. She was flawless and in total control of the baby grand piano. The audience was spellbound, as she played with energy and excitement in every note. Her little feet flew over the floor pedals, as her fingers limberly scaled the keys. She smiled, as she played, as if she had a guilty secret that she was busting to tell. When she finished, she slid off the piano bench and stood. The audience broke into clamorous applause, yells, and whistles. She picked up the rose and walked to the edge of the stage. She looked back at Gregory who was broadly smiling at her and clapping wildly. His pride in his sister's performance was obvious. She curtsied low until her knee touched the floor and she bowed her head. The audience went wild. They were all on their feet. Aretha slowly stood up, spotted Stacy on the first row with tears streaming down her face and clapping enthusiastically next to Benny. Aretha tossed the rose to Stacy and bowed again. Stacy caught the rose and was overcome with emotion. She buried her face in Benny's chest and he cradled her and rocked her in his arms.

Aretha grinned broadly and walked backward to the piano. The applause was still strong and raucous. People were yelling for an encore.

Aretha positioned herself on the piano stool, the audience hushed, and she began to play and sing the tune, "Do You Know" that Diana Ross had made famous. She played with such style and grace and sang with such emotion that eyes misted. Stacy and Benny were still holding on to each other. When Aretha finished, the applause was even more enthusiastic than before. She curtsied low again and tilted her head toward Gregory. They winked at each other and he gave her two thumbs-up. She rose and walked off the stage and Gregory closed the curtain.

When all of the performers were assembled on stage, Gregory opened the curtain again. They all stepped forward and bowed at the waist. The audience enthusiastically applauded. When they all stood up, Aretha winked at Stacy and she beamed.

The Good Sisters of the Churches had the Goodwill High School cafeteria smelling like the fabulous feast of the most renowned restaurants in the world. As people went through any one of four lines, the Good Sisters, dressed in their starched white uniforms with hairnets on their heads, dished up heaping spoonful's of food to each person. Ham, turkey, roast beef, fried chicken, fried fish, sweet potatoes, mashed potatoes, macaroni and cheese, rice and gravy, black beans, red beans, collard greens, string beans, squash, okra, kale, cauliflower and broccoli, steamed cabbage, peas and carrots and corn pudding. Salads of every type and description. The steam tables laden with foods seemed endless and the Styrofoam plates bent under the weight of the meal.

As people passed through the lines, the Good Sisters greeted each person by name (first and middle). As they emptied one large pan of food, another large pan of steaming hot food from the cafeteria kitchen ovens replaced the empty one. The Good Sisters never broke stride. They had the food service lines down to a fine science.

The Alexanders came through a line and then found seats where they could all sit together. Benny balanced two large plates full of food on his tray, as did Gregory and Bernard. Stacy was having trouble trying to balance one plate on her tray that was weighted down with quite a selection. She sat stuffing herself and her eyes lit up with appreciation for each mouthful. She moaned in ecstasy, as she tasted each selection on her plate and some that were on Benny's two plates. The Alexanders, never quieted as they ate, chatted animatedly, but they laughed loudly as Stacy sampled each dish. Her expressions were priceless,

Benny thought, as he gazed at her and fed her, laughing at the sparkle in her eyes that each mouthful brought.

Finally, after trying a little of each of seven desserts, Stacy gave up. She couldn't eat another bite. She leaned back in her chair, patting her stomach and proclaiming that she knew that she had died and gone to heaven. Everyone agreed. The Good Sisters of the Churches had done it again with genuine, down-home cooking.

Stacy glanced around the cafeteria at all of the people gathered, enjoying their meals and each other's company at the Sunday Afternoon Social. Some people went from table to table chatting with friends and relatives. Little children played carefully in their best Sunday-go-to-meeting clothes, and "good Sunday shoes." Men in their best suits with starched white shirts and ladies in their best dresses or suits, white laced gloves on their hands, and Sunday bonnets on their heads. It was such a simple, but joyous occasion, Stacy thought. She had witnessed large gatherings in the mess halls and aboard the aircraft carrier where she worked, but nothing compared to the spirit, joy and camaraderie which she experience in Goodwill, Summer County, South Carolina. Sensing that Benny was watching her, she turned her head toward him. He kissed her on the forehead and she laid her head on his shoulder.

"Dad, may I use the phone in your office? My cell needs charging." Benny asked.

"Sure, Son. I'll walk with you. I need a good stretch."

Bernard leaned over, gently kissed his wife, and winked. He put his hand on Benny's shoulder, as they walked along the school hallway.

"Son, I believe that love will cure everything and the love of a good woman has to be prized above all else. It's the glue that holds her man together and makes him strong. Stacy is a good woman and you can't go wrong loving her. I like her. She's very much like you. She has a sense of purpose and a dedication to duty. She can cure anything that ails you."

"She's very special to me."

"You know that we would be proud to have her in this family."

"I know. Everyone has made that abundantly clear. In fact, everyone in town seems to think that she's already a member of this family."

"With good reason, Son. You should have seen yourselves this morning when you came to the breakfast table. You two were glowing like neon lights and you're both still glowing now. Any two people who make each other glow like that deserve to be together. Everyone in town could see it."

"Stacy and I have a very close and intimate relationship beyond just being sexual partners, but we're nowhere near making a commitment beyond that. You're right though. We are very much alike and, I think, because of that, we understand each other. It's not that I don't want to be with her, because I do. Very much, but Stacy has a different agenda. It's not the way I want it to be, Dad, but that's the way Stacy wants it and I have to respect her decision." He waited a beat. "Dad, I know that you and mom talk all the time so this is probably not news to you. I explained to Mom that I'm seeing someone else who I believe I could make a part of my life."

"Yes, your mother told me…JeNelle Towson."

"Yes, Sir."

"You don't sound as sure of yourself about Ms. Towson, how you feel about her, and I don't see that same gleam in your eyes when I mentioned her name."

"It's different with JeNelle."

"What does she know about basketball?"

"Basketball?" Benny chuckled. "What does that have to do with anything?"

"Maybe nothing, but it's good when you find a woman who you can share everything with. You and JeNelle, you have something in common, do you?"

"When you meet her you'll see."

"And when will that be?"

"I'm not sure. JeNelle only wants a friendship for now, but I hope that in time, she'll change her mind. We've only known each other for a short time."

"And what about Stacy?"

"I have to admit, Dad, that I'm seeing Stacy from a different point of view. She makes me happy just being with her. We do that for each other. Being with her makes sense to me. Maybe it's because she's carrying our daughter or maybe it's that magic that comes from being at home around my family and friends. I'm always able to see things more clearly when I'm at home. It's that Southern exposure that works on all of us."

"Have you noticed that Stacy seems to be sad to be leaving today?"

"Yes, I know. That's why I'm planning a little surprise for her on the way back to San Diego, and why I need to make a few phone calls before we head to the airport."

"Then I'll leave you, Son, but I want you to think about something."

"What is it, Dad?"

"When you want to go somewhere, say you want to fly to a distant place, what do you have to do?"

Benny looked at his father quizzically. "You map and plan your route, but I don't understand what you're getting at, Dad."

"Son, first you have to decide where you're going. Like the song Aretha Grace sang today. Do you know where *you're* going? When you do, then you need to map your route. You may take a few detours along the way, but ultimately you know where you're going. Once you know where you're going, getting there is the easy part. You just map out the route and follow it. Know where you're going, Benjamin Staton, and know what to expect to find once you get there."

Benny embraced his father.

"I will, Dad."

Chapter 24

Vivian's family walked with her to her car and kissed her goodbye. Gregory's eyes misted. She promised that they would have good times in the summer in DC. Aretha gave Vivian a bear hug and promised that she would look after Gregory. Vivian knew that she would.

"Thank you, Benny, for being here for me," Vivian said, hugging him tightly. "I didn't think that I could have done this without you."

"You did just fine, Viv. Whenever you need me, you know what to do."

Vivian kissed everyone again and whispered in Stacy's ear. "I hope that you'll soon know that Benny is the man for you. When you do, I'll be proud to call you sister."

Stacy hugged Vivian and said, "No matter what happens, I'm proud to call you sister now."

Vivian drove away from Goodwill, Summer County, South Carolina, headed back to her life in Washington, DC, but she wasn't sad or unhappy. She still had to deal with the abortion, but it was necessary. She had no option. Still, being with her family had given her renewed strength.

* * *

"Hey, Viv. Welcome back!" Gloria yelled from the study room. "Did you have a good time at home with that hunk, Carlton?"

"It was an experience, Gloria," Vivian deadpanned. "One that I hope that I'll never forget."

"Well, Annie, I see you're back at the old homestead," Chuck said, as he lounged in the front living room before a roaring fire watching *Sleepless in Seattle* with Miguel and Angelique at his side. "Mosey on over here and sit her down."

Vivian went into the living room and sat down beside Chuck. She picked up Miguel, put him on her lap, and hugged him. Angelique got up and sat on Chuck's lap. She hugged Vivian and kissed her on the cheek.

"Chuck, I think that it's time for you to hang up your spurs, old pal. My brother told me that you were born and raised outside of Philadelphia, Pennsylvania, up in the Pocono Mountains. Not exactly bronco-busting territory, you know, partner."

"Well, Annie, I never said that I was a cowboy." He grinned.

"No you just let everyone believe that you were born to ride the range."

"I will someday, Annie. Someday I'm going to find me a piece of land, raise a house full of children, and work my ranch."

"Chuck, you're going to be a physician, not a veterinarian."

"You've got to have dreams, Annie. Dreams are the guide to the future. Without them, how would you know where you want to go?"

Miguel laid his head on Vivian's chest.

"You have to know where you came from before you know where you're going."

"You know where you came from, Annie, and I sense that you know where you're going."

"I do, Chuck. I not only know who I am, I also know *whose* I am. I have a family who love me unconditionally. I belong to them and they belong to me."

Vivian hugged Miguel again.

"Sounds like this weekend turned out to be more special than you expected."

"I can honestly say that it was the worst of times and it was the best of times, in that order."

Chuck lifted her left hand and rubbed his thumb over her bare, third finger. "Does the fact that you're not wearing Carlton's engagement ring contribute to this worst of times/best of times scenario?"

Vivian tingled from his touch, but taking a deep breath, she went on. "I'll explain that to you later, but now I need your help."

"Just name it, Annie," he said, raising his eyes to meet hers.

Again, Vivian took a deep breath before speaking. "Let's go somewhere so that we can talk privately."

Chuck arched an eyebrow, but rose with her to leave the house.

Vivian, Chuck, and the Snowman drove to East Potomac Park, just across the Anacostia River from National Airport and the Jefferson Memorial. As they walked along the riverbank, planes flew overhead and landed. Chuck listened unemotionally, as Vivian described what she found when she went to Carlton's apartment and what Benny told her about her supply of condoms.

"If Carlton has been as sexually active as you think, he has put you at risk for any number of different venereal diseases, not to mention HIV-AIDS. I don't understand men who risk the lives of the women they love."

"I don't understand a lot about what Carlton has done, but I can't dwell on that now. My family doesn't like what I have to do any more than I do, but they do support my decision to terminate this pregnancy. That's where you come in, Chuck."

"*Whoa*, Annie, I'm strictly pro-life. I don't perform abortions."

"I know you don't, but you must know at least one reputable doctor who does. I don't want to go to one of those clinics with a lot of fanatics standing around interfering with my right to decide what to do with my body."

"Are you sure that you want to do this? I mean, can't you give this decision some more thought? You're angry with Carlton now, but perhaps later on you and he can work this out."

"A baby is a powerful bond between two people. It's a lifelong commitment that two people share. I have no interest in sharing anything with Carlton, especially considering what he purposefully did to get me pregnant. I can't trust him so he's out of my life for good. After investing three years in the relationship with him, I'm going to have a hard time learning to live without him. I will not put myself through the pain and agony of carrying his child, raising it, and remembering for the rest of my life how that child was conceived. I understand and appreciate your position, Chuck. I can only hope that you can respect mine. If you can't or won't help me find someone to perform the procedure, then I'll respect that, too. One way or the other, I know what I have to do."

"I didn't say that I wouldn't help you find someone. I just think that someday you'll look back at this time in your life and regret what you've done. I know you well enough to know that that would tear you apart."

"I haven't done anything yet, and I already regret it. The decision that I have to make will be with me for the rest of my life. Nevertheless, I'm going through with it."

"I don't want to make this any harder on you, than it already is. I don't agree with your decision, but I do understand and respect it. I'll have a name for you tomorrow."

"Thanks, Chuck."

Chuck enveloped Vivian in his arms. He wanted to offer her another solution. To marry him and let him help her raise the child, but he sensed that she wouldn't be receptive to that idea. At least not now. She needed to regroup and he needed time to think of a way to change her mind.

The next day, he had lunch with his friend and colleague, Dr. Judith Kelly, a female obstetrics and gynecologist.

"Chuck, is this your baby that Ms. Alexander is carrying? Is that why you're trying so passionately to get me to talk her out of having an abortion? If so, I can tell her that there is no stigma attached to a Black woman having a baby fathered by a Caucasian man."

"Thanks, Judy, but Vivian is a very liberated woman and she's certainly no racist. She wouldn't let something as unimportant as my skin color force her into such a desperate act. Still, to answer your original question, no, it's not my baby. If it were, we wouldn't need to have this discussion. Vivian and I would be having the baby and I would be inviting you to our wedding ceremony. She is a very special woman though. I know that she didn't come to this decision easily. I just feel that she would regret this decision later on and that it would ruin any chance for her to be completely happy for the rest of her life."

"Abortion, for most women, is never the option or first choice, Chuck. You're right though. If she's the type of woman that you say, she will never forgive herself for making this choice. I'll do what I can to counsel her, but she's going to need strong, loving shoulders to lean on if she decides to go through with the procedure in the end."

"I'll be there for her, Judy, but I don't want her to know that we've had this discussion. She's a strong woman and very independent. She'd have my hide if she knew that I was trying to help her through this."

"I'm beginning to wonder why you're so interested in her myself, Chuck. You've said that you're not the father of her baby, but my instinct, listening to you talk about this proud and strong woman, makes me think that something else might be going on with you. Am I right?"

"Dr. Kelly, you're a top OB/GYN specialist," he said and laughed. "Are you trying to add psychiatry to your specialty?"

Judith just knowingly grinned at him.

"Just call me if or when she comes in for the procedure. I'll take care of her after that."

* * *

Vivian sat in the waiting room of the doctor's office, flipping nervously through the pages of a magazine.

"The doctor will see you now, Ms. Alexander," the kind nurse said quietly to Vivian.

The nurse led Vivian into an office where a collage of hundreds of pictures of babies graced the walls. A Black female physician looked up when Vivian came into the room.

"Ms. Alexander, I'm Dr. Kelly, Judith Kelly," the middle-aged doctor said, rising and extending her hand to Vivian. Then they both sat down. "Do you have any questions that you'd like to ask me before the procedure?"

"No, Dr. Kelly, I believe that I understand the process. My mother is a nurse and we have talked about it. Also, your assistant showed a video to me about the procedure and then thoroughly went over the details with me, too."

"Then do you have any other questions?"

"Other questions?"

"Yes, for example, are you questioning your decision to go through with this abortion? You've waited an inordinately long time to do this. You're almost at a point where I would be unable to perform this procedure."

"No, I've considered all of my options and I am committed to going through with this."

"Did anyone come with you today to take you home after the procedure?"

"No, I'll take a taxi home and I understand that I have to rest in bed for several days."

"What about the baby's father? Won't he be meeting you here?"

"No, Doctor, I'm completely alone."

"You're never completely alone, Ms. Alexander," Dr. Kelly said, with an expression of understanding. "We're here for you now and after the procedure if you need us and for as long as you need us."

"Thank you. I appreciate that, but I'm anxious to get this over with."

The doctor hesitated, as if in thought. Then lacing her fingers on her desk, she looked squarely at Vivian. "Ms. Alexander," she paused. "I don't know you, but I sense that this is a very difficult decision for you to make. If there is any reason why we should not proceed, I believe that we should discuss it now. I want to believe that you are making the right decision for you."

"I hope that I never have to make a decision that is as difficult and as emotionally draining as this one has been ever again in my life, but I'm confident that this is the right thing for me at this time. Though they are not here, I know that I have the love and support of my family to sustain me through this."

The doctor sighed. "All right, then, if you believe that you're ready, I'll have my nurse prepare you and I'll be in momentarily."

The nurse led Vivian to a cold, white, and sterile room with a gynecological table in the center of it. As instructed, Vivian undressed and lay on the table, as the nurse covered her in paper surgical garments. She felt a chill, as the nurse placed her legs in the stirrups and washed her with a cold solution. Vivian just lay there motionless, staring at the ceiling. Time seemed to be standing still. She could hear herself breathing. She could feel her heart pounding. Two nurses stood beside her quietly, as the doctor entered the room. Doctor Kelly came to Vivian's side.

The doctor put a comforting hand on Vivian's arms. "Ms. Alexander, it's not too late to change your mind. I certainly will not be offended if you don't want to go through with this."

Vivian continued to stare at the ceiling, fighting the tears that stung the back of her eyes, unwilling to meet the concern she sensed from the doctor.

"I'm ready, Doctor," Vivian said stoically.

The doctor patted Vivian's hand and went to a washbowl to scrub. A nurse covered the doctor's face with a surgical mask and shield, gloved her hands, and then the doctor moved into position at the end of the table. One of the two nurses assisted the doctor. Vivian heard the rubber gloves slip into place with a snap. The nurse then began passing the instruments to the doctor while the other nurse stood by Vivian, holding her hand and monitoring her vital signs.

Dr. Kelly talked with Vivian and explained to her what to expect before she proceeded with each step. Vivian felt the forceps inserting into her and open. She felt the heat from a high-powered lamp on her thighs, as it moved into position. Then she heard a machine turning on and a suctioning sound. The pressure on her abdomen, as the doctor worked was becoming unbearable.

With straying thoughts, Vivian felt the sharp instruments moving around inside her. To distract herself, she thought of the first time that she and Carlton made love. It was in her dormitory room at Spelman. She had not had a lot of experience with men and had never experienced an orgasm. Carlton was so gentle with her at the start, as he undressed her and kissed her. He carried her to the bed and lay beside her, gently stroking her body. He kissed her breasts and her nipples stood on end. She giggled with delight, as she felt the new sensations that he caused her to experience. He buried his head between her thighs and she felt the warmth of his tongue inside her. He hoisted her legs over his shoulders and held down her hands as she squirmed and heaved from one side to the other. It seemed like the sensations would never stop, overtaking her, flooding over her in torrents that she could not control. She was sweating profusely and breathing hard, as if she had run a twenty-mile marathon.

Then Carlton mounted her and penetrated her. She felt pain, as he jabbed himself into her, breaking the hymen each time, going deeper and deeper. She tried to move and to call out to him that he was hurting her. That he was too large and too long, but his mouth was covering hers. He was on top of her, pinning her down and jabbing her fast, hard, and furiously. The bed springs moaned and squeaked. He pinned her hands behind her back. He was so strong. She could not free herself. The sweat from his face dripped into her eyes and burned. She shut her eyes tightly and tried again to free herself from his grip. He mistook her frantic movement and efforts to call out for fits of passion. Flesh slapped against flesh. The more she tried to squirm away, the more violently he probed. Hot tears were flowing down her face and into her hair when his body contorted and the full weight of him pressed her heavily against the hard bed. All she could feel was the pain, as she laid there and silently cried. Carlton finally fell asleep and slowly released his grip on her. She managed to push him off her, as she rolled to her side. She curled herself into a fetal position and wept.

"Don't cry, dear," the nurse was saying, as she held Vivian's hand and wiped the tears from her face, "the doctor is almost finished."

It seemed as if a lifetime had passed.

"I'm through, Ms. Alexander," Doctor Kelly said, removing the bloody gloves from her hands, tossing them into the trash, and removing her surgical mask. "You'll be fine. You should not have any complications. I want to see you in my office again in two weeks. I want you to rest for a while before you leave. Then my nurse will come back and help you dress. She'll give you some instructions to follow for the next few days. Please call us if you have any additional questions."

One nurse cleaned up and then she and Doctor Kelly left the room. The other nurse removed Vivian's legs from the stirrups, covered her with fresh sheets, and then she left the room. Tears were still flowing down Vivian's face, but no sound would come out of her mouth. Later, the nurse helped her dress, as she sat on the side of the table.

"Here, dear," the nurse said, handing some tissues to Vivian, "you might want to blow your nose and wash your pretty face. It's all over now and, just as the doctor said, you'll be just fine."

An hour or so later, Vivian left the doctor's office and walked slowly down the long hallway to the elevator. She leaned her head against the wall and the tears flowed, but still no sound would come out. Entering the elevator, she wiped her eyes and hugged her body, as the elevator descended to the first floor. She walked slowly through the lobby. People she passed sympathetically looked at her. One man approached her and asked if she were all right or whether she needed assistance. She did not speak. She just shook her head and kept walking through the big glass doors into the bright sunlight. She looked around blankly. The cold air blew against her tears; she shivered.

"Hey! Georgetown! Can I give you a lift?"

Vivian looked up and saw Chuck leaning against his truck dressed in surgical greens and wearing a buckskin jacket, sunglasses, and Stetson. He looked at her and immediately came to her. As he took her in his arms, her body went limp and she cried aloud uncontrollably. She could not catch her breath, as he lifted her into his truck and moved into the driver's seat beside her. He continued to hold her as she cried.

"It's all right, Annie, let it all out. You're going to be fine. Let's get you home."

"No, Chuck," she sobbed. "No matter how many times someone says that, I'll never be fine again. Not ever."

Chuck held her close to him, as he drove through the streets of DC. He took her up the long steps to her room and helped her into bed. Covering her with a thick, downy comforter he sat on top of the covers, held her, as she wept and eventually fell off to asleep.

Chuck's pager sounded and woke Vivian.

"How long have I been asleep, Chuck?" Vivian lifted her head from his chest.

"Only about two hours, but you need the rest."

"You've been here all of that time? Aren't you on duty today?"

"C'mon, Annie, I can use the sleep."

He laid her head against his chest and leaned his head back against the headboard of the bed. He covered his face with his hat. His pager sounded again.

"You're on duty, Chuck." Vivian took Chuck's hat off his face and sat up in bed.

"C'mon, Annie," he whined. "Why is it that every time I try to catch a little shuteye, you want to talk?" He grabbed his hat and pulled her back into his arms. "Just close your eyes and your mouth and get some rest."

She leaned against him and hugged him. "How did you know that I was at the doctor's office today? I didn't tell anyone where I was going, not even my family."

"Get some rest, Annie."

"No, Chuck, I want to know how you found me."

"Sleep, Annie. Close your eyes and get some sleep."

Vivian sat up and took his hat off his face.

Chuck opened one eye and looked at her mutinous expression. She was staring at him with a determined look on her face. He took a deep breath. "All right, Annie," Chuck sighed. "Put away your whip. Holster your six shooters. It's no mystery. I asked Judy Kelly to call me when you came in for the procedure. She had her nurse call me as soon as you arrived. Now can we get some sleep?"

"You mean that you were waiting for me downstairs all the time that I was in Dr. Kelly's office?" Vivian asked, surprised.

"At least I got some sleep while I was waiting for you. More than I'm getting now. The nurse called me on my cell phone as soon as you left the office and told me that you were on your way down in the elevator. Now, let's get some sleep."

"You didn't have to do that. You're on duty and you've been away from the hospital for more than three hours."

"What is it going to take to get you to close your mouth and let a poor man sleep?"

"But, Chuck—"

Chuck bent his head and enveloped her mouth. The kiss was warm and calming. Vivian was surprised, but did not pull away. Her hand tentatively went to his chest and felt his strong, steady heartbeat. Then his pager sounded again.

"It must be a conspiracy!" Chuck grumbled, turning off his pager and abruptly getting off the bed. He pulled his cell phone from his jacket pocket and sat on Vivian's sofa. "This is Dr. Montgomery. What's the problem?" he asked tightly, combing his fingers over the stubble on his face and through his thick pelt of dark, silky hair. "No, I had an emergency outside the hospital. Dr. Dunn is covering for me.... His wife did *what?* She's in labor now? Who else is on the floor? Who's with Selznick? No, I'll be there." Chuck hung up.

He made a colossal mistake and he knew it. He wanted to kiss Vivian since the first day he met her and every day since, but this was the worst possible time to make the attempt. He knew that her emotions were very close to the surface and that her state of mind was embroiled in the devastation of the day's event. He wanted her, but he tamped down his need. What *she* needed was more important and he was a patient man. He would wait to tell her about his feelings for her. At the moment, he had to cover his behavior in the benign.

"Are you happy now? I'm awake and I'll probably have to pull a double shift because Jimmy Dunn's wife went into labor. All you had to do was close your eyes and your mouth and I could have had at least fifteen more minutes of sleep, but *noooo* you want to play twenty questions! What is it about a sleeping man that riles you, Ms. Oakley?"

Vivian sat beside Chuck on the sofa bed, hugged him, and wept. He put his arms around her and kissed her on the top of her head, her nose and then her mouth. He held back for as long as he thought humanly possible. Her face was turned up to him. Her sad, watery eyes tore at his gut. He had taken the Hippocratic Oath to preserve life, but he would gladly have taken Carlton's at that moment. Vivian didn't deserve the pain and suffering that Carlton had inflicted on her. Her soul was too forgiving. He wanted to help her forget, and he wanted her. The kiss was light, but meaningful to him. He held his breath to keep from taking it further. He sensed that she was not ready for him yet, not now in the midst of this terrible and devastating ordeal. There would be time later.

The surprise of Chuck's second kiss stunned Vivian momentarily. She did not feel it coming, but she did not stop him. Not the first or the second time. Her mind went in many directions at once, but Chuck, she sensed, was holding back. She appreciated that in him. He didn't or wouldn't take advantage of her. There were times when she felt a special chemistry between them, but she would not have acted on it because of her relationship with Carlton. Now that impediment was removed. There would be time later to ask the salient question: What did those kisses mean?

"No more water works for you, Ms. Oakley," he said tenderly. "Don't think that you're going to get on my good side with those tears. You've already cost me fifteen minutes of sleep," he said, guiding her back to bed and helping her to get in. "I've got to go, but you stay put! Don't go gallivanting around either. I'm giving Anna strict orders to keep you in bed and, if I hear that you've been up and around, I'll come back here, lasso you, and tie you to the bedpost! Are we clear, partner?" Chuck asked, putting on his hat and extended his hand.

"We're clear," Vivian said, shaking his hand and summoning a smile.

Chuck opened Vivian's bedroom door and the Snowman came galloping in. The dog jumped onto the foot of Vivian's bed and lay down. Chuck winked at Vivian.

"Now that the Snowman's on duty, I can leave."

"But, Chuck, why did you kiss—"

"Got to go, Annie. Remember our deal," he said hurriedly, as he left.

Vivian lay in her bed in total confusion for hours, watching the sun move across the sky when the telephone rang.

"Hello."

"Vivian, this is Kenneth. You sound strange. Are you all right?"

"Yes."

"You aren't convincing me, Viv. I don't like what I'm not hearing in your voice."

"I'm just a little tired, I guess. Nothing to worry about."

"I haven't heard from you in some time. Why haven't you called?"

"Just busy with classes and I know that you've got your hands full with your company."

"So you haven't called me because you've been too busy and you think that you'd be interrupting me?"

"Not just that, K.J. Carlton and I went through a bad time and we've decided not to see each other again."

"Is that something else that you weren't going to tell me about?"

"I don't understand."

"Apparently, you've been engaged since before New Year's and you never mentioned it."

"Oh, that."

"Yes, that."

"How did you find out about that?"

"Over a business lunch after Valentine's Day."

"Huh?"

"How I found out, young lady, is not important. The fact that you didn't tell me about it is very important to me."

"I'm sorry, K.J. It's just been a rough couple of months." Her voice quivered.

"Vivian, something is wrong. I can feel it."

She gathered herself. "I'll be just fine, Kenneth. This thing with Carlton has me feeling a little low."

"Are you sure that that's what has got you so upset?"

"Yes, I'm just not handling things very well right now. I'll be back on my feet soon."

"Uh huh. Okay, little sister. I'll talk with you again soon. I love you."

"I love you more, Kenneth." She hung up and the tears began to flow again. Lying to Kenneth wasn't getting any easier, but she wasn't prepared to face him yet.

It was dark outside when Vivian woke up again. She could see the stars through her bedroom windows. It was a clear night. No wind. No sounds except an occasional car passing along R Street. She lay on her side, curled her legs up close to her chest and wished on the stars that the day had been only a bad dream. Yet, as she lay there in her dark, silent room, she could still feel the doctor's instruments inside her. She could still hear the metal, as the doctor tossed instruments into a metal basin and then the heavy pressure from the machine in her abdomen. Then the rush of blood, as the doctor removed the fetus from her body. She could not hold back the tears. They clouded her view of the stars.

The Snowman raised his head and looked toward her bedroom door. Then he jumped down from the bed and began prancing and jumping around, wagging his tail and whining, as someone knocked on her door.

"Come in," Vivian called out, reaching for her tissues.

A man stood in her doorway, his body outlined by the light in the hallway behind him. He flipped on the light.

"Kenneth!" she screamed, sitting up in bed.

"Now, what were you saying about me being too busy?" he asked with a broad smile.

"What? How?" Vivian tried to speak, but she just stuttered and the tears kept getting in her way.

"You better watch that stuttering, Counselor. The jury might not understand what you're trying to say."

Kenneth sat on the side of the bed and Vivian wrapped her arms around him and cried.

"Now, I want you to tell me everything that's going on with you. You're hurting badly. I could hear it in your voice and I know that you haven't told me everything. I know you too well, Vivian Lynn Alexander. I'm your brother and I love you. You've been keeping things from me and I don't like it."

"You didn't need all of this emotional baggage right now, K.J. You've got your hands full with your company."

"Stop worrying about me and the company. I love you and I want to know about you, so start talking, little sister."

Kenneth held Vivian in his arms, as she began to tell him all that had happened. She sobbed through the entire story and he held her close to him and kissed her forehead.

"I knew that something was wrong. I could feel it. I don't know why you didn't let me help you go through this. You shouldn't have tried to do this alone."

"I've got to learn to stand on my own two feet sometime."

"This wasn't the time, baby. That's what family is for. We're there in the good times and the bad times. You should not have been alone."

"I wasn't alone. Chuck was with me after the procedure. He was there when I really needed someone desperately."

"I'd like to meet him and thank him for helping you. He sounds like a good friend. Not the skiing-cowboy, second-year, resident doctor that you described to me."

"I misjudged him. When I met him in the airport, all I saw was just another guy wearing a strange get-up and trying to hit on me. You sure can't judge every book by its cover. I don't know what I would have done without him."

The telephone rang. Kenneth picked it up.

"Kenneth, did I dial you by mistake?"

"No, Benny, I'm here in DC with Vivian. I just flew in a few hours ago."

"Is she all right? I've been worried about her."

"Physically, she seems fine."

"Should I come out there?"

"No, I'll stay with her, but I'm not happy with either of you for keeping this from me. You and I are going to have a little brother-to-brother sit down real soon over this."

Benny sensed that Kenneth was very angry with him for not telling him what was going on.

"Is there anything else that you and our sister are keeping from me? If so, I'd strongly suggest that you two speak on it now."

"Well, there is some good news that I was going to tell you about."

"Well, good! I could use some good news just about now. What is it?"

"You're going to be an uncle in September," Benny said cheerfully. "That's part of the reason that I went home with the mother of my child to meet the family," he rushed on. "I swear that I was going to call you about it."

Kenneth's heart stopped beating. He sat on the sofa and buried his face in his hand, as he listened to Benny describe the wonderful weekend in Goodwill. The blood rushed from his head. He closed his eyes.

"JeNelle is pregnant?" he asked slowly, the pain clawing him. "I thought that you two hadn't…I mean, you said that she only wanted a platonic relationship… uh…I mean, congratulations, Benny. I'm happy for you and JeNelle. Please give her my best wishes. She'll make a wonderful mother. Here's Vivian."

"Whoa, K.J. JeNelle's not pregnant, Stacy is. I haven't laid a finger on JeNelle—"

"Benny? Hi, it's Viv. Yes, I'm better now that K.J. is here with me. No, he didn't hear you, but I'll tell him what you said. I love you too, Benny. I'll call you in a couple of days."

Vivian hung up the telephone. She was watching her brother very closely. He stood leaning against her dresser before her mirror with his back to her. He grabbed the back of his neck. She could see his face in the mirror. He was in pain. He looked up into the mirror and saw her watching him. He noticed the concerned, but quizzical look on her face.

"That's good news about JeNelle and Benny, isn't it?" he asked, as he gathered himself.

"If you think that it's such good news, why do you look like your entire universe just collapsed?" Vivian asked, looking directly into his eyes.

He looked away from her. "I'm just tired from the long trip from San Francisco to DC. I've developed a headache. You and your brother have thrown me for a loop today."

Something began to dawn on Vivian. "Kenneth, what do you think of JeNelle Towson?" she asked. "Didn't you get to spend some time with her in San Francisco and again in Santa Barbara? I mean I saw those newspaper articles."

"I think she's very nice. Benny is lucky to have found her."

"I didn't like her at all. Too much flash, no substance. Body by Fischer, mind by Mattel."

Kenneth's eyes narrowed and she could see the fury rise in him.

"You're wrong," Kenneth said emphatically. "JeNelle is nothing like that. She's got more going for her than just a pretty face and a great body. She's got spirit and unbelievable energy. She's enthusiastic about her work and she does it extremely well. She has accomplished a great deal and is a successful businesswoman. She has a keen sense of fairness and she's intellectually superior to many people that I've met."

He began to pace, as he talked, his hands dug deep into his pockets. "She has developed great programs to help the young people in her area to find meaningful employment and careers. She has worked tirelessly on a program that the Governor is going to institute statewide to introduce youths in the state to more business and economic opportunities. She has real charisma.

"You should have heard her at the Chamber of Commerce Gala. She was flawless in her delivery of a very powerful, moving and heartfelt speech that still has people talking about it today." More animated now, he gestured with his hand, warming to his topic. "There have even been some extremely large grants and donations from many Fortune 500 companies for college scholarships to the young people who successfully complete the Youth in Business and Industry program. Those companies made it clear that it was her speech that created excitement about the Governor's program. Even some foreign dignitaries are offering exchange programs to the kids who finish college in business and/or economics and minor in certain languages.

"Somebody who has accomplished that can't be all flash." He stopped pacing, squaring his broad shoulders, he glared at his sister. "We're not talking about the same JeNelle Towson. She has captivated my entire staff with her warmth, charm, and kindness. Everyone thinks that she's the best thing since sliced bread and so do I. She's a shrewd businesswoman, but she's very compassionate and giving of herself and her time. She's no flash in the pan. She's well respected and loved by everyone she meets. I don't know how you formed your opinion of her, but you're wrong. Dead wrong. I respect and admire her and I'm sorely disappointed that you think she's only flash and no substance."

Vivian let out a long, audible breath. "Whew! Preach on, my brother!"

Kenneth frowned, his jaw knitted. "Don't be flippant."

"I'm not. K.J., you're doing to me just what you said you resented me doing to you," Vivian said sternly.

"What are you talking about? I'm giving you my perspective on JeNelle Towson. I'm just a little tired and I have a headache, so maybe I'm not expressing myself very well."

"Bull!" she exclaimed. "You were fine until Benny told you that he was going to be a father and then you looked like you were about to keel over dead. And don't try to tell me that you're 'just tired'. I'm not hearing it, my brother! When I attacked JeNelle, you lit into me like a lion protecting his pride. I've never heard you speak of anyone with such fervor before. Mom was right about your feelings for JeNelle. You're in love with her."

"JeNelle and I aren't involved. Benny's the one who she is involved with or didn't you know that she's carrying his child either?"

"JeNelle's not carrying Benny's child, Kenneth. Stacy Greene is. It was Stacy who Benny brought home to meet us, not JeNelle."

Kenneth's eyes widened and his tense body relaxed.

Vivian watched carefully the change in her brother's demeanor. "I've never met JeNelle. All I know about her is what I've heard from you, Benny, and Gloria. Of course, I've read the article about the 'Woman of the Year and Her

Man for All Seasons'. The pictures of the two of you, especially the one with you two dancing serenely in a single bright light, spoke a thousand words, Kenneth."

"That article was a complete fabrication of the facts," he tried to cover, gesturing offhandedly.

"Yeah, and if you think that I believe that one, I'm sure you've got a bridge in San Francisco and some swamp-front property in Florida that you can give me at real good price."

Kenneth looked at Vivian and realized what she had done to him—suckered him right into a trap.

"If you're suggesting that there's something going on between me and JeNelle, you're mistaken. In fact, I've been seeing someone lately. Her name is Lisa Lambert. Benny has already met her and he likes her. She's also a friend of JeNelle's. I'm not sure where my relationship with Lisa will go, but it's had a very interesting beginning."

Vivian was not convinced. She looked at Kenneth thoughtfully and remembered how he had sent money to her just because he *thought* that she needed it. She knew that he would not think twice about sacrificing his wants or desires if he thought that Benny was in love with JeNelle. That's who her brother is, someone who always sacrificed himself for his family. That's what their grandparents had taught them all to do. Family first. She decided to test her theory.

"How long have you known her? This Lisa Lambert person, I mean? You haven't mentioned her before."

"Not long. JeNelle introduced us. So you see there's nothing going on between me and JeNelle."

"I believe you wouldn't do anything that you thought might hurt Benny. I didn't say that there was anything going on between you and JeNelle. Mom thinks that you have strong feelings for her and based on your performance tonight, I know that Mom is right. Now when exactly did you say that you met this Lisa?"

"I didn't fly out here to talk about my relationship with Lisa, young lady," he glared. "I came to see my sister. Now let's get back to you and how I can help you get through this."

Vivian pointed an accusing finger at her brother. "Don't you try to change the subject. The witness is in contempt for failure to make a full disclosure and answer the question."

A corner of Kenneth's mouth tilted up in amusement. "Okay, Counselor, what's the question?" Kenneth asked to humor his sister.

"When did you meet the subject, Lisa Lambert?"

"It was Valentine's Day weekend."

"Did you meet the subject before or after the Santa Barbara Gala?"

"The same day as the Gala."

"And how many times have you seen the subject subsequent to the Gala in question?"

"Not very often, but that's only because she lives and works in Sacramento. She has a very busy schedule. She works for the Governor."

"Objection! Strike that remark from the record as unresponsive."

"Vivian," he exhaled in frustration, "Really?" but she pressed on.

"Did you meet the subject, Lisa Lambert, in a business or personal capacity?"

"Once for business and sometimes for racquetball."

"Have you been intimate with the subject, Lisa Lambert?"

"I refuse to answer on the grounds that my response is none of your business, Counselor."

"Guilty! You're not telling me everything! I rest my case!"

During the night, Kenneth lay awake on the sofa bed in Vivian's room while she slept. His thoughts would not let him rest. His muscles were tight. His head throbbed. He could not relax. He sat up and looked out the window at the stars. There it was again. That same vision that would seep into his head without warning or provocation. He tried to turn his thoughts elsewhere. Perhaps if he permitted himself to become more involved with Lisa, that haunting vision would disappear. Yet, what of Benny and JeNelle and now Stacy and a baby. He could not think of that. Benny had not talked with him about the situation. He didn't know what he would say to Benny when or if Benny discussed with him. Too much to think about.

Vivian began to whimper in her sleep. Kenneth got into bed with her and held her close to him. She clung to him. He felt her pain. How could Carlton do this to her? She didn't deserve this emotional devastation in her life. He remembered the happy little girl of their youth. Pigtails flopping, as she jumped rope. Or when she played with her miniature dolls' house, speaking the roles of each of the characters who lived in her dolls' house world. Or climbing into the hayloft and burying herself in the hay. Reading a bedtime story to her, as she fell asleep nestled in his arms. Hoisting her onto a horse and riding her around the barnyard, as she giggled and yelled to go faster and faster. Walking her to school on those cold winter mornings, as she wore her red snow suit and mittens. Teaching her to swim. Sitting and talking with her about all the things that she wanted to do and be when she grew up.

Now she was grown. He was proud of the woman that she had become. Only good things were supposed to happen to her. Not a traumatic and heart-wrenching nightmare that she was subjected to. She only deserved to be cherished, respected, and loved.

"Vivian, are you in there without me, again?" Bill Chandler joked, as he knocked on her bedroom door and then entered. He spotted a man in bed with Vivian. "Oh, I didn't know that you weren't alone."

"Bill, don't go spreading any malicious lies," Vivian said, as she awoke. "This is my brother, Kenneth."

"Your brother? I find you in the bed with another man and the best that you can come up with is he's your 'brother'? Is that 'brother' in the literal or figurative sense? Really, Vivian, I didn't think that you were into incest."

"Go away, Bill. Go far, far away. Pago Pago, perhaps."

"I'm going. I mean, we're all going shopping for Easter clothes and thought that you might want to join us, but since you're here alone with your 'brother'. Happy incest, you two," Bill said, closing the door behind him.

"Who was that character?" Kenneth asked, as he awoke.

"Bill Chandler. The lost link, I think. We're eventually going to return him to the Lost and Found and pay them to keep him."

"Is it safe to leave him loose on the unsuspecting public until then?" he said and laughed.

"He's harmless most of the time, but we keep him on a short leash."

They laughed and Vivian rolled into her brother's arms and hugged him tightly. "It's so good to have you here. Now, as I was saying last night, before you turned the light out on me, so you finally solved that water-bill problem, huh?"

"Oh no you don't, kid," Kenneth said, rolling out of bed and getting quickly to his feet. "We're not getting into that witness/prosecutor role again. I'm taking a long, hot shower and making breakfast for us."

Vivian sat up in the bed. "Okay, I'll help."

Kenneth shot a 'don't even try it' look at her. "Forget it, kid. It's breakfast in bed for you. Maybe you can come downstairs later, but for now, stay put!"

Vivian knew that searing look he gave her. She had seen it often enough on her father's face and Kenneth had inherited it honestly.

Vivian showered and lay in bed, trying not to think about the abortion. She tried to study, but her thoughts would not let her read the words on the pages of her books. She slammed the books closed, grabbed the latest copy of *Essence*, and flipped through it. Then she picked up *Black Enterprise*. Kenneth had been in the kitchen a long time, she thought. "Enough is enough! I can't just lay here looking at these four walls all day!" she huffed. She got out of bed, dressed, and crept down the steps. She could hear Kenneth on the phone in the kitchen, as she peeked in.

Kenneth spotted her. "Tom, I'll have to call you back later. I'm about to raise some hell around here," Kenneth said, looking angrily at Vivian, as he ended his call. "I thought that I told you to stay put?"

"K.J., I can't just lay around in the bed all day," she whined. "I tried, but it's not working. I'll just sit here at the kitchen table and I promise that I won't even move a muscle." She looked at him pleadingly.

Kenneth relented. "All right, you can stay here and have breakfast, but then it's back to bed for you."

Vivian hugged him and sat by the window wall. The Snowman was romping around in the backyard. The house was quiet. The sun was shining brightly. The smell of fresh brewed coffee was in the air.

"You know, the house looks great, Vivian. The pantry is well stocked and there aren't any science projects in the refrigerator."

"That's because of Anna. She keeps this place running like a well-oiled machine. She made us put our daily schedules up on the bulletin board. She has us up for breakfast by six o'clock in the morning, lunch is ready at twelve noon on the days that we're here, and dinner is served promptly at six o'clock in the evening. Since she's been here these last few months, we've saved a lot of money on the grocery bill. We rarely eat out anymore. She's a great cook and housekeeper. She even makes us separate our clothes before we wash them. You know, she even polishes the brass on the doors! The woman is amazing."

"How did you find her?"

"At the Family Homeless Shelter where I do volunteer work. She was brought there by one of the Shelter's van services during that big snow storm in December. I've been trying to help her find her husband. He's been missing for some time now. We filed a missing person's report with the police department, but, so far, no luck. I also talked to the fire department's investigators because the house where her husband was last known to be living burned down. The investigators told me that several people lost their lives in that fire, but they had not been able to identify all of the bodies yet. They promised to keep us posted. It's ironic, but Anna actually knew someone who is the subject of a case we were reviewing for a class on civil procedure."

"That is uncanny."

"Dad's been a big help. He signed as Anna's sponsor so that she could get her green card. She, her daughter and son are from Peru. My housemates, David, Alan and Melissa, are teaching Anna and the children to speak English and Anna is teaching them to speak Spanish. I'm teaching Angelique and Miguel to use a computer. You should see how Bill has furnished their apartment downstairs. They look like something out of *Better Homes* magazine. He and Melissa take them shopping at some of the best stores in town. Chuck takes care of the medical expenses for them and he's been following up with his friend, Derrick Jackson, on Angelique's and Miguel's medical care. Chuck took them all to the dentist and to have their eyes checked two weeks ago. Mr. Jones, next door, is giving Angelique piano lessons free of charge and David is giving Miguel violin lessons. The last few months have been interesting."

"Sounds like it has. I'm proud of you."

"I can't take the credit for all of this. Chuck Montgomery was the one who got us all involved, so we've adopted him, too. When he's not at the hospital, he's here doing something. He fixed the door and the plumbing downstairs. He took us all out in the country to chop wood for the fireplaces. He reads bedtime stories to Angelique and Miguel and he even has some ideas he wants to send to Benny about landscaping the backyard to include a vegetable garden. The man's incredible!"

"He's not married?"

"No, but I think that he and Melissa are seeing each other," she said, softly biting her bottom lip. "He comes from a big family in Pennsylvania in the Pocono Mountains. Seven boys and five girls. He and his sister, Joyce, are the youngest. His family has a farm, but his brothers work in the building trades. Each one of them has a different specialty: a welder, a brick layer, a painter, a plumber, an electrician, and a carpenter. He says that his sisters are the artistic ones in his family. One bakes cakes, pies, and other pastries for local stores. Another one makes draperies and curtains and reupholsters furniture. Someone else paints pictures and murals and another sister is a sculptor. His father is a mechanic by trade and his mother is a homemaker. He's the only one in his family who ever went to college and he's making plans for his younger sister, Joyce, to go, too. I think she's only fifteen or sixteen now."

Kenneth put breakfast on the table and sat down.

"You mentioned a Derrick Jackson. Is he the same guy who played professional basketball for Denver or Utah?"

"Denver."

"He's older than I am, Viv. Are you sure that you should become involved with someone that much older than you?"

"Yes, I'm sure. He's not out seeking the limelight. He's a pediatrician now. He and Chuck grew up together."

"I thought that you said Chuck grew up on a farm? I know, Jackson came out of a Philadelphia ghetto."

"Chuck's brothers used to go to work in Philly and in the summers they took Chuck along to help clean up their work sites. They lived in a big RV outside Philly in one of those mobile home parks. One summer they were working on a big urban renewal project in the inner city. During lunch breaks, Chuck would hang around the basketball court watching the neighborhood kids play. None of the boys would ask him to play, probably because he's white. Chuck said that one day Derrick came up to him and tossed a basketball to him. Chuck was only about nine or ten at the time, but big for his age. Derrick was a little older. Chuck had not played much basketball and really didn't have any skills. He was just a big country kid who liked to watch the games. Derrick started spending time with Chuck teaching him how to play. They were out on that court every day. Chuck said that, after a while, his brothers didn't even look for him. They knew exactly where he was. They had to give Derrick a job as the clean-up helper too just to get Chuck off the basketball court. After a while, Derrick started spending time on Chuck's family's farm on weekends or Chuck would spend time at Derrick's parent's place in the city. They've been best friends since then. Derrick is the reason that Chuck went to college, played in the pros, and went to medical school. Chuck is the reason why Derrick's family moved out of the city and now live in the country near the Montgomerys. One of Chuck's brothers, Bob, is married to one of Derrick's sisters, Sheila. They have three children and are working on a fourth. And we think that we've got a big family! Chuck already has twenty nieces and nephews. His parents both came from big families, too."

The front door opened and Vivian heard familiar footsteps in the hallway.

"Uh oh!" she said, as Chuck came into the kitchen.

"I knew it! The minute that Melissa told me that everyone, but you was going shopping, I knew you'd find an excuse to get out of bed and come downstairs."

Chuck glared at Vivian. "Can't turn my back on you for one minute, Annie Oakley, and you're off gallivanting around."

"Oh...uh...Hi, Chuck.... Uh...How are you? Uh...I just got up for a few minutes.... Uh...This is my brother, Kenneth, uh.... He made breakfast for me.... uh.... I haven't been on my feet.... I've just been sitting in one spot.... I didn't even move.... I swear!" Vivian was grinning sheepishly, but Chuck was not smiling.

"You must be Dr. Charles Montgomery. Vivian and I were just talking about you," Kenneth said, standing to shake Chuck's hand. "It's partly my fault. Vivian snuck down here and I let her stay. She's always had a problem with staying cooped up."

"I'm pleased to meet you, Kenneth, but call me Chuck," he said, smiling at Kenneth as he shook his hand, then frowning at Vivian he said, "They can use that Dr. Montgomery stuff when they acquit me for murdering your sister!"

"I know exactly what you mean, Chuck," Kenneth said and chuckled. "I felt a little homicidal myself last night toward Vivian and her partner-in-crime, Benjamin. I still may do something rash if she gives me any more trouble while I'm here."

"Get in line. I want the first crack at her and her doctor, Judy Kelly, will probably want to be next!"

"It's good to know that I'm not the only one who she's been giving a lot of grief."

"Ah, Man!" Chuck complained. "From the moment I met her in the Chicago airport she's been nothing but trouble. Hardheaded, obstinate, and that razor-sharp tongue of hers. I don't know how you all put up with her all those years."

"You think it's bad now. She's tame as compared to what she was in high school and her early years at Spelman. Bossing people around and making everybody jump through hoops. My parents stayed on the telephone with Spelman's faculty. Vivian had a habit of arguing with the university administration to change the curriculum, start some new program or hire more professors or lecturers that she had read about. My parents burned a lot of rubber driving to and from Atlanta to attend her basketball games or some production Vivian was involved in. She even created a student disciplinary board to review behavior problems on campus and you know who the judge was!"

"If she's tame now, the DC police department will never believe it. She had one investigator working overtime looking for Anna's husband. The sergeant told me that he hopes that he's retired before she becomes a judge in DC because she'll have everybody working double time."

Vivian sat looking anxiously between Chuck and Kenneth, as they talked about her. "Guys, you're talking about me like I'm not even in the room."

Kenneth and Chuck both leered at her and she immediately went back to eating her breakfast and said nothing more.

"How long are you going to be in town, Kenneth?"

"I'm not sure. I left San Francisco rather unexpectedly yesterday because my sister—what do you call her? Annie Oakley?—didn't sound right to me. I've talked to one of my partners and everything seems to be under control so I have some time."

"Annie, here, tells me that you're a hell of a ball player and I've already played against your brother, Benny the Bruiser. If you can swing it, let's go shoot around tomorrow. Some of the doctors and nurses at Georgetown have a game every day at one o'clock at McDonough Arena.

Kenneth laughed. "I haven't heard anyone call Benny, 'The Bruiser,' since he was in high school. Sounds like a plan. I usually work out every day that I can and I need the exercise."

"Annie tells me that you ski, too."

"I don't get to the slopes often. Benny and I try to get there at least once a season. I haven't been in a couple of years now, but I do enjoy it."

The telephone rang and Vivian made a move to get up to answer it. She quickly changed her mind when she looked at Kenneth's and Chuck's faces. Kenneth got up from the table and answered the telephone.

"Samson," a voice said on the other end.

"Delilah, this is a pleasant surprise." He smiled. "How are you?"

"Missing the hell out of you. How long will you be away?"

"Maybe a week. I'm not sure yet, why?"

"I wanted to schedule another racquetball session with you here in Sacramento."

"I can't promise anything now, but I'll see what I can do. Where's the racquet club?"

"My condo, bedroom level."

"Oh, that racquetball game," he said, grinning. "I'm not fully recovered from the last match."

"We'll just have to work harder on building up your endurance level and stamina. Let me know what your travel plans are so that I can arrange my schedule."

"I'll call you later in the week."

Kenneth hung up and returned to the table where Chuck and Vivian were sitting.

"Who was on the telephone, K.J.?" Vivian asked.

"Delilah," Kenneth said, with a straight face.

"Delilah? Who's Delilah, K.J.?"

Kenneth avoided Vivian's question. "How about some breakfast, Chuck?"

"Uh, no thanks, Kenneth, not for me. I ate at five-thirty this morning."

"Uh, do you want anything more for breakfast, Viv?" Kenneth asked.

"You're changing the subject again, Kenneth. Who's Delilah and how did she know that you were here?"

"There are some things that little sisters don't need to know. Now, it's back to bed for you."

"Can't I just lay on the sofa in the front living room? I don't want to go back up to my room yet."

Kenneth looked at Chuck who agreed that she should be fine on the sofa. Chuck escorted Vivian to the living room while Kenneth got a comforter and pillows. Chuck started a fire in the grate and Kenneth tucked Vivian in beneath the covers. They closed the doors to the living room and returned to the kitchen to talk.

Later, Chuck received a page from the hospital and got up to leave. He and Kenneth peeked in on Vivian. She was sound asleep. Chuck gently took her pulse, so as not to wake her, and nodded to Kenneth that she was fine.

"I'll see you tomorrow, Kenneth. Here are my pager number and cell number. Call me if you need me before then."

"Thanks, Chuck. You've been a good friend to Vivian. I appreciate everything that you have done for her."

"Your sister is a special lady, Kenneth," he said, with a warmth that Kenneth recognized went far beyond his words. "She's a handful, but I like her. She's a fighter. She'll get through this. I'll see to that."

He has some pretty deep feelings for Vivian, Kenneth surmised after Chuck left. He recognized the symptoms. Hell, he had those same feelings for JeNelle. Kenneth returned to the living room with his briefcase and laptop. He added some logs to the fire and watched it burn for a while. It started to rain hard, typical for March in Washington, and the raindrops caused the flames in the fireplace to sizzle. He took his plans for the CompuCorrect expansion out of his briefcase and worked on them for over two hours. Vivian was still asleep on the sofa. The rain was still pouring when he closed his briefcase, shut down his computer, and just listened to the wind blow and the raindrops beat against the window.

The house was quiet, as the rain poured outside. The Snowman lay on the floor beside the sofa where Vivian was sleeping, as if to guard her from any more harm. Kenneth closed his eyes and leaned back in the recliner. He knew that it would happen and it did. The vision. He did not fight it. He dozed off to sleep with the vision in his dream, the quiet house, and the rain beating down outside. He remembered how beautiful and exciting JeNelle looked when she opened the door to her home the night of the Gala. The light dancing in her eyes whenever she smiled. The touch of her soft hand in his. The feel of her body as they danced and after as he massaged her neck and shoulders. That vision was driving him crazy, but the thought of Benny's feelings for JeNelle usually brought him to his senses.

He was startled out of his dream by Vivian whimpering in her sleep. He went to the sofa, lifted her head to his shoulder and held her. She clung to him and sobbed. The Snowman sat up and put his big paw on her lap.

"I'm so glad that you're here, K.J.," she said, sobbing. "I can't seem to pull myself together."

"Don't be hard on yourself, Vivian. You've been through a traumatic experience. It's going to take time to get through this."

"I'm trying, K.J., but I hurt so much because of what I've done. Intellectually, I know that I've made the right decision, but emotionally, it's killing me."

"Chuck told me to expect that you would feel this way. He said, even some women who have babies experience postpartum depression. It usually passes."

"I know. Dr. Kelly's assistant told me that this might happen. So did Momma. Dr. Kelly gave me a prescription for some medication, but I don't want to take any pills."

"I'll be here for as long as you need me."

"You can't waste your time babysitting me for the rest of my life, K.J. I've got to get control of myself or I'll never get through this."

"You'll get through it, Vivian. Chuck's right. You're a fighter, but you'll have to let yourself heal physically and emotionally."

The telephone rang and Kenneth went into the kitchen to answer it.

"K.J., is that you?"

"Hey, Gregory. How's it going?"

"Okay, but what are you doing at Viv's place? Is she all right?" Gregory asked, concerned.

"She's going to be fine."

"Are you telling me everything? I'm not a little kid anymore, you know. I know about Vivian's pregnancy."

"I'm sorry, G. I sometimes forget how grown up you are. Vivian's pregnancy is over. She had an abortion yesterday. I flew into DC last night. I didn't know that she was pregnant until after I got here, and by then, it was all over with. But she seems fine physically. It's going to take some time for her to heal emotionally. I'm going to stay with her for a while until she feels stronger."

"I knew that something was up when she didn't call me this week. She always Skype or calls and talks to me and Aretha." Gregory's voice broke. "I hate that Carlton Andrews for what he did to her! I should have let Benny beat his brains out!"

"And how would that have helped Vivian?"

Gregory paused in contemplation. "It wouldn't have. That's why I stopped Benny. Carlton came to see Dad yesterday at school. I was working in the office when he came in."

"What did Carlton want with Dad?"

"I didn't hear all of the conversation, but Dad said that Carlton wanted to recruit me to play for Grand Strand University; something about keeping all of the talent in the family. He also wants Dad to talk to Vivian and get her to marry him because of the baby."

"What did Dad say?"

"A few choice words!" Gregory said and chuckled. "I did hear Dad tell Carlton that as far as he was concerned, Vivian was a grown woman capable of making her own decisions. She had made a decision about her relationship with Carlton and he and Mama weren't going to interfere on his behalf, so Carlton could just step off!"

Kenneth laughed. "Dad said that?" Kenneth asked, surprised.

"Yeah, that and a lot of other words that I didn't know Dad used."

Kenneth and Gregory laughed.

"Dad was cool about it though. He never raised his voice. You know how Dad can get his point across with a look."

"Yeah, I've seen that 'look' a few times myself. It usually means case closed and no further discussion."

"That's the 'look' all right. Carlton couldn't even look me in the face when he left. Has he tried to contact Vivian?"

"If he did, she didn't mention it."

"You would have been proud of her, K.J., if you could have seen how she handled Carlton after my game. She blew him off and dropped him like a bad habit. I was talking to some college recruiters, but I saw her handle him. She rode home with me and Aretha after the game and talked with us about what she decided to do about the pregnancy. I didn't want her to do it, but I knew that it was the right decision for her."

Gregory's voice broke again.

"I'm proud of her, too, G. She's resting now. Do you want to talk with her?"

"Naw. Now that I know you're there with her, I won't worry about her so much. Just tell her that I love her and that she can call me when she's feeling better."

"I'll tell her, G. Kiss Mom, Dad, and Aretha for me."

They hung up and Kenneth smiled. His brother was growing into a fine young man. He went back into the living room. Vivian was playing with the Snowman.

"Was that Delilah on the telephone again?"

"Delilah?" he asked, grinning. "No, that was G. He was worried about you because you hadn't been in touch with him and Aretha this week. He's fine now. He said to tell you that he loves you. He wants you to call him when you're feeling better."

"He and Aretha are trying to grow up on us, K.J. You would have been proud of G if you had seen him handle those college recruiters. You know how he sometimes acts when he's around his boys—his crew. Well, he reached into a different bag when he was talking to the recruiters. I almost didn't recognize him. Mom, Dad, and Aretha were standing with him, but they never said a word. There were at least ten recruiters asking him questions at one time. He was as smooth as silk, just like you, but he wouldn't commit to any of them. He told them that he and his family would make a decision at the end of his senior year and not before that. He also said that he would be looking at schools that offered academic excellence as well as athletic opportunity. You could have knocked me over with a feather, but Mom, Aretha, and Dad didn't even seem surprised at all. I'm looking forward to spending the summer with him."

"He's going to make all of us proud of him and so is Aretha," Kenneth said, with a smile.

"Now, tell me about Delilah, K.J."

"Delilah? Oh, you mean Lisa. Dr. Lisa Lambert."

"Oh, and I suppose you're Samson?" Vivian asked with a knowing smile.

Kenneth didn't answer. He just took a quick look at Vivian, grinned, and picked up his briefcase.

"You know what Delilah did to Samson?"

"Oh boy, do I ever!"

They both laughed.

"So you and Lisa are an item?"

"I wouldn't say that exactly."

"Well, what would you say…exactly?"

"I wouldn't say anything."

"Why not?"

"Because, at this point, there's nothing to say."

"Apparently, she has something to say. She tracked you down here, didn't she?"

"Lisa could find water on the moon if she wanted to. She's very, uh, resourceful."

"How does she compare with JeNelle Towson?"

"There's no comparison." Kenneth caught himself. "They are very different people, but they are friends as well as business associates. I told you, JeNelle introduced us, so you can stop trying to make something out of nothing. What do you want to eat for dinner?"

The front door opened and Gloria, Melissa, Anna, Bill, Alan, David, Miguel and Angelique came rushing in loaded with shopping bags. They shook the rain off their clothes.

"Where have all of you been all day long?" Vivian asked.

"Shopping, shopping and more shopping," Alan said, as he collapsed on the sofa beside Vivian.

"I'm beat!" David said. "I didn't know that there were that many stores in the whole world!"

"Yeah, and you should see what we all got," Melissa chirped. "Bill took us to these couture houses and they treated us like royalty! We bought all of these fabulous clothes at below market rates."

"And who do we have here?" Gloria asked in a sultry voice. "This has got to be another Alexander. You must be Kenneth," she said, as she sauntered over to him. "My God, your parents knew what they were doing when they made the men in your family, Vivian. Now I see what JeNelle is always talking about."

"Down, Gloria. You already have your hands full with Tony. Don't try to add another notch to your belt with K.J.," Vivian said dryly.

"I'm Melissa Charles and I'm free, single, and disengaged…oh, and available." She was grinning from ear to ear at Kenneth.

"You're not ready for K.J., yet, Melissa. You'll have to use Bill and his playthings to work up to my brother," Vivian said sarcastically without heat.

Bill snapped a look at Vivian. "You mean that he really *is* your brother?" Bill asked, surprised.

"Yes, Bill, that's what I told you this morning."

"Oh, open mouth and insert foot. I apologize, Kenneth, for that crack I made about incest. I thought that Vivian had found a boy toy to get over breaking up with Carlton."

"Incest?" Melissa asked. "Vivian I didn't think that you were into kinky stuff like that?"

"Melissa, come with me, dear," Bill said, guiding Melissa out of the living room. "Let's go into the kitchen and help Anna put the food on the table before we truly let our ignorance loose on a rampage."

"I was wrong, K.J. There must have been two lost links and I think that we've found both of them," Vivian said dryly.

Everybody laughed and Gloria, David, and Alan described every place that they had been. Alan was not as jubilant as Gloria. He was just glad to be home and off his feet. Gloria was busy tearing open her purchases and holding them up for everyone to see. David was impressed.

"Gloria, didn't you buy anything else except sexy underwear and negligees?" Vivian asked.

"Kenneth, don't you think that these are cute?" Gloria asked, holding up a particularly scant piece.

"Uh, Gloria, did you leave the rest of that in the store?" Kenneth asked with a smirk.

"It's not something my sister, JeNelle, would wear, Kenneth, but it's sure to get Tony's attention."

"And mine, too!" David enthusiastically added.

Kenneth didn't say anything, but Vivian saw his expression at the mention of JeNelle's name.

"Soups on!" Bill yelled, entering the room carrying a large tray filled with an assortment of Chinese foods. Melissa followed carrying another large tray and Anna brought in another of food that included the plates, forks and napkins.

"What did you do, Bill, buy up all the food in Chinatown?" Vivian asked.

"Anna and the kids have never eaten Chinese food before, so I got some of everything on the menu."

They feasted on every dish and went back for seconds. Eventually, they were stuffed to the gills.

"Anyone for dessert?" Bill asked.

They all groaned. Bill handed a plate full of fortune cookies to Miguel who walked to each person and handed them out. As everyone broke open their cookie, they read the fortune aloud.

"Focus on creativity, style, physical attraction, romance and your wedding announcement will follow. Beware of dark period," Gloria read.

"Fools rush in and underestimate your power, so respond accordingly," David read.

"The longstanding negotiations will result in an inheritance and what was surrendered will be returned to you," Alan read.

"You are fun to be with and people are reluctant to leave you because of your sense of humor, even at your own expense," Melissa read.

"Your physical attraction stirs the creative juices and amour in someone you find across a crowded room, so turn on the charm," Bill read.

"Dilemma will be resolved and you'll take charge of your own destiny with both love and success," Kenneth read.

"Intuitive intellect dominates, so heed inner voices and adhere to the unorthodox, but don't take individual for granted," Vivian read.

"The dark period will pass and you will pass into a new phase in your life. Stay put," Anna read.

"It's only the beginning. There is much, much more to come. Be prepared," Angelique read.

They all sat there momentarily trying to figure out what each reference meant. Then they all looked at each other and laughed uncontrollably.

Bill got up, called Melissa and Miguel out of the room, and closed the door. Melissa returned ten minutes later, put on Madonna's CD, *Vogue*, and stood in front of the fireplace.

"Ladies and Gentlemen, may I have your attention please?" Everyone looked at Melissa. "Presenting *GQ's* newest, and probably youngest, model, Mr. Miguel Luis Menendez-Gaza!"

Bill and Miguel entered the room dressed identically in Bill Blass attire from head to toe. They took up positions in front of the fireplace and began striking poses as Madonna's music played. The two of them had everyone clapping and singing along with the music. When it ended, Bill and Miguel took off their hats and bowed to their audience.

"That was a great show, Bill," Vivian said, "and these clothes are too cute for words!" She motioned for Miguel to come to her and he crawled up into her lap. "This is the real stuff, Bill. How did you find outfits alike in Miguel's size?"

"That's a part of the deal my agent cut. Miguel's going to be modeling the Bill Blass Collection with me in the fall edition of *GQ* so he gets to keep the clothes and a tidy five-figure check."

"You mean that you cut a deal for Miguel, too?"

"The client loved him! Miguel's been a real trooper. Chuck was with us. He had his attorney negotiate with my agent and set up a bank account for Miguel. Anna has the account in her name and Miguel's."

"Bill, you never said anything about it. I'm proud of you."

"Now don't go getting soft on me, Vivian. I can't take you being nice to me. It just makes me want to go do something bad just to whine you up."

"That's not all, Vivian," Melissa chirped up as she handed a large box to Vivian.

"I'm not the Bill Blass type, Melissa. What's in this box?"

"Open it and see," Gloria said, smiling.

Vivian opened the box and inside was a short buckskin jacket, buckskin skirt and cowgirl hat and boots. "You have got to be kidding!"

"It's from Chuck," Alan said. "He had us running all over town to find that outfit."

"Someone should check the hospital's supply of ether. Chuck must be using massive doses if he thinks that I'm going to be seen in public in this get-up." Vivian laughed so hard that her sides began to hurt.

"Didn't your fortune cookie say something about adhering to the unorthodox, Viv?" Kenneth asked, trying to stifle his amusement.

Vivian rolled her eyes and pursed her lips. She had no reply.

Kenneth turned out Vivian's light after talking with their parents and siblings, kissed her goodnight, and climbed onto the sofa bed. Vivian lay there in the dark listening to the rain pouring on the roof and beating against the windows. She thought of how happy she was at home with her family and her mother's comforting face and her father's strong and reassuring embraces when she told them what she had decided to do. She thought of all of the faces of her relatives. The look on Benny's face when their father announced that Benny would be a father in September. The tears of joy on Stacy's face as the family huddled around her. Sylvia had held her after the announcement. She and Stacy would have given birth at approximately the same time. Stacy had not wanted to have a child either, but because of all of them, she had relented and agreed. Still, although she loved her family, and they loved her, she had chosen a different course for herself without the knowledge or consent of her baby's father, Carlton Andrews.

She thought of the many days and nights that she and Carlton had spent together planning what their lives together would be like. Then she thought of the blissful days and nights that they had spent in that same bed where she now lay mourning the decision that she was forced to make because of him. Yet, those beautiful images were replaced by the sight of Carlton on the floor of his apartment having sex with another woman. Silent tears ran down Vivian's face. She thought that perhaps she could have handled the fact that Carlton was sleeping around. After all, they did live too far apart to be together very often. If that's what he wanted to do, then he could have just been honest with her. She would not have liked it, but she would have appreciated his honesty. She did not consider herself a jealous or possessive woman. She didn't have to accept the engagement ring. That could have waited until they were both ready to make a real commitment or not at all. *Why is it that our dreams aren't always in the place where we expect them to be? Do we dream the wrong dream or is it that we dream with the wrong person in mind?*

Chuck Montgomery came to her mind. Why did he kiss her? Twice?

Kenneth was saying something in his sleep and drew her attention from her restless thoughts. He tossed and turned. Vivian crept over to the sofa bed and heard Kenneth say JeNelle's name clearly several times. She started to wake him, but instead decided to crawl into bed and hold him as he had held her the night before. Was Kenneth dreaming the wrong dream?

* * *

A week later, Anna had lunch ready when Chuck and Kenneth came into the house after their basketball game. They had played each day at one o'clock for five days. Vivian looked up from her books that were spread out over the table in the library.

"Who won today?" she asked, as they passed the door where she sat.

"We did, of course," Chuck said, with a big smile. "I'd rather play with your brother than against him. I don't know how we're going to keep winning when Kenneth leaves tomorrow."

Vivian and Kenneth embraced and held each other. They looked into each other's eyes.

"You're not the only one who's going to miss him. We haven't spent this much time alone together since I graduated from high school. I went to California and stayed for a whole summer. Of course, it wasn't all fun and games. He put me to work in his office."

"It's been a good visit and I've enjoyed being here with you and meeting all of your new friends. You seem to be on the mend. Are you sure that you don't want me to stay longer?"

"I'm sure. I'm ready to get on with my life now. I'll never forget this experience, but I know now that I can cope with it."

"I'll keep an eye on Annie for you, Kenneth. I'll let you know if she strays off track," Chuck said.

"I'm counting on that, Chuck, and we're still going skiing next season, right?"

"You've got it, partner, but I'll be talking with you again long before the skiing season starts. I may even get to San Francisco sometime this year."

"If you do, you will have someplace to toss your hat and lay your head," Kenneth said.

"What time is your flight tomorrow, K.J.?" Vivian asked.

"It's at 9:00 A.M. from National Airport. I'll catch a cab from here in the morning."

"No, sir, you won't," Chuck said. "I'll pick you up at seven. It's only a fifteen minute ride from here."

"Thanks, Chuck. I appreciate that."

The next morning, Vivian kissed her brother goodbye and waved as he drove away with Chuck. She was feeling stronger.

Chapter 25

"Good morning, this is CompuCorrect. How may I direct your call please? No, I'm sorry, Judge Worthington, but Mr. Alexander is out of town. Could someone else help you? Well, I do have a telephone number where he can be reached in Washington, DC. Sure, the number is 202-555-8822. You're welcome, Judge Worthington, and thank you for calling CompuCorrect."

"Good morning, Sir. I'm sorry to have kept you waiting. May I help you?" Sara McDougal asked.

"Yes. I'm Colonel J. C. Baker. Is Kenneth Alexander available?"

"No, Sir, Colonel Baker, Mr. Alexander is out of town. Could someone else help you?"

"Uh, how about Tom Jenkins? Is he in the office?"

"Yes, Sir. If you'll have a seat, I'll tell him that you're here."

Sara dialed Tom who was meeting with some new CompuCorrect clients. He told Sara that he would be out shortly and to make Colonel Baker comfortable. Sara relayed Tom's message and offered Colonel Baker a cup of coffee, which he accepted. Sara left her desk to go to the lounge. Colonel Baker paced the reception area and looked at all of the framed articles that were hanging on the wall. One article in particular caught his eye. It was an article about JeNelle Towson and Kenneth Alexander, "The Woman of the Year and Her Man For All Seasons." Baker jotted down some notes as he read the article.

"Are you being helped?" Shirley Taylor asked.

Baker turned around and saw an attractive woman dressed in exercise gear with a towel around her neck and perspiration on her body and clothing.

"Yes," he said, eyeing her scantily clad and shapely body. "I'm waiting to see Tom Jenkins. I'm Colonel John Calvin Baker," he said extending his hand.

"Oh, yes, Colonel Baker. I'm Shirley Taylor, Tom's and Kenneth Alexander's business partner. Tom has mentioned you to me before," she said, with a smile and shaking his hand. She noticed him eyeing her attire. "Please pardon my appearance. I've been working out," Shirley said, attempting to withdraw her hand.

"I must say that you 'work out' rather well, Ms. Taylor. It is Miss Taylor, isn't it?" Baker asked with a suggestive look, still not releasing her hand.

She eased out of his grip. "Yes, Colonel, it is. Tom is meeting with some clients at the moment. Is there something that I or someone else can do for you?"

He eyed her body again. "You can join Tom and me for dinner tonight. I'm a personal friend of Kenneth Alexander's. It seems that Kenneth is away and Tom offered to take me to dinner the next time that I was in town."

"I don't know, Colonel. You and Tom may want to talk privately."

"Nothing that you can't be a part of, I'm sure. Besides, you're a partner in this company and a friend of Kenneth's, although I don't know how Kenneth could keep his mind on business with a lovely woman like you around."

"I'm not sure—"

Sara returned with Baker's coffee and handed it to him. The telephone began to ring.

Shirley overheard Sara McDougal answer a call from Lisa Lambert.

"Good morning, Dr. Lambert. No, Mr. Alexander is still out of town in Washington, DC. Yes, he's at his sister's house. Yes, that's the right telephone number. You're welcome, Dr. Lambert. Have a nice day."

Tom came out of his office, escorting the new clients to the door. He noticed Baker's furtive glances at Shirley. He chatted momentarily with the new clients until they left and then joined Shirley and Baker.

"J.C.," Tom interrupted, extending his hand to the man, "It's good to see you again. I see that you've met Shirley Taylor."

"Yes, I've been trying to persuade her to join us for dinner tonight. Perhaps you can convince her," J.C. said, shaking Tom's hand but still eyeing Shirley

"Dinner? Tonight? Well, I was scheduled to meet with some potential clients tonight, J.C., but I'll see whether I can rearrange my schedule. It's been a little hectic around here with Kenneth out of town."

"So, Ms. Taylor," Baker said, "Tom is willing to rework his schedule for a friend of Kenneth's. Are you going to disappoint me?"

Shirley overheard Sara McDougal answer the telephone and mention JeNelle's name.

"Oh, hi, JeNelle. It's so good to hear from you. No, Mr. Alexander is out of town, but I'll be happy to give him a message. Sure…If you want his number in Washington. Yes, he's at his sister's place. No I'm not sure when he'll be back. Tom is taking his calls…"

Shirley was about to reject Baker's offer, but then changed her mind.

"No, of course not. Any friend of Kenneth's is a friend of ours. I'd be delighted to have dinner with you and Tom."

"Then it's done, J.C.," Tom said. "Why don't we all meet at the Crown at seven o'clock tonight? That should give me ample time to meet my original obligation and then have dinner with you and Shirley."

"The Crown? You mean the one at the Fairmont?" Baker asked.

"Sure, is that all right with you?" Tom asked.

"You really know how to show a guy a good time, Tom. I'm sure this is going to be worth your while. I have some more GSA Requests for Proposals (RFPs) that I believe you'll be interested in. If you have a moment, I'd like to discuss them with you now so that we can all have a relaxing evening together."

"Sure, just let me check my messages with Sara and I'll be right with you."

Baker turned toward Shirley and leaned in close to her. "I'm glad that you've decided to join us tonight. If you're free, I'd like to see you for drinks before Tom joins us, say at about 6:00 P.M. at the Crown."

"All right, Colonel Baker, I'll see you at six."

Tom rejoined them. "Well, J.C., if you're ready, we can step into my office."

Tom and Baker went into Tom's office and closed the door. J.C. took ten RFPs out of his briefcase and handed them to Tom. They sat quietly until Tom finished reading.

"My God, J.C.! These all look great! I think that we can make a bid on all of them, but it's going to take a hell of a lot of work and right now we're flooded with clients and potential new projects. We've got more business coming in the door then I ever dreamed we'd have."

"Kenneth would not want to pass up any opportunity that comes your way."

"You're right, but I'd have to discuss it with him first before I wrote a bid on any of these. He's been preoccupied lately and now he's off in Washington visiting his sister. I'm not sure when he'll be back. I've been trying to hold down the fort and I haven't told him how chaotic things have been because he rarely gets away."

"I wouldn't bother Kenneth with these proposals if I were you. He probably needs the break and you have the authority to sign off on the bids. Of course, there are no guarantees that you will get any of the contracts, but I'm sure that Kenneth would be pleased that you made the effort for the company. You know how hard he's worked to get this company off the ground."

"Right again, J.C., but Kenneth is the real brain of this operation. I don't know how he does it, but he manages to keep everybody motivated to do the very best job that they can and to give our client's the best service possible. He's going to be even more occupied with the Governor's Youth in Business and Industry Blue Ribbon Panel," Tom said, proudly. "He's already been traveling all over the state meeting with junior high and high school kids, school boards and industry people to get a feel for what needs to be done. He's got a stack of requests on his desk from people who want him to speak at meetings, luncheons or conventions. He performs like there's nothing happening, when, in fact, he's the calm in the eye of a storm. How he keeps everything in his head has got to be the eighth wonder of the world."

"Well, then, Tom, you could really help Kenneth by handling this yourself. It sounds like his plate is full."

"Maybe I could bring in one or two of our new employees to actually write the bids for me and I could then just review and sign off on them without bothering Kenneth."

"That's the spirit. I'm sure that Kenneth will appreciate it in the end, but now tell me about Shirley Taylor."

"Shirley? She's great! She and I and Kenneth all worked together at Sandoval Anniston before Kenneth came up with the idea to start this business. Shirley has her CPA and MBA from Stanford. She joined Sandoval at about the same time that Kenneth and I did. She's an incredibly hard worker and she's dedicated to making this business a success."

"It's not her brain that I'm interested in, if you know what I mean," he said around a sly wink. "What about her private life? Is she seeing anyone? Is there anything going on between her and Kenneth...you know, a little office romance? She's got some kind of body!"

Tom's green eyes narrowed as he stared at Baker. "Shirley's not that kind of woman," Tom said sternly. "She's dedicated to Kenneth and to this business, but she nor Kenneth have ever..." He calmed himself and straightened his neck in his tie. "They have a purely platonic, business relationship. I think that your comment is out of line. I admire and respect Shirley and so does Kenneth."

"Calm down, Tom. I'm just making sure that the coast is clear." J.C. grinned disarmingly.

"Shirley isn't married and, to the best of my knowledge, she isn't involved with anyone, if that's what you're asking,"

"That's all I want to know. I'll take it from there," Baker said, with a sly smile.

J.C. Baker and Tom parted cordially, but when Baker was gone, Tom was still annoyed. He thought about Shirley. She was his friend and had comforted him during his separation from his children and his subsequent divorce from his wife. His wife left him over his decision to leave Sandoval Anniston and start a company with two Black people. Shirley was there for him. She even offered to help him pay for his children's private school education and spent time with him and his children helping him to entertain them on the weekends or during the summer. She was great with them and his children enjoyed being with her. They were so glad to see her at the Christmas party that they monopolized much of her time.

Tom denied his wife's allegations that he was having an affair with Shirley because he felt that, unfortunately, the accusations were not true. Still, he had worked late on many occasions with Shirley by his side. There were many late night suppers at a restaurant or at his place or hers, but they never dated. He wanted to ask Shirley out on a real date, but was afraid that she would turn him down because he wasn't a Black man. So he simply continued to find excuses to spend time with her. He knew that Shirley seemed to be infatuated with Kenneth. She often talked of no one else, but that was to be expected. Kenneth had many women in their office and business contacts interested in him. Yet, Kenneth never seemed to even notice the other women until JeNelle Towson came on the scene. Tom thought that Kenneth's obvious attraction to JeNelle and JeNelle's obvious attraction to Kenneth would dissipate Shirley's infatuation with Kenneth and leave her free to view him as a possible suitor. He was thrilled when he read the article about Kenneth and JeNelle and crushed when Kenneth denied its validity. Then he knew Kenneth well. Kenneth was telling the truth when he told them that there was nothing going on between him and JeNelle Towson, but he had seen them together. They were definitely suppressing some strong attractions, even from themselves. He didn't think that even Lisa Lambert's attentions to Kenneth would break the interest between Kenneth and JeNelle, but perhaps it would affect Shirley and he would be there to comfort her. J.C. Baker was not going to ruin his chances with Shirley, no matter what it took.

J.C. Baker sat in his chauffeur-driven military car outside CompuCorrect's office making phone calls.

"This is Colonel J.C. Baker. Get me a dossier on a JeNelle Elise Towson of Santa Barbara. She owns a company called 'INSIGHTS'. Fax it to me in my headquarters at the Presidio and mark it *Top Secret, Eyes Only*. I want it in two minutes and two seconds!" he barked. Then he dialed another number. "Get Lisa Lambert on the horn. This is Colonel J.C. Baker." A pause and then, "Look, Lisa, what's holding up your mission with Kenneth Alexander?" J.C. Baker sternly asked. "Why the hell do I have to do every damn thing myself?"

"Nothing's holding it up. I'm working on it as we speak, but Kenneth's not a man who is easily manipulated. You know that. It's going to take more time than we thought."

"You're almost out of time, Lisa! If you don't move your butt a lot faster, the Congressional Appropriations Committee is going to close a lot of military bases, many of them in this state. You'll have hundreds of thousands of people out of work and, need I remind you that there's an election year fast approaching! You weren't sent out here to be a social butterfly. Your mission is to get hundreds of contracts in place with local vendors so that the military budget won't be cut to the bone through sequestration and military bases won't be closed!"

"What's with this 'social butterfly' crap? I know what I was sent out here to do, Baker, and I'm doing it!"

"I saw your picture in the background of a newspaper clipping about some Santa Barbara Chamber of Commerce Gala."

"Look, Baker, when you failed, you gave me the toughest assignment—Kenneth Alexander—and you expect me to work miracles? The hell you say! I've been busting my butt on this. I was there to size up the man, not all the intel I gathered was sufficient to get good insight into who he is. I was doing my job, Baker! There were also a lot of people and companies represented there who do business with North Island Naval Air Station, Camp Pendleton and March Air Force Base. I've been coordinating the placement of more contracts in those areas, too. I have over five hundred potential military contracts out there that should account for at least seven to ten billion dollars in revenue for California out of the military budget. Kenneth Alexander is not the only iron I have in the fire at the moment!"

"What about this Towson woman? Is she going to be a problem or can she be used to distract Kenneth? I think I met her one night at Kenneth's place, but it was dark. I didn't get a clear look at her."

"I already thought of that. I instigated that story you read in the newspaper to see which way they would turn. I thought that JeNelle Towson would be instrumental in distracting Kenneth, but so far, it hasn't worked. She's not an easy woman to manipulate and she's not going to let anyone use her again. She had a bad marriage that's left her emotionally scarred, but I know that she has strong feelings for Kenneth Alexander. JeNelle's determined to stay free of all sexual involvements and she's not going to do anything that she thinks might hurt Kenneth personally or professionally.

"Kenneth is fighting his attraction to her too, but I've arranged it so that they'll be seeing a lot of each other over the next year. If my plan works, Kenneth will be so preoccupied with JeNelle that he won't have time to pay attention to what's going on in his office. He trusts his partners, Tom Jenkins and Shirley Taylor."

"This is taking too much time! Step up the plan!"

"That's not possible. I have to be very careful how I handle this. JeNelle has some powerful friends—Judge Worthington, for one. He can't be intimidated or used and he thinks that the sun rises and sets on JeNelle. When he was a District Attorney, he handled JeNelle's case against her former husband, Michel San Angeloe. He knows the whole story about her life."

"What's the other factor?"

"JeNelle's ex-husband's family—The San Angeloe Family in New York. They believe that they owe JeNelle a debt of gratitude because she did not have her husband incarcerated for what he did to her. She doesn't believe that they owe her anything, but she's still the owner of a restaurant, Michelangelo's in San Diego that her former husband gave her as a wedding gift. Her former husband's uncle, Milo San Angeloe, still runs it for her, even though she won't have anything to do with the business. Michel San Angeloe wants JeNelle back in his life, but his family is keeping a tight control on him where she's concerned. She has easy and unlimited access to his family anytime she wants. If she thinks that Kenneth is threatened by anything you and I are doing, she might not hesitate to use her relationship with the San Angeloe Family—and you know how Italian families regard a debt of gratitude. They take it seriously and personally. We'd cease to exist like Jimmy Hoffa!

"So don't try to twist me over this! I've got two people who are both strong-willed and independent types and who are not influenced or motivated by wealth, glory, greed or power. They are both that rare breed of animal—conscientious citizens—who think that they should try to make a difference. Hell, they're both so squeaky clean that they don't even cheat on their taxes. And they aren't the only ones. I've got a couple of hundred more just like them. If you want to keep your military appropriations healthy and inflated and those bases open just do your part and keep those RFPs flowing into the state!"

"That's what I'm doing. I just had a meeting with Tom Jenkins at CompuCorrect and I gave him ten RFP's; all of them were inflated, but Tom might not pick up on that since his background is public relations, sales and marketing. The problem might be this Shirley Taylor. She's a CPA and if she notices that the RFP's are inflated, she might bring it to Kenneth's attention. I'm having drinks with her and dinner with her and Tom tonight. If I can keep her distracted, and Tom doesn't notice what's going on, Kenneth won't find out about the RFP's until the Purchase Orders have been issued and the contracts come back signed, sealed and delivered. Kenneth's no fool though. You have to be careful with him."

"Tell me something that I don't already know. I've had to stay ten steps ahead of him all the way. I'll try to get him to Sacramento and keep him occupied until CompuCorrect gets those RFP's filed."

"Do whatever is necessary where this JeNelle and Kenneth situation is concerned, but you keep Kenneth occupied and away from his office for as long as you can. We may make it through this session of Congress unscathed, but the next Congress and this President are not going to look favorably on military appropriations when there is little or no threat of a war. We at the Joint Chiefs can't keep coming up with these little no-named countries to invade to keep the money in the military budget."

"I'll do what I have to, Baker, to keep this state's administration in power, but don't you ever call me again and try to manipulate me! I'm not one of your cunts that you can just ramrod at your discretion!"

Baker's tone lowered to a growl. "I remember a few nights back in Washington when we did some interesting maneuvers in my office at the Pentagon and on the boardroom table at the Heritage Foundation. Then there was that time on Capitol Hill in Senator—"

"That's ancient history, Baker. We're not going into that now!"

"You've still got ice water flowing through your body fueled by power. You screwed my brains out and you never felt a thing. You're one cold, Black—"

"Don't even think it, Baker! I got what I wanted out of you and you got as good as you gave! So don't try to run any guilt trip on me just because I'm not giving it up to you out of both panty legs! You're a good lay, Baker, but you're not the best I ever had! If I want you again, I'll just pucker up and whistle! You'll be there with your tongue hanging out of your mouth just like you always have! I'll send you a pair of my used panties the next time I screw Kenneth Alexander. So far he's the best lay that I've ever had! That ought to keep your dick at attention until I whistle!"

"Pucker up and blow then, Lisa! I'll collect that gift personally tonight! I'll reserve our usual suite at the Fairmont! You know which one it is! The Bentley Suite! Don't bother to dress!"

Lisa hung up and Baker sat back in the car seat.

"Take me to the Presidio!" he instructed the driver. "Lisa Lambert is one cold bitch," he said aloud to himself. However, he was looking forward to getting the pair of underwear she had promised. She was right. That did turn him on and so did she. He knew that Lisa would be at the Fairmont waiting for him when he finished dinner with Tom and Shirley.

Chapter 26

Kenneth sat in the airport waiting to board his flight back to San Francisco. People hustled and bustled around him. A woman passed him and he caught the whiff of a familiar perfume—JeNelle's perfume. He looked up and saw a woman who he thought...but she was quickly lost in the crowd. He gathered his coat, briefcase, and luggage and followed her. He called JeNelle's name. The woman turned around. It was not JeNelle. She smiled at him and he apologized.

"I thought that you were someone else," he said and smiled apologetically.

"I wish that I was whoever you thought I was," the woman said, with a broad smile. "Whoever she is, she's a lucky woman."

Kenneth smiled and returned to his departure gate. He stood looking out the window as the food service crew loaded the aircraft with provisions. Grabbing the back of his neck, he stretched. Suddenly, he picked up his luggage, coat, and briefcase and went back to the airline ticket desk.

Hours later, Kenneth sat in the kitchen of his parents' home in Goodwill, South Carolina, and stared out the window. He had been there for hours just sitting quietly and watching the wildlife in the backyard and in the forest beyond. It felt good to be home again. He enjoyed his life in California, but there was truly no place like home. Everywhere he looked had fond memories for him. Good friends and good family. The kitchen brought back special memories of his childhood with his paternal grandparents, Bernard, Senior and Emma Grace Alexander, teaching him and caring for him while his parents worked.

He wanted a little brother when Benny was born. He had someone who he could share adventures with and pal around with and teach the things that his grandparents and parents taught him. Benny was a daring little tyke. He'd go after something he wanted with a vengeance, but once he had it, whatever it was, lost its luster and he'd be off conquering something else. Kenneth could tell Benny that there was something that he couldn't do or something that he couldn't have, and Benny would always prove him wrong. He was tenacious. Benny was his little brother though, and he cared for him and watched over him because his grandparents told him that he was a precious commodity. Benny looked up to him as a role model, just as he looked up to his parents and grandparents.

Then Vivian was born. He taught Benny how to look after her as his grandparents had taught him. They were a happy threesome. Vivian was a handful for him and Benny. She was an independent little thing that would not be cooped up or corralled. Still, she would listen patiently to him and to Benny and she always had a comeback to any argument that they made. She had a sharp wit and mind, but a loveable disposition when it came to him and Benny. She would fiercely defend them, if she thought that they were under any threat of punishment by their parents or grands. She had her grandparents twisted around her little finger. They loved her spirit, wittiness, and ingenuity. Practicing law was clearly going to be the right career for her.

When Gregory came along, Kenneth was already a teenager soon to be leaving for college. He spent as much time as he could with Gregory over holiday weekends and summer vacations, but he depended on Benny and Vivian to watch over Gregory while he was away. The day that the Alexanders drove away, leaving him at Morehouse College, was one of the hardest times for him. He was excited about starting his college career, but Benny, Vivian and Gregory were heartbroken each year that he left home to return to school.

While he was away at school, Aretha was born. She became everyone's focal point. He could only spend short periods of time with her, but she was an amazing little girl. She was more like their grandparents than any of them. She ruled the roost and kept them spellbound with the insightful comments that she made.

Soon Benny would have a child and he worried that no one would be there to teach and protect Benny's baby the way that all of them had taught, nurtured, and protected each other. The newest Alexander might not ever learn the joy of growing up in Goodwill and swinging in the hammock and looking at the universe.

"Kenneth James!" Sylvia Alexander screamed joyfully as she came into her kitchen and found her eldest son sitting at the table. "I wondered whose rental car that was parked in the driveway. My God, it's good to see you!"

Sylvia was beaming, but she noticed sadness in her son's face and eyes.

"Mom, come here and give me your biggest and best hug and kiss," Kenneth said, as he cradled his mother in his arms.

Sylvia caressed his face, as she searched his eyes. "I think that you needed to come home a long time ago, Kenneth James. I could see it in your face in San Francisco and I could hear it in your voice. I told Bernie that something was up with you, but he thought that I was just being overprotective."

They sat down across from each other at the table. Sylvia held her son's hands in hers.

"I'm fine, Mom. I've just been sitting here remembering the good times. I'm probably just a little tired from the trip and ready for one of your good home-cooked meals."

"Kenneth James, you've never lied to me before and I won't forgive you if you lie to me now. It's this new thing with Benjamin Staton and JeNelle Towson that's got you hurting now so badly, isn't it?"

Not able to look into his mother's eyes, he tried to change the subject. "Mom, what's for dinner tonight? I'm starving, and when will Dad, Aretha and Gregory be home?"

"Kenneth James, I've known you since you were a gleam in your Daddy's eyes. Now, you look me in the eyes and tell me that it's not Benjamin Staton and JeNelle Towson."

Kenneth couldn't do it. He got up from the table and stretched. Feeling his mother's eyes on him, he knew that she was waiting for an answer and he knew that she would not be denied. He couldn't tell her everything. It would worry her if she knew he was in danger. He sat down at the table again and took his mother's warm hands in his.

"How did you know, Mom?"

She caressed his face with one hand. "No man looks at a woman and no woman looks at a man the way you two did in that picture in the newspaper without there being a strong chemistry going on between you. I know that look. Your father and I have looked at each other that same way for thirty-five wonderful years. I also heard it in your voice when you talked with us about JeNelle the week that she stayed with you in San Francisco. I've never heard you so excited about any woman before."

"I admit that I am attracted to JeNelle. I couldn't let myself admit it to anyone before now. I've tried to put her out of my head, but no matter what I do, thoughts of her are always with me. I remember her everywhere. At home. At the office. Places that we went in the city. The staff loves her and brings up her name or something that she said or did. Business associates mention her to me. Or I'll read something about her in the newspaper. It's been pure hell. It's driving me insane."

"Don't fool yourself, Kenneth James. You're not just attracted to JeNelle Towson. You're falling in love with her."

"I can't be in love with someone I have only seen a few times. It takes time to fall in love. You have to know a person very well before you can actually say that you're in love."

"Your Daddy and I knew, the minute that we saw each other for the very first time on Howard University's campus, that we were going to have something very special between us and we were right. It didn't take us years to know that."

"If I'm so much in love, Mom, how could I sleep with another woman? Someone who knows JeNelle?"

"I love your Daddy more than I love life, but if Sidney Poitier or Harry Belafonte had looked my way once before I was married, your last name might not have been Alexander. My father, mother, and grandparents knew both Poitier and Belafonte very well. I don't have to tell you that you don't have to be in love with someone to sleep with them. You've got two brothers who prove that theory all the time. Benjamin Staton told me about Lisa Lambert. You've never mentioned her in any of your letters or when we've talked with you on the telephone or in your e-mail or text messages. I'll bet that she is someone who you hardly knew and who caught you at a time that your brother, Benjamin Staton, would call 'an unguarded moment'. Was it heat that you felt for Lisa Lambert or passion?"

"Heat, Mom. I haven't been intimately involved for a long time. I've been working night and day to get the company on its feet, but JeNelle stirred something inside of me the first time I saw her that will not go away. If it had not been Lisa, it probably would have been someone else. Maybe even Shirley Taylor if she had been willing and the opportunity presented itself."

"Oh, Shirley would have been willing all right and she would have made the opportunity available if she even thought that she had a chance with you. The problem there is that you would have hurt not only Shirley, but also Tom Jenkins."

Kenneth looked at her quizzically. "Mom, what are you taking about? Tom and Shirley are not involved."

"Oh, Tom's involved all right. Right up to his pretty green eyes. But Shirley just thinks of him as a coworker, a business partner. She doesn't even think of him as being an eligible man maybe because he's not Black. She doesn't see herself as attractive enough for men to take notice. She's crazy about Tom's children though and they love her. If you weren't around, Tom might have a chance with Shirley."

"How could you possibly know all of this? You've only met Shirley three or four times, tops."

"Son, you weren't surprised when I said that Shirley is interested in you, were you?"

"No, because I've heard that from more than one source and her behavior has been rather erratic lately."

"Then don't doubt me now when I tell you that Tom is interested in Shirley. Tess Braxton and I weren't just sitting in that corner at the Christmas party knitting. There was a lot going on that we saw from our point of view than you'll ever believe. Even Tess spotted the dynamics between her daughter, Juan's twin sisters, and Gregory Clayton. We were batting a thousand with our predictions and observations. If Tess' husband had pinched Sara McDougal on the fanny one more time, Tess said that she was going to use my knitting needles on him," she said, giggling. "Poor Benjamin Staton was trying hard to get something going with Shirley, but she wasn't buying it. She was too busy trying to get you to notice her. Still, if that young thing from your paper supply associate had rubbed up against your daddy one more time, Tess Braxton wouldn't have been the only one finding new uses for knitting needles," she said and chuckled. "Yet your daddy was cool. He knew what that young thing was trying to do and he quickly got out of her line of fire. I don't know what it is about those Alexander genes that drive sane people crazy, but if I could bottle it, I'd sell it and make a mint for my grandbabies."

"Speaking of grandbabies, Mom," Kenneth said cautiously.

Sylvia exhaled slowly. "I thought you'd get around to that eventually. Are you thinking about Vivian Lynn or Benjamin Staton?"

"Vivian was so demoralized when I got to DC, but each day she seemed to get better. She's a strong woman, Mom, just like you."

"Vivian will be fine. I never worry about her. She's got a good head on her shoulders. Your daddy and I wanted her to stay here and have the procedure at home, but she refused. I know that she didn't want us to see the emotional pain that she would be going through. She was especially worried about Gregory. She didn't think that he could take it and she was scared to death to tell you about any of it. She didn't want you to be disappointed in her after all that you had tried to teach her about nurturing, loving, and trusting family."

Kenneth exhaled slowly and held his mother's hands in his. "I know. We have had some long talks this past week. Maybe I raised the standard too high and didn't leave room for anything less than giving their very best for the investment that our grandparents and you and Dad have made in each one of us."

Sylvia gently squeezed his hands. "No, you haven't, Kenneth James. You didn't raise the standard too high for your sisters and brothers. You raised it too high for yourself. You've beaten yourself nearly to death to set a good example for your brothers and sisters and here you are beating yourself again because you think that Benjamin Staton is in love with JeNelle Towson. You've never denied your sisters or brothers anything that they wanted or needed from you. You're even willing to deny your feelings for JeNelle so that Benjamin Staton can succeed with her." Sylvia smiled knowingly and shook her head. "Well, Kenneth James, you're wasting your time and energy where Benjamin Staton is concerned. He's so much in love with Stacy Greene that it's a shame. And she's in love with him, too. The poor babies don't even know it yet or if they do they can't or won't admit it. Someday they will." She winked.

Kenneth's brow furrowed. "How do you know that Benny is not in love with JeNelle? He's done everything that he can think of, including turn my life upside down, for her on more than one occasion."

A grin lifted the corners of her mouth and put a sparkle in her doe-like eyes. "The look, baby. He and Stacy look at each other the same way you and JeNelle looked at each other in that picture. The same way that me and your daddy look at each other. That's not just heat that they generate, it's real intimacy, passion and love. Benjamin Staton said that he and Stacy are only good friends who enjoy having sex together. Well, your daddy and I heard them making love every night and every morning and twice on Sunday." She giggled. "They weren't in there just knocking boots, as Gregory Clayton would put it. You should have seen them when they were here. They were glowing like a honeymoon couple. They would catch a look at each other whenever they thought that the other one wasn't looking. Then they couldn't stay away from each other for two minutes. Benjamin Staton was hovering over Stacy and keeping all of his eligible cousins and friends away from her."

Kenneth shook his head slowly. "You haven't met JeNelle yet. Wait until you see how he looks at her. There's real love there."

"Huh!" Sylvia intoned. "That's real lust—not love. How does JeNelle look at Benjamin Staton?"

Kenneth's eyes narrowed in thought. "I never really noticed. I've only seen them together a few times."

"If she felt anything more than friendship for him, you would have felt it, too." She smiled warmly. "Still you and JeNelle didn't even need that beam of light to glow on you two. You two would have ignited the room, if you had just let yourselves go and stopped fighting the feelings."

Kenneth stood abruptly and paced. Turning to his mother and spraying his hands in supplication. "What if you're wrong and Benny is in love with JeNelle? I can't hurt him by permitting myself to become involved with her."

Sylvia stood and took his outstretched hands in hers, squeezing gently. "Kenneth James, stop playing 'what if' games with yourself. You may have been able to pull the wool over Benjamin Staton's eyes thus far, but you're not going to be able to keep him or anybody else in the dark for much longer. I'm not worried about Benjamin Staton and JeNelle Towson. There's never going to be anything but friendship between them. I know your brother has a reputation as an extraordinary ladies' man, but Stacy Greene and their daughter, Whitney, will change Benjamin Staton. He'll have the two most important ladies in his life in them. What you may have to resolve is what has happened in JeNelle Towson's life that has made her so resistant to intimate relationships." She tapped a finger to her temple. "That may be a more difficult problem to resolve than anything you've faced so far." Sylvia hugged him briefly, but warmly. "Now I'm going to change out of my uniform and start dinner, but I want you to think about what I've said to you."

She kissed her son on the cheek and went to her bedroom to change.

Kenneth sat in the kitchen alone. He wanted to believe what his mother said about Benny and Stacy, but he had never met Stacy. All that he knew about her was what Benny told him. He talked about how much he respected, admired, and enjoyed Stacy Greene, but he had never professed to love any woman that he knew of—only JeNelle. He remembered Benny's face the night that he burst through the door of his office convinced that something was going on between him and JeNelle. Would his brother take off on the spur of the moment and fly to San Francisco to confront him if his feelings for JeNelle weren't deep and abiding? But what about JeNelle? Just as his mother had proffered, he never witnessed anything between them, except friendship. That's all that JeNelle ever said was between them. He remembered the night of the Gala and how uncomfortable JeNelle seemed at the thought of wearing the expensive earrings that Benny gave her. She only agreed to wear them because he asked her to. He also remembered how adamant JeNelle was about dissolving her friendship with Benny if Benny blamed him for the conclusions that the press had drawn. He would have to consider these matters more carefully if he were ever to begin putting his life back together again.

* * *

"Kenneth James," Aretha yelled from the front door. "You have a telephone call."

"Thanks, Retha," he answered as he wiped the grease from his hands. He was helping Gregory change the oil in his car. "I'll be right back, G. Don't let that oil drip on the ground."

"Okay, K.J. I've done this before, you know."

He entered the house and picked up the cordless telephone in his father's study. "Hello."

"Kenneth, I'm glad I finally caught up with you. This is Johnston Worthington."

"How are you, Judge Worthington?" Kenneth asked somewhat confused and surprised that Judge Worthington would track him down.

"I'm fine, Kenneth, but please call me Johnston. We're going to be working closely together over the next few months."

"Then a decision has been made about the proposal that we submitted to revamp the intrastate judicial computer network system?"

"Yes, the State Budget and Finance Director has signed off on your proposal, but I have a few things that I need to clear up with you."

"Certainly, Johnston. I'll call my office and have Tom Jenkins get right on it."

"No, no, Kenneth. I'd like to talk with you about this matter, in person. Is it possible for you to fly into Santa Barbara on your way back to San Francisco?"

"I believe that I can arrange that, Johnston, but is there any reason why we can't discuss this matter over the phone?"

"I like to look a man in his eyes when we talk. It's an old practice of mine and it has served me well over the years."

"Well, there is always Skype, but, all right, I'll fly into Santa Barbara. I'm spending a few days with my family. Is there any urgency?"

"No, no, Kenneth. It'll take time to set this...uh, I mean, take all the time you need. Just let me know when you are arriving and I'll have someone meet you at the airport," he said jovially.

"Fine, Johnston. I'll talk with you soon."

They hung up and Kenneth called Tom Jenkins. "How are things going, Tom?"

"Just great, Kenneth. We don't even miss having you around getting in our way while we're being creative."

Kenneth laughed. "Maybe I'd better come back immediately. You sound like you're trying to make my position obsolete."

"We're not ready to put you out to pasture quite yet, old man, but we're considering the purchase of a rocking chair for you."

"Now I know that it's time to come back!" Kenneth and Tom laughed. "Since you don't seem to need me around anyway, I'm going to fly into Santa Barbara on my way back to see—"

"The lovely JeNelle Towson, I hope," Tom interrupted.

"Stop putting words in your mouth that you can't speak or swallow, Tom," Kenneth joked. "I'm going to see Judge Worthington. He called me today and said that the communications network deal for the California Court System has been approved, but he has some questions. Do you have any idea what might be on his mind?"

"No, I don't, but I have the proposal somewhere here on my desk."

Kenneth heard Tom shuffling through papers. He also heard what he thought was a lamp crash to the floor and Tom issue an expletive.

"Here it is, Kenneth. It looks fairly straightforward. Shirley's cost projections on the job seem to be right on target. In fact, we came in under budget on the hardware and software packages. Since it's all in-state, the travel expenses to do the installations in every state courthouse can be kept to a minimum. Manufacturing and Production seem to have the equipment ready on schedule and after installation the training staff have scheduled in the in-house educational programs. Finally, a month after the installation goes operational, the Feedback Team goes out to each site to evaluate the success of the project. I don't see why Judge Worthington would have any problems with the project plan whatsoever. We're saving the judicial court network a nice piece of change under the projected cost."

"E-mail a copy of the proposal to me. I'll go over it on my way to Santa Barbara... Oh, and Tom?"

"Yes, Kenneth?"

"Find yourself a secretary or assistant before I get back, please, before you demolish the building. We've got a big expansion project underway and I want the construction company to have something left to start with."

Tom laughed. "Okay, Kenneth, I'll find someone to assist me."

"Good, Tom. I feel safer already. I'll call you when I know more about my plans."

They hung up and Kenneth made another call.

"Dr. Lambert, please. This is Kenneth Alexander."

"Samson," she cooed.

"Lisa...."

"All right, I get it," she sighed. "Well, hello, Kenneth. Why are we being so formal? Are you calling me to tell me that you're ready for that racquetball game?"

"No, in fact, it doesn't appear that I'm going to get up to Sacramento after all. I have some business to attend to in Santa Barbara on my way back to San Francisco."

"Don't tell me that I've already lost one match to JeNelle Towson." She laughed.

"No, I'm not going to see JeNelle."

"Well, that's good news. When do you plan to be back in San Francisco?"

"I'm not sure. Perhaps another three or four days, why?"

"Listening to your voice on the telephone is making me more anxious to see you."

"Uh, Lisa...I'll call you after I get back to San Francisco and clear up whatever is on my desk. Then maybe we can schedule something that fits both of our schedules. Perhaps something less demanding than your version of racquetball."

"But, Kenneth, I thought that you enjoyed our matches."

"I told you, Lisa. I was younger then. I've aged considerably since our first encounter. Let's try something a little different. I'll call you next week."

"Sure, Kenneth, I'll talk to you next week."

They hung up.

"Sounds like you're planning to go back to work, Son," Bernard said, as he came into his study.

"No, Dad, not quite yet. I haven't soaked up enough of Goodwill to recharge my batteries yet. I'll be here a few more days. I want to at least see Gregory play in the championship tournament. He's been beating up on me on the basketball court too much since I got home. And Aretha is playing in a recital over in Dillard. From what I hear, she is quite a little child progeny reminiscent of Mama's family and Aunt Mariah."

"It's good to have you home, Son. Your mama and I miss having you around here from time to time and so do Gregory Clayton and Aretha Grace. They've been showing you off to all of their friends, I hear."

Kenneth laughed. "Yes, they have. I didn't realize how much I missed being here. I promise that I'll be home more often from now on."

Bernard clamped a hand on Kenneth's shoulder and guided him to a chair. They sat forward across from each other, resting their arms on their knees.

"Son, you sound much better than you did when you got here a couple of days ago."

"Southern exposure. I can clear my mind here. Put things in their proper perspective and function better."

"You've accomplished a lot in your life, Kenneth James. You've far exceeded all of our high expectations for you. We're very proud of the man that you are. Your grandparents taught you well and we've never been disappointed in the decisions that you've made. But—"

"But what, Dad?"

"You do tend to carry too much of the burden for your brothers and sisters. You need to loosen up, Son, and live a little for yourself."

"That's what Mom said," Kenneth said, knotting his hands before him.

"She's right, Son. Your mama knows what she's talking about. I've loved your mama for more than thirty-five years. She's a handful, but she's never disappointed me or let me down. She's always right on target."

Kenneth looked up into his father's eyes. "Is that the secret of your happiness with Mom?"

A sparkle lit his eyes and a knowing grin lifted the edges of his mouth. "Man, it's the look in her eyes whenever she sees me. She makes me feel like it's the first time that we met. She smiles at me with those beautiful eyes of hers and I fall in love with her all over again."

"Yeah," Kenneth snorted. "You two have been keeping me and Gregory awake at night and in the morning. Doesn't seem to bother Aretha though."

Bernard smiled at his son. "Son, there is nothing in this universe better than being with a woman who loves you. I keep praying that being with your mama couldn't get any better. But it always is. Someone's not listening to my prayers. Sometimes during the day, I'll see a vision of your mother in my mind and I'll call her just so I can hear her voice. Or sometimes she'll surprise me and drive over to the high school to have lunch with me. Then I can't wait to come home to her and hold her in my arms. Or we'll be sitting at the kitchen table folding the laundry and she'll give me a special smile. Sometimes I take your mama out to dinner and dancing in Columbia on date night, and we'll end up spending the weekend at one of those big hotels with room service." Bernard smiled to himself. "We're still discovering things about each other every day— and every night." Bernard's smile broadened. "These might not sound like big, earthshaking moments to you, Kenneth James, but it's those little things that happen every day that are the secret to our happiness."

"People don't often find what you and Mom have, Dad. It's a rare commodity."

"Benny and Stacy have found it. They just haven't found each other yet. You'll find it, too. You won't settle for anything less. It's not just physical love making—it's emotional and mental loving, too. It's passion. You put everything that you are into it and hold back nothing and you get back everything that your partner is. I like to call it unadulterated loving. Nothing fazes it."

"I hope you're right, Dad. I'm beginning to feel like I want someone in my life."

"Maybe JeNelle Towson?"

Kenneth slumped back in his seat, shaking his head. "I can't think like that, Dad. Benny would be destroyed if he thought that I would betray him in that way. Still, you're right, JeNelle excites me like no other woman I've ever known. I don't mean just physical excitement, because I've never approached her in that way. I've had to take a hell of a lot of cold showers though since I met her. I've even been sleeping with someone else in the hope that I could put JeNelle out of my head and not let Benny or anyone else know how I've been feeling. Yet, whenever I think of JeNelle, there's that physical, intellectual and emotional excitement. I want to see her. Talk with her. Make love—" Kenneth caught himself and buried his face in his hands momentarily, stood up, and stretched. He looked back over his shoulder at his father. "You know what I mean, Dad. I want to know what's going on with her. I want her to trust me and share her confidences with me. I want to know what fuels that fire that burns inside of her. What's buried behind her beautiful eyes, but I can't.

"Since I've been home, I've decided that I'm going to give this relationship with Lisa a real chance to develop. I'm going to distance myself from Benny and JeNelle and let them develop whatever there is between them."

Bernard shook his head. "I think that you're being too hard on yourself and demanding too much from yourself. You've always looked after your sisters and brothers. They are mostly grown now. It's time for you to look after yourself. Give yourself a break. Your brother may think that he's falling in love with JeNelle Towson, but I know better. I've seen him with Stacy Greene. He's a happy man and it's not just because Stacy's carrying their baby either. I know that just as surely as your mama does. Benjamin Staton is in love with Stacy Greene and she's in love with him."

"Dad, I love you and Mom and I respect both of you and your opinions, but I won't take the chance that you and Mom might be wrong."

"Trust in the principles that our ancestors laid down for this family. You won't be disappointed." He sat back in his chair. "Now, tell me what else it is that you've been trying to handle on your own."

Kenneth looked into his father's determined face and knew he couldn't hide it any longer. He sat with him for hours and revealed the facts.

* * *

When the plane landed at the Santa Barbara airport, a man wearing a chauffeur's uniform met Kenneth. Before long, the limousine stopped in front of Maison's and a doorman opened the car door as Kenneth got out. He jolted at the memory of having lunch there with JeNelle the day that she introduced him to Lisa. He prayed that JeNelle would not be there that day, but, with his luck, another prayer probably wouldn't be answered.

"Good afternoon, Mr. Alexander. It's good to see you again," Jerrod said, as Kenneth entered. "Judge Worthington is waiting for you. Peter will show you to the table."

The waiter showed him into the dining room. Kenneth scanned the room. He was relieved that JeNelle was not there. Well, maybe this time one of his prayers was being answered. People stopped him along the way and shook his hand, greeted him, or handed a business card to him and asked him to call them. He finally reached Judge Worthington's table.

"Well, hello, Kenneth," Judge Worthington said, with a broad smile as he rose from the table and extended his hand.

"Johnston, it's a pleasure to see you again, Sir."

"You, too, Kenneth. Did you have a good visit with your family?"

"Yes, it's always good to go home to Goodwill. Living is still simple and easy in the South."

"You look happy, Kenneth. What's your secret?"

"My parents," Kenneth said, smiling to himself.

"Your parents? I don't understand."

"They do what all good parents do. They try to raise their children to new levels of understanding."

"They must be very proud of you, Kenneth."

"More importantly, they love me unconditionally. However, you didn't ask me to come here to discuss life in Goodwill, Summer County, South Carolina. I've gone over the proposal that my company submitted and I have been unable to determine where there might be any problems."

"Oh, uh, that. Uh, that can wait," he said dismissively with a wave of his hand. "Let's order lunch."

The Judge buried his face in his menu, but occasionally he looked up and furtively scanned the dining room. Kenneth decided what he was going to order for lunch and sat patiently waiting for the Judge to make his selection. The Judge was taking an extraordinarily long time, Kenneth thought, as he checked his watch a few times. Finally, the Judge, apparently, saw what he was looking for, but it wasn't on the menu.

"JeNelle, how are you, my dear?" the Judge asked, with a broad, warm smile as he rose from the table. "You look lovely."

Kenneth's stomach took a high dive. Without warning, there she was at his side. He looked at the Judge and then JeNelle, before he got to his feet.

"Kenneth," JeNelle said slowly narrowing her eyes, her heart doing a fast fox trot, "this is a pleasant surprise. I didn't know that you were in town." As Kenneth's body unfolded, she marveled again at how devastating handsome he was. His mere presence sent her senseless.

"Uh, hello, JeNelle. Uh, I just flew in a few hours ago. Judge Worthington asked me to stop by on my way back to San Francisco. We're discussing the overhaul of the state judicial computer network." He felt awed by her presence. She was so beautiful, so alluring. He wanted to devour her cinnamon-colored mouth in his, rake his fingers through her silky, bronze hair, taste her… He blinked, fighting the tightening in his tailored slacks.

JeNelle looked at Johnston and Johnston looked away. "Well, Kenneth, Johnston asked me here for a drink. I'm meeting Paul Garrett here for lunch."

"Why don't you sit down, JeNelle?" Johnston asked, quickly pulling out a chair for her. She looked at him as she was seated.

The Judge looked away from her and motioned for the waiter. "A bottle of Au Bon Climat, Chardonnay '92 or '93, please," the Judge said, as the waiter approached then turning back to JeNelle and Kenneth. "Well, isn't this a coincidence. I must have completely confused my calendar. I really must be getting up in years." The Judge chuckled nervously.

Kenneth and JeNelle just sat back in their seats and looked at Johnston. They both wondered whether the Honorable Judge orchestrated this accidental-on-purpose meeting, but neither broached the topic.

"Oh, excuse me for a moment, please," the Judge said, rising from the table, "I need to speak to Judge Milton over there for a few minutes."

Kenneth rose from the table as the Judge left. When he sat down again, JeNelle was smiling at him.

"Kenneth, do you have the same impression that I do that something's afoot here?"

"I'm beginning to believe that the Honorable Johnston White Worthington is a sly old fox," Kenneth answered.

"I had nothing to do with this subterfuge. I'm as surprised as you are."

"I believe you, but I don't understand why Johnston has gone to the trouble to arrange this rendezvous."

"He's been acting strangely since the night of the Gala. He's been pumping me for information about you. I thought that he was just evaluating you and your company for the work that the judges need to have done on their intrastate court network, but I'm beginning to believe that he had something else in mind. What that is, I haven't got a clue."

"That newspaper article about us still has a lot of people talking, including my parents."

"I know," she said almost sadly. "My parents and friends won't let it rest either." She looked away from his warm eyes. "I called your office last week and Sara told me that you were in Washington visiting your sister. Then I spoke with Gloria and she said that Vivian seemed to have been ill. How is she doing?"

"Vivian and her fiancée broke off their long-term relationship. She was going through a very bad time. She's much better now. Why did you call me?"

JeNelle couldn't think of a plausible explanation. She couldn't tell him the truth. That she just wanted to hear his voice. Wanted to know what he was doing. Fortunately, she didn't have to explain her uncharacteristic behavior.

The waiter brought a telephone to the table.

"Mr. Alexander, there's a telephone call for you."

"Thank you," Kenneth said, with some surprise. "Hello."

"Samson."

"Oh, hello."

"You must not be able to talk right now."

"That's right."

"Are you with JeNelle?"

"Yes, but why do you ask?"

"Just curious about whether she's won the match."

"It's not what you're thinking."

"Well, that's good news. I've decided that if Samson won't come to Delilah, then Delilah will simply have to come to Samson."

"I don't understand."

"I'll be at the San Francisco Airport to pick you up. What time are you getting in?"

"Uh, I need to go straight to the office. I've been away for nearly two weeks. Can we reschedule for later next week?"

"Remember, Kenneth, I'm doing this for you. If Benjamin finds out that you're with JeNelle, he might not be as easily dissuaded the next time."

"I see your point. All right, I should be there around 7:00 P.M. I'll let you know if my plans change."

"That's better. I'll see you then."

Kenneth hung up. His mood changed. He didn't like the emotional blackmail game that Lisa was playing. He liked even less the uncomfortable feeling that she might be having him watched. It was too much of a coincidence that he would be sitting with JeNelle in a Santa Barbara restaurant at the very moment that she called.

"Kenneth, is something wrong?"

"Uh, no, JeNelle," he said, shaking off his concerns for the moment.

She wasn't convinced. She saw the expression on his face. "Benny tells me that you've been dating Lisa Lambert."

Kenneth's stomach did another high dive.

"I saw a few pictures in the newspaper of you two with the Governor at a Manufactures Association's dinner and you two are the talk of the business community these days."

"How is Benny? I haven't spoken with him this week."

"I'm sure he's fine. He seems to have been very busy since he got back from Goodwill. We've only talked on the telephone a few times."

"I'm sure he'll be getting himself back on track soon, JeNelle. Be patient with him."

"Kenneth James Alexander, how many times do I have to tell you that your brother and I are not involved?" she bristled.

Her reaction took Kenneth by surprise. He was about to follow up, but Paul Garrett came to the table.

"Oh, Paul, you remember Kenneth Alexander, don't you?" JeNelle asked, as she rose from her seat.

Kenneth rose as well and shook Paul's hand.

"Oh, yes, Kenneth, we met at the Expo in San Francisco," Paul said.

"Yes, Paul, I do remember. Garrett Printing and Engraving, isn't it?" Kenneth asked.

"Yes, you have a good memory. I've been reading good things about CompuCorrect. I'm glad to see another brother doing so well."

"Thank you, Paul."

"Well, JeNelle, our table is ready. It was good to see you again, Kenneth. Keep up the good work," Paul said.

Kenneth shook Paul's hand again before he turned away to escort JeNelle to their table directly across the room.

Judge Worthington returned to the table with Kenneth and sat down. He looked sheepishly at Kenneth. Kenneth sat back in his chair, folded his arms across his chest, and waited for an explanation.

"Now, don't be angry with me," Johnston said, noticing Kenneth's demeanor.

"What are you up to? There was nothing wrong with CompuCorrect's proposal, was there?"

"No, the proposal sailed through without a hitch. Your company did an excellent job and everyone is pleased with the plan."

"Then why did you get me here? And this had better be good."

"I know that this is presumptuous on my part, but I've known JeNelle Towson for some time now. She's like a daughter to me. I'm sure that you'll agree that she's a wonderful, bright, and enchanting woman. She's a dynamic businesswoman and she works hard. She simply doesn't give herself a break. She doesn't take any time to be just a woman again—"

"Johnston," Kenneth impatiently interrupted.

"Please, Kenneth, just hear me out."

Kenneth relented.

"The night of the Gala, JeNelle was radiant. I have never seen her so happy, so alive, and I haven't seen that same sparkle since, until today, when she saw you here. You should have seen your own face, too, Kenneth. It's obvious to me that you two feel something for each other. JeNelle deserves to be happy and excited about life again and I think that you do that for her and that she does that for you. I had to see whether I was right and now I'm sure that I am."

Kenneth held up his hand, silencing Johnston. "You don't understand. JeNelle is involved with my brother, Benjamin. This little rendezvous that you've arranged has put us both in an awkward position."

"I've talked with JeNelle about her relationship with your brother. I'm convinced and she has confirmed that there's nothing going on there but friendship. However, you mean something more to her than your brother does."

"Have you met my brother yet? If not, you need to know that he's a fine man and he's crazy about JeNelle." He didn't know whether to be angry, amused or intrigued by what Johnston was saying, so he just listened.

Johnston's pale-blue eyes looked solemn to Kenneth. "Your brother isn't what JeNelle needs in her life. She's had the fast-paced, razzle-dazzle kind of existence and it nearly got her…I can't go into all of the details, but I can tell you that JeNelle was an aspiring young pianist, a virtuoso, at the Julliard School of Music in New York. She went to dinner at an Italian restaurant with some friends of hers after one of her recitals one night. Michel San Angeloe, a wealthy man, much older than JeNelle, spotted her and arranged to pay the tab for everyone in her party. He was infatuated by her beauty and began this whirlwind romance with her. She was only seventeen, first time away from home, very little of life's experiences. In sum, she was just a beautiful, talented and bright teenager. This man showered her with gifts and flowers every day, just like your brother does. Four months later, they were married and two years later, they were divorced. JeNelle suffered a great deal as a result of that experience and she does not need to be reminded of that period in her life. She has not dated seriously since then. Apparently, your brother has been waging an all-out campaign for JeNelle's attention. She likes your brother, as a friend, but his approach to her is reminiscent of the beginning of her relationship with Michel San Angeloe. I don't want to see her suffer any more pain and disappointment."

Kenneth listened, a myriad of thoughts and emotions tangling and then something came to mind. "The night of the Gala, I saw you in, what appeared to be, a heated argument with three men who were talking with JeNelle. Was that related to her former husband?"

"Yes it was and JeNelle was very shaken by the experience. She's a strong woman, Kenneth, but she needs someone in her life who loves her not just because of her beauty, but in spite of it. Someone who's solid and dependable. Not that your brother isn't a nice guy, but I don't think that your brother is the person for JeNelle." He paused searching Kenneth's face thoughtfully before he spoke again. "I'm convinced that you are that person. I could see it the night of the Gala. You two were pure magic!"

Kenneth looked into Johnston's face. There was such compassion there. It reminded him of his feelings as he held Vivian after her abortion. Johnston looked away toward the window and stared blankly with his head resting on the palm of his hand.

"No one should ever be in so much pain," he said, still staring out of the window.

Kenneth glanced at the table where JeNelle and Paul were sitting and caught JeNelle looking at them. She quickly averted her eyes.

"I'm not sure what it is that you want me to do. I consider myself a friend of JeNelle's. I can talk with my brother and suggest that he tone down his advances, but I won't interfere beyond that."

"You two will be working very closely together over the next year on the Governor's Blue Ribbon Panel. Perhaps you could spend more time together doing things that aren't related to your tasks. JeNelle told me how much she enjoyed touring San Francisco with you. She actually giggled a few times. Something about a big floppy hat."

It wasn't just the hat, he reminisced to himself. *It was JeNelle and how adorable she was—and still is,* he thought, glancing at her quickly. His gut tightened at the thought of her with any other man, including his brother. He had to rein in his emotions though. Benny was falling in love with her even if she was not ready to accept Benny's affection now, that didn't mean that she never would.

"Do you understand what you're asking of me? I love my brother. He's my best friend. You're asking me to spend time with the woman who he says he loves. My brother is exceptionally bright and he's usually a reasonable and understanding man, but even I couldn't justify this to him. And what about JeNelle? She might misunderstand my spending so much time with her. And what about me? I'm involved with someone, too. No, Johnston, I don't think that this is a good idea at all."

"You think about it, Kenneth. As I said before, I know that this is very presumptuous on my part, but you're a very resourceful man. I'm sure that you'll find some way to handle this situation."

Johnston signaled for the waiter and they ordered lunch. Kenneth barely touched his food. He was too deep in thought and the sight of JeNelle in the same room was too disconcerting. Something akin to jealously gripped him as Paul Garrett reached across the table and took JeNelle's hand in his.

"JeNelle, have you heard a word that I've been saying?"

"Oh, I'm sorry, Paul. I've got something on my mind. What were you saying?"

"You've got *someone* on your mind. You've been starring at Johnston Worthington and Kenneth Alexander since we sat down. Now, what's going on?"

"Nothing, Paul. Let's get back to the discussion about the new brochures for INSIGHTS. I like what you did on the layouts. The colors were very clear and vivid. I think that I'll start with 1,000 and see how that goes and then—"

"JeNelle, I delivered five thousand of those brochures to you a week ago, remember? You said that you wanted to talk about the new line of art that you bought at the Expo in San Francisco."

"Oh, oh, that's right. I don't know where my mind is today."

"Still on Kenneth Alexander, I see."

"Why would you say that? Kenneth Alexander and I are just barely acquainted."

"JeNelle, remember me? I'm the man who tried to take you out for lunch or dinner while we were in San Francisco at the Expo. I'm also the man who has been trying for months to take you out since we've been back in Santa Barbara. Remember me? I was in San Francisco at the Expo and at the Gala when you received the 'Woman of the Year' award. In all of the time that we've been meeting over business matters, you've never once looked at me the way that I've seen you look at Kenneth Alexander."

"You're wrong. Kenneth is seeing someone, a business acquaintance of mine."

"Oh, you mean Lisa Lambert, the Black Ice Queen. Yeah, I've seen the pictures in the newspapers of them together at various social events. She's attractive all right, but you make her look like last year's news."

"You're sweet, but Lisa is a very attractive and formidable woman. She and Kenneth make a very handsome couple. Lisa just has a unique style about her."

"Don't get me wrong, JeNelle. I respect Kenneth Alexander. The brother's on the one, up front—honest type. A good business head on his shoulders, but Lisa Lambert is a whole nother breed of animal. Remember, I was her escort for the Gala. She was on a mission and Kenneth Alexander was the target. She locked her sights on him all evening long, but he clearly had you on his agenda. He barely knew that she or anyone else was in the room, but whatever Lisa wants, Lisa gets. Believe me when I tell you that, in this case, I wish her well with Kenneth. Maybe then you'll go out with me."

"You've been a good friend and I really like the work that we've done together. I've been telling everyone that I know that Garrett Printing and Engraving is the best kept secret in town—"

"Here comes the *'but'* part."

"Yes, Paul, *but* I haven't made room in my life for social affairs."

"I'm not interested in a one-night stand with you, although at this point, I'll take whatever time you want to give me. No, I'm looking for something with some substance to it. You know, spending some quality time, getting to know each other."

"You're a very handsome man. Charming, witty, and you have a great sense of humor—"

"However, my name isn't Kenneth Alexander."

"Let's just get back to the business at hand. What have you come up with for the art layouts?"

"You can run, but you can't hide. I'm going to keep asking you out until we're both old and grey, but here's how I see the art work layouts...."

She had a hard time keeping her mind on business that day at lunch with Paul. In her view, Kenneth's presence in the restaurant filled the room. She lamented the fact that Kenneth and Lisa apparently were involved in an intimate relationship. She knew Lisa well. She was cunning and relentless when they played racquetball together. Focused on her objective and goal-oriented. If Lisa had set her sights on Kenneth, she knew that Paul was right. It would be game, set, and match. Advantage, Lisa.

After lunch with Johnston, the limo dropped Kenneth at the Santa Barbara airport. He started toward his departure gate, changed his mind, and took his cell phone from his pocket.

"Benny, this is Kenneth. Are you busy today?"

"No, Stacy and I just got back from her doctor's office, why, K.J.?"

"Meet me at the airport in San Diego. I'm taking the shuttle now. I should be there in about an hour."

"What's up, K.J.? Is something wrong?"

"I'll tell you when I see you."

He hung up and dialed another number. The voice mail came on.

"Lisa, I apologize, but I've had another change in my plans. I won't be in until much later tonight. I'll call you next week."

He hung up, changed his reservation to San Francisco, and bought a ticket for the shuttle to San Diego.

Benny was waiting for Kenneth at the shuttle gate. They embraced and Kenneth led Benny by the arm to a secluded area of the airport.

"Whoa, brother, what's going on?" Benny asked.

"Are you in love with JeNelle Towson?" Kenneth asked straightforwardly.

Benny's eyes bunched into a quizzical smile. "It's not that cut and dry, K.J. I mean, I want to be with her.... She's very special. She's not just someone—"

"Benjamin, either you're in love with JeNelle or you're not!" Kenneth said sternly.

Benny studied his brother's expression before he answered. "Yes, I think I am. Why? What's this all about, Kenneth?" he asked without expression.

"What about Stacy? How do you feel about her?" His impatience was showing.

"We're good friends and lovers, but I've told you that before. Is this about Mom's and Dad's belief that I'm in love with Stacy?"

"No, Benny, it's about JeNelle and you."

"What about us, K.J.? You're acting real strange. What is it?"

Kenneth handed a card to Benny. "This is Judge Johnston Worthington's telephone number in Santa Barbara. You call him and arrange to meet with him as soon as you can. Tomorrow, if possible. If you love JeNelle, you'll listen to what this man has to say."

"A judge? What does this have to do with me and JeNelle?"

"Judge Worthington will explain it to you. I've got to go. I'm on the next flight to San Francisco."

"But, K.J., I don't understand what's going on."

"You will. I love you, Benny."

Kenneth walked quickly toward the departure gate for his flight to San Francisco. Benny stood holding Judge Worthington's business card in a state of confusion.

It was dark when Kenneth's flight landed at the San Francisco Airport and he was weary. He caught a taxicab and leaned his head back against the headrest as he was driven through the streets. His father's words came back to him, *You carry too much of the burden for your brothers and sisters. You have to live a little for yourself.* How could he do that when he had just given up any chance to be with the one woman he could love? Initially he planned to tell Benny how he felt about JeNelle, but when Benny admitted that he loved her, he couldn't bring himself to do it. No matter how he felt about her, he would never compete with his brother for JeNelle's love. It just wasn't to be. Now he had to let go and get on with the rest of his life.

It was nearly 9:00 P.M. when he reached his office, but the lights were still on and Tom's car was still parked in the lot next to Kenneth's van. Tom was sitting at his desk, resting his face on his hands, but looked up when Kenneth walked in. Mountains of papers were everywhere.

"Kenneth, what are you doing here?" Tom asked, as he suddenly stood.

"I could ask you the same question, Tom. It's after nine."

"Well, as you can see, I'm trying to catch up on a few details, but I'm getting nowhere fast."

"Then get out of here and go home or to a movie, or to a club and party. Call Shirley, maybe she'll go with you."

Tom looked dejected. "Shirley had a date tonight. She left early."

Kenneth felt sorry for Tom. "Then let's go have a drink or something, Tom."

Tom looked up. His green eyes had no sparkle, but he managed a slight smile.

"Pardon me, Kenneth. You're cute, but you're not my type. I like my companions a little less hairy and a lot less muscular."

Kenneth laughed. "You don't trip my trigger either, Tom. Let's go anyway. It's late and tomorrow is another day."

Tom grabbed his coat and briefcase, and shuffled out of his office. They went to a local sports bar and had a sandwich and a beer. Kenneth insisted that they not talk about business, but just enjoy a boys' night out. They had a few good laughs and talked about sports, politics, and the price of butter in China. Afterwards, Kenneth walked Tom to his car. As Tom got in, he rolled down his window. Kenneth leaned in.

"Don't worry, Tom. I have it from an unimpeachable source that you'll have your chance with Shirley," Kenneth said, with a smile and a wink.

Tom's green eyes widened and his jaw dropped. "How? What? Kenneth, who told you?"

"Good night, Tom," Kenneth said, with a smirk as he got into his van, started the engine, and drove away.

Kenneth pulled into his driveway. As he got out of his van, he smelled smoke coming from one of the chimneys of his house. He went inside and saw logs still burning in the living room fireplace. He put down his luggage and briefcase in the vestibule and hung up his overcoat. As he passed the dining room, he saw the table set for two with the candles still burning. He took off his jacket, loosened his tie, and unbuttoned his shirt at the neck. As he proceeded to his bedroom, he saw the glow of many candles through the partially opened door. He slung his jacket over his shoulder, leaned against the doorjamb, and slowly pushed the door open.

"Samson, I was beginning to think that you'd never get here," Lisa said, smiling, seductively reclining in a suggestive position on Kenneth's bed. She poured two glasses of champagne.

Kenneth didn't speak a word, but his body betrayed him. He felt free of JeNelle at last. He had made the right decision. He laid his jacket on a chair, removed his tie, loosened the French cuffs and buttons on his shirt, unbuttoned the fly on his slacks, slipped out of his shoes, removed his slacks and his socks, and removed his watch. Watching Lisa with longing and purpose in mind, this time he would satisfy himself. As he undressed, she smiled ever so broadly as he removed each piece of clothing. No matter what her agenda was, Lisa was there for him and he needed and wanted to be there for her. He would not hold back. Standing over her, he took the champagne glasses from her hands, and slowly poured them one by one over her nude body. Lisa moaned with delight as he licked the champagne from her breasts, her navel and her thighs. *No more JeNelle Towson,* he promised himself. In that moment, as he covered Lisa's body with his, he wished that it were JeNelle in his bed.

In the early morning, Kenneth showered and was dressed, standing before his full-length mirror, putting on his tie when Lisa awoke. The candles were mere memories of their former lives. The magnum of champagne was turned upside down in the ice bucket beside the bed and the champagne glasses lay on their sides on a nightstand. Lisa slowly tried to lift her head from the pillow, but couldn't. She blew the hair out of her eyes when the muscles in her arms would not respond. She tried to roll over, but her body went limp. She gave up and slumped against the mattress. She was spent.

"Good morning. How do you feel?" Kenneth cheerfully asked, as he straightened his tie and reached for his suit jacket.

"Like Delilah after Samson," she groaned, trying to summon the energy to move.

"Well, Delilah, I have just what you need to get your strength back." Kenneth brought a breakfast tray to the bed. "Hot coffee, warm croissant, and frozen melon balls."

"How appropriate," she quipped, dryly. "What time is it, Kenneth?" She struggled to sit up in bed and accept the breakfast tray.

"About 6:00 A.M."

"Six o'clock in the morning?" she groaned. "And you're already dressed?"

"And out the door," he added, quickly kissing her on the forehead and grabbing his watch. He headed for the bedroom door and then turned. "Ah, Lisa, I think that you already know that you don't have to lock the door when you leave. It's always open."

He smiled, winked, and closed the bedroom door behind him.

Chapter 27

"Well, JeNelle," Johnston said at a reception at his palatial estate in Montecito, "I've been hearing some extraordinary things about Kenneth Alexander, but since I've been working with him closely over the last few months I'm totally impressed with him and his company. He seems to be well respected in a lot of circles not only for his business acumen, but also for his integrity and his skill as a professional industrial engineer."

"This is not news and you know it," she said and laughed. "You probably had your contacts check him out from A to Z."

Johnston laughed, too. "I did and he comes up aces! So what have you two got going on?"

"Not a thing, Johnston Worthington, and you stop trying to play cupid. I don't think that a state Supreme Court judge would go over very well in pink tights and you're certainly no angel," JeNelle said, laughing.

"I think that you're smitten with Mr. Kenneth J. Alexander and he is with you."

"Not likely or haven't you been reading the society pages lately? Kenneth's one of the most eligible bachelors in California and number one on a lot of women's top ten list, but Lisa Lambert is on the top of his list—not me, so stop trying to make something out of nothing. Besides, as you can see my escort tonight is Benjamin Alexander."

"JeNelle Towson, remember who you're talking to now. I've seen you when there was no fire in your eyes. I've watched you build a small business into a Santa Barbara icon. I know everyone in this town and you're one of the most respected business and community leaders around. I know when I see this new light in your eyes that Kenneth Alexander is the reason for it. You don't shine like that for his brother."

"The flame is out, Johnston," she deadpanned.

"We'll see about that," Johnston said assuredly. "In the meantime, what do you want to do about Michel San Angeloe?"

"Nothing. He hasn't bothered me recently. I spoke with his uncle, Milo San Angeloe, and told him that Michel has been harassing me. Milo assured me that Michel would not bother me again."

"Michel has ignored his family's warnings before. He's very rich and powerful, JeNelle. He has the resources to do virtually anything that he wants to. You could put a stop to this tyranny and harassment. Just say the word and I'll have the US Attorney bring Michel San Angeloe up on criminal charges and reopen the case on civil grounds."

"No, Johnston, please. I don't want to have to relive that era of my life. It's over and done."

"You're making a big mistake, JeNelle. Michel isn't going to stop trying to get you to come back to him. From what I know of that man, he's ruthless and relentless, but I'll abide by your decision…this time. I do believe that you'll regret your decision one day."

"Thank you, Johnston. You've been a good friend."

"Now about Benjamin Alexander."

"What is it with all of these questions?"

"I'm interested in your welfare."

"You and my parents ought to get together and form a committee for the preservation of the social order. Just because I'm thirty and unmarried doesn't mean that the whole societal structure is about to collapse. When being single and thirty becomes a problem for women, I'll recommend that they seek counseling from your committee."

* * *

JeNelle didn't see Kenneth again until the first meeting of the Governor's Blue Ribbon Panel on Youth in Business and Industry in May in Sacramento. The Panel consisted of representatives from both large and small businesses. There were both men and women represented on the Panel and people from all major ethnic groups.

Kenneth's was the first face that she looked for as she entered the crowded room. When he finally arrived, he shook hands with the other Panel members and they all took seats around the large conference tables.

"JeNelle, isn't that Kenneth Alexander over there?" Florence Ewing asked.

"Yes, Florence, don't you know him?"

"No, but I sure would like to. Look at the body on that man!"

"Yes, he does look nice in his clothes."

"It's what's in his clothes that I'm thinking about. He could press my grapes anytime he had a notion! Uh, JeNelle, weren't you two an item some time ago?"

"No, we're just friends. I stayed at his home during the Small Business Expo in San Francisco back in the winter and he was my escort, by default, at the Santa Barbara Chamber of Commerce Gala."

"How is he in bed?"

"We weren't intimate."

"What's wrong with you? You stayed at his house and you didn't taste the fruit?"

"We're at this conference to talk about the Governor's Youth in Business and Industry Program and your wine bottling company in the Napa Valley is going to play a major role in helping young people in that region of the state learn about your industry."

"Everyone here knows that this program was your idea and that you've let the Governor and Lisa Lambert take the credit for it. I'll get serious when we start this meeting, but right now, I'd like to get busy with that Kenneth Alexander. Are you sure that you can't give me any details on his pillow talk?"

"I haven't got a clue. Ask Lisa. They've been seeing each other. Maybe she can fill you in."

"I'm a woman lusting after a man's body. Lisa's not going to tell me jack about Kenneth Alexander."

"Not that I know anything, but I'm a woman. What makes you think that I'd tell you anything?"

"You and I have known each other since you joined the Business and Professional Women's League over five years ago. You never once treated me in any way other than as a colleague and as a friend. The fact that I'm white never was an issue to you. That's why you were elected President of the Santa Barbara Chapter and for the very same reason you're going to be elected California State Business and Professional Women's League President. You've practiced what Doctor King preached. You've judged people by the content of their character and not by the color of their skin. You treat everyone as if they have no color. You have dealt fairly and equitably with everyone no matter whom or what they were. Because of your leadership, we have more women from other ethnic groups as members and officials. That's an accomplishment that we have all been proud of."

"I'm still not going to make Kenneth Alexander the new girls' locker room gossip, Florence. I have a lot of respect for him."

"I've read some articles recently about him and his company. He's well respected by his peers. My company is talking to him about redesigning our internet network to beef up our security system. Everyone says that he's done some very creative and impressive work for the Presidio and for the San Francisco County school and library systems. My husband said that CompuCorrect did an excellent job on the judicial intrastate network, too. Floyd's law firm can actually find cases now without sending a legion of paralegals over to the court house to do the research manually."

"And what would Floyd think about you lusting after Kenneth Alexander? Floyd's a very good criminal attorney, you know."

"Yeah, but what he lacks in his bedside manner is criminal and he leaves a lot to be desired."

"I don't want to know about your sex life with Floyd."

"What's to know? It's rated 'G' for general audiences. Invite the kids, bring the dog, the grandparents, too. That's about how exciting it is, but now if Floyd looked like that Kenneth Alexander, I could get real creative with him and some powdered sheets!"

JeNelle laughed. "Control yourself. Remember you're a happily married woman with two wonderful children and a husband who thinks that the sun rises and sets on you."

"There must be something wrong with your hormonal system. Have you had it tuned lately? I'll bet you lunch that if I took a poll of every woman on this Panel, Kenneth Alexander would be at the top of every woman's 'TO DO' list. You've got to admit that the man has sex appeal."

"I've told you, Florence, Kenneth is a friend of mine and I respect him."

"Then introduce me to him. I'll find out whether he can respect me in the morning—not that I'd give a damn if he didn't!"

"I'm not going to contribute to the delinquency of an adult." She chuckled. "If you want to meet him, then there he is, but I'd suggest that you not try to walk over Lisa to get to him. I know that she plays a mean game of racquetball and she has a lethal backhand."

The governor opened the conference with a broad outline of what he expected the Panel to accomplish over the next year. During the conference, which lasted three days, Lisa had monopolized most of Kenneth's time.

"Kenneth, I have barely had an opportunity to say hello to you," JeNelle said, standing beside him.

"How are you, JeNelle?" he asked neutrally.

"I'm fine. How have you been? I haven't seen you since the Judge arranged that accidental-on-purpose meeting between us."

"Busy as usual. I hope that the computer system that we installed is working out well."

"Yes, Juan has done an excellent job and—"

"The meeting will come to order," Lisa said.

She and Kenneth took their seats and did not speak to each other again.

On the final day of the first conference, Kenneth and Lisa entered the conference room last. Lisa immediately called the meeting to order and worked out assignments for the Panel members. They broke up into groups of five. JeNelle and Kenneth were in the same group. He didn't look at her as she spoke, but she was looking at him as he outlined his thoughts on their topic of discussion. JeNelle couldn't understand why he seemed to be so distant, so cool, toward her. He was behaving as if they had never met. She felt a sense of loss and hurt.

As she was leaving the conference room, she saw Lisa wrap herself in Kenneth's arms and kiss him very passionately. Her disappointment grew as she saw Kenneth holding Lisa. He had treated her distantly and she tried desperately to put Kenneth out of her mind, to stop having those dreams and amorous feelings about him. He was clearly having a love affair with her friend and business associate, she kept telling herself. It didn't help the ache.

Chapter 28

"It's a girl!" Benny yelled, pulling off the green scrubs and rushing into his mother's arms. "I told you, Mom," he said, lifting her off the floor in the waiting room of the military hospital. "Seven pounds, six ounces and twenty-two inches long!" he exclaimed. He was beaming with excitement for three o'clock in the morning.

"Congratulations, Son," Sylvia said, as he lowered her to the floor. "How is Stacy doing?"

"She's fine, Mom, and she handled it like a champ! She did call out a few words that questioned my heritage, but other than that, there were no complications. She's very tired and they're taking her to the recovery room. But you should see our daughter, Mom! She's beautiful! She has hair on her head and she's got the cutest smile…after she stopped screaming, that is. Her hands are so tiny, but she's already got fingernails and big feet just like mine."

Benny was flustered. He was ranting and flailing his arms as he talked.

"Sit down, Benjamin Staton, and take a few deep breaths," Sylvia said, smiling and guiding him to a chair.

"Mom, you just should have seen her. I watched her head come out. They didn't even have to use forceps and they let me cut the cord. She's just so beautiful. She even opened her eyes after they cleaned her up and weighed her. Mom, do all babies have blue eyes? She was making such a racket that—"

"Put your head between your legs, Benjamin Staton," Sylvia calmly said. "That's right. Now take some deep breaths…. Good!"

Benny sat up and put his hands over his face. His eyes were red and watery. He took more deep breaths, sat back in the seat and put his arms around his mother, pulling her close to him. He thought about Stacy and the special times that they had spent together planning for the arrival of their daughter.

It had been a long, hot summer in San Diego. Stacy had blossomed early and could no longer wear her petite Navy uniform. She ordered larger ones, but before she had them for very long, they were too small. By the eighth month of her pregnancy, Stacy was huge. She could barely rise from a sitting position without assistance and her back ached as she tried to navigate around the small apartment that she rented just off the naval base. She had rejected Benny's pleas for her to move into his condo with him.

On almost a daily basis, he and Stacy would walk the short distance to the dock at the Naval Air Station. The Navy ships pulled in and out of the San Diego Bay port; the largest naval air station on the West Coast and the headquarters for the Navy's Pacific Fleet operation. Stacy would look at the communications arrays above the hulking vessels as they turned in all directions. Some of her former shipmates and officers waved to them as they departed for new voyages. Navy aircraft flew overhead and Stacy would tell Benny exactly what the communications officers on board the aircraft carriers far out at sea were doing. She had handled communications traffic for most of her career. They would walk through the naval base, no matter what the time of day or temperature, just to be near the things that she loved and so that she could feel a part of it all again. She was sad he remembered as the ships and aircraft disappeared from her view across the wide ocean.

Benny recalled that he was often away for days at a time and how he hated not being there with her. He had leased a van when Stacy was too large and uncomfortable to ride in his two-seater Mercedes Benz. He tried to spend nights with her as often as he could, but it was usually late in the evening when he arrived and early in the morning when he had to leave. His trips to Santa Barbara were few and far between. He was getting very little rest, but when he had mandatory crew-rest days, he and Stacy spent time alone sailing, going to the movies, or to the beach. They took advantage of the pool, spa, exercise equipment, and other amenities in Benny's building. They did some sightseeing like tourists do when they visit a new place. They spent a day at Balboa Park and listened to the 100-bell carillon as it chimed in the California Tower.

He smiled to himself as he recalled how he pleaded with Stacy to visit the San Diego Aerospace Museum and see the replica of Lindbergh's Spirit of St. Louis. As a compensation for her patience, he took her to the Maritime Museum to see the 1863 tall ship, Star of India. They both felt saddened by the animals caged at the San Diego Zoo. They ate dinner out often and took long midnight strolls when Stacy could not sleep. Whenever he could be there with her, he would cook meals. He was actually getting quite good at it and he made a mean tossed green salad with baked chicken slices.

They rented videos, played cards, backgammon or chess. They practiced Lamaze and he showered with Stacy loving the sight and feel of her rising belly. Her navel nearly disappeared. He washed her hair and rubbed her stomach with cocoa butter. When her breasts were full and ached, he placed cool towels on them. He slept with Stacy close to him with his hand on her large belly.

Having sex had become an interesting experience, but they discovered new and interesting ways to make it work. Stacy and now Whitney Ivy Alexander were the most important two people in his life.

Benny kissed his mother's forehead and smiled as he recalled how she flew to San Diego three days before Whitney arrived. Whitney was early. They were all sitting in Stacy's apartment and had just finished dinner. Stacy had risen from the table to waddle to the bathroom, but before she took her first step, she felt a pain that doubled her over. Fluid rushed down her legs and onto the floor. He had dropped the dishes, rushed to her and lifted her in his arms. Sylvia checked her pulse and timed her contractions all the way to the hospital. When they arrived at the hospital, Stacy's contractions were five minutes apart.

Benny didn't realize that tears were streaming down his face until Sylvia wiped them. "I'll be back," she smiled.

Sylvia had set up a conference call while Benny was in the labor room with Stacy. Sylvia returned and guided Benny to the telephone and instructed the operator to make all of the connections. Kenneth picked up first, then Vivian, and then Bernard, Aretha, and Gregory.

"It's a girl!" Benny yelled into the telephone, as he sat hugging his mother at the waist.

Everyone cheered as he gave them all the details. Vivian cried, but she assured them all that they were mostly tears of joy and not of sorrow. Benny talked so rapidly and so demonstratively that he was nearly out of breath. He managed to tell them all how much he loved them. Sylvia took the telephone from her son, as he buried his face in his hands.

"I thought Benjamin Staton was about to pass out when Stacy's water broke," Sylvia said chuckling, "but he did just fine. She was only in labor for nine hours and Benjamin Staton says that she's doing fine."

They all tried to talk at once and Sylvia had to calm them all down. They asked questions in rapid succession for more than thirty minutes. Finally, they knew as much as Sylvia could tell them. Kenneth said that he'd fly down to San Diego on the first available flight. Vivian begged to have scads of pictures of Stacy and Whitney sent to her by e-mail. Bernard, Aretha, and Gregory seconded that request and Sylvia agreed to comply as she rubbed her son's back and kissed him for all of them.

"Captain Alexander, you may see your daughter now," a male Navy nurse said, ushering him and Sylvia into an area outside of the nursery.

Benny sat in a chair and another nurse handed Whitney to him. He didn't speak for a while. He just looked at Whitney's tiny face as she slept in his arms. Sylvia peeked at Whitney over Benny's shoulder and rubbed his back.

"She's a beautiful little girl, Benjamin Staton," Sylvia said softly.

"I know, Mom. Just like her mother," he answered quietly.

Later that morning, Kenneth arrived at Benny's condo. His mother opened the door and he hugged her and lifted her off the floor.

"Kenneth James, you put me down!" she said, giggling.

Kenneth smiled and she cupped his face in her hands.

"You look better."

"I am better, Mom. The trip home was good for me. I'm looking forward to the holidays."

Benny came out of his bedroom and down the steps dripping wet with towels wrapped around his waist and shoulders. He hugged his brother tightly for a long time. When he released Kenneth, his clothes were damp, but Kenneth didn't care.

"So when do I get to see my niece?" Kenneth asked, with a broad smile.

"We just got home from the hospital, Kenneth James. Give us a few minutes to catch our breath. Nobody's had any sleep or any breakfast," Sylvia said.

"She's beautiful, K.J.," Benny said, with a broad, reverent smile.

"I know, Benny. I heard you the first hundred times that you told me." Kenneth grinned. "How is Stacy?"

"She was sleeping when we left the hospital. She should be awake later this morning. The hospitals usually have the mothers on their feet and in the shower shortly after the baby is born," Sylvia answered.

"You two look beat. Why don't you catch a nap and I'll make something to eat," Kenneth said.

Sylvia agreed and went into a spare bedroom to rest, but Benny was still too pumped up. He followed Kenneth into the kitchen and sat at the table by the sliding glass door. He stared out of the window and smiled. Kenneth made coffee and brought two cups to the table. He sat across from his brother.

"I've never felt anything like this before, K.J. I've got such a rush and I can't come down."

"I can tell, Benny. You should see yourself. I think that's going to be a permanent smile on your face."

Benny leaned back in his chair. Water was still dripping off his body.

"I love her, K.J.," Benny said looking out into the distance.

"Of course, you do. I haven't even seen her yet and I love her, too. It's only natural."

Benny turned his head toward Kenneth. "Natural?"

"Sure. She's yours. How could you not love her?"

"K.J., you don't understand. I'm talking about Stacy. I love her."

Kenneth smiled. "Of course you love her. She's your friend and the mother of the most beautiful baby girl ever born."

Benny narrowed his eyes. "I'm in love with Stacy. I want to be her husband, not just the father of our daughter."

Suddenly the full weight of what Benny was saying began to dawn on Kenneth.

"What is this, Benny, some kind of peek-a-boo romance? Now you see it, now you don't? When I met you at the airport months ago, you told me that it was JeNelle that you were in love with! Now you tell me that it's Stacy? Do you have a clue who it is that you're really in love with? Do you even know what being in love is?" he raged.

Benny looked away. "I've learned a lot about myself, K.J. I know that I haven't handled the truth very well, especially when it hurts. Life is about growth and sometimes growing up hurts. I never realized how fragile my ego was, until I met Stacy. I've always been eager to explore life and live it to its fullest, but we all have defense mechanisms that come into play when someone gives us another point of view that's contrary to the ones that we hold. Stacy does that for me. She forces me to grow up and to deal with the real world. I didn't want to deal with the fact that Stacy still wanted to have her freedom, the choice to see other men while we were together. Or the fact that I was not the only man who could satisfy her sexually or emotionally. Stacy operates on a different level though. She's always honest with me, but she's never condescending or denigrating. She tells me how much she values my opinion and our relationship. We worked on our platonic relationship first and that made it easy to work on all other aspects of our liaison.

"With other women I went from hello to where's my condom at 900 knots. Not with Stacy. We help each other reach for and achieve our goals. We talk about sensitive issues and give each other permission to give feedback even when we may not like what was being said. It's an unwritten agreement between us and we realize that our relationship has a purpose; not just something that we stumbled into and take for granted.

"When I got back after the Christmas holiday in San Francisco, Stacy tried to warn me that I was taking our friendship for granted. That I was focusing too much on our sexual bond. Even after I told her about JeNelle she suggested that we go back to having a platonic link. I wasn't willing to do that, but Stacy began to make herself scarce. She was taking on more difficult and challenging assignments. I had to support her views on what she was doing and the goals that she had set for herself. We have a powerful rapport because we could share each other's points of view even when they were vastly different. The only argument that Stacy and I have ever had was over whether to have Whitney. Even then, we gave each other permission to disagree.

"It wasn't about winning or losing. It was about sharing. I know a lot of women. They all have special qualities and talents, but you don't meet a Stacy Greene every day. We get below the surface and I like what I see there. We reached new heights and I like what I found there too. I love Stacy on more than just a sexual level, that's what I'm going to tell her today when I see her. I'm going to tell her that I'm in love with her and that I want her to marry me. I can't and I won't lose her. I won't let her go. I've been fooling myself that Stacy's decisions were hers alone to make. I'm a part of her and she knows it. She's been backing away to give me space. Well, I'm about to close that gap."

Kenneth slumped in his seat. There was now no doubt in his mind that Benny was deeply in love with Stacy just as his parents and Vivian had proffered. Still, was he also in love with JeNelle? Could a man be in love with two women at the same time? He shook off his troublesome questions. It wasn't his dilemma to solve and he knew that he had to stay out of Benny's life to save his own sanity. Whom Benny loved or didn't love was not his decision to make. He had his own life to contend with and Lisa.

Kenneth and Benny talked quietly together before Kenneth finally convinced Benny to rest. Then Kenneth went out onto the terrace to read the newspaper and have another cup of coffee. There, on the front page, was an article about the Governor's new Youth in Government and Industry program and a picture of the Governor with the Blue Ribbon Panel members. Kenneth noted, with mixed emotions, that he was standing next to Lisa and JeNelle stood apart from him on the other side of the Governor.

Kenneth looked at the picture closely. JeNelle was smiling. They all were. He remembered the first Panel meeting in May in Sacramento. JeNelle was the first face that he saw as he entered the crowded room. She looked more gorgeous than he had remembered. He shook hands with the other Panel members as they all began to take their seats around the large conference tables. He sat a distance away from JeNelle as Lisa called the meeting to order and the governor made his remarks.

During a break, Lisa approached him and monopolized most of his time. He saw JeNelle looking at them as they talked. During the noon break, the Panel received a catered lunch. He sat at a table with four other business people. He caught glimpses of JeNelle as she sat at another table. When the meeting broke up for the day, Lisa whisked him away. Later, as he and Lisa returned to the hotel after dinner, he spotted JeNelle in the lobby cocktail lounge sitting with other Panel members. JeNelle was watching them as he and Lisa entered the elevator and the doors closed.

That night he and Lisa made love, but knowing that JeNelle was in the same hotel, he ended their intimacy feigning a headache. It wasn't far from the truth. It was his heart that ached.

The next morning as he and Lisa were leaving his suite, JeNelle was leaving hers only a few doors away. The moments standing at the elevator while JeNelle and Lisa chatted were pure hell. On another day, he and Lisa sat at a table for two for breakfast in the hotel breakfast room, when he saw JeNelle enter carrying her briefcase and a newspaper. She did not approach them, but instead opted to sit alone in a distant part of the room. He noticed that she had a light breakfast and left. When he and Lisa approached the meeting room, several Panel members were milling around snacking on a continental breakfast. JeNelle was already seated at the conference table having coffee and talking with Panel members. She looked up when he and Lisa entered the room together and his gut wrenched. He put his briefcase on the conference table and went to one of the large coffee urns to get another cup of coffee. Then it happened.

"Kenneth, I've barely had an opportunity to say hello to you," JeNelle said, suddenly by his side.

"How are you, JeNelle?" he asked dryly not looking into her eyes.

"I'm fine."

"And your parents?"

"My mother is well, but my father is going to need heart by-pass surgery."

"When?"

"We're not sure yet."

"I like your parents very much. Let me know if there is anything that I can do."

"You've been so busy, Kenneth. I've been following your activities in the headlines."

"I'm never too busy if you or your parents need me."

"The meeting will come to order," Lisa had said.

He and JeNelle took their seats and did not speak to each other again throughout the day. That evening, as he and Lisa were dressed for a formal business event and getting into a chauffeured limousine, JeNelle and some of the other panel members were returning to the hotel. He felt JeNelle's eyes on them as they drove away.

On the final day of that conference, he and Lisa entered the conference room last. Lisa immediately called the meeting to order and worked out assignments for the panel members. The Panel broke up into groups of five and the luck of the draw had him and JeNelle in the same group. He could barely look at her as she spoke, but he knew that she was looking at him as he outlined his thoughts on the topic under discussion. He didn't want to embarrass Lisa in front of the Panel who all seemed to know that they were dating. He had to respect the relationship that they were developing even though it started out as a ruse to hide his attraction to JeNelle from Benny. Nevertheless, he wasn't the type of man to play around. Lisa was committing a lot of her time and attention to him and he would respect her even if in his heart, he knew that he was, without question, falling in love with JeNelle.

By five o'clock that afternoon the conference was over. Panel members were packing up their briefcases and shaking each other's hands. Lisa was talking with some of the Panel members, including JeNelle. When Lisa finished saying her goodbyes to the Panel members, they began to leave the room. He waited behind. JeNelle gathered her briefcase and approached him.

"It was good to see you again, Kenneth," she said, extending her hand.

"Take care of yourself, JeNelle, and give my best to your parents. Have a safe trip home."

JeNelle was leaving as Lisa approached him and kissed him on the lips. He shivered, but not from Lisa's kiss. Rather it was from the display of affection in front of JeNelle. The kiss made him feel uncomfortable. He'd rather have been kissing JeNelle.

"You did very well, Samson," Lisa said at the time, snaking her arms around his neck. "If I didn't know better, that cool act that you put on would have convinced even me."

He didn't answer her. His head was pounding. He eased out of her grasp.

"I've got a plane to catch. Do you want to have dinner before I go?" he asked a bit too testy for his own comfort.

"I can't tonight, Kenneth, but do you have to go back to San Francisco tonight? Couldn't you leave in the morning?" she cooed, rubbing his chest and kissing his neck.

He backed away from her. "No, I have appointments early tomorrow morning. I'll have to go tonight." He kissed her on the lips. "Until the next time, Delilah," he whispered.

The Blue Ribbon Panel met for three days each month all during the summer. He never changed his behavior toward JeNelle, although it was killing him to act so coolly toward her. He knew that it was for the best for all concerned. There would be many more three-day meetings before it was over.

As he sat on the terrace of Benny's condo, Kenneth prayed that he would continue to have the strength to get through them.

The telephone rang taking Kenneth's thoughts away from his pain, but only momentarily.

"Kenneth, is that you? This is JeNelle."

His heart lurched at the sound of her voice. "Good morning, JeNelle. Benny is taking a nap at the moment. Do you want me to wake him or have him call you when he gets up?"

There was a long pause. "Kenneth, are you angry with me about something?"

There was a note of concern in her voice. The question startled him. His heart was beating a fast rhythm. He tried to sound unemotional…cool.

"No, of course not."

"Then why have you been acting like we're complete strangers at the conferences?"

"The sessions have been very intense."

"I've seen you handle much more intense situations than these conferences have been. Are you sure that that's all that it is?"

"Yes. Now, should I wake Benny for you?" he clipped.

"No," she sighed. "Just let him know that I returned his call."

"Sure, JeNelle. I'll tell him when he wakes up."

Kenneth hung up the telephone and buried his face in his hands. Just hearing her voice on the telephone was unnerving, but it was Benny she wanted to talk with, not him.

"Still carrying that load for your brother, I see, Kenneth James," Sylvia said.

He had not heard his mother come onto the terrace. He tried to recover his composure. She sat down on the end of the chaise lounge where he was sitting.

"No, Mom. I've put it all behind me. Whatever happens between JeNelle and Benny is strictly between them. Dad was right. I have a life to live, too."

"Then you're not in love with JeNelle anymore?"

Kenneth didn't answer. He just looked into his mother's eyes.

"Uh huh, that's what I thought," Sylvia said knowingly, as she patted her son's face. "Well, where's that meal you promised me? It's nearly noon and I'm hungry."

Kenneth set the table on the terrace and then went to see whether Benny was awake. He was still sleeping, but Kenneth noticed that there were several more pictures of JeNelle in Benny's bedroom. He walked to the dresser, picked up one of them, and gazed at it for a while.

"Beautiful, isn't she, Kenneth?" Benny asked, as he awoke and found his brother standing in his bedroom.

"Yes, she is, Benny. She called you, but she didn't want me to wake you."

"Stacy says that I can tell JeNelle about Whitney now."

"How do you think she's going to handle it?"

"I don't know, but Johnston Worthington knows about me and Stacy and he agrees that I should tell her as soon as possible."

"Then you did meet with him?"

"Yes, the day after you told me to call him. He was surprised to hear from me, but he helped me to understand why JeNelle is reluctant to get involved with me. I haven't put any pressure on her since then. We've spent time together when it was convenient for her. It's been difficult while Stacy was carrying Whitney. Still, Johnston thought that the time was adequate. JeNelle's very happy for you and Lisa, though. She says that you two are always together."

Kenneth's heart beat faster. "We've been seeing each other, of course, but the relationship was becoming too much of a distraction. I've been juggling a lot of tasks. The Panel is taking up a lot more of my time than I thought it would. I've been on the road more than I've been in my office and we're working on plans for the next Expo." Kenneth tried to change the subject. "The company's expansion plan is completed. We have a lot more clients down here in the Southern part of the state. The staff in San Francisco has doubled. We're even looking at the possibility of opening a second office somewhere in this area."

"JeNelle thinks that you and Lisa might be falling in love. Is she right?"

Kenneth's head was beginning to pound. "I don't know, Benny. We haven't known each other very long and we haven't spent a lot of time together. But that's enough questions about me. Let's eat so that I can see my beautiful niece."

"I'll be there in a minute. I'm going to call JeNelle."

Kenneth closed the door behind him as he left Benny's bedroom and returned to the terrace where his mother was having lunch.

"JeNelle, would you come to San Diego tomorrow around three o'clock?"

"Why, Benny? What's going on?"

"There are some special people who I want you to meet."

"I think that I can arrange that. Aren't you going to give me any more details?"

"Oh no. Just meet me here at my place."

"Okay, Benny, I'll see you tomorrow."

They hung up and Benny made a number of other calls before he joined his mother and brother.

When Kenneth, Sylvia, and Benny arrived at the hospital, the nurse told them that Stacy was sleeping and suggested that they not wake her because she had not rested well. Benny ached to be with her, to tell her that he was in love with her, but they went to the nursery to see Whitney instead. The nurse led them into an anteroom and gave Whitney to Benny to feed. Sylvia began snapping pictures as Benny held his daughter in his arms. Kenneth took video pictures of the proud father and his daughter. They were there all afternoon until visiting hours were over. The nurse shooed them away before they could see Stacy, but she confirmed that Stacy received the flowers and balloons that Benny sent.

That evening they went to Michelangelo's for dinner and Benny pointed out the prominently displayed picture of himself and JeNelle. Kenneth recalled the conversation that he had with Johnston Worthington about Michel San Angeloe. The fact that JeNelle owned Michelangelo's and had once been married to Michel San Angeloe was intriguing, but not enough for him to delve into the situation further. Benny apparently didn't know that JeNelle owned the restaurant and he didn't feel compelled to tell him. Benny had done as Johnston had asked and Kenneth had not interfered.

The next day they arrived at the hospital at eleven o'clock in the morning to pick up Whitney and Stacy. When they entered Stacy's room, it was empty and the bed stripped. Benny approached one of the nurses.

"Nurse, where is Lieutenant Stacy Greene?" he asked. "She isn't in her room."

"Lieutenant Greene? She's gone, Captain Alexander. She left around 0800 this morning," the nurse answered.

Something as devastating as a shark attack grabbed Benny in the pit of his stomach.

"Gone?" Benny asked in disbelief. "What do you mean, she's gone? Where did she go?"

"I don't know, Captain," the nurse said, snapping to attention under his glare, "but your daughter is in the nursery waiting for you," she added timidly.

"At ease!" he barked.

"Yes, sir. Thank you, sir." The nurse saluted and scurried away.

Benny was stunned. The knot in his stomach tightened. He thought that his heart had stopped beating. He couldn't gather his thoughts. He didn't understand why Stacy would leave the hospital before he arrived. He went to a telephone and dialed the number at Stacy's apartment. His body tensed when the operator confirmed that the number had been disconnected. Then he dialed the number for her commanding officer.

"This is Captain Alexander, Commander Morris. I want a confirmation on whether Lieutenant Stacy Greene is on the base or in her quarters!"

"I can confirm that Lieutenant Greene is not on the base, Sir. She requested and received a transfer, Captain. She's currently on leave status, Sir."

"Where is she billeted, Commander?"

"I don't have that information, Captain. The orders came directly from Command at the Pentagon. Her current location and new duty station are classified by order of Admiral Gordon at the Office of the Joint Chiefs, Sir."

Benny hung up abruptly and called J.C. Baker at the offices of the Joint Chiefs of Staff.

"J.C., I'm trying to locate a Lieutenant Stacy Greene, Navy. She's under Admiral Gordon's command."

"Greene? Isn't that that fine young thing that you met here several years ago?"

"Yes, J.C., she's the same woman. Lieutenant Stacy Greene."

"Hold one, Benny," Baker said, as he keyed up the personnel records on his computer. He came back to the telephone. "She's classified, Benny. I can't access her without a higher security clearance. She must have some powerful connections."

"Can you get anything on her, J.C.?" he asked sternly, but anxiously.

"I'll try, Benny, but what's so important about one lieutenant? You must have a whole harem full of them out there in San Diego," he said, laughing.

"Just see what you can come up with, J.C. This is very important to me."

"All right, Benny, but this is going to take some time. This classification is so high up that maybe only the President can access it."

"Thanks, J.C. Get back to me as soon as possible when you've got something."

"Sure, Benny, but she must be a damn good lay, if you're this hot for her," he laughed.

"Damn it, J.C.! Just find her!" Benny said angrily and hung up the telephone.

Sylvia and Kenneth were standing beside him and tried to calm him. Benny tried to think of where Stacy might go. He knew that she was from Chicago, the old Cabrini Green area, but he didn't know where her family lived or any of her friends. He called Cecil and Janice at their offices, but they had not heard from Stacy and didn't know how he could reach her family. They didn't even know that she had already given birth. She had not talked about her family members by name or, if she had, he didn't remember them. He knew that she had graduated from the Naval Academy in Annapolis, Maryland. He searched his memory for any contacts that he had there.

"Come on, Benny," Kenneth said. "Let's get my niece home and then you can look for Stacy."

Benny reluctantly agreed and they went to the nursery. Sylvia spoke to the charge nurse.

"Has Lieutenant Greene been nursing Whitney Alexander?" Sylvia asked.

"No, ma'am," the nurse said, "she never saw the baby. She asked for a non-nursing room after Whitney was born."

They all looked at each other. Benny sat down and grabbed the back of his neck. His head was pounding.

"Why would she do that? Why didn't she even want to see our daughter?"

"Your daughter, Benjamin Staton," Sylvia said, gently, as she sat down beside her son and rubbed his back. "Remember, Stacy never wanted to have a baby. She told you that in no uncertain terms. She told me in Goodwill that she was going to have Whitney for you. That she couldn't raise your daughter, but that she wasn't going to deny you the opportunity to raise her."

"She sounds like quite a woman, Benny," Kenneth added, as he sat down next to his brother. "That's a hell of a special gift for one friend to give another. You're lucky to have a friend who cares enough about you to make that kind of a sacrifice."

Benny just sat there trying to sort out his thoughts, but his feelings kept getting in the way. That ache in his gut; that fear that he would not find Stacy. The fear that he might not ever see Stacy again.

"I know. Stacy's always been up front and honest with me."

The nurse brought Whitney wrapped and ready to go. They took Whitney home to Benny's condo. Kenneth held her in his arms while Sylvia prepared her bassinet and bottles. Benny went to Stacy's apartment.

When Benny arrived, the apartment door was unlocked. Everything was neat and tidy, but empty, except for the baby clothes, toys, and other things that they had purchased together over the last seven months. Attached to the huge bear, that he had insisted on buying, was a note addressed to him. He immediately opened it.

To Whitney Ivy Alexander's father and my best friend—

Only you, Benny, can be there now to hold Whitney when she cries as you have held me, to feed her when she's hungry, and to teach her in the ways that you learned as a child. She is the most precious gift that I can give to you, my dear friend. I know that you and your family will love and cherish her. Teach her to be an explorer just like her father and, most importantly, how to love family. I thank you for sharing your family with me. I will never forget them and you.

Stacy

Benny searched frantically everywhere in the apartment for any clue as to where Stacy might be. Finally, he sat down by the window and buried his face in his hands. The sense of loss was brutal. His fears were realized. She had walked away from him—from their child—from the love they should have shared together as a family. He could not imagine a sensation more painful than the knowledge that he might never see Stacy again. Images of them together flooded over him. He closed his eyes tightly, hoping to block out those images and to stop the pain. He had lost a part of himself and he knew that he would never be a whole person again without Stacy in his life.

Kenneth was enjoying every minute with Whitney. She was awake and moving her tiny hands as Kenneth began to tell her about her great-grandparents, her grandparents, her uncles, her aunts, her cousins, and their home in Goodwill, Summer County, South Carolina. Whitney dozed off a few times, but Kenneth continued to tell her the stories. He had just finished telling her about Gregory and Aretha when the doorbell rang. Kenneth got up with Whitney still in his arms to answer it.

His heart stopped beating when he opened the door.

"JeNelle, uh…uh, Benny's not here at the moment, but he should be back at any time…. uh, was he expecting you? Uh, I mean…. uh…. Come in…. "

JeNelle looked confused as she entered the condo and saw Kenneth holding a baby.

"Hi, Kenneth," she said slowly, "you and Lisa must have worked fast on this one," she said jokingly, still puzzled.

Kenneth laughed and flashed that million-dollar, polar-ice-cap-melting smile that she had missed seeing on his face.

"Oh, no. This is my niece, Ms. Whitney Ivy Alexander. Whitney, I want you to meet a friend of your dad's, Ms. JeNelle Elise Towson."

"Benny's daughter?" JeNelle asked, surprised.

"Yes, she's mine," Benny said, entering the condo carrying bags of baby things and a huge bear. "She's two days old today."

He was smiling, but Kenneth could sense that there must have been disappointing news about Stacy.

"So, Ms. Whitney is the special person that you wanted me to meet?"

"Yes, and my mother, Sylvia Benson Alexander," Benny said, as Sylvia appeared on the balcony and came down the steps. "Mom, this is JeNelle Elise Towson."

"It's a pleasure to meet you at last, JeNelle. Both of my sons have talked about you a great deal."

"And you too, Mrs. Alexander," she said, smiling. "They brag about you shamelessly. However, let me be among the first to congratulate you on your beautiful granddaughter. I know that you must be very proud and happy."

"I am, JeNelle, but please call me Sylvia. I feel as if I know you that well and I hope that we'll get to know each other even better."

"Thank you, Sylvia, I'd like that very much, but where is Whitney Ivy's mother? I'd like to congratulate her, too."

JeNelle saw a sudden sadness come over Benny's face.

"She's not here, JeNelle. It's just me and Whitney Ivy. And, of course, the rest of our wonderful family," Benny said, with his arm around his mother and looking at his brother.

Whitney started to whimper and Benny took her from Kenneth, kissed her, and checked her diaper.

"Okay, Ms. Whitney. Your dad's an old pro at changing diapers. Your aunts, Vivian and Aretha, and Uncle Gregory can tell you all about it when you meet them."

He took Whitney upstairs to the nursery next to his bedroom and Sylvia excused herself and followed with the camera. She had already taken scads of pictures and she was working on many more.

Kenneth and JeNelle were suddenly alone in the living room. The void between them was beginning to grow wider.

"Uh, can I offer you something to drink, JeNelle?" Kenneth asked, as he went to the wet bar.

"Yes, I think that I need a drink. A double, in fact."

JeNelle sat on a barstool.

"You like Amaretto, neat, don't you, JeNelle?"

"Yes, Kenneth. I'm surprised that you remembered," she said, with a hint of harshness in her voice.

He didn't comment, but he looked at her in the mirror as he poured a double Amaretto. He noticed that she was looking at him, too. Her beautiful face seemed full of concern and questions. He could not determine how she was taking the news about Whitney.

"Kenneth, why didn't you tell me about Whitney?" JeNelle asked, as he handed the drink to her.

"It was up to Benny to do that."

"We're friends too, aren't we, Kenneth?"

"Sure, JeNelle, but—"

"But nothing, Kenneth. You introduced me to Whitney as a friend of her dad's. I don't want to feel like I'm only Benny's friend."

JeNelle was clearly annoyed, he noted.

"I'm sorry, JeNelle. Of course we're friends, too."

Kenneth could not look at JeNelle. He turned his back to her and walked toward the terrace door. He looked out as he sipped his glass of wine. He could feel JeNelle's eyes on him, but he could not turn around to face her. He grabbed the back of his neck and stretched. He wanted her. He wanted her in his arms to kiss the worry from her face and tell her that he loved her, but he held back. He gritted his teeth. His temples were throbbing.

Benny came out of the nursery and stood at the railing overlooking the living room at Kenneth and JeNelle. Something was strange about the way they were avoiding contact with each other. He had not seen them together since the day that he picked her up in San Francisco and that had only been a brief encounter. Something about seeing them together now was curious.

"Would you excuse me for a moment, JeNelle?" he asked, as he came down the stairs. "My daughter has a healthy appetite."

"I'll do that, Benny," Kenneth said. "You should stay here and keep JeNelle company. Whitney is my niece. You've got a lifetime to feed her. I'll feed her now and again at 10:00 P.M."

"Oh, no, big brother. You got a chance to hold her all afternoon. It's my turn now," Benny said.

"No, you can give her that 2:00 A.M. feeding. She's all yours until 6:00 A.M. Then it's my turn again," Kenneth said.

"Why don't you take the 2:00 A.M. feeding and I'll take the one at 6:00 A.M.?" Benny asked.

"I'm the oldest and your big brother. I get to choose first," Kenneth said jokingly.

JeNelle was laughing at them arguing over who was going to do what with Whitney until Sylvia came onto the balcony holding Whitney and issuing her orders.

"Kenneth James, you feed Whitney now. Benjamin Staton you go to the store and get more milk and diapers. JeNelle, would you mind helping me prepare dinner?"

JeNelle was still laughing at Kenneth and Benny as they followed their mother's instructions.

"I'd love to help you, Sylvia," JeNelle said.

Kenneth positioned himself on the sofa with Whitney while Benjamin handed the bottle to him.

"Hold the bottle down a little more, K.J., so that she can see me while she's eating," Benny said.

"I know how to hold a bottle, Benny. I fed you, didn't I?"

"Yeah, and I probably couldn't see anything while you were holding me."

"You saw plenty—"

"Benjamin Staton! Kenneth James!" Sylvia scolded from the kitchen.

They both immediately continued on their appointed rounds. Benny kissed Whitney.

"I'll be back in a minute, Whitney. Uncle Kenneth will take care of you until I get back."

The brothers looked at each other and smiled.

Sylvia and JeNelle were talking as they prepared dinner. JeNelle made a fresh tomato, asparagus and onion salad and watched as Sylvia prepared Chicken Florentine. JeNelle microwaved large white baking potatoes, cored them, whipped the meat of the potato with sour cream, cream cheese, and chives and put the mixture back into the potato shells. She sprinkled sharp, grated cheese over top and put them back into the microwave ready to heat. Sylvia was watching her closely as she worked.

"You sure know your way around a kitchen, JeNelle," Sylvia commented approvingly.

"So do you. That Chicken Florentine looks like it's going to be delicious."

"I enjoy cooking for my family."

"You have quite a family. Benny and Kenneth are both fine men," JeNelle said, as she sipped her Amaretto.

"But you're not in love with Benny, are you?"

The question took JeNelle by surprise. She almost choked on her drink. She looked into Sylvia's eyes and felt comforted. She smiled. "No, Sylvia, I'm not in love with Benny and he's not in love with me."

The next question really threw JeNelle for a loop.

"Then, are you in love with Kenneth?"

JeNelle couldn't look Sylvia in the face. She blanched and took another sip of her drink and a deep breath. "I'm friends with both of your sons."

"Uh huh, I thought so," Sylvia said, satisfied.

They were all seated at the dining room table, including Whitney who seemed to be enchanted by the flickering candles on the table. Sylvia noticed that although they were all having a lively conversation, Kenneth never looked directly at JeNelle. Benny noticed it, too. When the telephone rang, Benny gave Whitney to Kenneth and got up to answer the telephone. He returned to the dining room.

"Kenneth, I think it's the lovely Lisa. She thought that I was someone called Samson. Need I ask who Delilah is?" Benny asked with a grin and a wink as he handed the telephone to Kenneth.

Sylvia looked at JeNelle's face and saw the light dim in her eyes as Kenneth took the call and went into the kitchen with Whitney still in his arms. Kenneth's conversation could still be faintly heard in the dining room.

"No, Lisa, I'm sorry I won't be able to make it. No, I'm spending some time with my family. We've had a new addition to the Alexander clan. Maybe three or four days. I'm not sure, why? Racquetball? Uh, no, Delilah, I have to conserve what little strength you've left me for my niece. I'll call you when I'm back in San Francisco. I'll see what I can do, Lisa, but I'm not going to make any promises that I don't intend to keep. No, Lisa, that's the best that I can do at the moment. Sure…next week. Goodbye."

Kenneth hung up the telephone and returned to the dining room with Whitney.

"So, Kenneth, is it true what they said about Delilah cutting off Samson's—"

"Benjamin Staton!" Sylvia interjected, sternly.

"I was going to say hair, Mom."

Kenneth didn't answer Benny.

"Dessert anyone?" JeNelle asked, abruptly rising from the table and gathering up the dinner dishes.

Sylvia had been watching JeNelle's expression as Kenneth talked on the telephone. She was very satisfied with what she saw. She couldn't wait to talk with her husband.

After coffee and dessert, Sylvia instructed Kenneth to give Whitney a bath and to get her ready for bed while she and Benjamin cleaned the kitchen. JeNelle was holding Whitney and she offered to help Kenneth. Kenneth handled Whitney like a professional nurse. He knew exactly what to do. JeNelle watched in amazement as Kenneth set about his task. He talked to Whitney as he bathed her. Her little hands and feet were flailing in the air as she listened to the deep, melodious sound of his voice. Her little face moved from side to side searching for his voice.

"Looks like you've done this a few times before, Kenneth," JeNelle said, smiling at Whitney and passing supplies to Kenneth as he worked.

"Many times before. I helped my grandparents take care of Benny, so by the time Vivian came along, I had my master's degree in diaper changing and my Ph.D. in baby washing when Gregory and Aretha came along. Babies are my favorite little people. One day, I'd like to have a house full of them just like Whitney."

JeNelle looked at Kenneth. He was smiling so warmly at the baby. The kindness that JeNelle remembered so vividly when she first met Kenneth had returned. He was such a study in the dichotomy of the human species. On the one hand, the dynamic business persona and on the other hand, the adoring uncle. He did not feel distant to her standing there with his niece. The walls seemed to be crumbling.

"You'll be a great father, Kenneth."

Kenneth didn't comment. He was so engrossed with Whitney that he had momentarily let his guard down with JeNelle.

Kenneth and JeNelle dressed Whitney, as she yawned and fell asleep. They placed her in the bassinet beside Benny's bed. Kenneth turned on the baby monitor that he brought with him and installed in several rooms of Benny's condo. JeNelle noticed the pictures of herself in Benny's bedroom, but she did not comment.

Since it was late, JeNelle stayed the night, but rose early to begin her journey back to Santa Barbara. Benny walked JeNelle to the condo lobby desk to wait for the valet to bring her car. They sat in the lobby as he explained to JeNelle about his relationship with Stacy and her disappearance. He showed Stacy's note to her.

"She must be very much in love with you, Benny," JeNelle said holding his hand and talking with him warmly as a good friend would do. "She's a career naval officer with the potential for a very successful career ahead of her. No woman in her position would put herself through the ordeal of a pregnancy and giving birth, if the feelings didn't go very deep, far beyond friendship. You're a warm, sensitive, and affectionate person. Those qualities are very rare in a man. I'm surprised that you didn't see how deep the feeling must have been for Stacy and you must have some strong feelings for her too, I believe. I see how deeply hurt you are that Stacy's not here with you and Whitney."

"I've wanted to tell you about Stacy and our baby from the beginning, but Stacy wouldn't permit it. I've been trying to balance what I felt were obligations to two close friends, you and Stacy."

"I've never lied to you. I've said consistently that I cannot offer you anything more than friendship. That's all that I can give and, no doubt, all that you need from me. I'm your friend, Benny, and I want to do everything that I can do for you and Whitney, but you were never in love with me and I think that now you realize that, too."

"Yes, I know that now, but Stacy doesn't and that's who I want to see and tell the truth to most of all. I want her to know that I love her. That I've always loved her. I've been a total and absolute idiot. I just hope that it's not too late. I should have told her the truth when we were in Goodwill. Maybe then, she would have listened to me. Maybe she wouldn't have left the way that she did."

JeNelle left and Benny watched as her car moved out of sight. He realized that what JeNelle said was true. He was never in love with her. He waged an all-out campaign for JeNelle's attention just as he had done with other women before her. Was it her resistance to his advances that made him even more determined to have her? What if she had not been so unobtainable? Would he have felt the same way about her? Or was it out of his own frustration because Stacy chose her career over him? That pain still wrenched his gut. Stacy was a real challenge, too. She still was. He knew that he had to find her. Not because she was a challenge, but in spite of it.

Something else began to dawn on Benny. He remembered the photo of JeNelle and Kenneth dancing in a beam of light; how JeNelle reacted when Lisa Lambert called Kenneth; the tension in the air that he observed between JeNelle and Kenneth in his living room. Something was out of sync.

* * *

Weeks later, Benny sat alone in his kitchen looking out at the lights of the city and the dark ocean beyond. For hours, he had been looking at a picture album. Pictures of him and Stacy together. Only the accent lights of the kitchen illuminated Stacy's face, but she was etched in his mind.

"Benjamin Staton, why are you sitting here in this dim light? It's two o'clock in the morning. You should get some rest," Sylvia said, as she entered the kitchen and flipped on the ceiling light.

"I came downstairs to warm a bottle for Whitney, Mom. She should be waking up soon."

"You don't look like you've been to bed. You've got to learn to sleep when she does. Have you had any rest?"

"I'll sleep later. I'm not tired."

Sylvia went to the table and sat down across from her son. She noticed the empty coffee cup sitting before him, a small picture album, and a note that he had clutched in his hand.

"How long have you been sitting here, Benjamin Staton?"

"I'm not sure, Mom. I lost track of time," he said listlessly, rubbing his face forcefully with both hands.

"What's in the album?"

"Pictures of Stacy. I was just looking at them and remembering how we met."

"You never told me about it. How did you two meet?"

Benny began to describe how he and Stacy met at the Pentagon. He spoke in slow, reflective tones as if he did not want to leave out one detail. He was expressionless. No excitement in his voice or demeanor. Almost a solemn mood of someone in mourning at the loss of a loved one.

"....So the next day I called Stacy and invited her out for a drink. She told me that she was busy and asked me if I wanted to have lunch instead. J.C. and I had been out partying all night with three women we met at a club in DC. I didn't think that I was in any shape to face daylight hours after what we had to drink the night before, but I wanted to see Stacy again, so I agreed to have lunch with her.

"We met at Port-of-Call, a small restaurant in Crystal City, Virginia. A lot of other military, mostly Navy personnel were there when I arrived. I was early and decided to have the 'hair-of-the-dog' to try to refocus my eyes. It was raining pretty hard outside. Stacy came in wearing her dark blue uniform and carrying her briefcase. She looked beautiful in her uniform. She had that clean, crisp smile and pearl white teeth, but you've seen her so you know that. She didn't have an umbrella, her uniform was damp, and she was shaking the water off her top coat and cap when she spotted me at the bar. Some of the Navy officers spoke to her when she came in. Some asked her to have lunch with them. She thanked them and spoke to them for a few minutes and told them that she was meeting me for lunch. They teased her for passing them up to have lunch with a 'Fly Boy', an Air Force pilot. It didn't seem to faze her in the least. She just gave them a look that made them all shut up." Benny smiled to himself and continued the story.

"I'm sorry that I'm late, Captain Alexander. I hope that you haven't been waiting long."

"No, Lieutenant, not long. Looks like you're catching a little flack from the Navy for having lunch with the enemy."

"They'll just have to cope. I decide who I will or won't have lunch with."

"I'm glad that you decided that it would be me. I'd hate to be in those other guys' shoes being turned down by a beautiful and sensuous woman like you."

"Stacy's eyes narrowed and I sensed that I had said the wrong thing. I hadn't tried to make a pass at her during our accidental meeting in the cafeteria. She said that she thought that I was different from the other men who often made passes at her. She said that perhaps she was wrong." Benny continued.

"Captain, I really don't have the time or the inclination to sit and play games with you. I've got about thirty minutes to eat and then I've got to get back to work. So let's cut to the chase. Why did you want to see me today?" Stacy asked, signaling for the waiter.

"There's no mystery. You're a very attractive woman and...."

"And you thought that I'd be a quick lay—another notch in your belt, huh, Captain?"

"We're both adults, free, single and disengaged...."

"You're a handsome man, Sir. Built like a Greek God and all that. Looks like you probably know your way around a bedroom, too. You're probably even a damn good lay, but guys like you are a dime a dozen in the Navy. I'm not looking for a bed warmer. My electric blanket works just fine. So if that's why we're here, you can scrub this mission, Fly Boy. You just crashed and burned."

"Stacy startled me. She was direct. No push. No pull. No bull. She shot me down cold. I sensed that she meant what she said. That she wasn't just trying to play hard to get or any other game. She started to leave just as the waiter came to the table. I stopped her, apologized for coming on to her so hard, and convinced her not to leave. She sat down again and we ordered lunch. I enjoyed talking with her. She really didn't say much. I had to do most of the talking. I couldn't determine whether she even liked me. She kept checking her watch periodically."

"Captain, it's been interesting talking with you, but I have to go."

"Go? You just got here, Lieutenant. Doesn't the Navy give their people time for a decent lunch?"

"Sure, but there's a seminar on new sonar equipment that I want to sit in on and it starts in about twenty minutes."

"You mean that you'd rather be sitting in a seminar than having lunch with me?"

"Sorry, Captain. First things first."

"She got up from the table, paid her part of the check, and was out of the door. That took me by surprise. My ego wasn't just bruised, it needed major surgery. That had never happened to me before. I thought that I would just chalk that one up to experience and move on, but there was something about her that I liked.

I called her and left messages, but she didn't return my calls. I sent flowers to her and still nothing. The day before I was scheduled to leave, I decided to stop by the Pentagon to see her. She wasn't in her office, but her secretary told me that I could find her in the library."

"Captain Alexander, what are you doing here?"

"Looking for you, Lieutenant Greene. You're a hard person to catch up with. Didn't you get my messages or my flowers?"

"Yes, Captain, I got them."

"Then why didn't you call?"

"Captain, I really don't have time to spend.... Look, you're a nice man, but—."

"But what, Lieutenant?"

"But I'm not interested."

"Whoa, Lieutenant, I could begin to take this personally."

"Don't, Captain. It's business, not personal. You're the type of man who women could get real personal with—you're dangerous. I'm sure that you're not lacking for female companionship. Any woman in her right mind, I'm sure, would jump at the chance to spend time with you."

"But you're not just any woman, Lieutenant. I'd like to get to know you better. More importantly, I'd like for you to get to know me better."

"Why?" she asked.

"'Why'? What do you mean 'why'?"

"Captain, I didn't stutter. Why do you want to get to know me better? And don't give me any of the usual lines. Believe me, I've heard them all."

"I was caught flat, but somehow I said, 'Options'. She looked at me quizzically."

"All right, Captain, meet me at the Japanese Embassy at 1800. Wear your dress blues and please be prompt. I've got to go now, but I'll see you at 1800."

"When I arrived at the Embassy there must have been five hundred people there. Security had my name on a list and told me to go in and enjoy myself. I knew some of the military people there, but it took a while to find Stacy. When she spotted me she came over and introduced me to the daughter of General Paul Bates, Paulette. She was an attractive woman, All right, but not what I had in mind. Stacy left us together and she went back to talk with the other guests. She speaks fluent Japanese and Admiral Gordon kept her busy most of the night. I watched Stacy work the crowd with Admiral Gordon and the rest of his entourage. She was spectacular. Bright, eager, energetic, resourceful. It was obvious that the Admiral relied on her and her keen sense of diplomacy to keep him on tract. I finally got a moment alone with her.

"Are you having a good time, Captain? Where is Paulette Bates?"

"No, I don't know, and I don't care, I said to her."

"What?"

"Lieutenant, I thought that we, you and I, were going to spend some time together getting know each other. I don't think that it's happening, do you? At least not with five hundred other people around. So you have three options."

"Options?"

"Yes, Lieutenant, options."

"All right, Captain, what are my options?"

"You can have a lover, a friend or whatever is behind curtain number three."

"I'll take whatever is behind curtain number three."

"Good, then get your coat, say goodnight, Gracy, and let's get out of here now."

"But what's behind curtain number three?"

"I'll tell you later."

"We drove to the Naval Observatory. A friend of mine arranged to get us in after closing. The place was deserted except for the night guard. We looked through the telescope and gazed at the stars. We had a great time. I told her about all of you and she listened closely. We lost track of time. It was 0500 when the guard finally told us that we had to go.

I gave Stacy my contact information and asked her to call. She never did. Then I got an unexpected message from her saying that she would be in San

Diego with Admiral Gordon. She said that she would call later and maybe we could get together for a drink. I didn't hear from her for a while and I thought that maybe her plans had changed, but then she called and asked whether I wanted to go sailing. I agreed and she suggested that I bring a date, so I did. I took Janice and Cecil. About twelve of us met early one morning at Shelter Island. Stacy was with a Lieutenant Commander Bruce Payton who was stationed at the USN Amphibious Base. He had a sail boat and was teaching Stacy how to sail. The rest of us ended up being her crew. She caught on quickly. She sailed us from Shelton Island to one of the Mission Bay Islands and we found a deserted cove to drop anchor. We had a picnic lunch, did some scuba diving and fishing. We cooked the fish on the beach. We sailed back into San Diego late and I overheard Stacy tell someone else that she would be stationed in San Diego for two years and was looking forward to more sailing trips. Admiral Gordon, her commanding officer, had been given command of the Pacific Fleet and Stacy was his XO, his Executive Officer.

"I started running in to her at different clubs and parties. She could really dance and she enjoyed it. We danced together a lot and I asked her out on a real date. She agreed. I knew that she was not easily impressed, so I didn't try to impress her. I took her on a dinner and dance cruise. We had a great time. After that we started seeing each other more regularly, but not exclusively. It was purely platonic until Janice and Cecil gave me a surprise birthday party here at the condo pool. Since they had met Stacy, she helped them arrange it. It was a great party. When it was over, I waited in the lobby with Stacy for the valet to bring her car. The valet said that the car wouldn't start, so I suggested that Stacy spend the rest of the night and get someone from the Navy's motor pool to fix her car in the morning. She agreed and we came back here to my condo. It was all quite innocent."

"Benny, are you sure that this is not an imposition? I can take a cab back to base and have someone from the motor pool pick up the car for me later."

"It's late. We've been partying all night. You, Janice, and Cecil really put one over on me. I didn't have a clue what was going on. This is my way of saying thank you to one of my good friends."

"Okay, Benny, but if any of those women who were after you tonight come up here to give you a special present, I'm going over the terrace. They'll never tear me apart trying to get to you."

"Maybe you didn't notice, Lieutenant, but there was only one person who had my full attention tonight and it wasn't Cecil or Janice."

"I noticed, Captain, but I told you before that I'm not looking to fall in love. You're the dangerous type, remember? The type of man who women go insane for and fall head over heels in love with. Insanity does not run in my family, and I'm not putting myself in harm's way."

"We've been seeing each other for some time now. I know that you're not interested in falling in love. You've made that abundantly clear, but I have to tell you the truth. I want more than just a platonic relationship with you. I have for some time. That string that you call a bikini would make a blind man see. Make the Pope give up religion! Wake up the dead and it makes me.... Well, I think that you get the picture."

"Stacy actually blushed." "I'll be truthful with you too, Benny. Your swimming trunks ought to be designated a lethal weapon. I've spent more than a few nights wondering what all the women on base are talking about. When we went dancing that night on the dinner cruise, I began to feel something, and it wasn't the motion of the ocean."

"So, why don't we...."

"Hold on, Fly Boy, I think that we've got a good relationship going. We've become good friends and I don't want to ruin that."

"I think that taking this friendship to another level can only make it better. I want to be with you, not just because you're the most sensual woman I know, but because I care about you. I respect what you're doing and I admire you and what you've accomplished. Not many military personnel become the Executive Officer to a high-ranking person like Admiral Gordon at such a young age. You're a very special lady, Stacy Greene, and the type of woman that I would want to take home to meet my family, if we were to get to that point. But, I know that you're not ready for that and neither am I. I understand and respect your independence. I know that your career goals are the most important part of your life now. I would not want to interfere with that. If we take this relationship to the next level, it will be on any terms that you want. With or without the sex. I don't want to lose what we have either."

Benny ended the story of his early relationship with Stacy there.

"That was the first time that we made love, Mom."

"Benjamin Staton, did you hear what you just said?"

"Yes, Mom, that's what I've been sitting here thinking about and why I've been looking at these pictures of me and Stacy together over the last two years. I've been on an emotional roller coaster since Stacy left three weeks ago. I never thought that she would not be an important part of my life. I realize now how much I love her, need her, and miss her."

"And what about JeNelle Towson? She's been coming to see you quite frequently. You thought that you were in love with her at one point not too long ago."

"JeNelle enjoys spending time with Whitney, Mom. She's not in love with me and I'm not in love with her. I'm not proud of how I've behaved where JeNelle is concerned."

"What do you mean, Benjamin Staton?"

"Do you remember how as a kid K.J. would challenge me to get me to perform?"

"Sure, that was sometimes the only way that he could get you to live up to your potential."

"Well, that's what JeNelle was to me...a challenge. I began to realize that after Stacy and I got back from Goodwill. Dad told me to first figure out where I was going, then map out my route. He also said that I might make some detours along the way, but at least I knew where I was headed. That wasn't the first time that I had heard that. Stacy said the very same thing to me. I realize now that Stacy was where I was going all along, and JeNelle and the other women I've known were the detours."

Benny got up from the table and poured another cup of coffee. He didn't look at his mother.

"Benjamin Staton, you are a good man. Your father and I could not be more proud of you and how you have grown. The fact that you can look at yourself clearly, speaks well for what we and your grandparents tried to teach you and your sisters and brothers. Your first responsibility is still to be the best person that you can be. Growing up is a perpetual process. It doesn't stop when you reach eighteen or twenty-one or even when you reach my age. You're still on the right track. Your next responsibility is to Whitney Ivy to be the best parent that you can be for her. I'm confident that you'll do a wonderful job as her father. As for Stacy, well, she'll be back. When she does come back though, I know that you will make the right choices about your relationship with her. She loves you, Son. I'm sure of that, but she has different dreams for herself and her career just like Vivian Lynn does. You'll have to be ready to make some sacrifices and adjustments when the time comes, but if it's right for both of you, and I believe that it will be, then it will all be worth it."

Sylvia and Benny heard Whitney crying.

"I'll take care of Whitney Ivy, Son. You get some rest."

"Thanks, Mom, but I want to spend as much time with Whitney as I can. She helps me to get through the days and nights without Stacy. I have so much that I have to tell Whitney about her mother."

Chapter 29

Vivian was studying in her room when Chuck knocked on her opened door.

"Hey! Annie! You need a break!" Chuck grinned broadly at her.

Vivian looked up from her books and laptop to see Chuck leaning against the door jamb, wearing his full cowboy outfit, with his Stetson pulled down so low on his face she couldn't see his devilish brown eyes. She smiled at him. "I've got a lot of work to do, Chuck." She continued working.

"C'mon, Annie," he entreated. "You've been cooped up all summer long and most of the fall, too. If it weren't for the fact that Gregory was here this summer, you probably would have been in the house the entire time. It's Saturday night, Annie. Me and the posse are going over to the Red, Hot and Blue for a real footstomping hoedown. I even washed for this. C'mon and get up from there, put on some girl clothes, and let's mosey on down to the Red Hot. Derrick wants to join us over there and he's been asking about you."

That got Vivian's attention. "*Derrick?* You mean Derrick Jackson?" Vivian's eyes brightened. "Uh, maybe this brief can wait until tomorrow, but do I really have to wear that cowgirl stuff? I've got this red body dress—"

"Naw, Annie! Try something different. Stretch out with your feelings, feel the force," Chuck teased.

"Don't you start with me, Charles Montgomery. I'm a Trekie and I'm proud of it. The *Star Wars* saga are the best movies ever made," she retorted.

"Holster those six shooters, Annie. You haven't seen the movie, *Pure Country*, yet. Let's get that hitch out of your get-a-long and mosey on outta here."

"All right, Chuck, I'm a comin'," she teased. "Now you shoo so that I can get dressed. I'll be down shortly."

"That-a-girl, Annie!"

Vivian showered and dressed in the cowgirl outfit that Chuck gave to her. She felt foolish as she stood before her full-length mirror, sure that Derrick Jackson, the Denzel Washington double, would probably prefer a woman with a more sophisticated look. She tried different poses and then gave up. "I'm about as sophisticated as a bowl of prunes," she said aloud to herself. "Well, Dr. Jackson, this is all there is. Like it or not."

"C'mon, Annie!" Chuck yelled from the bottom of the stairs as he stood with the other housemates preparing to leave. "You're holding up progress."

Vivian could barely contain her laughter as she galloped down the stairs and glimpsed the motley crew. Even Angelique, Miguel, and Anna were dressed in Country and Western fashion. David looked like a refugee from Central Casting. Melissa had her hair up in two ponytails, complete with bow ribbons. Gloria was much more conservative in her black satin embroidered western shirt and short western skirt and cowgirl boots. Alan had an Indian band around his forehead with one feather that stood straight up out of the back of the headband, a buckskin jacket, leather vest, buckskin pants and moccasins. Vivian had never noticed how well built he was, but, apparently, Melissa had. She was buzzing around him like a bee making honey. Mr. *GQ*, Bill Chandler, took the prize with his full-body, black leather get-up and black leather Stetson. All he needed was a cape and he could have tested for the role of Zorro. *Whoa, did he have sex appeal or what?* Vivian thought.

Chuck beamed as Vivian came down the stairs. "All right, posse, let's head 'em up and move 'em out!" he instructed.

The Red, Hot and Blue was already crowded when the Georgetown posse arrived. People were all over the dance floor doing the Down and Dirty, Country Slide, Achy-Breaky and other steps this posse was unaccustomed to, but Chuck was truly in his element. Before they were even seated, Chuck was on the dance floor stepping in a line dance with the best of them. For a big, tall man, he was surprisingly light on his feet with well-coordinated dance moves. He didn't miss a beat. He looked right at home in the crowd and the women were on his trail. David and Bill got up to try some of the steps in the line dance, but when the women started pressing Bill, he pulled Vivian onto the dance floor as his dance partner. Vivian didn't protest. Bill looked too good in that leather outfit and both men and women were watching him move. In less than an hour, all of the housemates were dancing to the upbeat western tunes as if they had been born listening to them all of their lives. Even Angelique and Miguel had the steps down pat. They were all yelping and calling with every step.

Vivian was dancing the Texas two-step to a slow tune on the crowded dance floor with Bill when Bill spotted Derrick Jackson come in the door. Vivian didn't see Derrick immediately, but she felt Bill's nature start to rise. She looked at him quizzically, leaned in, and whispered, "If you even think it, you'll be modeling for *House and Garden* when I'm through with you."

Bill gave Vivian a questioning look. Vivian looked down toward the bulge in his tight, leather pants. He looked at her and grinned.

"That's not for you this time, Vivian," he said, with a wink. "I'm saving it for that vision over there."

He nodded toward the entrance and Vivian craned her neck to follow his gaze. There she saw Derrick looking totally correct and edible.

Vivian leaned into Bill again and whispered, "Same goes. Remember, *House and Garden* if you even blink at him."

Derrick looked so sexy with his tight-fitting blue jeans, plaid shirt open at the collar, and dark brown cowboy hat, Vivian thought. Standing with his thumbs stuck down in his low riding jeans and that Denzel Washington smile, he watched Vivian and Bill dance. Something stirred in Vivian that she had not felt since she was with Carlton. Yet, this feeling had nothing to do with Carlton. She liked what she was feeling and she noticed that she wasn't the only one. Gloria batted her eyes and approached Derrick. So did Melissa. Chuck joined them and Derrick greeted them all cordially, but she noticed that he never took his eyes off her and Bill on the dance floor. As the music ended, Derrick excused himself and strode toward them.

"Well, Ms. Alexander, it's about time that I got to meet you under those better circumstances that I've been waiting for."

Vivian's heart was racing. Bill hunched her in her back. She ignored him.

"It's good to see you again, Dr. Jackson. I've been looking forward to this too."

Bill hunched her again. She finally relented and made the introductions.

"Dr. Derrick Jelon Jackson, this is one of my housemates and a fellow law school student, William Anthony Chandler. Bill, this is the famous basketball player, Dunk and Jam Jackson. Dr. Jackson took care of Angelique when she had Scarlet Fever."

"Bill, it's a pleasure to meet you, but your face is very familiar. Have we met before?" Derrick asked, extending his hand.

"I don't believe so. I'm sure that I would have remembered if we had," Bill said, taking Derrick's hand and wearing a curious smile.

"Still, I know I've seen you somewhere before," Derrick said, trying to remember where.

"Probably in *GQ, Esquire,* or some other less notable trade magazine ads," Vivian said, noticing Bill's expression. "Like you, Bill is multitalented. He's also a professional model. He's been in magazine ads or on billboards nearly every month for the last eight years. He did a Calvin Klein ad on television. The ad must run about fifty times a day on different channels."

"That's where I've seen you," Derrick said, with a broad Denzel smile, "in television ads. I've never met a professional model before, Bill. It seems like an interesting career. You'll have to tell me how you manage to juggle such a demanding law school schedule and a professional modeling career at the same time."

"It would be a pleasure to learn more about what you do, too, Derrick. With Miguel and Angelique around, we need good medical advice."

The music started again and Derrick asked Vivian to dance. She was thrilled and pushed Bill toward the maddening crowd that was stalking him. Derrick, she found, was a smooth dancer even with the two-step tempo of the western tunes, and he glided her around the dance floor as if she were a feather floating in a gentle breeze. They talked as they danced close to each other.

"You look great tonight, Ms. Alexander. That outfit adds a whole new dimension to your persona," Derrick said, with a suggestive smile. "I was very impressed with you when we first met, but Chuck told me that you were engaged."

"That was then, Dr. Jackson. I'm no longer engaged to do anything, except finish law school and start a career."

"I'm very happy to hear that. I'd like to call you sometime very soon. Perhaps we could catch a show, have dinner or lunch. Whatever your schedule permits."

"I'd like that. Perhaps a basketball game. Chuck tells me that you taught him everything that he knows about the game."

"Apparently, I didn't teach him quite enough. He told me how you and your brother, Gregory, used him to wipe the pine regularly this past summer. He also said that quite a few doctors on staff at Georgetown lost their shirts to you."

"Oh, that," she blushed, "I may have hit a few shots, purely by chance, of course. You know how Chuck is given to overstatement."

"Chuck wasn't the only one that I heard this from. I still play a little ball myself from time to time with some of the other doctors and nurses and some of them also told me not to bet against you. They said that you have the deadliest three-point shots that they have ever seen."

"Occasionally, I try to rise to the level of the competition. I hit a few lucky shots that my brothers taught me."

"I remember your brother, 'Benny the Bruiser'. I watched him wipe out Chuck at the Boston Shootout many years ago. I had hoped to see him in the pros, but I understand from Chuck that he's a jet pilot in the Air Force. He must be pretty smart to fly jets."

"He is, but now he's a brand new father. He has a daughter, Whitney Ivy. Benny is no longer a 'Bruiser'. Whitney is the center of his existence. I'm looking forward to seeing my new niece during the holidays."

"I understand that you also have another brother who's a very good ball player, too. He and Chuck got to know each other very well last spring. I think they're scheduled to do some skiing together this coming season."

"Oh, that's Kenneth, my oldest brother."

"Kenneth Alexander? The Executive Director of CompuCorrect, Inc., in California? He's your brother, too?"

"Yes, but how did you know about his company?"

"You can't read the *Wall Street Journal, Forbes, Fortune, Black Enterprise Magazine* and the Business Section of the *Washington Post* and not read about one of the best managed, fastest growing small businesses in America today. I like to follow the careers of men who are doing well. There have been several articles lately about your brother and a Blue Ribbon Panel on Youth in Business and Industry. I'm very interested in the program. I'd like to see something like that for youth in science, technology and medicine. I didn't make the connection between you and Kenneth Alexander, until now. That means that you're also related to Don Dixon."

"Yes, he's my cousin. He has a twin brother, James," she said, with some surprise. "How do you know Donny?"

"He was at MIT when I was at Boston College. We used to shoot around together. You certainly are a family of overachievers."

"Ha! Overachievers! You haven't met my sister, Aretha. Now she's the overachiever in our family."

"Chuck thinks that you're going to be a great attorney one day. He's also betting that you'll be sitting on a state or federal court bench before you're thirty. I know not to bet against him...or you."

"Chuck's been a good friend, considering how I treated him when we met."

"Chuck's one of a kind. His whole family is like that."

"I know. He told me that you two grew up together."

"He's my best friend. Meeting Chuck and his family was one of the best days of my life. We've been friends since we were little kids. I couldn't have designed a better person if someone had given me all the parts that I wanted and told me to put a whole person together. He's one of the most unselfish, big-hearted men I know. He thinks no man is his enemy and he makes every man his friend. Now I have something else to thank him for."

"Oh, what's that?" she asked innocently.

"For introducing me to you," he said; his voice dropped to a lower register.

Vivian blushed and nodded toward where Chuck was sitting at the bar surrounded by young, attractive women. "Every woman seems to want to be his friend, too. Just look at all those women over there just hanging on every word he speaks. He's got Melissa mesmerized, too."

"Yeah, Chuck's what some women call 'a hunk' all right. Never had any problem with the ladies, but he's not a shallow person and he doesn't mistreat women, or anyone else for that matter. He's a real country gentlemen under all that cowboy get-up."

"Speaking of 'hunks', Dr. Jackson....uh...are you seeing.... I mean, are you involved with anyone?"

Derrick laughed. "Hunk? Well, I don't know about that, but I hope to be involved very soon, if you're willing to see me again."

The thermometer in Vivian's body was rising while she and Derrick danced and talked, but that comment blew the mercury right out of the thermometer. *Would I see him?!* she thought. *Does a bear go in the woods?! Does the Pope wear a beanie?! Hell yes!* was what she wanted to scream. *Every day of the week and twice on Sunday! He can ring my bell anytime!*

"Yes, that would be very nice," Vivian said demurely.

The music ended and another tune started. Derrick didn't let Vivian sit down. They danced nearly every dance together and spent time talking alone about his life and hers. He had quite a good sense of humor, she thought. He was easy to talk with—very open and affable. He was quite a bit older than she was, maybe ten years or so, in his thirties, about Kenneth's age, maybe thirty-four or thirty-five. Nevertheless, after a while they were so in tuned with each other that they were beginning to finish each other's sentences and thoughts. They agreed about their positions on a multitude of issues from politics to pictures. They started talking about movies and television shows that they liked. They liked a lot of the same ones. Derrick loved the *Star Wars* movies and he was a Trekie, too.

"You know, Ms. Alexander, you remind me of that actress, uh, Jada, Jada Pinkett-Smith. You not only look like her, but you have her type of openness, her energy, her style, but much, much more."

"You mean that she looks like me, don't you, Dr. Jackson? You mean that she has my openness, my energy and my style, but less. I loaned the kid those qualities, but she's still a work-in-progress," Vivian teased flippantly with a wry smile.

"I stand corrected, Counselor. Ms. Pinkett-Smith couldn't hold a candle to you," Derrick said, pretending to be ashamed of his *faux pas*.

They both laughed.

"Well, Dr. Jackson, I'm sure that I'm not the first person to mistake you for Denzel Washington."

"Is he one of your favorite actors?"

"Sure, he's very talented and handsome. A real craftsman."

"Then I'm glad that he looks like me. Just so long as you can tell us apart."

They both laughed.

"*Touché*, Dr. Jackson."

Later that night, the group left Red, Hot and Blue and bought at least ten different flavors of ice cream from Baskin-Robbins in Georgetown. They took the ice cream home and ate it as they sat around the living room laughing, talking and listening to Chuck's CD's of Charlie Pride, Ray Charles, Aaron Nevel and Cleve Francis. Chuck told funny stories about Derrick when they were younger and Derrick told even funnier stories about Chuck when they were older.

As Vivian and Derrick sat next to each other on the floor, they exchanged quick glances and smiles throughout the evening. They were both enjoying each other's company tremendously. Vivian didn't want the evening to end, but it was already two-thirty in the morning.

Derrick got up from the floor and told everyone how much he enjoyed the evening with them and how he hoped that he would be invited to join them again very soon. He looked down at Vivian with a broad smile and extended his hand to help her to her feet. Her heart was pounding in her throat. They left the living room hand-in-hand and Derrick closed the living room doors behind them for a little privacy. He took Vivian's hands in his and smiled.

"I hope you know that I had a great time with you this evening, Ms. Alexander. I know that your life in law school is probably very chaotic now, but I'd like for you to fit me into your regular schedule, if that's possible."

"That can be arranged," she said, feeling a warm tingling sensation rising up her spine.

"Is later today too soon?" He looked into her eyes.

"What did you have in mind?" Vivian tried to conceal the excitement bursting inside her.

"I'm meeting some friends for a Wizards' game. They're playing the Miami Heat. Our medical practice has a box at the arena. I thought that you and I could see the game and then have a late dinner alone together afterwards."

Vivian wondered whether Derrick was a mind reader. She had high hopes that he would want to see her again very soon.

"That would fit into my schedule just fine, Dr. Jackson."

"I have rounds at Children's Hospital in the morning and I'm scheduled to be on emergency call, so I'll have to call you about the time."

"I'll be waiting to hear from you. I'm looking forward to seeing you again, too."

Derrick leaned over and kissed Vivian softly on the forehead. She thought she would faint. Every fiber in her body tingled.

"The name is Derrick, Counselor," he whispered.

She stood on her tiptoes and kissed his cheek. "Only if you'll call me Vivian."

"We should seal this deal with a kiss," he smiled, capturing her mouth softly.

The kiss left them both smiling at each other. Derrick left and Vivian waved goodbye to him as he drove away. She closed the door, leaned back against it, squeezed herself and yelled "Yes!" with much emotion and enthusiasm. She pushed open the living room doors and playfully staggered into the room, holding her hand over her heart. She tossed her cowgirl hat into the air and playfully collapsed in the middle of the floor.

Her housemates laughed at her antics, but Chuck's expression was stoic.

"Whoa, Vivian, that is some good-looking hunk there!" Gloria squealed. "I think I could learn to love his bedside manner real easy!"

Vivian shot a deadly look at Gloria. "Don't you even try it, Gloria Towson!" Vivian said sternly. "You're already wearing that diamond mine on your finger that you and Tony call an engagement ring. And that brand new Lexus sitting out front that Tony gave you for an engagement present should be enough to keep you in check. Tony's got you on total lock down, remember? So don't you worry about Derrick Jackson's bedside manner. I'll handle that myself, personally."

"A woman can still look, can't she?" Gloria asked.

"Or a man can," Bill added glibly.

"Chandler, I don't want any competition from you either. Don't think that I didn't notice how you tried to get his attention all night. You keep that up and you'll be making a career-ending decision."

"I think that as long as a man is free, single and disengaged, he's fair game," Melissa chirped up.

Vivian gave Melissa a serious 'you're-dead-meat' look.

"Maybe not," Melissa said, glimpsing Vivian's menacing expression.

Chuck rose abruptly. "I'm outta here," he said, putting on his hat and grabbing his coat.

"Good night, Chuck," everyone said in unison.

Chuck didn't answer.

The housemates talked about what a great time they had at Red, Hot and Blue. It was unlike anything that any of them had ever experienced. Vivian said that although she was a country girl, she didn't realize how many Black people were involved in country music. They vowed to make that place one of their regular hangouts because, they all agreed, it was just plain, pure fun.

Later that next morning, Vivian woke up early. She had new energy. She lay in the bed smiling to herself and hugging her pillow as she recalled the evening before with Derrick Jackson. She was almost giddy. She grabbed the telephone and hit the speed dial.

"Benny!" she yelled in her excitement when he answered.

"Vivian, this had better be good. It's three-thirty in the morning out here."

"Did I catch you at a bad time? I mean, are you alone or do you have company?"

"I'm never alone with Ms. Whitney around, but if you're asking me whether I'm with a woman, the answer is no. I'm not seeing anyone."

Vivian's excitement suddenly disappeared. She could hear the subtle hint of pain in her brother's voice. He was trying to hide it, but she knew her brother too well.

"How is my niece?"

"More beautiful than ever." His tone brightened considerably. "She's teething so she's biting everything that she can get her hands on, including me." He laughed. "She likes to play at the oddest hours. I just put her back in her crib. She decided that she wanted to play 'let's-roll-over-on-daddy-tonight' for two hours."

"She's just a little baby, Benny, and she's rolling over already?"

"Yeah, that and a few other tricks that Mrs. Tyler says that she's learned."

"Who's Mrs. Tyler?"

"She's my next door neighbor. She takes care of Ms. Whitney while I'm working. She even cooks for me when I'm here and we have dinner together. It's like having Mom around."

"She sounds perfect."

"She is. She told me how much she used to enjoy watching me entertain female friends. That blew me away. She knew more about what I was doing than I did."

He laughed.

"But aren't you seeing anyone now?"

"No, no one. It's just me and Ms. Whitney Ivy, and I like it that way."

"Still no word from Stacy?"

She sensed Benny's mood had changed. He seemed more somber and her heart went out to him.

"Nothing yet. I've talked with Senator Abraham Makin, the Senator who recommended Stacy to the Naval Academy. He remembered her, but when he tried to locate her family, he reached a dead end. Her family moved out of the Cabrini Green area and he couldn't find out where they've gone. I've also talked with people at the Naval Academy and at the Pentagon who know Stacy, but no one has heard from her."

"What are you going to do?" Vivian asked, concerned.

"J.C. Baker and a few others are still working on finding her. In the meantime, I'm going to hope that Mom and Dad are right that Stacy does love me enough that she'll come back when her deployment ends." What he didn't say was how afraid he was for Stacy. After 911, any deployment she was on that was top secret had to be dangerous.

Vivian could hear the pain and frustration in her brother's voice.

"You didn't call me at this ungodly hour to talk about me. What's got you so excited?"

"Derrick Jelon Jackson," she said, with joy in her voice.

"DJ Jackson, 'Dunk and Jam' Jackson, the basketball player?"

"The former ball player. Remember, I told you about him before? He's a pediatrician here in D.C. and he's wonderful."

"I can tell by your voice. You sound like you're feeling a hell of a rush."

"I am. I could hardly sleep. I've had a perpetual smile on my face."

"Sounds like you're completely over Carlton."

"I am. I do think about him sometimes."

"He's called me a few times and asked me to talk with you for him. He says that he still loves you and still wants to marry you under any terms or conditions that you want."

"I know. He's called me, written long letters, sent cards and flowers. He's talked to almost everyone I know. I forgave him for deceiving me about the women he was seeing, but I told him that I would never forget what he put me through. I won't be with someone who doesn't respect me, no matter how much I love him."

"You sound confident in your decision not to see him again."

"I am, and for the first time in a very long time, I'm excited about a new friendship."

"It's good to hear you sound so happy again. I know that it's been tough on you."

"It has been tough putting my life back together, but it was great having Gregory around all summer. He really got me through the roughest periods. Our little brother is quite a man."

"Yeah, a ladies man," Benny snorted.

"You don't have to tell me that. I was constantly trying to keep my housemates, Gloria and Melissa, and a lot of other women at Georgetown Law off of him. Chuck Montgomery and I had to get the kid out of town a lot. We took him to visit different colleges and universities in the area. We thought that we could breathe easy once when we took him to the University of Virginia for a tour of the campus. Chuck and I left him with members of the men's basketball team and the campus tour group while we went to visit Monticello, Thomas Jefferson's home. There's a new exhibit there about Jefferson Black mistress, Sally Heming's and the six children they had together. When Chuck and I got back on campus, we looked for Gregory everywhere. We walked The Lawn until we saw a crowd of young ladies at the Rotunda. I knew immediately that it had to be Gregory and I was right. We found him sitting on the steps of the Jefferson Library surrounded by young women. We got some dirty looks from those young women when we finally dragged Gregory away."

Vivian and Benny both laughed.

"But no matter where I went or what I did, Gregory was right by my side. We had some great times together. I'm really looking forward to going home on Tuesday for Thanksgiving, but for today, I'm looking forward to my date with Derrick Jackson!"

"Take it easy on a brother, Viv. He's older than I am, I think. He may even be older than K.J. Don't throw that little red body dress of yours at the poor man yet. He's a little older than the men you usually date. You could send him into cardiac arrest or give him a stroke in that dress," Benny teased.

"Are you a mind reader or what?"

"Oh, no, Viv. I know you and I've seen how men react to you when you wear that dress. Remember, you wore it when we went to the Officer's Club at the Navy Yard. J.C. Baker and I almost had to call in the MPs to keep those officers and gentlemen in line. No. No. Derrick's not ready for that red dress yet. He'll have to work up to that. Just make sure that you have a medical emergency team standing by the first time he sees you in that dress."

"Good night, Benjamin Staton!" Vivian said sternly in a joking manner. "I don't think that I want to talk to you any more today."

Benny was laughing loudly. "Good night, Viv. I love you, and Whitney Ivy and I will see you at home for Thanksgiving."

Vivian laughed, too. "I love you, too, Benny. Kiss my niece for me."

They hung up.

Vivian stretched and hugged herself as she lay in the bed. She was grinning from ear to ear. She felt wonderful. She hopped out of bed and began studying. She had been at it for more than two hours when the telephone rang. She wondered who would be calling her so early in the morning.

"Hello."

"Good morning, Vivian."

A deep, melodic voice engulfed her and she began to tingle from head to toe. She caught her breath. "Derrick . . .uh...Good morning.... uh.... I didn't expect to hear from you this early. Are you at the hospital already?"

"No, I just woke up and I wanted to be the first person to say good morning to you."

Vivian's heart leaped from her chest.

"I'll call you later when I know my schedule and, if your schedule permits, I'd like to pick you up earlier than we had originally planned."

"But I thought that you had rounds at the hospital this morning and that you were on emergency call today."

"I am going on rounds, but I've taken myself off emergency call. I don't want anything to interfere with our plans for today."

Not only did Vivian's heart leap from her body, it was doing somersaults like an Olympic acrobat.

"I'm looking forward to it, too," she said quietly. "Just give me a call when you're ready."

"Vivian, I'm ready now, but I do have to pretend to put in a few hours of work, so I'll call you very soon."

They hung up.

"Okay! Okay!..... .That did it!" she yelled, hopping cheerfully from her seat, flailing her arms in the air. "It's the red body dress! That's what I'm going to wear!"

She slid an old Whitney Houston CD into the player, went directly to her favorite selection, and turned the music up loud. The music was jarring the room. Vivian was singing *I'm Every Woman* along with Whitney Houston at the top of her lungs and trying on the red dress. She was pantomiming the words to the music and looking at herself in the full view mirror when Bill burst through her bedroom door. He was half-asleep, wearing only his loose-fitting, silk Calvin Klein jockeys.

"Vivian, what the hell—" He stopped in his tracks and his eyes widened when he saw Vivian in the red dress. *"Whoa, baby!* Who are you trying to hurt wearing that dress?!" He turned down Vivian's loud music.

"Derrick," Vivian said in a sultry voice.

"Oh, no, Vivian, you can't do that to the man on a Sunday. He'll have to go to confession all week for lusting after you in his heart. Besides, I can't compete when you wear that dress!"

"I'm warning you, Chandler! Don't you even smile in Derrick's direction!" Vivian said, with a homicidal tone.

Bill didn't retort. He went to her closet and started looking through it.

"Let's see what we have to work with here," he said, pulling out a few outfits and threw them on her bed. "Not much here. Don't you wear anything but jeans and sweats? I knew that I should have taken you shopping."

"I'm not really into high fashion," she quipped.

"Low fashion either, by the looks of things," he retorted. "It looks more like no fashion."

He gave up looking through her closet, dialed Gloria and Melissa's bedrooms, and told them that they had a lot of work to do. They both dragged themselves out of their beds and shuffled up the stairs to Vivian's bedroom. They worked on dressing her in different outfits for nearly two hours before they gave up. Clothes were stacked everywhere around the room. Bill picked up the telephone and made a few calls.

"Bring the brown suede with the beige blouse in a size 10 and 12. Yes and the blue silk. No, the one with the matching suede shoes, size 7 and 9. And the teal outfit. Yes, that's the one. I'm not sure. Let me check. Vivian, are you a 36B or C cup?"

Vivian rolled her eyes at Bill and said quietly, "B."

Melissa and Gloria broke up into laughter and Gloria said to Bill, "Make that a C cup, Bill."

"Make it a C cup. Now let's see, that's about twenty complete outfits with accessories, isn't it? Okay, I'll see you in an hour."

Bill hung up the telephone. Vivian stared at him apprehensively. "What are you up to?" Vivian stood in the middle of her bedroom floor with her arms akimbo, wearing only her bra and panties.

Bill didn't say anything. He just walked around her eyeing her body quizzically. Vivian rolled her eyes and put her hands on her hips. Bill started issuing orders. "Melissa, you do the manicure and pedicure. Gloria, you do the facial and makeup. I'll do her hair. Vivian, uh.... you just go take a long, hot jacuzze and put some of that Aveno skin softener in the water."

Bill clapped his hands and Melissa and Gloria scurried to their rooms to get the heavy artillery ready. Vivian stared at Bill. He noticed that she hadn't moved. He leaned in close to her and whispered very slowly, but deliberately, "We can do this your way or we can do this my way. But I want to warn you, Alexander, my way includes me getting into the Jacuzzi with you and scrubbing every inch of your body...and I do mean every inch."

"Uh, I'll do it my way, Chandler. Did you say use the Aveno?"

"You got it, Alexander!"

Vivian disappeared into the bathroom and soaked in the Jacuzzi for more than thirty minutes until Melissa and Gloria showed up and disturbed her peace and quiet. Gloria started putting a facial mask on Vivian's face while Melissa grabbed Vivian's foot out of the water and started giving her a pedicure. They poked and prodded her for nearly an hour before they snatched her out of the Jacuzzi and returned her to Bill who was waiting for her in her bedroom. He was joined by two men who were showing him various women's haute couture outfits—beautiful and expensive outfits, Vivian noted. Bill had her try on each outfit in the wardrobe.

The telephone rang while Melissa was polishing Vivian's toenails and Gloria was applying Vivian's makeup. Bill answered the telephone.

"Chandler's Couture," he said flippantly.

"Bill, is that you?" Derrick questioned.

"Oh, yes, Derrick. It's me."

"Uh, is Vivian around?"

"Yes, Derrick, but she's indisposed at the moment. May I give her a message for you?"

"Yes, tell her I'll be there to pick her up at three o'clock."

"I'll tell her, Derrick."

Vivian nearly jumped out of her seat, but Melissa and Gloria threatened bodily harm if she moved before they were finished with her. When Bill, Gloria, and Melissa finished their work, they all stood back observing their finished product. They were very satisfied. Bill put on the Whitney Houston tune, "Queen of the Night." Vivian finally got a chance to look at herself in the full-length mirror as the music played.

"Is that me?" she exclaimed in total disbelief.

Bill had selected a medium brown, soft suede, two-piece pants and jacket set, a magenta, silk-layered Carmeuse blouse with a draped V-neck that closed at the waistline. A color-blocked brown and black suede swing coat completed the ensemble. Her gold chain that read FAMILY hung around her neck and gold stud earrings graced her earlobes. Her makeup was shades of earth tones that enhanced her brown eyes and her full lips. Her face looked soft and smooth. Her nail polish matched her redwood lipstick. Her hair was moussed back away from her face in soft, flowing lines. Bill hung a small Gucci purse from her shoulder that had a scarf tied to the strap. It was an entirely new, more sophisticated look for Vivian, yet youthful. Melissa, Bill, and Gloria were giving each other high-fives.

"Chandler, when you're good, you're good!" Gloria said emphatically, admiring Bill's handiwork with Vivian. "You can get me started now on my new look for Tony."

"Me, too, Bill," Melissa added. "Talk about turning a sow's ear into a silk purse! If you can make Vivian look like she just stepped off of the cover of *Vogue*, you could do wonders for me and not have to work nearly as hard."

Vivian glared at them all, but she did have to admit that she liked her new look. She even selected a lot of the other outfits to keep for future occasions.

Chuck, Alan, and David were sitting in the kitchen finishing their second pieces of Anna's peach pie when the doorbell rang. They all looked at each other.

"Your turn, Chuck," Alan said, as he scooped up another piece of pie with ice cream.

Chuck grumbled and got up from the table. "C'mon guys, I don't even live here and you've got me answering the door. What do I look like, the butler?"

"You just don't pay rent here, Chuck," David said. "But you sure live here all right."

Chuck grumbled and went to the front door. When he opened it, Derrick walked in wearing a huge smile. Chuck noticed that Derrick was smartly dressed in a Calvin Klein shearling car coat and cashmere V-neck sweater, a pair of Wilke-Rodriguez casual slacks, and Mauri Italian shoes. Chuck was still complimenting Derrick on his threads when he saw Derrick's face really light up. He turned and looked over his shoulder toward the staircase. He saw a very sophisticated-looking woman, who resembled Vivian, descending the staircase very slowly with Bill, Melissa, and Gloria bringing up the rear. His heart started beating wildly in his chest.

"*Whoa!*" Chuck said loudly, as Vivian approached. "Annie, is that you?"

David and Alan heard the commotion in the hallway and followed Anna out of the kitchen door.

"*Au chiwawa!*" Anna exclaimed when she saw Vivian descending the stairs.

"May the Saints be praised!" David blurted out, as he made the sign of the cross.

"There is a God!" Alan said slowly, but expressively.

Everyone stood in silence admiring Vivian. She blushed.

"Don't mind them, Derrick. They act like I'm a teenager going to my high school prom," said Vivian.

Derrick swallowed the lump in his throat. His mouth was dry and his heart was pounding. He approached the beauty and revered her. "No, Vivian, they're just admiring perfection. I know exactly how they feel," Derrick said, extending his hand. "Shall we go, Ms. Alexander?"

"Yes, Dr. Jackson, I believe that we should," Vivian said, putting her hand in his and giving him a radiantly charming smile.

Derrick opened the door of his black, custom-built Citroën Maserati and helped Vivian in. He slid in under the steering wheel and reached across her to fasten her seatbelt.

"I can't let anything happen to you," he said and smiled.

Derrick was so close to her that she could smell the intoxicating aroma of his Adventurer cologne. He started the car and the hydraulic lifters moved into action.

"Where are we going, Derrick? The game doesn't start until eight o'clock."

"I have a special young girlfriend that I have to see. Her name is Linda."

"This is a first. You're taking me to meet your girlfriend?" she asked with one raised brow.

"A very special girlfriend. You don't mind, do you? We'll only be there for a little while."

"Do I look intimidated?"

"No, you look absolutely stunning."

Vivian was not sure what to make of this turn of events, given her experiences with Carlton, but for some inexplicable reason, she didn't feel intimidated by

Derrick's "young girlfriend." And the way that he was looking at her gave her even more reason to feel confident and comfortable. They drove through the streets of Washington, DC, continuing the lively repartee that they had begun the night before. They arrived at the Children's National Medical Center and drove into the doctors' parking area. Derrick opened the door for her and helped her to her feet. Then he opened the trunk of the car and removed a long, oblong box covered with birthday wrapping paper. He reached for Vivian's hand and they went inside. A bevy of beautiful nurses greeted him warmly as she and Derrick walked hand-in-hand down the hospital corridors into a cheerfully decorated party room. There were about thirty children sitting in the room who showed great enthusiasm as Derrick entered.

"Hello, Dr. DJ," the children all chorused cheerfully in unison.

Derrick introduced Vivian to the children and they all said hello to her. Then Derrick went to the young girlfriend who he was there to see. She was lying in a bed with splints on both legs and with her head bandaged.

"Linda Lewis, do you have a special hug for me today?" Derrick asked with a broad, endearing smile.

Linda blushed and covered her face with her hands. Then she peeked through her fingers and grinned at him, her two front teeth missing.

"You've been talking about Doctor DJ all day, Linda, and now you're hiding from him," a nurse said, smiling, standing by Linda's bed.

"Is that your wife?" Linda asked, pointing innocently at Vivian.

"I thought that you were going to marry me, Linda?" Derrick asked.

"I am, but she's pretty," Linda said, smiling bashfully.

"Yes, Linda, she is very pretty, but so are you. I promised to wait for you to get older, remember? And today you're a whole year older and I have something special just for you."

Linda's little eyes widened as Derrick put the box on her bed beside her. He and the nurse helped Linda open it. It was a big, cuddly doll with big brown eyes. Linda giggled with delight and hugged the doll tightly. The other children ooed and ahhed. She smiled at Derrick and reached for him. They hugged each other securely. Another nurse came into the room carrying a big birthday cake with seven candles. They all sang "Happy Birthday" to Linda, but none sang more enthusiastically than Derrick. Linda made her secret wish and Derrick helped Linda blow out the candles and cut the first piece of cake. The nurses took pictures of the happy event and several pictures of Vivian and Derrick. Derrick took out his cell phone and one of the nurses took pictures of him and Vivian.

Vivian enjoyed watching Derrick interact with all of the little people. They truly loved him and he flashed that Denzel Washington million-megawatt smile for nearly two hours. He was truly in his element, she thought.

Derrick and Vivian were about to leave, but Linda wanted to kiss Vivian goodbye. Vivian leaned over Linda's bed, and hugged and kissed her.

"You can marry Dr. DJ first and then I'll marry him second," Linda said in a loud whisper.

"Linda, I really think that Dr. Jackson wants to marry you first, but we'll talk about that the next time that I see you," Vivian said in an equally loud whisper.

Derrick beamed.

Vivian kissed Linda again on the nose and Linda giggled as Derrick reached for Vivian's hand. Several children rushed to Derrick so that he could hug them and say goodbye. Derrick took the time to say a special goodbye to each one of the children. Vivian's heart was full of joy at the warmth Derrick gave so freely to the little ones. The thought of her own child came to mind, but she forced it to pass.

Vivian and Derrick walked to his car and Derrick opened Vivian's door. Before he helped her inside, he pulled her into his arms and kissed her gently on the lips. Vivian was surprised, but pleased as she gazed up into his dark, enchanting eyes.

"I like the way that you handled yourself in there, Ms. Alexander. Thank you."

"There's nothing wrong with your bedside manner either, Dr. DJ."

They were grinning at each other shamelessly before Derrick lowered his head again and this time captured her mouth in an even more mind-bending kiss. Only a low, constant whistle from another doctor passing by broke the union.

As they drove from the hospital toward the arena, Derrick explained that Linda Lewis was in a head-on collision caused by a drunk driver. Linda's only known living relatives, her mother and her little brother, were both killed in the accident. Her father died in the war. Linda was seriously injured and hospitalized for over a year. She underwent a series of operations and still had more to go.

"And I think that this accident, although not preventable, would have been far less serious if Linda's family had been wearing their seatbelts. I believe that any parent caught riding with children in the car, who are not in a seatbelt or safely seat, ought to be forced to come to the trauma unit of any hospital and see the damage that their child could suffer."

"You're very passionate about the issue of child safety."

"I am. I love children. They're so open and trusting. I'd love to have many children of my own someday."

"A child like Linda," Vivian said and smiled. "I think you'd make an excellent father."

"I hope so. I'm looking forward to it."

They smiled at each other.

"You're passionate about children and seatbelts and I'm passionate about drunk drivers. My family lost my Uncle Rick and Aunt Beatrice Johnson, my father's sister and brother-in-law to an accident caused by a drunk driver. They lived in Los Angeles and had nine children. The children were like stair steps. Fortunately all were in school or daycare at the time and weren't involved in the accident. My grandfather and grandmother went to California to take care of the funeral arrangements, close up their home, settle their estates and brought the children back to Summer County to live. They are all grown now, but this drunk driver devastated nine children, my grandparents, parents, uncles, aunts, and cousins just because he wanted to drink a twenty-dollar bottle of alcohol. That wasn't his first offense either. He was not only driving under the influence, he was also driving without a license. The Court had already suspended his license.

Derrick put his hand on her and gently squeezed in solidarity with her passion.

The skybox at the arena was very plush and well stocked with food and beverages. Four, large flat-screens hung on the walls in the room. Comfortable lounge chairs and a large bar made the room complete. Two waitresses and a bartender worked diligently to assure that everyone was comfortable. They attended to everyone's slightest desire. Derrick introduced Vivian to the twenty or so guests, as they mingled with the crowd together hand-in-hand before the game began. They separated occasionally and talked with other people, but they kept stealing quick glances at each other no matter where they were in the skybox. They sat together to eat and chat.

Chuck came into the skybox at the beginning of the second half. Vivian was sitting at the bar sipping a glass of white wine surrounded by admirers who were awed by her obvious sophistication and insightful knowledge of the game of basketball. When Chuck approached her, Vivian almost choked on her wine. Of course, she, like any other red-blooded female noticed how drop-dead handsome Chuck was, but tonight he looked more appealing and sensual in his black Ralph Lauren jacket, burgundy crew neck sweater, gray athletic cut Ralph Lauren slacks, and black Gussini loafers. His dark, curly hair was pulled back and tied at the nape of his neck, the gold stud in his left earlobe somehow lending a rakish appearance. He wore a black leather hat low, just above his eyes. For a nearly seven-foot man, he did wonders for his attire. Something stirred in her and her heart skipped a beat or two. She shook her head and blinked, surprised by the hot flash that moved over her.

"Good evening, Ms. Alexander," Chuck said, with a very debonair demeanor.

Vivian had to force herself to speak around the large lump that had lodged in her throat.

"Dr. Montgomery, it's a pleasure to see you again so soon. I'm sorry to see that Ms. Charles did not accompany you to the game tonight. You look especially handsome this evening," Vivian said particularly awestruck by his appearance.

Chuck grinned at Vivian, as he shook hands with the other guests who were surrounding Vivian, but he kept his smiling eyes on her. Derrick came to Vivian's side.

"Chuck, is that you?" Derrick asked, surprised by Chuck's *GQ* attire. "I'm surprised to see you here. I thought that you said that you couldn't join us this evening."

"I had a change in my plan and I decided to see how the other half lived."

They all laughed, but Vivian was still struck by the transformation.

Derrick monopolized most of Vivian's time during the second half of the game, but she had no complaints. They were looking at each other more than looking at or listening to the basketball game. Vivian's eyes were shinning and TNT couldn't have blasted the smile off her face. It would have taken a large load of nitroglycerin to remove Derrick's smile, too. Finally, Derrick leaned across the small round table that separated him from Vivian and took her hand in his.

"Would you mind if we left early?" Derrick asked, gazing into Vivian's eyes.

"No, Derrick, of course I wouldn't mind. Do you have to go back to the hospital?"

"No, you have a lot of admirers and I don't want to share you with anyone else tonight."

Vivian beamed. She felt a warm sensation flooding over her body. "I thought that you'd never ask," she said, demurely.

Derrick took Vivian's hand and they waved goodnight to the other people in the skybox. Vivian winked and smiled broadly at Chuck, who she thought had a curious look on his face as she and Derrick left. Something about the way Chuck was looking at her caused her heart to quiver.

Derrick drove to Déjà Vu, a cozy little restaurant in Georgetown. They had a delicious meal, although neither of them finished their dinners. They were too busy talking to each other, gazing into each other's eyes, and playing finger games across the table. After dinner, they drove to East Potomac Park and walked along the picturesque waterfront.

"This is one of my favorite spots to look at the stars," Derrick said, as they strolled along. "When you look up, you realize how immense the universe is...."

"And how insignificant we and our lives are," Vivian said, as she once again finished a statement that Derrick had started.

Derrick gazed at her and a lazy smile bowed the corners of his mouth. "You know, we've been doing that quite a lot over the last twenty-four hours."

"I noticed. What do you think that we ought to do about it?" she asked, the smile reaching her eyes.

"Keep it up. If it's not broken...."

"Don't fix it," Vivian added.

Derrick suddenly stopped walking and caressed Vivian's face. His eyes were feasting on every detail of her lovely countenance. He was oblivious to everything around them, as he kissed her on the forehead.

"For a former, all-pro basketball player, Derrick, your aim is a little off," Vivian said, looking up into his eyes.

"There's nothing wrong with my aim," Derrick answered in a deeper, husky voice. "I wanted to be sure that my timing wasn't off."

She smiled, dropping her eyes to his chest. But Derrick raised her chin and bent slowly by degrees until he gently touched down on her lips. He kissed her softly at first, sending erotic signals to his nature. His breathing was quick and uneven and his body grew taut with desire as he devoured her mouth.

Vivian returned his passion, holding her breath less she explode with desire. He held her gently against his body. She couldn't help the moan of pleasure that escaped her when she put her arms around him beneath his open coat and spread her fingers as she pressed the tightly woven muscles in his back. He enveloped her inside his coat. His kiss was warm and sensuous she felt. She could feel his heart beating rapidly in his chest and it caused her to quiver when he deepened his kiss. Her heart quickened when she felt the prominent ridge of hard muscle pressed against her. Her nipples hardened and pressed against his chest. The rhythmic movement of his hands on her back sent warm, thrilling sensations up her spine. She felt his nature rising more, pulsating against her, adding to her passion. She moaned quietly with delight and moved closer to him. She parted her lips slightly and accepted his tongue. He placed one hand on the back of her head and guided his tongue into her mouth slanting his lips over hers. She felt his muscles flex around her. She rolled her tongue over his lips. His breathing quickened more. She stroked his face and he moaned slightly as their tongues danced together for what felt like an eternity. When they finally tried to separate, they were both breathless. Derrick leaned his head back with his face to the stars and tried to catch his breath. His chest was heaving. She could still feel his rock-hard muscle against her body. Vivian leaned her forehead against his chest, trying to get control of her breathing and the sensations that were flooding her body.

They did not speak until they were almost in control of themselves. Derrick lazily stroked the back of Vivian's head. She looked up at him and traced the outline of his lips with her fingertips. He kissed her fingers and then her even more passionately than before. She closed her eyes and was lost in the wonderment of their union.

Later that night, they sat on the sofa at her Georgetown house before a roaring fire, sipping brandy and listening to Luther Vandross singing on the CD player. Derrick placed his arm on the back of the sofa. Vivian sat facing him with her bare feet curled up under her. Their fingers intertwined. He placed his brandy on the coffee table and then hers. He removed her jacket and stroked her arms and shoulder. He uncurled one of Vivian's legs and placed it across his hip. He pulled her toward him and kissed her gently on the lips. Then he suddenly stopped.

"Something special is happening between us, Vivian," Derrick said, caressing her face.

"I know. I feel it, too."

"I don't want to rush you into anything, but I like what I've been feeling. I like it very much. I want this special feeling to grow slowly, but steadily, carefully. I don't want to miss one minute as it grows. I'm older than you, too old to play games. If I let myself go any further tonight, I would want to make love with you, right here, right now. I don't think that we're ready for that step yet, but I do want to know what you think, and feel, and want."

She looked away and smiled. Derrick noticed.

"You don't agree?" he asked.

She looked back into his eyes. "Yes, I do agree."

"Then I don't understand. Why are you amused?"

"That wasn't amusement that you were reading on my face. I was thinking about something that my brother, Benny, told me about taking it easy and unguarded moments. I want this special feeling between us to blossom slowly, too. I don't want to go too far too fast. I have to admit that I haven't had sex with anyone in a very long time and it would be very easy for me to have sex with you, but it would spoil what we have started. I think that we will know when the time is right. That time is not here and it's not now."

"You're a very beautiful and a very desirable woman, Vivian, and you don't make it easy on a man who also hasn't been sexually active in a very long time to maintain his composure. It's not going to be easy on my constitution, but there's a level of intimacy that I think we can reach without the physical act. I want to get to know you very well. I haven't given my heart to anyone before, but I'm willing to now if you are. I want your body, but more importantly, I want your respect and your trust."

"That's what I want from you, Derrick. I've trusted before and I was deeply disappointed. I don't want to bring that emotional baggage into this relationship. You're a very handsome man. Even my housemates were thinking of trying to capture your attention. I need to know what I'm up against before I trust fully again."

"Your housemates will learn very quickly that I don't play around. I'm too old for that game. I've had opportunities before and still do, but I haven't acted on them. I want you to have complete confidence in me before we make any sexual commitments, so take your time and get to know me completely. I want to warn you though that I'm going to take full advantage of every opportunity that I can find to spend time with you. I want to carry your books home from school or quiz you on a test, take you to the market or for a walk or have a quick lunch with you. Spend long days doing whatever makes you happy and long evenings together talking about anything and everything going on in our lives, with our families or friends or just sitting looking at a video or the flames in the fireplace."

"How do you like your popcorn?" she asked, grinning.

"With hot sauce." He smiled back at her.

"And no butter."

Derrick's broad smile beamed back at her as he nodded in agreement.

"Why am I not surprised? So do I."

Later, after Derrick left, Vivian snuggled into her bed replaying the enchanted evening in her head. Her mind stumbled over Chuck and how impressive he looked. Something seemed to have changed about him, she thought. Maybe it was her imagination, but he seemed angry when she and Derrick left the arena. Stuffing her pillow under her head, she recalled that Chuck had seemed miffed the night before. It was unlike him to leave so abruptly without a word. The telephone rang, taking her thoughts away from Chuck. The name on the caller ID surprised her.

"Derrick, is everything okay?"

"Yes, I just wanted to be the last one to say goodnight to you."

Chapter 30

It was the Wednesday before Thanksgiving. Everyone was heading home for the holiday weekend. Vivian had left on Tuesday night. Chuck was headed home to Pennsylvania after he took Melissa to the airport, but as he and Melissa were about to leave, the house telephone rang indicating a familiar ID.

"Hi, Mrs. Alexander, how are you?"

"I'm fine, Melissa. Is Vivian there? I want to know what time to expect her."

Melissa's brow furrowed with concern. Vivian should have already arrived in Goodwill, but she didn't want to worry Mrs. Alexander.

"No, Mrs. Alexander, Vivian isn't here at the moment, but I'll tell her to call you."

"Thanks, Melissa, and you have a Happy Thanksgiving with your folks."

Melissa hung up and turned to Chuck. She was near tears.

"Chuck, Vivian's not home yet and she got on the road yesterday. Her family thinks that she hasn't left here yet. What should I do? I'm really beginning to worry," she said, nervously.

"Did Vivian say anything about stopping anywhere? Maybe to see a friend before she went home?"

"No, she was real excited about going straight home to see her new niece. She and Derrick were at his place early Tuesday for breakfast before he left to go home for the holidays. She wasn't going to stop anywhere else. She was going to drive straight through. It's about a nine-hour drive. She should have been at home early this morning, at least by six o'clock. Now it's nearly 5:00 P.M. and she's not at home yet."

"Don't worry, Melissa. Let me get you to the airport or you'll miss your flight. I'll see what I can find out about Vivian."

"Are you sure, Chuck? Shouldn't I stay here in case she or her family calls?" she worried.

"No, Melissa, I've got the time to do this. I'm not on duty this week. I'll get in touch with her family, if I have to, but let's get you on your way."

Chuck took Melissa to National Airport in time for her flight to Providence, Rhode Island, and then he immediately started calling the highway patrol in Virginia, North Carolina, and South Carolina from his cell phone. There were no reports of any accidents involving a black Toyota 4Runner with tags that read EXPLORE. He was already packed and ready to go home for the holiday, but he decided to try to locate Vivian first. He knew that Kenneth and Benny were probably already in the air headed for South Carolina. He had talked with Kenneth the day before and knew that he was flying to San Diego to meet Benny and help him with Whitney on their flight home to Goodwill.

Chuck decided to call Gregory while he started driving down Interstate 95 South. To his way of thinking, it was the only logical route that Vivian would take home. He knew that, if anything, Vivian was pure logic. She was tenacious, too. He marveled at the way that she went after information concerning Anna's husband's tragic death. She had both the DC Police Department and the Fire Department marching in lock step to help. She was tremendously persistent when she felt that they were not doing all that they could, but she wasn't going to be denied, and she wasn't. She had been through a lot herself with the emotional devastation that having an abortion reeks on a woman. But she didn't sit and sulk and feel sorry for herself. Oh no, Chuck thought, as he drove, she got on her feet and started working with young high school-aged women and men to help stem the epidemic number of teenage pregnancies. She was at work at the DC Police Boys and Girls Club talking to young people about their career objectives and what they wanted out of life. She was never dictatorial with those young people. That's why the kids responded to her so well. She just found ways of speaking their language and helping them to understand how important they are to society. Vivian Lynn Alexander had true grit, Chuck thought, but she could be stubborn and independent, too. If she needed help or was in trouble, she'd never ask. She'd try to handle it herself. That's what had him worried.

"Hey, Gregory, this is Chuck Montgomery. How are you doing there, partner?"

"Sup, Chuck? I haven't talked with you since last summer. I enjoyed spending all that money that me and Vivian won off of you and those other doctors," he said, laughing.

"Well, you know, bad knees and all. I can't move on a basketball court the way I used to," Chuck prevaricated with a laugh. "I'd be telegraphing my moves if I did."

"Ah, man! You told me that you saw that old movie *White Men Can't Jump*."

"Well back in my prime I could."

"That was then, Chuck. This is now," he teased.

"We'll see when you come up to DC next summer. I've got a whole new bag of moves I haven't used on you yet."

"I just love taking your money, Chuck, but you're not calling just to schedule me to run another clinic on you. What's up?"

"I need to talk with your sister. When she gets there, tell her that it's real important that I talk with her. She should call me on my cell phone no matter what time it is. She has the number."

"Okay, Chuck, I'll tell her as soon as she gets here."

They hung up.

Chuck knew after talking with Gregory that Vivian still had not arrived at home, but if she did, he'd get a call from her. In the meantime, Chuck continued his drive on Interstate 95 South.

The holiday traffic moving in both directions on the highway was heavy. He stopped at every parked highway patrol car he saw along the way and asked about any accidents that the highway police may have heard about. He talked to the truckers via his CB radio as he drove along. He knew that no trucker would leave a woman stranded on the highway.

"Breaker, Breaker, one-nine. This is the City Cowboy to anybody who's got their ears on. I'm looking for a little lost filly, south bound on I-95. Come Back."

"This is the Lonesome Dove, City Cowboy. Whereabouts did you lose this filly? Come Back."

"Somewhere between Washington, DC and Columbia, South Carolina, Lonesome Dove. Come Back."

"It's a big country, City Cowboy. When did you lose this filly? Come Back."

"Sometime between 9:00 P.M. Tuesday and 6:00 A.M. Wednesday, Lonesome Dove. Come Back."

"Breaker, breaker, one-nine. This is the Tree Stomper, eighteen-wheeler, City Cowboy. What's this little filly pushing? Come Back."

"She's in a late model, 4Runner. Black on black, in black. Tag: EXPLORE. Tree Stomper. Come Back."

"I'll give a holler out, City Cowboy. Keep your ears on. This is the Tree Stomper Out."

"Ten-four, good buddy. The City Cowboy's got his ears on."

All night long Chuck talked with the truckers who regularly ran the I-95 corridor and other north/south routes. The CBer's had a two-hundred-fifty-mile radius range and were talking all night to other drivers, cars equipped with CB radios, and the State Police who usually monitored Channel 19, the Emergency CB Radio Channel. He pulled into each truck stop along the route and talked with the truckers.

Chuck was approaching the South of the Border tourist and truck rest stop on the North Carolina-South Carolina boarder. It would be morning soon on Thanksgiving Day and Vivian had not yet called. He knew that he would have to call her family if he failed to find her in the next few hours. Every CB base and mobile radio station had been putting out the call for the lost filly in the black 4Runner. Chuck sat in the parking lot of South of the Border drinking coffee as the early twilight hour approached.

"Breaker, Breaker, one-nine. This is the Roadrunner looking for the City Cowboy. You got your ears on, City Cowboy? Come back."

"Affirmative. This is the City Cowboy, Roadrunner. Come back."

"This little lost filly you looking for have a dog called Snowman, City Cowboy? Come back."

"That's the one, Roadrunner! Come back!" Chuck said excitedly.

"City Cowboy, I got your little lost filly Tuesday night Wednesday morning at mile one-forty south bound. That 4Runner made venison out of an old buck at about two o'clock in the morning. Tore up the front end of that 4Runner, busted the radiator, but your little lost filly was fine when I left her. Mad as a wet hen, she was, City Cowboy. Come back."

"Where'd you leave the little lost filly, Roadrunner? Come back!"

"Towed her up to mile one-twenty-nine at North Carolina State Road 74, near Maxton. She should still be holed up there, City Cowboy. That front end's gonna take a heap of fixin', but your little lost filly bagged herself one hell of a big ten-point buck for her trouble! Come back."

"*Yahoo!*" Chuck yelled. "Roadrunner this is the City Cowboy! I thank you kindly for your trouble! Come back!"

"Sorry, I didn't get the shout out to you sooner, City Cowboy, but I'm hauling out of Miami headed for Maine. Just put my ears on outside Jacksonville and heard the call. You mosey on up to Maxton, City Cowboy, and you'll find your little lost filly. Come back."

"I wanna thank y'all mighty much! This is the City Cowboy rolling! I'm out!"

Chuck wheeled out of the parking lot and headed for Maxton, a small country town forty miles off I-95. As he rolled through the tiny town, he asked about auto repair garages in the area. There was only one in town. As he pulled into the garage lot, he saw the black 4Runner. His heart was leaping with joy.

His prayers had been answered. She was safe. Snowman was standing guard. Chuck could see the figures of two people working under the front end of the 4Runner. He got out of his truck, pulled his hat low over his eyes, crossed his arms, and leaned against his truck. Snowman galloped over to Chuck, jumping and wagging his tail.

"Hey! Georgetown! You need a ride?" Chuck yelled, trying to contain his excitement.

Vivian rolled out from under the 4Runner and looked at Chuck. She was covered with grease and dirt.

"Charles Patrick Montgomery, I'm not even going to ask you how the hell you found me out here in no man's land!" she said, with great surprise at seeing him.

"Well, Annie, I may have bad knees, but I've got good ears," he said, with a smirk.

"I don't understand, Chuck," she said, quizzically.

"I'll tell you later, Annie, but you sure don't look as good as you did at the basketball game. Right now, you need a good wash before you get in my truck. Then I've got to get you home. Your family's waiting for you. They don't know that you were missing."

"Missing? I'm not missing, Chuck. I'm right here. I had to pull that radiator out of the truck and try to fix it. It took me and the garage mechanic all day to pull out the grill so that I could get to the radiator and—"

Chuck couldn't hold it any longer. He grabbed her and tightly hugged her against his body. He lost the battle not to kiss her and sensed Vivian's surprise when his lips silenced her. Her knees slightly buckled while he held her. He released her and smiled. "Where's your bunkhouse?"

She shook her head in disbelief and dismissed his exuberant kiss as his relief at finding her. But that kiss seemed to say more than mere exuberance, and, what was even more unnerving, was the fact that she liked it. Maybe it was gratitude. Chuck seemed to have a knack for coming to her aid when she needed him most.

She took Chuck to the small motel, next to the garage, where she had spent the night waiting for parts to be delivered to fix the 4Runner. She explained that the parts had not arrived and were not likely to be delivered on Thanksgiving Day. Vivian went into the bathroom and started the shower. She left the door slightly ajar while she talked with Chuck and explained what she was doing working under the 4Runner. Steam filled the bathroom and fogged the mirror, but Chuck could still see the outline of Vivian's body as he sat on the bed playing tug on a hank of rope with Snowman and talking with her. The sight of her nude body gabbed at his groin and he felt his nature rising.

"Hey! Annie! I'm going to go put your things in my truck."

"Thanks, Chuck. I should be ready in about ten minutes," Vivian yelled from the bathroom.

Chuck bit back an expletive as he left Vivian's motel room. He took off his Stetson and, with his forearm, wiped the perspiration from his brow. One more moment alone with her and he might not have handled it like a gentleman. He was tempted to join her in the shower, but opted to leave the room and let the cold November air cool his rising nature. *Why did she have to be so beautiful and alluring?* he wondered. *Yet and still, why did he let his best friend, Derrick, beat him to the punch with expressing his interest in her?*

As they pulled into the yard of the Alexanders' home some hours later and saw all the cars gathered there, Chuck remarked at how much this resembled his parents' home during the holidays. Everyone was already there, seated at the tables when Vivian and Chuck came into the house. They could hear people laughing and talking as they approached the dining room. Suddenly, there was a moment of dead silence when Chuck entered. Gregory broke the uneasy calm.

"Well, look who's coming to dinner!" he said, slowly, but jokingly.

Everybody laughed and Sylvia made another place for Chuck at the table.

Thanksgiving dinner was usually a lively event in the Alexander household and this one was even more so as Chuck described his search for Vivian, the poor dead deer she had bagged, and the law school student turned greasy mechanic he found under the truck fixing the front end of EXPLORE. Chuck's comical story led to the telling of other humorous stories about the Alexander children. After dinner, Benny, Kenneth, Gregory, and the Dixon twins and Chuck went outside for a game or two of basketball. Of course, Aretha was the referee. They wouldn't let Vivian play with them, claiming that they were broke and were not going to go into debt because they lost to her again. She offered to take charge cards and even checks or IOUs, but they refused.

Sylvia corralled Vivian in the kitchen to wash the dishes since she was not there to help set up before dinner. Sylvia sat in the kitchen feeding Whitney, who was wide-awake and cooing at everything that was going on around her. She was getting pretty big for a three month old girl, and she was the apple of everyone's eye. People argued over whom would hold her until Bernard made them all take a number. Of course, however, he would be number one and nobody dared argue with the proud grandfather.

Vivian was raving to her mother about Derrick Jackson as she stored the leftovers in the refrigerator. She and Derrick had been seeing each other almost daily and talking on the telephone at least twice a day. Vivian showed her mother pictures of herself and Derrick together.

"Tell me about Chuck, Vivian Lynn," Sylvia blithely asked.

"Chuck?" Vivian asked, surprised. She shrugged. "What you see is what you get."

"Have you known him very long?"

Vivian began to tell her mother the story of how she met Chuck at O'Hare airport nearly a year earlier and the ride home; the fact that he saved Angelique's life; how he had helped with getting her new tenants; giving her moral support before and after the abortion and a myriad of other small kindnesses that he performed for her and her housemates. She also told her mother about Chuck's relationship with her new main squeeze, Derrick, and what she knew about Chuck's family in Pennsylvania. Sylvia listened closely to her daughter as she talked.

"Still, he drove all night and half the day looking for you, Vivian?"

"That's Chuck, Mom. He'd do that for anyone."

"Uh huh," Sylvia knowingly intoned under her breath.

After all the dishes were cleared away and the basketball games ended, the Alexander family sat around the living room catching up on everyone's news. Gregory and Benny sat at opposite ends of the sofa with Vivian stretched out between them. She had her head on Gregory's lap and her feet on Benny's lap and Whitney nestled in her arms. Chuck, Kenneth, and Aretha sat on the floor in front of the sofa with Aretha perched on Kenneth's lap. They constantly peeked at Whitney and gave her lots of kisses as she smiled, kicked her little feet in the air, and cooed.

Kenneth talked about looking for a southern California city to open CompuCorrect South, since they now had a large contingent of clients in that part of the state. He believed that the new year would be even better than the previous years. The Blue Ribbon Panel had many success stories to report and they only had one more conference before the Christmas break. He told his family that he already had his round trip ticket home for the Christmas and New Year's holidays and that he was planning to leave straight from the December conference in Sacramento and would be at home for at least two weeks.

Gregory announced that although he had received twenty-seven invitations to visit different colleges and universities, he was only considering three schools seriously. He said that although Georgetown was one of the schools he was considering, it was at the bottom of the list because Vivian and Chuck had watched him like hawks during the summer in DC. He said that they had him busy every minute of every day and that he never got to Howard University's campus once during the whole time that he was there. At the top of his list, however, was the University of Virginia. Everyone was very surprised until Gregory explained that UVA had a good ACC basketball team, a top ranked Darden School of Business, and some of the sweetest hunnies he had ever seen. Bernard mentioned that so far that semester, Gregory was carrying a 4.0 GPA in his core courses with no sweat and got a high SAT score. Gregory attributed his academic improvement to Aretha's domineering personality and the fact that she threatened to tell about all his hunnies if he didn't study harder. The Georgetown coach was also an influence because he stressed academic success over athletic ability. Everyone seconded the motion on that point.

Vivian began her update by raving about Derrick Jackson. Everyone praised her on her new, more sophisticated look. She told them that it was about time that she got more serious about her appearance, especially because of Derrick. She noted that she still had her basketball gear though if anyone wanted to play a little one-on-one. There were no takers. She also announced that she was asked to work parttime for a Senate Subcommittee beginning in January. She said that she was recommended by Professor Fahey, a former senator, now retired, but who was teaching a Civil Procedure class that she found particularly interesting. She was a research assistant for Professor Fahey over the previous summer and learned a lot from him in the process. They were all saddened, however, by the news that Anna's husband was positively identified as one of the victims of a house fire. Anna, her children, Alan, Bill, and David flew to Peru during Thanksgiving to scatter her husband's ashes on his native soil. She was happy to announce though that although Miguel's bank account and investment portfolio now reached into the six digits, thanks in large part to Bill Chandler, Anna was perfectly happy right where she was and had no intention of leaving the housemates. In fact, she was taking classes to become a U.S. citizen.

Chuck announced that the plan for the Youth in Business and Industry Program would be instituted in Pennsylvania in the New Year and that Kenneth's discussions with the Pennsylvania state officials were the catalyst that got things going. He also said that Georgetown Hospital offered a position on staff to him after his residency was over, but that he was looking for an opportunity to start his own practice somewhere in the rural or suburban areas outside of Washington, DC.

Benny also had good news that he was promoted and that he was now Major Alexander, which meant that he could pick his own duty station and was seriously considering Shaw Air Force Base in Columbia, South Carolina. He wanted Whitney to grow up in Goodwill with her family. Everyone was surprised that he would be willing to give up life in San Diego—everyone except Sylvia, that is, who didn't seem surprised at all. They were even more surprised when he said that he might leave the Air Force if he were asked to take any more long term, overseas assignments. He was considering starting a charter air carrier business that would keep him closer to home and his daughter. He also reported that J.C. Baker had failed in his efforts to locate Stacy.

"Your father and I have had a note from Stacy," Sylvia announced.

Everyone looked at Sylvia in astonishment.

"Where is she, Mom? I've got to talk with her," Benny implored.

"I don't know where she is, Benjamin Staton. There was no postmark on the envelope and she didn't mention anything about her location in the note."

"What did she say?" Benny asked anxiously.

"She thanked me for sending pictures of you and Whitney to her."

"Did she say anything about me and Whitney?"

"She said that she knew that you would be an excellent father to Whitney and hoped that you would soon find a good mother for her. She thought that JeNelle Towson would make an excellent choice for you and Whitney."

"JeNelle?" Benny said, frowning. "She and I are only friends and that's all it's ever going to be between us."

Kenneth was startled at Benny's remark. Vivian and Sylvia were watching Kenneth closely.

"How did you get pictures to Stacy? Her duty station is classified top secret."

"I sent a little note to that nice Admiral Gordon and asked him to make sure that the pictures got to Stacy."

"You're unbelievable. No one knows how to find Stacy and you get pictures to her through the top brass in the Navy?" Benny asked, astonished.

"I've been sending pictures every month since Whitney was born. I've got a hunch that your father and I will be hearing from Stacy again."

Benny lifted Whitney in his arms. A silence hung as he left the room to put her to bed.

Bernard and Sylvia looked into each other's eyes and interlaced their fingers, squeezing gently.

Then Sylvia announced that she was considering early retirement from the hospital, if Benny decided to move back home to Goodwill. She wanted to spend all or most of her time with Whitney, teaching her the things that Bernard's parents had taught the Alexander children.

Bernard was pleased to announce that a new Goodwill town restoration project was approved that would include the old loading dock and train station in town. He and other members of the Goodwill Town Council had found that the old train station loading dock and other places around the town were considered historic preservation sites and would be eligible for federal and state restoration funding. He also announced that he was approached about running for public office. The State Senate seat for his district would be vacant in the next election and his supporters believed that he would be a shoo-in even if he was a political independent.

Aretha announced that she would be competing in a statewide piano competition. She didn't like the idea of competing, but she was going to do it because Gregory asked her to. She was twelve now and thought that she should focus her attention on her teenage years, being an aunt, and her other career opportunities.

That's what Thanksgiving was about in the Alexander household. Like a video postcard. Caring and sharing the things that happened in each person's life. That's what families were for.

The rest of the weekend was eventful as Vivian and her family toured the area introducing Chuck to their friends and family. Aretha sang at the Thanksgiving Pageant and Cotillion at the high school, of course receiving a standing ovation from the audience, her family and Chuck. Gregory's basketball team was in a Thanksgiving Tournament, which the Alexander family and Chuck attended in Columbia. The Goodwill High team won the championship game. The deer that Vivian brought would be served at Christmas when all the family members would again be gathered together in Goodwill.

On Sunday morning, Chuck drove Vivian back to Maxton to pick up the 4Runner. He installed the brand new CB radio that Bernard purchased for his daughter and she rode with a new cell phone that Kenneth bought. Benny gave her money to pay for the repairs and Gregory gave her a road emergency kit just in case. Aretha gave her a $10.00 off newspaper coupon to have her eyes checked at any Pearle Vision Center. Vivian was well prepared for her journey back to Washington, DC, with Chuck following her every step of the way.

"You know, Chuck. It's going to take some time for me to learn this CB radio jargon," Vivian said, as she drove the 4Runner on I-95 North talking with Chuck on the radio.

"Don't worry, Annie. The truckers already know about Annie Oakley. Your reputation is now legendary, far and wide. Come back."

Chapter 31

Benny, Kenneth, and Whitney also left Goodwill for San Diego on Sunday. Kenneth had won the toss on who would get to carry Whitney and who would get to carry all of her baggage, of which there was plenty, including a car seat, diaper bag, clothing bag, toy bag, and food bag. They were taking no chances with this little Southern Belle. She would be dressed to the nines no matter what mishaps might occur.

They arrived in San Diego on one of those rare days when the sun was not shining brightly in the sky. It was raining when Benny landed the plane at the airport. They caught a taxicab to Benny's condo and Fred greeted them as they arrived.

"The Brothers Alexander are back at last, I see. And how is Ms. Whitney Ivy, today?" Fred asked, reaching for Whitney and cradling her in his arms. He left Kenneth and Benny to carry the bags as he went to the elevator.

Kenneth visited with Benny and Whitney frequently on the weekends and he would come to babysit if Benny had to be away for a few days. He marveled at how much Whitney grew between his visits. He spent many hours just talking to her and holding her. Benny enjoyed having his brother visit with them. They spent many evenings talking together about the family and planning for Whitney's future. On this visit, as it was with others, Kenneth bathed Whitney and put her to bed for the night. Then he went to look for Benny.

Benny stood on the terrace of his condo sipping a Corona and watching the lights of the city flicker. The rain had subsided and left a grey mist settling over the city and the ocean. He crossed his arms across his chest and felt a flood of emotion pass over him. He looked to the sea and thought of Stacy. He closed his eyes. He could see her face before him. He could feel her body next to his. The visions of her making love with him were overpowering.

He recalled their trip from Goodwill to Vail, Colorado. It seemed like only yesterday, but more than nine months passed since then. He had just cleared the runway and started up through the clouds. Stacy sat beside him in the cockpit. She was relatively quiet on the drive to the airport and as they waited for clearance to take off. She put on her sunglasses to shield her eyes from the late afternoon sun, rested her head against the headrest, and gazed out of the side window. Her hair was swept up under her US Navy baseball cap. She was wearing her US Navy warm-ups, sox, and a pair of tennis shoes. Benny could not read her mood. She had been radiant all day. In fact, they both had been, he recalled, but something seemed to be overshadowing that exuberance that he had witnessed before. She was expressionless as she sat next to him. She kept twisting her Naval Academy ring around on her finger.

"Are you feeling all right, Stacy?" he asked, as they leveled off and headed west. *"You aren't feeling air sick are you?"*

"No, Benny, I'm fine," Stacy answered without emotion.

"You've been quiet since we left Goodwill."

"I've been going over the weekend in my head. I don't ever want to forget the time that we spent there."

"We'll come back again, especially for the 4th of July family reunion and again after Whitney is born."

Stacy hadn't answered him. She had simply looked out of the window. Then she said, *"You have a very special family. I liked each and every one of your zillion cousins, aunts, and uncles. I even liked your first girlfriend, Caroline Ann. Goodwill is rich in unity and togetherness. I've never experienced anything like it. Everyone enjoys just being together doing the simple things that make life have real meaning and purpose. Going to a high school basketball game, having an impromptu picnic, going for a walk and seeing faces smiling back at you from people you don't even know. Watching your little sister play the piano with such insight into what she was producing. It seems so wonderful, somehow surreal."*

"Southern exposure, Stacy. I told you. It isn't the life that you see in the movies."

"No, it's certainly not what I expected, but neither was your family. They're wonderful. I'll bet that you and Vivian were as close as Aretha and Gregory are. They take good care of each other."

"Vivian and I are still that close. She can be a real piece of work, but her heart's always in the right place."

"Will she be okay?" Stacy seemed concerned. *"She told me that she's decided to go through with the abortion."*

"She'll never forget it, but she's strong and she's a fighter. She'll find a way to deal with this just as she found a way to say goodbye to Carlton. She's not alone and she knows it."

Stacy relaxed and looked ahead.

"I know, Aretha told me." Stacy smiled and looked at him. He could not see her eyes through her sunglasses. She had looked at the rose pinned to her sweatshirt that Aretha tossed to her.

"My youngest sister is quite a handful herself."

"She's more than a notion," Stacy said, with a broad smile.

"She wants me to teach her to fly."

"Why am I not surprised? She's going to be great at anything that she decides to do. She'll be a great mother someday too, just like Sylvia."

They talked about the relatives and Stacy was beginning to make real progress at figuring out who was related to whom and how. Then she began to notice that they seemed to be flying in the wrong direction.

"Benny, are we off course?"

"No," he said nonchalantly.

"We seem to be flying northward and not southward."

"Really? Why don't you take the controls and I'll check the map."

"Me? I'm not a flyer, I'm a sailor. I do my best work on the sea, not in the air!"

"I can't fly and look at the map at the same time," he said to her hiding his sly smile. *"So, since you're my copilot, it's up to you. It's easy to fly one of these Cessna Citation Mustangs. They practically fly themselves. Put your hands on the wheel and hold her steady the way you hold me,"* he said and grinned.

"Are you serious? You want me to fly this plane?" Stacy asked with great concern.

"Sure, all you have to do…"

He gave a short flying lesson to her and in no time she had the aircraft under control. He pretended to be checking the map for their exact location. Then he checked the gauges, his watch, their air speed which was four hundred miles per hour and mileage of eleven hundred fifty nautical miles on fuel consumption. Their elevation was forty thousand feet. He knew exactly where they were. He had been flying since he hit puberty and soloed before his thirteenth birthday. He loved the sense of space that flying gave him. Stacy was having so much fun piloting the plane that she didn't even offer to relinquish the controls. She was the pilot for nearly two hours when he instructed her on how to slow her air speed. He put on the headset and talked with the tower. He instructed her to bank to the right to get into a landing pattern. He turned on the landing lights and instructed her on how to lower the wheels and the flaps. When the tower signaled that they were cleared for landing, he told her to bank to the left and to line up the jet with the dials on the cockpit indicators. She saw the landing strip lights before her as she brought the plane in for a smooth landing. He was watching the excitement on her face as she landed. He knew that look. She was feeling a rush; a thrill that went all through her body. As she taxied the aircraft to where the ground crew led her and she released the controls, she sat back in her seat and gazed at him. She was glowing and her eyes were sparkling. She didn't say a word, but she reached for and passionately kissed him.

One of the ground crew opened her door and she climbed out onto the aircraft wing and then climbed down to the ground. She shivered as she looked around and saw the snow on the mountains around her.

"Benny, this is not San Diego!" she said, hugging her body and shivering.

"We have to refuel," he said, wrapping his coat around her, "and I'm hungry."

"Hungry? How can you possibly be hungry? We just ate five hours ago."

"I'm a country boy, remember?"

Stacy shook her head and looked around for the ladies room. When she returned, he was leaning against a taxicab smiling.

"Where are we going, Benny?"

"The cab driver told me about an excellent restaurant. Get in, he's going to take us there."

Stacy quizzically looked at him, but she complied and got into the cab. She talked all the way about her flying experience until the cab driver pulled up to the front door of a snow-covered building. Night had fallen and the lights were burning inside. Stacy said that it didn't look like any restaurant that she had ever seen and that there didn't appear to be a parking lot or a restaurant sign either.

"We're here," he said to her as he helped her from the cab.

Stacy looked around the remote, isolated location and saw the smoke coming from the chimney. Tire tracks led away from the building, but there didn't seem to be any other signs of life. Just pure unblemished snow. More snow started to fall and Stacy looked up at him narrowing her brow.

"We're where…exactly?" she asked.

"Here," he said to her with a broad smile as he guided her up the steps and into the house.

When he opened the door, Stacy's mouth dropped open. There were flowers strategically placed throughout the beautifully decorated room. The floor was thickly carpeted and the living room was beautifully furnished with soft black velvet-like covering. A roaring fire was burning in the fireplace and dinner for two was set at a small black lacquer dining room ensemble with the candles already lit. Bottles of sparkling cider were tucked into an ice bucket. The curtains were drawn closed behind a large round bed that was covered with black satin sheets and a matching comforter. A large Jacuzzi was in another part of the room with the water churning and bubbling. Towels and different scents of bath salts were stacked beside the Jacuzzi. A small kitchenette was tucked in another part of the room and they could see a large bathroom down a short hallway past some closet doors. He was pleased with the arrangements that he had secretly made from his father's office before they left the Sunday Social at Goodwill High.

The cab driver brought the luggage in, Benny paid him, and he left. When he turned around Stacy was standing with her hands on her hips and a menacing look on her face.

"You tricked me, Benjamin Alexander! What are you up to?"

He approached her and put his arms around her bringing her up against his body. A devilish grin crossed her lips as she put her arms around his neck. He remembered exactly how he had kissed her moving her smoothly into a dance with Seal crooning in the background. Her tongue creating wicked sensations in his mouth.

"I thought that we'd try to go back to wherever it was that we were this morning. Vail, Colorado, seems to be about as good of a place to start," he remembered breathing heavily against the hollow of her neck as they continued to dance. *"We've got five days to find that place or any reasonable facsimile thereof."*

He remembered kissing her again and how she responded to him raising his passion for her. They didn't bother to unpack. They turned out the lights and undressed each other by firelight and danced slowly in the buff. The firelight danced in her eyes when she raised her head to kiss his lips.

"You're going to have to walk the plank for tricking me, Captain," she said softly.

He knew that he was in for it.... and he eagerly welcomed what he knew she could do to him.

"Stacy, if this is a taste of the punishment, I'll take it like a man," he had groaned deep into the hot cavern of her mouth. His heart rate was rushing ahead of him as Stacy found that sensitive place near his left ear; the spot that sent his body into ecstasy. She had teased and taunted him feathering her velvet tongue across that spot when he least expected it and then retreating only to attack again without warning and to blow cool streams of air across his heat. She trailed hot, wet lips along the tendons of his neck.

"If you keep that up, Stacy, I'm not going to be the only one in trouble," he said raggedly.

Her eyes suddenly laughed with the challenge. *"You asked for it, Fly Boy."*

"Am I going to get it, Navy?" he had grinned.

"Yes, Sir. You sure are, Sir."

Then before he had sensed what was coming, she flipped him on his face onto the bed, pinned his hands behind his back and mounted him. She had him roped and hog tied in a New York second. He groaned from deep within his core when she began her strategic maneuver starting at that erogenous zone and working her way down his neck to his shoulders and back. He sucked in his breath through gritted teeth as she reached the hollow at the base of his spine, and brushed her hardened nipples against the back of his thighs. His engorged phallus could have lifted him from the bed. Her reconnoiter not ended, she turned him over and began her forced march up his torso teasing and taunting every nerve ending in his well over six-foot frame. Not touching her while she smothered his body with her tongue sent him into an inverted dive pulling G's beyond the scale. They made love in the large Jacuzzi, on the rug before the fireplace and in the round bed. Each time seemed more exciting than the time before. He remembered reaching new levels of passion—more than they had every reached before. They ignored the dinner that had been set up for their arrival and feasted only on each other.

In the late morning, he drew open the draperies behind the round bed and revealed a panoramic view of the ski slopes. He recalled how beautiful Stacy looked when she woke and saw the mountains looming before her.

"*Benny, I didn't know that you could ski,*" she said, yawned.

"*Kenneth taught me,*" he told her mesmerized by how beautiful she was in the morning light.

"*I hope that you don't expect me to go up there and ski down that slope. If so, you really don't have all of your oars in the water. I can't ski,*" she stretched her body sending his imagination on a long slow trip along her torso.

"*I'm not taking any chances with you and our baby. You can just watch, but yesterday you thought that you couldn't fly an airplane. Last week, you didn't think that we could have our daughter. Before that you thought that you couldn't learn to sail a 60-foot sailboat. There's nothing that you can't do, Stacy, and I'm proud of you and our relationship. You'll be skiing like a champ after our daughter is born, but right now skiing is not what's on my mind.*"

He remembered that he couldn't stop her from trying the beginners' slopes while he went off to tackle the higher ranges. She learned quickly and easily how to maneuver. She was very athletic and her muscles well-toned. Before long, she was skiing by his side. She told him with glee that there wasn't anything that a man could do that a woman couldn't except stand up and pee. He agreed. They were blissfully happy, he thought, each day and each night.

On the last night of their trip, he recalled sitting on the deeply carpeted flooring leaning back against the sofa with Stacy sitting between his legs leaning back against his chest. He had been sitting there holding her in his arms as they watched the flames in the fireplace and listened to an old Luther Vandross CD. Stacy felt a twinge of movement in her belly. She was not sure what it was, she told him, but the twinge kept fluttering. She placed his hand over the spot and he felt the movement, too. Then she smiled up at him with sparkling eyes.

"Benny, I think that your daughter is beginning to communicate with you."

The memories of those days in Goodwill and in Vail with Stacy many months before were now entrenched in his mind. He took a deep breath, grabbed the back of his neck, and stretched. The grey, rain soaked night added to his malaise.

"Are you tired, little brother?" Kenneth asked, as he came onto the terrace and found his brother deep in thought.

"No, I'm in agony. You know how that feels, don't you, Kenneth? It's a familiar pain to you, too, isn't it?" Benny asked, turning toward Kenneth and handing a glass of wine to him.

"'Agony?'" Kenneth took the glass of wine. "I don't understand."

"I'm in agony because I nearly destroyed the lives of people who are most important to me."

"You're not making any sense. You would never destroy anyone's life. Especially not anyone you care about," Kenneth said, with great concern. "Who are you talking about?"

"For starters, you. You and JeNelle."

Kenneth was startled and took a quick sip of the wine, trying not to show his surprise, but Benny was looking at him directly in his eyes. Benny didn't appear tense or angry to him. Rather, his body seemed relaxed. He was calm, but solemn.

"I don't know what you're thinking, but I swear to you that there is nothing going on between me and JeNelle. I've told you that before," Kenneth said calmly.

"That's only because you wouldn't permit it and JeNelle is in too much pain to respond to you."

"I—"

"Don't bother to deny it. You've been in agony for a long time. Probably since the day you first met JeNelle. You've done everything in your power to deny your feelings for her and to protect me just as you've always done since we were little. I've seen you do it on more than one occasion."

"You're misreading the situation. JeNelle is a wonderful woman. You're a lucky man—"

"I saw the videotape of the Gala. Cecil and Janice showed it to me months ago. I knew, as I watched JeNelle speak, with you beside her. I watched you two dancing together in that beam of light. I knew then that you were falling in love with each other, but I didn't want to believe it. Then you were seeing Lisa and I thought that maybe I was wrong, but I saw the agony you were feeling clearly here after we brought Whitney home from the hospital. You couldn't even look at or talk to JeNelle. You were standing with your back to her once when I came down the steps to the living room. All through dinner on that same day, you never looked at her once. Mom noticed it, too. Then when JeNelle told me how distant you were acting toward her, I knew that you were in agony over your feelings. JeNelle has been fighting her feelings for you, too. Initially, I couldn't understand why she was hurt by your distancing yourself from her. I could hear it in her voice. Then it came to me when I saw the light go out of her eyes after Lisa called you here. JeNelle is in agony, but not because of her feelings, or lack thereof, for me. She has something else to resolve in her life. Still, I've watched her face when we've talked about you. It's a familiar pain that I've seen in her eyes."

Kenneth turned away from Benny. "You know that I've been involved with Lisa. We have had a satisfying, intimate relationship."

"No doubt you have had sex with her. Having sex with women and making love to a woman are as different as day and night. I know what I'm talking about. I'm an expert at it. I learned the difference when Stacy and I spent that week at Vail. I still thought that Stacy and I were only having a friendly roll in the hay, so to speak, something just between good friends, friends with benefits. I was a fool. I desired Stacy even when I thought that I was falling in love with JeNelle. Sometimes I ached to be with Stacy, not just physically, but emotionally. She and I shared the same excitements. The same rush. Mom told me months ago that I was in love with Stacy. I didn't believe her. Now, I may have lost her and I can't feel anything but agony. I'm not a whole person without her. I have no desire to be with another woman. Not even JeNelle. Intimate relationship," he snorted. "Sex is easy. Intimacy is the tough part." Benny looked away from Kenneth, leaned against the terrace wall, and looked toward the sea. "Mom thinks that Stacy will come back because she loves me.

I won't doubt Mom again and you shouldn't either. Until Stacy comes back, I have a small part of her in Whitney Ivy. Don't make the same mistakes that I have, Kenneth. If you're in love with JeNelle, and I believe that you are, don't let it slip away from you."

Denying his feelings toward JeNelle was no longer possible. Kenneth embraced his brother for a long time. They shared each other's pain. It was a familiar pain. They both loved women who were outside of their reach.

Chapter 32

Kenneth flew back to San Francisco from San Diego late in the evening on the next day. The stars shone brightly in the late evening sky. One star shone more brightly than the rest. It was a pure white beam of light. Thoughts flooded his mind. He thought of his brother and their pain.

Kenneth spent a restless night. He tossed and turned trying to relax and clear his mind. He finally gave up and got out of bed. He put on a robe and went to the living room. It was two-thirty in the morning when he lit a fire in the grate and stood over it as it began to burn. Lisa, he thought. Where were they going with their relationship? Initially, it was only a subterfuge to cover up his feelings for JeNelle or was there more? It had only been a physical relationship. Purely technical. No warmth or feeling. Had he put enough effort into it to make it work out? Could he? He had difficulty when he thought of taking Lisa to Goodwill to meet his family. The image simply didn't fit. That's not to say that it might not ever work out, only that what was happening between them so far didn't seem to have grown or changed since the first night that they spent together.

And JeNelle, he wondered. *What about JeNelle?* He could see the vision of JeNelle sitting in the stillness of the darkened living room gazing into the fireplace. She seemed so fragile, so alone, so much in her own silent pain. He remembered how serene she was as they sat in Scoma's in Sausalito. How she wished that the Expo was not ending and that she could bottle the calmness and take it home with her. He remembered talking with Benny as they stood watching JeNelle at the end of the Expo. He knew then that something he could not discern fueled a fire within her—a quiet storm, he had called it at the time. Why didn't he ask her about the men at the Gala? Why wouldn't she open up to him?

All of these seemingly inconsequential incidents were coming together in his mind. Dawn was breaking and the logs in the fireplace were mere cinders. Kenneth rose from his sofa and went to his bedroom to shower and dress. It was 6:00 A.M. and he had not slept, but he had finally made certain crucial decisions about his life. He needed to get to the office. There was much work that he needed to get done.

Kenneth was not the first to arrive. Tom was already in his office when Kenneth entered.

"Good morning, Tom. How was your holiday?"

"What holiday? You mean we had a holiday? Why didn't anyone tell me?" he asked jokingly.

"Sounds like you've been working too hard. Why are you here so early?"

"I've been going over these bids and something just isn't adding up."

"Which bids, Tom?" Kenneth asked, putting down his briefcase and walking toward Tom's desk.

"These bids that I submitted to GSA for different computer service contracts."

"What's wrong with them?"

"Nothing's wrong with them, Kenneth."

"Tom, it's a bit early in the morning for me. You said that something wasn't adding up. What were you referring to?"

"While you were away last spring, I received ten different notices that the government released Requests For Proposals. I had Eugene, Mallory, and Todd in sales and marketing prepare CompuCorrect's bids on the requests and I signed off on them. Last week, while you were away for the holiday, all ten proposals that I sent in were accepted and here are the government's Purchase Orders. We got all of them!"

"*What?*" Kenneth asked, stunned. "That's not possible. We couldn't have beaten out other companies on ten proposals!"

"That's what I mean. It doesn't add up. I've been here all weekend going over these proposals with a fine-toothed comb and I can't shake the feeling that something is wrong. I expected that we might win one or two contracts. Maybe even three. I'm good at what I do, Kenneth, but even I don't believe that I sold the government on ten proposals."

"You're right, Tom, that is highly improbable," Kenneth said leafing through the Purchase Orders."

"Wait, there's more," Tom said, rising from his seat and pacing his office. He turned to face Kenneth. "We've been subpoenaed to appear in Washington before a special Congressional committee that's investigating irregularities in the grant of military contracts. We're not the only ones. I've been talking to other companies that do business with the military. Every contract is being reviewed by the federal Government Accountability Office (GAO)."

Kenneth's thoughts raced at the speed of light. Realization dawning like the rising sun. He turned to face Tom's worried face. "You haven't done anything illegal, Tom. I'm confident of that."

"I should not have acted on these RFPs without your approval, but I thought that I was doing the right thing."

"There's no need for you to apologize to me. You've helped to make this company what it is today. No one could have been a better partner or friend." Then bunching his brow he asked, "Did Shirley check the numbers on the proposals?"

"No," Tom said slowly, "she had her new assistants do it. She's been preoccupied with J.C. Baker lately."

"Baker? Baker's been seeing Shirley?"

"Yeah, it happened while you were away in Washington late last winter. He's been coming to town regularly and, whenever he's here, Shirley's been leaving work early and coming in late."

Something else began to dawn on Kenneth. "Tom, where did these RFPs come from?"

"J.C. Baker gave them to me."

"Damn!" Kenneth bit out in disgust.

"Don't be angry with Shirley, Kenneth," Tom implored. "She works very hard for this company. She deserves to take a break every now and then."

"It's not Shirley that I'm angry with, it's Baker!"

"Baker? I thought that you and Baker were friends. Don't tell me that you're jealous of his relationship with Shirley."

Kenneth looked Tom directly in the eyes. "No, Tom, I'm not jealous of Baker, but you should be as mad as hell."

Tom was startled. His green eyes widened. "Why? Uh…What do you mean? Uh…Why should I be angry?"

"Because you care more than a little about Shirley, that's why! Tom, you can sell ice to Eskimos. You're one of the best sales and marketing men in the business! Why the hell haven't you sold Shirley on you?"

Tom's mouth dropped open, then he turned away from Kenneth, pacing his office. He stopped pacing and looked at Kenneth.

"Because she's crazy about you, Kenneth," he said slowly.

"And you let that stand in your way? We've been together for more than seven years, Tom. You know what my relationship has been with Shirley. I respect her as a person and I care about her as a friend, but I have never made any advances toward her."

"You don't have to tell me that. I know what kind of person you are."

"Then I don't understand the problem. Why haven't you told Shirley how you feel about her?"

"I was afraid that she would reject me because I'm not a Black man. Not that I think that Shirley is prejudice or anything. She's been great with my kids and they think the world of her, but she just doesn't see me or look at me the way that she looks at you. I think that she's angry with you now though. First because of JeNelle Towson and now Lisa Lambert. I think that's why she's seeing J.C. Baker."

"Look, Tom, I've learned something about familiar pain. We can't afford to live our lives in it. Life's entirely too short. I'm not going to let unimportant, inconsequential issues interfere with my life again and I suggest that you do the same. Tell Shirley how you feel about her. Don't hide your feelings out of fear and anguish over what might happen. That kind of pain eats away at you and makes you do very foolish things. I'm speaking as an expert on that score. As for Baker, I'll take care of that. Shirley's going to need someone to lean on when I'm finished with him and that person won't be me."

Kenneth took the files from Tom and went to his office. He was still reviewing the Purchase Orders when Shirley knocked on his opened door.

"I'm glad to see you're back, Kenneth," she said, smiling as she entered. "Your family must have enjoyed having you home for Thanksgiving. You've been away quite a bit this past year."

"Yes, Shirley, and I'll probably be away even more this coming year, but I'll discuss that with you and Tom later. Right now you and I need to talk about these military Purchase Orders."

"What about them?"

"Did you review the RFP figures closely before you signed off on them?"

"I had the new accounting assistants do it. It all seemed to be consistent with other bids that we've submitted."

"I'm not talking about our bids, Shirley. Those are right on target. What I'm referring to are the RFPs. That's what seems to be out of line."

Shirley took the RFP's from Kenneth's hands. She began to scan them quickly. Her eyes began to widen as she went to the computer on Kenneth's desk and began entering data. She rechecked the figures. Then she looked up at Kenneth with a stricken expression.

"Did we win all ten of these contracts?" she asked in disbelief.

"Yes and the GAO is auditing these accounts. We've also been subpoenaed to testify before a Congressional committee."

"These figures on the RFP's, they're substantially higher than normal costs for the type of work the government is asking us to perform," she said, the reality and fear beginning to grip her. "I should have caught this before we submitted our bids. There are millions of dollars in hidden, unnecessary transactions. Our costs would not run nearly as high as the RFP's require even after factoring in a reasonable profit. This more than triples what we would usually bill a customer for these services. It's like stealing from the government," she said, with panic growing. "My God, what have I done?! What are we going to do?!"

"Don't worry," he said calmly. "I've already taken steps to handle this situation. That's what partners are for."

Shirley began to wring her hands. "I don't know what to say. I haven't been paying close attention to my work lately. If I had, this never would have happened. I'm sorry. I'm so sorry," she said, anguished.

"I understand that you've been seeing J.C. Baker."

Shirley's worried face lifted to search Kenneth's eyes. "Yes, but how did you know? You haven't been around much lately. I mean, you've been away quite a bit and you've been dating pretty heavily."

"Tom told me about it and he's more than a little hurt because of it."

"Tom? Why would Tom be hurt because I'm seeing someone?"

"Because he cares about you, Shirley, and for you."

"Tom and I are just business partners...I mean, we're friends, too. We've had to work together a lot closer while you've been away, but he's never said anything about...well you know...wanting to have something more than a business relationship."

"Still, if he had, Shirley, how do you think you would have responded to him?"

Shirley drew back, silenced momentarily by the question. "Tom's a fine man, Kenneth, you know that. He's caring, responsible, and affectionate with his children. I have a great deal of confidence in him, and I respect him and his judgment, but he's not...."

"He's not what?" Kenneth asked, soberly. "Were you going to say that he's not me?"

Shirley stood up and walked toward Kenneth's window. Wrapping her arms around her waist, she took a deep breath. Without turning, she said quietly, "Yes, he's not you."

Kenneth sat on the edge of his credenza, looking at Shirley. He took her hands in his. She looked down, but she would not meet his eyes.

"I'm the last person who should tell someone how to feel or who to love, so I'm not going to try to convince you of anything about Tom, but I am going to share something with you about me. I've been a walking, talking example of emotional confusion, but of this, I am sure; you deserve to have someone who can love you completely and who you can love. Not someone who won't answer your needs and won't return your affection. You deserve the very best. You have a lot to offer a man, but one who deserves you. I'm not that man."

Shirley looked at Kenneth squarely. "You're in love, aren't you, Kenneth?" she asked softly.

"Yes, Shirley, I am."

She removed her hands from Kenneth's and wrapped them around her body again. She stared blankly out of the window.

"It's JeNelle Towson, isn't it?" she asked quietly.

Kenneth didn't answer her.

"What is it that she or any other woman can offer you that I can't?"

"Nothing. It's what I can offer."

Later, Kenneth sat in his office making calls all afternoon. He called a commercial real estate broker, a few construction companies and some headhunters. He also called Johnston Worthington. By late afternoon, Kenneth had finished with all of his tasks. It was a beautiful day. His mind was clear. His plans were in the works. He decided to do a little Christmas shopping.

* * *

"Hi, Daddy. This is a pleasant surprise," JeNelle Towson said. "Come in. Is Mama with you?"

"No, I just got off from work and I thought that I'd stop by and see you before you left for Sacramento. Your mama and I have been worried about you."

"I'm fine, but how are you feeling? Have the doctors scheduled your heart bypass surgery yet?"

"Yes, it's scheduled for tomorrow."

"Tomorrow! I wanted to be there for your operation."

"You go to your meeting, JeNelle. Those doctors that you found for me know what they're doing. I'll be back on my feet by the New Year."

"What about Mama? She's going to need somebody with her while you're in surgery."

"Your mama's twin sister and your Uncle Forrest are already here. They'll be with your mama, but I didn't come here to talk about my operation."

"What is it, Daddy?"

"You, baby. I want to know what's wrong with you?"

"Nothing's wrong with me. I'm fine."

"You can't fool an old war horse like me. You haven't been yourself since you came back from San Francisco last winter. After that, you were so happy until the night of the Gala and now every time you come back from Sacramento and these panel meetings you've been depressed. Is it Michel again? Is he still bothering you?"

At that moment, JeNelle wanted to tell her father the truth—that Michel scared her. The night of the Gala came back to her. She could still hear Michel's voice. *"Bella,"* a voice, low and laced with vile seduction said behind her. She knew who it was, without turning.

She had tried to walk away, but two men blocked her path. Then she remembered who the men were. They were bodyguards and every muscle in her body tensed.

"Michel, I have nothing to say to you," she said, not turning to look at him.

"Bella, you are more beautiful than ever."

"Please leave me alone!" she said through clenched teeth, trying not to show fear.

"But you are my wife. It is time for you—"

"Stop it! I'm not your wife! We're divorced! You know that!"

"You act like a petulant child. You think that it is over because of a piece of paper? That someone, anyone can keep us apart!"

"I don't love you, Michel! I don't want to be with you ever again!"

"You can say that, but you have not looked at me. Look at me!" he demanded. She had turned to see those dark penetrating eyes, smooth olive complexion, and impeccably dressed Michel Alverez San Angeloe. His hair was graying at the temples, but his distinguished exterior had not hidden his black heart from her. It was his glare that she could not withstand. The eyes that had silenced her and struck fear in her heart. A debilitating fear. No one crossed Michel. He had a presence that made the hair on her neck stand on end. She had witnessed strong, confident men—congressmen and statesmen, captains of industry, and others—dissolve into tears under that glare without so much as a word falling from his lips. She could not look into his face. She fixed her stare on the cross that hung from his neck below his black tie. A small cross of unusual design and beauty. She remembered that he never took it off. It was a reminder of how he hurt her, humiliated her. How it swung from his neck when he was on top of her—hurting her so badly that she had prayed for sweet death.

His words were venomous and syrupy. *"What will it take, Bella? Must I show you a sign of who I am, is that what you want to force me to do? Who shall it be, Bella? Who do you love most? Your father? Your mother? How about your little sister, Gloria? The one I held on my knee. Must you force me to take her from you before you realize that I am your husband? That no other man will ever have you? I am the only one in your life!"*

"What is this? What are you saying to her? You dare to threaten her?" Johnston suddenly interrupted, standing beside her his body shaking with anger.

Michel did not flinch. She could still feel his steely eyes on her.

"Leave her alone, San Angeloe! If you continue to harass her I'll have you back in court so fast—"

"Old man," he had said still staring at her, *"Is she not beautiful, my wife. A Madonna. My Madonna! Hair spun by the Gods. The face of my Madonna—"*

"I'm not afraid of you, San Angeloe! I'll find a way to take you back into court! You'll lose everything! Remember, the court warned you that if you harassed JeNelle even once—"

"The court?" he laughed tightly with a mixture of amusement and disdain, *"what can the court do?"*

"Then your father!"

That got Michel's attention, she knew. Michel's eyes finally left her and were locked on Johnston.

Their war of words was on. Threats and counter threats. Finally, she couldn't take anymore.

"Johnston, please, let's just go. I don't want to make a scene," she recalled pleading.

"Remember, Bella. I will come for you," he had said. *"No matter what you do, or who you see, you are mine. You are my wife until death!"*

"JeNelle?"

The sound of her father's voice brought her back to the present.

"No, Daddy, Michel hasn't bothered me. After I talked to his Uncle Milo, I haven't heard from him. Michel's sister, Maria, called me to say that Millos, their father, sent Michel back to Italy. She said that she didn't think that Michel was ever going to bother me again."

"Then what is it? Is it Benny Alexander? I haven't seen him around here in a long time."

"No it's not him and he hasn't been around. Benny has a daughter. She's a beautiful little girl. That's who's occupying Benny's time."

"Benny's married?"

"No, he's not married. He and a very good friend of his had an unguarded moment. She's a highly placed Navy lieutenant. She wanted to have an abortion, but Benny refused to even consider it. She sacrificed her career to have his baby for him. I think that they are very much in love."

"So now they're getting married."

"No. She was redeployed, left on a mission, shortly after their baby was born. Benny's raising his daughter alone."

"Well, if it isn't Michel and it isn't Benny, then who is making you so unhappy? Oh, wait a minute. It's the other Alexander boy...Kenneth. That's his name, isn't it?"

"Yes, Daddy, but we're just friends. He hasn't done anything to me."

"And he hasn't done anything *with you* either, now has he?"

"What do you mean?"

"I haven't seen you as happy as you were the night of that Gala when you were with Kenneth. He's on this Blue Ribbon Panel with you, too, isn't he?"

"Yes, but we're not involved or anything."

"Then that's the problem, isn't it? Did you two have some type of lover's quarrel? Can't you patch things up between you? I really liked him."

"Daddy, I told you that Kenneth Alexander and I haven't been involved. He's seeing someone else."

"I talked with Kenneth a long time the night of the Gala. Unless I miss my bet, that man's crazy about you and, from the look on your face, you're crazy about him, too. Are you still letting what Michel did to you ruin your life? Kenneth didn't strike me as the type of man who would just walk away from you because of what Michel did to you. Both of those Alexander boys seemed like real decent people."

"They're all very decent people. Especially their mother, Sylvia. I've never met a nicer and more loving and understanding family. I've only talked with Vivian on the telephone, but I really like her. She's a good influence for Gloria. I haven't met their father, or little brother or sister, but Benny and Kenneth both have this glow about them when they talk about their relatives."

"Then what happened between you and Kenneth, or maybe I should ask what *didn't* happen?"

"I don't know. Kenneth avoids me, I think. Maybe he still believes that there's something going on between me and Benny. Or maybe he's in love with Lisa Lambert. Or maybe I'm just not his type. I don't really know."

"Don't you think that it's about time that you found out? Does he know about Michel and what he did to you?"

"I told Kenneth that I had been married before, but I couldn't tell him about what happened to me. I can't talk about that to anyone. It's still too painful."

"Men sometimes find it hard to express their true feelings to a woman."

"You never seem to have that problem with Mama."

"No, because I know that your mama loves me and that she's never going to try to hurt me. Even if we don't agree on something, she has never attacked me or made me feel like less than a man. Your mama's a beautiful woman inside and outside. She could have done better than just marrying a city bus driver."

"You're a wonderful man, too, Daddy, and the best father that a girl could have. Mama knew what she was doing when she married you thirty-three years ago."

"What about Kenneth Alexander? What kind of man is he?"

"He's a good man, just like you. He has an open mind. As far as I know, he doesn't have any hang-ups. He works smart and hard. He's very intelligent and he loves to laugh. He's got good common sense, but his mind goes into overdrive when he's working on a project. His thoughts are crystal clear and right to the point. He respects other peoples' opinions and works within the framework that is best for everyone involved. He's a consensus builder, but he knows how to take a leadership role whenever it's necessary and appropriate. He doesn't get bogged down in the minutia either. He doesn't even know how special and unique he is.

"His staff loves him and they respect him and his opinions. In the years since he has been in operation, no one has ever left his company. There aren't even any disgruntled employees on his staff. He makes everyone feel valuable to the company. He doesn't stand over anyone to make them work. The employees set their own schedules and goals and he's never had a disciplinary problem. The employees enjoy what they are doing and they work incredibly long hours getting the job done, but nobody complains. They all seem to care about each other and they help each other. Does that tell you what kind of man he is, Daddy?"

"Just as I thought. He's a decent individual. The kind of man that you need in your life."

"It just doesn't seem like it's meant to be."

* * *

It was nearly Christmas and Kenneth was planning to leave directly from the Panel Conference in Sacramento to go home to Goodwill for the Christmas and New Year's holidays. He arrived early at the hotel in Sacramento and found a message from Lisa waiting for him at the Reservations Desk when he checked in. He was to call her when he arrived so that they could meet for dinner. He sent his luggage and briefcase to his room, and then he went to the bar.

The hotel bar was nearly empty, just a few people scattered around. Kenneth sat down on a barstool. The bartender put down the glass that he was wiping and came over to Kenneth.

"Good afternoon, Sir. What will you have?" asked the redheaded, middle-aged man with a thick Irish brogue.

"Scotch, straight. Make it a double."

The bartender did a double take and proceeded to pour a double shot of Pinch. He placed a doily under the glass, placing it on the bar in front of Kenneth.

"Woman problems, huh?" the bartender asked conversationally, leaning an elbow on the bar and regarding Kenneth with a knowing stoic expression. "Should I run a tab?"

Kenneth looked up at the bartender and grinned slightly. "What, are you a psychic, too?"

"Naw, in this business, you get to know the look."

"What look?"

"The look of a man who orders a double scotch at three-thirty in the afternoon, but doesn't ask for a brand name. You don't even look like a scotch man." He leaned back and sized up Kenneth. "No, you're definitely not a scotch man. I'd guess maybe wine."

Kenneth laughed. "Sometimes. How can you tell?"

"You work out. Broad shoulders. Clean cut appearance. You look like a ball player. Take care of your body. No wrinkles on your face. You handle your problems. You don't find answers in the bottom of a scotch glass."

"You are psychic," Kenneth said and snorted, "and a very good one."

"Let me pour your usual drink. What'll you have?"

"Brandy, but make it a double."

The bartender took the scotch away and brought back the brandy. "Okay, how many women are we working with here?" the bartender asked.

Kenneth laughed. "You know, you missed your calling. You could do wonders on Wall Street."

The bartender laughed. "Naw, I leave that to you business types. I like my life—nice and uncomplicated. I use the KISS method."

"What's the KISS method?"

"Keep It Simple, Stupid."

"That's the KISS method?"

"Yeah, works every time. So, tell me, how many women have you—a prosperous-looking businessman—sitting on my bar stool at this time of the day?"

Kenneth took a sip of the brandy. "Two," he said quietly.

"Uh huh, and I assume that they are both attractive, probably beautiful, aggressive, independent types. Got a lot on the ball. Know how to handle themselves. But they're very different—probably extremely different women."

"Have you ever considered handicapping races at the track?"

The bartender laughed. "Guess I'm on the right track. Which one can pass the MOM test?" the bartender asked.

"What's the MOM test?"

"Which one can you take home to meet your mother and the rest of your family?"

Kenneth laughed loudly. "You must have met my mother. Nothing gets by Sylvia Benson Alexander. Sometimes I think that *she's* psychic."

"Mothers usually know what they're talking about. They can read us like a book and they know every chapter verbatim."

"The one who has passed your 'MOM test' isn't even under consideration."

"Then what's the problem?"

"I'm trying to decide whether to take my relationship with the other one to another level."

"Forget it! If you have to think about it, it ain't happening. Work on the one who already passed the MOM test. She's the right one."

"It's not that simple," Kenneth said, taking another sip of his brandy.

"Oh hell yes it is! Use that KISS test and you'll find out just how simple it can be," the bartender said. "I never let the facts get in the way of my feelings. Complicates things too much. If you know it in your gut, then it's the right move."

Kenneth downed the rest of his brandy and stood up. "What's your name?" Kenneth asked, reaching for his money clip.

"Joe, Joe Grayson."

"You're kidding, right? Joe the Bartender?" Kenneth asked, amused.

"Joe's my name, bartending is my game," he quipped with a smile.

"Well, Joe Grayson, here's my business card. If you ever want to walk on the wild side, give me a call. You've got a job with my company anytime you're ready," Kenneth said, placing a twenty-dollar bill in Joe's hand with his business card.

The bartender looked at the card. "Thanks, Mr. Alexander, you take care of yourself and remember the KISS MOM methods."

Kenneth smiled, left the bar and went to his suite. He started to dial Lisa's telephone number, but changed his mind. He wasn't ready to talk with her yet. He still had some things to work out in his own mind. Instead, he went into the bedroom, took off his clothes, and unpacked his bag. He stepped into the bathroom and started to shave. He turned on the shower and heard the telephone ringing. When he reached for it, it stopped. He waited to see whether the message light would come on, but when it didn't, he returned to the bathroom and stepped into the shower. He had been there for a while when he heard a knock on the door. Turning off the shower, he wrapped a towel around his body and answered the door.

"Room service!" the bellhop said, as he wheeled in a table set for two with food in hot containers underneath.

"I didn't order room service. You must have the wrong room," Kenneth said, as the man went past him.

"You didn't, but I did," Lisa cooed, as she stepped into the suite behind the bellhop.

The waiter started to set up the table. Lisa eyed Kenneth's partially covered body with water dripping off his face, chest and legs.

"I'll do that," Lisa said, as she handed money to the waiter who then left the room.

Lisa flipped on the Do-Not-Disturb light and kicked off her shoes. She took off her jacket and began unbuttoning her blouse and then her skirt.

Kenneth stopped her. "Lisa, I think that we should talk," he said, as she continued to disrobe.

"We can talk later." Her skirt fell to the floor.

"No, Lisa, let's talk now."

She ignored him and removed her thigh-high stockings. She was not wearing panties. She slipped out of her bra and Kenneth approached her.

"Lisa," he said, grabbing her arms, "this is not working."

Again, she ignored him as she released his towel and moved close to his body. She began kissing his chest and stroking his flaccid muscle. Kenneth didn't respond, his body rigid and unyielding. He backed away from her, picked up his towel, and placed it around his waist.

Lisa looked at him with frustration evident in her demeanor. "All right, Kenneth, what do you want to talk about?" she asked, annoyed.

"Us, Lisa. What are we doing?"

"'What we're doing?'" she bristled. "We're not *doing* anything! You just stopped me or didn't you notice?"

"Don't be obtuse. You know what I'm talking about."

"For weeks now you've been avoiding me. You don't return my calls and you've broken several dates. Now you ask me what we're doing. Same question, same answer. We're not *doing* anything! Now ask me what I *want* to do! That I can answer!"

"I want this relationship to work between us, but what do you want out of this?"

"I want you in the bed! That's what I want out of this relationship!"

"Is that all you want? Just sex?"

"Of course! That's simple enough to understand, isn't it? What else is there? I'm not looking for love or commitment. I'm not JeNelle Towson."

"No, Lisa, you're not and I'm not just some sex machine that you can turn on or off at your discretion. I want to be with someone who feels something for me other than just what we do in bed."

"Someone like JeNelle, I presume."

"This isn't about JeNelle. This is about us—you and me."

"Kenneth, there is no 'you and me'! I'm a woman and you're a man. I enjoy having sex with you, that's all."

"If that's how you feel, that's not enough for me. When I take someone to bed, I don't want to feel like it's a racquetball match. I compete in the boardroom, not in the bedroom."

"What's gotten into you? What's all this stuff about *feelings*? Feelings are highly overrated, you know. Can't we just pick up where we started before? If you want to *feel* something, let's stop talking and let me touch you."

"I won't do that. Not anymore."

Lisa looked at him with searching eyes. She was trying to read him. He did not blink. She approached him.

"If you want me to pretend that I'm in love with you to turn you on, I can do that," she said, stroking his body.

He grabbed her hands. "I don't want you to *pretend* anything. If you don't feel it, don't force it. Game, set, match, Lisa. It's over."

Kenneth wasn't budging. He pinned Lisa with his eyes. She walked away and put on her clothes.

"It's not over yet, Kenneth," Lisa said, as she opened the door to leave. "You still need me to keep anyone, including your precious little brother, Benjamin, from suspecting how you feel about JeNelle."

"No, Lisa, I'm going to use the KISS method from now on. Goodbye," Kenneth said sternly.

The next day, the Blue Ribbon Panel began assembling at 8:00 A.M. Kenneth was seated making some notes as Lisa entered the conference room. She didn't approach him and he didn't look up at her. JeNelle entered the room, spoke with some of the other panel members, and got a cup of coffee. She seated herself at the opposite end of the table from Kenneth.

Lisa called the meeting to order and they began their work. They had been underway for nearly three hours when a bellhop came into the room and handed a message to JeNelle. As she read the message, Kenneth noticed the color drain from her face and the light go out of her eyes. She grabbed her purse and bolted from the room. Tears were streaming down her face. Kenneth leaped from his seat and followed her. She was at the bank of elevators frantically pushing the buttons when he reached her. She slumped against the marble wall. Kenneth reached for her and she fell into his arms, sobbing uncontrollably.

"JeNelle, what's wrong? What's got you so upset?" he demanded.

She could not speak, but handed the note to him. It said that her sister was in the Intensive Care Unit at Georgetown University Hospital in Washington, DC, and that she should come immediately. Kenneth led JeNelle to a bench by the elevators and sat her down. He went back to the conference room, gathered his briefcase and hers, and returned to JeNelle. He took her to his suite and called the hospital. He asked for Chuck Montgomery when the nurse answered. JeNelle was still sobbing on the sofa in Kenneth's suite. He sat down beside her and held her close to him while he waited for Chuck to answer.

"Kenneth, this is Chuck."

"Chuck, I'm calling about Gloria Towson. What's her condition?"

"It's touch and go, Kenneth. I've been with her all night since she was brought into Emergency."

"What happened to her?"

"She's been badly beaten and she's in a coma. Tests show that she had GHB, aka Rohypnol, the date-rape drug, in her system. The police have arrested Tony Jamerson and charged him with assault and battery. They'll charge him with murder, if she dies. I've called her parents, but her father is very ill. He's undergoing open-heart surgery and her mother doesn't want to leave him. I've been trying to reach her sister, JeNelle, but she's away on business. Someone from Gloria's family needs to be here."

"Is Vivian there or any of the other housemates?"

"No, Vivian and everyone else left to go home yesterday before this happened. I called Vivian and told her about it, but I asked her not to drive back and I told her that I would keep her posted."

"I'm with Gloria's sister now in Sacramento. I'll bring her to DC as soon as possible."

"I'd hurry, if I were you, Kenneth. Things don't look very good. I'm trying to be optimistic, but she's in very bad shape."

"We'll be there, Chuck."

Kenneth called Housekeeping and had them pack JeNelle's clothes. He called Executive Air and made arrangements for a private, nonstop flight to Washington, DC. Within an hour, they were at the airport.

JeNelle tried to compose herself. She clung to Kenneth's hand as if her life depended on it. They sat in the VIP lounge of the private jetway waiting to board a chartered Adventurers Executive private airline flight. He held her in his arms and tried to comfort her. She was fighting back the tears, but her body trembled with emotion.

When they arrived at the hospital in Washington, DC, reporters were lined up outside. They snapped pictures and shouted questions at JeNelle as she and Kenneth got out of the taxicab. Kenneth protected her from the press and media and led her directly to the Intensive Care Unit. He had Chuck paged and he soon arrived at the unit.

"I'm glad that you got here so fast, Kenneth."

"This is Gloria's sister, JeNelle Towson. How is Gloria?"

"She's holding her own, but she's still comatose."

"Can we see her, Chuck?" Kenneth asked.

"Ms. Towson doesn't look like she can handle seeing her sister right now. Gloria's pretty badly—"

"Please, I want to be with her," JeNelle interrupted, summoning her courage. "I'll handle it."

"All right, but just for a moment," Chuck said to JeNelle. He turned to Kenneth. "I think that you ought to go in with her."

Kenneth agreed and held JeNelle as they entered Gloria's room. A nurse sat next to her bed. Chuck motioned for the nurse to leave. JeNelle approached the bed. She saw all the tubes and wires connected to her sister. Machines were flashing and monitors were recording her vital signs.

JeNelle sat by her sister and kissed her bruised and swollen hand. Tears were streaming down her face, but she did not cry out.

Heavily bandaged around the head and face, Gloria's jaw was swollen and wired. Her ribs were taped. Her hip immobilized. One arm was in a cast and one of her legs was elevated in a splint. JeNelle stood up, surveyed her sister's badly bruised body, and started to whimper. Kenneth grabbed her from behind and held her against his body. Her body was trembling and started to fall. Kenneth caught her and led her out of the room. She began to cry and fell against his chest. Her arms fell to her sides and her knees buckled.

Chuck and Kenneth led her to a chair. She buried her face in Kenneth's chest and clung to his neck. He kissed the top of her head and held her tightly, rocking her gently. Chuck suggested that he give her something to calm her.

"No! No pills!" she stated firmly. "I just need to know that my sister will be all right. Please, just tell me that she'll be okay," JeNelle pleaded through her tears.

"We are doing everything that we can for her, Ms. Towson. The next couple of days are going to be pivotal, but I've got to believe that she's going to pull through this. I'll stay with her every step of the way." Chuck knelt before JeNelle. He held JeNelle's hand. "I've known Gloria for nearly a year. She's tough. We're going to make sure that she pulls through this."

He was looking into her eyes. She felt comforted and put her hand on top of his. She was too emotional to speak, but she nodded and stopped sobbing.

Kenneth and JeNelle sat in the Intensive Care Unit waiting room for hours. He held her the entire time until Chuck came back. They both bolted from their seats when Chuck approached.

"Kenneth, I think that you should take Ms. Towson out of here. There's been no change in Gloria's condition since you arrived. She's still in a coma. The reporters are still outside trying to get a story and the police want to talk to Ms. Towson. Jameson's lawyers and the football team's lawyers are here, too. I've told the police and the lawyers that both Gloria and JeNelle are under my medical care and that neither can be questioned today. I've got my truck standing by at the service elevator so that we can get her out of here without seeing the police, lawyers or the reporters."

Kenneth agreed, but JeNelle wanted to see Gloria again before she left.

"I think she can handle it now, Chuck," Kenneth said.

Chuck led JeNelle back into Gloria's room. She leaned over and kissed Gloria's fingers, whispered something to her, and left.

Chuck took them to the house in Georgetown. There were no reporters around and the house was empty. As Chuck had said, everyone had left for the holiday. Chuck put the luggage upstairs in Vivian's bedroom while Kenneth took JeNelle to the living room. Kenneth took off JeNelle's coat, removed her shoes, and laid her on the sofa. Chuck brought a pillow and a blanket to cover her.

"I'm going back to the hospital, Kenneth. If you need me, just page me."

"Thanks, Chuck, I appreciate everything that you've done."

"We just have to get Gloria back. That will be thanks enough."

Chuck knelt beside JeNelle and said, "You rest and call me if you need to at any time."

"Thank you, Dr. Montgomery," JeNelle said softly.

Chuck talked with Kenneth privately and left. The telephone rang.

"Yes, Benny, she's here. She's resting."

"Let me speak to her please, K.J."

"All right, Benny, but she's feeling a little shaky."

Kenneth took the cordless telephone to JeNelle.

"Hello," JeNelle said quietly.

"JeNelle, I've heard about Gloria. Vivian and I are in South Carolina and we want to fly up there tomorrow."

"No, Benny. There's nothing you and Vivian can do."

"We can be with you. Help you to get through this."

"You and Vivian stay with Whitney. This is her first Christmas. It's a special time for families. Maybe you'll hear from Stacy."

"I want to help if I can."

"I know that you do, but right now everything that can be done is being done. I know that you'll be there for me when I need you."

"All right, JeNelle, we won't come now, but you keep your head up. Gloria's going to come through this."

"Thank you, Benny. I'm going to be fine and so will Gloria. Dr. Montgomery is taking very good care of her and me."

She gave the telephone back to Kenneth.

"K.J., are you sure that we shouldn't come there?"

"Yes, Benny, I'm sure. I'll stay with JeNelle. You give Whitney a big kiss from me. I'll keep you all posted on Gloria and JeNelle. Tell the folks that I love them and that I'll come home when I can."

They hung up.

"Your family is very special, Kenneth, and so are you. I don't know what I would have done without you. I can't seem to get control of myself."

He held her hand. "You're going to be fine, JeNelle, but Chuck thinks that you're in shock. I want you to rest now. You're going to need your strength to get through this crisis."

He kissed her on the forehead and she touched his face with the palm of her hand. He covered her with the blanket and she closed her eyes.

Kenneth took off his suit jacket, unbuttoned his shirt at the neck and loosened his tie. He loosened his shirt cuffs and rolled up his sleeves. He lit the logs in the fireplace and went to the kitchen to check the refrigerator. He made sandwiches, cut up some melons, and brewed some tea. He took it into the living room. JeNelle opened her eyes and sat up as he placed the tray on the coffee table.

"Can you eat something? You haven't had anything to eat all day, I'll bet."

"I'll try, but I'm not really very hungry."

"I'm not really a very good cook, so if this isn't very appetizing, I'm apologizing in advance. There wasn't that much to work with in the refrigerator."

A slight smile crossed JeNelle's face, as she reached for a sandwich. She didn't eat it all, but she ate most of it, the fruit and drank the tea. Kenneth sat beside her on the sofa and she leaned back into his arm and gazed at the fire.

"What makes a person do something like that, Kenneth? I just don't understand a man who could hurt a woman like that," she said, tears forming in her eyes.

Kenneth placed his cheek on the top of her head and held her close to him.

"There's no excuse or explanation for it, JeNelle. No man should ever touch a woman in anger."

"Yet, it happens all the time. You read about battered women every day." JeNelle began to cry. "It happened to me when I was seventeen."

Kenneth held her tighter. "No matter what the circumstances, you didn't deserve to be beaten and neither did Gloria. No woman deserves that."

"Still, Michel was my husband. I should have known something, done something."

"A marriage license doesn't give a man a right to beat his wife. No one can predict how a relationship or a marriage will end up. There are no warning labels that keep you from harm. It wasn't your fault. You're not to blame for his ignorance and stupidity or his violence just as Gloria is not to blame."

JeNelle began to cry again as Kenneth held her even closer. *Could Michel have made good on his threat?* JeNelle wondered. Was he behind this attack on her sister? Did he pay or coerce this Tony Jamerson into beating her? What she remembered about Tony didn't seem to mesh with what had happened to Gloria. Was Michel trying to intimidate her through her sister? It was just the type of thing that he would do. If so, who would be next? Her parents? Kenneth? His family? The fears gripped her and grew more frightening.

Later that night, Kenneth took JeNelle to Vivian's bedroom instead of Gloria's so that he could watch over her. He tucked her into bed, took off his shirt, sox and shoes, and sat on the sofa bed preparing to keep a vigil over her throughout the night. He watched JeNelle while she slept. She looked so fragile and helpless lying there. Her sleep was restless. She tossed, turned, and whimpered. Kenneth went to her, sat on the bed, and cradled her in his arms. Her hair and face lay against his bare chest. She put her arm across his waist and pressed him close to her in her sleep. She began to rest more peacefully while he held her.

Kenneth recalled holding Vivian the same way after Carlton hurt her so deeply. His body tensed as he thought of how badly the three women had suffered. They might recover from the immediate pain, but none would recover from the experience, he thought, as he slept with JeNelle in his arms.

JeNelle woke and could see the early traces of daylight begin to come through the windows. Kenneth was still sleeping. She lifted herself from his arms and looked at him as he lay on top of the covers beside her. He was not wearing a shirt and the gold chain around his neck shone brilliantly. The soft wooly hair on his chest curled down as far as she could see to his abdomen. His slacks were unbuttoned.

JeNelle quietly got out of bed and showered. She went to the kitchen, made coffee, and sat staring out of the windowed wall. Her hair was still wet and hung down her back dripping onto her terrycloth robe. She did not hear Kenneth come down the steps or notice him standing at the kitchen doorway.

"I was worried when I woke up and you weren't there," Kenneth said. "Why didn't you wake me?"

JeNelle turned and looked at him. The gold chain around his neck sparked against his brown skin. His muscular body flexed as he put on his watch.

"You needed to sleep, too, Kenneth. If nothing else, we're jet lagged. It's only five-thirty in the morning, East Coast time. That's two-thirty West Coast time. You were awake half the night. I could feel you holding me together every time I had a bad dream."

Kenneth walked across the kitchen and took a coffee cup from the rack. JeNelle could not help but look at his finely sculptured physique. His slacks were still unbuttoned and hung low on his narrow waist. She looked away from him into the backyard and Rock Creek Park beyond. Kenneth poured a cup of coffee and sat at the table across from her.

"How are you feeling this morning?"

"Better, Kenneth," she answered not looking at him.

"Do you want to be alone?"

"No," she said quietly still not looking in his direction. "I'm scared and I hate my fear. I don't want to be alone."

He reached across the table and put his hand on hers. She turned and looked at him.

"I still think that you need to rest, JeNelle. I've paged Chuck Montgomery and after he calls, I want you to lie down for a while longer."

She shook her head. "I wouldn't be able to sleep."

"I know, but you need to relax. I'll take you to the hospital later."

She looked into his eyes. "Kenneth, you have a business to run and a life to live. I can't keep imposing on your kindness."

"I'll decide what I can and cannot do, JeNelle. This is not an imposition. You need to have someone with you and I've elected myself for the job, but if you want Benny—"

"No, I don't want Benny to come, but, Kenneth, it's the holiday season. You should be with your family or Lisa."

"You're stuck with me, JeNelle Towson, until Gloria is out of danger. That's what friends are for."

JeNelle smiled at Kenneth. Tears formed in her eyes and rolled down her soft cheeks. He wiped her tears with his thumbs and caressed her face. She kissed the palm of his hand and held his hand in hers. They sat there as the sun came up over the horizon. She never looked more beautiful to him than she did at that moment.

The morning newspaper was full of the story of Gloria's beating at the hands of her superstar fiancée. There were also pictures of Kenneth and JeNelle arriving at the hospital and a story about JeNelle Towson-San Angeloe and her former husband, Michel. One of the articles read:

A Horror Revisited.

Tragedy literally has again struck a fierce blow at the Towson family of Santa Barbara, California. JeNelle Towson rushed to the bedside of her sister, Gloria, at Georgetown University Hospital after Ms. Gloria Towson was found beaten in the

Washington Hotel. Her condition is listed as 'critical'. Her fiancée, Tony Jamerson, a prominent sports figure and a wide receiver with a San Diego team, has been arrested and charged with assault and battery. He has denied any involvement in the beating and claims that he would never hurt the woman he loves.

Ms. JeNelle Towson was escorted to Washington by her fiancé, Kenneth J. Alexander, Executive Director of CompuCorrect, Inc., a prosperous computer network company in San Francisco.

JeNelle Towson, former wife of Michel San Angeloe of the New York San Angeloe Family, is reported to have suffered a similar fate at the age of eighteen. Eyewitness accounts disclosed that Michel San Angeloe beat and raped his former wife outside of the popular San Diego restaurant, Michelangelo's, that he had given to her as a wedding present. JeNelle Towson-San Angeloe withdrew the charges against Michel San Angeloe for the alleged assault and refused to be a witness for the prosecution.

Reliable sources report that the incident at the restaurant was one of many brutal beatings JeNelle Towson-San Angeloe sustained at the hands of her former husband during their brief, but stormy, marriage. JeNelle Towson was alleged to have been pregnant at the time that she was reported to have been brutally raped and beaten. Subsequent to the alleged assault, she spent six months in recuperation and rehabilitation at an undisclosed location.

JeNelle Towson-San Angeloe later filed a petition for divorce in California. Michel San Angeloe vigorously contested the divorce proceedings claiming that, although he believed that his wife was having numerous affairs and that he was not the father of her unborn child, he was willing to forgive her and wanted to reconcile their marriage. He denied claims that he raped and beat her in the parking lot of the restaurant and stated for the record that they were simply having a lover's quarrel. He further claimed that the allegations had been exploited and exaggerated by the press because of their bias against people with Sicilian backgrounds.

Divorce Court records indicate that Ms. Towson refused any alimony or other remuneration and insisted that she only wanted her freedom from an untenable marriage. California is a community property state and provides that a spouse is entitled to half of the property held in the marriage. Michel San Angeloe is reported to be one of the wealthiest men in the world whose vast holdings are diverse. The judge overruled Ms. Towson's request for no remuneration and ruled that she be given the restaurant and an undisclosed amount of money. The judge granted Ms. Towson's petition for divorce and instructed that Michel San Angeloe seek counseling.

In an unusual move, the Court issued a Writ of Attachment stating that if Michel San Angeloe was found in the vicinity of his former wife, all of his property would come under the control of the Court and his holdings would be divided equally between him and his former spouse.

In the spring of this year, Ms. JeNelle Towson-San Angeloe was named the Woman of the Year by the Santa Barbara Chamber of Commerce. She is now a respected businesswoman in San Diego and is the owner of INSIGHTS, the third largest bookstore, art emporium and novelty boutique in that city; the President of the Business and Professional Women's League; a member of a California Blue Ribbon Panel on Youth in Business and Industry; and a member of the Board of Directors of the Santa Barbara Chamber of Commerce.

Ms. Towson-San Angeloe and her current fiancée could not be reached for comment. They have apparently gone into seclusion at some undisclosed location to await the outcome of her sister's fate.

Statistics today indicate that more than....

Kenneth closed the newspaper and buried his face in his hand. Now he knew and understood that JeNelle had not only suffered the atrocity of being beaten by her husband, but that she had also been publicly raped and humiliated. This was what Johnston Worthington was trying to tell him, but could not. This was what he had seen in her eyes. This is why she feared relationships and why this courageous woman, who he respected, admired, and fell in love with, buckled under the pressure of her sister's beating. Obviously, the similarities between the two atrocities befalling two sisters were devastating.

JeNelle came out of the kitchen and saw Kenneth standing in the hallway with his face buried in his hand.

"Kenneth, what is it? What's wrong? Is it Gloria?" she asked almost panic stricken.

Kenneth tried to recover. "No, no, JeNelle, everything's fine."

"Then why do you look like that, Kenneth? Something is definitely wrong." She approached him. She saw the newspaper in his hand. "Is it something in the newspaper?"

He looked at her and gathered her into his arms.

"Kenneth, you're scaring me! What is it?"

He released her and handed the newspaper to her. As she read, her eyes filled with tears. She cupped a hand over her mouth.

"Oh, no! God no! Please no!" she shrieked in agony. "Will this nightmare never end?"

She looked up at Kenneth and began to cry uncontrollably. He took her in his arms and held her face against his bare chest. Her tears ran down his chest and her body trembled and shook with emotion. He kissed the top of her damp hair and caressed her face. She put her arms around him and clung to him as he rocked her. She let the newspaper fall to the floor.

Later that morning, the telephone rang and Kenneth answered it.

"Kenneth, I got your page, but I have been busy. Gloria seems to be coming out of the coma. She's been in and out of consciousness and I think that you should bring her sister to the hospital as soon as possible. This is a good sign, good buddy! Gloria's not out of the woods yet, but I'm even more hopeful than before."

"That's great news, Chuck! I'll bring JeNelle to the hospital immediately!"

JeNelle's eyes brightened as Kenneth told her the news. When they arrived at the hospital, Chuck took them straight to Gloria. Gloria's eyes were open, but sad. Tears rolled down her battered face, but she could not move or speak. JeNelle held her hand and kissed her fingers.

"You're going to be fine, baby. I promise you. You're going to come through this. I'm here and I'm going to stay with you," JeNelle said, smiling at her sister with tears rolling down her cheeks.

Gloria mouthed the words "I love you," and JeNelle reached for Kenneth's hand and he reached for hers. There was strength and tenderness in that touch.

Later, Kenneth and JeNelle left the ICU and stood with Chuck in the waiting room. Chuck was beside himself with joy. He was almost giddy.

"Dr. Montgomery," an elderly nurse said, "I've been looking all over this hospital for you. I know that you've been on duty for thirty-six hours, but your handwriting is still horrible. You ought to get more sleep, young man."

Chuck leaned over close to the elderly nurse. "How about your place, Judy? Say about fifteen minutes from now? You can tuck me in."

"Dr. Montgomery!" she huffed sternly.

He grabbed her and gave her a big, sloppy kiss on her lips.

"You called, Judy?" he asked with a sly smile and a twinkle in his eye.

Nurse Judy recovered. "Well! Doctor Montgomery, I never!" she huffed again more sternly, straightening the cap on her head.

"I haven't either, Judy. At least, not in a very long time, but I'm yours for the asking," he teased.

Nurse Judy straightened her uniform and looked at Chuck sternly with her grey eyes flashing. Then a slight smile crept over her lips. Using the clipboard in her hand, she popped him on his butt. Chuck winked at her.

"That's a start, Judy," he said, grinning. "Give me a few minutes and we can finish."

The elderly nurse cupped her hands over her mouth, giggled like a school girl, and scurried away.

JeNelle smiled and Kenneth chuckled. Kenneth and Chuck embraced, and then Chuck playfully pushed Kenneth away.

"Move aside, Alexander, you're not my type, but I'll take a big hug from this lovely lady of yours."

JeNelle complied and hugged Chuck tightly. Chuck cupped JeNelle's smiling face in his hands and kissed her forehead.

"All right, Montgomery," Kenneth said, as he playfully pushed Chuck away from JeNelle and put his arms around her. "You go catch up with Nurse Judy over there. She's more your speed."

They all laughed as JeNelle put her arm around Kenneth and laid her head against his chest.

"Okay, okay. Engaged, huh? I got the picture, Alexander," Chuck said, playfully raising his hands in the air. "You two kids get out of here now. I'll call you when you can see Gloria again."

Kenneth and JeNelle did not bother to correct Chuck, as they walked the long hallway, hugging each other around the waist.

By Christmas Eve, Gloria was out of danger. Kenneth and JeNelle returned from another long day at the hospital. JeNelle kicked off her shoes and collapsed on the sofa. Kenneth brought an Amaretto to her and sat at the other end of the sofa, sipping a brandy. JeNelle stretched, let her hair loose from a bun on top of her head, and let her hair fall to her shoulders. Kenneth put her feet in his lap and massaged them.

JeNelle smiled. "As I recall, Mr. Alexander, you charge handsomely for that service."

"Oh, yes, and I must be paid well for this talent."

"And just what price are you going to exact from me for your services?"

Kenneth glimpsed JeNelle's face and grinned. "I'll tell you later," he said, as he continued to massage her feet.

JeNelle smiled at him quizzically, but Kenneth didn't offer any other explanation.

After dinner, they called Sylvia Alexander to wish her a happy birthday. They talked to everyone in the house, including Whitney Ivy who cheerfully cooed on the telephone.

"You sound happy, Kenneth James," Sylvia said.

"I am, Mom. I really am," he said, as he watched JeNelle clear away the dinner dishes and load the dishwasher.

"JeNelle sounds good, too," Sylvia said, with a little lift in her voice.

He chuckled. "She's doing fine. Gloria is recovering very well. She'll have to be in therapy for several months, but she's going to be all right."

"That's not what I mean, Kenneth James, and you know it."

Kenneth avoided his mother's obvious question. "How is Benny doing, Mom?"

"He's still hurting over Stacy, but Whitney Ivy keeps a perpetual smile on his face."

"Did he hear from Stacy?"

"No, not yet, but I haven't given up hope."

"She's got to come back to him."

"She will, Kenneth James. When she does, then both of my sons will be happy again."

"I love you, Mom."

"I love you more, Kenneth James."

They hung up.

JeNelle could see the sadness on Kenneth's face as he sat at the kitchen table. She went to him and cupped his face in her hands.

"Benny is a good man, Kenneth. Stacy will realize that one day. No woman can walk away from a man like him and a beautiful daughter like Whitney. She'll be back."

Kenneth put his arms around JeNelle's waist. She pulled his head to her breast and kissed the top of his head.

"I hope so, JeNelle. I really hope that she loves him enough to come back to him. He and Whitney need her in their lives. No man is whole without the woman he loves."

JeNelle rocked Kenneth in her arms. "Now," she said happily, as she released him, went to the refrigerator, and bent over searching the shelves, "what do you want for dessert?"

Kenneth was eyeing her shapely bottom. When he did not answer, JeNelle looked over her shoulder and caught a gleam in his eyes. "Uh, surprise me," he said, with a naughty grin.

JeNelle put one hand on her hip, pursed her lips, and shook her head in amusement.

Later that night they sat quietly on the living room floor before a roaring fire sipping brandy. She had her arms wrapped around her legs and her knees pulled up against her chest just as she had done at his home almost a year ago, he remembered. Her hair was loose and trailed down over her shoulders and her back. Her face was illuminated only by the firelight. She put one hand on her face and her fingers into her hair.

"I've misjudged you, Kenneth," she said unexpectedly, "and I'm ashamed of myself for what I thought of you."

Kenneth looked at her questioningly. "I don't understand."

JeNelle looked away from the fire and directly at him. Kenneth saw a strange sadness in her eyes. She began to tell him about her marriage to and divorce from Michel San Angeloe. As she talked, tears came into her eyes, but she did not falter. When she got to the part about the rape and the beating at the restaurant, she took a deep breath before she spoke.

"I was playing a piece on the piano in the restaurant. I usually played there on nights when Michel was away or busy. Besides, I really loved the atmosphere in the club and the restaurant. I finished a set and went to the bar. Three men who were regular customers were talking with me about my music when Michel came in. All he saw was me laughing and talking with three customers. These men had never even made a pass at me. They were all just nice people who enjoyed the music as much as I did. I was excited and very happy because I had just learned that I was pregnant. Michel came over to me and pulled me off the barstool and out into the parking lot. He was so angry. I knew what was coming. He had hit me before, but each time he promised that it would never happen again. Then he'd buy some expensive trinket for me or take me on an expensive holiday as if that would appease me. As soon as we were outside, I began pleading with him and telling him how much I loved him. When I told him that I was pregnant with his child, I thought that he would stop hurting me, but instead he began beating me and calling me a whore and a slut. He dragged me by my hair over to his Rolls Royce and kept kicking me in the stomach. I tried to get away, but he was too strong. He tore off my skirt and bent me over his car. He held his hand over my mouth and raped and sodomized me. People were coming out of the restaurant trying to get to me to help me, but Michel's bodyguards kept them back at gunpoint. He kept slamming my face against the car as he violated me. I remember seeing his uncle, Milo San Angeloe, grab Michel and pull him off me. That's all I remembered until I woke up in the hospital three days later. Milo was sitting next to my bed. He had been there the whole time. He never left my side. He cried when he told me that I had lost my baby and he promised that he would never let Michel hurt me again. Milo took care of me until I was on my feet again. He was with me every day.

"One day when I was better, Michel's father, Millos, came to see me. He told me that I could have anything that I wanted if I would not bring criminal charges against Michel. I told him that I didn't want anything from the San Angeloes except my freedom from his son. He told me that he would arrange it; that he would always be in my debt; and that if ever I needed anything, I only had to ask.

"After the divorce, I wouldn't touch any of Michel's money or operate the restaurant. Milo told me that he understood and that he would take care of everything for me. I didn't want to go back to Julliard or New York, so I stayed in California and went to San Diego State University. I worked in San Diego after I graduated until my parents asked me to move back to Santa Barbara. Gloria was getting to be a handful and they wanted my help with her. Gloria missed the things that I was able to do for her when I was married to Michel. She was only eleven or twelve at the time. She blamed me for the divorce and said that one day she would have all of the things that I had thrown away. I had to find a way to show her that possessions were not the measure of who you are.

"My father won a big accident case and gave part of his money to me to start INSIGHTS. We sent Gloria to the best schools hoping that she would get her life on track, but when she was a runner up in the Miss California contest, she started dating guys with big money and fast cars. I tried to help her understand that she had to rely on herself, if she was going to be successful in any career that she wanted. I tried to show her by example that she could make it on her own and wait for the right man to come into her life, but that, even if she never found anyone, she could be happy. We were still having that argument when his happened.

"When I first met you at the airport, you and Benny had already taken control of my life. You orchestrated everything that was to happen. Where my booth at the Expo would be located, what computer services I would receive, even where I would be staying and what I would be doing while I was in San Francisco. It wasn't a big thing to you, but no one had taken that type of control over me or my life since I left Michel. You were overwhelming. I couldn't say no to you just as I couldn't say no to Michel. He has a very strong, forceful personality just like yours. I had let him dictate what I would wear, who I could see, what I could do. He didn't want me to go to school after we married or to have any type of career other than being at his beck and call, twenty-four seven. I had lost sight of who I was while I was married to him, that I was a person. I no longer valued myself. After the divorce, I went through therapy and joined a women's focus group for battered spouses. I had to refocus my life and, because of Gloria, I was determined that no one would ever hurt her in the same way and that no one else would ever control me again.

"Michel has harassed me since the divorce. That was him who you saw talking to me at the Gala. It brought the whole ugly scenario back to me. You and Michel are as different as day and night, but all that I could see initially were similarities in your strong, dominate personalities. But then, during the week that I spent with you, I noticed how people responded to you. People responded to Michel out of fear, but people respond to you out of respect and caring. There was a huge difference between you.

"I was frightened the night that you argued with Colonel Baker. It was such a violent argument, unlike what I had witnessed before in your demeanor. Again it was reminiscent of Michel and I judged you in that light. Later, you were so kind and helpful to me. You weren't even angry about the article in the newspaper, but I was panic stricken. You were only concerned about how it would affect your brother. After my experience with Michel, I was afraid to trust my own judgment. Then when the Panel meetings started, you were so cold and distant toward me that I was confused. I was even more confused when I saw you with Whitney. How gentle you are with her and how much you love her and your family. And now you've taken care of me and supported me through one of the most stressful periods in my life and you've done it with such kindness and caring.

"Women sometimes make the mistake of comparing men in their lives to one another. In this case, I was wrong. I'm pleased with the person that I am now."

All the time that she talked, tears were flooding her face. Kenneth listened closely to her, wiped her tears with his fingers, and held her.

"None of this is your fault, JeNelle. You have nothing to apologize to me for. You did everything that you could do to protect Gloria. You did everything that you could do to protect yourself."

"I know, Kenneth. This is the first time that I've been able to talk about this to anyone except Johnston. He was the District Attorney who was going to try the case against Michel. He was furious with me when I withdrew the charges against Michel and refused to be a witness. Later, Johnston and I became friends and he's been my mentor and protector ever since." She looked at Kenneth. "I don't know why I've told you all of this, but somehow I felt that I owed an explanation to you. You've been a good friend to me, Kenneth. You've been coming to my aid for nearly a year when I've needed someone the most. I've got to find words better than just 'thank you' to show you my appreciation."

"There's a different point of view from which to look at this, JeNelle. I've been guilty of giving you mixed signals, but we'll be friends for a long time. We will both find a few new words to say to each other when the time comes."

Chapter 33

Christmas in Goodwill was in the family picture albums and the video had been copied and distributed to each family member. Benny rolled over in his bed and spotted his duffle bag already packed and ready to go. His suit bag was hanging on the back of the door. He turned over again, this time on to his stomach and closed his eyes. He stretched his hand out to feel the space where Stacy had once slept next to him. That space in the bed was permanently hers, he thought. He had slept with so many women in other spaces, but this space in his bed, in his bedroom, in his parents' home, in Goodwill, Summer County, South Carolina, belonged to her. It belonged to Lieutenant Stacy Greene, United States Navy on duty at that very moment somewhere in the world.... but where? Where was she?

It wasn't time to get up yet, but the roosters were crowing. He turned his head to the other side and tried to take his thoughts off Stacy. He was not successful doing that all night, he thought. Why should the morning be any different? The dawn broke and he was still tossing and turning. He opened his eyes and saw the glimmer of the sun on the condensation dripping down the window. He wondered what Stacy was doing at that very same moment and where? Whether she had celebrated Christmas with someone? He remembered that it had almost been exactly a year ago that she first said that she loved him. *What a difference a year makes,* he thought. He remembered the sun coming through the window in Vail that very same way while Stacy slept. The sunlight had awakened her when he opened the drapes to look at the pristine newly fallen snow on the North Slope of the mountain range.

He recalled standing before the picture window and feeling her arms slip around him, her warm, wet kisses on his back, and her hands stroking his chest and abdomen. They did not speak, just touched. He recollected placing his hands on the condensated window, leaning forward to brace himself, and then putting his forehead against the chilled glass while Stacy found creative ways to heat his blood. He wasn't fighting the feeling she was creating in him, instead he surrendered to her skillful touch stroking him and arousing him. Drawing him out to a full, thick length. She knew his body better than he did. She covered his back with her mouth while still exercising his muscle. His knees wanted to buckle.

"You're driving me crazy, Navy. I don't want to even leave the villa today to do any skiing. All I want to do is make love with you," he panted.

"You can't have it both ways, Fly Boy. We can only have sex. Making love is what you do when you're with JeNelle."

He could not see her face, but her words still cut deep into his heart. She was wrong. When they were together, they did make love, not just have sex.

Benny brought his mind back to the present, but still recalled the feel of Stacy's soft but powerful hands as his knees finally buckled, his body had trembled uncontrollably, his hands and head slid down the window and the sounds that grew from his groin through his throat expelled with his bated breath.

He couldn't take remembering anymore!

Benny sat on the side of the bed momentarily disturbed by the memory until his heart rate slowed to a normal pace. He grabbed a tissue from the nightstand to erase the signs of his loneliness. He tossed the tissue in the trash can and rubbed his face in frustration. He got to his feet, stretched, and yawned. He had to work out for at least fifteen minutes to relieve the tightness in his muscles, he knew. He put on his jogging shoes and clothes and quietly left the house.

The air was chilled and he could see his breath as he jogged along a deserted back road. A breeze caught the trees and the dried leaves that still clung to the branches rustled in the wind. His running was even paced. On he ran further out into the countryside far from the farmhouse and the support of his family. The road ended and a path showed no signs that anyone had recently passed that way. The ground was hard and crusty from the previous night's frost. The grassy patches crunched beneath his feet and his muscles and legs began to burn more with each step. The chilled wind caused his eyes to water, he thought, but when the tears began to blur his vision in the rising sun, he slowed his pace to an unsteady walk in the wilderness. His chest ached as his heart pounded against it. Minutes later, he finally stopped in the stillness of the wilderness turning around and around unsure of what to do with his gut-wrenching sense of loss and pain. His knees buckled him to the cold, hard ground, and his heaving chest expelled the air that formed the name that exploded from his mouth, and shattered the stillness.

"Stacy!!!"

"Mom, where's Benny?" Vivian asked, yawning as she shuffled into the kitchen.

Sylvia quickly wiped her tears. "He's out running," she said quietly blowing her nose into the tissue. "He's been gone for over an hour. He usually only runs for thirty minutes."

Vivian noticed her mother's dismay and came to her. "Mom, it's going to be all right," she said putting her arms around her mother and holding her.

"Oh, baby, it's just got to be," she lamented. "He's hurting so badly." She fought back the tears taking a deep calming breath. "He's trying so hard, but he's our son. Your daddy and I can see the pain that he's going through. If he only knew where Stacy was, maybe that would help. It's the not knowing whether she's safe or just—" she cut off her thought and took another deep fortifying breath. "No, I'm not going to give into that way of thinking. She's in the Navy. So she can't be in any kind of danger. Besides, they don't let women do anything dangerous in the Navy," she reassured herself.

Vivian took a deep breath. "Mom, I don't want to worry you more, but whatever Stacy is doing, isn't routine. She's a highly qualified and highly trained, senior executive officer. I suspect that the level of security surrounding her mission means that it's possibly dangerous. You're right though, the most dangerous missions usually involve duty on nuclear submarines or participation with super-secret intelligence operations like the Navy SEALs. Women have been excluded from those careers up 'til now, but...."

"But what, baby?" Sylvia asked.

"Well, female activists groups have been working for years to remove those barriers and end job discrimination in all aspects of military life, particularly after September 11. Women can't adhere to the old 'don't ask, don't tell' bury-your-head-in-the-sand kind of avoidance of the real issues. Stacy's been at the forefront of that battle since she first put on a Navy uniform. She's a moving force in the struggle and a person who throws herself into the fray full force. She's among the highest ranking female officers in military service."

"You don't mean to say that she'd do something like that.... I mean, put herself in harm's way, do you?" Sylvia asked, concerned.

Vivian threw up her hands in frustration. "I don't know, Mom, but, if I had to guess, I'd say, yes, she would. She grew up having to be tough. She hasn't lost that edge, but she's also smart and resourceful."

"Still, they wouldn't let her do that, would they? I mean, wouldn't there have to be some type of announced policy about this? Wouldn't the President and the Congress have to debate the issue publicly before they would allow something like that to go into effect? Get public response and consider it in their decision making process?"

"A lot that goes on in Washington doesn't end up as a sound bite or talking head on political talk shows or the six o'clock news. For that matter, a lot that goes on around the world doesn't either."

"I'm not naïve, Vivian Lynn, but shouldn't there be an open debate on the matter of women serving in life-threatening military positions?"

"Mama, women have served in life-threatening positions before, even when they were restricted to mostly clerical jobs or nursing. There's no position in the military that's bulletproof and even if there were, Stacy wouldn't be in it. Benny knows that. He also knows that Stacy's probably risking her life wherever she is. That's why he's so worried."

Sylvia looked up and out through the window. She saw her son walking back toward the house across the barren field.

"Heaven help me, I want Stacy to do anything and everything that she wants in her life, and I can support that fully, but I just want Benjamin Staton to have just one chance to say what's in his heart to her. Just one chance. Then I think that he could cope better with her decision. He needs to tell her that he's in love with her."

"That wouldn't be enough for him, Mom. He wants a commitment from her and I don't know whether Stacy could give him what he needs now. At least not until she knows what she needs. I hope she realizes that she needs him in her life as much as he needs her."

Benny still didn't hear Whitney when he returned to the house. He went into the bathroom, showered, and shaved. When he finished, he dressed partially and went into Aretha's bedroom. Whitney was wide-awake, playing quietly with her hands and feet.

"Good morning, sunshine." He smiled down at her.

His daughter's big, bright smile revealed the budding teeth in her pink gums. He changed her diaper and lifted her from her crib onto his shoulder as they went to the kitchen carrying on their usual morning conversation. The chain around his neck still fascinated her. She tried to finger it while he walked around the kitchen preparing her cereal and fruit. He put warm water in a pot to knock the chill off her bottle and started the coffeemaker.

As he propped her in his arm and spooned the food into her mouth, she ate, and giggled and laughed while he talked with her.

"You two are a wonderful sight," Bernard said, smiling from the kitchen door.

"You do that real well, Benjamin Staton," Sylvia said from behind the video cam.

"Your grandparents are at it again, Whitney Ivy," he said, smiling and propping her up so that his mother could get a clear view. "You're probably the most photographed baby in this hemisphere."

"These times are too precious to miss," Bernard said, lifting Whitney from Benny's arms. "Sure you don't want to leave her with us while you go up to DC with Vivian Lynn?"

"I haven't had any time with her since we got here," Benny said, smiling. "Everyone in the family has spent more time with her than I have."

Bernard tested the warmth of the milk by dropping some on the inside of his wrist. He sat with his first grandchild in his arms, helping her to hold her bottle. Sylvia was still videotaping as if it were a major event.

"Well, I guess I'm elected to cook breakfast," Benny said, rising from the kitchen table.

His parents' attention never left Whitney. He got the flat iron skillet from the cupboard and the eggs and French bread from its bin. Thirty minutes later the French toast was piping hot and heaped on an oblong plate, the sausage and bacon were situated around the sides of the French toast and the eggs were fluffy and heaped in the bowl. He turned from the refrigerator with the milk and orange juice in his hands and closed the refrigerator door with his foot. He looked up into his family's eyes as they began to applaud.

"Well done, Benjamin Staton," Sylvia beamed. "I'm going to have to write another letter to Stacy just to tell her about this."

"She already knows, Mom," Benny said. "She taught me how to cook while she was carrying Whitney."

"Way to go, Stacy!" Aretha interjected. "I knew she had what it takes!"

They smiled, joined hands and looked toward Bernard.

"We come together in the unity of the mind, body and spirit of this family whether near or far," Bernard said.

"We will continue to be dedicated to the careers that we have chosen to learn and to master," Vivian said.

"We will continue to work toward our collective endeavors and take responsibility for our failures as well as our successes," Benny said.

"We will continue to contribute our collective means and gains toward the perpetuation of the family," Aretha said.

"We will continue to foster the purpose that has been set for us by the ancestors," Gregory said.

"We will continue the creative spirit that has helped us to seek the high ground," Sylvia said.

"If Kenneth James were here in body, he would remind us to continue to have faith in each other," Bernard said, "and the future generations embodied in our child, Whitney Ivy," he ended.

They smiled at each other and began to eat the breakfast that Benny had made.

"Benjamin Staton, you're doing an excellent job raising Whitney Ivy." Bernard beamed, as he dug into the succulent French toast.

"Thanks, Dad, but the credit belongs to you and Mom. I'm just doing what I was taught by you two."

"You've learned well, son. Continue to build the bond between you and our granddaughter and she'll be fine and so will you."

"Dad, what are the most important things you can teach a child?" Gregory asked.

"There's only one, Gregory Clayton," Aretha said, crunching on a piece of bacon.

"And what is that?" Vivian asked.

"Truth," Aretha answered. "If you know that you will always hear the truth from your parents and family, everything else falls into place."

"She's right," Benny said. "That's what I'm teaching Whitney. No fairy tales about Tooth Fairies, Santa Clauses or Easter Bunnies. People tell their children that kind of stuff and then they wonder why their children don't believe in them or believe them on the important things."

"How could any child believe in a parent once that child discovers that the parent has lied to them?" Vivian asked rhetorically. "It's the little, supposedly benign, white lies that lead to the big ones and the lack of trust that develops. Lying comes too easily. It becomes the norm rather than the exception. You can't build a healthy relationship with someone who couldn't even trust his or her parents to tell the truth."

Everyone looked at Vivian.

"God, am I glad I grew up in this family," she said, smiling slightly, looking around the table.

Everyone smiled and nodded in agreement.

"When that happens.... When you run into someone who has no truth or trust to offer because they haven't learned it, they have to unravel their history or they'll never get beyond that point," Bernard said, looking at Benny.

"I overlooked so much when I dealt with women. It never occurred to me to question their early socialization. That's how naïve I've been. I've grown up with role models who are complete and who I thought were the norm: self-sufficient, self-reliant, and self-motivated."

"Stacy is a complete woman, Benjamin Staton," Sylvia said, "she just has a different agenda. You shouldn't try to put her into your timetable for life's events. She's given you all she thought you wanted from her: your daughter. Now you have to give her what she thinks she needs: her freedom. When her need to have her freedom, her career, becomes less important than her need to be loved and cherished, she'll come home to you."

Vivian was sitting in the backseat playing with Whitney as Benny drove the 4Runner up Interstate 95 North.

"How are you handling this new friendship with Derrick Jackson, Viv?"

"Carefully," she answered. "Very carefully. I don't want to rush into anything just because I'm still on the rebound from Carlton. I think I've made a pretty good start at trying to get over him and all the things that happened between us before I started this relationship with Derrick, but I haven't learned to trust again. Not yet anyway."

"You certainly have changed your style. I like the new look, but I liked the old look, too."

"You're my brother," she said and laughed. "It's in the Brother Book: thou shall like thy sister's look."

"Funny, I never read that chapter," he said and smiled.

"What about you, Benny?"

"What about me?"

"Your relationships, how are you handling them?"

"Still rated General Audiences. I'm not seeing anyone."

"What about JeNelle?"

"She's not on the agenda. Unless I miss my guess, K.J.'s life will soon be rated Restricted Audiences, restricted to him and JeNelle only." He was glad that he could now smile at the thought of JeNelle and Kenneth together.

"You okay with that?"

"Yes. What I feel for JeNelle is only friendship. What she feels for K.J., I believe, is an entirely different matter."

"Think they're going to get together?"

"If they haven't already, bet money on it. They've been alone together since Gloria was assaulted."

"Yeah, in Benny's Bordello."

Benny laughed. "You can call it Benny's Bed and Breakfast from now on."

"You know, you've changed, too, Benny."

"I suppose I have. Love makes you do foolish things."

"Foolish? You were never foolish. Horny yes, foolish no."

"You're my sister. It's written in the Sister Book: thou shalt accept all thy brother's shortcomings."

"Funny, I never read that chapter," she said and smiled. "I guess you're still waiting to exhale."

"I have to. Stacy's the only woman that can get me there and I can't and won't lose her."

"What did K.J. say on the telephone?"

"He said that he traced Stacy's father and mother through his Internet connections using their Social Security numbers and job records. Stacy's mother is in Illinois and her father is in North Carolina."

"How did he get their Social Security numbers?"

"From her application to the Naval Academy."

"Leave it to K.J. to figure out how to help."

"I wish he'd figure out what to do with these upcoming hearings. I lived in Washington long enough to know that politics, the military industrial complex, and big pots of money spell trouble."

"So have I. I'll be working part time on Capitol Hill this semester. I'm going to do everything I can to help him."

"We all are, Viv. That is if he'll let us. That's part of the reason I decided to come back to Washington with you. I'm going to sniff around the Pentagon and see what's in the wind."

"And to see Admiral Gordon, too, I'll bet."

"Armed with mom's homemade, deep-dish apple pie, you'd win that bet."

Chapter 34

Vivian came down the steps and checked her watch. As she passed the front door, someone knocked. She smiled broadly, as she opened the door.

"You're late again," she said and smiled until the man standing at her door turned around. "Carlton?" The smile slipped from her face. "What are you doing here?"

"My team's coming to town to play… Look, do I have to stand in the cold? Can't I come in?"

Vivian didn't answer. She walked away from the door and he walked in closing the door behind him. He leaned toward her to kiss her and she coldly turned away from him.

"God, you look good! A whole new look!" He grinned, walking around her and looking at her from all angles. "But then, you always did look good to me." He eased up to her and slipped his arms around her.

She pushed away from him. "What do you want, Carlton?"

"To see my lady and our baby, of course. I came up a day early just so that we could get some things cleared up between us. Start the New Year off right with a clean slate. Is the baby upstairs?"

Vivian froze momentarily and then walked into the front living room. Carlton followed her. She turned to face him, bracing herself against the back of the sofa. "There is no baby, Carlton."

"No baby? What are you talking about, Vivian? You were pregnant, right? You'd never lie to me about anything and certainly not about something as important to me as that," he said searching her eyes. "Are you trying to deny me my rights as a father? Are you still that angry with me over that little misunderstanding? I've tried to do everything that I can to apologize. I thought that I'd give you a little space and a little time. I love you, Vivian. I want us back the way we were. I want us to be a family. I promise it will be different. I'll be different. You can't still be jealous because I've seen other women? I was just sowing a few wild oats before we settled down. Now I just want to make it right between us."

"Don't you understand? Nothing can make it right between us, Carlton. It hasn't been right between us for a very long time. I refused to believe it though.

I kept telling myself that all I had to do was be there for you, be patient. Help you with your career goals and love you as much as humanly possible, but you kept proving me wrong. When I went to all that trouble to arrange that party for those men you thought were going to help your career and—"

"Not that again! I told you, they went a little too far, that's all. Why do you want to bring up old stuff?"

"A little too far? You were going to let them use me like a prostitute and all you can say is that 'they went a little too far'?"

"Is that why you want to hurt me? I didn't let them touch you. That's why those other women were there. I told you that deal didn't mean anything to me! It's you I love!

"I sent money and gifts to you for the baby! I even started a college fund for our child! You sent everything back to me. I tried to call you and you hung up on me. I've tried to see you, but your housemates kept telling me that you were away. I even tried to talk to your family. No one would listen to me. Chuck Montgomery, of all people, was the only one who would even talk to me. He even got me some interviews with some pro teams."

"I wonder what my family and friends would have said if I had told them about you and that poor kid you humiliated at the party you took me to a couple of summers ago. You and your frat brothers made that kid's life hell. Then you tell me that you have to go make a run for more beer and I find you in your car sodomizing that same kid."

"He was gay! He begged me to do it! What damn difference does it make who I screwed when you weren't around? Look, baby, I used a condom every time! I never tried to butt fuck you, did I?"

Vivian narrowed her eyes.

"Well, it was just that one time, Vivian! I was high and besides you damn near took my head off! Look, baby, all that's behind us now. We have a baby and a future together to think about, not the past. Now I'm asking you to tell me what's going to make this happen between us, for our baby's sake?"

"I told you! Nothing is going to make it right between us ever again, Carlton! There is no baby! I had an abortion!" she screamed. "Now get out! I don't ever want to see you again!"

Carlton stared at her in disbelief, rage building in him. "No! No! You wouldn't do that! You're lying to me! Why are you lying to me, Vivian?!" he yelled, grabbing her arms and shaking her.

"I'm not lying to you!" she screamed, jerking away from him. "I had an abortion! Do you hear me? Do you know what that does to a woman? Do you have any idea what you put me through? Get out, Carlton, and don't ever come back!"

"I'm not leaving until I get some answers!" he yelled. "Why did you do this to me? Why would you kill my child? Who talked you into doing this to me? I know it wasn't your family. Who—" Carlton narrowed his eyes at Vivian. "Chuck. Was it Chuck? You're screwing him, aren't you? That's it! That's why he helped me! I knew it! I could tell from the way he looked at you that he wanted you! Always hanging around you, looking at you when you weren't looking. He wanted you and now you're fucking him! You did it to get back at me! Because of those college cunts!"

"Chuck had nothing to do with my decision! He tried to talk me out of it. He never even told me that he helped you!"

"You're lying to me, Vivian! You were probably fucking him all along while I was making love to you! What's wrong, Vivian, white dick taste better than mine?!"

"That's enough!" an angry voice flew at them from the doorway.

Chuck strode into the living room with his teeth gritted and eyes flashing.

Carlton looked from him to Vivian.

"Now I see it clearly! I had to damn near beg you to get in here and he's got a damn key!" Carlton roared. "Now ain't that the shit? The slave givin' a key to the massa! I heard that you brought him home with you for Thanksgiving. Sitting at your parents' house in *my* place. Then I heard that you took him all over Summer County with you and a baby, a little girl. A light-skinned baby! Maybe it wasn't my baby you were carrying after all! Maybe it—"

SMACK!!!

Vivian's hand whipped across Carlton's face before she realized what she was doing. "You have no right to speak to me or him like that! Chuck is my friend!" she said through gritted teeth. "He is *not* my lover!"

Carlton rubbed his face. "Looks like I've touched a nerve. Who would have thought that a sistah like you would lay down for whitey? You livin' up here with all these white folks in your damn house! Wouldn't move back to South Carolina with me when I asked you to. Now I know why! I should have known you'd turn your back on a Black man!"

"I said that's enough, Andrews!" Chuck railed.

"Stay out of this, Montgomery! This is between me and my woman!"

"I'm not *your* woman, Carlton, and I want you to leave!"

"You heard the lady, Andrews! Get out!"

"Deny it, Montgomery! Tell me to my face that you don't want my woman! Say it out loud! Tell me that her cocoabutter skin doesn't turn you the fuck on!" Carlton backed up toward the door. "It's not over between us, Vivian! You remember that when you get tired of this white bread and want me back! You think about it while you're oozing all your chocolate syrup all over him and remember what it was like between us! What it felt like to make love to a Black man! How good we were together! A white man can't love you the way I have! You remember that!"

Carlton slammed the door so hard that the windows rattled.

Vivian slumped and tears rolled down her cheeks. Chuck engulfed her in his arms.

"C'mon, Annie, don't let him get to you like this."

"He's angry, Chuck," she said, sobbing. "I aborted his seed. He doesn't know what to do with his anger," she sobbed.

"I don't give a good damn what he's feeling! That's no excuse for him lashing out at you like that!"

"He's hurting," she moved out of Chuck's embrace, "but he should never have said those things to you. I tried to tell him how hard you worked to persuade me to keep his baby. How you told me that I would regret that decision one day."

Chuck embraced her again. "You've been hurting, too, for too long, Vivian. Every day, I've watched you try to put that abortion behind you. You can't let Carlton make you the villain when you were the victim. I know what this has done to you. He doesn't," He squeezed her tightly against his chest.

Vivian hugged him and cried. They stood for a while and then Vivian looked up at him and tried to smile.

"Don't you ever get tired of rescuing damsels in distress?"

"Naw, Annie, that's the cowboy way." He smiled, as he wiped her tears with his thumbs.

She saw something in his eyes. The way he looked at her with warmth. Was Carlton right? Did Chuck have feelings to her? She looked into his eyes again, as his head began to descend. She remembered his mesmerizing kisses and snapped out of her thoughts.

"God, I must look like warmed over death," she said, trying to gather herself. "Derrick should be here any minute. I'm going to wash my face and—"

"Uh, that's why I came over, Annie. Derrick has an emergency. He asked me to pick you up. He gave a list to me of things that he wants us to pick up from the market for the party tonight."

"Oh, I thought that you were here looking for Melissa."

"No, she'll be back in town later. I'll pick her up at the airport around nine. Now you go get ready and let's go."

Vivian came to him and kissed him on the cheek. "Melissa is a very lucky lady, Chuck Montgomery."

"Uh uh, Derrick's a very lucky man." He smiled.

* * *

The porters at The Watergate Hotel and Condo Complex loaded the groceries onto a conveyance and followed Vivian and Chuck into the lobby.

"Ms. Alexander, Dr. Montgomery, a Happy New Year to you both."

"Thanks, Joshua," Vivian said, smiling. "How are things going for you here?"

"Just great. I can't thank you and Dr. Montgomery enough for getting me this job and finding a place for me and my family to live. My wife loves her new job as a switchboard operator at the hospital, too."

"I'm happy for all of you," Vivian said, smiling. "Kiss the kids for me."

"I will, Ms. Alexander. We didn't have a prayer before you and Dr. Montgomery helped us move out of the Family Homeless Shelter. How can I repay your kindness?" He gushed.

"Help someone else in need," Vivian said. "The people at the shelter need all the help they can get."

"I'll do that, Ms. Alexander." He shook her outstretched hand.

"Is Dr. Jackson here yet?" Chuck asked.

"Yes, sir, he is. He went up to his condo about an hour ago. Said you two would be coming soon. He's expecting you." He leaned in close to Chuck. "I don't want to alarm Ms. Alexander, but being that you're a doctor and everything, Doc Jackson, he wasn't looking like himself. Kinda down or something. Started to get his mail and then he just left it. I asked him if he needed help. Just said he'd be fine in a minute. Didn't look good to me at all, Dr. Montgomery."

"Thanks, Joshua," Chuck said hurriedly, as he quickly stepped toward the elevators and inserted an electronic key.

Vivian, surprised and concerned by his sudden haste, asked, "Chuck, what is it?"

"Uh, nothing, Annie," he said hastily.

When the elevator doors opened on Derrick's floor, Chuck nearly sprinted down the hallway. Vivian followed him at a trot. When they reached the door, Chuck inserted the key and rushed in.

"DJ! DJ!" he yelled somewhat frantically. "DJ, where are you?!"

"In here, Chuck. I'm in the study."

Chuck went in hurriedly. Vivian followed, alarmed by Chuck's haste and demeanor.

"What is it, DJ?" Chuck asked, as he approached Derrick.

Derrick was sitting in a leather recliner with his feet up.

"I'm fine, Chuck! Stop worrying about me!" he railed.

Vivian approached Derrick. "What is it? Are you all right, Derrick?" she asked, looking from Chuck to Derrick.

Derrick smiled at her. "Yes, even better now that you're here," he said, standing and pulling her into his embrace.

She sensed that something passed between Derrick and Chuck over her shoulder in a moment of uneasy silence as Derrick held her. When she turned around to look at Chuck, he turned his back to her, grabbed the back of his neck, and stretched, she thought, in frustration.

"Don't mind him," Derrick said, with a smile, noticing her confused expression.

"Something's going on, Derrick," she said. "I know Chuck well enough to tell when something is bothering him—"

"It's nothing, Vivian. Really," he said looking at Chuck and then back at her. "I just had a tough case today. That's why I asked Chuck to fill in for me, pick you up, and run those errands, that's all."

The doorbell rang.

"I'll get it," Chuck said. "It's probably Joshua with the party stuff."

He bounded from the room and Vivian turned to Derrick still confused.

"I could use one of your life-giving kisses, Counselor," he said, pulling her into his arms.

"Is that what the doctor ordered?" she asked, grinning.

"That's what's on the prescription. Daily doses of your kisses administered by mouth frequently."

She put her arms around him, stood on tiptoes, and kissed him with passion.

"Now that will put color in any man's cheeks," he said and smiled at her as she held him.

Vivian looked into his eyes. "Derrick, are you sure you're all right? Is there something going on between you and Chuck that I should know about?"

"Us? No. Chuck's just being himself. Now about my next dose of your medicine," he joked, sitting on the edge of his desk and pulling her toward him between his thighs.

She took his face in her hands and searched his eyes. "You look tired, Derrick. We won't last long, if we can't talk with each other. If we can't tell each other the truth and have confidence in each other."

He pulled her closer to him, resting his head on her shoulder and kissing her neck. She put her arms around him, stroked his hair and his back. He lifted his head and looked her in the eyes.

"I trust you, Vivian. It's just this case that came in this morning. A girl. Thirteen years old. She tried to give herself an abortion. She didn't want her parents to know that she was pregnant," he said, with anguish. "I couldn't save—" he choked. He stood up abruptly, released Vivian, grabbed the back of his neck and paced his den slowly.

"She died?" Vivian asked. "Is that it? No one's blaming you, are they?"

"No, nothing like that. The girl will be fine. I couldn't save the baby."

"But you said that she was only thirteen. She's too young—"

"There's no excuse for this!" he angrily flared. "That girl had a life growing inside of her! A human life! She gave up her rights to be a child the moment that life was conceived!"

Vivian was stunned at his forcefulness and fervor. "Surely you believe that, when there are extenuating circumstances, the woman, or child in this case, has a right to choose whether to have a baby or not?"

Derrick looked at Vivian and narrowed his eyes. "No, I don't. When it comes to a question of whether a woman should have an abortion, in my mind there are no extenuating circumstances. If it were up to me, abortions would be illegal."

"Illegal? Derrick, you can't mean that."

"Of course, I mean it. Vivian, I'm a pediatric surgeon. I have the privilege of holding little golden nuggets every day. Children are very important to me, like Linda Lewis. She's in so much pain, yet she can still smile at me and I can use my skills to reduce her suffering and to help her smile every day. She deserves that."

"Still, Linda isn't pregnant with a child that she can't take care of emotionally or financially."

"Oh, you mean my patient shouldn't have a child because she can't afford it or isn't emotionally ready for it? Well that's where you and I agree, but this was not the first pregnancy for this girl. She has a one-year-old boy. I've been treating her since the first pregnancy and her little boy. She has a serious problem. She refuses to get professional help. She refuses to use any type of contraception.

She comes from, what appears to be, a wholesome home environment with loving and understanding parents. She and her eighteen-year-old boyfriend wanted me to perform an abortion and when I refused she stuck metal in her—" He closed his eyes and rubbed his face in frustration. "I don't hate, but I can't abide abortion!"

Vivian felt the blood rushing from her head. She closed her eyes tightly. She took a deep breath. "Derrick, I think that there's something that you ought to know—"

"DJ, I've put the groceries in the kitchen," Chuck interrupted. "Your florist is here and the caterer is on the way up. You're having a New Year's Eve party tonight, remember?"

"Oh, yeah, thanks, little brother," he said to Chuck. "Vivian, can we talk about this later? I need to take care of a few things."

"This is important, Derrick." She tried to detain him.

"But it can wait, Annie, can't it?" Chuck interjected forcefully.

Vivian looked up at him and then at Derrick. "Yes, it can wait," she said reluctantly.

Derrick kissed her quickly and hurried out the door to see the florist and caterers.

Vivian started to follow, but Chuck held her back.

"I know that you were about to tell him about your abortion, weren't you?"

"I have to tell him the truth. I won't lie to him."

"Don't do it. Not now. Not today. You've suffered enough. What good would it accomplish? It happened before you two became involved. Derrick is my best friend. We've known each other nearly all of our lives. His feelings about abortion go very deep. I'm asking you as your friend and his. Don't do this to yourself or to him."

"Your feelings about abortion are very strong as well, but you were still there for me."

"Derrick doesn't know you yet the way I do. Give him time."

"And are you going to tell me what was going on between you two earlier? I'm not blind. You were very upset about something and I don't believe that it was about Derrick's patient."

Chuck looked away. "That's an entirely different issue. It's personal, Annie, between me and DJ. I can't talk with you about it. Do you trust me?"

"Yes, but—"

"No buts, Annie. Just trust me."

Vivian reluctantly relented, and they joined Derrick in the living room as the caterer and florist went about their tasks.

Later, Vivian watched as Derrick and Chuck made magic in the kitchen. The spacious thirty-five-hundred-square-foot, four-bedroom, three-and-a-half-bath condo was teaming with activity. The band came in and set up their equipment. The bartenders were racking glasses and setting up kegs of beer, slicing fruit for the drinks in the media room. Hostesses were assisting with the preparations of the table under a bubble canopy that was installed on the terrace. The florists were testing the release mechanism on the balloons and sparkling confetti over the living room, dining room, family room and library.

"This is going to be some event," Vivian said, as she sat watching Derrick and Chuck preparing even more food. "But what do you need me around for?"

"You're my inspiration," Derrick said. "Besides, I went to a lot of trouble just to get you to come back to town for New Year's Eve." He smiled and kissed her mouth quickly.

"All you had to do was ask me," she said, and smiled back at him. "You didn't have to resort to subterfuge."

"All right. The party's off. Everyone can go home," he said to all the workers.

"Derrick!" Vivian fussed.

"Oh, so you want them to stay?" He grinned.

"Of course," she said, flustered. "Look at this place. You've invested a mint in this party and you've got an army of people working on this."

"Okay, everyone back to work," he said. "She said you can stay."

Vivian rolled her eyes and pursed her lips. Derrick came to the center-post counter where she was sitting, put her arms around his neck, and kissed her again, but this time with more enthusiasm.

Vivian blushed when he released her mouth.

"See what I'm willing to do to make sure that I'm in your arms at midnight?" He smiled, popping a fresh strawberry in her mouth.

She cocked her head to the side and smiled at him. "Oh? So, if I were to leave, you'd call the party off, I presume?"

"Chuck, she doesn't believe me," he said, cocking his head to the opposite side in a similar motion.

"He'd cancel it, Annie, without further thought," Chuck confirmed. "Let's not test him on this one. I'm a great chef and I'm making myself hungry."

"You're a second best chef, Chuck. I'm better," Derrick said.

"Oh yeah? Who's Eggs Benedict—"

"Not as good as mine and you know it," he retorted. "But we'll let Vivian be the judge of that in the morning." He grinned.

"Save it, guys. I'm not looking to be a judge quite yet."

The band began to tune up and started practicing with an upbeat tune. Derrick released Vivian and tapped Chuck on the shoulder.

"May I have this last dance of the year, my dear?" Derrick demonstratively asked Chuck.

"Why certainly, my darling," Chuck said and curtseyed.

They jostled, trying to decide who would lead and then they started waltzing around the kitchen, popping fresh fruit into each other's mouths. Vivian was laughing hysterically at the sight of two giant former basketball players waltzing and not to the beat of the music. The workers thought that it was comical, too, but two obviously gay waiters were beside themselves with excitement.

"Mmm, I'd like to make either one of them my New Years' resolution," Vivian overheard one man saying to the other.

"Get's my vote," the other responded, "but they look like they've been lovers a long time. I don't think we have a chance."

"One can dream, can't one?" the other man answered.

The two waiters swooned in unison.

Vivian smiled and shook her head.

Later, Chuck left to pick up Melissa and Vivian went into a spare bedroom to shower and dress for the party. She sat before a mirror in her robe applying her makeup and thinking about what Chuck had asked of her and wondered what was between him and Derrick. Someone knocked on the door and interrupted her thoughts.

"Yes," she called out.

Derrick peeked in. "I was about to go and get dressed and remembered that I haven't had my hourly dose of you," he said.

"Then maybe you need a double dose now."

Derrick came into the room and closed the door slightly behind him. She rose from the vanity bench and wrapped her arms around his neck. He kissed her and lifted her, carrying her to a sofa. He sat with her on his lap nibbling at her lips.

"Mmm, you feel good," he whispered, burying his face under her neck.

She found his mouth and kissed him, and then she stopped and looked into his eyes. "Derrick, about you and Chuck—"

He started kissing her neck and shoulders under her robe.

"What about us?" he whispered between kisses.

"I mean, I've read *Invisible Life* and *Just As I Am*, and I understand that sometimes things aren't always what one might expect, uh, but you two aren't bisexual, are you?"

Derrick leaned back from her, narrowed his eyes, and turned his head toward her.

"What?" he asked in disbelief.

"You and Chuck, are you...?"

A grin bowed his mouth and then a smile. Soon he was laughing so hard that tears were forming in his eyes.

"Derrick, why are you laughing? I'm serious," she said, flustered.

Derrick laughed louder, grabbing his stomach.

Vivian got up from his lap and looked at him. He was roaring in laughter. Chuck knocked on the door and peeked in.

"What the hell are you laughing about, DJ? I could hear you halfway down the hall."

Derrick was laughing so loud and hard that he couldn't catch his breath to answer.

"What got into him, Annie?" Chuck asked, bunching his brow.

"I asked him a question," Vivian said in exasperation, looking at Derrick rolling around on the sofa, still uproariously laughing.

"What did you ask him?"

"I just asked him whether he was bisexual, Chuck. I thought that maybe you and he—"

"That we what? That we were lovers?" he asked in confused amusement.

"Yes, I don't understand what's—"

Chuck started laughing and soon tears were rolling down his face, too.

Vivian looked at the two of them laughing. Chuck's face and Derrick's eyes were red.

"What's going on in here?" Bill asked, as he came into the room and saw Chuck and Derrick falling over and laughing at the top of their lungs.

They looked at Bill and laughed louder.

"I asked Derrick whether he and Chuck were bisexual and they've been hysterical ever since."

"Them? Bisexual? I wish!" Bill retorted. "They're too straight for public television. Trust me, Vivian. I'm bisexual. I know these things," he quipped.

"Thanks, Bill," Chuck said, trying to gain his composure.

Derrick was wiping his eyes. He and Chuck looked at each other and burst out laughing again.

Vivian turned on her heels and strode into the bathroom, slamming the door. Derrick followed.

"I'm sorry, Vivian," he said, still trying to compose himself. He washed his face and grabbed a towel to dry.

"I was serious, Derrick!" Vivian flashed.

"I know." He smiled pulling her close to him and hugging her. "That's what made it even more laughable. Wait until our parents hear this one."

"Your parents?" she flashed. "You're going to tell your parents what I said?"

"Yeah, this really will make them laugh. Chuck's parents, too. They've caught us in a lot of compromising positions, when we were younger, but we were never into each other," he said, smiling. "There were always several girls in the mix. Too many, according to our parents. Nothing's changed since then. Chuck and I have had a checkered past, but no, we're not bisexual or gay. I'm glad that you felt comfortable enough to ask me about it though. I hope you're not disappointed."

"Derrick!" she fussed.

He smiled at her and sat on the edge of the bathroom counter, bringing her closer to him between his thighs. "Look, Counselor, I don't know what brought you to that point, but—"

"I've watched you and Chuck together. You two have this kind of non-verbal communication going on all the time."

"Like Sayers and Piccolo?"

"Yes, like you know what the other one is thinking or feeling all the time."

"I guess we do, but you and I have been picking up on each other's vibes since we met at Red, Hot and Blue, haven't we?"

"Yes, but—"

He kissed her. "Can you tell what I'm thinking?" he asked with a grin and a gleam in his eyes. "If not, I'll give you a clue." He moved her hand to his full erection.

"Oh," she said, shyly. "Point well taken."

"Not yet, it hasn't been. That didn't come from thinking about Chuck. I don't think that I have anything to prove, but if you're not fully convinced that I'm totally heterosexual—"

"I get the picture, Derrick," she said, before he reached for his zipper. "You don't have to prove anything to me."

"Good. Sex isn't a game to me, Vivian. I'm not trying to see how many times I can score. I do want to sleep with you and wake with you in the morning. You're driving me crazy just thinking about you, but Chuck mentioned that you had an unwelcome visitor from your past today and that he upset you. I want to make love with you, not just have sex. Right now I know that you're still not ready for that kind of commitment, but we've waited this long and I'll continue to wait until you are ready. Until you can make love with me without letting the past spoil it for us and our future together."

"I like taking it easy better than rushing into something just because the heat is turned up."

"So do I. See how easily we communicate?"

The kiss that she planted on him communicated even more, she thought. She was beginning to feel free of Carlton.

Vivian dressed in a strawberry red, shimmering floor-length body sheath that Bill found for her and walked out into the living room. The combo was already playing when she entered. All the commotion was finished and Derrick stood near the entrance hall welcoming his guests as they arrived. He turned and looked at her.

"*Whoa!*" he said quickly and expressively appraising her with admiration.

"'Whoa', yourself,'" she exclaimed and smiled broadly. "You sure know how to wear a tux."

"Careful, Counselor. You're going to make it melt right off my back," he said, eyeing her suggestively.

"Don't start something that I can't finish."

"You already have," he whispered. "Dance with me before I embarrass myself before our guests," he said, taking her hand.

He motioned for a butler to greet guests as they arrived and led her into the spacious living room. Chuck and Melissa were already there when they entered.

"Way to go, Annie!" Chuck said and whistled.

"Vivian, look at you!" Melissa gasped.

"See what I mean, Counselor," Derrick grinned, as he took her in his arms.

Vivian smiled up at him as they danced and talked. After a few minutes, his face was all she could see and his voice was all that she could hear.

The party was comfortably packed when Kenneth, JeNelle, and Benny arrived together.

"Is this our little sister?" Benny asked Kenneth.

"Looks like her, I think, but I've never seen her sparkle like that before," Kenneth joked.

"Must be the dress, huh, K.J.?"

"I don't know, Benny. There's this light in her eyes that I've never seen before."

"You think?" he asked, looking into her eyes. "What do you think, DJ? You think it's the dress?"

"She could wear a potato sack and look like new money," Derrick said, seriously.

"I don't know whether our parents have ever seen her dressed to kill like that before."

"You two boys want to play a little round ball, two on one?" Vivian quipped with a devilish grin and arms open wide in invitation. "I'll spot you boys ten points and I'll even wear this dress and the high heel shoes."

"No bet," Benny and Kenneth said in unison.

"Stop picking on your sister, you two," JeNelle said, laughing. "You're making her blush. You look stunning, Vivian."

"Thank you, JeNelle. So do you," she said, taking JeNelle's arm and turning up her nose playfully at her brothers.

"How's Gloria, JeNelle? I didn't get to see her today."

"She's healing physically. David is with her."

"Yes, I figured as much. He has a huge crush on her."

"Speaking of crushes," JeNelle segued. "You do look particularly radiant tonight. So does Derrick."

"He is this side of perfection," she sighed, glancing at him across the room, "but we don't seem to be the only ones lighting up this party." She grinned at JeNelle.

JeNelle blushed. "You do have two very handsome brothers, Vivian."

"Still, you're only falling in love with one of them, and I bet I can guess which one."

"You are your mother's daughter."

"Thanks, I'll take that as a compliment because my mother is never wrong. Me, on the other hand," she shrugged, "let's just say I haven't reached her level of perfection yet."

"You will. I hope she's right about Stacy. I hope she's going to come back to Benny."

"Like I said. She's never wrong."

The party was a roaring success. As the clock wound down on the end of the year, Vivian and Derrick found each other through the crowded rooms.

"Happy New Year, Counselor," Derrick said.

"Happy New Beginnings, Doctor," she said back at him.

Derrick took a small gift-wrapped box from his jacket and handed it to her. Vivian looked at him quizzically.

"What's this?"

"Something I want you to have obviously."

Vivian pursed her lips and opened the box. She lifted the electronic key from the box and gazed into Derrick's eyes.

"This is a key to your place. Are you sure you want me to have this?"

"No, I don't just want you to have it; I want you to use it anytime you want. It opens the garage where you have a parking space next to mine, the elevators and the front door. No restrictions. No questions. Come whenever you want. You, my dear, Vivian Lynn Alexander, soon to be Esquire, have unlimited access."

Vivian took his hand and led him to where her purse lay on a table. She lifted a small gift from her purse and handed it to Derrick. He narrowed his eyes.

"What's this?" he asked, as he opened the gift.

"It's dangerous how we keep reading each other's mind."

Derrick lifted the keys to her house from the box. They hung on a heart-shaped key ring.

"Touché, Counselor," he said, as he kissed her deeply and they swayed to the music.

Kenneth held JeNelle in his arms as the clock struck twelve. The band began to play *Auld Lang Syne* and they sang the words gazing into each other's eyes.

"Happy New Year, guys," Melissa said, kissing Chuck and then Benny.

She breezed away as quickly as she came.

"So, Chuck, what's with this crush you've got on my sister?" Benny asked.

Chuck looked away. "What makes you think that I've got something on for Annie?"

"My mother told me and I've been watching you with her. You haven't been able to take your eyes off her all evening. Believe me. I've been there. Two men falling for the same woman."

"I thought your mother was suspicious of my feelings when I was there for Thanksgiving, but no matter what anyone thinks, it's Vivian who decides, not me."

"Yeah, but you didn't give her any options, did you?"

Chuck looked away again. "I was trying to give her time and space to get past the pain Carlton caused her."

"Look, Chuck, both Kenneth and I like you and DJ and we both love our sister. She deserves to be happy. She's a lucky lady no matter how you cut it, but she can't operate in a vacuum. A very special woman told me once that *there are places in a woman's soul that not just any man can reach; no matter how much love and attention he's willing and able to give. Men are no different. Reaching below the surface into the very soul is a scary proposition. It's not for the faint-hearted. You have to be ready and able to deal well with what you find there.*"

"That 'special woman' is Stacy Greene, isn't it?"

"Yes. I made the tragic mistake of not telling her that I was in love with her before she made the decision to leave. Don't make the same mistake with my sister, Chuck."

"It may be too late already, Benny," he said, nodding toward the middle of the floor where Vivian and Derrick stood passionately kissing. "I'm a day late and a dollar short."

Chapter 35

News of the upcoming US Congressional fact-finding hearings were in all the newspapers and all of the political cable television networks were on hand to cover them gavel to gavel. A number of companies, both large and small, who did business with the military installations nationwide, were subpoenaed to testify before a special Congressional Committee composed of members from both Houses of Congress. A Special Prosecutor was selected to investigate and pursue any criminal charges that might be brought. CompuCorrect, Incorporated, was one of the many companies subpoenaed. Tom, Shirley, and Kenneth flew to Washington, DC, several days before they were scheduled to testify.

Vivian was furious when Kenneth told her that he was not going to be represented by legal counsel, but he was adamant. Tom and Shirley could not budge him either. Her complaints to her family about it seemed to have fallen on deaf ears, too. It was his position that CompuCorrect had nothing to hide and had done nothing illegal. In light of Kenneth's decision, Vivian rallied all of the housemates who dropped everything to lend assistance. They started burning the midnight oil to do the legal research on previous hearings of the same nature and precedent setting cases. They staked out their own territory and went to work.

Bill went to Capitol Hill to talk with Congressional legal staff members and other Congressional investigators. He could get more out of the young Congressional staffers than anyone. All he needed to do was smile at them.

Melissa and Alan researched cases in the Congressional Record, at the Library of Congress, and at Georgetown's law library. They performed military budget comparisons and prepared cost breakdowns for contracted services year-to-year over a twenty-year period.

David and Vivian prepared the testimony that they thought that Kenneth should use in his opening statement. They stayed up all night working on briefs based on the research that had been done during the day between classes, volunteer work, and their individual jobs and other obligations.

JeNelle was worried about all of the negative publicity that the companies were receiving. She wrote several editorials for her blog, lambasting the press and media for false, misleading or biased reporting. The press and media were crucifying the companies and Kenneth's name and CompuCorrect's were mentioned prominently in connection with the names of other companies that had received a large number of very lucrative government contracts totaling in the billions. She was petrified when Sylvia Alexander told her that Kenneth refused legal representation. She and Sylvia talked frequently on the telephone after JeNelle returned to Santa Barbara.

Once released from the hospital, Gloria stayed in Washington at the National Rehabilitation Center, a physical therapy center. Chuck was taking personal care of her recovery and the housemates were working with her on what she had missed in class. Derrick would stop in to visit her when he made his rounds of the children's wards.

Many of the Alexander family members were assembled in Washington to give Kenneth moral support. There were cots and beds all over the Georgetown house. Anna had more than a few hands at work in the kitchen, helping her to prepare meals.

Gregory and Aretha refused to be left at home while Kenneth testified. Their parents reluctantly agreed to take them along. After all, witnessing a branch of Congress at work first hand would be a learning experience for them. Gregory was in the middle of his senior year and his basketball season was in full swing. Aretha had an upcoming statewide piano competition. She had won every piano competition that she had entered, which was of little or no consequence to her, but it made Gregory very happy, so she kept entering competitions for him. She did enjoy playing duets with Angelique Menéndez-Gaza though.

Benny and Whitney flew in from California. Benny made calls and visits to a number of his contacts at the Pentagon and other military offices, many of whom were women with whom he had intimate relations in the past. He was even more appealing to some of the women now when they met his daughter. He wondered what it was about a single man, raising his daughter alone that drove women into such states of aggressive sexual overtures and advances toward him. He was not accepting any of the invitations that were being advanced in unbelievable volumes. He also found time to visit Admiral Gordon personally.

"Come in, Major Alexander," Admiral Gordon said. "It's a pleasure to meet you," he said extending his hand. "I'm sorry that I was unavailable the last time you stopped by."

"Admiral," Benny acknowledged, first with a salute and then a handshake.

"That's why I made an appointment this time. Thank you for taking the time to see me."

Admiral Gordon smiled at Whitney. "May I?" he asked reaching for the little girl.

Benny released his daughter to the Admiral who walked around his large spacious office bouncing Whitney in his arms.

"Fine looking recruit you have here, Major," the Admiral said gruffly and smiled.

"Thank you, Admiral, but if you don't mind—"

"Sure, sure, Major, I know why you've come. As I've told you before, I'm not at liberty to discuss Lieutenant Greene's mission."

"With all due respect, Admiral, it is imperative that I speak with her."

The Admiral moved toward a sofa in his office and propped Whitney on his knee. He motioned for Benny to sit down and he complied. Once seated, the Admiral looked solemnly from Whitney to Benny.

"In love with her, aren't you, Major?" the Admiral asked more as a statement than a question.

"Yes, Sir, I am," Benny answered, sitting forward and resting his arms on his knees.

"That's what I thought," the Admiral acknowledged. "Well, Major, I understand your plight fully. Been married to the same wonderful woman for forty-two years now. I don't believe that I could live without her, but," he looked at Benny, "she's career Army Ranger. We've had far less time living in the same house together since we've been married. Either she's out of the country or I am. We managed to raise seven children though and now we have five grands, so I know what you're going through." He smiled and hugged Whitney.

"Admiral, it's not just for our daughter that I want to see her. Lieutenant Greene left with some unfinished business between us. I want a chance to talk with her. Let her know what she means to me and—"

"And try to talk her out of her mission," the Admiral finished.

Benny stood abruptly and slowly paced the Admiral's office.

"Can you tell me honestly that you wouldn't try to influence her to abandon her mission, Major? Use every tool at your disposal to convince her to change her mind and accept some soft, cushy job behind a desk? Something safe and secure as she did when she was my XO?"

Benny exhaled in frustration. He turned to face the Admiral. "Yes, Sir, I would try to influence her even if I had to resort to kidnapping her," he admitted.

"I've spoken to the Air Force brass about you. Everyone, to a man, gives you One A top of your class. Smart, resourceful, intuitive and a damn fine airman. They tell me that you'll make colonel ahead of schedule. Would you be willing to give up your commission in the Air Force, if Lieutenant Greene asked you to?"

"I'd resign this second if it meant that I could have her back, Sir," Benny answered quickly and confidently, his jaw set resolutely.

The Admiral could see the determination in Benny's eyes. "Somehow, Major, I believe you, but—"

"But what, Sir?" Benny asked anxiously.

"But would Lieutenant Greene ask you to do that for her?"

Benny blew out a frustrated breath, shook his head slowly and looked into the Admiral's eyes. "No, she wouldn't," he answered quietly.

The admiral nodded his head in agreement and rose from his seat, handing Whitney back to Benny.

"Commitment to principles, Major. I believe that we both understand Lieutenant Greene's motivation, and we both must respect it and her. I need not tell you that she has sacrificed a great deal for her vision, and that she is an inspiration to all who know her. She reminds me most of my wife. The General has sacrificed much for this country and that's sometimes hard for a man to cope with—that his spouse, and in your case, the woman you love, has chosen to put commitment to her country ahead of her commitment to a relationship and family, but in so doing, she raises the level of dedication to duty, and the standard of selflessness. I believe your course is clear, Major. Lieutenant Greene needs and deserves your support."

"She has it, Admiral, but I give you fair warning, I won't give up until I find her."

The Admiral smiled slightly. "I'm not at all surprised, Major. From the intel I've gathered on you, failure is not in your vocabulary."

Benny started toward the door and then turned toward the Admiral. "Sir, how long is her deployment expected to last?"

The Admiral stroked Whitney's golden brown locks of hair. "Lieutenant Greene is calling the shots, Major. She designed this mission, but if I had to guess, I'd say your daughter will be well into her school years if the mission goes as the Lieutenant has designed it."

The realization jolted Benny. Whitney was barely six months old now. He extended his hand to the Admiral. "Thank you, Admiral Gordon, for taking the time to see me."

"Good luck to you, Major, and if you're ever interested in a career change, the Navy would welcome you aboard."

Benny left and the Admiral picked up the secure red telephone.

"Yes, Admiral, have you completed your meeting with Major Alexander?"

"Yes, Mr. President, he just left, and I agree with your assessment of him. He is a credit to the uniform he wears."

"Seems the whole family is made of the right stuff."

"Yes, Sir, I agree."

"Any chance that OPERATION: EXPLORERS will not succeed?"

"No, Sir, no chance. Lieutenant Greene has selected eleven other women to participate. They're all near the end of the first six months of training at different global locations. So far, Lieutenant Greene is scoring in the ninety percentile of all recruits, both men and women. No one knows that she's a woman though. She's ahead of schedule for deployment."

"Lebanon?"

"No, Sir, Iraq and then Iran."

"Thank you, Admiral. Keep me posted on her progress."

"Sir?"

"Yes."

"What are you going to do about Major Alexander? He's got Washington leaking information like the Titanic. He's got a lot of friends in high places."

"Yes, I know, and family, too."

"Yes, Sir, you mean Delta Dawn, don't you, Sir?"

"Yes, but we can't discuss Delta over this line. Neither of us is in a secure skiff at the moment. You know the rules, Admiral. Needless to say, I've had a number of personal calls on the Major's behalf. Johnny Worthington called me breathing fire and so did Gus Fahey. I've got plans for the young Major, but first I've got to deal with this Congressional hearing. Kenneth Alexander is surfacing as a formidable force."

"Yes, Sir. I'm not surprised at all, Sir."

"Neither am I. Carry on, Admiral."

"Thank you, Mr. President."

The Georgetown house was the center of activity.

Vivian had not found the time to spend with Derrick, but he told her that he understood. He called every morning when he woke up just to tell her good morning and every evening before he went to bed to tell her good night. He visited the house on a number of occasions and Vivian's female cousins went into tailspins every time Derrick smiled. Vivian was accustomed to women nearly fainting or otherwise turning cartwheels whenever she and Derrick were together. Derrick told her that he didn't think that he would ever get accustomed to the men who were leering, ogling or otherwise undressing her with their eyes, but Vivian was totally unaware of and unimpressed by anyone else's glances except Derrick's.

Two days before Kenneth was scheduled to testify, the crowd inside the Georgetown house was at a fever pitch. Calls were placed to anybody that might have even a sliver of information that might help Kenneth. There were more cell phones in operation in the house than at an electronics convention. Kenneth, however, was his usual calm-in-the-eye-of-a-hurricane. He often smiled and shook his head at all of the commotion.

Kenneth talked with JeNelle at least once every day after he left her in Washington after the holidays. He was looking forward to each conversation they had. He took Whitney Ivy to Vivian's room, bathed her and put her in the bed beside him while he called JeNelle at home. He was surprised when her answering machine came on. He then tried to reach her at the store although it was long after closing time. Felix Olsen, her Art Manager, was still at the store, but JeNelle had left early that morning without saying where she was going or when she would return. Felix told Kenneth that JeNelle and all of the employees were upset by the newspaper accounts of the Congressional investigations and Felix assured him that he had the whole-hearted support of all of the members of the Santa Barbara Chamber of Commerce. Kenneth told Felix that he appreciated the support, but was more concerned about JeNelle. Felix promised to locate her for him and have her call him the next day.

The following day, Kenneth waited impatiently for JeNelle to call. When she finally did, he breathed a sigh of relief.

"I'm fine, Kenneth. You shouldn't worry about me so much. I'm a big girl. I can take care of myself…most of the time," she said jokingly. "You didn't have to send out the National Guard to find me."

"I only made a few telephone calls, JeNelle. Can I help it if Santa Barbara swings into action when its Woman of the Year comes up missing for a few hours?"

"Kenneth Alexander, you had people camping on my doorstep when I got home. I'd say you made more than just 'a few' telephone calls. Johnston left the bench when I called to say that I was fine and scolded me unmercifully."

"You're very important and precious to a lot of people, JeNelle. Especially to me."

"I didn't mean to worry anyone, Kenneth, especially not you. You've got a lot going on with the Congressional hearing tomorrow. I wish that you'd let me come and be with you and help you get through this."

"No, JeNelle, it's pure chaos here. My family is everywhere in this house and the city. Vivian, her housemates, and their study group, the Legal Dream Team, have turned this place into a bastion of legal roadblocks and obstacle courses. Tom and Shirley were saying a bunch of Hail Mary's this morning. I don't want you to be caught up in all of this confusion. It's all going to work out fine and it will all be over very soon."

"The press reports are vicious and slanderous. There are rumors flying all over the place, linking these allegations to people high up in NSA and even to the Governor's office. This could hurt you personally and professionally. I can't help it. I'm concerned for you, especially since you won't even hire legal representation to defend yourself. Everyone else who was subpoenaed called out the biggest legal guns that they could find."

"As if you haven't been busy yourself, Ms. Towson. I've been reading your comments in the Letters to the Editor section of the newspaper. Did you really have to be so graphic about where the reporters could stick their poison pens?" he mused. "CompuCorrect has done nothing wrong, JeNelle. You'll simply have to trust me on that point."

"I'd trust you with my life, Kenneth. It's the politicians and the Fifth Estate who I don't trust. And, yes, they deserved every word. I even toned it down a notch or two." She laughed.

"I'm glad to hear you say that."

"Say what, Kenneth? That I don't trust the politicians or the press?"

"That you'd trust me with your life."

"It's true, Kenneth. You're the most trustworthy, honest, upstanding, responsible—"

"Are you trying to finesse your way out of the payment that you owe me for my massage services?"

"Kenneth Alexander, how can you joke with me at a time like this?" she fussed.

"Temper, temper, Ms. Towson. Remember, you'll have to trust me."

"You won't let me help you. You won't let me come there. I've got to find a way to repay you for all that you've done for me and for Gloria. Writing a few letters to the newspapers isn't nearly enough. At least, if I were there, I could find a way to say more than just thank you."

"If you were here, I'd be spending all of my time just looking at you. I wouldn't be able to focus on anything or anyone else. I need for you to stay put…for now. Later, I'll help you find some new words to say."

"You said that before. What did you mean by that? Have you thought of something that I can do to help or a way to say thank you?"

"Uh huh, but I'll tell you later," he said smugly.

"You know, there are times that you can be the most exasperating person I know. Have you always been this stubborn?"

"I'm sometimes an acquired taste. You'll get used to it."

Later that evening, while the housemates worked diligently trying to prepare defense strategies for Kenneth, Melissa and Alan were returning from the law library. As Alan got out of his car, a limousine screeched to a halt beside him. Someone, sitting in the back seat of the limo, let down the window slightly. Without a word, an envelope was passed to Alan, and then the car sped away. Alan noted that the New York license plates on the car read SANGELO.

Melissa rushed to him. "Alan!" she screamed. "Are you all right? Did they hurt you?" she asked, checking his body for any sign of injury.

"No…I'm not hurt," he said slowly, thoughtfully.

"It happened so fast! I didn't see them coming! What did they want, Alan?" Melissa asked in a near hysterical state.

"I don't know," he said calmly, looking down at the envelope in his hand. He flipped it over and read the name: Alexander.

"C'mon, Alan," Melissa said, grabbing his arm and pulling him out of the street. "Let's go inside before anything else bizarre happens. That was really scary."

Alan was somewhat bewildered by the event, but Melissa was upset, so he followed her into the house. As soon as they entered, she ran to the other housemates and recounted what had just occurred. They jumped to their feet and rushed to Alan to assure that he was not injured. He handed the envelope to Vivian. She tore it open and looked inside. There was single sheet of paper with the word "Yeager" typed on it.

"Yeager?" Vivian repeated over and over trying to remember where she had heard the word before. "Yeager? Yeager?" she said still trying to make the connection.

Everyone was looking at her.

"What's a Yeager?" David asked.

"Beats me," Melissa answered. "Google it. It has to mean something."

Gregory strolled into the room, eating a huge hero sandwich. He plopped down in one of the overstuffed armchairs and hung a long leg over the thick armrest.

"What's up?" he asked.

No one acknowledged his presence. The housemates were standing around, scratching their heads. Gregory shrugged and continued eating his sandwich.

"Yeager?" Vivian said in a barely audible voice still trying to make the connection.

"Sam Yeager," Gregory said, as he bit down on his sandwich again.

Suddenly all heads snapped toward him. He was about to take another bite of his sandwich when he noticed that everyone's eyes were on him.

"What?" he asked quizzically, feeling as if he had said a bad word and was about to be attacked.

"What did you say, Gregory?" Vivian asked, as she approached him in what he thought was a menacing way.

Gregory's eyes grew large as saucers as he looked at her. "Sam Yeager," he repeated, his eyes darting from one person to the next. "You said 'Yeager', didn't you?"

"Yes, but who is Sam Yeager?"

"Oh, that's J.C. Baker's right hand man. Baker takes him everywhere with him."

Gregory started to take another bite of his sandwich. Vivian stopped him.

"How do you know this Sam Yeager?"

"I worked with him last summer at the Pentagon. We shot around in the gym some, too. You know him, V. Sam said that Baker sent him over here to check on you once after a big snowstorm. Big guy from Holly Hill, South Carolina."

That reference threw the switch in Vivian's head and she snapped her finger. She got very excited.

"Corporal Yeager! I didn't make the connection until now. It's not a thing. It's a he. Where does this Sam Yeager live, G?"

"Fort Myers in Virginia," Gregory said, as he started to take another bite.

Vivian grabbed him and yanked him out of the chair. His sandwich went flying in a different direction.

"Come on!" she yelled to her housemates as she dragged Gregory through the door. The housemates grabbed their coats and followed. They took two cars and raced through the streets of Washington across the district line toward Fort Myers in Arlington, Virginia. As they drove, Vivian explained her theory that Corporal Yeager must know something about the investigation. That was the only plausible explanation for the manner in which his name was delivered, although she didn't understand why. Alan got them through the security point with his Veteran's ID card. Gregory directed them to the barracks where Corporal Yeager lived. They entered the barracks like gangbusters, looking around wildly for Sam Yeager. Soldiers, who were scantily clad or nude, scurried out of the way of the attacking posse. Melissa took the time to look around, grin at the half dressed solders, and do a little finger wave, but Alan grabbed her, put his hands over her eyes, and guided her forward.

Corporal Yeager was reclining on his bunk wearing only a pair of jockey underwear. He jumped to his feet when he saw the posse approach.

"What did I do?" he yelled, as the posse reached his bunk. "Oh, it's you, G, but who are all of these other people? Oh, hi, Vivian."

"Corporal Yeager," Vivian said, with a suspicious tone and a broad, equally suspicious smile. "I think we need to have a little talk."

The posse took Yeager into another room and interrogated him. They were shooting questions at him as if he was the man who shot John F. Kennedy. He was giving them all of the right answers. David and Melissa started writing, as Yeager talked. Alan, Vivian and Bill kept up the questioning. It was nearly 6:00 A.M. when they finished. They took Yeager and headed for Professor Gustafson "Gus" Fehey's, a former senator's residence. The professor was not particularly happy to see his scholars' program students, the posse at six-thirty in the morning, but he admitted them to his house and listened to what they had to say.

"All right, calm down," Professor Fehey said. "If you want to get this soldier's affidavit on the record, you've got to get to one of the congressmen or senators on the committee before nine o'clock this morning. That's the only way that this testimony will be heard."

"But, Professor, who can we go to?" Melissa asked. "We don't know any of these congressmen or senators. Believe me, we've tried to get in to see everyone on the committee with no luck."

"I may still have a few contacts on The Hill. Let me make a few calls."

Professor Fehey made his calls and returned to the posse.

"See Geraldine Dukakis in Senator Marshall's office. I wasn't able to reach her personally, but she may be able to get this information in to the session.

I remind you that, although you have gathered sufficient circumstantial information, there are no guarantees that it will have probative value or be pivotal to the course of the hearing."

When the posse tore out of Professor Fehey's home and headed for Capitol Hill, he went to his security phone and dialed. Shortly, he heard, "What is it, Gus?"

"I think you need to get Johnny in on this discussion. The shit's about to hit the fan, Mr. President."

"Ah, hell. Hold on."

It was 8:00 A.M. and the traffic was bumper to bumper on Constitution Avenue. The hearing was scheduled to start at nine o'clock. When the posse arrived at the Senate Office Building, they tore through the long, wide halls looking for Senator Marshall's office. When they found it, they barged right in.

"Are you Geraldine Dukakis?" Vivian asked, nearly out of breath.

The redheaded, middle-aged woman scowled at them over the top of her cat-eye glasses.

"Yes, but I'm not buying anything or donating to any more causes," she said, annoyed.

"We're not selling anything. We need to see Senator Marshall immediately. It's urgent."

"The Senator sees constituents only on Wednesday mornings between 9:00 A.M. and 11:00 A.M. by appointment only. I can put you on his schedule for three months from now."

"We're not constituents," Vivian said. "We have some information that's vital to the hearing."

"I'm sorry, young lady, but anything concerning the hearings must be submitted in writing, in triplicate, twenty-four hours before the start of the session. No other *ex parte* contacts are allowed."

"But this information is crucial to the investigation! Senator Marshall has got to see us!" Vivian demanded.

"No, young lady, he doesn't! Now you and your crew move along or I'll have to call security!" The woman huffed.

Vivian was getting angry when Bill stepped forward and moved in close to the Congressional aide.

"Mrs. Dukakis or is it *Ms.* Dukakis, I hope?" Bill asked, exuding all the charm and sex appeal he exhibited in his photographs.

"Uh, why yes, young man. It is Ms. Dukakis," the woman said and blushed. Her eyes began to shine and a broad smile came over her otherwise dour face as she patted her beehive-styled hair.

"Ms. Dukakis…uh…may I call you Geraldine? That's such a pretty name for such a sophisticated, young woman," Bill crooned, as he touched her arm and guided her away to another room.

The housemates looked at each other in confusion. They knew Bill could melt steel with his charm. A short time later, Bill returned with Geraldine on his arm. She was flushed in the face and straightening her disheveled hair and her dress as they approached.

"I'll take this matter directly to the Senator in the Hearing Room myself, personally," Geraldine said, assuming her former stately manner. She gave a naughty glance at Bill who winked at her as she giggled and scurried away.

The posse all looked at him in disbelief and puzzlement.

"I'll tell you later," he said glibly and headed out of the door whistling. They all still followed, scratching their heads.

Meanwhile, back at the house in Georgetown, the Alexander clan prepared to leave for the Congressional hearings.

"Mom, where are Vivian and the rest of the Legal Dream Team?" Kenneth asked.

"I don't know. They went running out of here last night and they haven't been back. Wherever they are they've got Gregory Clayton with them."

"Do you think that I should try to track them down?" Benny asked.

"No," Kenneth mused, "If I know our sister, she's up to something…and it's big."

"Son, you're awfully calm considering the fact that you're getting ready to give testimony before a joint Congressional Committee investigating irregularities in contracts you've accepted. This could be very damaging to your company and to your reputation as well," Bernard said, with concern.

Kenneth smiled at both of his parents and his brother. "Dad, you and Mom are the best parents a son could have. I love you for all of the things that you've taught me over the years and for all of the things that I'm still learning from you both. If I lost everything that I have, I'd still have your love and the love of my brothers, sisters, and family. With one exception, that's all that I would need to be the richest man in the world."

"What's the one exception, Son?" Bernard asked.

"I'll tell you later, Dad," Kenneth said, with a smile.

Sylvia cupped Kenneth's face in her hands. They gazed into each other's eyes for a moment. A knowing smile grew on Sylvia's face. "Well, I guess we'd better go get this over with," Sylvia said glibly. "Has anyone seen my knitting?"

"I don't understand why everyone is so worried about Kenneth James," Aretha said absently, while playing with her hand-held brain-buster computer game. "You should know that Kenneth James has got this whole thing all mapped out and nailed down." She shook her head and proceeded out of the door. They all looked after her in amazement. She stopped, turned, and looked at them. "Well, what are you all standing there looking at? We've got better things to do with our time. Let's go get this thing done!" she said confidently.

They all shook their heads and followed her.

The Georgetown house emptied and all of the family members piled into cars and vans and headed for Capitol Hill.

The Congressional chamber was packed. Television cameras from CNN, CSPAN, MSNBC and all of the major networks, ABC, CBS, NBC and PBS were there, including the print media and blogosphere. The Alexander family entered and took seats reserved for them directly behind the table where Kenneth sat alone. Shirley and Tom entered the hearing room nervously and sat with the Alexanders. J.C. Baker sat with other high-ranking, military officials in the hearing room attired in his full-dress uniform. He started to approach Kenneth, but when he pinned Baker with his eyes, Baker turned away. Kenneth also noted that Lisa Lambert was in the hearing room. She turned a cold gaze on him, but she did not attempt to approach him.

The Senators and Congressmen entered the chamber and took their seats on the dais. Chairman Marshall called the Committee to order with a large gavel. The throngs of people went silent. The Chairman announced the purpose of the fact-finding investigative hearing and then turned to the first witness of the day, Kenneth James Alexander.

"Mr. Alexander would you state your name and address for the record?" Chairman Marshall asked.

Silence fell over the cavernous chamber.

"I am Kenneth James Alexander, formerly of Goodwill, South Carolina, currently residing in San Francisco, California," Kenneth said in a clear, cool, and crisp voice.

"And your occupation, Mr. Alexander?"

"I am an industrial electronics engineer and the Executive Director of CompuCorrect, Inc."

Just then, the posse arrived creating quite a commotion as they entered. They quickly took seats with the rest of the family members behind Kenneth.

"Mr. Alexander, are you represented here today by legal counsel?"

"No, Mr. Chairman, I am not."

The audience gasped.

"Well, Mr. Alexander, do you have an opening statement that you would like to read into the Congressional Record?"

"No, Mr. Chairman, I do not."

Another audible gasp rose from the audience.

"Mr. Alexander, this is highly irregular. You're not represented by legal counsel and you have no statement for the record. Either you're very confident of your position or you've made a fool's mistake."

"My parents did not raise fools, Mr. Chairman."

The audience chuckled. Even the Congressmen laughed, but Kenneth sat straight and confidently in his chair without flinching. The Congressmen began to ask questions in the order that the Chairman called their names. Kenneth answered each question clearly and concisely. The cameras captured him from every angle as other reporters snapped pictures of him. He was in full control.

"Mr. Alexander, did your company recently bid on ten military contracts and were you the successful bidder on all ten?" Chairman Marshall asked.

"Yes, to both questions, Mr. Chairman."

"Isn't it highly unlikely that a small company like yours should be so favored as to have received all of the contracts that it bid for?"

"No, Mr. Chairman, CompuCorrect is a growing company with highly trained, competent, qualified, and energetic people. I would expect our government to be searching for companies that have highly qualified people on whom the government can depend to produce a high-quality product."

"But weren't these contract costs inflated, Mr. Alexander?"

"Yes, they were, Mr. Chairman."

The audience gasped again. Reporters pulled out cell phones and started calling in their stories. The video media took close-up views of Kenneth. J.C. Baker shifted uncomfortably in his seat and whispered something to the other military officers. Murmurs were heard throughout the cavernous chamber. The Chairman banged his gavel and the noise level decreased.

"Mr. Alexander, are you admitting to wrongdoing in the acceptance of these contracts?"

"Absolutely not, Mr. Chairman."

Shirley grabbed Tom's hand, her face stricken. Tom patted her hand to comfort her. Kenneth's words were still hanging in the air when Geraldine Dukakis came into the chamber, handed Chairman Marshall a copy of some papers and whispered something in his ear. The Chairman covered his microphone, looked over the papers while Geraldine handed a copy of the papers to each member of the Committee. There was a flurry of activity from the congressional aides as their Congressmen and Congresswomen conferred with them. The Chairman came back to the microphone.

"Would William Anthony Chandler, David Berham Carter, III, Alan Lightfoot, Melissa Bernice Charles, and Vivian Lynn Alexander please rise if you are in this Chamber?" Chairman Marshall asked.

They all rose.

"Mr. Alexander, do you know these people?"

A slight smile crossed Kenneth's face. "Yes, Mr. Chairman, I do know them."

"Have you authorized them to act on your behalf, Mr. Alexander?"

"No, Mr. Chairman, but I will take full responsibility for whatever they have done."

"Thank you, Mr. Alexander. You young people may be seated," Chairman Marshall said. Then, "Mr. Alexander, you are excused momentarily while we examine certain new information which has just been brought to this Committee's attention."

Kenneth got up and sat next to his parents.

"This Committee calls a Corporal Samuel Yeager to the witness table."

The crowd began to murmur loudly. Reporters started looking around the chamber to see the witness. J.C. Baker it appeared nearly leaped out of his skin. The Committee room doors opened and Corporal Yeager marched in. He was attired in his spit and polish, full-dressed military uniform. At the front of the chamber, the Clerk swore him in, and he took a seat at the witness table.

"Corporal Yeager, I'm holding an affidavit which appears to have your signature affixed and notarized," Chairman Marshall said. The Clerk handed a copy of the document to Corporal Yeager. "Is that your signature?"

"Yes, Sir!" Corporal Yeager said sharply.

"Son, would you tell us in your own words what is contained in this document?"

"Yes, Sir. I've been a military driver for the brass for several years now, Sir. I've been Colonel John Calvin Baker's assistant and driver since he came to the Pentagon, Sir. During that time, Colonel Baker and other military officials have been on a mission to assure that the military budget was not cut. Seems the brass has some resorts that they use for what they call 'high-level planning' that are funded from a slush fund in the budget. You Congressmen and women been threatening to give the President a line-item veto and the Colonel was ordered to make sure that there was more than enough money in the military budget to keep the resorts opened. That's what he's been doing, all right. Just what he was ordered. He started a long time ago and it was working until he attempted to coerce Mr. Alexander into inflating the costs of some projects while he was working for Sandoval Anniston Corporation. Mr. Alexander kept giving them a lot of flak and refused to do what they wanted. Then he resigned and left the company. Then sequestration happened and the military budget considerably dried up. Since then, Colonel Baker's been trying to get these contracts out to all of these companies. He worked with people like Dr. Lisa Lambert to distract Mr. Alexander while he slipped some RFPs through Mr. Alexander's new company."

Kenneth's expression did not change as Corporal Yeager continued, but Lisa twisted uncomfortably in her seat.

"He, I mean, Colonel Baker, was real afraid that Mr. Alexander would find out about it so he did it real slow like. Then Colonel Baker was concerned that Ms. Shirley Taylor, a partner of Mr. Alexander's, might discover the overpricing and alert Mr. Alexander, so he started this affair with her to keep her from finding out and to keep tabs on what Mr. Alexander was doing."

Shirley flushed and glared at Baker, but Baker wouldn't make eye contact.

"Colonel Baker instructed Dr. Lambert to use Ms. JeNelle Towson or anyone else to distract Mr. Alexander. They were concerned about using Ms. Towson because they thought that, if she found out what was going on, she'd tell Mr. Alexander. They were also concerned about her relationship with California State Supreme Court Judge Johnston White Worthington and about the San Angeloe Family in New York; people who they thought wouldn't permit themselves to be used either. They've been pushing these inflated RFPs into California and other states so that the military budget could not be cut and so that military bases would not be closed. Colonel Baker and other military officers have had their intelligence operations going in each state similar to the one in California for years. In Florida and Texas...."

The audience sat immobile in absolute amazement and silence as Corporal Yeager spoke for nearly an hour and gave highlights and details of other transactions that he had witnessed. When Corporal Yeager finished, pandemonium broke loose.

The Chairman loudly banged the gavel several times.

"Corporal Yeager, do you have anything else to add to your testimony?"

"Well I left out the part about Dr. Lambert and Colonel Baker having sex in your office on your desk, Sir, and the Heritage Foundation Board Room, but I'll put that all in my book when it's published," Yeager said proudly.

Pandemonium broke out again and the Chairman banged the gavel again.

"In my office? On my desk?" the Chairman yelled, nearly rising in visible anger from his seat. "Son, do you have any evidence to back up these allegations?"

"Well, Sir, you have my word, but I am from Holly Hill, South Carolina, Sir, and in South Carolina a man's word is his bond."

The audience laughed.

"I'm sure that that's true, Son, but we can't charge highly decorated officers of our military, state government officials, and respected captains of industries with these unspeakable acts without proof."

"I have proof, Mr. Chairman," Kenneth said, as he stood and walked to the witness table.

The audience hushed. Kenneth took his pager off his waist and placed it before the microphone. He flipped a switch and his voice and Baker's could be heard arguing over many of the facts that Yeager had testified to.

Baker: *Kenneth, I didn't know that you had company. Not a bad looking piece, either, from what I could see.*

Alexander: *Watch it, Baker! I won't tolerate you talking about JeNelle Towson that way! She's someone who I respect and admire! Now, I didn't invite you here and, in fact, I told you that we have nothing to say to each other. So you tell me why you're sitting in front of my home at this time of the night and then get the hell out of here!*

Baker: *Calm down, Kenneth. I didn't know that she meant that much to you. You and I haven't seen that much of each other lately. I just thought that I'd stop by and talk with you about taking on some more government contracts.*

Alexander: *There's a reason we have not kept in touch! It's no mystery! You know the reason as well as I do! And as for your military contracts, you can take them and shove them and I don't have to tell you where! So, if that's why you're here, we can end this conversation now!*

Baker: *You're making a big mistake! You've always been hard headed and stubborn. Thought you could do it your way! You could have had it all! You could have been at the top! But no! You threw it all away because of your damn principles! How many Black men do you think get to where you were in a major corporation like Sandoval Anniston making big, stupid money like you did? All you had to do was go along! Sign off on a few projects! Show everybody that you were a team player! Everything would have worked out just fine for everyone concerned.*

Alexander: *I'm going to tell you again for the very last time! I can't be bought by big business, big government or anyone else. Yes, I am a Black man and I am proud of it! But what you and the people you work for forgot is that I'm a man first! Regardless of my color! I'm a part of the human race! I'm not going to do anything against the human race! What you and others are trying to do does nothing to enhance our lives on this planet. You said that all that I had to do was just 'go along' with the program. My parents and my grandparents didn't raise me to just 'go along'! I won't compromise myself or my principles, their teachings, or my obligations to the rest of the human race under any circumstance!*

Baker: *There you go again thinking that you can make a difference! Your whole family is like that! Benny thinks that there are ways to avoid wars and have peace everywhere! Vivian thinks that you can just work with people and give them a helping hand and everything is going to work out just fine! What crap! Well the world isn't made up like that! There are those who take and those who get taken! You can't change human nature! The government has big bucks and deep pockets! What do you think all those people are going to do if those military bases are closed?! They are going to get taken because they are going to lose their jobs. Then the economy is going to tank! What happens to your lofty ideals then?! Are you going to feed those hungry families? Are you going to get them a job and put clothes on their backs?!*

Alexander: *You're not doing this to save anyone's job but your own, Baker, so don't come at me with that crap! You don't give a tinker's damn about people working for the government or the military. You want to keep the military budget inflated so that you can build some new toy or cover up something that you've already done. Some other way to kill and maim human beings! The bigger the bomb the better. What you seem to forget is that the people you're blowing up are a part of the human race, too! They are a part of the family of man! We all came from the same seed! The more bombs you drop on our family anywhere in the world the more dangerous you make it for the part of that family that lives in this hemisphere. I'd take it real personal if someone decided to drop a bomb on Goodwill, Summer County, South Carolina.*

Baker: *You act like we were asking you to commit a crime or something! All you had to do was sign, saying that the projects you were working on cost more than they did! That Congress should appropriate more money in the budget if it wants to keep this country strong!*

Alexander: *This country is strong! It's strong because of the strength that came from its forefathers, my grandparents, great grandparents and millions like them across this country and around the world. If you want to keep this country strong with its people, then find a way to build a new high-speed rail system! Find a solution to acid rain! Clean up the rivers, streams, and oceans! Stop the dumping of toxic waste into the soil! Stop the devastation of our youth in the streets of this country! Rebuild our cities, road, bridges and tunnels! Find a cure for HIV/AIDS and cancer and a myriad of other deadly diseases! Improve the quality of education! Find a way to end homelessness and the feeling of helplessness, which pervades too many citizens of this country! But don't you ever come to me, anyone at CompuCorrect or anyone else that I know with your traitorous plans for bilking this government—our government—out of billions of dollars that can be used to solve people problems. I won't tolerate it!*

When the tape ended, Kenneth opened his briefcase and displayed many tapes on the witness table.

"These tapes are copies of conversations that I have had with officials both at Sandival Anniston and with various government agencies over the past seven years. I'm sure that this august body will find these tapes to be very enlightening.

"On the day after Colonel Baker's visit to me in January of last year I turned over a complete record of these recordings and a statement under oath to the California State Attorney General's office and the US Attorney for the San Francisco District. Using the contacts I made on the California governor's blue ribbon panel on youth, I subsequently contacted other small businessmen and businesswomen around the state who I was aware consistently contracted with the military bases throughout the state. We met secretly with the State Attorney General and the US Attorney identifying any activity that had the hint or the appearance of impropriety. I believe that there are other people and companies throughout this country who will come forward to demonstrate their support for the values that our forefathers have instilled in all of us."

Throughout our history, when people have looked for new ways to solve their problems, and to uphold the principles of this nation, many times we have turned to our politicians. What is it about the political system that makes it the instrument that people use when they search for ways to shape their future? Well I believe the answer to that question lies in our concept of governing. Our concept of governing is derived from our view of people. It is a concept deeply rooted in a set of beliefs firmly etched in the national conscience of all of us.

He went on to speak for thirty minutes.

When Kenneth finished his remarks, his words and no doubt his demeanor enthralled the audience. He spoke without benefit of notes or a prepared script. Kenneth's voice was confident, clear, and stalwart. Thunderous applause broke out instantaneously. People leaped to their feet. Clamorous roars went up with great fervor filling the cavernous enclave. Even some of the Congressmen and women stood and applauded. Kenneth seemed unaffected by it all as cameras flashed in his face.

Lisa and Baker stormed toward Kenneth.

"You'll pay for this!" Lisa hissed. "You'll regret the day you ever laid eyes on me!"

"I already do, Lisa. Game's over," Kenneth reminded her and then turned his attention to Baker. "I wasn't the only one who had it made, Baker."

"Watch your back, K.J.," he said through gritted teeth.

"No, Baker, you watch your face because I'll be dead in it if you try anything like this again!"

"You forget, K.J., Benny is still under my command."

"Not for long, J.C.," Kenneth grinned and then leaned in close to Baker. "And if anything happens to him or anyone else in my family, grab your ass, J.C. and kiss it goodbye. Dismissed!" He hissed, turned away from Baker coolly and went to greet his family.

The entire Alexander clan solidly engulfed him.

"You are one cool character under fire, my brother!" Benny said, beaming with pride.

Vivian hugged Kenneth. "K.J., have you ever considered running for public office? I might enjoy calling you Congressman Alexander or Senator Alexander," Vivian bubbled.

"How about Governor Alexander or even President Alexander," Gregory added. "Imagine how many hunnies I could get if my brother was the President of the United States!"

"Uh, come here, little brother," Benny said. "Maybe we need to have a little brother-to-brother talk after all. For starters, you hold Whitney. Does that suggest to you what we're going to talk about?"

Gregory happily took Whitney from Benny and kissed her. He grinned at Benny. "Yeah, brother, but I actually remember to wear my condoms and I've got a lifetime supply thanks to my family!"

Vivian and Kenneth laughed. Benny playfully grabbed Gregory around the neck and pulled him toward him.

"Son, your mother and I have never been more proud of you than we are today. I wish that your grandparents could have been here to see and hear you."

"They were with me, Dad. They're always with me. So are you and Mom."

Bernard embraced his son and kissed him on the cheek. He looked at Kenneth with such pride and love.

"I know, Son, I could hear it in every word you spoke. Your grandparents taught you well."

Sylvia stood beside Bernard. Tears were in her eyes, but she did not cry. Kenneth looked at his mother, cupped her face in his hands, and kissed her gently on her forehead. They did not speak. They simply gazed into each other's eyes and smiled.

"Kenneth Alexander, I don't know how you do it, but you always do it with class!" Tom said, beaming as he extended his hand and then embraced Kenneth. "I'm proud to be your partner."

"He's not the only man here with real class," Shirley said, as she took Tom's arm.

Tom looked at Shirley, as he felt her arm slip into his. A smile began to grow on Tom's face and his green eyes began to sparkle.

Kenneth craned his neck looking for Aretha. He found her sitting outside of the fray focusing on her computerized chess game. He separated himself from the melee and went to her. "Well, little one, how did I do?" he asked, sitting beside her and putting his arm around her shoulder.

Aretha continued to concentrate on the chess game. "Not bad for starters," she said not looking up at him. "Still, it's not over yet and you know it, don't you, Kenneth James?"

"I know, yes," he quietly said, hugging her.

"You don't have to worry, Kenneth James. You're going to win."

"I'm glad that you have confidence in me."

"I love you, Kenneth James, but I'm not the only one. Now when are you going to make JeNelle Towson my sister-in-law and give me some more nephews and nieces?"

Kenneth grinned broadly and ruffled his little sister's thick hair. She had the insight and wisdom of the ancestors.

Everyone crowded in around Kenneth and his family. Reporters were asking questions fast and furiously. Other businessmen greeted and congratulated him warmly. Many shook his hand and patted him on his back. Spectators rushed to him asking for his business card or an autograph. The crowds kept him there for more than two hours. His family and friends gave interviews of their own to the reporters, telling the stories of their youth. Then they all left Capitol Hill for the house in Georgetown.

Derrick and Chuck were waiting at the house with Anna and the children when the Alexander family arrived. Darrick ordered a lavish buffet lunch to be served. Vivian spotted them as she came through the door. Derrick was smiling at her broadly and she rushed into his open arms. Then she went to Chuck and he kissed her with such passion that it took her breath away. When he released her, her heart was pounding and her head was spinning like never before. She had communicated something too as she returned his passion. That kiss caused her nature to rise. She looked into his warm, dark brown eyes and felt a force growing within her. She was momentarily dazed and confused, but her family's jubilation took her away from him.

"Good work, Annie," he said softly and winked at her. "I knew you could do it."

Derrick turned and reached for her hand, snapping her attention back. He held her as she formerly introduced him to the rest of her family. Each one shook his hand and greeted him warmly. Occasionally, she glimpsed Chuck across the room as he interacted effortlessly with her family many of whom he already met. She was seeing him from a different point of view. She tried to shake off her feelings, but couldn't. Her mind began to wonder back to the beginning of their relationship and over the past year. The chance meeting in O'Hare Airport, his friendliness to three stranded people in a blizzard, his compassion toward Anna and her children, his support for her during her crisis, his good-natured camaraderie with her and Gregory over the summer, his relentless search for her when she was stranded on the road, and how he was always there when she needed someone, especially with Carlton. The many times they had been together and the joy and excitement she felt when she was with him. His quick wit and easy manner. How sexy he looked in his cowboy duds. She liked the way that only he called her Annie Oakley. For some odd reason she recalled the fortune cookie's prophecy: *"Intuitive intellect dominates, so heed inner voices and adhere to the unorthodox, but don't take individual for granted."*

"Kenneth, I'm very proud of what you said. Chuck and I watched you on television today," Derrick said, with a broad smile. "I think you spoke—for all people—words that have not been said, but needed to be heard,"

"Thank you, Derrick, but a lot of the credit belongs to my little sister. How she came up with Sam Yeager is beyond me. She really saved the day. Vivian? Hey kid, you with us or what?" Kenneth asked snapping his finger in front of her face.

Vivian snapped out of her haze.

"What? Oh, I'm sorry, what did you say?" she asked Kenneth.

"I just told Derrick that you and the Legal Dream Team saved the day," he said, smiling curiously at her. "You look like you were a million miles away. What are you thinking about?"

She touched her lips lightly remembering Chuck's kiss.

"Me? Oh, a prophecy, uh, I mean, I'm just a little tired. I haven't had any sleep, you know. I mean, uh, I wish that I could take credit for being a brilliant investigative attorney, K.J., but, actually, we don't know who put us on to Sam Yeager or why. I didn't have time to tell you about it, but someone with a New York license plate and the letters 'SANGELO' nearly ran Alan down in front of the house last night. They handed Alan an envelope and were gone before he could ask any questions. The only thing in the envelope was Yeager's name. It's all a big mystery to me, but it worked."

"SANGELO?" Kenneth repeated, confused. "I wonder who...." Something began to dawn on Kenneth. He remembered Yeager's remarks about JeNelle and the San Angeloe family and her mysterious disappearance a few days earlier. She never did say where she went that day he remembered. SANGELO SAN ANGELO The San Angelo, nee Santangelo family. JeNelle's former in-laws. Her former father-in-law who feels that he and his family are in her debt for not having his son, Michel, incarcerated. JeNelle must have reached out to them for him.

"Kenneth, what are you smiling about? You look like you just won the lottery," Vivian said

"I just did," Kenneth said. "I'm the richest man in the universe."

Vivian and Derrick looked at him quizzically.

"What are you talking about, K.J.?" Vivian asked, still confused by his obviously controlled elation.

"I'll explain it to you later," he said, barely able to control his excitement. "But now I have to get back to San Francisco. I've got a lot of work to do."

Chapter 36

It was a crisp, clear day in San Francisco. The sun was shining brightly, but it was unusually quiet inside the offices of CompuCorrect, Inc. Kenneth stood before his partners and the entire CompuCorrect staff as he described the changes in the company that had been in the works over the many weeks since the hearing in Washington. The group was somber. Sara McDougal was crying and there were tears forming in the eyes of other staff members. Shirley briefly turned her back so as not to appear overly emotional as Kenneth spoke to them all. Tom's expression was stoic. He comforted Shirley as Kenneth was ending his remarks.

"....And I want you all to know how much I have enjoyed working closely with each and every one of you. I'm proud of what we have accomplished together. You have been the driving force in bringing this company to this point. My partners and I could not have made it this far without you, but change has to come at some point in everyone's life and it has come to the life of this company. I will remember each of you no matter where I am."

Kenneth shook each person's hand. He took a last look around the office of CompuCorrect, picked up the last of his bags, and started for the door. He spotted the newspaper article hanging on the wall with the tag across it that said, "IT'S NOT TRUE." He took a pen from his jacket and blackened the word "NOT." The staff began to cheer and clap wildly as he left. Kenneth placed the last of his luggage into his already loaded truck and drove away from CompuCorrect, Inc. Beside him in the passenger seat was a beautifully wrapped square box. He glanced at it occasionally as he drove South on the Pacific Coast Highway and smiled.

* * *

It was late afternoon and JeNelle was leading a discussion with her student trainees about the extraordinary progress that they made running the new mail-order business for INSIGHTS. As a part of the Youth in Business and Industry Project, JeNelle had personally selected twenty young people who the schools and social workers characterized as youths-at-risk. She was demonstrating the levels of progress that they had achieved over the many months that they had been working in the business. She was using the software package that Kenneth's company designed for her business. It was absolutely perfect for their operation. They weren't as big as L.L. Bean or Amazon, yet, she had said, but sales were up primarily because of the many good ideas and suggestions that the students had not only contributed, but had actually made a reality. She was very proud of each of them and the hard work that they had put into making the business a success.

They were having some difficulty talking because of the noise and racket that the construction crews were making as they worked on refurbishing an old, warehouse building across the street from INSIGHTS. The construction company had been at it for weeks. Although she was glad to see new businesses move into the area, her patience with the noise was beginning to wear thin. She decided that she would have to speak to the construction foreman on the job site about the noise first thing in the morning.

"Ms. Towson, would you come to the front desk? You are wanted on the telephone and you have a special delivery," Wanda said over the store intercom.

JeNelle was a little annoyed with Wanda. She had asked Wanda not to interrupt her when she was meeting with her student trainees. She excused herself and went to the front of the store. It was quite a walk since the store had now doubled in size because of the backroom operation. The finishing touches were also being made on yet another project next door to INSIGHTS for the opening of another small business venture. She and her new partners would unveil the new business at an open-house celebration over an upcoming holiday weekend. JeNelle and her parents had gone into partnership in TOWSON & TOWSON COUTURE. Her mother taught a group of young people to design and make clothing that they sold to their customers, some of whom were very wealthy, like Mrs. Johnston White Worthington, who had become a regular customer and who had brought many of her friends to the shop. Others were teenagers looking for the newest and hottest styles that the young at-risk student workers were creating. JeNelle's father was the manager of the shop and was working with some of the young people, showing them what he had learned about how to manage a business.

"Wanda, I thought that I asked you not to disturb me when I'm working with our new employees, unless it is very important?"

"I know, Ms. Towson, but this seems to be very important," Wanda said apologetically. "Mrs. Worthington is on line three and you have a special delivery."

JeNelle looked at Wanda's very apologetic demeanor, smiled at her, and shook her head. She took a deep breath and answered the telephone.

"Constance, I'm sorry to keep you waiting," JeNelle said cheerfully. "How can I help you this afternoon?"

"Oh, I know how busy you are, JeNelle, and I won't take up much of your time. I just need to get a few details cleared up."

"All right, Constance. If this is about TOWSON & TOWSON COUTURE, what do you need to know?"

"Well, I've got the announcements and invitations all worked out. I've been working with that nice young man, Paul Garrett at Garrett Printing and Engraving. He really selected a beautiful beige onionskin paper and the raised embossed printing in script is simply divine. He thought that you might like that. He's worked with you before and I think that he's captured your spirit—and Kenneth's, of course. Well, anyway, the guest list is completed. It's just going to be a small affair with just your family and Kenneth's and three hundred of your closest friends. Johnston and I are so glad that you and Kenneth agreed to let us host your engagement party. The catering is all arranged, but I need to know what color scheme you're going to have at the wedding so that I can incorporate those colors into the decorations for the engagement party. Kenneth didn't say. All he said was that you would tell me later. I know that he's just as busy as you are with his new office, but color schemes are very important too."

As Constance Worthington spoke, JeNelle's eyes grew wide and her mouth dropped open. She didn't believe what she was hearing, but then there was that noise from the construction going on across the street. Or had Constance finally gone 'round the bend'! She wondered whether Johnston knew that his wife had flipped her wig.

"Engagement party? Color scheme? Catering? Invitations? Constance, are we talking about the opening of TOWSON & TOWSON COUTURE?"

"Oh, JeNelle, I know that these are not things that you have a lot of time to deal with right now, but since the announcement is already in this afternoon's newspaper, I thought that I'd better get it all cleared up before we're swamped with calls and acceptances. So you just think about it, dear, and give me a call later when you and Kenneth have made a decision."

Constance hung up and JeNelle was left in total bewilderment. Wanda quickly placed a stool behind JeNelle and helped her to sit down. She handed a copy of the Style Section of the afternoon newspaper to JeNelle and stepped back, far back. Wanda remembered the last time that JeNelle got news from the newspaper. She was not taking any chances this time. She was completely innocent.

"It wasn't me, Ms. Towson. I swear!" Wanda said, holding her hands up in the air.

JeNelle began to read the article.

"Dr. and Mrs. Bernard Alexander of Goodwill, South Carolina, are pleased to announce the engagement of their eldest son, Kenneth James Alexander, formerly of San Francisco, to Ms. JeNelle Elise Towson, daughter of Mr. and Mrs. Harvey Towson of Santa Barbara. Ms. Towson is the owner of INSIGHTS, and TOWSON & TOWSON COUTURE of Santa Barbara and is a leading citizen of the Santa Barbara community. She was named Woman of the Year last year by the Santa Barbara Chamber of Commerce.

Mr. Kenneth Alexander, the Executive Director of CompuCorrect, Incorporated, stated in an exclusive interview that he and his lovely bride-to-be will reside most of the year in Santa Barbara where Mr. Alexander is opening his new offices, but that they would also maintain a home in Goodwill, Summer County, South Carolina.

Judge and Mrs. Johnston White Worthington, III, will host the happy couple's engagement party at their estate on Valentine's Day. Mr. Alexander stated that the date of the engagement party was chosen carefully to coincide with the one-year anniversary of their love for each other. The wedding date has not yet been disclosed, according to Mr. Alexander, but he stated that he would prefer a short engagement since the couple is planning to have a very large family.

It was nearly one year ago that this reporter covered the selection of Ms. Towson as the recipient of the prestigious Chamber of Commerce award. The question then was, 'Who would move for love'? It appears that Mr. Alexander has answered that question loudly and clearly. We wish the happy couple well."

Just as JeNelle finished reading the article and looked up, the noise from the construction stopped and she saw a sign being hoisted on the building across the street. The sign read in bold letters,

FUTURE HOME OF COMPUCORRECT, INC.
SOUTHERN DIVISION
KENNETH J. ALEXANDER, EXECUTIVE DIRECTOR

JeNelle blinked rapidly. She couldn't believe what she was seeing.

"First Constance, then the article, now this? What is going on?" she asked aloud.

"You forgot about your special delivery, Ms. Towson," a very familiar, deep, melodic voice spoke to her.

JeNelle turned to see Kenneth leaning against the bookshelves in that same sexy stance of his, wearing that same warm, million-dollar, polar-ice-cap-melting smile. He walked toward her, took a box from behind his back, and handed it to her. JeNelle gazed at Kenneth quizzically, still dazed by the events.

"Kenneth, what—"

He kissed her open mouth softly, loving the feel. Her bewilderment grew.

"Open the box, JeNelle," he whispered, smiling into her eyes.

JeNelle took the box and started to open it. She kept looking at Kenneth as she fumbled with the pretty ribbon and paper. As she unfurled the tissue paper inside the box, she saw the beautiful covered Waterford crystal jewelry box that she had admired at Tiffany & Company in San Francisco. Her eyes began to water. It was more beautiful than she remembered.

"Kenneth, how—"

He kissed her mouth again.

"Open it, JeNelle," he said.

JeNelle looked at him questioningly, as she removed the lid of the crystal box. The aromatic scent of rose pedals glided out of the container and floated in the air. A red satin box sat in the middle of the white rose pedals. JeNelle looked up at Kenneth.

"Kenneth, who—"

He kissed her mouth again.

"Open it, JeNelle," he whispered.

JeNelle opened the box and caught her breath. Tears began rolling down her cheeks as she lifted a magnificent, star-diamond, engagement ring with many beams of light from its holder.

"Now, if you're ready for your vocabulary lesson, Ms. Towson, repeat after me: Kenneth James Alexander, I love you as much as you have loved me. We will love each other more tomorrow than we do today. We will love each other and our children—"

JeNelle didn't let him finish. She leaped from the stool into his arms and kissed Kenneth with all of the passion that she had locked away for far too many years.

"And the sleigh bed?" She laughed through her joyous tears. "Did you finish it yet?"

"I had it shipped. It should be here tomorrow, but tonight—"

She kissed him passionately. "Tonight will take care of itself." She beamed.

Wanda, the other staff members, her student trainees, and customers in the store cheered and clapped as Kenneth and JeNelle stood lost in their love for each other.

* * *

The sun was setting on another glorious San Diego day. Benny carried Whitney out onto the terrace and cradled her in his arms, as he looked out across the wide, blue Pacific Ocean. His daughter was grabbing for the gold chain around his neck and cooing in her own baby-talk conversation. She was beginning to look more like Stacy, he thought. The same beautiful light brown eyes and hair color. *Stacy should see her now,* he thought. "Your mother should see how beautiful you are," he spoke aloud, smiling at Whitney.

Whitney clapped her hands and smiled broadly. Benny rubbed his nose against hers and she giggled.

"You're getting heavy, young lady." He smiled, lifting her to his shoulder and gently rubbing her back. When she let out the air that was worrying her stomach, Benny again cradled her in his arms, picked up the book that sat on the table beside him—a book that JeNelle gave to him as a gift. He began to read aloud to Whitney again.

"*Some women...have more influence than others. They're more persistent, persuasive, in a way of speaking. Give you more confidence. I see women as an inspiration, something to work for. It don't take a whole lot to satisfy a man. A woman gives a man something to go on, otherwise he's like a ship without a rudder with nobody to lead him on and give him inspiration.*' John Van Der Zee said that," he said to Whitney. "That's how your daddy feels, sweetheart, like a ship without a rudder, like a jet with only one wing."

Whitney's little hands gripped his face and she gave him a big sloppy kiss. He smiled broadly at her and then raised his eyes toward the sea again. He closed his eyes and thought of Stacy. She consumed his every waking moment.

Later, while Whitney slept, Benny called his uncle and aunt in Goodwill.

"Honey, we know you're hurting, but...." Olivia Alexander Dixon said.

"Please, Aunt Olivia, get in touch with Donald. I need his help. I don't know what he does, but I'm sure that if anyone can tell me where Stacy is he can."

"But, Benjamin Staton, you know that he can't tell you where she is if—"

"Please, Aunt Olivia, try. I need to talk with Donald."

Olivia sighed. "All right, honey, I'll try to get a message to him.

"Thanks, Aunt Olivia."

"Don't thank me yet," she said, as she hung up.

*   *   *

Vivian wound her way through the nearly deserted halls of Georgetown Medical Center in the dead of night. The lights were low and few people were about. Quiet filled the hallway, but her heart pounded fiercely in her chest. Her tennis shoes were silent and she walked cautiously, her eyes searching for someone, anyone who could give her some direction.

She tried to sleep after Derrick called to say goodnight, but visions kept her awake. Visions that disturbed and excited her simultaneously. She could no longer deny what she was feeling, confused and wary among other emotions that she didn't know what to do with. Finally, she had gotten out of bed, dressed, and left the house, walking in search of answers. She found herself in front of the Emergency Room entrance. Now she knew she had to ask the questions that had been nagging at the recesses of her mind.

"Hi, Viv," a cheery voice said to her.

Vivian turned and smiled at her sorority sister from Spelman, Dr. Savannah Logan. "Hi, Savannah."

Savannah narrowed her eyes. "You looking for Derrick?" she asked.

"Uh, is he around?"

Savannah looked at her watch and then checked the roster of doctors on duty.

"No, he wasn't scheduled for coverage tonight, but I'll have him paged if you want. He usually doesn't work the graveyard shift, especially since you two have been seeing each other," she said and smiled.

"Uh, no, don't bother," Vivian said. "I'll talk with him some other time."

Savannah shrugged. "Well, okay, Viv. If I see him, I'll tell him that you're looking for him."

"Thanks," Vivian said, as she turned to leave.

"Vivian, I just remembered. Chuck is here. I saw him in the Doctor's Lounge a few minutes ago. He was going over his patients' charts. He may know whether Derrick is in the hospital." Savannah motioned toward the lounge and then returned to her work.

Vivian moved slowly toward the door that would lead to the answers she sought. As she slipped inside the lounge, she noticed that it was empty except for one, lone figure—Chuck. His back was toward her, as she stood in silence, watching him while he poured over medical charts. His thick, dark brown, curly hair was tied with a piece of rawhide at the nape of his neck. His broad, strong shoulders flexed as he flipped pages or made notes. His long, tall, agile frame sat comfortably with his legs propped up on another chair and crossed at the ankles. Vivian wasn't sure what she was going to say or whether she should say anything at all. Maybe she should just leave, she thought. Then he closed the chart that he was reviewing, put it on the table before him, and rubbed his face with the palms of his hands.

"How long are you going to stand there, Vivian?" Chuck asked, without turning.

She wondered how he knew that she was in the room. She was rooted to the spot.

Chuck stood, shoved his hands into his pants pockets and turned to face her.

"Chuck, we have to talk," she said quietly.

Chuck inhaled. "Yes, it's time that we did that. In fact, it's a confession that's long overdue."

* * *

In the early morning, Kenneth stood on the deck of JeNelle's home looking at the magical beginning of a new day and the peaceful ocean as it rolled gently onto the shore. He folded his arms across his bare chest and looked up at the last glimmer of the stars as day began to overtake night. He said a silent prayer and felt alive. The fortune cookie prophecy had come true. He knew now what his parents shared between them. He now understood unadulterated love. He knew what Benny and Vivian were facing, too. It would not be an easy year for either of them, he knew, but he would be there for them if they needed him.

JeNelle came onto the deck from the bedroom where she and Kenneth had shared their first night together. She kissed his bare back, put her arms around his strong, muscular body, and stroked the hard plain of his chest and his abdomen. She laid her cheek against his back and pressed her scantily clad body against his. He kissed her fingers and the ring on the third finger of her left hand.

"I missed you when I woke up and you weren't there," JeNelle said, as she held Kenneth.

"I came out here to talk with my ancestors about Vivian and Benny. I want their lives to be as full and happy as mine is now. I also wanted to thank my grandparents and ancestors for bringing me to this point. I'm in love for the first time in my life."

JeNelle moved around to face Kenneth. She put her arms around his neck, raised to her tiptoes, and kissed him passionately. She was glowing as she looked into Kenneth's eyes.

"I want to thank your ancestors, too, for bringing you to this point because I'm in love for the last time in my life."

Kenneth lowered his head and captured her mouth, kissing her gently.

They heard the telephone ringing, but they ignored it. The answering machine picked up.

"At the sound of the tone, please leave your message."

"JeNelle, this is Michel. It's not over!"

THE END

OR MAYBE NOT. I'LL TELL YOU LATER.

AUTHOR BIO

Ann Jeffries is a native of Washington, D. C. She is an only child who enjoyed the benefits of a private school education at Allen in Asheville, NC, and a public education at the University of Maryland. She began writing fiction for her own amusement.

Ann is the recipient of many awards for leadership and public service. A speaker at colleges and universities and conferences and conventions, she has extensively traveled the North American continent, Asia and Europe. Among other things, she is an entrepreneur, an avid viewer of public television and a voracious reader of fiction.

Ms. Jeffries' pride and joy are her family, particularly her Fabulous Four grands. She lives in Maryland and South Carolina.

Made in the USA
Charleston, SC
17 June 2014